The Eternal Champion

The Eternal Champion
Phoenix in Obsidian
The Dragon in the Sword

MICHAEL MOORCOCK

Edited by John Davey

Copyright © Michael and Linda Moorcock 1970, 1986
Revised versions Copyright © Michael and Linda Moorcock 2013
All characters, the distinctive likenesses thereof, and all related
indicia are ™ and © 2013 Michael and Linda Moorcock

All rights reserved

The right of Michael Moorcock to be identified as the author
of this work has been asserted by him in accordance with the
Copyright, Designs and Patents Act 1988.

This edition published in Great Britain in 2013 by
Gollancz
An imprint of the Orion Publishing Group
Orion House, 5 Upper St Martin's Lane,
London WC2H 9EA

An Hachette UK Company

1 3 5 7 9 10 8 6 4 2

A CIP catalogue record for this book is
available from the British Library

ISBN 978 0 575 09265 5

Typeset by Jouve (UK), Milton Keynes

Printed and bound by CPI Group (UK) Ltd, Croydon, CR0 4YY

The Orion Publishing Group's policy is to use papers
that are natural, renewable and recyclable products and
made from wood grown in sustainable forests. The logging
and manufacturing processes are expected to conform to
the environmental regulations of the country of origin.

www.multiverse.org
www. sfgateway.com
www.gollancz.co.uk
www. orionbooks.co.uk

Introduction to
The Michael Moorcock Collection
John Clute

H E IS NOW over 70, enough time for most careers to start and
end in, enough time to fit in an occasional half-decade or so
of silence to mark off the big years. Silence happens. I don't think
I know an author who doesn't fear silence like the plague; most of
us, if we live long enough, can remember a bad blank year or so,
or more. Not Michael Moorcock. Except for some worrying
surgery on his toes in recent years, he seems not to have taken
time off to breathe the air of peace and panic. There has been no
time to spare. The nearly 60 years of his active career seems to
have been too short to fit everything in: the teenage comics; the
editing jobs; the pulp fiction; the reinvented heroic fantasies;
the Eternal Champion; the deep Jerry Cornelius riffs; NEW WORLDS;
the 1970s/1980s flow of stories and novels, dozens upon dozens
of them in every category of modern fantastika; the tales of the
dying Earth and the possessing of Jesus; the exercises in postmodernism that turned the world inside out before most of us had
begun to guess we were living on the wrong side of things; the
invention (more or less) of steampunk; the alternate histories; the
Mitteleuropean tales of sexual terror; the deep-city London riffs:
the turns and changes and returns and reconfigurations to which
he has subjected his oeuvre over the years (he expects this new
Collected Edition will fix these transformations in place for good);
the late tales where he has been remodelling the intersecting
worlds he created in the 1960s in terms of twenty-first-century
physics: for starters. If you can't take the heat, I guess, stay out of
the multiverse.

His life has been full and complicated, a life he has exposed and hidden (like many other prolific authors) throughout his work. In *Mother London* (1988), though, a nonfantastic novel published at what is now something like the midpoint of his career, it may be possible to find the key to all the other selves who made the 100 books. There are three protagonists in the tale, which is set from about 1940 to about 1988 in the suburbs and inner runnels of the vast metropolis of Charles Dickens and Robert Louis Stevenson. The oldest of these protagonists is Joseph Kiss, a flamboyant self-advertising fin-de-siècle figure of substantial girth and a fantasticating relationship to the world: he is Michael Moorcock, seen with genial bite as a kind of G.K. Chesterton without the wearying punch-line paradoxes. The youngest of the three is David Mummery, a haunted introspective half-insane denizen of a secret London of trials and runes and codes and magic: he too is Michael Moorcock, seen through a glass, darkly. And there is Mary Gasalee, a kind of holy-innocent and survivor, blessed with a luminous clarity of insight, so that in all her apparent ignorance of the onrushing secular world she is more deeply wise than other folk: she is also Michael Moorcock, Moorcock when young as viewed from the wry middle years of 1988. When we read the book, we are reading a book of instructions for the assembly of a London writer. The Moorcock we put together from this choice of portraits is amused and bemused at the vision of himself; he is a phenomenon of flamboyance and introspection, a poseur and a solitary, a dreamer and a doer, a multitude and a singleton. But only the three Moorcocks in this book, working together, could have written all the other books.

It all began – as it does for David Mummery in *Mother London* – in South London, in a subtopian stretch of villas called Mitcham, in 1939. In early childhood, he experienced the Blitz, and never forgot the extraordinariness of being a participant – however minute – in the great drama; all around him, as though the world were being dismantled nightly, darkness and blackout would descend, bombs fall, buildings and streets disappear; and in the morning, as though a new universe had taken over from the old one and the world had become portals, the sun would rise on glinting rubble, abandoned tricycles, men and women going about their daily tasks as though nothing had happened, strange shards of ruin poking into altered air. From a very early age, Michael Moorcock's security reposed in a sense that everything might change, in the blinking of an eye, and be *rejourneyed* the next day (or the next book). Though as a writer he has certainly elucidated the fears and alarums of life in Aftermath Britain, it does seem that his very early years were marked by the epiphanies of war, rather than the inflictions of despair and beclouding amnesia most adults necessarily experienced. After the war ended, his parents separated, and the young Moorcock began to attend a pretty wide variety of schools, several of which he seems to have been expelled from, and as soon as he could legally do so he began to work full time, up north in London's heart, which he only left when he moved to Texas (with intervals in Paris) in the early 1990s, from where (to jump briefly up the decades) he continues to cast a Martian eye: as with most exiles, Moorcock's intensest anatomies of his homeland date from after his cunning departure.

But back again to the beginning (just as though we were rimming a multiverse). Starting in the 1950s there was the comics and pulp work for Fleetway Publications; there was the first book (*Caribbean Crisis*, 1962) as by Desmond Reid, co-written with his early friend the artist James Cawthorn (1929–2008); there was marriage, with the writer Hilary Bailey (they divorced in 1978), three children, a heated existence in the Ladbroke Grove/Notting Hill Gate region of London he was later to populate with Jerry Cornelius and his vast family; there was the editing of NEW WORLDS, which began in 1964 and became the heartbeat of the British New Wave two years later as writers like Brian W. Aldiss and J.G. Ballard, reaching their early prime, made it into a tympanum, as young American writers like Thomas M. Disch, John T. Sladek, Norman Spinrad and Pamela Zoline found a home in London for material they could not publish in America, and new British writers like M. John Harrison and Charles Platt began their careers in its pages; but before that there was Elric. With *The Stealer of Souls* (1963) and *Stormbringer* (1965), the multiverse began to flicker into view, and the Eternal Champion (whom Elric parodied and embodied) began properly to ransack the worlds in his fight against a greater Chaos than the great dance could sustain. There was also the first SF novel, *The Sundered Worlds* (1965), but in the 1960s SF was a difficult nut to demolish for Moorcock: he would bide his time.

We come to the heart of the matter. Jerry Cornelius, who first appears in *The Final Programme* (1968) – which assembles and coordinates material first published a few years earlier in NEW WORLDS – is a deliberate solarisation of the albino Elric, who was himself a mocking solarisation of Robert E. Howard's Conan, or rather of the mighty-thew-headed Conan created for profit by Howard epigones: Moorcock rarely mocks the true quill. Cornelius, who reaches his first and most telling apotheosis in the four novels comprising *The Cornelius Quartet*, remains his most distinctive and perhaps most original single creation: a wide boy, an agent, a *flaneur*, a bad musician, a shopper, a shapechanger, a trans, a spy in the house of London: a toxic palimpsest on whom and through whom the *zeitgeist* inscribes surreal conjugations of 'message'. Jerry Cornelius gives head to Elric.

The life continued apace. By 1970, with NEW WORLDS on its last legs, multiverse fantasies and experimental novels poured forth; Moorcock and Hilary Bailey began to live separately, though he moved, in fact, only around the corner, where he set up house with Jill Riches, who would become his second wife; there was a second home in Yorkshire, but London remained his central base. *The Condition of Muzak* (1977), which is the fourth Cornelius novel, and *Gloriana; or, The Unfulfill'd Queen* (1978), which transfigures the first Elizabeth into a kinked Astraea, marked perhaps the high point of his career as a writer of fiction whose font lay in genre or its mutations – marked perhaps the furthest bournes he could transgress while remaining within the perimeters of fantasy (though *within* those bournes vast stretches of territory remained and would, continually, be explored). During these years he sometimes wore a leather jacket constructed out of numerous patches of varicoloured material, and it sometimes seemed perfectly fitting that he bore the semblance, as his jacket flickered and fuzzed from across a room or road, of an illustrated man, a map, a thing of shreds and patches, a student fleshed from dreams. Like the stories he told, he seemed to be more than one thing. To use a term frequently applied (by me at least) to twenty-first-century fiction, he seemed equipoisal: which is to say that, through all his genre-hopping and genre-mixing and genre-transcending and genre-loyal returnings to old pitches, *he was never still*, because 'equipoise' is all about *making stories move*. As with his stories, he cannot be pinned down, because he is not in one place. In person and in his work, it has always been sink or swim: like a shark, or a dancer, or an equilibrist...

The marriage with Jill Riches came to an end. He married Linda Steele in 1983; they remain married. The Colonel Pyat books, *Byzantium Endures* (1981), *The Laughter of Carthage* (1984), *Jerusalem Commands* (1992) and *The Vengeance of Rome* (2006), dominated these years, along with *Mother London*. As these books, which are non-fantastic, are not included in the current *Michael Moorcock Collection*, it might be worth noting here that, in their insistence on the irreducible difficulty of gaining anything like true sight, they represent Moorcock's mature modernist take on what one might call the rag-and-bone shop of the world itself; and that the huge ornate postmodern edifice of his multiverse *loosens* us from that world, gives us room to breathe, to juggle our strategies for living – allows us ultimately to escape from prison (to use a phrase from a writer he does not respect, J.R.R. Tolkien, for whom the twentieth century was a prison train bound for hell). What Moorcock may best be remembered for in the end is the (perhaps unique) interplay between modernism and postmodernism in his work. (But a plethora of discordant understandings makes these terms hard to use; so enough of them.) In the end, one might just say that Moorcock's work as a whole represents an extraordinarily multifarious execution of the fantasist's main task: which is to *get us out of here*.

Recent decades saw a continuation of the multifarious, but with a more intensely applied methodology. The late volumes of the long Elric saga, and the Second Ether sequence of meta-fantasies – *Blood: A Southern Fantasy* (1995), *Fabulous Harbours* (1995) and *The War Amongst the Angels: An Autobiographical Story* (1996) – brood on the real world and the multiverse through the lens of Chaos Theory: the closer you get to the world, the less you describe it. *The Metatemporal Detective* (2007) – a narrative in the Steampunk mode Moorcock had previewed as long ago as *The Warlord of the Air* (1971) and *The Land Leviathan* (1974) – continues the process, sometimes dizzyingly: as though the reader inhabited the eye of a camera increasing its focus on a closely observed reality while its bogey simultaneously wheels it backwards from the desired rapport: an old Kurasawa trick here amplified into a tool of conspectus, fantasy eyed and (once again) rejourneyed, this time through the lens of SF.

We reach the second decade of the twenty-first century, time still to make things new, but also time to sort. There are dozens of titles in *The Michael Moorcock Collection* that have not been listed in this short space, much less trawled for tidbits. The various avatars of the Eternal Champion – Elric, Kane of Old Mars, Hawkmoon, Count Brass, Corum, Von Bek – differ vastly from one another. Hawkmoon is a bit of a berk; Corum is a steely solitary at the End of Time: the joys and doleurs of the interplays amongst them can only be experienced through immersion. And the Dancers at the End of Time books, and the Nomad of the Time Stream books, and the Karl Glogauer books, and all the others. They are here now, a 100 books that make up one book. They have been fixed for reading. It is time to enter the multiverse and see the world.

September 2012

Introduction to
The Michael Moorcock Collection
Michael Moorcock

B Y 1964, AFTER I had been editing NEW WORLDS for some months and had published several science fiction and fantasy novels, including *Stormbringer*, I realised that my run as a writer was over. About the only new ideas I'd come up with were miniature computers, the multiverse and black holes, all very crudely realised, in *The Sundered Worlds*. No doubt I would have to return to journalism, writing features and editing. 'My career,' I told my friend J.G. Ballard, 'is finished.' He sympathised and told me he only had a few SF stories left in him, then he, too, wasn't sure what he'd do.

In January 1965, living in Colville Terrace, Notting Hill, then an infamous slum, best known for its race riots, I sat down at the typewriter in our kitchen-cum-bathroom and began a locally based book, designed to be accompanied by music and graphics. *The Final Programme* featured a character based on a young man I'd seen around the area and whom I named after a local green-grocer, Jerry Cornelius, 'Messiah to the Age of Science'. Jerry was as much a technique as a character. Not the 'spy' some critics described him as but an urban adventurer as interested in his psychic environment as the contemporary physical world. My influences were English and French absurdists, American noir novels. My inspiration was William Burroughs with whom I'd recently begun a correspondence. I also borrowed a few SF ideas, though I was adamant that I was not writing in any established genre. I felt I had at last found my own authentic voice.

I had already written a short novel, *The Golden Barge*, set in a nowhere, no-time world very much influenced by Peake and the surrealists, which I had not attempted to publish. An earlier auto-biographical novel, *The Hungry Dreamers*, set in Soho, was eaten by rats in a Ladbroke Grove basement. I remained unsatisfied with my style and my technique. *The Final Programme* took nine days to complete (by 20 January, 1965) with my baby daughters sometimes cradled with their bottles while I typed on. This, I should say, is my memory of events; my then wife scoffed at this story when I recounted it. Whatever the truth, the fact is I only believed I might be a serious writer after I had finished that novel, with all its flaws. But Jerry Cornelius, probably my most successful sustained attempt at unconventional fiction, was born then and ever since has remained a useful means of telling complex stories. Associated with the 60s and 70s, he has been equally at home in all the following decades. Through novels and novellas I developed a means of carrying several narratives and viewpoints on what appeared to be a very light (but tight) structure which dispensed with some of the earlier methods of fiction. In the sense that it took for granted the understanding that the novel is among other things an internal dialogue and I did not feel the need to repeat by now commonly understood modernist conventions, this fiction was post-modern.

Not all my fiction looked for new forms for the new century. Like many 'revolutionaries' I looked back as well as forward. As George Meredith looked to the eighteenth century for inspiration for his experiments with narrative, I looked to Meredith, popular Edwardian realists like Pett Ridge and Zangwill and the writers of the *fin de siècle* for methods and inspiration. An almost obsessive interest in the Fabians, several of whom believed in the possibility of benign imperialism, ultimately led to my Bastable books which examined our enduring British notion that an empire could be essentially a force for good. The first was *The Warlord of the Air*.

I also wrote my *Dancers at the End of Time* stories and novels under the influence of Edwardian humourists and absurdists like Jerome or Firbank. Together with more conventional generic books like *The Ice Schooner* or *The Black Corridor*, most of that work was done in the 1960s and 70s when I wrote the Eternal Champion supernatural adventure novels which helped support my own and others' experiments via NEW WORLDS, allowing me also to keep a family while writing books in which action and fantastic invention were paramount. Though I did them quickly, I didn't write them cynically. I have always believed, somewhat puritanically, in giving the audience good value for money. I enjoyed writing them, tried to avoid repetition, and through each new one was able to develop a few more ideas. They also continued to teach me how to express myself through image and metaphor. My Everyman became the Eternal Champion, his dreams and ambitions represented by the multiverse. He could be an ordinary person struggling with familiar problems in a contemporary setting or he could be a swordsman fighting monsters on a far-away world.

Long before I wrote *Gloriana* (in four parts reflecting the seasons) I had learned to think in images and symbols through reading John Bunyan's *Pilgrim's Progress*, Milton and others, understanding early on that the visual could be the most important part of a book and was often in itself a story as, for instance, a famous personality could also, through everything associated with their name, function as narrative. I wanted to find ways of carrying as many stories as possible in one. From the cinema I also learned how to use images as connecting themes. Images, colours, music, and even popular magazine headlines can all add coherence to an apparently random story, underpinning it and giving the reader a sense of internal logic and a satisfactory resolution, dispensing with certain familiar literary conventions.

When the story required it, I also began writing neo-realist fiction exploring the interface of character and environment, especially the city, especially London. In some books I condensed, manipulated and randomised time to achieve what I wanted, but in others the sense of 'real time' as we all generally perceive it was more suitable and could best be achieved by traditional nineteenth-century means. For the Pyat books I first looked back to the great

German classic, Grimmelshausen's *Simplicissimus* and other early picaresques. I then examined the roots of a certain kind of moral fiction from Defoe through Thackeray and Meredith then to modern times where the picaresque (or rogue tale) can take the form of a road movie, for instance. While it's probably fair to say that Pyat and *Byzantium Endures* precipitated the end of my second marriage (echoed to a degree in *The Brothel in Rosenstrasse*), the late 70s and the 80s were exhilarating times for me, with *Mother London* being perhaps my own favourite novel of that period. I wanted to write something celebratory.

By the 90s I was again attempting to unite several kinds of fiction in one novel with my Second Ether trilogy. With Mandel-brot, Chaos Theory and String Theory I felt, as I said at the time, as if I were being offered a chart of my own brain. That chart made it easier for me to develop the notion of the multiverse as representing both the internal and the external, as a metaphor and as a means of structuring and rationalising an outrageously inventive and quasi-realistic narrative. The worlds of the multi-verse move up and down scales or 'planes' explained in terms of mass, allowing entire universes to exist in the 'same' space. The result of developing this idea was the *War Amongst the Angels* sequence which added absurdist elements also functioning as a kind of mythology and folklore for a world beginning to under-stand itself in terms of new metaphysics and theoretical physics. As the cosmos becomes denser and almost infinite before our eyes, with black holes and dark matter affecting our own reality, we can explore them and observe them as our ancestors explored our planet and observed the heavens.

At the end of the 90s I'd returned to realism, sometimes with a dash of fantasy, with *King of the City* and the stories collected in *London Bone*. I also wrote a new Elric / Eternal Champion sequence, beginning with *Daughter of Dreams*, which brought the fantasy worlds of Hawkmoon, Bastable and Co. in line with my realistic and autobiographical stories, another attempt to unify all my fic-tion, and also offer a way in which disparate genres could be reunited, through notions developed from the multiverse and the Eternal Champion, as one giant novel. At the time I was finishing the Pyat sequence which attempted to look at the roots of the Nazi Holocaust in our European, Middle Eastern and American cultures and to ground my strange survival guilt while at the same time examining my own cultural roots in the light of an enduring anti-Semitism.

By the 2000s I was exploring various conventional ways of story-telling in the last parts of *The Metatemporal Detective* and through other homages, comics, parodies and games. I also looked back at my earliest influences. I had reached retirement age and felt like a rest. I wrote a 'prequel' to the Elric series as a graphic novel with Walter Simonson, *The Making of a Sorcerer*, and did a little online editing with FANTASTIC METROPOLIS.

By 2010 I had written a novel featuring Doctor Who, *The Coming of the Terraphiles*, with a nod to P.G. Wodehouse (a boyhood favourite), continued to write short stories and novellas and to work on the beginning of a new sequence combining pure fantasy and straight autobiography called *The Whispering Swarm* while still writing more Cornelius stories trying to unite all the various genres and sub-genres into which contemporary fiction has fallen.

Throughout my career critics have announced that I'm 'abandoning' fantasy and concentrating on literary fiction. The truth is, however, that all my life, since I became a professional writer and editor at the age of 16, I've written in whatever mode suits a story best and where necessary created a new form if an old one didn't work for me. Certain ideas are best carried on a Jerry Cornelius story, others work better as realism and others as fantasy or science fiction. Some work best as a combination. I'm sure I'll write whatever I like and will continue to experiment with all the ways there are of telling stories and carrying as many themes as possible. Whether I write about a widow coping with loneliness in her cottage or a massive, universe-size sentient spaceship searching for her children, I'll no doubt die trying to tell them all. I hope you'll find at least some of them to your taste.

One thing a reader can be sure of about these new editions is that they would not have been possible without the tremendous and indispensable help of my old friend and bibliographer John Davey. John has ensured that these Gollancz editions are definitive. I am indebted to John for many things, including his work at Moorcock's Miscellany, my website, but his work on this edition has been outstanding. As well as being an accomplished novelist in his own right John is an astonishingly good editor who has worked with Gollancz and myself to point out every error and flaw in all previous editions, some of them not corrected since their first publication, and has enabled me to correct or revise them. I couldn't have completed this project without him. Together, I think, Gollancz, John Davey and myself have produced what will be the best editions possible and I am very grateful to him, to Malcolm Edwards, Darren Nash and Marcus Gipps for all the considerable hard work they have done to make this edition what it is.

Michael Moorcock

Contents

The Eternal Champion

A Fantastic Romance

To the memory of Douglas Fairbanks,
the greatest hero of them all

Prologue

THEY CALLED FOR ME.

That is all I really know.

They called for me and I went to them. I could not do otherwise. The will of the whole of humanity was a strong thing. It smashed through the ties of time and the chains of space and dragged me to hell.

Why was I chosen? I still do not know, though they believed they had told me. Now it is done and I am here. I shall always be here. And if as wise men tell me, time is cyclic, then I shall one day return to part of the cycle I knew as the twentieth century, for (it was no wish of mine) I am immortal.

Chapter One
A Call Across Time

B ETWEEN WAKEFULNESS AND sleeping we have most of us had the illusion of hearing voices, scraps of conversation, phrases spoken in unfamiliar tones. Sometimes we attempt to attune our minds so that we can hear more, but we are rarely successful. These illusions are called 'hypnagogic hallucinations' – the beginning of the dreams we shall later experience as we sleep.

There was a woman. A child. A city. An occupation. A name: John Daker. A sense of frustration. A need for fulfilment. Though I loved them. I know I loved them.

It was in the winter. I lay miserably in a cold bed and I stared through the window at the moon. I do not remember my exact thoughts. Something to do with morality and the futility of human existence, no doubt. Then, between wakefulness and sleeping, I began every night to hear voices...

At first I dismissed them, expecting to fall immediately asleep, but they continued and I began trying to listen to them, thinking, perhaps, to receive some message from my unconscious. But the most commonly repeated word was gibberish to me:

Erekosë... Erekosë... Erekosë...

I could not recognise the language, though it had a peculiar familiarity. The closest language I could place it with was the language of Sioux Indians, but I knew only a few words of Sioux.

Erekosë... Erekosë... Erekosë...

Each night I redoubled my efforts to concentrate on the voices and gradually I began to experience much stronger hypnagogic hallucinations, until one night it seemed that I broke free from my body altogether.

★

*Had I hung for an eternity in limbo? Was I alive – dead? Was there a
memory of a world that lay in the far past or the distant future? Of
another world which seemed closer? And the names? Was I John Daker
or Erekosë? Was I either of these? Many other names – Corum Jhaelen
Irsei, Aubec, Seaton Begg, Elric, Rackhir, Ilian, Oona, Simon, Bastable,
Cornelius, the Rose, von Bek, Asquiol, Hawkmoon – fled away down the
ghostly rivers of my memory. I hung in darkness, bodiless. A man spoke.
Where was he? I tried to look but had no eyes with which to see...*

'*Erekosë the Champion, where are you?*'
   Another voice: '*Father... it is only a legend...*'
   '*No, Iolinda. I feel he is listening. Erekosë...*'

I tried to answer, but I had no tongue with which to speak.

   Then there were swirling half-dreams of a house in a great city
of miracles; a swollen, grimy city of miracles, crammed with
dull-coloured machines, many of which bore human passengers.
There were buildings, beautiful beneath their coatings of dust,
and there were other, brighter buildings not so beautiful, with
austere lines and many windows. There were screams and loud
noises.

   There was a troop of riders galloping over undulating countryside, flamboyant in armour of lacquered gold, coloured pennants
draped around their blood-encrusted lances. Their faces were
heavy with weariness.

   Then there were more faces, many faces. Some of them I half-
recognised. Others were completely unfamiliar. Many of these
were dressed in strange clothes. I saw a white-haired man in middle age. He wore a tall, spiked crown of iron and diamonds upon
his head. His mouth moved. He was speaking...

'*Erekosë. It is I – King Rigenos, Defender of Humanity...*'
   '*You are needed again, Erekosë. The Hounds of Evil rule a third of
the world and humankind is weary with the war against them. Come to
us, Erekosë. Lead us to victory. From the Plains of Melting Ice to the*'

Mountains of Sorrow they have set up their corrupt standard and I fear they will advance yet farther into our territories.

'Come to us, Erekosë. Lead us to victory. Come to us, Erekosë. Lead us...'

The woman's voice:

'Father. This is only an empty tomb. Not even the mummy of Erekosë remains. It became drifting dust long ago. Let us leave and return to Necranal to marshal the living peers!'

I felt like a fainting man who strives to fight against dizzy oblivion but, however much he tries, cannot take control of his own brain. Again I tried to answer, but could not.

It was as if I wavered backwards through Time, while every atom of me wanted to go forward. I had the sensation of vast size, as if I were made of stone with eyelids of granite that measured miles across – eyelids which I could not open.

And then I was tiny: the most minute grain in the universe. And yet I felt I belonged to the whole far more than did the stone giant.

Memories came and went.

The panorama of the twentieth century, its discoveries and its deceits, its beauties and its bitterness, its satisfactions, its strife, its self-delusion, its superstitious fancies to which it gave the name of Science, rushed into my mind like air into a vacuum.

But it was only momentary, for the next second my entire being was flung elsewhere – to a world which was Earth, but not the Earth of John Daker, not quite the world of dead Erekosë...

There were three great continents; two close together were divided from the third by a vast sea containing many islands, large and small.

I saw an ocean of ice which I knew to be slowly shrinking – the Plains of Melting Ice.

I saw the third continent, which bore lush flora, mighty forests, blue lakes and which was bound along its northern coasts by a towering chain of mountains – the Mountains of Sorrow. This

I knew to be the domain of the Eldren, whom King Rigenos had called the Hounds of Evil.

Now, on the other two continents, I saw the wheatlands of the West on the continent of Zavara, with their tall cities of multicoloured rock, their rich cities – Stalaco, Calodemia, Mooros, Ninadoon and Dratarda.

There were the great sea-ports – Shilaal, Wedmah, Sinana, Tarkar – and Noonos with her towers cobbled in precious stones.

Then I saw the fortress cities of the continent of Necralala, with the capital city Necranal chief among them, built on, into and about a mighty mountain, peaked by the spreading palace of its warrior kings.

Now I began to remember as, in the background of my awareness, I heard a voice calling, '*Erekosë, Erekosë, Erekosë...*'

The warrior kings of Necranal, kings for two thousand years of a humanity united, at war, and united again. The warrior kings of whom King Rigenos was the last living – and ageing now, with only a daughter, Iolinda, to carry on his line. Old and weary with hate – but still hating. Hating the unhuman folk whom he called the Hounds of Evil, mankind's age-old enemies, reckless and wild; linked, it was said, by a thin line of blood to the human race – an outcome of a union between an ancient queen and the Evil One, Azmobaana. Hated by King Rigenos as soulless immortals, slaves of Azmobaana's machinations.

And, hating, he called upon John Daker, whom he named Erekosë, to aid him with his war against them.

'Erekosë, I beg thee answer me. Are you ready to come?' His voice was loud and echoing, and when, after a struggle, I could reply, my own voice seemed to echo, also.

'I am ready,' I replied, 'but seem to be chained.'

'*Chained*?' There was consternation in his voice. 'Are you, then, a prisoner of Azmobaana's frightful minions? Are you trapped upon the Ghost Worlds?'

'Perhaps,' I said. 'But I do not think so. It is Space and Time which chain me. I am separated from you by a gulf without form or dimension.'

'How may we bridge that gulf and bring you to us?'

'The united wills of Humanity may serve the purpose.'

'Already we pray that you may come to us.'

'Then continue,' I said.

I was falling away again. I thought I remembered laughter, sadness, pride. Then, suddenly, more faces. I felt as if I witnessed the passing of everyone I had known, down the ages, and then one face superimposed itself over the others – the head and shoulders of an amazingly beautiful woman, with blonde hair piled beneath a diadem of precious stones which seemed to light the sweetness of her oval face. 'Iolinda,' I said.

I saw her more solidly now. She was clinging to the arm of the tall, gaunt man who wore the crown of iron and diamonds: King Rigenos.

They stood before an empty platform of quartz and gold and resting on a cushion of dust was a straight sword which they dared not touch. Neither did they dare step too close to it, for it gave off a radiation which might slay them.

It was a tomb in which they stood.

The tomb of Erekosë. My tomb.

I moved towards the platform, hanging over it.

Ages before, my body had been placed there. I stared at the sword, which held no dangers for me, but I was unable in my captivity to pick it up. It was my spirit only which inhabited that dark place – but the whole of my spirit now, not the fragment which had inhabited the tomb for thousands of years. That fragment had heard King Rigenos and had enabled John Daker to hear it, to come to it, to be united with it.

'Erekosë!' called the king, straining his eyes through the gloom as if he had seen me. 'Erekosë! We pray.'

Then I experienced the dreadful pain which I supposed must be like that of a woman experiencing childbirth, a pain that seemed eternal and yet was intrinsically its own vanquisher. I was screaming, writhing in the air above them. Great spasms of agony – but an agony complete with purpose – the purpose of creation.

I shrieked. But there was joy in my cry.

I groaned. But there was triumph there.

I grew heavy and I reeled. I grew heavier and heavier and I gasped, stretching out my arms to balance myself.

I had flesh and I had muscle and I had blood and I had strength. The strength coursed through me and I took a huge breath and touched my body. It was a powerful body, tall and fit.

I looked up. I stood before them in the flesh. I was their god and I had returned.

'I have come,' I said. 'I am here, King Rigenos. I have left nothing worthwhile behind me, but do not let me regret that leaving.'

'You will not regret it, Champion.' He was pale, exhilarated, smiling. I looked at Iolinda, who dropped her eyes modestly and then, as if against her will, raised them again to regard me. I turned to the dais on my right.

'My sword,' I said, reaching for it.

I heard King Rigenos sigh with satisfaction.

'They are doomed now, the dogs,' he said.

Chapter Two
'The Champion Has Come!'

THEY HAD A sheath for the sword. It had been made days before. King Rigenos left to get it, leaving me alone with his daughter.

Now that I was here, I did not think to question how I came and why it should have been possible. Neither, it seemed, did she question the fact. I was there. It seemed inevitable.

We regarded one another silently until the king returned with the scabbard.

'This will protect us against your sword's poison,' he said.

He held it out to me. For a moment I hesitated before stretching my own hand towards it and accepting it.

The king frowned and looked at the ground. Then he folded his arms across his chest.

I held the scabbard in my two hands. It was opaque, like old glass, but the metal was unfamiliar to me – or rather to John Daker. It was light, flexible and strong.

I turned and picked up the sword. The handle was bound in gold thread and was vibrant to my touch. The pommel was a globe of deep red onyx and the hilt was worked in strips of silver and black onyx. The blade was long and straight and sharp, but it did not shine like steel. Instead, in colour, it resembled lead. The sword was beautifully balanced and I swung it through the air and laughed aloud, and it seemed to laugh with me.

'Erekosë! Sheathe it!' cried King Rigenos in alarm. 'Sheathe it! The radiation is death to all but yourself!'

I was reluctant now to put the sword away. The feel of it awakened a dim remembrance.

'Erekosë! Please! I beg you!' Iolinda's voice echoed her father's. 'Sheathe the sword!'

Reluctantly I slid the sword into its scabbard. Why was I the only one who could wear the sword without being affected by its radiation?

Was it because, in that transition from my own age to this, I had become constitutionally different in some way? Was it that the ancient Erekosë and the unborn John Daker (or was it vice versa?) had metabolisms which had adapted to protect themselves against the power which flowed from the sword?

I shrugged. It did not matter. The fact itself was enough. I was unconcerned. It was as if I was aware that my fate had been taken almost entirely out of my own hands. I had become a tool.

If only I had known then to what use the tool would be put, then I might have fought against the pull and remained the harmless intellectual, John Daker. But perhaps I could not have fought and won. The power that drew me to this age was very great.

At any rate, I was prepared at that moment to do whatever Fate demanded of me. I stood where I had materialised, in the tomb of Erekosë, and I revelled in my strength and in my sword.

Later, things were to change.

'I will need clothes,' I said, for I was naked. 'And armour. And a steed. I am Erekosë.'

'Clothes have been prepared,' said King Rigenos. He clapped his hands. 'Here.'

The slaves entered. One carried a robe, another a cloak, another a white cloth which I gathered had to serve for underwear. They wrapped the cloth around my lower quarters and slipped the robe over my head. It was loose and cool and felt pleasant on my skin. It was deep blue, with complicated designs stitched into it in gold, silver and scarlet thread. The cloak was scarlet, with designs of gold, silver and blue. They gave me soft boots of doeskin to put on my feet, and a wide belt of light brown leather with an iron buckle in which were set rubies and sapphires, and I hung my scabbard on this. Then I gripped the sword with my left fist.

'I am ready,' I said.

Iolinda shuddered. 'Then let us leave this gloomy place,' she murmured.

With one last look back at the dais on which the heap of dust still lay, I walked with the King and the Princess of Necranal out of my own tomb and into a calm day that, while warm, had a light breeze blowing. We were standing on a small hill. Behind us the tomb, apparently built of black quartz, looked time-worn and ancient, pitted by the passing of many storms and many winds. On its roof was the corroded statue of a warrior mounted on a great battle charger. The face had been smoothed by dust and rain, but I knew it. It was my face.

I looked away.

Below us a caravan was waiting. There were the richly caparisoned horses and a guard of men dressed in that same golden armour I had seen in my dreams. These warriors, however, were fresher-looking than the others. Their armour was fluted, embellished with raised designs, ornate and beautiful but, according to my sparse reading on the subject of armour, coupled with Erekosë's stirring memory, totally unsuitable for war. The fluting and embossing acted as a trap to catch the point of a spear or sword, whereas armour should be made to turn a point. This armour, for all its beauty, acted more as an extra danger than a protection.

The guards were mounted on heavy warhorses, but the beasts that knelt awaiting us resembled a kind of camel from which all the camel's lumpen ugliness had been bred. These beasts were beautiful. On their high backs were cabins of ebony, ivory and mother-of-pearl, curtained in scintillating silks.

We walked down the hill and, as we walked, I noticed that I still had on my finger the ring that I had worn as John Daker, a ring of woven silver that my wife had given me. My wife – I could not recall her face. I felt I should have left the ring behind me, on that other body. But perhaps there is no body left behind.

We reached the kneeling beasts and the guards stiffened their backs to acknowledge our arrival. I saw curiosity in many of the eyes that looked at me.

King Rigenos gestured towards one of the beasts. 'Would you care to take your cabin, Champion?' Though he himself had summoned me, he seemed to be slightly wary of me.

'Thank you.' I climbed the little ladder of plaited silk and entered the cabin. It was completely lined with deep cushions of a variety of hues.

The camels climbed to their feet and we began to move swiftly through a narrow valley whose sides were lined with evergreen trees which I could not name – something like spreading monkey-puzzle trees, but with more branches and broader leaves.

I had laid my sword across my knees. I inspected it. It was a plain soldier's sword, having no markings on the blade. The hilt fitted perfectly into my right hand as I gripped it. It was a good sword. But why it was poisonous to others I did not know. Presumably it was also lethal to those whom King Rigenos called the Hounds of Evil – the Eldren.

As we travelled through the soft day I drowsed on my cushions, feeling strangely weary, until I heard a cry and pushed back the curtains of my cabin to look ahead.

There was Necranal, the city which I had seen in my dreams.

Far away still, it towered upwards so that the entire mountain upon which it was built was hidden by its wondrous architecture. Minarets, steeples, domes and battlements shone in the sun and above them all loomed the huge palace of the warrior kings, a noble structure, many-towered, the Palace of Ten Thousand Windows. I remembered the name.

I saw King Rigenos peer from his own cabin and cry: 'Katorn! Ride ahead and tell the people that Erekosë the Champion has come to drive the Evil Ones back to the Mountains of Sorrow!'

The man he addressed was a sullen-faced individual, doubtless the Captain of the Imperial Guard. 'Aye, sire,' he growled.

He drew his horse out of line and galloped speedily along the road of white dust which wound now down an incline. I could see the road stretching for many miles into the distance towards Necranal. I watched the rider for a while but wearied of this eventually and instead strained my eyes to make out details in that great city structure.

The cities of London, New York or Tokyo were probably bigger in area, but not much. Necranal was spread around the base of the mountain for many miles. Surrounding the city was a high wall upon which turrets were mounted at intervals.

So, at last, we came to the great main gate of Necranal and our caravan halted.

A musical instrument sounded and the gates began to swing open. We passed through into streets packed with jostling, cheering people who shouted so loudly I was forced, at times, to cover my ears for fear they would rupture.

Chapter Three
The Eldren Threat

Now the cheering gradually fell away as the little caravan ascended the winding road to the Palace of Ten Thousand Windows. A silence settled and I heard only the creak of the howdah in which I sat, the occasional jingle of harness or the clatter of a horse's hoof. I began to feel discomfited. There was something about the mood of the city that was not altogether sane and which could not be explained away in conventional terms. Certainly the people were afraid of enemy attack; certainly they were weary with fighting. But it seemed to me that this mood held something morbid – a mixture of hysterical elation and melancholic depression that I had sensed only once before in my previous life, during my single visit to a mental hospital.

Or perhaps I was merely imposing my own mood on my surroundings. After all, it could be argued that I was experiencing classic paranoid-schizophrenic symptoms! A man with two or more well-defined identities who also happened to be considered in this world the potential saviour of mankind! For a moment I wondered if in fact I had not gone completely insane, if this were not some monstrous delusion, if I were not *actually* at this moment in the very madhouse I had once visited!

I touched the draperies, my scabbarded sword; I peered out at the vast city now stretched out below me; I stared at the huge bulk of the Palace of Ten Thousand Windows above me. I attempted to see beyond them, deliberately assuming that they were an illusion, expecting to see the walls of a hospital room, or even the familiar walls of my own apartment. But the Palace of Ten Thousand Windows remained as solid as ever. The city of Necranal had none of the qualities of a mirage. I sank back in my cushions. I had to assume that this was real, that I had been trans-ported somehow across the ages and through space to this Earth of which there were no records in any history book I had ever read (and I had read many) and of which there were only echoes in myths and legends.

I was no longer John Daker. I was Erekosë – the Eternal Champion.

A legend myself, come to life.

I laughed then. If I were mad, then it was a glorious madness, a madness which I would never have considered myself capable of inventing!

At length our caravan arrived at the summit of the mountain and the jewelled gates of the palace opened for us and we passed inside a splendid courtyard in which trees grew and fountains played, feeding little rivers spanned by ornamental bridges. Fish swam in the rivers and birds sang in the trees as pages came for-ward to make our beasts kneel down and we stepped out into the evening light.

King Rigenos smiled with pride as he gestured around the great courtyard. 'You like this, Erekosë? I had it built myself, shortly after I came to the throne. The courtyard was a gloomy sort of place until then – it did not fit with the rest of the palace.'

'It is very beautiful,' I said. I turned to look at Iolinda, who had joined us. 'And not the only beautiful thing you have helped create – for here is the most beautiful adornment to your palace!'

King Rigenos chuckled. 'You are a courtier as well as a warrior, I see.' He took my arm and Iolinda's and guided us across the courtyard. 'Of course, I have little time these days to consider the creation of beauty. It is weapons we must create now. Instead of plans for gardens, I must concern myself with battle plans.' He sighed. 'Perhaps you will drive the Eldren away for ever, Erekosë. Perhaps, when they are destroyed, we shall be able to enjoy the peaceful things of life again.'

I felt sorry for him at that moment. He only wanted what every man wanted – freedom from fear, a chance to raise children with a reasonable certainty that they would be allowed to do the same, a chance to look forward to the future without the knowledge that any plans made might be wrecked for ever by some sudden act of violence. His world, after all, was not so different from the one I had so recently left.

I put my hand on the king's shoulder. 'Let us hope so, King Rigenos,' I said. 'I will do what I can.'

He cleared his throat. 'And that will be a great deal, Champion. I know it will be a great deal. We shall soon rid ourselves of the Eldren menace!'

We entered a cool hall whose walls were lined with beaten silver over which tapestries were draped. It was a pleasant hall, though very large. Off the hall led a wide staircase and down the staircase now descended a whole army of slaves, servants and retainers of all kinds. They drew themselves up in ranks at the bottom and knelt to greet the king.

'This is Lord Erekosë,' King Rigenos told them. 'He is a great warrior and my honoured guest. Treat him as you would treat me – obey him as you would obey me. All that he wishes shall be his.'

To my embarrassment, the assemblage fell to its knees again and chorused: 'Greetings, Lord Erekosë.'

I spread my hands. They rose. I was beginning to take this sort of behaviour for granted. There was no doubt that part of me was used to it.

'I shall not burden you with ceremony for tonight,' Rigenos said. 'If you would like to refresh yourself in the apartments we have set aside for your use, we shall visit you later.'

'Very well,' I said. I turned to Iolinda and put out my hand to take hers. She extended it after a moment's hesitation and I kissed it. 'I look forward to seeing you both again in a little time,' I murmured, looking deep into her marvellous eyes. She dropped her gaze and withdrew her hand, and I allowed the servants to escort me upstairs to my apartments.

Twenty large rooms had been set aside for my use. These contained quarters for a staff of some ten personal slaves and servants and they were most of them extravagantly furnished with an eye to luxury that, it seemed to me, the people of the twentieth century had lost. 'Opulent' was the word that sprang to mind. I could not move but a slave would come forward and take my surcoat or help me pour a glass of water or arrange the cushions of a divan. Yet I was still somewhat uneasy and it was a relief, on exploring the apartments, to come upon more austere rooms. These were weapon-lined warriors' rooms, without cushions or silks or furs, but with solid benches and blades and maces of iron and steel, brass-shod lances and razor-sharp arrows.

I spent some time in the weapons rooms and then returned to eat. My slaves brought me food and wine and I ate and drank heartily.

When I had finished, I felt as if I had been asleep for a long time and had awakened invigorated. Again I paced the rooms, exploring them further, taking more interest in the weapons than in the furnishings, which would have delighted even the most jaded sybarite. I stepped out onto one of the several covered balconies and surveyed the great city of Necranal as the sun set over it and deep shadows began to flow through the streets.

The faraway sky was full of smoky colour. There were purples, oranges, yellows and blues and these colours were reflected in the domes and steeples of Necranal so that the entire city seemed to take on a softer texture, like a pastel drawing.

The shadows grew blacker. The sun set and stained the topmost domes scarlet and then night fell and fire flared suddenly all around the distant walls of Necranal, the yellow and red flames leaping upward at intervals of a few yards and illuminating much of the city within the walls. Lights appeared in windows and I heard the calls of nightbirds and insects. I turned to go in and saw that my servants had lit lamps for me. It had grown colder, but I hesitated on the balcony and decided to stay where I was, thinking deeply about my strange situation and trying to gauge the exact nature of the perils which Humanity faced.

There came a sound behind me. I looked back into the apartments and saw King Rigenos entering. Moody Katorn, Captain of the Imperial Guard, was with him. Instead of a helmet, he now wore a platinum circlet on his head and, instead of a breastplate, a leather jerkin stamped with a design in gold, but the absence of armour did not seem to soften his general demeanour. King Rigenos was wrapped in a white fur cloak and still wore his spiked crown of iron and diamonds. The two men joined me on the balcony.

'You feel rested, I hope, Erekosë?' King Rigenos enquired almost nervously, as if he had expected me to fade into air while he was away.

'I feel very well, thank you, King Rigenos.'

'Good.' He hesitated.

'Time is valuable,' Katorn grunted.

'Yes, Katorn. Yes, I know.' King Rigenos looked at me as if he hoped I already knew what he wished to say, but I did not and could only stare back, waiting for him to speak.

'You will forgive us, Erekosë,' said Katorn, 'if we come immediately to the matter of the Human Kingdoms. The king would outline to you our position and what we require of you.'

'Of course,' I said. 'I am ready.' I was in fact very anxious to learn the position.

'We have maps,' said King Rigenos. 'Where are the maps, Katorn?'

'Within, sire.'

'Shall we…?'

I nodded and we entered my apartments. We passed through two chambers until we came to the main living room, in which was a large oak table. Here stood several of King Rigenos's slaves with large rolls of parchment under their arms. Katorn selected several of the rolls and spread them, one on top of the other, on the table. He drew his heavy dagger to weight one side and picked up a metal vase studded with rubies and emeralds to hold the other side.

I looked at the maps with interest. I already recognised them. I had seen something similar in my dreams before I had been called here by King Rigenos's incantations.

Now the king bent over the maps and his long, pale index finger traced over the territories shown.

'As I told you in your – your tomb, Erekosë, the Eldren now dominate the entire southern continent. They call this continent Mernadin. There.' His finger now hovered over a coastal region of the continent. 'Five years ago they recaptured the only real outpost we had on Mernadin. Here. Their ancient sea-port of Paphanaal. There was little fighting.'

'Your forces fled?' I asked.

Katorn came in again. 'I admit that we had grown complacent. When they suddenly swept out of the Mountains of Sorrow, we were unprepared. They must have been building their damned armies for years and we were unaware of it. We could not be expected to know their plans – they're aided by sorcery and we are not!'

'You were able to evacuate most of your colonies, I take it?' I put in.

Katorn shrugged. 'There was little evacuation necessary. Mernadin was virtually uninhabited since human beings would not live in a land which had been polluted by the presence of the Hounds of Evil. The continent is cursed. Inhabited by fiends from Hell.'

I rubbed my chin and asked innocently: 'Then why did you drive the Eldren back to the mountains in the first place if you had no need of their territories?'

'Because, while they had the land under their control, they were a constant threat to Humanity!'

'I see.' I made a tiny gesture with my right hand. 'Forgive me for interrupting you. Please continue.'

'A constant threat –' began Katorn.

'That threat is once again imminent,' the king's voice broke in. It was thick and trembling. His eyes were suddenly full of fear and hatred. 'We expect them at any moment to launch an attack upon the Two Continents – upon Zavara and Necralala!'

'Do you know when they plan this invasion?' I asked. 'How long have we to ready ourselves?'

'They'll attack!' Katorn's bleak eyes came to life. The thin beard framing his pale face seemed to bristle.

'They'll attack,' agreed King Rigenos. 'They would have overrun us now if we did not constantly war against them.'

'We have to keep them back,' added Katorn. 'Once a breach is made, they will engulf us!'

King Rigenos sighed. 'Humanity, though, is battle-weary. We needed one of two things – though ideally both – fresh warriors to drive the Eldren back or a leader to give the warriors we have new hope.'

'And you can train no fresh warriors?' I asked.

Katorn made a short, guttural sound in his throat. I took this to be a laugh. 'Impossible! All mankind fights the Eldren menace!'

The king nodded. 'So I called you, Erekosë – though believing myself to be a desperate fool willing to think a mirage reality.'

Katorn turned away at this. It seemed to me that this had been his private theory – that the king had gone mad in his desperation. My materialisation seemed to have destroyed this theory and made him in some way resentful of me, though I did not think I could be blamed for the king's decision.

The king straightened his shoulders. 'I called you. And I hold you to your vow.'

I knew of no vow. I was surprised. 'What vow?' I said.

Now the king looked astonished. 'Why, the vow that, if ever the Eldren dominated Mernadin again, you would come to decide the struggle between them and Humanity.'

'I see.' I signed to a slave to bring me a cup of wine and I sipped it and stared at the map. As John Daker, I saw a meaningless war between two ferocious, blindly hating factions, both of whom seemed to be conducting a racial jihad, one against the other. Yet my loyalties were clear. I belonged to the human race and should use all my powers to help defend my kind. Humanity had to be saved.

'The Eldren?' I looked up at King Rigenos. 'What do they say?'

'What do you mean?' Katorn growled. '*Say*? You speak as if you do not believe our king.'

'I am not questioning the truth of your statements,' I told him. 'I wish to know the exact terms in which the Eldren justify their war against us. It would help if I had a clearer idea of their ambitions.'

Katorn shrugged. 'They would wipe us out,' he said. 'Is that not enough to know?'

'No,' I said. 'You must have taken prisoners. What do the prisoners tell you?' I spread my hands. 'How have the Eldren leaders justified their war against Humanity?'

King Rigenos smiled patronisingly. 'You have forgotten a great deal, Erekosë, if you have forgotten the Eldren. They are not human. They are clever. They are cold and they have smooth, deceitful tongues with which they would lull a man into a false sense of tranquillity before tearing his heart from his body with their bare fangs. They are brave, though, I'll give them that. Under torture they die, refusing to tell us their true plans. They are cunning. They try to make us believe their talk of peace, of mutual trust and mutual help, hoping that we will drop our defences long enough so that they may turn and destroy us, or get us to look them full in the face so that they can work the evil eye upon us. Do not be naïve, Erekosë. Do not attempt to deal with an Eldren as you would deal with a human being, for if you did so, you would be doomed. They have no souls, as we understand souls. They have no love, save a cold loyalty to their cause and to their master Azmobaana. Realise this, Erekosë – the Eldren are demons. They are fiends to whom Azmobaana in his dreadful blasphemy has granted something like a human form. But you must not be blinded by the form. That which is inside an Eldren is *not* human – it is everything, in fact, that is unhuman.'

Katorn's face twisted.

'You cannot trust an Eldren wolf. They are treacherous, immoral and evil. We shall not be safe until their whole race is destroyed. Utterly destroyed – so that not a fragment of their flesh, not a droplet of their blood, not a splinter of their bone, not a strand of their hair is left to taint the Earth. And I speak literally, Erekosë, for whilst one finger-clipping of an Eldren survives upon our world, then there is the chance that Azmobaana can re-create his servants and attack us again. That demon brood must be burned to the finest ash – every man, every female and every youngling. Burned – then cast to the winds, the clean winds. That is our mission, Erekosë, the mission of Humanity. And we have the Good One's blessing for that mission.'

Then I heard another voice, a sweeter voice, and I glanced towards the door. It was Iolinda.

'You must lead us to victory, Erekosë,' she said candidly. 'What Katorn says is true – no matter how fiercely he declaims it. The facts are as he tells you. You must lead us to victory.'

I looked again into her eyes. I drew a deep breath and my face felt hard and cold.

'I will lead you,' I said.

Chapter Four
Iolinda

THE NEXT MORNING I awoke to the sounds of the slaves preparing my breakfast. Or was it the slaves? Was it not my wife moving about the room, getting ready to wake up the boy as she did every morning?

I opened my eyes expecting to see her.

I did not see her. Nor did I see my room in my apartment where I had lived as John Daker.

Nor did I see slaves.

Instead, I saw Iolinda. She was smiling down at me as she prepared the breakfast with her own hands.

I felt guilty for a moment, as if I had betrayed my wife in some obscure way. Then I realised that there was nothing I could be ashamed of. I was the victim of Fate – of forces which I could not hope to understand. I was not John Daker. I was Erekosë. I realised that it would be the best for me if I were to insist on that. A man divided between two identities is a sick man. I resolved to forget John Daker as soon as possible. Since I was Erekosë now, I should concentrate on being Erekosë only. In that I was a fatalist.

Iolinda brought a bowl of fruit towards me. 'Would you eat, Lord Erekosë?'

I selected a strange, soft fruit with a reddish yellow skin. She handed me a small knife. I tried to peel it, but since the fruit was new to me, I was not sure how to begin. She gently took it from me and began to peel it for me, sitting on the edge of my low bed and concentrating rather excessively, in my opinion, on the fruit she held.

At last the fruit was peeled and she quartered it and placed it on a plate and handed the plate to me, still avoiding my direct gaze, but smiling a little mysteriously as she looked about her. I picked up a piece of the fruit and bit it. It was sharp and sweet at the same time and very refreshing.

'Thank you,' I said. 'It is good. I have never had this fruit before.'

'Have you not?' She was genuinely surprised. 'But the *ecrex* is the commonest fruit in Necralala.'

'You forget I am a stranger to Necralala,' I pointed out.

She put her head on one side and looked at me with a slight frown. She pushed back the flimsy blue cloth that covered her golden hair and made a great play of arranging her matching blue gown. She really did seem to be puzzled. 'A stranger...' she murmured.

'A stranger,' I agreed.

'But –' she paused – 'but you are the great hero of Humanity, Lord Erekosë. You knew Necranal as it was in its greatest glory – when you ruled here as the Champion. You knew Earth in ancient times, when you set it free from the chains the Eldren had bound around it. You know more of this world than I do, Erekosë.'

I shrugged. 'I admit that much of it is familiar – and growing increasingly familiar. But until yesterday my name was John Daker and I lived in a city very different from Necranal and my occupation was not that of warrior or, indeed, anything like it. I do not deny that I am Erekosë – the name is familiar and I am comfortable with it. But I do not know *who* Erekosë was, any more than do you. He was a great hero of ancient times who, before he died, swore that he would return to decide the issue between Eldren and Humanity if he were needed. He was placed in a rather gloomy tomb on a hillside along with his sword, which only he could wield.'

'The sword Kanajana,' murmured Iolinda.

'It has a name, then?'

'Aye – Kanajana. It – it is more than a name, I believe. It is some sort of mystic description – a description of its exact nature – of the powers it contains.'

'And is there any legend that explains why only I can bear that blade?' I asked her.

'There are several,' she said.

'Which do you prefer?' I smiled.

Then, for the first time that morning, she looked directly at me and her voice lowered and she said: 'I prefer the one that says that you are the chosen son of the Good One, the Great One – that your sword is a sword of the gods and that you can handle it because you are a god – an Immortal.'

I laughed. 'You do not believe that?'

She dropped her gaze. 'If you tell me that it is not true, then I must believe you,' she said. 'Of course.'

'I admit that I feel extremely healthy,' I told her. 'But that is a long way from feeling as a god must feel! Besides, I think I would know if I were a god. I would know other gods. I would dwell in some plane where the gods dwell. I would count goddesses amongst my friends.' I stopped. She seemed disturbed.

I reached out and touched her and said softly: 'But then perhaps you are right. Perhaps I am a god – for I am certainly privileged to know a goddess.'

She shrugged off my hand. 'You are making mock of me, my lord.'

'No. I swear it.'

She got up. 'I must appear foolish to such a great lord as yourself. I apologise for wasting your time with my chatter.'

'You have not wasted my time,' I said. 'You have helped me, in fact.'

Her lips parted. 'Helped you?'

'Yes. You have filled in part of my somewhat peculiar background. I still do not remember my past as Erekosë, but at least I know as much about that past as anyone here. Which is not a disadvantage!'

'Perhaps your centuries-long sleep has washed your mind free of memory,' she said.

'Perhaps,' I agreed. 'Or perhaps there have been so many other memories during that sleep – new experiences, other lives.'

'What do you mean?'

'Well, it seems to me that I have been more people than just John Daker and Erekosë. Other names spring to mind – strange names in unfamiliar tongues. I have a vague – and perhaps stupid – notion that while I slept as Erekosë, my spirit took on other shapes and names. Some in the future, some in the past, some – elsewhere...' I could not explain, but added lamely: 'Perhaps that spirit cannot sleep, but must forever be active.' I stopped. I was getting deep into the realms of metaphysics – and I had never possessed any great predilection for metaphysics. I considered myself a pragmatist, in fact. Such notions as reincarnation I had always scoffed at – still scoffed at, really, in spite of the evidence, such as it was.

But Iolinda pressed me to continue what I considered to be pointless speculation. 'Go on,' she said. 'Please continue, Lord Erekosë.'

If only to keep the beautiful girl beside me for a short while longer, I did as she asked.

'Well,' I said, 'while you and your father were attempting to bring me here, I thought I remembered other lives than this one as Erekosë or the other one, as John Daker. I remembered, very dimly, other civilisations – though I could not tell you whether they existed in the past or in the future. In fact, the idea of past and future seems meaningless to me now. I have no idea, for instance, whether this civilisation lies in the "future" that I know as John Daker or in the "past". It is here. I am here. Perhaps there is only ever "the present"? There are certain things that I will have to do. That is all I can say.'

'But these other incarnations,' she said. 'What do you know of them?'

I shrugged. 'Nothing. I am attempting to describe a dim feeling, not an exact impression. A few names which I have now forgotten. A few images which have almost completely faded away as dreams fade. And perhaps that is all they ever were – just dreams. Perhaps my life as John Daker, which in its turn is beginning to fade in my memory, was merely that, a dream. Certainly

I know nothing of any supernatural agencies of whom your father and Katorn have spoken. I know of no "Azmobaana", no Good and Great One, no demons or, indeed, angels. I know only that I am a man and that I exist.'

Her face was grave. 'That is true. You are a man. You exist. I saw you materialise.'

'But from where did I come?'

'From the Other Regions,' she said. 'From the place where all great warriors go when they die, and where their women go to join them, to live in eternal happiness.'

Again I smiled, but then smothered the smile for I did not wish to offend her beliefs. 'I remember no such place,' I said. 'I remember only strife. If I have been away from here, it was not in some land of eternal happiness – it was in many lands, lands of eternal warfare.'

Suddenly I felt depressed and weary. 'Eternal warfare,' I repeated and I sighed.

Her look became sympathetic. 'Do you think that this is your fate – to war for ever against the enemies of Humanity?'

I frowned. 'Not quite, for I seem to remember times when I was not human as you would understand the word. If I have a spirit, as I said, that inhabits many forms, then there have been times when it has inhabited forms that were – different.' I rejected the thought. It was too difficult to grasp, too frightening to tolerate.

It disturbed Iolinda. She rose and darted a look of incomprehension at me. 'Not – not as an...'

I smiled. 'An Eldren? I do not know. But I do not think so, for the name is not familiar to me in that respect.'

She was relieved. 'It is so hard to trust...' she said sadly.

'To trust what? Words?'

'To trust anything,' she said. 'I once thought I understood the world. Perhaps I was too young. Now I understand nothing. I do not know whether I shall even be alive next year.'

'I think that may be described as a common fear to all we mortals,' I said gently.

'"We mortals"?' Her smile was without humour. 'You are not mortal, Erekosë!'

I had not up to now considered it. After all, I had been summoned into existence in thin air! I laughed. 'We shall soon know whether I am or not,' I said, 'when we have joined battle with the Eldren!'

A little moan escaped her lips then. 'Oh!' she cried. 'Do not consider it!' She moved towards the door. 'You *are* immortal, Erekosë! You *are* invulnerable! You *are* – eternal! You are the only thing of which I can be sure, the only person I can trust! Do not joke so! Do not joke so, I beg you!'

I was astonished at this outburst. I would have risen from the bed to hold her and comfort her, but I was naked. Admittedly she had seen me naked once before, when I had originally materialised in Erekosë's tomb, but I did not know enough of the customs of these people to guess whether it would shock her or not.

'Forgive me, Iolinda,' I said. 'I did not realise…'

What had I not realised? The extent of the poor girl's insecurity? Or something deeper than that?

'Do not go,' I begged.

She stopped by the door and turned, and there were tears in her huge, wide eyes. 'You are eternal, Erekosë. You are immortal. You can never die!'

I could not reply.

For all I knew I would be dead in the first encounter with the Eldren.

Suddenly I became aware of the responsibility I had tacitly agreed to assume – a responsibility not just to this beautiful woman but to the whole human race. I swallowed hard and fell back on my pillows as Iolinda rushed from the room.

Could I possibly bear such a burden?

Did I wish to bear such a burden?

I did not. I had no great faith in my own powers and there was no reason to believe that those powers were any more potent than, say, Katorn's. Katorn was, after all, far more experienced in warfare than I. He had a right to be resentful of me. I had taken over his rôle, robbed him of his power and of a responsibility which he had been prepared to shoulder – and I was unproven. Suddenly I saw Katorn's point of view and sympathised with it.

What right had I to lead Humanity in a war that could decide its very existence?

None.

And then another thought came to me – a more self-pitying thought.

What right had Humanity to expect so much of me?

They had, let us say, awakened me from a slumber which I had earned, leading the quiet, decent life of John Daker. And now they were imposing their will upon me, demanding that I give back to them the self-confidence and – yes – self-righteousness that they were losing.

I lay there in the bed and for a while I hated King Rigenos, Katorn and the rest of the human race – including the fair Iolinda, who had been the one to bring this question to my mind.

Erekosë the Champion, Defender of Humanity, Greatest of Warriors, lay wretched and snivelling in his bed and felt very sorry for himself indeed.

Chapter Five
Katorn

I AROSE AT last and dressed myself in a simple tunic, having been washed and shaved – much to my embarrassment – by my slaves. I went by myself into the weapons rooms and there took down my sword from where it hung in its scabbard on a peg.

I unsheathed the blade and again a sort of exultation filled me. Immediately I forgot my qualms and scruples and laughed as the sword whistled around my head and my muscles flexed with the weight of it.

I feinted with the sword and it seemed that it was part of my very body, that it was another limb whose presence I had been unaware of until now. I thrust it out at full reach, pulled it back, swung it down. It filled me with joy to wield it!

It made me into something greater than I had ever felt I was before. It made me into a man. A warrior. A champion.

And yet, as John Daker, I had handled swords perhaps twice in my life – and handled them most clumsily, according to those friends of mine who had considered themselves experts.

At last I reluctantly sheathed the sword as I saw a slave hovering some distance away. I remembered that only I, Erekosë, could hold the sword and live.

'What is it?' I said.

'The Lord Katorn, master. He would speak with you.' I put my sword back on its peg. 'Bid him enter,' I told the slave.

Katorn came in rapidly. He appeared to have been waiting some time and was in no better a mood than when I had first encountered him. His boots, which seemed to be shod with metal, clattered on the flagstones of the weapons room.

'Good morning to you, Lord Erekosë,' he said.

I bowed. 'Good morning, Lord Katorn. I apologise if you were made to wait. I was trying out that sword.'

'The sword Kanajana.' Katorn looked at it speculatively.

'The sword Kanajana,' I said. 'Would you have some refreshment, Lord Katorn?' I was making a great effort to please him, not only because it would not do to have so experienced a warrior as an enemy when plans of battle were being prepared, but because I had, as I said, come to sympathise with his situation.

But Katorn refused to be mollified. 'I broke my fast at dawn,' he said. 'I have come to discuss more pressing matters than eating, Lord Erekosë.'

'And what are those?' Manfully I restrained my own temper.

'Matters of war, Lord Erekosë. What else?'

'Indeed. And what specific matters would you wish to discuss with me, Lord Katorn?'

'It seems to me that we should attack the Eldren before they come against us.'

'Attack being the best form of defence, eh?

He looked surprised at this. He had plainly not heard the phrase before. 'Eloquently put, my lord. One would think you an Eldren yourself, with such a way with words.' He was deliberately trying my temper. But I swallowed the insinuation.

'So,' I said, 'we attack them. Where?'

'That is what we shall have to discuss with all those concerned in planning this war. But it seems there is one obvious point.'

'And that is?'

He wheeled and strode into another chamber, returning with a map which he spread on a bench. It was a map of Mernadin, the third continent, the one entirely controlled by the Eldren. With his dagger he stabbed at a spot I had seen indicated the night before.

'Paphanaal,' I said.

'While it is the logical point of an initial attack in a campaign of the sort we plan, it seems to me unlikely that the Eldren will expect us to make so bold a move, knowing that we are weary and under strength.'

'But if we are weary and weak,' I said, 'would it not seem a good idea to attack some less important city first?'

'You are forgetting, my lord, that our warriors have been heartened by your coming,' Katorn said dryly.

I could not help grinning at this cut. But Katorn scowled, angry that I had not taken offence.

I said quietly: 'We must learn to work together, my lord Katorn. I bow to your great experience as a warrior leader. I acknowledge that you have had much more recent knowledge of the Eldren than have I. I need your help surely as much as King Rigenos believes he needs mine.'

Katorn seemed slightly comforted by this. He cleared his throat and continued.

'Once Paphanaal, province *and* city, are taken, we shall have a beachhead from which other attacks inland can be made. With Paphanaal again in our hands, we can decide our own strategy – initiate action rather than react to the Eldren's strategy. Only once we have pushed them back into the mountains will we have the wearying task of clearing them all out. It will take years. But it is what we should have done in the first place. That, however, will be a matter for ordinary military administration and will not concern us directly.'

'And what kind of defences has Paphanaal?' I asked.

Katorn smiled. 'She relies almost entirely on her warships. If we can destroy her fleet, then Paphanaal is as good as taken.' He bared his teeth in what I gathered was a grin. And he looked at me, his expression changing to one of sudden suspicion, as if he had revealed too much to me.

I could not ignore the expression. 'What is on your mind, Lord Katorn?' I asked. 'Do you not trust me?'

He controlled his features. 'I must trust you,' he said flatly. 'We all must trust you, Lord Erekosë. Have you not returned to fulfil your ancient promise?'

I gazed searchingly into his face. 'Do you believe that?'

'I must believe it.'

'Do you believe that I am Erekosë the Champion returned?'

'I must believe that also.'

'You believe it because you surmise that, if I am not Erekosë – the Erekosë of the legends – then Humanity is doomed?'

He lowered his head as if in assent.

'And what if I am not Erekosë, my lord?'

Katorn looked up. 'You must be Erekosë – my lord. If it were not for one thing, I would suspect...'

'What would you suspect?'

'Nothing.'

'You would suspect that I were an Eldren in disguise. Is that it, Lord Katorn? Some cunning unhuman who had assumed the outer appearance of a man? Do I read your thoughts correctly, my lord?'

'Too correctly.' Katorn's thick brows came together and his mouth was thin and white. 'The Eldren are said to have the power to probe minds. But human beings do not possess that power.'

'And are you, then, afraid, Lord Katorn?'

'Of an Eldren? By the Good One, I'll show you...' and Katorn's heavy hand rushed to the hilt of his sword.

I raised my own hand and then pointed at the sword that hung sheathed on the peg on the wall. 'But that is the one fact that does not fit your theory, isn't it? If I am not Erekosë, then how is it that I can handle Erekosë's blade?'

He did not draw his sword, but his grip remained on the hilt.

'It is true, is it not, that no living creature – human or Eldren – can touch that blade and live?' I said quietly.

'That is the legend,' he agreed.

'Legend?'

'I have never seen an Eldren try to handle the sword Kanajana.'

'But you must assume that it is true. Otherwise...'

'Otherwise, there is little hope for Humanity.' The words were dragged from his lips.

'Very well, Lord Katorn. You will assume that I am Erekosë, summoned by King Rigenos to lead Humanity to victory.'

'I have no choice but to assume that.'

'Good. And there is something that I, too, must assume, for my part, Lord Katorn.'

'You? What?'

'I must assume that you will work *with* me in this enterprise. That there will be no plots behind my back, that there will be no information withheld from me that might prove vital, that you will not seek to make allies against me within our own ranks. You see, Lord Katorn, it could be your suspicions that might wreck our plans. A man jealous and resentful of his leader is capable of doing more harm than any enemy.'

He nodded his head and straightened his shoulders, the hand falling away from his sword. 'I had considered that question, my lord. I am not a fool.'

'I know you are not a fool, Lord Katorn. If you were a fool, I should not have bothered to have had this conversation.'

His tongue bulged in his cheek as he mulled over this statement. Eventually he said: 'And you are not a fool, Lord Erekosë.'

'Thank you. I did not suspect that you judge me that.'

'Hmph.' He removed his helmet and ran his fingers through his thick hair. He was still thinking.

I waited for him to say something further, but then he replaced his helmet firmly on his head, dug his thumb into the side of his mouth and picked at a tooth with the nail. He withdrew the thumb and stared at it intently for a moment. Then he looked at the map and murmured, 'Well, at least we have an understanding. With that, it will be easier to fight this stinking war.'

I nodded. 'Much easier, I think.'

He sniffed.

'How good is our own fleet?' I asked him.

'It's a fine fleet still. Not as large as it was, but we are remedying that, too. Our shipyards work night and day to build more and larger men-o'-war. And in our ironworks up and down the land we forge powerful guns with which to arm those ships.'

'And what of men to crew them?'

'We are recruiting all we can. Even women are used in certain tasks – and boys. You were told that, Lord Erekosë, and it was true – the *whole* of Humanity fights the Eldren warriors.'

I said nothing, but I had begun to admire the spirit of this people. I was less divided in my mind concerning the rights or wrongs of what I did. The folk of this strange time and place in which I found myself were fighting for nothing more nor less than the survival of their species.

But then another thought came to me. Could not the same be said of the Eldren?

I dismissed the thought.

At least Katorn and I had that in common. We refused to concern ourselves with speculation on moral and sentimental issues. We had a task to perform. We had assumed the responsibility for that task. We should do it to the best of our ability.

Chapter Six

Preparing for War

A<small>ND SO</small> I talked with generals and with admirals. We pored over maps and discussed tactics, logistics, available men, animals and ships, while the fleets massed and the Two Continents were scoured for warriors, from boys of ten years old to men of fifty or older, from girls of twelve to women of sixty. All were marshalled beneath the double banner of Humanity which bore the arms of Zavara and Necralala and the standards of their king, Rigenos, and their war champion, Erekosë.

As the days passed, we planned the great land–sea invasion of Mernadin's chief harbour, Paphanaal, and the surrounding province, which was also called Paphanaal.

When not conferring with the commanders of the armies and navies, I practised weaponry, riding, until I became skilled in those arts.

It was not a question of *learning* so much as *remembering*. Just as the feel of my strange sword had been familiar, so was the sensation of a horse between my legs. Just as I had always known my name was Erekosë (which, I had been told, meant 'The One Who Is Always There' in some ancient tongue of Humanity which was no longer used) so I had always known how to pull an arrow on a bowstring and let fly at a target as I galloped past on horseback.

But Iolinda – she was not familiar to me. Though there was some part of me that seemed able to travel through Time and Space and assume many incarnations, they were plainly not the same incarnations. I was not living an episode of my life over again, I had merely become the same person again, going through a different series of actions, or so it seemed. I had a sense of free will, within those terms. I did not feel that my fate was preordained.

But perhaps it was. Perhaps I am too much of an optimist. Perhaps I am, after all, a fool and Katorn was wrong in his assessment of me. The Eternal Fool.

Certainly I was willing to make a fool of myself where Iolinda was concerned. Her beauty was almost unbearable. But with her I could not be a fool. She wanted a hero, an Immortal – and nothing less. So I must play the hero for her, to comfort her, though it went ill with my preferred manner, which has always been pretty casual. Sometimes, in fact, I felt more like her father than her would-be lover and, with my pat twentieth-century notions of human motivation, wondered if I were really nothing more than a substitute for the strong father she expected in Rigenos.

I think that she secretly despised Rigenos for not being more heroic, but I sympathised with the older man (older? I think it is I who am older, infinitely older – but enough of that) for Rigenos bore a great responsibility and bore it pretty well as far as I could make out. After all, he was a man who would rather plan pleasant gardens than battles. It was not his fault that he had been born a king without a close male successor to whom he could have, if he had been luckier, transferred responsibility. And I had heard that he bore himself well in battle and never backed away from any responsibility. King Rigenos was meant for a gentler life, maybe – though he could be fierce enough when it came to hating the Eldren. I was to be the hero that he felt incapable of being. I accepted that. But I was much more reluctant to be the father that he could not be. I wanted to enjoy a much healthier relationship with Iolinda or, so I told myself, I would not enjoy one at all!

I am not sure I had a choice. I was mesmerised by her. I would probably have accepted her on any terms.

We spent whatever time we could together, whenever I could get away from the military men and my own martial training. We would wander arm in arm along the closed balconies which covered the Palace of Ten Thousand Windows like a creeping plant, winding from top to bottom of the great palace and containing a superb variety of flowers, shrubs and caged and uncaged birds that fluttered through the foliage of these spiralling passages and perched amongst the branches of the vines and the small trees and sang to us as we wandered. I learned that this, too, had been King Rigenos's idea, to make the balconies more pleasant.

But that had been before the coming of the Eldren.

Slowly the day approached when the fleet would gather together and sail for the distant continent where the Eldren ruled. I had begun by being impatient to get to grips with the Eldren, but now I was becoming more and more reluctant to leave – for it would mean leaving Iolinda and my lust for her was growing quite as strongly as my love.

Although I gathered that day by day the society of humankind was becoming less and less open, more and more bound by unpleasant and unnecessary restrictions, it was still not considered wrong for unwed lovers to sleep together, so long as they were of an equal social standing. I was much relieved when I discovered this. It seemed to me that an Immortal – as I was assumed to be – and a princess were quite decently matched. But it was not the social conventions that hampered my ambition – it was Iolinda herself. And that is one thing that no amount of freedom or 'licence' or 'permissiveness' or whatever the old fogies call it can cope with. That is the odd assumption found in the twentieth century (I wonder if you who read this will know what those two stupid words mean?): that if the laws that man makes concerning 'morality' – particularly sexual morality – are done away with, then one huge orgy will begin. It forgets that people are, generally speaking, only attracted to a few other people and only fall in love with one or two in their whole lives. And there may be many other reasons why they may not be able to make love, even if their love is confirmed.

Where Iolinda was concerned, I hesitated because, as I have said, I did not wish to be merely a substitute for her father – and she hesitated because she needed to be absolutely sure she could 'trust' me. John Daker would have called this a neurotic attitude.

Perhaps it was, but on the other hand, was it neurotic for a relatively normal girl to feel a bit peculiar about someone she had only lately seen materialise from thin air?

But enough of this. All I should say is that, although we were both deeply in love at this point, we did not sleep together – we did not even discuss the matter, though it was often on the tip of my tongue.

What, in fact, began to happen was, oddly, that my lust began to wane. My love for Iolinda remained as strong as ever – if not stronger – but I did not feel any great need to express it in physical terms. It was not like me. Or perhaps I should say that it was not like John Daker!

However, as the day of departure came closer, I began to feel a need to express my love in some way and, one evening as we wandered through the balconies, I paused and put my hand under her hair and stroked the back of her neck and gently turned her to face me.

She looked sweetly up at me and smiled. Her red lips parted slightly and she did not move her head as I bent my own lips to hers and kissed her softly. My heart leaped. I held her close against me, feeling her breasts rise and fall against my chest. I lifted her hand and held it against my face as I looked down at her beauty. I thrust my hand deep into her hair and tasted her warm, sweet breath as we kissed again. She curled her fingers in mine and opened her eyes and her eyes were happy – truly happy for the first time. We drew apart.

Her breathing was now much less regular and she began to murmur something, but I cut her off short. She smiled at me expectantly, with a mixture of pride and tenderness.

'When I return,' I said softly, 'we shall be married.'

She looked surprised for a moment and then she realised what I had said – the significance of what I had said. I was trying to tell her that she could trust me. It was the only way I could think of to do it. Perhaps a John Daker reflex, I don't know.

She nodded her head, drawing off her hand a wonderfully

worked ring of gold, pearls and rose-coloured diamonds. This she placed on my little finger.

'A token of my love,' she said. 'An acceptance of your proposal. A charm, perhaps, to bring you luck in your battles. Something to remind you of me when you are tempted by those unhuman Eldren beauties.' She smiled when she made this last retort.

'It has many functions,' I said, 'this ring.'

'As many as you wish,' she replied.

'Thank you.'

'I love you, Erekosë,' she said simply.

'I love you, Iolinda.' I paused, then added, 'But I am a crude sort of lover, am I not? I have no token to give you. I feel embarrassed and a bit inadequate.'

'Your word is enough,' she said. 'Swear that you will return to me.'

I looked at her nonplussed for a second. Naturally I would return to her.

'Swear it,' she said.

'I'll swear it. There is no question.'

'Swear it again.'

'I'll swear it a thousand times if once is not enough. I swear it. I swear that I will return to you, Iolinda, my love, my delight.'

'Good.' She seemed satisfied.

There came the sound of hurried footsteps along the balcony and we saw a slave I recognised as one of my own rushing towards us.

'Ah, master, there you are. King Rigenos has asked me to bring you to him.'

It was late. 'And what does King Rigenos want?' I asked.

'He did not say, master.'

I smiled down at Iolinda and tucked her arm in mine. 'Very well. We shall come.'

Chapter Seven
The Armour of Erekosë

THE SLAVE LED us to my own apartments. They were empty of anyone save my retinue.

'But where is King Rigenos?' I asked.

'He said to wait here, master.'

I smiled at Iolinda again. She smiled back. 'Very well,' I said. 'We shall wait.'

We did not wait long. Presently slaves began to arrive at my apartments. They were carrying bulky pieces of metal wrapped in oiled parchment and they began to pile it in the weapons room. I watched them with as little expression as possible, though I was greatly puzzled.

Then at last King Rigenos entered. He seemed much more excited than usual and Katorn was not, this time, with him.

'Greetings, Father,' said Iolinda. 'I…'

But King Rigenos raised a hand and turned to address the slaves. 'Strip off the coverings,' he said. 'Hurry.'

'King Rigenos,' I said. 'I would like to tell you that…'

'Forgive me, Lord Erekosë. First, look at what I have brought. It has lain for centuries in the vaults of the palace. Waiting, Erekosë – waiting for you!'

'Waiting?'

Then the oiled parchment was torn away and lay in curling heaps on the flagstones, revealing what was to me a magnificent sight.

'This,' said the king, 'is the armour of Erekosë. Broken from its tomb of rock deep beneath the palace's lowest dungeons so that Erekosë can wear it again.'

The armour was black and it shone. It was as if it had been

forged that day and forged by the greatest smith in history, for it
was of exquisite workmanship.

I picked up the breastplate and ran my hand over it.

Unlike the armour worn by the Imperial Guard, this was smooth,
without any kind of raised embellishment. The shoulder pieces
were grooved, fanning high and away from the head, to channel a
blow of sword, axe or lance from the wearer. The helmet, breastplate, greaves and the rest were all grooved in the same manner.

The metal was light, but very strong, like that of the sword.
But the black lacquer shone. It shone brightly – almost blindingly.
In its simplicity, the armour *was* beautiful – as beautiful as only
really fine craftsmanship can be. Its sole ornament was a thick
plume of scarlet horsehair which sprang from the crest of the helmet and cascaded down the smooth sides. I touched the armour
with the reverence one has for fine art. In this case it was fine art
designed to protect my life and my reverence was, if anything,
that much greater!

'Thank you, King Rigenos,' I said, and I was honestly grateful.
'I will wear it on the day we set sail against the Eldren.'

'That day is tomorrow,' said King Rigenos quietly.

'What?'

'The last of our ships has come in. The last member of the
crew is on board. The last cannon has been fitted. It will be a good
tide tomorrow and we cannot miss it.'

I glanced at him. Had I been misled in some way? Had Katorn
prevailed upon the king not to let me know the exact time of sailing? But the king's expression showed no sign of a plot. I dismissed
the idea and accepted what he said. I turned my gaze to Iolinda.
She looked stricken.

'Tomorrow,' she said.

'Tomorrow,' confirmed King Rigenos.

I bit my lower lip. 'Then I must prepare.'

She said: 'Father...'

He looked at her. 'Yes, Iolinda?'

I began to speak and then paused. She glanced at me and was

also silent. There was no easy way of telling him and suddenly it was as if we should keep our love, our pact, a secret. Neither of us knew why.

Tactfully the king withdrew. 'I will discuss last-minute matters with you later, Lord Erekosë.'

I bowed. He left.

Somewhat stunned, Iolinda and I stared at each other and then we moved into each other's arms and we wept.

John Daker would not have written this. He would have laughed at the sentiments, just as he would have scoffed at anyone who considered the arts of war important. John Daker would not have written this, but I must:

I began to feel a rising sense of excitement for the coming war. The old exultant mood started to sweep through me again. Overlaying my excitement was my love for Iolinda. This love seemed to be a calmer, purer love, so much more satisfying than casual, carnal love. It was a thing apart. Perhaps this was the chivalrous love which the peers of Christendom are said to have held above all other.

John Daker would have spoken of sexual repression and of swordplay as a substitute for sexual intercourse.

Perhaps John Daker would have been right. But it did not seem to me that he was right, though I was well aware of all the rationalist arguments that supported such a view. There is a great tendency for the human race to see all other times in its own terms. The terms of this society were subtly different – I was only dimly aware of many of the differences. I was responding to Iolinda in those terms. It is all I can say. And later events, I suppose, were also played out in those terms.

I took Iolinda's face in my two hands and I bent and I kissed her forehead and she kissed my lips and then she left.

'Shall I see you before I leave?' I asked as she reached the door.

'Yes,' she said. 'Yes, my love, if it is possible.'

When she had gone, I did not feel sad. I inspected the armour once again and then I went down to the main hall, where King

Rigenos stood with many of his greatest captains, studying a large map of Mernadin and the waters between it and Necralala.

'We start here in the morning,' Rigenos told me, indicating the harbour area of Necranal. The River Droonaa flowed through Necranal to the sea and the port of Noonos, where the fleet was assembled. 'There must be a certain amount of ceremony, I fear, Erekosë. Various rituals to perform. I have already sketched them to you, I believe.'

'You have,' I said. 'The ceremony seems more arduous than the warfare.'

The captains laughed. Though somewhat distant and a trifle wary of me, they liked me well enough, for I had proved (to my own astonishment) to have a natural grasp of tactics and the war-like arts.

'But the ceremony is necessary,' Rigenos said, 'for the people. It makes a reality for them, you see. They can experience something of what we shall be doing.'

'We?' I said. 'Am I wrong? I thought you implied that you were sailing, too.'

'I am,' Rigenos said quietly. 'I decided that it was necessary.'

'Necessary?'

'Yes.' He would say no more, particularly in front of his marshals. 'Now, let us continue. We must all of us rise very early tomorrow morning.'

As we discussed these final matters of order and tactics and logistics, I studied the king's face as best I could.

No-one expected him to sail with his armies. He would lose no face at all by remaining behind in his capital. Yet he had made a decision which would put him in a position of extreme danger and cause him to take actions for which he had no palate.

Why had he made the decision? To prove to himself that he could fight, perhaps? Yet he had proved it already. Because he was jealous of me? Because he did not altogether trust me? I glanced at Katorn, but saw nothing in Katorn's face to indicate satisfaction. Katorn was merely his usual surly self.

Mentally I shrugged. Speculation at this point would get me nowhere. The fact was that the king, not an altogether robust man now, was coming with us. It might give extra inspiration to our warriors, at least. It might also help control Katorn's particular tendencies.

Eventually we dispersed and went our ways. I went straight to my bed and, before I slept, lay there peacefully, thinking of Iolinda, thinking of the battle plans I had helped hatch, wondering what the Eldren would be like to fight – I still had no completely clear idea of how they fought (save 'treacherously and ferociously') or even what they looked like (save that they resembled 'demons from the deepest pits').

I knew I would soon have some of the answers, at any rate. Soon I was asleep.

My dreams were strange dreams on that night before we sailed for Mernadin.

I saw towers and marshes and lakes and armies and lances that shot flames and metallic flying machines whose wings flapped like those of gigantic birds. I saw monstrously large flamingoes, strange masklike helmets resembling the faces of beasts.

I saw dragons – huge reptiles with fiery venom, flapping across dark, moody skies. I saw a beautiful city tumbling in flames. I saw unhuman creatures that I knew to be gods. I saw a woman whom I could not name, a small red-headed man who seemed to be my friend. A sword – a great, black sword more powerful than the one I now owned – a sword that perhaps, oddly, was myself!

I saw a world of ice across which strange, great ships with billowing sails ran and black beasts like whales propelled themselves over endless plateaux of white.

I saw a world – or was it a universe? – that had no horizon and was filled with a rich, jewelled mosaic atmosphere which changed all the time and from which people and objects emerged only to disappear again. It was somewhere beyond the Earth, I was sure. Yes – I was aboard a spaceship – but a ship that travelled through no universe conceived of by Man.

I saw a desert through which I stumbled weeping and I was alone – lonelier than any man had ever been.

I saw a jungle – a jungle of primitive trees and gigantic ferns. And through the ferns I saw huge, bizarre buildings and there was a weapon in my hand that was not a sword and was not a gun, but it was more powerful than either.

I rode strange beasts and encountered stranger people. I moved through landscapes that were beautiful and terrifying. I piloted flying machines and spaceships and I drove chariots. I hated. I fell in love. I built empires and caused the collapse of nations and I slew many and was slain many times. I triumphed and was humiliated. And I had many names. The names roared in my skull. Too many names. Too many...

And there was no peace. There was only strife.

Chapter Eight
The Sailing

NEXT MORNING I awoke and my dreams went away and I was left in an introspective mood and there was only one thing that I desired.

That thing was an Upmann's Coronas Major cigar.

I kept trying to push the name from my mind. To my knowledge John Daker had never smoked an Upmann's. He would not have known one cigar from another! Where had the name come from? Another name came into my head – Jeremiah. And that, too, was vaguely familiar.

I sat up in bed and I recognised my surroundings and the two names merged with the other names I had dreamed of and I got up and entered the next chamber where slaves were finishing preparing my bath. With relief I got into the bath and, as I washed my body, I began to concentrate once again on the problem at hand. Yet a sense of depression remained with me and again for a moment I wondered if I were mad and involved in some complicated schizophrenic fantasy.

When the slaves brought in my armour I began to feel much better. Again I marvelled at its beauty and its craftsmanship.

And now the time had come to put it on. First I donned my underclothes, then a sort of quilted overall and then I began to strap the armour about me. Again it was easy to find the appropriate straps and buckles. It was as if I had clad myself in this armour every morning of my life. It fitted perfectly. It was comfortable and no weight at all, though it completely covered my body.

Next, I strode to the weapons room and took down the great sword that hung there and I drew the belt of metal links around my waist and settled the poisonous sword in its protecting scabbard against my left hip, tossed back the scarlet plume on my helmet, lifted the visor and was ready.

Slaves escorted me down to the Great Hall, where the peers of Humanity had assembled to make their final leave-taking with Necranal.

The tapestries which had earlier hung on the walls of beaten silver had now been removed and in their place were hundreds of bright banners. These were the banners of the marshals, the captains and the knights, who were gathered there in splendid array, assembled according to rank.

On a specially erected dais the throne of the king had been placed. The dais was hung with a cloth of emerald green and behind it were the twin banners of the Two Continents. I took my place before the dais and we waited tensely for the arrival of the king. I had already been coached concerning the responses I was to make in the forthcoming ceremony.

At last there came a great yelling of trumpets and beating of martial drums from the gallery above us and through a door came the king.

King Rigenos had gained stature, it seemed, for he wore a suit of gilded armour over which was hung a surcoat of white and red. Set into his helmet was his crown of iron and diamonds. He walked proudly to the dais and ascended it, seating himself in his throne with both arms stretched along the arms of the seat.

We raised our hands in salute:

'Hail, King Rigenos!' we roared.

And then we kneeled. I kneeled first. Behind me kneeled the little group of marshals. Behind them were a hundred captains, behind them were five thousand knights, all kneeling. And surrounding us, along the walls, were the old nobles, the ladies of the Court, men-at-arms at attention, slaves and squires, the mayors of the various quarters of the city and from the various provinces of the Two Continents.

And all watched Rigenos and his champion, Erekosë.

King Rigenos rose from his throne. I looked up at him and his face was grave and stern. I had never before seen him look so much a king.

Now I felt that the attention of the watchers was on myself alone. I, Erekosë, Champion of Humanity, was to be their saviour. They knew it.

In my confidence and pride, I knew it, also.

King Rigenos raised his hands and spread them out and began to speak:

'Erekosë the Champion, Marshals, Captains and Knights of Humanity – we go to wage war against unhuman evil. We go to fight something that is more than an enemy bent on conquest. We go to fight a menace that would destroy our entire race. We go to save our two fair continents from total annihilation. The victor will rule the entire Earth. The defeated will become dust and will be forgotten – it will be as if he had never existed.

'This expedition upon which we are about to embark will be decisive. With Erekosë to lead us, we shall win the port of Paphanaal and its surrounding province. But that will only be the first stage in our campaigns.'

King Rigenos paused and then spoke again into the almost absolute silence that had fallen in the Great Hall.

'More battle must follow fast upon the first so that the hated Hounds of Evil will, once and for all, be destroyed. Men and women – even children – must perish. We drove them to their holes in the Mountains of Sorrow once, but this time we must not let their race survive. Let only their memory remain for a little while – to remind us what evil is!'

Still kneeling, I raised both my hands above my head and clenched my fists.

'Erekosë,' said King Rigenos. 'You who by the power of your eternal will made yourself into flesh again and came to us at this time of need, you will be the power with which we shall destroy the Eldren. You will be Humanity's scythe to sweep this way and that and cut the Eldren down as weeds. You will be Humanity's spade to dig up the roots wherever they have grown. You will be

Humanity's fire to burn the waste to the finest ash. You, Erekosë, will be the wind that will blow those ashes away as if they had never existed! You will destroy the Eldren!'

'I will destroy the Eldren!' I cried and my voice echoed through the Great Hall like the voice of a god. *'I will destroy the enemies of Humanity! With the sword Kanajana I will ride upon them with vengeance and hatred and cruelty in my heart and I will vanquish the Eldren!'*

From behind me now came a mighty shout:

'WE SHALL VANQUISH THE ELDREN!'

Now the king raised his head and his eyes glittered and his mouth was hard.

'Swear it!' he said.

We were intoxicated by the atmosphere of hate and rage in the Great Hall.

'We so swear!' we roared. *'We will destroy the Eldren!'*

Hatred seared from the king's eyes, trembled in his voice:

'Go now, Paladins of Mankind. Go – *destroy the Eldren offal. Clean our planet of the Eldren filth!'*

As one man, we rose to our feet and yelled our battle-cries, turned in precision and marched from the Great Hall, out of the Palace of Ten Thousand Windows and into a day noisy with the swelling cheers of the people.

But as we marched, one thought preyed on my mind. Where was Iolinda? Why had she not come to me? There had been so little time before the ceremony and yet I would have thought she would have sent a message at least.

Down the winding streets of Necranal we marched in glorious procession. Through the cheering day with the bright sun shining on our weapons and our armour and our flags of a thousand rich colours waving in the wind.

And I led them. I, Erekosë, the Eternal, the Champion, the Vengeance Bringer – I led them. My arms were raised as if I were already celebrating my victory. Pride filled me. I knew what glory was and I relished it. This was the way to live – as a warrior, a leader of great armies, a wielder of weapons.

On we marched, down towards the waiting ships which were ready on the river. And a song came to my lips – a song that was in an archaic version of the language I now spoke. I sang the song and it was taken up by all the warriors who marched behind me. Drums began to beat and trumpets to shout, and we cried aloud for blood and death and the great red reaping that would come to Mernadin.

That is how we marched. That is how we felt.

Do not judge me until I have told you more.

We reached the wide part of the river where the harbour was and there were the ships. There were fifty ships stretched along both quays on either side of the river. Fifty ships bearing the fifty standards of fifty proud paladins.

And these were only fifty. The fleet itself waited for us to join it at the port of Noonos. Noonos of the Jewelled Towers.

The people of Necranal lined the banks of the river. They were cheering, cheering – so that we became used to their voices as men become used to the sounds of the sea, scarcely hearing them.

I regarded the ships. Richly decorated cabins were built on the decks and the ships of the paladins had several masts bearing furled sails of painted canvas. Already oars were being slipped through the ports and dipped into the placid river waters. Strong men, three to a sweep, sat upon the rowing benches. These men were not, as far as I could see, slaves, but free warriors.

At the head of this squadron of ships lay the king's huge battle-barge – a magnificent man-o'-war. It had eighty pairs of oars and eight tall masts. Its rails were painted in red, gold and black, its decks were polished crimson, its sails were yellow, dark blue and orange and its huge carved figurehead, representing a goddess holding a sword in her two outstretched hands, was predominantly scarlet and silver. Ornate and splendid, the deck cabins shone with fresh varnish which had been laid over pictures of ancient human heroes (I was among them, though the likenesses were poor) and ancient human victories, of mythical beasts and demons and gods.

Detaching myself from the main force that had drawn itself up on the quayside, I walked to the tapestry-covered gangway and strode up it and boarded the ship. Sailors rushed forward to greet me.

One said: 'The Princess Iolinda awaits you in the Grand Cabin, excellency.'

I turned and then paused, looking at the splendid structure of the cabin, smiling slightly at the representations of myself painted upon it. Then I moved towards it and entered a comparatively low door into a room which was covered, floor, walls and ceiling, with thick tapestries in deep reds and blacks and golds. Lanterns hung in the room, and in the shadows, clad in a simple dress and a thin, dark cloak, stood my Iolinda.

'I did not wish to interrupt the preparations this morning,' she said. 'My father said that they were important – that there was little time to spare. So I thought you would not want to see me.'

I smiled. 'You still do not believe what I say, do you, Iolinda? You still do not trust me when I proclaim my love for you, when I tell you that I would do anything for you.' I went towards her and held her in my arms. 'I love you, Iolinda. I shall always love you.'

'And I shall always love you, Erekosë. You will live for ever, but…'

'There is no proof of that,' I said gently. 'And I am by no means invulnerable, Iolinda. I sustained enough cuts and bruises in my weapons practice to realise that!'

'You will not die, Erekosë.'

'I would be happier if I shared your conviction!'

'Do not laugh at me, Erekosë. I will not be patronised!'

'I am not laughing at you, Iolinda. I am not condescending to you. I only speak the truth. You must face that truth. You must.'

'Very well,' she said. 'I will face it. But I feel that you will not die. Yet, I have such strange premonitions – I feel that something worse than death could befall us.'

'Your fears are natural, but they are baseless. There is no need for gloom, my dear. Look at the fine armour I wear, the powerful sword I bear, the mighty force I command.'

'Kiss me, Erekosë.'

I kissed her. I kissed her for a long time and then she broke from my arms and ran to the door and was gone.

I stared at the door, half thinking of running after her, of reassuring her. But I knew that I could not reassure her. Her fears were not really rational – they reflected her constant sense of insecurity. I promised myself that later I would give her proof of security. I would bring constants into her life – things she could trust.

Trumpets sounded. King Rigenos was coming aboard.

A few moments later the king entered the cabin, tugging off his crowned helm. Katorn was behind him, as sullen as ever.

'The people seem enthusiastic,' I said. 'The ceremony seemed to have the effect you desired, King Rigenos.'

Rigenos nodded wearily. 'Aye.' The ritual had plainly taken much from him and he slumped into a hanging chair in the corner and called for wine. 'We'll be sailing soon. When, Katorn?'

'Within the quarter-hour, my lord king.' Katorn took the jug of wine from the slave who brought it and poured Rigenos a cup without offering one to me.

King Rigenos waved his hand. 'Would you have some wine, Lord Erekosë?'

I declined. 'You spoke well in the hall, King Rigenos,' I said. 'You fired us with a fine bloodlust.'

Katorn sniffed. 'Let us hope it lasts until we get to the enemy,' he said. 'We have some raw soldiers sailing on this expedition. Half our warriors have never fought before – and half of those are boys. There are even women in some detachments, I've heard.'

'You seem pessimistic, Lord Katorn,' I said.

He grunted. 'It is as well to be. This finery and grandeur is all right for cheering up the civilians, but it's best you don't believe it yourself. You should know, Erekosë. You should know what real war is all about – pain, fear, death. There's nothing else to it.'

'You forget,' I said. 'My memory of my own past is clouded.'

Katorn sniffed and gobbled down his wine. He replaced the cup with a clatter and left. 'I'll see to the casting off.'

The king cleared his throat. 'You and Katorn...' he began, but broke off. 'You...'

'We are not friends,' I said. 'I dislike his surly, mistrustful manner – and he suspects me of being a fraud, a traitor, a spy of some sort.'

King Rigenos nodded. 'He has hinted as much to me.' He sipped his wine. 'I told him that I saw you materialise with my own eyes, that there is no question you are Erekosë, that there is no reason not to trust you – but he persists. Why, do you think? He is a sane, sensible soldier.'

'He is jealous,' I said. 'I have taken over his power.'

'But he was as agreed as any of us that we needed a new leader who would inspire our people in the fight against the Eldren!'

'In principle, perhaps,' I said. I shrugged. 'It does not matter, King Rigenos. I think we have worked out a compromise.'

King Rigenos was lost in his own thoughts. 'There again,' he murmured, 'it could have nothing to do with war, at all.'

'What do you mean?'

He gave me a candid look. 'It might concern matters of love, Erekosë. Katorn has always been pleased by Iolinda's manner.'

'You could be right. But again there is nothing I can do. Iolinda seems to prefer my company.'

'Katorn might see it as mere infatuation with an ideal rather than a real person.'

'Do you see it as that?'

'I do not know. I have not talked to Iolinda about it.'

'Well,' I said, 'perhaps we shall see when we return.'

'*If* we return,' said King Rigenos. 'In that, I must admit, I'm in agreement with Katorn. Overconfidence has often been the main cause of many defeats.'

I nodded. 'Perhaps you are right.'

There came shouts and cries from outside and the ship lurched suddenly as the ropes were cast off and the anchors hauled in.

'Come,' said King Rigenos. 'Let us go out on deck. It will be expected of us.' Hastily he finished his wine and placed his crowned helmet upon his head. We left the cabin together and, as we came out, the cheering on the quayside swelled louder and louder.

We stood there waving to the people as the drums began to pound out the slow rowing rhythm. I saw Iolinda seated in her carriage, her body half-turned to watch as we left. I waved to her and she raised her own arm in a final salute.

'Goodbye, Iolinda,' I murmured.

Katorn darted me a cynical look from the corner of his eye as he passed to supervise the rowing.

Goodbye, Iolinda.

The wind had dropped. I was sweating in my war-gear, for the day was oppressed by a great flaming sun, blazing in a cloud-less sky.

I continued to wave from the stern of the swaying vessel, keeping my gaze on Iolinda as she sat there erect in her carriage, and then we had rounded a bend in the river and saw only the rearing towers of Necranal above and behind us, heard only the distant cheering.

We beat down the Droonaa River, moving fast with the current towards Noonos of the Jewelled Towers – and the fleets.

Chapter Nine

At Noonos

*O*H THESE BLIND *and bloody wars…*

'Really, Bishop, you fail to understand that human affairs are resolved in terms of action.'

Brittle arguments, pointless causes, cynicism disguised as pragmatism.

'Would you not rest, my son?'

'I cannot rest, Father, while the Paynim horde is already on the banks of the Danube.'

'Peace…'

'Will they be content with peace?'

'Perhaps.'

'They won't be satisfied with Vietnam. They won't be content until the whole of Asia is theirs… And after that, the world.'

'We are not beasts.'

'We must act as beasts. They act as beasts.'

'But if we tried…'

'We have tried.'

'Have we?'

'Fire must be fought with fire.'

'Is there no other way?'

'There is no other way.'

'The children…'

'There is no other way.'

A gun. A sword. A bomb. A bow. A vibrapistol. A flame lance. An axe. A club.

'There is no other way.'

On board the flagship that night, as the oars rose and fell and the drum continued its steady beat and the timbers creaked and the waves lapped at the hull, I slept poorly. Fragments of conversations. Phrases. Images. They tumbled in my tired brain and refused to leave me in peace. A thousand different periods of history. A million different faces. But the situation was always the same. The argument – made in myriad tongues – did not change.

Only when I rose from my bunk did my head clear and at length I resolved to go on deck.

What sort of creature was I? Why did it seem that I was forever doomed to drift from era to era and act out the same rôle wherever I went? What trick – what cosmic joke had been played upon me?

The night air was cool on my face and the moonlight struck through the light clouds at regular intervals so that the beams looked like the spokes of some gigantic wheel. It was as if the chariot of a god had sunk through the low cloud and become imbedded in the coarser air beneath.

I stared at the water and saw the clouds reflected in it, saw them break to reveal the moon. It was the same moon I had known as John Daker. The same bland face could be made out staring down in contentment at the antics of the creatures of the planet it circled. How many disasters had that moon witnessed? How many foolish crusades? How many wars and battles and murders?

The clouds moved together again and the waters of the river grew black as if to say that I would never find the revelation I sought.

I looked to the banks. We were passing through a thick forest. The tops of the trees were silhouetted against the slightly lighter darkness of the night. A few night animals voiced their cries from time to time and it seemed to me that they were lonely cries, lost cries, pitiful cries. I sighed and leaned against the rail and watched the water creamed grey by the slashing oars.

I had better accept that I must fight again. Again? Where had I fought before? What did my vague memories mean? What significance had my dreams? The simple answer – the pragmatic answer (or certainly one that John Daker could have best understood) – was that I was mad. My imagination was overwrought. Perhaps I had never been John Daker. Perhaps he, too, was another crazed invention.

I must fight again.

That was all there was to it. I had accepted the rôle and I must play it to the finish.

My brain began to clear as the moon set and dawn lightly touched the horizon.

I watched the sun rise, a huge scarlet disc moving with steady grandeur into the sky, as if curious to discover the sounds that disturbed the world – the beat of the drum, the crack of the oars.

'You are not sleeping, Lord Erekosë. You are eager, I see, to do battle.'

I felt I did not need Katorn's banter added to the burden. 'I thought I would enjoy watching the sun rise,' I said.

'And the moon set?' Katorn's voice implied something that I could not quite grasp. 'You seem to like the night, Lord Erekosë.'

'Sometimes,' I said. 'It is peaceful,' I added as significantly as I could. 'There is little to disturb a man's thoughts in the night.'

'True. You have something in common with our enemies, then.'

I turned impatiently, regarding his dark features with anger. 'What do you mean?'

'I meant only that the Eldren, too, are said to prefer the night to the day.'

'If it is true of me, my lord,' I said, 'then it will be a great asset to us in our war with them if I can fight them by night as well as by day.'

'I hope so, my lord.'

'Why do you mistrust me so, Lord Katorn?'

He shrugged. 'Did I say that I did? We struck a bargain, remember?'

'And I have kept my part of it.'

'And I mine. I will follow you, do not doubt that. Whatever I suspect, I will still follow you.'

'Then I would ask you to discontinue these little jibes of yours. They are naïve. They serve no purpose.'

'They serve a purpose for me, Lord Erekosë. They ease my temper – they channel it into a suitable area.'

'I have sworn my oath to Humanity,' I told him. 'I will serve King Rigenos's cause. I have my own burdens to bear, Lord Katorn.'

'I am deeply sympathetic.'

I turned away. I had come close to making a fool of myself – appealing to Katorn for mercy, almost, by claiming my own problems as an excuse.

'Thank you, Lord Katorn,' I said coldly. The ship began to turn a bend in the river and I thought I could see the sea ahead. 'I am grateful for your understanding.' I slapped at my face. The ship was passing through a cloud of midges hovering over the river. 'These insects are irritating, are they not?'

'Perhaps it would be best if you did not allow yourself to be subjected to their intentions, my lord,' Katorn replied.

'Indeed, I think you are right, Lord Katorn. I will go below.'

'Good morrow, my lord.'

'Good morrow, Lord Katorn.'

I left him standing on the deck and staring moodily ahead.

In other circumstances, I thought, *I would slay that man.*

As it was, there seemed a growing chance that he would do his utmost to slay me. I wondered if Rigenos were correct and Katorn was doubly jealous of me – jealous of my reputation as a warrior, jealous of Iolinda's love for me.

I washed and dressed myself in my war-gear and refused to bother myself with all these pointless thoughts. A little later I heard the helmsman shout and went on deck to see what his call signified.

Noonos was in sight. We all crowded the rails to get a glimpse of this fabulous city. We were half blinded by the glare from the towers for they were truly jewelled. The city flared with light – a great white aura speckled with a hundred other colours, green and violet and pink and mauve and ochre and red, all dancing in the brighter glow created by a million gems.

And beyond Noonos lay the sea – a calm sea gleaming in the sunshine.

As Noonos came closer, the river widened until it was clear that this was where it opened into the ocean. The banks became more and more distant and we kept closer to the starboard bank, for that was the bank on which Noonos was built. There were other towns and villages dotted amongst the wooded hills over-looking the river mouth. Some of them were picturesque, but they were all dominated by the port we were approaching.

Now seabirds began to squeal around our topmast and, with a great flapping of wings, settle in the yards and squabble, it appeared, for the best spot in the rigging.

The rhythm of the oars became slower and we began to back water as we approached the harbour itself. Behind us the squadron of proud ships dropped anchor. They would join us later when the pilot had come out to give them their mooring order.

Leaving our sister ships behind, we rowed slowly into Noonos, flying the standard of King Rigenos and the standard of Erekosë – a black field supporting a silver sword.

And the cheering began again. Held back by soldiers in armour of quilted leather, the crowds craned their necks to see us as we disembarked. And then, as I walked down the gangplank and appeared on the quayside, a huge chanting began that startled me at first when I realised what the word was that they were chanting.

'*EREKOSË! EREKOSË! EREKOSË! EREKOSË!*'

I raised my right arm in salute and almost staggered as the noise increased until it was literally deafening. I could barely refrain from covering my ears!

Prince Bladagh, Overlord of Noonos, greeted us with due cere-mony and read out a speech that could not be heard for the shouting and then we were escorted through the streets towards the quarters we were to use while making our brief stay in the city.

The jewelled towers were not disappointing, though I noticed that the houses built closer to the ground made a great contrast. Many of them were little better than hovels. It was quite plain where the money came from to encrust the towers with rubies, pearls and emeralds.

I had not noticed this great disparity between the rich and the poor in Necranal. Either I had been too impressed by the newness of the sights or the royal city took pains to disguise any areas of poverty, if they indeed existed.

And there were ragged people here, to go with the hovels, though they cheered as loudly as the rest, if not louder. Perhaps they blamed the Eldren for their misery.

Prince Bladagh was a sallow-featured man of about forty-five. He had a long, drooping moustache, pale, watery eyes and his gestures were those of an irritable but fastidious vulture. It emerged, and I was not surprised, that he would not be joining us in our expedition but would remain behind 'to protect the city' – or his own gold most likely, I thought.

'Ah, now, my liege,' he muttered as we reached his palace and the jewelled gates swung back to admit us (I noticed that they would have shone better if they had been cleaned). 'Ah, now – my palace is yours, King Rigenos. And yours, too, Lord Erekosë, of course. Anything you need.'

'A hot meal – and a simple one,' King Rigenos said, echoing my own sentiments. 'No banquets. I warned you not to make a large ceremony of this, Bladagh.'

'And I have not, my liege.' Bladagh looked relieved. He did not seem to me to be a man who enjoyed spending money. 'I have not.'

The meal *was* simple, though not particularly well-prepared. We ate it with Prince Bladagh, his plump, stupid wife, Princess Ionante, and their two scrawny children. Privately I was amused at the contrast between the city seen from a distance and the appearance and way of life of its ruler.

A short while later the various commanders who had been

assembling in Noonos for the past several weeks arrived to confer with Rigenos and myself. Katorn was among them and was able to outline very succinctly and graphically the battle plans we had worked out between us in Necranal.

Among the commanders were several famous heroes of the Two Continents – Count Roldero, a burly aristocrat whose armour was as workmanlike and free from decoration as my own; also there was Prince Malihar and his brother, Duke Ezak, both of whom had been through many campaigns; Earl Shanura of Kara-koa, one of the farthest provinces and one of the most barbaric. Shanura wore his hair long, in three plaits that hung down his back. His pale features were gaunt and criss-crossed with scars. He spoke seldom and usually to ask specific questions. The variety of the faces and the costumes surprised me at first. At least, I thought ironically, Humanity was united on this world, which was more than could be said for the world John Daker had left. But perhaps they were only united for the moment, to defeat the common enemy. After that, I thought, their unity might well suffer a setback. Earl Shanura, for instance, did not seem too happy about taking orders from King Rigenos, whom he probably considered soft.

I hoped that I could keep so disparate a group of officers together in the battles that were to follow.

At last we were finished with our discussions and I had spoken a word or two with every commander there. King Rigenos glanced at the bronze clock that stood on the table and which was marked with sixteen divisions. 'It will be time to put to sea soon,' he said. 'Are all ships ready?'

'Mine have been ready for months,' Earl Shanura said gruffly. 'I was beginning to feel they would rot before they saw action.'

The others agreed that their ships would be able to sail with little more than an hour's notice.

Rigenos and I thanked Bladagh and his family for their hospitality and they seemed rather more cheerful now that we were leaving.

Instead of marching from the palace, we now hurried in coaches to the quayside and rapidly boarded our ships. The king's flagship was called the *Iolinda*, a fact which I had not noticed before, my thoughts being full of the woman who bore that name. Our other ships from Necranal were now in port and their sailors were refreshing themselves in the short time they had, while slaves took on board the last provisions and armaments that were needed.

There was still a mood of slight depression hanging over me from my strange half-dreams of the previous night, but it was beginning to disperse as my excitement grew. It was still a month's sailing to Mernadin, but already I was beginning to relish the chance of action. At least action would help me forget the other problems. I was reminded of something that Pierre told Andrei in *War and Peace* – something about all men finding their own ways of forgetting the fact of death. Some womanised, some gambled, some drank and some, paradoxically, made war. Well, it was not the fact of death that obsessed me – indeed, it seemed that it was the fact of eternal existence that was preying on my mind. An eternal life involving eternal warfare.

Would I at some stage discover the truth? I was not sure that I wanted to know the truth. The thought frightened me. Perhaps a god could have accepted it. But I was not a god. I was a man. I knew I was a man. My problems, my ambitions, my emotions were on a human scale, save for the one abiding problem – the question of how I came to exist in this form, of how I had become what I was. Or was I truly eternal? Was there no beginning and no end to my existence? The very nature of Time was held in question. I could no longer regard Time as being linear, as I had once done as John Daker. Time could not be conceived of any longer in spacial terms.

I needed a philosopher, a magician, a scientist to help me on that problem. Or else I could forget it. But could I forget it? I would have to try.

The seabirds squawked and circled as the sails smacked down

and swelled in the sultry wind that had started to blow. The timbers creaked as the anchors were weighed and the mooring ropes cast off from the capstans and the great flagship, *Iolinda*, heaved herself from the port, her oars still rising and falling, but making faster speed now as she sailed towards the open sea.

Chapter Ten
First Sight of the Eldren

T HE FLEET WAS huge and contained great fighting ships of many kinds, some resembling what John Daker would have called nineteenth-century tea clippers, some that looked like junks, some with the lateen rig of Mediterranean craft, some that were very like Elizabethan caravels. Sailing in their separate formations, according to their province of origin, they symbolised the differences and the unity of mankind. I was proud of them.

Excited, tense, alert and confident of victory, we sailed for Paphanaal, gateway to Mernadin and conquest.

Yet I still felt the need to know more of the Eldren. My cloudy memory of the life of an earlier Erekosë could only conjure an impression of confused battles against them and also, perhaps, somewhere a feeling of emotional pain. That was all. I had heard that they had no orbs to their eyes and that this was their chief distinguishing non-human characteristic. They were said to be inhumanly beautiful, inhumanly merciless, and with inhuman sexual appetites. They were slightly taller than the average man, had long heads with high cheekbones and slightly slanting eyes. But this was not really enough for me. There were no pictures of Eldren anywhere on the Two Continents. Pictures were supposed to bring bad luck, particularly if the evil eyes of the Eldren were depicted.

As we sailed, there was a great deal of ship-to-ship communication, with commanders being rowed or hauled in slings to and from the flagship, depending on the weather. We had worked out our basic strategy and had contingency plans in case it should prove impossible to exercise. The idea had been mine and seemed a new one to the others, but they soon grasped it and the details had now all been decided upon. Each day the warriors of every

ship were drilled in what they were to do when the Eldren fleet
was sighted, if it was sighted. If it was not, we should dispatch
part of the fleet straight to Paphanaal and begin the attack on the
city. However, we expected the Eldren to send out their defence
fleet to meet us before we reached Paphanaal and it was on this
probability that we based our main plan.

Katorn and I avoided each other as much as possible. There
were, in those first few days of sailing, none of the verbal duels of
the sort we had had in Necranal and on the Droonaa River. I was
polite to Katorn when we had need to communicate and he, in his
surly way, was polite to me. King Rigenos seemed to be relieved
and told me that he was glad we had settled our differences. We
had not, of course, settled anything. We had merely waived those
differences until such time as we could decide them once and for
all. I knew eventually that I must fight Katorn or that he would try
to murder me.

I took a liking to Count Roldero of Stalaco, though he was perhaps the most bloodthirsty of all when it came to discussing the
Eldren. John Daker would have called him a reactionary, but he
would have liked him. He was a staunch, stoical, honest man who
spoke his mind and allowed others to speak theirs, expecting the
same tolerance from them as he gave. When I had once suggested
to him that he saw things too plainly in black and white, he smiled
wearily and replied:

'Erekosë, my friend, when you have seen what I have of the
events that have taken place in my lifetime on this planet of ours,
then you will see things quite as clearly in black and white as I do.
You can only judge people by their actions, not by their protesta-
tions. People act for good or they act for ill and those who do
great ill are bad and those who do great good – they are good.'

'But people may do great good accidentally, though with evil
intentions – and conversely people may do great evil though having the best of intentions,' I said, amused by his assumption that
he had lived longer and seen more than I had – though I think his
assumption was meant in jest.

'Exactly!' Count Roldero replied. 'You have only repeated my point. I do not care, as I said, what people protest their intentions to be. I judge them by the results they achieve. Take the Eldren…'

I raised my hand, laughing. 'I know how wicked they are. Everyone has told me of their cunning, their treachery, their black powers.'

'Ah, you seem to think I hate Eldren individuals. I do not. For all I know they may be kind to their own children, love their wives and treat their animals well. I do not say that they are, as individuals, monsters. It is as a force that they must be considered. It is what they do that must be judged. It is on the threat of their own ambitions that we must base our attitude towards them.'

'And how do you consider that force?' I asked.

'It is not human, therefore its interests are not human. Therefore, in terms of its own self-interest, it needs to destroy us. In this case, because the Eldren are not human, they threaten us merely by existing. And, by the same token, we threaten them. They understand this and would wipe us out. We understand this and would wipe them out before they have the chance to destroy us. You understand?'

The argument seemed convincing enough to the pragmatist that I considered myself to be. But a thought came to mind and I voiced it.

'Are you not forgetting one thing, Count Roldero? You have said it yourself – the Eldren are *not* human. You are assuming that they have human interests.'

'They are flesh and blood,' he said. 'They are beasts, as we are beasts. They have those impulses, just as we have them.'

'But many species of beast seem to live together in basic harmony,' I reminded him. 'The lion does not constantly war with the leopard; the horse does not war with the cow; even among themselves they rarely kill each other, no matter how important the issue to them.'

'But they would,' said Count Roldero, undaunted. 'They would if they could anticipate events. They would if they could work out the rate at which the rival animal is consuming food, breeding, expanding its territory.'

I gave up. I felt we were both on shaky ground now. We were seated in my cabin, looking out at a beautiful evening and a calm sea through the open porthole. I poured Count Roldero more wine from my dwindling store (I had taken to drinking a good deal of wine shortly before I went to bed, to insure myself of a rest not broken by visions and memories).

Count Roldero quaffed the wine and stood up. 'It's getting late. I must return to my ship or my men will think I've drowned and be celebrating. I see you're running short of wine. I'll bring a skin or two on my next visit. Farewell, friend Erekosë. Your heart's in the right place, I'm sure. But you're a sentimentalist, for all you say to the contrary.'

I grinned. 'Goodnight, Roldero.' I raised my half-full wine-cup. 'Let's drink to peace when this business is over!'

Roldero snorted. 'Aye, peace – like the cows and the horses! Goodnight, my friend.' He left laughing.

Rather drunkenly, I removed my clothes and fell into my bunk, chuckling foolishly at Roldero's parting remark. 'Like the cows and the horses. He's right. Who wants to lead a life like that? Here's to war!' And I flung the wine-cup through the open port-hole and fell to snoring almost before my eyes had closed.

And I dreamed.

But this time I dreamed of the wine-cup I had hurled through the porthole. I imagined I saw it bobbing on the waves, its gold and jewels glittering. I imagined I saw it caught by a current and borne far away from the fleet – out to a lonely place where ships never sailed and land was never in sight, tossed for ever on a bleak sea.

For the whole month of our sailing, the sea was calm, the wind good and the weather, on the whole, fine.

Our spirits rose higher. We took this to be a sign of good luck. All of us were cheerful. All, that is, save Katorn, who grumbled that this could well be the calm before the storm, that we must expect the worst of the Eldren when we eventually engaged.

'They are tricky,' he would say. 'Those filth are tricky. Even now they could know of our coming and have planned some manoeuvre we are not expecting. They might even be responsible for the weather.'

I could not help laughing openly at this and he stalked off up the deck in anger. 'You will see, Lord Erekosë,' he called back. 'You will see!'

And the next day the opportunity came.

According to our charts, we were nearing the coasts of Merna-din. We posted more lookouts, arranged the fleets of Humanity in battle order, checked our armament and cut our speed.

The morning passed slowly as we waited, the flagship in the forefront rocking on the waves, its sails reefed, its oars raised.

And then, around noon, the lookout in our topmast yelled through his megaphone:

'Ships for'ard! Five sails!'

King Rigenos, Katorn and I stood on the foredeck, staring ahead. I looked at King Rigenos and frowned. 'Five ships? Five ships only?'

King Rigenos shook his head. 'Perhaps they are not Eldren ships.'

'They'll be Eldren craft,' Katorn grunted. 'What else could they be in these waters? No human merchants would trade with the creatures!'

And then the cry of the lookout reached us again.

'Ten sails now! Twenty! It's the fleet – the Eldren fleet! They are sailing fast upon us!'

And now I thought I glimpsed a flash of white on the horizon. Had it been the crest of a wave? No. It was the sail of a ship, I was sure.

'Look,' I said. 'There.' And I pointed.

Rigenos screwed up his eyes and shielded them with his hand. 'I see nothing. It is your imagination. They could not be coming in so fast.'

Katorn, too, peered ahead. 'Yes! I see it, too. A sail! They are that swift! By the Sea God's scales – slimy sorcery aids them! It is the only explanation.'

King Rigenos seemed sceptical. 'They are lighter craft than ours,' he reminded Katorn, 'and the wind is in their favour.'

Katorn, in turn, was not convinced. 'Maybe,' he growled. 'Perhaps you are right, sire.'

'Have they used sorcery before?' I asked him. I was willing to believe anything. I had to if I was to believe what had happened to me!

'Aye!' spat Katorn. 'Many times. All kinds! Ooph! I can smell sorcery on the very air!'

'When?' I asked him. 'What kind? I wish to know so that I can take counter-measures.'

'They can make themselves invisible sometimes. That's how they took Paphanaal, so it's said. They can walk on water, sail through the air.'

'You have seen them do this?'

'Not myself. But I've heard many tales, tales I can believe from men who do not lie.'

'And these men have experienced this sorcery?'

'Not themselves. But they have known men who did.'

'So their use of sorcery remains a rumour,' I said.

'Ach! Say what you like!' Katorn roared. 'Do not believe me – you who are the very essence of sorcery, who owes his existence to an incantation. Why do you think I supported the notion to bring you back, Erekosë? Because I felt we needed sorcery that would be stronger than theirs! What else is that sword at your side but a sorcerous blade?'

I shrugged. 'Let us wait, then,' I said, 'and see their sorcery.'

King Rigenos called up at the lookout. 'How big's the fleet you see?'

'About half our size, my liege!' he shouted back, his words distorted by the megaphone. 'Certainly no larger. And I think it is their whole fleet. I see no more coming.'

'They do not seem to be drawing any closer at this moment,' I murmured to King Rigenos. 'Ask him if they're moving.'

'Has the Eldren fleet hove to, master lookout?' called King Rigenos.

'Aye, my liege. It no longer speeds hither and they seem to be furling their sails.'

'They are waiting for us,' Katorn muttered. 'They want us to attack them. Well, we shall wait, too.'

I nodded. 'That is the strategy we agreed.'

And we waited.

We waited as the sun set and night fell and far away on the horizon we caught the occasional glimpse of silver that could have been a wave or a ship. Hasty messages were sent by swimmers back and forth among the vessels of the fleet.

And we continued to wait, sleeping as best we could, wondering when, if at all, the Eldren would attack.

Katorn's footsteps could be heard pacing the deck as I lay awake in my cabin, trying to do the sensible thing and preserve my energy for the next day. Of all of us, Katorn was the most impatient to engage the enemy. I felt that, if it had been up to him, we should even now be sailing on the Eldren, having thrown our carefully worked-out battle plans overboard.

But luckily it was up to me. Even King Rigenos did not have the authority, except under exceptional circumstances, to countermand any of my orders.

I rested, but I could not sleep. I had had my first glimpse of an Eldren craft, yet I still did not know what the ships really looked like or what my impression of their crews would be.

I lay there, praying that our battle should soon begin. A fleet of only half our size! I smiled without humour. I smiled because I knew we should be victorious.

When would the Eldren attack?

It might even be tonight. Katorn had said that they loved the night.

I would not care if it was at night. I wanted to fight. A huge battle-lust was building within me. I wanted to fight!

Chapter Eleven
The Fleets Engage

A WHOLE DAY passed and another night and still the Eldren remained on the horizon.

Were they deliberately hoping to tire us, make us nervous? Or were they afraid of the size of our fleet? Perhaps, I thought, their own strategy depended on our attacking them.

On the second night I did sleep, but not the drink-sodden slumber I had trained myself to. There was no drink left. Count Roldero had never had a chance to bring his wineskins on board.

And the dreams, if anything, were worse than ever.

I saw entire worlds at war, destroying themselves in senseless battles.

I saw Earth, but this was an Earth without a moon, an Earth which did not rotate, which was half in sunlight, half in a darkness relieved only by the stars. And there was strife here, too, and a morbid quest that as good as destroyed me. A name – Clarvis? Something of the sort. I grasped at these names, but they almost always eluded me and, I suppose, they were really the least important parts of the dreams.

I saw Earth – a different Earth again, an Earth which was so old that even the seas had begun to dry up. And I rode across a murky landscape, beneath a tiny sun, and I thought about Time.

I tried to hang on to this dream, this hallucination, this memory, whatever it was. I thought there might be a clue here to what I was, what had begun it all.

Another name – the Chronarch. Then it faded. There seemed to be no extra significance to this dream than to the rest.

Then this dream had faded and I stood in a city beside a large car and I was laughing and there was a strange sort of gun in my hand and

*bombs were raining from planes and destroying the city. I tasted an
Upmann's cigar.*

I woke up, but was almost at once dragged back into my dreams.

*I walked, insane and lonely, through corridors of steel and beyond the
walls of the corridors was empty space. Earth was far behind. The steel
machine in which I paced was heading for another star. I was tormented.
I was obsessed with thoughts of my family. John Daker? No – John.*

*And then, as if to confuse me further, the names began. I saw them. I
heard them. They were spelled in many different forms of hieroglyphics,
chanted in many tongues.*

*Aubec. Byzantium. Cornelius. Colvin. Bradbury. London. Melniboné.
Hawkmoon. Lanjis Liho. Powys. Marca. Elric. Muldoon. Dietrich. Arflane.
Simon. Kane. Begg. Corum. Persson. Ryan. Asquiol. Pepin. Seward. Men-
nell. Tallow. Hallner. Köln. Carnelian. Bastable. Von Bek...*

The names went on and on and on.

I awoke screaming.

And it was morning.

Sweating, I got out of my bunk and splashed cold water all over
my body.

Why did it not begin? Why?

I knew that, once the fighting started, the dreams would go
away. I was sure of it.

And then the door of my cabin burst open and a slave entered.
'Master –'

A trumpet voiced a brazen bellow. There were the sounds of
running men all over the ship.

'Master, the enemy ships are moving.'

With a great sigh of relief I dressed myself, buckling on my
armour as quickly as I could and strapping my sword about me.

Then I ran up on deck and climbed to the forecastle where
King Rigenos stood, clad in his own armour, his face grim.

Everywhere in the fleet the war signals were being flown and voices called from ship to ship, trumpets snarled like metallic beasts and drums began to beat.

Now I could see for certain that the Eldren ships were on the move.

'Our commanders are all prepared,' Rigenos murmured tensely. 'See, our ships are already taking their positions.'

I looked with pleasure as the fleet began to form itself according to our much rehearsed battle plan. Now, if only the Eldren would behave as we had anticipated, we should be the victors.

I looked forward again and gasped as the Eldren ships drew closer, marvelled at their rare grace as they leaped lightly over the water like dolphins.

But they were not dolphins, I thought. They would rend us all if they could. Now I understood something of Katorn's suspicion of everything Eldren. If I had not known that these were our enemies, that they intended to destroy us, I would have stood there entranced at their beauty.

They were not galleons, as most of our craft were. They were ships of sail only – and the sails were diaphanous on slim masts. White hulls broke the darker white of the surf as they surged wildly, without faltering, towards us.

I studied their armament intently.

They mounted some cannon, but not as many as ours. Their cannon, however, were slender and silver and, when I saw them, I feared their power.

Katorn joined us. He was snarling with pleasure. 'Ah, now,' he growled. 'Now. Now. See their guns, Erekosë? Beware of them. There is sorcery, if you do not believe me!'

'Sorcery? What do you mean?'

But he was off again, shouting at the men in the rigging to hurry their work.

I began to make out tiny figures on the decks of the Eldren ships. I caught glimpses of eldritch faces, but still could not, at that distance, discern any special characteristics. They moved swiftly about their ships as they swam speedily towards us.

Now our own fleet's manoeuvres were almost complete and the flagship began to move into position.

I myself gave the orders to heave to and we rocked in the sea, awaiting the Eldren ships rushing towards us.

As planned, we had manoeuvred to form a square that was strong on three sides, but weak on the side facing the Eldren fleet.

Some hundred ships were at the far end of the square, set stem to stern with cannon bristling. The two other strong sides also had about a hundred ships each and were at a far enough distance from each other so that their cannon could not accidentally sink one of their own craft. We had placed a thinner wall of ships – about twenty-five – at the side of the square where the Eldren were drawing in. We hoped to give the impression of a tightly closed square formation, with a few ships in the middle flying the royal colours, to give the impression that this was the flagship and its escorts. These ships were bait. The true flagship – the one on which I stood – had temporarily taken down its colours and lay roughly in the middle of the starboard side of the square.

Closer and closer now the Eldren ships approached. It was almost true what Katorn had said. They did seem to fly through the air rather than through the waves.

My hands began to sweat. Would they take the bait? The plan had struck the commanders as original, which meant that it was not the classical manoeuvre it had been in some periods of Earth's history. If it did not work, I would lose Katorn's confidence still further and it would not make my position any better with the king, whose daughter I hoped to marry.

But there was no point in worrying about that. I watched.

And the Eldren took the bait.

Cannon roaring, the Eldren craft smashed in a delta formation into the thin wall and, under their own impetus, sailed on to find themselves thickly surrounded on three sides.

'Raise our colours!' I shouted to Katorn. 'Raise the colours! Let them see the originator of their defeat!'

Katorn gave the orders. My own banner went up first – the

black field with the silver sword – and then the king's. We moved to tighten the trap, to crush the Eldren as they realised they had been tricked.

I had never seen such highly manoeuvrable sailing craft as the slender ships used by the Eldren. Slightly smaller than our men-o'-war, they darted about seeking an opening in the wall of ships. But there was no opening. I had seen to that.

Now their cannon bellowed fiercely, gouting balls of flame. Was this what Katorn had meant by 'sorcery'? The Eldren ammunition was fire-bombs rather than solid shot of the sort we used. Like comets, the fireballs hurtled through the noonday air. Many of our ships were fired. They blazed, crackling and groaning as the flames consumed them.

Like comets they were and the ships were like flashing sharks.

But they were sharks caught in a net that could not be broken. Inexorably we tightened the trap, our own guns booming heavy iron that tore into those white hulls and left black, gaping wounds; that ripped through those slim masts and brought the yards splintering down, the diaphanous sails flapping and fading like the wings of dying moths.

Our own monstrous men-o'-war, their heavy timbers clothed in brass, their huge oars churning the water, their dark, painted sails bulging, drew in to crush the Eldren.

Then the Eldren fleet divided into two roughly equal parts and dashed for the far corners of the net of ships – its weakest points. Many Eldren craft broke through, but we were prepared for this and with monumental precision our ships closed around them.

The Eldren fleet was now divided into several groups and it made our work easier. Implacably we sailed in to crush them.

The skies were filled with smoke and the seas with flaming wreckage and the air was populated by screams, yells and war-shouts, the whine of the Eldren fireballs, the roar of our own shot, the shattering bellowings of the cannon. My face was covered by a film of grease and ash from the smoke and I sweated in the heat from the flames.

From time to time I caught a glimpse of a tense Eldren face and I wondered at their beauty and feared that perhaps we had been overconfident in our assumption of our victory. They were clad in light armour and moved about their ships as gracefully as trained dancers and their silver cannon did not once pause in their bombardment of our craft. Wherever the fireballs landed, the decks or rigging became instantly alight with a shrieking, all-consuming flame that burned green and blue and seemed to devour metal as easily as it did wood.

I gripped the rail of the foredeck and leaned forward, trying to peer through the stinging smoke. All at once I saw an Eldren ship side-on immediately ahead of us.

'Prepare to ram!' I yelled. 'Prepare to ram!'

Like many of our ships, the *Iolinda* possessed an iron-shod ram lying just below the waterline. Now was our chance to use it. I saw the Eldren commander on his poop deck shout orders to his men to turn the ship. But it was too late even for the speedy Eldren. We bore down on the smaller craft and, our whole ship reverberating with the mighty roar, we drove into its side. Iron and timber screamed and ruptured, and foam lashed skyward. I was thrown back against the mast, losing my footing, and, as I clambered to my feet, I saw that we had broken the Eldren craft completely in two. I looked on the sight with a mixture of horror and exultation. I had not guessed the brutal power of the *Iolinda*.

On either side of our flagship I saw the two halves of the enemy ship rear in the water and begin to go down. The horror on my own face seemed matched by that on the Eldren commander's as he fiercely strove to hold himself erect on his sloping poop deck while his men threw up their arms and leaped into the dark, surging sea that was already full of smashed timbers and drifting corpses.

Swiftly now the sea swallowed the slim ship and I heard King Rigenos laughing behind me as the Eldren drowned.

I turned. His face was smeared by soot and his red-rimmed eyes stared wildly out of his haggard skull. The helmet-crown of iron and diamonds was askew on his head as he continued to laugh in his morbid triumph.

'Good work, Erekosë! The most satisfying method of all when dealing with these creatures. Break them open. Send them to the depths of the ocean so that they can be that much closer to their master, the Lord of Hell!'

Katorn climbed up. His face, too, was exultant. 'I'll give you that, Lord Erekosë. You have proved you know how to kill Eldren.'

'I know how to kill many kinds of men,' I said quietly. I was disgusted by their response. I had admired the way in which the Eldren commander had died. 'I merely took an opportunity,' I said. 'There is nothing clever in a ship of this size crushing lighter craft.'

But there was no time to dispute the issue. Our ship was moving through the wreckage it had created, surrounded by orange tongues of flame, shrieks and yells, thick smoke which obscured vision in all directions so that it was impossible to tell how the fleets of Humanity fared.

'We must get out of this,' I said. 'Into clearer sea. We must let our own ships know that we are unharmed. Will you give the orders, Katorn?'

'Aye.' Katorn went back to his duties.

My head was beginning to throb with the din of the battle. It became one great wall of noise, one huge wave of smoke and flame and the stench of death.

And yet – it was all familiar to me.

Up to now my battle tactics had been somewhat notional – intellectual rather than instinctive. But now it did seem that old instincts came into play and I gave orders without working them out first.

And I was confident that the orders were good. Even Katorn trusted them.

Thus it had been with the order to ram the Eldren craft. I had not stopped to think. It was probably just as well.

Its oars pulling strongly, the *Iolinda* cleared the worst of the smoke and her trumpets and drums announced her presence to the rest of the fleet. A cheering went up from some of the nearby ships as we emerged into an area relatively free of smoke, wreckage and other ships.

A few of our craft had begun to single out individual Eldren vessels and were hurling out their grappling irons towards the shark-ships. The savage barbs cut into the white rails, ripped through the shining sails, bit into flesh and tore off arms and legs. The great men-o'-war dragged the Eldren craft towards them, as whalers haul in their half-dead prey.

Arrows began to fly from deck to deck as archers, their legs twisted in the rigging, shot at enemy archers. Javelins rattled on the decks or pierced the armour of the warriors, Eldren and human, and threw them prone. The sound of cannon could still be heard, but it was not the steady pounding it had been. The shots became more intermittent and were replaced by the clash of swords, the shouts of warriors fighting hand to hand.

Smoke still formed acrid blossoms in the air above that watery battlefield. And when I could see through the murk to the green, wreckage-strewn ocean itself, I saw that the foam was no longer white. It was red. The sea was covered by a slick of blood.

As our ship beat on to join battle once again, I saw upturned faces staring at me from the sea. They were the faces of the dead, both Eldren and human, and they seemed to share a common expression – an expression of astonished accusation.

After a while, I tried to ignore the sight of those faces.

Chapter Twelve
The Broken Truce

TWO MORE SHIPS fell to our ram and we sustained hardly any damage at all. The *Iolinda* moved through the battle like a dignified juggernaut, as if assured of her own invulnerability.

It was King Rigenos who saw it first. He screwed up his eyes and pointed through the smoke, his open mouth red in the blackness of his soot-covered face.

'There! See it, Erekosë? There!'

I saw a magnificent Eldren ship ahead of us, but I did not know why Rigenos singled it out.

'It is the Eldren flagship, Erekosë,' Rigenos said. 'It could be that their leader himself is aboard. If that cursed servant of Azmobaana does ride his own flagship and if we can destroy him, then our cause will be truly won. Pray that the Eldren prince rides her, Erekosë!'

Katorn snarled from behind us: 'I would like to be the one to bring him down.' He had a heavy crossbow in his mailed hands and he stroked its butt as another man might stroke a favourite kitten.

'Oh, let Prince Arjavh be there. Let him be there,' hissed Rigenos thirstily.

I paid them little heed, but shouted the order for grappling irons to be readied.

Luck, it seemed, was still with us. Our huge vessel reared up on a surging wave at exactly the right moment and we rode it down upon the Eldren flagship, our timbers scraping its sides and turning it so that it lay in a perfect position for our grapples to seize it. The iron claws snaked out on thick ropes, clamped in the rigging, stabbed into the deck, snatched at the rails.

Now the Eldren craft was bound to us. We held it close, as a lover holds his mistress.

And that same smile of triumph began to cross my face. I had the sweet taste of victory on my lips. It was the sweetest taste of all. I, Erekosë, signed for a slave to run forward and wipe my face with a damp cloth. I drew myself up proudly on my deck. Just behind me was King Rigenos, on my right. On my left was Katorn. I felt a comradeship with them suddenly. I looked proudly down on the Eldren deck. The warriors looked exhausted. But they stood ready, with arrows strung on bows, with swords clenched in white fists and shields raised. They watched us silently; they did not attempt to cut the ropes, they waited for us to make the first move.

When two flagships locked in this way, there was always a pause before fighting broke out. This was to enable the enemy commanders to speak and, if both desired it, decide a truce and the terms of that truce.

Now King Rigenos bellowed across the rail of his high deck, calling out to the Eldren who looked up at him, their strange eyes smarting with the smoke as much as ours did.

'This is King Rigenos and his champion, the immortal Erekosë, your ancient enemy come again to defeat you. We would speak with your commander for a moment, in the usual truce.'

From beneath a canvas awning on his poop deck, a tall man now emerged. Through the shifting smoke I saw, dimly at first, a pointed, golden face with blue-flecked milky eyes staring sadly from the sockets of the slanting brow. An eldritch voice, like music, sang across the sea:

'I am Duke Baynahn, commander of the Eldren fleet. We will make no complicated peace terms with you, but if you let us sail away now, we will not continue to fight.'

Rigenos smiled and Katorn snorted. 'How gracious! He knows he is doomed.'

Rigenos chuckled at this. Then he called back to Duke Baynahn. 'I find your proposal somewhat naïve, Duke Baynahn.'

Baynahn shrugged wearily. 'Then let us finish this,' he sighed. He raised his gloved hand to order his men to loose their arrows.

'Hold a moment!' Rigenos shouted. 'There is another way, if you would spare your men.

Slowly Baynahn lowered his hand. 'What is that?' His voice was wary.

'If your master, Arjavh of Mernadin, is aboard his own flagship – as he should be – let him come out and do battle with Lord Erekosë, Humanity's champion.' King Rigenos spread out his palms. 'If Arjavh should win, why, you will go in peace. If Erekosë should win, then you will become our prisoners.'

Duke Baynahn folded his arms across his chest. 'I have to tell you that our Prince Arjavh could not get to Paphanaal in time to sail with our fleet. He is in the west – in Loos Ptokai.'

King Rigenos turned to Katorn.

'Kill that one, Katorn,' he said quietly.

Duke Baynahn continued: 'However, I am prepared to fight your champion if...'

'No!' I cried to Katorn. 'Stop! King Rigenos, that is dishonourable – you speak during a truce.'

'There is no question of honour, Erekosë, when exterminating vermin. That you will soon learn. Kill him, Katorn!'

Duke Baynahn was frowning, plainly puzzled at our muted argument, striving to catch the words.

'I will fight your Erekosë,' he said. 'Is it agreed?'

And Katorn brought up the crossbow and the bolt whirred and I heard a soft gasp as it penetrated the Eldren speaker's throat.

His hands went up towards the quivering bolt. His strange eyes filmed. He fell.

I was enraged at the treachery shown by one who so often spoke of treachery in his enemies. But now there was no time to remonstrate for already the Eldren arrows were whistling towards us and I had to ensure our defences and prepare to lead the boarding party against the betrayed crew of the enemy ship.

I grasped a trailing rope, unsheathed my glowing sword and let the words come from my lips, though I was still full of anger against Katorn and the king.

'For Humanity!' I shouted. 'Death to the Hounds of Evil!'

I swung down through the heated air that slashed against my face in that swift passage and I dropped, with howling human warriors behind me, among the Eldren ranks.

Then we were fighting.

My followers took care to stay away from me as the sword opened pale wounds in the Eldren foes, destroying all whom it even lightly cut. Many Eldren died beneath Kanajana, but there was no battle-joy in me as I fought, for I was still furious with my own people's actions and there was no skill needed for such slaying – the Eldren were shocked at the death of their commander and they were plainly half-dead with weariness, though they fought bravely.

Indeed, the slender ships seemed to hold more men than I had estimated. The long-skulled Eldren, well aware that my sword touch was lethal, flung themselves at me with desperate and ferocious courage.

Many of them wielded long-hafted axes, swinging at me out of reach of my sword. The sword was no sharper than any ordinary blade and, although I hacked at the shafts, I succeeded only in splintering them slightly. I had constantly to duck, stab beneath the whirling axe blades.

A young, golden-haired Eldren leaped at me, swung his axe and it smashed against my shoulder plate, knocking me off balance.

I rolled, trying desperately to regain my footing on the blood-smeared deck. The axe smashed down again, onto my breastplate, winding me. I struggled up into a crouching position, plunged forward beneath the axe and slashed at the Eldren's bared wrist.

A peculiar sobbing grunt escaped his lips. He groaned and died. The 'poison' of the blade had done its work yet again. I still did not understand how the metal itself could be poisoned, but there was no doubting its effectiveness. I straightened up, my bruised body throbbing as I stared down at the brave young Eldren who now lay at my feet. Then I looked about me.

I saw that we had the advantage. The last pocket of fiercely fighting Eldren was on the main deck, back to back around their banner – a scarlet field bearing the silver basilisk of Mernadin.

I stumbled towards the fray. The Eldren were fighting to the last man. They knew they would receive no mercy from their human enemies.

I stopped. The warriors had no need of help from me. I sheathed my sword and watched as the Eldren were engulfed by our forces and, although all badly wounded, continued to fight until slain.

I looked about me. A peculiar silence seemed to surround the two locked ships, though in the distance the sound of cannon could still be heard.

Then Katorn, who had led the attack on the last Eldren defenders, snatched down their basilisk banner and flung it into the flowing Eldren blood. Insanely he began to trample the flag until it was completely soaked and unrecognisable.

'Thus will all the Eldren perish!' he screamed in his mad triumph. 'All! All! All!'

He stumbled below to see what loot there was.

The silence returned. The drifting smoke began to dissipate and hang higher in the air above us, obscuring the sunlight.

Now that the flagship was ours, the day was won. Not a single prisoner would be taken. In the distance the victorious human warriors were busy firing the Eldren vessels. There seemed to be no Eldren ships left uncaptured, none fleeing over the horizon. Many of our own ships had been destroyed or were sinking in flames. Both sides' craft were stretched across a vast expanse of water and the ocean itself was covered by so great and thick a carpet of wreckage and corpses that it seemed as if the remaining ships were embedded in it.

I, for one, felt trapped by it. I wanted to leave this scene as soon as possible. The smell of the dead choked me. This was not the battle I had expected to fight. This was not the glory I had hoped to win.

Katorn re-emerged with a look of satisfaction on his dark face.

'You're empty-handed,' I said. 'Why so pleased?'

He wiped his lips. 'Duke Baynahn had his daughter with him.'

'Is she still alive?'

'Not now.'

I shuddered.

Katorn stretched up his head and looked around him. 'Good. We've finished them. I'll give orders to fire the remaining vessels.'

'Surely,' I said, 'that is a waste. We could use their ships to replace those we have lost.'

'Use these cursed craft? Never.' He spoke with a twist of his mouth and strode to the rail of the Eldren flagship, shouting to his men to follow him back to their own vessel.

I came reluctantly, looking back to where the corpse of the betrayed Duke Baynahn still lay, the crossbow bolt projecting from his slender neck.

Then I clambered aboard our ship and I gave the orders to save what grapples we could and cut away the rest.

King Rigenos greeted me. He had taken no part in the actual fighting. 'You did well, Erekosë. Why, you could have taken that ship single-handed.'

'I could have,' I said. 'I could have taken the whole fleet single-handed.'

He laughed. 'You are very confident! The whole fleet!'

'Aye. There was one way.'

He frowned. 'What do you mean?'

'If you had let me fight Duke Baynahn – as he suggested – many lives and many ships would have been saved. Our lives. Our ships.'

'You surely did not trust him? The Eldren will always try some trick like that. Doubtless, if you had agreed to his plan, you would have stepped aboard his ship and been cut down by a hundred arrows. Believe me, Erekosë, you must not be deceived by them. Our ancestors were so deceived – and look how we suffer now.'

I shrugged. 'Maybe you are right.'

'Of course I am right.' King Rigenos turned his head and called to our crew. 'Fire the ship! Fire that cursed Eldren craft! Hurry, you laggards!'

He was in a good humour was King Rigenos. A great good humour.

I watched as blazing arrows were accurately shot into bales of combustible materials which had been placed in strategic parts of the Eldren ship.

The slender vessel soon caught. The bodies of the slain began to burn and oily smoke struck upward to the sky. The ship drifted away, its silver cannon like the snouts of slaughtered beasts, its glistening sails dropping in flaming ribbons to the already flaming deck. It gave a long shudder suddenly as if expiring the last of its life.

'Put a couple of shots below the waterline,' Katorn shouted to his gunners. 'Let's make sure the thing sinks once and for all.'

Our brazen cannon snarled and the heavy shot smashed into the Eldren flagship, sending up gouts of water and crashing through the timbers.

The flagship yawed, but still seemed to be trying to stay upright. Her drifting went slower and slower as she settled lower in the water until she had stopped altogether. And then all at once she sank swiftly and was gone.

I thought of the Eldren duke. I thought of his daughter.

And something in me envied them. They would know eternal peace, just as it seemed I should know nothing but eternal strife.

Our fleet began to reassemble.

We had lost thirty-eight men-o'-war and a hundred and ten smaller craft of different types.

But nothing remained of the Eldren fleet.

Nothing but the burning hulks which we left, sinking, behind us as we sailed, in battle-thirsty glee, for Paphanaal.

Chapter Thirteen
Paphanaal

FOR THE REST of our sailing towards Paphanaal, I avoided both Katorn and King Rigenos. Perhaps they were right and the Eldren could not be trusted. But should we not set some kind of example?

On the second night of the voyage after the big battle with the Eldren, Count Roldero visited me.

'You did well there,' he said. 'Your tactics were superb. And I hear you accounted well for yourself in the hand-to-hand fighting.' He looked about him in mock fear and whispered, jerking his thumb at a vague spot above him, 'But I hear Rigenos decided that it was best he did not put the royal person in danger, lest we warriors lose heart.'

'Oh,' I said, 'Rigenos has a fair point. He came with us, don't forget. He could have stayed behind. We all expected him to. Did you hear of the order he gave while the truce was on with the enemy commander?'

Roldero sniffed. 'Had him shot by Katorn?'

'Yes.'

'Well…' Roldero grinned at me. 'You make allowances for Rigenos's cowardice and I'll make allowances for his treachery!' He burst into gusty laughter. 'That's fair, eh?'

I could not help smiling. But later, more seriously, I said: 'Would you have done the same, Roldero?'

'Oh, I expect so. War, after all…'

'But Baynahn was prepared to fight me. He must have known his chances were slim. He must have known, too, that Rigenos could not be trusted to keep his word.'

'If he did, then he would have acted as Rigenos acted. It was just that Rigenos was quicker. Merely tactics, you see – the trick is to gauge the exact moment to be treacherous.'

'Baynahn did not look like one who would have acted treacherously.'

'He was probably a very kind man and treated his family well. I told you, Erekosë, it is not Baynahn's character I dispute. I just say that, as a warrior, he would have tried what Rigenos succeeded in doing – eliminating the enemy's chief. It is one of the basic principles of warfare!'

'Do you say so, Roldero?'

'I do say so. Now drink up.'

I did drink up. And I drank deep and I drank myself stupid. Now there were not merely the dream memories to contend with, but much more recent memories, too.

Another night came before we reached the harbour city of Paphanaal and we lay at anchor, a sea league or so offshore.

Then, in the shifting dawn of the morrow, we upped anchors and rowed in towards Paphanaal, for there was no wind to fill our sails.

Nearer we came to land.

I saw cliffs and black mountains rising.

Nearer.

I saw a flash of brighter colour to the east of us.

'Paphanaal!' shouted the lookout from his precarious perch in the top trees.

Nearer.

And there was Paphanaal.

She was undefended as far as we could make out. We had left her defenders on the bottom of the ocean, far behind.

There were no domes on this city, no minarets. There were steeples and buttresses and battlements, all close together. They made the city seem like one great palace. The materials of their construction were breathtaking. There was white marble veined with pink, blue, green and yellow. Orange marble, veined with black. Marble faced with gold, basalt and quartz and bluestone in abundance.

It was a shining city.

As we came closer, we saw no-one on the quaysides, no-one in the streets or on the battlements. I assumed that the city had been deserted.

I was wrong.

We put in to the great harbour and disembarked. I formed our armies into disciplined ranks and warned them of a possible trap, although I did not really believe there could be one.

The warriors had spent the rest of the voyage repairing their clothes and their armour, cleaning their weapons and making repairs to their ships.

All the ships crowded the harbour now, their flags waving in the light breeze that had come up almost as soon as we set foot on the cobblestones of the quay. Clouds came in with the breeze and made the day grey.

The warriors stood before King Rigenos, Katorn and myself. Rank upon rank they stood, their armour bright, their heavy banners moving sluggishly.

There were seven hundred divisions, each hundred divisions commanded by a marshal, who had as his commanders his captains, who controlled twenty-five divisions each, and his knights, who controlled one division.

The wine had helped fade the memory of the battle and I felt the return of my old pride as I stood looking at the paladins and armies of Humanity assembled before me. I addressed them.

'Marshals, Captains, Knights and Warriors of Humanity, you have seen me to be a victorious war leader.'

'Aye!' they roared, jubilant.

'We shall be victorious here and elsewhere in the land of Mernadin. Go now, with caution, and search these buildings for Eldren. But be careful. This city could hide an army, remember!'

Count Roldero spoke up from the front rank.

'And booty, Lord Erekosë. What of that?'

King Rigenos waved his hand. 'Take what booty you desire. But remember what Erekosë has said – be wary for such things as poisoned food. Even the wine-cups could be smeared with poison. Anything in this damned city could be poisoned!'

The divisions began to march past us, each taking a different direction.

I watched them go and I thought that, while the city received them into its heart, it did not welcome them.

I wondered what we would find in Paphanaal. Traps? Hidden snipers? Everything poisoned, as Rigenos had said?

We found a city of women.

Not one Eldren man had remained.

Not one boy over twelve. Not one old man of any age.

We had slain them all at sea.

Chapter Fourteen
Ermizhad

I DID NOT know how they slew the children. I begged King
Rigenos not to give the order. I pleaded with Katorn to spare
them – to drive them from the city if he must, but not to kill
them.

But the children were slain. I do not know how many.

We had taken over the palace which had belonged to Duke Baynahn
himself. He had, it transpired, been warden of Paphanaal.

I shut myself in my quarters while the slaughter went on outside. I reflected sardonically that for all their talk of the Eldren
'filth', they did not seem to mind forcing their attentions on the
Eldren women.

There was nothing I could do. I did not even know if there was
anything I should do. I had been brought here by Rigenos to fight
for Humanity, not to judge it. I had agreed to answer his summons, after all – doubtless with reason. But I had forgotten any
reason.

I sat in a room that was exquisitely furnished with delicate furniture and fine, light tapestries on walls and floor. I looked at the
Eldren craftsmanship and I sipped the aromatic Eldren wine and I
tried not to listen to the cries of the Eldren children as they were
butchered in their beds in the houses in the streets beyond the thin
palace walls.

I looked at Kanajana, which I had propped in a corner, and I
hated the poisoned thing. I had stripped myself of my armour
and I sat alone.

And I drank more wine.

But the wine of the Eldren began to taste of blood and I tossed the cup away and found a skin that Count Roldero had given me and sucked it dry of the bitter wine it contained.

But I could not get drunk. I could not stop the screams from the streets. I could not fail to see the flickering shadows on the tapestries I had drawn over the windows. I could not get drunk and therefore I could not even begin to try to sleep, for I knew what my dreams would be and I feared those almost as much as I feared thinking of the implications of what we were doing to those who were left in Paphanaal.

Why was I here? Oh, why was I here?

There was a noise outside my door and then a knock.

'Enter,' I said.

No-one entered. My voice had been too low.

The knock sounded again.

I rose and walked unsteadily to the door and flung it open.

'Can you not leave me in peace?'

A frightened soldier of the Imperial Guard stood there. 'Lord Erekosë, forgive me for disturbing you, but I bear a message from King Rigenos.'

'What's the message?' I said without interest.

'He would like you to join him. He says that there are still plans to discuss.'

I sighed. 'Very well. I will come down shortly.'

The soldier hurried off along the corridor.

At last, reluctantly, I rejoined the other conquerors. All the marshals were there, lounging on cushions and celebrating their victory. King Rigenos was there and he was so drunk that I envied him. And, to my relief, Katorn was not there.

Doubtless he was leading the looters.

As I came into the hall, a huge cheer went up from the marshals and they raised their wine-cups in a toast to me.

I ignored them and walked to where the king was seated alone, staring vacantly into space.

'You wish to discuss further campaigns, King Rigenos,' I said. 'Are you sure?'

'Ah, my friend Erekosë. The Immortal. The Champion. The saviour of Humanity. Greetings, Erekosë.' He put a hand drunkenly on my arm. 'You disapprove of my unkingly insobriety, I see.'

'I disapprove of nothing,' I said. 'I have been drinking much myself.'

'But you – an Immortal – can contain your –' he belched – 'can contain your liquor.'

I took pains to smile and said: 'Perhaps you have stronger liquor. If so, let me try it.'

'Slave!' screamed King Rigenos. 'Slave! More of that wine for my friend Erekosë!'

A curtain parted and a trembling Eldren boy appeared. He was bearing a wineskin almost as large as himself.

'I see you have not slain all the children,' I said.

King Rigenos giggled. 'Not yet. Not while there are uses for them!'

I took the wineskin from the child and nodded to him. 'You may go.' I held the skin and put the opening to my lips and began to drink deeply. But still the wine refused to dull my brain. I hurled the skin away and it fell heavily and slopped wine over the tapestries and cushions covering the floor.

King Rigenos continued to giggle. 'Good! Good!'

These people were barbarians. Suddenly I wished that I was John Daker again. Studious, unhappy John Daker, living his quiet, cut-off life in the pursuit of pointless learning.

I turned to leave.

'Stay, Erekosë. I'll sing a song. It's a filthy song about the filthy Eldren.'

'Tomorrow.'

'It's already tomorrow!'

'I must rest.'

'I am your king, Erekosë. You owe your material form to me. Do not forget that!'

'I have not forgotten.'

The doors of the hall burst open then and they dragged in the girl.

Katorn led them and he was grinning like a sated wolf.

She was a black-haired girl. Her alien features were composed against the fear she felt. She had a strange, shifting beauty which was always there but which seemed to change with every breath she took. They had torn her garments and bruised her arms and face.

'Erekosë!' Katorn followed his men in. He, too, was very drunk. 'Erekosë – Rigenos, my lord king – *look*!'

The king blinked and looked at the girl with distaste. 'Why should we take interest in an Eldren wanton? Get hence, Katorn. Use her as you will – that is your private decision – but be sure she is not still alive when we leave Paphanaal.'

'No!' laughed Katorn. 'Look! Look at her!'

The king shrugged and inspected the wine swilling in his cup.

'Why have you brought her here, Katorn?' I asked quietly.

Katorn rocked with laughter. His thick lips opened wide and he roared in our faces. 'You know not who she is, that's plain!'

'Take the Eldren wench away, Katorn!' The king's voice rose in drunken irritation.

'My lord king – this – this is *Ermizhad*!'

'What?' The king leaned forward and stared at the girl. 'What? Ermizhad, that whore! Ermizhad of the Ghost Worlds!'

Katorn nodded. 'The same.'

The king grew more sober. 'She's lured many a mortal to his death, so I've heard. She shall die by torture for her lustful crimes. The stake shall have her.'

Katorn shook his head. 'No, King Rigenos – at least, not yet. Forget you that she's Prince Arjavh's *sister*?'

The king nodded in a mockery of gravity. 'Of course. Arjavh's sister.'

'And the implications, my lord? We should keep her prisoner, should we not? She will make a good hostage, eh? A good bargaining counter, should we need one?'

'Ah, of course. Yes. You did right, Katorn. Keep her prisoner.' The king grinned a silly grin. 'No. It is not fair. You deserve to enjoy yourself further this night. Who does not wish to enjoy himself?' He looked at me. 'Erekosë – Erekosë who cannot get drunk. She shall be put in your charge, Champion.'

I nodded. 'I accept the charge,' I said. I pitied the girl, whatever terrible crimes she had committed.

Katorn looked at me suspiciously.

'Do not worry, Lord Katorn,' I said. 'Do as the king says – continue to enjoy yourself. Slay some more. Rape some more. There must be plenty left.'

Katorn drew his brows together. Then his face cleared a little.

'A few maybe,' he said. 'But we've been thorough. Only she will live to see the sun rise, I think.' He jabbed a thumb at his prisoner, then signed to his men. 'Come! Let's finish our task.'

He stalked out.

Count Roldero got up slowly and came towards me as I stood looking at the Eldren girl.

The king looked up. 'Good. Keep her from harm, Erekosë,' he said cynically. 'Keep her from harm. She'll be a useful piece in our game with Arjavh.'

'Take her to my apartments in the east wing,' I told the guards, 'and make sure she's unmolested and has no chance to escape.'

They took her away and, almost as soon as she had left, King Rigenos made to stand up, swayed and fell with a crash to the floor.

Count Roldero gave a slight smile. 'Our liege is not himself,' he said. 'But Katorn is right. The Eldren bitch will be useful to us.'

'I understand her usefulness as a hostage,' I said, 'but I do not understand this reference to "the Ghost Worlds". I've heard them spoken of once before. What are they, Roldero?'

'The Ghost Worlds? Why, we all know of them. I should have thought that you would, too. But we do not often speak of them.'

'Why so?'

'Humankind fear Arjavh's allies so much that they will rarely mention them, in terror of conjuring them up by their words, you understand.'

'I do not understand.'

Roldero rubbed his nose and coughed. 'I am not superstitious, Erekosë,' he said. 'Like yourself.'

'I know. But what are the Ghost Worlds?'

Roldero seemed nervous. 'I'll tell you, but I'm uncomfortable about doing so in this cursed place. The Eldren know better than we what the Ghost Worlds are. We had thought, at first, that you yourself were a prisoner there. That was why I was surprised.'

'Where are they?'

'The Ghost Worlds lie beyond Earth – beyond Time and beyond Space – linked to Earth only by the most tenuous of bonds.'

Roldero's voice dropped, but he whispered on.

'There, on the torn Ghost Worlds, dwell the many-coiled serpents which are the terror and the scourge of the eight dimensions. Here, also, live ghosts and men – those who are manlike and those who are unlike men – those who know that their fate is to live without Time, and those who are unaware of their doom. And there, also, do kinfolk to the Eldren dwell – the halflings.'

'But what *are* these worlds?' I asked impatiently.

Roldero licked his lips. 'They are the worlds to which human sorcerers sometimes go in search of alien wisdom, and from which they draw helpers of horrible powers and disgusting deeds. It is said that within those worlds an initiate may meet his long-slain comrades, who may sometimes help him; his dead loves and his dead kin, and particularly his enemies – those whom he has caused to die. Malevolent enemies with great powers – or wretches who are half-souled and incomplete.'

His whispered words convinced me, perhaps because I had drunk so much. Was it these Ghost Worlds that were the origin of my strange dreams? I wanted to know more.

'But what are they, Roldero? Where are they?'

Roldero shook his head. 'I do not concern myself with such

mysteries, Erekosë. I have never been much of a mystic. I believe – but I do not probe. I know of no answer to either of your questions. They are worlds full of shadow and gloomy shores upon which drab seas beat. The populace can sometimes be summoned by powerful sorcery to visit this Earth, to haunt, to help – or to terrorise. We think that the Eldren came, originally, from these half-worlds if they were not, as our legends say, spawned from the womb of a wicked queen who gave her virginity to Azmobaana in return for immortality – the immortality which her offspring inherited. But the Eldren are material enough, for all their lack of souls, whereas the Ghost Armies are rarely solid flesh.'

'And Ermizhad?'

'The Wanton of the Ghost Worlds.'

'Why is she called that?'

'It is said that she mates with ghouls,' muttered Count Roldero. He shrugged and drank more wine. 'And in return for giving her favours to them, she receives special powers over the halflings who are friends with the ghouls. The halflings love her, I'm told, as far as it's possible for such creatures to love.'

I could not believe it. The girl seemed young. Innocent. I said as much.

Roldero gestured dismissively. 'How do you tell the age of an Immortal? Look at yourself. How old are you, Erekosë? Thirty? You look no older.'

'But I have not lived for ever,' I said. 'At least, not in one body, I do not think.'

'But how do you tell?'

I could not answer him, of course. 'Well, I think there's a great deal of superstition mixed up in your tale, Roldero,' I said. 'I would not have expected it of you, old friend.'

'Believe me or not,' Roldero muttered. 'But you would do better to believe me until I am proved a liar, eh?'

'Possibly you're right.'

'I sometimes wonder at you, Erekosë,' he said. 'Here you are owing your own existence to an incantation, and you are the most sceptical man I know!'

I smiled at this. 'Yes, Roldero. I should indeed believe more.'

'Come,' said Roldero, moving towards the prone king, who lay on his face in a pool of wine. 'Let's get our lord to bed before he drowns.'

Together we picked up the king and called for a soldier to help us as we hauled Rigenos up the stairs and dumped him on his bed.

Roldero put a huge hand on my shoulder. 'And stop brooding, friend. It will do no good. Think you that I enjoy the slaughter of children? The rape of young girls?' He rubbed his mouth with the back of his hand as if to rid it of a foul taste. 'But if it is not done now, Erekosë, it will be done at some time to our children and to our young girls. I know the Eldren are beautiful. But so are many snakes. So are some kinds of wolf that prey on sheep. It is braver to do what has to be done than it is to pretend to yourself that you are not doing it. You follow me?'

We stood in the king's bedchamber staring at each other.

'You are very kind, Roldero,' I said.

'It's well-meant advice,' he told me.

'I know it is.'

'It was not your decision to slaughter the children,' he said.

'But it was my decision to say little of it to King Rigenos,' I replied.

At the mention of his name, the king stirred and began to mumble in his stupor.

'Come,' grinned Roldero. 'Let's get out of here before he remembers the words of that dirty song he promised to sing us.'

We parted in the corridor outside the chamber. Count Roldero looked at me with some concern. 'These actions must be made,' he said. 'It has befallen us to be the instruments of a decision made some centuries ago. Do not bother yourself with matters of conscience. The future may see us as bloody-handed butchers. But we know we are not. We are men. We are warriors. And we are at war with those who would destroy us.'

I said nothing, but put my hand on his shoulder, then turned and walked back to my lonely apartments.

In my mental discomfort, I had all but forgotten the girl until I saw the guard at my door.

'Is the prisoner secure?' I asked him.

'There is no way out,' the guard said. 'No way, at least, Lord Erekosë, that a human could take. But if she were to summon her halfling allies…'

'We'll concern ourselves with those when they materialise,' I told him. He unlocked the door for me and I entered.

There was only one lamp burning and I could barely see. I took a taper from a table and with it lit another lamp.

The Eldren girl lay on the bed. Her eyes were closed, but her cheeks were stained with tears.

So they cry like us, too, I thought.

I tried not to disturb her, but she opened her eyes and I thought I saw fear in them, though it was difficult to tell, for the eyes really were strange – without orbs and flecked with gold and blue. Seeing those eyes, I remembered what Roldero had told me and I began to believe him.

'How are you?' I asked inanely.

Her lips parted, but she did not speak.

'I do not intend to harm you,' I said weakly. 'I would have spared the children if I could. I would have spared the warriors in the battle. But I have only the power to lead men to kill each other. I have no power to save their lives.'

She frowned.

'I am Erekosë,' I said.

'Erekosë?' The name was music when she spoke it. She pronounced it more familiarly than I did myself.

'You know who I am?'

'I know who you were.'

'I am reborn,' I said. 'Do not ask me how.'

'You do not seem happy to be reborn, Erekosë.'

I shrugged.

'Erekosë,' she said again. And then she voiced a low, bitter laugh.
'Why do you laugh?'

But she would not speak again. I tried to converse with her further. She closed her eyes. I left the room and went to the bed next door.

The wine had worked at last – or something had – for I slept without dreaming.

Chapter Fifteen
The Returning

NEXT MORNING I arose, washed myself, dressed and knocked on Ermizhad's door.

There was no reply.

Thinking that she had, perhaps, escaped and that Katorn would be instantly suspicious that I had helped her, I flung open the door and entered.

She had not escaped. She still lay on the bed, but now her eyes were open again as she stared at the ceiling. Those eyes were as mysterious to me as the star-flecked depths of the universe.

'Did you sleep well?' I asked.

She did not reply.

'Are you ill?' was my next, rather stupid question. But she had plainly decided to communicate with me no further. I made one last attempt and then left, going down to the great hall. Here Roldero was waiting for me and there were a few other marshals, looking the worse for wear, but King Rigenos and Katorn were not present.

Roldero's eyes twinkled. 'There are no drums beating in your skull by the look of you.'

He was right. I had not considered it, but I suffered no aftereffects from the huge quantities of wine drunk the night before.

'I feel very good,' I said.

'Ah, now I believe you are an Immortal!' he laughed. 'I have not escaped so lightly. Neither, it seems, have King Rigenos and Lord Katorn, or some of the others who were enjoying themselves so much last night.' He drew closer and said quietly: 'And I hope you are in better spirits today, my friend.'

'I suppose that I am,' I said. I felt drained of emotion, in fact.

'Good. And what of that Eldren creature? Still safe?'

'Still safe.'

'She did not try to seduce you?'

'On the contrary, she will not speak to me at all!'

'Just as well.' Roldero looked around impatiently. 'I hope they get up soon. There's much to discuss. Do we carry on inland or what?'

'I thought we agreed that the best plan was to leave a good force here, strong enough to defend the city, and get back to the Two Continents to re-equip and to check any attempt to invade us while our fleet's at Paphanaal.'

Roldero nodded. 'It's the most sensible plan. But I do not like it very much. While it has logic, it does not suit my impatience to get at the enemy as soon as possible.'

I agreed with him. 'I would like to have done with this as soon as I am able,' I told him.

But we had little clear idea where the rest of the Eldren forces were marshalled. There were four other major cities on the continent of Mernadin. The chief of these was Loos Ptokai, which lay near to the Plains of Melting Ice. This was Arjavh's headquarters and, from what the Eldren on the flagship had said, he was either there now or marching to recapture Paphanaal. It seemed to us that he would attempt this, because Paphanaal was the most important position on the coast. With it in our hands, we had a good harbour in which to bring our ships and land our men.

And if Arjavh did march against us, then all we had to do was save our energy and wait. We thought that we could leave our main force in Paphanaal, return to our own base at Noonos, bringing back the divisions of warriors who, because of insufficient ships, had been unable to come with us on the preliminary expedition.

But Roldero had something else on his mind. 'We must not forget the sorcerous fortresses of the Outer Islands,' he told me. 'They lie at World's Edge. The Outer Islands should be taken as soon as possible.'

'What exactly are the Outer Islands? Why are they so strategic?' I asked him. 'And why haven't they been mentioned before in our plans?'

'Ah,' said Count Roldero. 'Ah, it is because of our reluctance, particularly when at home, to discuss the Ghost Worlds.'

I made a sign of mock despair. 'The Ghost Worlds again!'

'The Outer Islands lie in the gateway to the Ghost Worlds,' Roldero said seriously. 'From there the Eldren can summon their ghoulish allies. Perhaps, now Paphanaal is taken, we should concentrate on smashing their strength in the west – at World's Edge.'

Had I been wrong to be so sceptical? Or was Roldero overestimating the power of the Ghost World denizens? 'Roldero, have you ever seen these halflings?' I asked him.

'Oh, yes, my friend,' he replied. 'You are wrong if you believe them legendary beings. They are, in one sense, real enough.'

I became more convinced. I trusted Roldero's opinions more than most.

'Then perhaps we should alter our strategy slightly,' I said. 'We can leave the main army here to wait for Arjavh to march against the city and waste his strength trying to take it from the land side. We return to Noonos with the large portion of the fleet, add any new ships that are ready to our force, take fresh warriors aboard – and sail against the Outer Islands while, if we are right, Arjavh expends his own force trying to retake Paphanaal.'

Roldero nodded. 'It seems a wise plan to me, Erekosë. But what of the girl, our hostage? How shall we use her to our best advantage?'

I frowned. I did not like the idea of using her at all. I wondered where she would be safest.

'I suppose we should keep her as far away from here as possible,' I said. 'Necranal would be best. There is little chance of her people being able to rescue her and she would have a difficult time getting back if she managed to escape. What do you think?'

Roldero nodded. 'I think you are right. That's sensible.'

'We must discuss all this with the king, of course,' I said gravely.

'Of course,' said Roldero, and winked.

'And Katorn,' I added.

'And Katorn,' he agreed. 'Especially Katorn.'

It was well after noon before we had the chance to speak with Katorn or the king. Both were pale-faced and were quick to agree with our suggestions as if they would agree to anything as long as they were left alone.

'We'll establish our position here,' I told the king, 'and set sail back to Noonos within the week. We should waste no time. Now that we have gained Paphanaal, we can expect savage counter-attacks from the Eldren.'

'Aye,' muttered Katorn. He was red-eyed. 'And you are right to try to block off Arjavh's summoning of his frightful Ghost Armies.'

'I am glad you approve of my plan, Lord Katorn,' I said.

His smile was twisted. 'You're proving yourself, my lord, after all. Still a little soft towards our enemies, but you're beginning to realise what they're like.'

'I wonder,' I said.

There were minor details of the plan to discuss and, while the victorious warriors continued to pleasure themselves on Eldren spoils, we talked of these matters until they were completely settled.

It was a good plan.

It would work if the Eldren reacted as we expected. And we were sure that they would.

We agreed that King Rigenos and I would return with the fleet, leaving Katorn to command the army at Paphanaal. Roldero also elected to return with us. The bulk of the warriors would remain behind. We had to hope that the Eldren did not have another fleet in the vicinity, for we would be sailing back with just the min-imum crews and would be hard-pressed to defend ourselves if attacked at sea.

But there were risks to all the different possibilities and we had to decide which actions the Eldren were most likely to take and act accordingly.

The next few days were spent in preparation for the voyage back and soon we were ready to sail.

We sailed out of Paphanaal on a dawn tide, our ships moving sluggishly through the water, for they groaned with captured Eldren treasure.

Begrudgingly the king had agreed to give Ermizhad decent quarters next to mine. His attitude towards me seemed to have changed since the first drunken night in Paphanaal. He was reserved, almost embarrassed by my presence. Doubtless he remembered vaguely that he had made some sort of fool of himself. Perhaps he resented my refusal to celebrate our victory; perhaps the glory that I had won for him made him jealous, though the gods knew I wanted nothing of that tainted glory.

Or perhaps he sensed my own disgust with the war I had agreed to fight for him and was nervous that I might suddenly refuse to be the champion he felt he so desperately needed?

I had no opportunity to discuss this with him and Count Roldero could offer no explanation save to say, in the king's favour, that the slaughter might have wearied Rigenos just as it had wearied me.

I was not sure of this, for Rigenos seemed to hate the Eldren even more than before, as was made evident by his treatment of Ermizhad.

Ermizhad still refused to speak. She hardly ate and she rarely left her cabin. But one evening, as I strolled on deck, I saw her standing at the rail and staring down into the sea as if she contemplated hurling herself into its depths.

I increased my pace so that I should be near if she did attempt to throw herself overboard. She half-turned as I approached and then looked away again.

At this point the king emerged on the poop deck and called down to me.

'I see you've taken pains to make sure the wind's behind you when you get near to the Eldren bitch, Lord Erekosë.'

I stopped and looked up. At first, I hardly understood the reference. I glanced at Ermizhad, who pretended not to have heard the king's insult. I, too, pretended I had not understood the significance of the remark and gave a slight, polite bow.

Then, deliberately, I walked past Ermizhad and paused near the rail, staring out to sea.

'Perhaps you have no sense of smell, Lord Erekosë,' the king called. Again I ignored the remark.

'It seems a pity that we must tolerate vermin on our ship when we took such pains to scrub our decks free of their tainted blood,' the king went on.

At last, furious, I turned around, but he had left the poop deck. I looked at Ermizhad. She continued to stare into the dark waters as they were pierced by our oars. She seemed almost mesmerised by the rhythm. I wondered if she really had not heard the insults.

There were several more occasions of that kind on board the flagship *Iolinda* as we sailed for Noonos. Whenever King Rigenos got the opportunity, he would speak of Ermizhad in her presence as if she were not there; speak disdainfully of her and his disgust for all her kind.

Increasingly, I found it harder to control my anger, but control it I did, and Ermizhad, for her part, showed no sign that she was offended by the king's crude references to her and her race.

I saw less of Ermizhad than I wished but, in spite of the king's warnings, came to like her. She was certainly the most beautiful woman I had ever seen. Her beauty was different from the cool beauty of Iolinda, my betrothed.

What is love? Even now, now that the whole pattern of my particular destiny seems to have been fulfilled, I do not know. Oh, yes, I still loved Iolinda, but I think that, while I did not know it, I was falling in love with Ermizhad, too.

I refused to believe the stories told about her and esteemed her, though, at that time, I had no thought of letting this affect my attitude towards her. That attitude had to be of a jailer for his prisoner – an important prisoner, at that. A prisoner who could help decide the war against the Eldren in our favour.

I did pause, once or twice, to wonder about the logic of keeping her as a hostage. If, as King Rigenos insisted, the Eldren were cold-hearted and unhuman, then why should Arjavh care that his sister would be murdered by us?

Ermizhad, if she were the creature King Rigenos believed her to be, showed no signs of her evil. Rather, she seemed to me to exhibit a singular nobility of soul that was in excellent contrast to the king's rude banter.

And then I wondered if the king realised the affection I felt for Ermizhad and was afraid that the union between his daughter and his immortal champion was threatened.

But I remained loyal to Iolinda. It did not occur to me to question that we should not be married on my return, as we had agreed.

There must be countless forms of love. Which is the form which conquers the rest? I cannot define it. I shall not try.

Ermizhad's beauty had the fascination of being an unhuman beauty, but close enough to my own race's ideal to attract me.

She had the long, pointed Eldren face that John Daker might have tried to describe as 'elfin' and failed to do justice to its nobility. She had the slanting eyes that seemed blind in their strange milkiness, the slightly pointed ears, the high angular cheekbones and a slender body that was almost boyish. All the Eldren women were slender like this, small-breasted and narrow-waisted. Her red lips were fairly wide, curving naturally upwards so that she always seemed to be on the point of smiling when her face was in repose.

For the first two weeks of our voyage, she continued to refuse to speak, although I showed her elaborate courtesy. I saw that she had everything for her comfort and she thanked me through her guards, that was all. But one day I stood outside the set of cabins where she, the king and myself had our apartments, leaning over the rail and looking at a grey sea and an overcast sky, and I saw her approach me.

'Greetings, Sir Champion,' she said half-mockingly as she came out of her cabin.

I was surprised.

'Greetings, Lady Ermizhad,' said I. She was dressed in a cloak of midnight blue flung around a simple smock of pale blue wool.

'A day of omens, I think,' she said, looking at the gloomy sky which boiled darkly now above us, full of heavy greys and dusty yellows.

'Why think you?' I enquired.

She laughed. It was lovely to hear – crystal and gold-strung harps. It was the music of heaven, not of hell. 'Forgive me,' she said. 'I sought to disturb you – but I see you are not so prone to suggestion as others of your race.'

I grinned. 'You are very complimentary, my lady. I find their superstitions a trifle tedious, I must admit. As are their insults.'

'One is not troubled by those,' she said. 'They are sad little insults, really.'

'You are very charitable.'

'We Eldren are a charitable race, I think.'

'I have heard otherwise.'

'I suppose you have.'

'I have bruises that prove otherwise!' I smiled. 'Your warriors did not seem particularly charitable in the sea-fight beyond Paphanaal.'

She bowed her head. 'And yours were not charitable when they came to Paphanaal. Is it true? Am I the only survivor?'

I licked my lips. They were suddenly dry. 'I believe so,' I said quietly.

'Then I am lucky,' she said, her voice rising a little.

There was, of course, no reply I could make.

We stood there in silence, looking at the sea.

Later she said quietly: 'So you are Erekosë. You are not like the rest of your race. In fact, you do not seem wholly of that race.'

'Aha,' I replied. 'Now I know you are my enemy.'

'What do you mean?'

'My enemies – the Lord Katorn in particular – suspect my humanity.'

'And are you human?'

'I am nothing else. I am sure of that. I have the uncertainties of any ordinary mortal. I am as confused as the rest, though my problems are, perhaps, different. How I came here, I do not know. They say I am a great hero reborn, come to aid them against your people. They brought me here by means of an incantation. But then it sometimes seems to me, in dreams, at night, that I have been many heroes.'

'And all of them human?'

'I am not sure. I do not think my basic character has altered in any of those incarnations. I have no special wisdom, no special powers, so far as I know. Would you not think that an Immortal would have gathered a great store of wisdom?'

She nodded slightly. 'I would think so, my lord.'

'I am not even sure where I am,' I continued. 'I do not know if I came here from the far future or from the far past.'

'The terms mean little to the Eldren,' she said. 'But some of us believe that past and future are the same – that Time moves in a circle, so that the past is the future and the future is the past.'

'An interesting theory,' I said. 'But a rather simple one, is it not?'

'I think I would agree with you,' she murmured. 'Time is a subtle thing. Even our wisest philosophers do not fully understand its nature. The Eldren do not think very much about Time – we do not have to, normally. Of course, we have our histories. But history is not Time. History is merely a record of certain events.'

'I understand you,' I said.

Now she came and stood by the ship's rail, one hand resting lightly upon it.

At that moment I felt the affection that I suppose a father might have for a daughter, a father who delights in his offspring's assured

113

innocence. She could not have been, I felt, much more than nineteen. Yet her voice had a confidence that comes with knowledge of the world, her carriage was proud, also confident. I realised then that Count Roldero might well have spoken the truth. How, indeed, could you gauge the age of an Immortal?

'I thought at first,' I said, 'that I came from your future. But now I am not sure. Perhaps I come from your past – that this world is, in relation to what I call the "twentieth century", in the far future.'

'This world is very ancient,' she agreed.

'Is there a record of a time when only human beings occupied Earth?'

'We have no such records,' she smiled. 'There is an echo of a myth, the thread of a legend, which says that there was a time when only the Eldren occupied Earth. My brother has studied this. I believe he knows more.'

I shivered. I did not know why, but my vitals seemed to chill within me. I could not, easily, continue the conversation, though I wanted to.

She appeared not to have noticed my discomfort.

At last I said: 'A day of omens, madam. I hope to talk with you again soon.' I bowed and returned to my cabin.

Chapter Sixteen
Confrontation with the King

T HAT NIGHT I slept without my usual precaution of a jug of
wine to send me into deeper slumber. I did it deliberately,
though with trepidation.

'EREKOSË...'
*I heard the voice calling as it had called once before to John Daker. But
this time it was not the voice of King Rigenos.*
'Erekosë...'
This voice was more musical.
*I saw green, swaying forests and great, green hills and glades and
castles and delicate beasts whose names I did not know.*
*'Erekosë? My name is not Erekosë,' I said. 'It is Prince Corum. Prince
Corum – Prince Corum Jhaelen Irsei in the Scarlet Robe – and I seek my
people. O, where are my people? Why is there no cessation to this quest?'*
*I rode a horse. The horse was mantled in yellow velvet and hung about
with panniers, two spears, a plain round shield, a bow and a quiver hold-
ing arrows. I wore a conical silver helm and a double weight of chainmail,
the lower layer of brass and the upper of silver. And I bore a long, strong
sword that was not the sword Kanajana.*
'Erekosë.'
'I am not Erekosë.'
'Erekosë!'
'I am John Daker!'
'Erekosë!'
'I am Jerry Cornelius.'
'Erekosë!'
'I am Konrad Arflane.'
'Erekosë!'

'What do you want?' I asked.

'We want your help!'

'You have my help!'

'Erekosë!'

'I am Karl Glogauer!'

'Erekosë!'

'I seek lost Tanelorn.'

The names did not matter. I knew it now. Only the fact mattered. The fact that I was a creature incapable of dying. A creature eternal. Doomed to have many shapes, to be called many names, but to be forever battling.

And perhaps I had been wrong. Perhaps I was not truly human, but only assumed the characteristics of a human being if I were caught in a human body.

It seemed to me that I howled in misery then. What was I? What was I, if I were not a man?

The voice was still calling, but I refused to heed it. How I wished I had not heeded it before, as I lay in my comfortable bed, in the comfortable identity of John Daker.

I awoke and I was sweating. I had found out nothing more about myself and the mystery of my origin. It seemed I had only succeeded in confusing myself further.

It was still night, but I dared not fall asleep again.

I peered through the darkness. I looked at the curtains pulled across the windows, the white coverlet of the bed, my wife beside me.

I began to scream.

'EREKOSË – EREKOSË – EREKOSË.'

'I am John Daker!' I screamed. 'Look – I am John Daker!'

'EREKOSË.'

'I know nothing of this name, Erekosë. My name is Elric, Prince of Melniboné. Elric Kinslayer. I am known by many names.

Many names – many names – many names...

How was it possible to possess dozens of identities all at the same time? To move from period to period at random? To move away from Earth itself, out to where the cold stars glared?

'I seek Tanelorn and peace. Oh, where lies Tanelorn?'

There was a rushing noise and then I plunged through dark, airless places, down, down, down. And there was nothing in the universe but drifting gas. No gravity, no colour, no air, no intelligence save my own – and perhaps, somewhere, one other.

Again I screamed.

And I refused to let myself know further.

Whatever the doom upon me, I thought next morning, I would never understand it. And it was probably for the best.

I went on deck and there was Ermizhad, standing in the same place at the rail, as if she had not moved all night. The sky had cleared somewhat and sunlight pushed thick beams through the clouds, the rays slanting down on the choppy sea so that the world was half-dark, half-light.

A moody day.

We stood for a while in silence, leaning out over the rail, watching the surf slide by, watching the oars smash into the waters in monotonous rhythm.

Again, she was the first to speak.

'What do they plan to do with me?' she asked quietly.

'You will be a hostage against the eventuality of your brother, Prince Arjavh, ever attacking Necranal,' I told her. It was only half the truth. There were other ways of using her against her brother, but there was no point in detailing them. 'You will be safe – King Rigenos will not be able to bargain if you are harmed.'

She sighed.

'Why did not you and the other Eldren women flee when our fleets put in to Paphanaal?' I asked. This had puzzled me for some time.

'The Eldren do not flee,' she said. 'They do not flee from cities that they build themselves.'

117

'They fled to the Mountains of Sorrow some centuries ago,' I pointed out.

'No.' She shook her head. 'They were driven there. That is the difference.'

'That is a difference,' I agreed.

'Who speaks of difference?' A new, harsher voice broke in. It was King Rigenos. He had come silently out of his cabin and stood behind us, feet apart on the swaying deck. He did not acknowledge Ermizhad but stared directly at me. He did not look well.

'Greetings, sire,' I said. 'We were discussing the meaning of words.'

'You've become uncommon friendly with the Eldren bitch!' he sneered. What was it about this man who had shown himself kind and brave in many ways that, when the Eldren were concerned, he became an uncouth barbarian?

'Sire,' I said, for I could no longer be polite. 'Sire, you speak of one who, though our enemy, is of noble blood.'

Again he sneered. 'Noble blood! The vile stuff which flows in their polluted veins cannot be termed thus! Beware, Erekosë! I realise that you are not altogether versed in our ways or our knowledge, that your memory is hazy – but remember that the Eldren wanton has a tongue of liquid gold which can beguile you to your doom and ours. Pay no heed to her!'

It was the most direct and most portentous speech he had made thus far.

'Sire,' I said.

'She'll weave such a spell that you'll be a fawning dog at her mercy and no good to any of us. I tell you, Erekosë, beware. Gods! I've half a mind to give her to the rowers and let them have their way with her before she's thrown over the side!'

'You placed her under my protection, my lord king,' I said angrily. 'And I am sworn to protect her against all dangers!'

'Fool! I have warned you. I do not want to lose your friendship, Erekosë – and more, I do not want to lose our war champion. If she shows further signs of enchanting you, I shall slay her. None shall stop me!'

'I am doing your work, my king,' I said, 'at your request. But remember *you* this – I am Erekosë. I have been many other champions. What I do is for the human race. I have taken no oath of loyalty to you or to any other king. I am Erekosë, the War Champion, Champion of Humanity – not Rigenos's Champion!'

His eyes narrowed. 'Is this treachery, Erekosë?' It was almost as if he hoped it were.

'No, King Rigenos. Disagreement with a single representative of Humanity does not constitute treachery to mankind.'

He said nothing, but just stood there, seeming to hate me as much as he hated the Eldren girl. His breathing was heavy and rasped in his throat.

'Give me no reason to regret my summoning of thee, dead Erekosë,' he said at length and turned away, going back into his cabin.

'I think it would be for the best if we discontinued our conversation,' said Ermizhad quietly.

'Dead Erekosë, eh?' I said, and then grinned. 'If I'm dead, then I'm strangely prone to emotion for a corpse.' I made light of our dispute, yet events had taken a turn which caused me to fear that he would not, among other things, allow me the hand of Iolinda – for he still did not know that we were betrothed.

She looked at me strangely and moved her hand as if to comfort me.

'Perhaps I am dead,' I said. 'Have you seen any creatures like me on the Ghost Worlds?'

She shook her head. 'Not really.'

'So the Ghost Worlds do exist?' I said. 'I had been speaking rhetorically.'

'Of course they exist!' She laughed. 'You are the greatest sceptic I have ever met!'

'Tell me about them, Ermizhad.'

'What is there to tell?' She shook her head. 'And if you do not believe what you have heard already, then there's little point if I tell you more that you will not believe, is there?'

I shrugged. 'I suppose not.' I felt she was being unduly secretive, but I did not press the matter.

'Answer one thing,' I said. 'Would the mystery of my existence be found on the Ghost Worlds?'

She smiled sympathetically. 'How could I answer that, Erekosë?'

'I don't know. I thought the Eldren knew more of – of sorcery…'

'Now you are showing yourself to be as superstitious as your fellows,' she said. 'You do not believe…'

'Madam,' I said, 'I do not know what I should believe. The logic of this world – both human and Eldren – is, I fear, a mystery to me.'

Chapter Seventeen
Necranal Again

ALTHOUGH THE KING refrained from further outbursts against either myself or Ermizhad, it could not really be said that he warmed to me again, though he grew more relaxed as the shores of Necralala drew closer.

And eventually Noonos was sighted and we left the better part of the fleet there to refit and reprovision, and sailed back up the River Droonaa to come again to Necranal.

The news of our great sea victory was already in Necranal. Indeed, it had been amplified and it seemed that I had sunk some score of ships and destroyed their crews single-handedly!

I did nothing to deny the truth of this. I was worried King Rigenos would begin to work against me. The adulation of the people, however, meant that he could not be seen to deny me anything. My power had grown. I had achieved a victory, I had proved myself the champion the people wanted.

It now seemed that, if King Rigenos acted against me, he would arouse the wrath of the people against *him* – and that wrath would be so great it could lose him his crown – and his head.

This did not mean, of course, that he had to like me, but in fact, when we had once again reached the Palace of Ten Thousand Windows, he was almost in an affable mood.

Exhaustion makes us see threats from outside when really the threat is from within – the signals of failing physical powers: I think he had begun to see me as a threat to his throne, but the sight of his palace, his people and his daughter, the promise of rest and security, reassured him that he was still the king and would always be the king. I was not interested in his crown. I was interested only in his daughter.

Guards escorted Ermizhad away to her quarters when we arrived. She had departed before Iolinda came running down the stairs into the Great Hall, her face radiant, her carriage graceful, kissing first her father and then myself.

'Have you told Father of our secret?' she asked.

'I think he knew before we left.' I laughed, turning to Rigenos, upon whose face there had come something of an abstracted look. 'We would be betrothed, sire. Do you give us your consent?'

King Rigenos opened his mouth, wiped his forehead and swallowed before nodding. 'Of course. My blessings to you. This will make our unity even stronger.'

A slight frown came to Iolinda's brow. 'Father – you are pleased, are you not?'

'Of c... yes, naturally I am pleased... naturally. But I am weary with travelling and with fighting, my dear. I need to rest. Forgive me.'

'Oh, I am sorry, Father. Yes, you must rest. You do not look well. I will have the slaves prepare some food for you and you can dine in bed.'

'Yes,' he said, 'yes.'

When he had gone, Iolinda looked at me curiously. 'You, too, seem to have suffered from the fighting, Erekosë. You are not hurt?'

'No. The battle was bloody. And I did not enjoy much of what we had to do.'

'Warriors must kill. That is the way.'

'But must they kill women, Iolinda? Must they kill children? Babies?'

She moistened her lips with her tongue. Then she said: 'Come. Let's eat in my apartments. It is more restful there.'

When we had eaten, I felt better, but was still not completely at ease.

'What happened?' she asked. 'At Mernadin?'

'There was a great sea-fight. We won it.'

'That is good.'

'Yes.'

'You took Paphanaal. You stormed it and took it.'

'Who told you we "stormed" it?' I asked in astonishment.

'Why, you do – the returning warriors. We heard the news shortly before you came back.'

'The city gave no resistance,' I told her. 'There were some women in Paphanaal and there were some children in Paphanaal and they were butchered by our troops.'

'A few women and children always get harmed in the storming of a city,' said Iolinda. 'You must not blame yourself if…'

'We did not storm the city,' I repeated. 'It was undefended. There were no men there. Every one of the male inhabitants of Paphanaal had sailed with the fleet we destroyed.'

She shrugged. Evidently she could not visualise the true picture. Perhaps it was just as well. But I could not resist one further comment:

'And, although we would have won anyway, part of our sea victory was due to our treachery,' I said.

'You were betrayed, did you say?' She looked up eagerly. 'Some treachery of the Eldren?'

'The Eldren fought honourably. We slaughtered their commander during a truce.'

'I see,' she said. Then she smiled. 'Well, we must help you forget such terrible things, Erekosë.'

'I hope you can,' I said.

The king announced our betrothal the next day and the news was received with joy by the citizens of Necranal. We stood before them on the great balcony overlooking the city. We smiled and waved but, when we went inside again, the king left us with a curt word and hurried away.

'Father really does seem to disapprove of our match,' Iolinda said in puzzlement, 'in spite of his consent.'

'A disagreement about tactics while at war,' I said. 'You know how important we soldiers think these things. He will soon forget.'

But I was perturbed. Here was I, a great hero, loved by the people, marrying the king's daughter as a hero should, and something was beginning to strike me as being not quite right. I had had the feeling for some time, but I could not trace the source. I did not know whether it was to do with my peculiar dreams, my worries concerning my origin or merely the crisis which seemed to be building between the king and myself. There again, I was still very weary and probably my anxiety was baseless.

Iolinda and I now went to the bridal bed together, as was the custom in the Human Kingdoms.

But, that first night, we did not make love.

Halfway through the night I felt my shoulder being touched and I straightened up almost instantly.

I smiled in relief.

'Oh, it is you, Iolinda.'

'It is I, Erekosë. You moaned and groaned so in your sleep that I thought it better to wake you.'

'Aye…' I rubbed my eyes. 'I thank you.' My memory was unclear, but it seemed to me that I had been experiencing the usual dreams.

'Tell me something of Ermizhad,' Iolinda said suddenly.

'Ermizhad?' I yawned. 'What of her?'

'You have seen much of her, I heard. You conversed with her. I have never conversed with an Eldren. Usually we do not take prisoners.'

I smiled. 'Well, I gather it's heresy to say so, but I found her quite – human.'

'Oh, Erekosë. That's a joke in bad taste. They say she's beautiful. They say she has a thousand human lives to account for. She's evil, is she not? She has lured many men to their deaths.'

'I did not ask her about that,' I said. 'Mainly we discussed broad matters of philosophy.'

'She is very clever, then?'

'I do not know. She seemed almost innocent to me.' Then I added hastily, diplomatically: 'But perhaps that's her cleverness – to seem innocent.'

Iolinda frowned. 'Innocent! Ha!'

I was disturbed. 'I only offer my impression, Iolinda. I have no opinions, really, concerning Ermizhad. Or for that matter the rest of the Eldren.'

'Do you love me, Erekosë?'

'Of course.'

'You would not betray me?'

I laughed and took her in my arms. 'How could you fear such a thing?'

We fell again into sleep.

Next morning, King Rigenos, Count Roldero and myself got down to the serious business of planning our strategy. Concerning ourselves with maps and battle plans, the tensions between us began to relax. Rigenos was almost cheerful. We were in unison about what should be done. By now it was likely Prince Arjavh would be attempting to retake Paphanaal – and assuredly failing. Probably he would lay siege to it, but we could bring in supplies and weapons by ship, so he would waste his time. Meanwhile, our expedition to the Outer Islands would attack Eldren positions there and, Roldero and Rigenos assured me, make it impossible for them to call on their halfling allies.

The plan, of course, depended on Arjavh's attacking Paphanaal.

'But he would have been already on his way when we sailed in,' Rigenos reasoned. 'It would be pointless for him to turn back. What could he achieve by doing that?'

Roldero agreed. 'I think it's pretty certain that he'll concentrate on Paphanaal,' he said. 'Another two or three days and our fleets will be ready to sail again. We'll soon have the Outer Islands subdued, then we move on to Loos Ptokai itself. With luck, Arjavh will still have his main force concentrated on Paphanaal. By the end of this year, every Eldren position will have fallen to us.'

I was a trifle cynical about his overconfidence. Katorn at least would have been less sure. I half-wished, in fact, that Katorn was here. I respected his advice as a soldier and strategist.

Next day, while we still pored over maps, the news came.

It astonished us. It altered every plan we had made. It made nonsense of our strategy. It put us in a frightening position.

Arjavh, Prince of Mernadin, Ruler of the Eldren, had not attacked Paphanaal. A great proportion of our troops waited there to greet him, but he had not deigned to pay them a visit.

Perhaps he had never intended to march on Paphanaal.

Perhaps he had always planned to do what he had done now and it was we who were the dupes! We had been outma-noeuvred!

'I said that the Eldren were clever,' said King Rigenos when we received the news. 'I told you, Erekosë.'

'I believe you now,' I said softly, trying to grasp the enormity of what had happened.

'Now how do you feel about them, my friend?' Roldero said. 'Are you still divided?'

I shook my head. My loyalties lay with Humanity. There was no time for conscience, no point in trying to understand these unhuman people. I had underestimated them and now it seemed that Humanity itself might have to pay the price.

Eldren ships had beached on the coasts of Necralala, on the eastern seaboard and reasonably close to Necranal. An Eldren army was pushing towards Necranal herself and, it was said, none could stand against It.

I cursed myself then. Rigenos, Katorn, Roldero, even Iolinda had all been right. I had been deceived by their golden tongues, their alien beauty.

And there was hardly a warrior in Necranal. Half our available force was in Paphanaal and it would take a month to bring them back. The fleet Eldren craft had probably crossed the ocean in half that time! We thought we had defeated their fleet at Paphanaal. We had only defeated a fraction of it!

There was fear on all our faces as we made hasty contingency plans.

'There's no point in recalling the troops in Paphanaal at this stage,' I said. 'By the time they got here, the battle would have been decided. Send a fast messenger there, Roldero. Tell them what has happened and let Katorn decide his own strategy. Tell him I trust him.'

'Very well,' Roldero nodded. 'But our available warriors are scarce in number. We can get a few divisions from Zavara. There are troops at Stalaco, Calodemia and some at Dratarda. Perhaps they can reach us in a week. Then we have some men at Shilaal and Sinana, but I hesitate to recommend their withdrawal.'

'I agree,' I said. 'The ports must be defended at all costs. Who knows how many other fleets the Eldren have?' I cursed. 'If only we had some means of gathering intelligence. Some spies…'

'That's idle talk,' Roldero said. 'Who among our people could disguise himself as an Eldren? For that matter who would be able to stomach their company long enough?'

Rigenos said: 'The only large force we have is at Noonos. We'll have to send for them and pray that Noonos is not attacked in their absence.' He looked at me. 'This is not your fault, Erekosë. We expected too much of you.'

'Well,' I promised him, 'you can expect more of me now, King Rigenos. I'll drive the Eldren back.'

Rigenos scowled thoughtfully. 'There's one thing we have to bargain with,' he said. 'The Eldren bitch – Arjavh's sister.'

And then an idea began to dawn on me. We had thought Prince Arjavh must certainly march on Paphanaal and he had not. We had never expected him to invade Necralala. But he had. Why?

'What of her?' I said.

'Could we not use her now? Tell Arjavh that, if he does not retreat, we will slay her?'

'Would he trust us?'

'That depends on how much he loves his sister, eh?' King Rigenos grinned, his spirits rising. 'Yes. Try that, anyway, Erekosë.

But do not go to him in weakness. Take all the divisions you can muster.'

'Naturally,' I said. 'I have a feeling that Arjavh will not let sentiment stop him while there is a chance he can capture the capital.'

King Rigenos ignored this. Even I wondered about the truth of it, particularly since I was beginning to think there might be something more to Arjavh's decision.

King Rigenos put his hand on my shoulder. 'We have had our differences, Erekosë. But now we are united. Go. Do battle with the Hounds of Evil. Win the battle. Kill Arjavh. This is your opportunity to strike the head from the monster that is the Eldren. And if battle seems impossible – use his sister to buy time for us. Be brave, Erekosë, be cunning – be strong.'

'I will try,' I said. 'I will leave at once to rally the warriors at Noonos. I'll take all available cavalry and leave a small force of infantry and artillery to defend the city.'

'Do as you think fit, Erekosë.'

I went back to our apartments and said farewell to Iolinda. She was full of sorrow.

I did not call on Ermizhad and tell her what we planned.

Chapter Eighteen
Prince Arjavh

I RODE OUT in my proud armour at the head of my army. My lance flaunted my banner of a silver sword on a black field, my horse pranced, my stance was confident and I had five thousand knights at my back and no idea of the size of the Eldren army.

We rode from Noonos eastwards to where the Eldren were said to be marching. We planned to cut them off before they reached Necranal.

Well before we met Arjavh's forces, we heard stories of their progress from fleeing villagers and townspeople. Apparently the Eldren were marching doggedly for Necranal, avoiding any settlements they came to. There were no reports, so far, of Eldren atrocities. They seemed to be moving too fast to bother to waste time on civilians.

Arjavh appeared to have only one ambition – to reach Necranal in the shortest possible time. I knew little of the Eldren prince save that he was reputedly a monster incarnate, a slayer and torturer of women and children. I was impatient to meet him in battle.

And there was one other rumour concerning Prince Arjavh's army. They said it was partly comprised of halflings – creatures from the Ghost Worlds. This story had terrified my men, but I had tried to assure them that the rumours were false.

Roldero and Rigenos were not with me. Roldero had returned to supervise the defence of Necranal, should we be unsuccessful, and it was in Necranal that Rigenos also stayed.

For the first time now, I was on my own. I had no advisors. I felt I needed none.

*

The armies of the Eldren and the forces of Humanity saw each other at last when they reached a vast plateau known as the Plain of Olas, after an ancient city that had once stood there. The plateau was surrounded by the peaks of distant hills. It was green and the hills were purple and we saw the banners of the Eldren as the sun set and those banners shone as if they were flags of fire.

My marshals and captains were all for rushing upon the Eldren as soon as morning came. To our relief it seemed that their numbers were smaller than ours and it now looked likely we could defeat them.

I felt relieved. It meant that I did not need to use Ermizhad for bartering with Arjavh and I could afford to stand by the Code of War which the humans used among themselves but refused to extend to the Eldren.

My commanders were horrified when I told them, but I said: 'Let us act well and with nobility. Let us set an example to them.' Now there was no Katorn, no Rigenos – not even Roldero – to argue with me and tell me that we must be treacherous and quick where Eldren were concerned. I wanted to fight this battle in the terms that Erekosë understood, for I was following Erekosë's instincts now.

I watched our herald ride into the night under a flag of truce. I watched him ride away and then, on an impulse, spurred after him.

My marshals called after me: 'Lord Erekosë – where do you go?'

'To the Eldren camp!' I called back, and laughed at their consternation.

The herald turned in his saddle, hearing the hoofbeats of my horse. 'Lord Erekosë?' he said questioningly.

'Ride on, herald – and I'll ride with you.'

And so, together, we came at last to the Eldren camp, and we stopped as the outer guards hailed us.

'What would you here, humans?' some low-ranking officer asked, peering with his blue-flecked eyes through the gloom.

The moon came out and shone silver. I took my banner from

where it lay against my horse's side. I raised it and I shook it out. The moon picked up the motif.

'That is Erekosë's banner,' said the officer.

'And I am Erekosë,' I said.

A look of disgust crossed the Eldren's face. 'We heard what you did at Paphanaal. If you were not here under the truce flag, I would...'

'I did nothing at Paphanaal I am ashamed of,' I said.

'No. You would not be ashamed.'

'My sword was sheathed during the whole stay at Paphanaal, Eldren.'

'Aye – sheathed in the bodies of babes.'

'Think what you will,' I said. 'Lead me to your master. I'll not waste time with you.'

We rode through the silent camp until we came to the simple pavilion of Prince Arjavh. The officer went inside.

Then I heard a movement in the tent and from it stepped a lithe figure, dressed in half-armour, a steel breastplate strapped over a loose shirt of green, leather hose beneath leg greaves, also of steel, and sandals on his feet. His long black hair was kept away from his eyes by a band of gold bearing a single great ruby.

And his face – his face was beautiful. I hesitate to use the word to describe a man, but it is the only one that will do justice to those fine features. Like Ermizhad, he had the tapering skull, the slanting, orbless eyes. But his lips did not curve upwards as did hers. His mouth was grim and there were lines of weariness about it. He passed his hand across his face and looked up at us.

'I am Prince Arjavh of Mernadin,' he said in his liquid voice. 'What would you say to me, Erekosë, you who abducted my sister?'

'I came personally to bring the traditional challenge from the hosts of Humanity,' I said.

He raised his head to look about him. 'Some plot, I gather. Some fresh treachery?'

'I speak only the truth,' I told him.

There was melancholy irony in his smile when he replied. 'Very well, Lord Erekosë. On behalf of the Eldren, I accept your gracious challenge. We will battle, then, shall we? We will kill each other tomorrow, shall we?'

'You may decide when to begin,' I said. 'For it is we who made the challenge.'

He frowned. 'It has been perhaps a million years since the Eldren and Humanity fought according to the Code of War. How can I trust you, Erekosë? We have heard how you butchered the children.

'I butchered no children,' I said quietly. 'I begged that they be spared. But at Paphanaal I was advised by King Rigenos and his marshals. Now I control the battle forces and I choose to fight according to the Code of War. The Code of War, I believe, that I originally drew up.'

'Aye,' Arjavh said thoughtfully. 'It's sometimes called Erekosë's Code. But you are not the true Erekosë. He was a mortal like all men. Only the Eldren are immortal.'

'I am mortal in many respects,' I said shortly, 'and immortal in others. Now, shall we decide the terms of battle?'

Arjavh spread his arms. 'Oh, how can I trust all this talk? How many times have we agreed to believe you humans and have been betrayed time after time? How can I accept that you are Erekosë, the Champion of Humanity, our ancient enemy whom, even in our legends, we respect as a noble foe? I wish to believe you, you who calls himself Erekosë, but I cannot afford to.'

'May I dismount?' I asked. The herald glanced at me in astonishment.

'If you will.'

I clambered from the back of my armoured horse and unbuck-led my sword and hung it over the pommel of the saddle and I pushed the horse to one side and walked forward and stood there confronting Prince Arjavh face to face.

'We are a stronger force than you,' I said. 'We stand a good chance of winning the battle tomorrow. It is possible that within a week even the few who escape the battle will be dead at the hands of our soldiers or our peasants. I offer you the chance to fight a noble battle, Prince Arjavh. A fair battle. I suggest that the terms can include the sparing of prisoners, medical treatment for all captured wounded, a counting of the dead and of the living.' I was remembering it all as I spoke.

'You know Erekosë's Code well,' he said.

'I should.'

He looked away and up at the moon. 'Is my sister still alive?'

'She is.'

'Why did you come thus with your herald to our camp?'

'Curiosity, I suppose,' I told him. 'I have spoken much with Ermizhad. I wanted to see if you were the devil I heard you were – or the person Ermizhad described.'

'And what do you see?'

'If you are a devil, you are a weary one.'

'Not too weary to fight,' he said. 'Not too weary to take Necranal if I can.'

'We expected you to march on Paphanaal,' I told him. 'We thought it logical that you would try to recapture your main port.'

'Aye – that's what I planned. Then I learned that you had abducted my sister.' He paused. 'How is she?'

'Well,' I said. 'She was placed under my protection and I have seen to it that she has been treated with courtesy wherever possible.'

He nodded.

'We come, of course, to rescue her,' he said.

'I wondered if that was your reason.' I smiled a little. 'We should have expected it, but we did not. You realise that they will, should you win tomorrow's battle, threaten to kill her if you do not retreat.'

Arjavh pursed his lips. 'They will kill her, anyway, will they not? They will torture her. I know how they treat Eldren prisoners.'

I could say nothing to the contrary.

'If they kill my sister,' Prince Arjavh said, 'I will burn down

Necranal though I am the only one left to do it. I will kill Rigenos, his daughter, everyone.'

'And so it goes on,' I said softly.

Arjavh looked back at me. 'I am sorry. You wished to discuss the terms of battle. Very well, Erekosë, I will trust you. I agree to all your proposals – and offer a term of my own.'

'That is?'

'Deliverance of Ermizhad from captivity if we should win. It will save you and us many lives.'

'It would,' I agreed, 'but it is not for me to make that bargain. I regret it, Prince Arjavh, but it is the king who holds her. If she were my prisoner and not just under my protection, I would do as you suggest. If you win, you must go on to Necranal and lay siege to the city.'

He sighed. 'Very well, Sir Champion. We shall be ready at dawn tomorrow.'

I said hurriedly: 'We outnumber you, Prince Arjavh. You could go back now – in peace.'

He shook his head. 'Let the battle be fought.'

'Until dawn, then, Prince of the Eldren.'

He moved his hand tiredly in assent. 'Farewell, Lord Erekosë.'

'Farewell.' I mounted my horse and rode back to our camp in a sorrowful mood, the puzzled herald at my side.

Once again I was divided. Were the Eldren so clever they could deceive me so easily?

Tomorrow would tell.

That night in my own pavilion I slept as badly as ever, but I accepted the dreams, the vague memories, and I did not attempt to fight them, to interpret them. It had become clear to me that there was no point to it. I was what I was – I was the Eternal Champion, the Everlasting Wager of War. I would never know why.

Before dawn our trumpets warned us to awake and make ourselves ready. I buckled on my armour, my sword and my lance's cover was ripped off to reveal the long, metal-shod spear.

I went out into the chill of the dying night. The day was not yet with us. Silhouetted against what little light we had, my cavalry was already mounting. There was a cold, clammy sweat on my forehead. I wiped it with a rag time after time, but it remained there. I raised my helm and brought it down over my head, strapping it to my shoulder plates. My squires handed me my gauntlets and I pulled them on. Then, stiff-legged in my armour, I stalked towards my steed, was helped into the saddle, was handed my shield and my lance, and cantered up the line to the head of my troops.

It was very quiet when we began to move – a steel sea lapping at the coast that was the Eldren camp.

As the watery dawn broke, our forces sighted each other. The Eldren were still by their camp but, when they saw us, they too began to move. Very slowly, it seemed, but implacably.

I lifted my visor to get a wider view of the surroundings. The ground seemed good and dry. There appeared to be no places with superior advantages.

The horses' hoofs thumped the turf. The arms of the riders clattered at their sides. Their armour clashed and their harness creaked. But in spite of this a silence seemed to fill the air.

Nearer we came and nearer.

A flight of swallows flew high above us and then glided away towards the far-off hills.

I closed my visor. The back of the horse jogged beneath me. The cold sweat seemed to cover my body and clog my armour. The lance and the shield were suddenly very heavy.

I smelled the stink of other sweating men and horses. Before long, I would smell their blood, too.

Because of our need for speed, we had brought no cannon. The Eldren, also wishing to travel rapidly, had no artillery either. Perhaps, I thought, their siege machines were following behind at a slower pace.

Nearer now. I could make out Arjavh's banner and a little cluster of flags that were those of his commanders.

I planned to depend upon my cavalry. They would spread out on two sides to surround the Eldren while another arrowhead of horsemen pierced the centre of their ranks and pushed through to the rear so that we would surround them on all sides.

Nearer still. My stomach grumbled and I tasted bile in my mouth.

Close. I reined in my horse and raised my lance and gave the order for the archers to shoot.

We had no crossbows, only longbows, which had greater range and penetrating power and could shoot many more arrows at a time. The first flight of arrows screamed overhead and thudded down into the Eldren ranks and then were almost instantly followed by another flight and then another.

Our shafts were answered by the slim arrows of the Eldren. Horses and men shrieked as the arrows found their marks and for a moment there was consternation among our men as their ranks became ragged. But then, with great discipline, they re-formed.

Again I raised my lance on which fluttered my black-and-silver pennant.

'Cavalry! Advance at full gallop!'

The trumpets shouted the order. The air was savaged by the sound. The knights spurred their war-steeds forward and began, line upon line of them, to fan out on two sides while another division rode straight towards the centre of the Eldren host. These knights were bent over the necks of their fast-moving horses, lances leaning at an angle across their saddles, some held under the right arm and aimed to the left and others secure under left arms, aimed at the right. Their helmet plumes fluttered behind them as they bore down on the Eldren. Their cloaks streamed out, and their pennants waved and the dim sunlight gleamed on their armour.

I was almost deafened by the thunder of hoofs as I kicked my charger into a gallop and, with a band of fifty picked knights behind me, they themselves surrounding the twin standards of Humanity, rode forward, straining my eyes for Arjavh whom, at that moment, I hated with a terrible hatred.

I hated him because I must fight this battle and possibly kill him.

With a fearful din made up of shouts and clashing metal, we smashed into the Eldren army and soon I was oblivious to all but the need to kill and defend my life against those who would kill me. I broke my lance early on. It smashed right through the armoured body of an Eldren noble and split with the impetus. I left it in him and drew my sword.

Now I hewed about me with savage intensity, seeking sight of Arjavh. At last I saw him, a huge mace swinging from his gauntleted hand, battering at the infantrymen who sought to pull him from his saddle.

'Arjavh!'

He glimpsed me from the corner of his eye as I waited for him. 'A moment, Erekosë, I have work here.'

'Arjavh!' The name I screamed was a challenge, nothing else.

Arjavh finished the last of the foot soldiers and he kicked his horse towards me, still flailing around him with his giant mace as two mounted knights came at him. Then the men drew back as they saw we were about to engage.

We came close enough to fight now. I aimed a mighty blow at him with my poisoned sword, but he pulled aside in time and I felt his mace glance off my back as I leaned so far forward in my saddle after the wasted blow that my sword almost touched the churned ground.

I brought the sword up in an underarm swing and the mace was there to deflect it. For several minutes we fought until, in my astonishment, I heard a voice some distance away.

'RALLY THE STANDARD! RALLY, KNIGHTS OF HUMANITY!'

We had not succeeded in our tactics! That was obvious from the cry. Our forces were attempting to consolidate and attack afresh. Arjavh smiled and lowered his mace.

'They sought to surround the halflings,' he said and laughed aloud.

'We'll meet again soon, Arjavh,' I shouted as I turned my horse back and spurred it through the press, forcing my way through the milling, embattled men towards the standard which swayed to my right.

There was no cowardice in my leaving and Arjavh knew it. I had to be with my men when they rallied. That was why Arjavh had lowered his weapon. He had not sought to stop me.

Chapter Nineteen
The Battle Decided

Arjavh had mentioned the halflings. I had noticed no ghouls amongst his men. What were they, then? What kind of creatures could not be surrounded?

The halflings were only part of my problem. Fresh tactics had to be decided upon hurriedly or the day would be soon lost. Four of my marshals were desperately trying to get our ranks re-formed as I came up to them. The Eldren enclosed us where we had planned to enclose them and many groups of our warriors were cut off from the main force.

Above the noise of the battle I shouted to one of my marshals: 'What's the position? Why did we fail so quickly? We outnumber them.'

'It's hard to tell what the position is, Lord Erekosë,' the marshal answered, 'or how we failed. One moment we had surrounded the Eldren and the next moment half their forces were surrounding us – they vanished and reappeared behind us! Even now we cannot tell which is material Eldren and which halfling.' The man who answered me was Count Maybeda, an experienced old warrior. His voice was ragged and he was very much shaken.

'What other qualities do these halflings possess?' I asked.

'They are solid enough when fighting, Lord Erekosë, and they can be slain by ordinary weapons – but they can disappear at will and be wherever they wish on the field. It is impossible to plan tactics against such a foe.'

'In that case,' I decided, 'we had best keep our men together and fight a defensive action. I think we still outnumber the Eldren and their ghostly allies. Let them come to us!'

The morale of my warriors was low. They were disconcerted

and were finding it difficult to face the possibility of defeat when victory had seemed so certain.

Through the milling men I saw the basilisk banner of the Eldren approaching us. Their cavalry poured in swiftly with Prince Arjavh at their head.

Our forces came together again and once more I was doing battle with the Eldren leader.

He knew the power of my sword – knew that the touch of it could slay him if it fell on a break in his armour – but that deadly mace, wielded with the dexterity with which another would wield a sword, warded off every blow I aimed.

I fought him for half an hour until he showed signs of dazed weariness and my own muscles ached horribly.

And again our forces had been split! Again it was impossible to see how the battle went. For most of the time I was uncaring, oblivious to the events around me as I concentrated on breaking through Arjavh's splendid guard.

Then I saw Count Maybeda ride swiftly past me, his golden armour split, his face and arms bloody. In one red hand he carried the torn banner of Humanity and his eyes stared in fear from his wounded head.

'Flee, Lord Erekosë!' he screamed as he galloped past. 'Flee! The day is lost!'

I could not believe it, until the ragged remnants of my warriors began to stream past me in ignominious flight.

'Rally, Humanity!' I called. 'Rally!' But they paid me no heed. Again Arjavh dropped his mace to his side.

'You are defeated,' he said.

Reluctantly I lowered my sword.

'You are a worthy foe, Prince Arjavh.'

'You are a worthy foe, Erekosë. I remember our battle terms. Go in peace. Necranal will need you.'

I shook my head slowly and drew a heavy breath. 'Prepare to defend yourself, Prince Arjavh,' I said.

He shrugged, swiftly brought up the mace against the blow I

aimed at him and then brought it down suddenly upon my metal-gauntleted wrist. My whole arm went numb. I tried to cling to the sword, but my fingers would not respond. It dropped from my hand and hung by a thong from my wrist.

With a curse, I flung myself from my saddle straight at him, my good hand grasping at him, but he turned his horse aside and I fell, face forward, in the bloody mud of the field.

I attempted once to rise, failed and lost consciousness.

Chapter Twenty

A Bargain

WHO AM I?
You are Erekosë, the Eternal Champion.
WHAT IS MY REAL NAME?
Whatever it happens to be.
WHY AM I AS I AM?
Because that is what you have always been.
WHAT IS 'ALWAYS'?
Always.
WILL I EVER KNOW PEACE?
You will sometimes know peace.
FOR HOW LONG?
For a while.
WHERE DID I COME FROM?
You have always been.
WHERE WILL I GO?
Where you must.
FOR WHAT PURPOSE?
To fight.
TO FIGHT FOR WHAT?
To fight.
FOR WHAT?
Fight.
FOR WHAT?

I shivered, aware that I was no longer clad in my armour. I looked up. Arjavh stood over me.

'I wonder why he hated me then,' he was murmuring to himself. Then he realised I was awake and his expression altered. He gave a light smile. 'You're a ferocious one, Sir Champion.'

I looked into his moody, milky eyes.

'My warriors,' I said, 'what...?'

'Those that were left have fled. We released the few prisoners we had and sent them after their comrades. Those were the terms, I believe?'

I struggled up. 'Then you are going to release me?'

'I suppose so. Although...'

'Although?'

'You would be a useful bargaining prisoner.'

I took his meaning and relaxed, sinking back onto the hard bed. I thought deeply and fought the idea which came to me. But it grew too large in me. At length I said, almost against my will: 'Trade me for Ermizhad.'

His cool eyes showed surprise for an instant. 'You would suggest that? But Ermizhad is such a strong hostage for Humanity.'

'Damn you, Eldren. I told you to trade me for her.'

'You're a strange human, my friend. But with your permission granted, that is what I shall do. I thank you. You really do remember the old Code of War, don't you? I think you are who you say you are.'

I closed my eyes. My head ached.

He left the tent and I heard him instructing a messenger.

'Make sure the people know!' I shouted from the bed. 'The king may not agree, but the people will force his hand. I'm their hero! They'll willingly trade me for an Eldren – no matter who that Eldren is.'

Arjavh instructed the messenger accordingly. He came back into the tent.

'It puzzles me,' I said at length. He was sitting on a bench on the other side of the tent. 'It puzzles me that the Eldren have not conquered Humanity before now. With those halfling warriors, I should think you'd be invincible.'

He shook his head. 'We rarely make use of our allies,' he said. 'But I was desperate. You can understand that I was prepared to go to almost any measures to rescue my sister.'

'I can,' I told him.

'We would never have invaded,' he continued, 'had it not been for her.' It was said so simply that I believed him. I had already been fairly certain of that.

I took a deep breath. 'It is hard for me,' I said. 'I am forced to fight like this, with no clear idea about the rights or the wrongs of that fighting, with no true knowledge of this world, with no opinions of those who inhabit it. Simple facts turn out to be lies – and unbelievable things turn out to be true. What are the halflings, for instance?'

Again he smiled. 'Sorcerous ghouls,' he said.

'That is what Count Roldero told me. It is no explanation.'

'What if I told you they were capable of breaking up their atomic structure at will and assembling again in another place? You would not understand me. Sorcery, you would say.'

I was surprised at the scientific nature of his explanation. 'I would understand you better,' I said slowly.

He raised his slanting eyebrows.

'You *are* different,' he said. 'Well, the halflings, as you have seen, are related to the Eldren. Not all the dwellers on the Ghost Worlds are our kin – some are more closely related to men, and there are other, baser forms of life.

'The Ghost Worlds are solid enough, but exist in an alternate series of dimensions to our own. There are many such series, our philosophers believe – possibly an infinite series. On the worlds we know, the halflings have no special powers – no more than we have – but here they have. We do not know why. They do not know why. On Earth different laws seem to apply for them. More than a million years ago we discovered a means of bridging the dimensions between Earth and these other worlds. We found a race akin to our own who will, at times, come to our aid if our need is especially great. This was one of those times. Sometimes, however, the bridge ceases to exist when the Ghost Worlds move into another phase of their weird orbit, so that any halflings on Earth cannot return and any of our people are in the same position if they are on the Ghost Worlds. Therefore, you will understand, it is dangerous to stay on either side overlong.'

'Is it possible,' I asked, 'that the Eldren came originally from these Ghost Worlds?'

'I suppose it is possible,' he agreed. 'There are no records, though.'

'Perhaps that is why the humans hate you as aliens,' I suggested.

'That is not the reason,' he told me, 'for the Eldren occupied Earth for ages before humankind ever came here.'

'What!'

'It is true,' he said. 'I am an immortal and my grandfather was an immortal. He was slain during the first wars between the Eldren and Humanity. When the humans came to Earth, they had incredible weapons of terrible destructive potential. In those days we also possessed similar weapons. The wars created such destruction that the Earth seemed like a blackened ball of mud when the wars were ended and the Eldren defeated. So terrifying was the destruction that we swore never again to use our weapons, whether we were threatened with extermination or not. We could not assume the responsibility for destroying an entire planet.'

'You mean you still have these weapons?'

'They are locked away, yes.'

'And you have the knowledge to use them?'

'Of course. We are immortal. We have many people who fought in those ancient wars, some even built new weapons before our decision was made.'

'Then why…?'

'I have told you. We swore not to.'

'What happened to the humans' weapons – and their knowledge of them? Did they make the same decision?

'No. The human race degenerated. Wars occurred among

themselves. At one time they almost wiped themselves out completely, at another they were barbarians, and at another they seemed to have matured, to have conquered their monstrous egos and found self-respect at last, to be at peace with their own souls and with one another. During one of those stages they lost the knowledge and the remaining weapons. In the last million years they have climbed back from absolute savagery – the peaceful years were short, a false lull – and I'd predict they'll sink back again soon enough. They seem bent on their own destruction as well as ours. We have wondered if the humans, who must surely exist in other planes, are the same. Perhaps not.'

'I hope not,' I said. 'How do you think the Eldren will fare against the humans?'

'Badly,' he said. 'Particularly since the humans are inspired by your leadership and the gateway to the Ghost Worlds is due soon to close again. Previously Humanity was split by quarrels, you see. King Rigenos could never get his marshals to agree and he was too uncertain of himself to make the large decisions. But you have made decisions for him and you have united the marshals. You will win, I think.'

'You are a fatalist,' I said.

'I am a realist,' he said.

'Could not peace terms be arranged?'

He shook his head. 'What use is it to talk?' he asked me bitterly. 'You humans, I pity you. Why will you always identify our motives with your own? We do not seek power – only peace. But that, I suppose, this planet shall never have until Humanity dies of old age.'

I stayed with Arjavh for a few more days before he released me, on trust, and I rode back towards Necranal. It was a long, lonely ride and I had a great deal of time to think.

I was hardly recognised this time, for I was dusty and my armour was battered and the people of Necranal had become used to seeing beaten warriors returning to the city.

I reached the Palace of Ten Thousand Windows. A gloomy quiet had settled on it. The king was not in the Great Hall and Iolinda was not in her quarters.

In my old apartments, I stripped off my armour. 'When did the Lady Ermizhad leave?' I asked a slave.

'Leave, master? Is she not still here?'

'What? Where?'

'In the same quarters, surely.'

I still had my breastplate on and I donned my sword as I strode through the corridors until I got to Ermizhad's apartments and brushed past the guard on the door.

'Ermizhad – you were to be traded for me. Those were the terms. Where is the king? Why has he not kept his word?'

'I knew nothing of this,' she said. 'I did not know Arjavh was so close, otherwise...'

I interrupted her. 'Come with me. We'll find the king and get you on your journey back.'

I half dragged her from room to room of the palace until at last I found the king in his private apartments. He was in conference with Roldero as I burst in upon them.

'King Rigenos, what is the meaning of this? My word was given to Prince Arjavh that Ermizhad was to leave here freely upon my release. He allowed me to leave his camp on trust and now I return to find the Lady Ermizhad still in captivity. I demand that she be released immediately.'

The king and Roldero laughed at me.

'Come now, Erekosë,' said Roldero. 'Who needs to keep his word to an Eldren jackal? Now we have our war champion back and still retain our chief hostage. Forget it, Erekosë. There is no need to regard the Eldren as human!'

Ermizhad smiled. 'Do not worry, Erekosë. I have other friends.' She closed her eyes and began to croon. At first the words came softly, but the volume rose until she was giving voice to a weird series of harmonies.

Roldero jumped forward, dragging out his sword.

'Sorcery!'

I stepped between them.

Roldero said urgently: 'Erekosë! The bitch invokes her demon kind!'

I drew my own sword and held it warningly in front of me, protecting Ermizhad. I had no idea what she was doing, but I was going to give her the chance, now, to do whatever she wanted.

Her voice changed abruptly and then stopped. Then she cried: 'Brethren! Brethren of the Ghost Worlds – aid me!'

Chapter Twenty-One

An Oath

Q UITE SUDDENLY THERE materialised in the chamber some dozen or so Eldren, their faces but slightly different from others I had seen. I recognised them now as halflings.

'There!' shouted Rigenos. 'Evil sorcery. She is a witch. I told you! A witch!'

The halflings were silent. They surrounded Ermizhad until all their bodies touched hers and one another's. Then Ermizhad shouted: 'Away, brethren – back to the camp of the Eldren!'

Their forms began to flicker so that they seemed half in our dimension, half in some other. 'Goodbye, Erekosë,' she cried. 'I hope we shall meet in happier circumstances.'

'I hope so!' I shouted back. And then she vanished.

'Traitor!' cursed King Rigenos. 'You aided her escape!'

'You should die by torture!' added Roldero, disgusted.

'I'm no traitor, as well you know,' I said evenly. 'You are traitors – traitors to your words, to the great tradition of your ancestors. You have no case against me, you stupid – stupid brutes.'

I stopped, turned on my heel and left the chamber.

'You lost the battle – War Champion!' screamed King Rigenos after me as I stalked out. 'The people do not respect defeat!'

I went to find Iolinda.

She had been walking in the balconies and had now returned to her apartments. I kissed her, needing at that moment a woman's friendly sympathy, but I seemed to meet a block. She was not, it seemed, prepared to give me help, although she kissed me dutifully. At length I ceased to embrace her and stood back a little, looking into her eyes.

'What's wrong?'

'Nothing,' she said. 'Should there be? You are safe. I had feared you dead.'

Was it me, then? Was it? I pushed the thought from me. But can a man force himself to love a woman? Can he love two women at the same time? I was desperately clinging to the strands of the love I had felt for her when first we met.

'Ermizhad is safe,' I blurted. 'She called her halfling brothers to her aid and, when she returns to the Eldren camp, Arjavh will take his forces back to Mernadin. You should be pleased.'

'I am,' she said, and then: 'And you are pleased, no doubt, that our hostage escaped!'

'What do you mean?'

'My father told me how you'd been enchanted by her wanton sorcery. You seemed to be more anxious for her safety than ours.'

'That is foolish talk.'

'You seem to like the company of the Eldren, too. Holidaying with our greatest enemy…'

'Stop!'

'I think my father spoke true, Erekosë.' Her voice was subdued now. She turned from me.

'But, Iolinda, I love you. You alone.'

'I do not believe you, Erekosë.'

What is it in me that I should become what I became then? At that moment I gave an oath which was to affect all our destinies. Why, as my love for her began to fade and I saw her as a selfish, grasping fool, did I yet protest a greater love for her?

I do not know. I only know that I did it.

'I love you more than life, Iolinda!' I said. 'I would do anything for you!'

'I do not believe you!'

'I do. I will prove it!' I cried in agony.

She turned. There was pain and reproach in her eyes. There was a bitterness that went so deep it had no bottom. There was anger and there was revenge.

'How will you prove it, Erekosë?' she said softly.

'I swear I shall kill all the Eldren.'

'All?'

'Every single Eldren.'

'You will spare none?'

'None! None! I want it to be over. And the only way I can finish it is to kill them all. Then it will be over – only then!'

'Including Prince Arjavh and his sister?'

'Including them!'

'You swear this? You swear it?'

'I swear it. And when the last Eldren dies, when the whole world is ours, then I will bring it to you and we shall be married.'

She nodded. 'Very well, Erekosë.' She went swiftly from the room.

I unstrapped my sword and flung it savagely to the floor. I spent the next few hours fighting my own agony of spirit.

But I had made the oath now.

Soon I became cold. I meant what I had said. I would destroy all the Eldren. Rid the world of them. Rid myself of this continual turmoil in my mind.

Chapter Twenty-Two
The Reaving

THE LESS OF a man I became, and the more of an automaton, so the dreams and half-memories ceased to plague me. It was as if they had deliberately driven me into this mindless rôle; so long as I continued to be a creature without remorse or conscience they would reward me with their absence. If I again showed signs of ordinary humanity, then they would punish me with their presence.

But that is a notion. It is no nearer the truth, I suppose, than any other. One might also argue that I was about to achieve the catharsis that would rid me of any ambivalence; banish my nightmares; cleanse my psyche.

In the month I spent preparing for the great war against the Eldren, I saw but little of my betrothed and, finally, ceased to seek her out, concentrating instead on the plans for the campaigns we intended to fight.

I developed the strictly controlled mind of the soldier. I allowed no emotion, whether it was love or hate, to influence me.

I became strong. And in my strength I became virtually inhuman. I knew people remarked upon it – but they also saw in me the qualities of a great battle leader and, while all avoided my company socially, they were very glad that Erekosë led them.

Arjavh and his sister returned to their ships and in their ships went back to their own land. Now, doubtless, they awaited us, readying themselves for the next battle.

We continued with our original plans and at length were ready to sail for the Outer Islands at World's Edge. The gateway to the Ghost Worlds which we intended to close.

Then we sailed.

It was a long and arduous sailing, that one, before we sighted the bleak cliffs of the Outer Islands and prepared ourselves for the invasion.

Roldero was with me. But it was a grim Roldero, a silent Roldero who had made himself, as I had, into nothing but an instrument of war.

Warily we sailed in. The Eldren, however, had known of our coming and had all but deserted their towns. This time there were no women and no children, nought but a few handfuls of Eldren warriors whom we slew. And of halflings there were none. Arjavh had spoken the truth when he said the gates were closing to the Ghost Worlds.

We ripped the towns to rubble, burning and pillaging as a matter of course, but without lust. We tortured captured Eldren to discover the meaning for this desertion and they told us nothing intelligible; but secretly I knew the meaning. Our troops became morose, possessed of a sense of anticlimax and, though we left no building standing, no Eldren alive, the men could not rid themselves of the notion that they had been thwarted in some inexplicable way – as an ardent lover is innocently thwarted by a coy maiden.

And, because of the Eldren's refusal to give them a mighty battle, our soldiers grew to hate the Eldren that much more.

When our work was done in the Outer Islands, and every building was dust, every Eldren a corpse, we sailed almost immediately for the continent of Mernadin and put into Paphanaal, which was still held by our forces under the Lord Katorn. But, in the meantime, King Rigenos had joined them and was waiting for us to arrive. We landed our troops and pushed outwards across the continent, bent on conquest.

I remember few incidents in detail. Days merged one into the other and wherever we went we slew Eldren. There was no Eldren fortress which could withstand our grim thrusting.

I was tireless in my murdering; insatiable in my bloodlust. Humanity had wanted such a wolf as I, and now they had him and they followed him, and they feared him.

It was a year of fire and steel and ruined flesh; Mernadin seemed at times to be nothing but a sea of smoke and blood. The troops were all physically weary, but the spirit of slaughter was in them and it gave them a horrible vitality.

A year of pain and death. Everywhere that the banners of Humanity met the standards of the Eldren, the basilisk standards would be torn down and trampled.

We put all we found to the sword. We mercilessly punished deserters in our own ranks, we flogged our troops to greater endurance.

We were the horsemen of death, King Rigenos, Lord Katorn, Count Roldero and myself. We grew as gaunt as hungry dogs and it seemed we fed on Eldren flesh, drank only Eldren blood. Fierce dogs we were. Wild-eyed and panting dogs, sharp-fanged dogs forever restless for the scent of fear and death.

Towns burned behind us, cities fell and were crushed, stone by stone, to the ground. Eldren corpses littered the countryside and the fairest of our camp followers were fat carrion birds and sleek-coated jackals. A year of bloodshed. A year of destruction. But was it Mernadin I wished to destroy, or was it myself? If I could not force myself to love, then I could force myself to hate; and this I did. All feared me, humans and Eldren alike, as I turned beautiful Mernadin into a funeral pyre on which I sought, in terrible bewilderment and grief, to burn the decaying vestiges of my own humanity.

I cannot justify my actions. Roldero had said that men must be judged by their deeds, not their motives. I offer such speculation only in the hope that by understanding our motives we may thus control our deeds.

It was in the Valley of Kalaquita, where stood the garden city of Lakh, that King Rigenos was killed.

The city looked peaceful and deserted, and we rode down upon it with little caution. We howled one great, concerted war-cry and, in place of the disciplined army which had landed at Paphanaal, we were one mass of blood-encrusted armour and dust-ingrained flesh, waving our weapons and galloping wildly upon that garden city of Lakh.

It was a trap.

The Eldren were in the hills and had used their beautiful city as bait. Silver-snouted cannon suddenly shouted from surrounding copses and sent a searing shower of shot into our astonished soldiers' midst! Slender arrows whistled in a wave of sharp-tipped terror as the hidden Eldren archers took their vengeance with their bows.

Horses fell. Men screamed. We turned in confusion. But then our own bowmen began to retaliate, concentrating not on the enemy archers, but on their cannoneers. Gradually the silver guns went silent and the archers melted back into the hills, retreating again to one of their few remaining fortresses.

I turned to King Rigenos, who sat beside me on his big war-steed. He was rigid, staring up at the sky. And then I saw that an arrow had pierced his thigh and imbedded itself in his saddle, pinning him to his horse.

'Roldero!' I shouted. 'Get a doctor for the king if we have one.'

Roldero rode up from where he had been taking account of our dead. He pushed back the king's visor and shrugged. Then he stared significantly at me. 'He has not breathed for several minutes by the look of him.'

'Nonsense. An arrow in the thigh doesn't kill. Not normally, at any rate – and not so quickly. Get the doctor.'

A peculiar smile crossed Roldero's bleak features. 'It was the shock, I think, that killed him.' Then he laughed brutally and pushed at the armoured corpse with his hand so that it tilted over, wrenching the arrow free, and crashed into the mud. 'Your betrothed is queen now, Erekosë,' said Roldero, still laughing. 'I congratulate you.'

My horse stirred as I stared down at Rigenos's corpse. Then I shrugged and turned my steed away.

It was our habit with the dead to leave them, no matter who they had been, where they lay.

We took Rigenos's horse with us. It was a good horse.

The loss of the king did not worry our warriors much, though Katorn himself seemed a little perturbed, perhaps because he had had such great influence over the monarch. But the king had possessed no real authority in this last year, for Humanity followed a grimmer chief, who some thought might be Death Himself.

Dead Erekosë is what they called me. The vengeful, mindless Sword of Humanity.

I did not care what they called me – Reaver, Bloodletter, Berserker – for my dreams no longer plagued me, my own hypocrisy did not disturb me, and my ultimate goal came closer and closer.

It was the last fortress of the Eldren left undefeated. I dragged my armies behind me as if by a rope. I dragged them towards the principal city of Mernadin, by the Plains of Melting Ice, Arjavh's capital – Loos Ptokai.

And at last we saw its looming towers silhouetted against a red evening sky. Of marble and black granite, it rose mighty and seemingly invulnerable above us.

But I knew we should take it.

I had Arjavh's word for it, after all. He had told me we should win.

The night after we had camped beneath the walls of Loos Ptokai, I sprawled in my chair and could not sleep. Instead I stared into the darkness. This was not my habit. Normally I would now slump into my bed and snore till dawn, wearied by the day's killing.

But tonight I brooded.

And then, at dawn the next day, my features cold as stone, I rode beneath my banner as I had ridden a year before into the camp of the Eldren, with my herald at my side.

We came close to the main gate of Loos Ptokai and then we stopped. A few Eldren looked down from distant battlements but I could not read their expressions.

My herald raised his golden trumpet to his lips and blew an eery blast upon it which echoed among the black and white towers of Loos Ptokai.

'Eldren prince!' I called in my dead voice. 'Arjavh of Mernadin, I have come to slay you.'

Then on the battlements directly over the great main gate I saw Arjavh appear. He peered down at me and there was a sadness in his strange eyes.

'Greetings, old enemy,' he called. 'You will have a long siege before you break this, the last of our strength.'

'So be it,' I said, 'but break it we shall.'

Arjavh paused. Then he said: 'We once agreed to fight a battle according to the Erekosian Code of War. Do you wish to discuss terms again?'

I shook my head. 'We shall not stop until every Eldren is slain. I have sworn an oath, you see, to rid Earth of all your kind.'

'Then,' said Arjavh, 'before the battle commences, I invite you to enter Loos Ptokai as my guest and refresh yourself. You would seem in need of refreshment.'

At this I bridled, but then my herald sneered. 'They become ingenuous in their defeat, master, if they think they can deceive you by such a simple trick.'

My mind had once again suddenly become a battleground of conflicting emotions. 'Be silent!' I ordered the herald. I took a deep breath.

'Well?' called Arjavh.

'I accept,' I said hollowly. And then I added: 'Is the Lady Ermizhad therein?'

'She is – and is eager to see you again.' There was an edge to Arjavh's voice as he answered this last question. For a moment I was again suspicious; did I detect the threat of treachery?

Arjavh must have been aware of my own affection for his sister:

the affection I did not admit, but which secretly contributed to my decision to enter Loos Ptokai.

The herald said in astonishment: 'My lord, surely you cannot be serious? As soon as you are inside the gates, you will be slain. There were stories once that you and Prince Arjavh were on not unfriendly terms, for enemies, but after the havoc you have caused in Mernadin, he will kill you immediately. Who would not?'

I shook my head. I was in a new and quieter mood. 'He will not,' I said. 'And this way I can find an opportunity to judge the Eldren strength. It will be useful to us.

'But disastrous for us, if you should die.'

'I will not die,' I said, and then, incredibly, all the ferocity, the hate, the mad battle-anger, rushed out of me, leaving me, as I turned away from the herald so he should not see, with tears in my eyes.

'Open your gates, Prince Arjavh,' I called in shaking tones. 'I come to Loos Ptokai as your guest.'

Chapter Twenty-Three
In Loos Ptokai

I RODE MY horse slowly into the city, having left my sword and lance with the herald, who was now, in astonishment, galloping back to our own camp to give the news to the marshals.

The streets of Loos Ptokai were silent, as if in mourning. And when Arjavh came down the steps from the battlements to greet me, I saw, that he, too, wore the expression which showed upon my own harsh features. His step was not so lithe and his voice not quite so lilting as when we had first met a year before.

I dismounted. He gripped my arm.

'So,' he said in attempted gaiety, 'the barbarian battlemonger is still material. My people had begun to doubt it.'

'I suppose they hate me,' I said.

He seemed a little surprised. 'The Eldren cannot hate,' he said as he led me towards his palace.

I was shown by Arjavh to a small room containing a bed, a table and a chair of wonderful workmanship, all slender and seemingly of precious metal but in fact of cunningly wrought wood. In one corner was a sunken bath with water steaming in it.

When Arjavh had gone, I stripped off my blood- and dust-encrusted armour and climbed out of the underclothes I had worn for much of the past year. Then I sank gratefully into the water.

Since the initial emotional shock I had received when Arjavh had issued his invitation, my mind had become numbed. But now, for the first time in a year, I relaxed, mentally and physically, washing all the grief and hatred from me as I washed my body. So suddenly did the tension leave me that it might have been the result of Eldren sorcery; but I think now that I relaxed because I did not have to deceive myself in Loos Ptokai.

I was almost cheerful as I donned the fresh clothes which had been laid out for me and, when someone knocked at my door, called lightly for them to enter.

'Greetings, Erekosë.' It was Ermizhad.

'My lady.' I bowed.

'How are you faring, Erekosë?'

'In war, as you know, I am faring well. And personally I feel better for your hospitality.'

'Arjavh sent me to bring you to the meal.'

'I am ready. But first tell me how you have fared, Ermizhad.'

'Well enough – in health,' said she. Then she came closer to me. Involuntarily I leaned back slightly. She looked at the ground and raised her hands to touch her throat. 'And tell me – are you now wed to Queen Iolinda?'

'We are still betrothed,' I told her.

Deliberately, then, I looked into Ermizhad's eyes and added as levelly as I could: 'We are to be married when...'

'When?'

'When Loos Ptokai is taken.'

She said nothing.

I stepped forward so that we were separated by little more than an inch. 'Those are the only terms on which she will accept me,' I said. 'I must destroy all the Eldren. Your trampled banners will be my wedding gift to her.'

Ermizhad nodded and gave me a queer, sad and sardonic look. 'That is the oath you swore. You must abide by it. You must slay every Eldren. Every one.'

I cleared my throat. 'That is the oath.'

'Come,' she said. 'The meal grows cold.'

At dinner, Ermizhad and I sat close together and Arjavh spoke wittily of some of the stranger experiments of his scientist ancestors and for a little while we managed to drive away the knowledge of the forthcoming battle. But later, as Ermizhad and I talked softly to one another, I caught a look of pain in Arjavh's eyes and for a moment he was quiet. He broke into our conversation suddenly:

'We are beaten, as you know, Erekosë.'

I did not want to speak of these things any more. I shrugged and tried to continue the lighter talk with Ermizhad. But Arjavh was insistent.

'We are doomed, Erekosë, to fall beneath the swords of your great army.'

I drew a deep breath and looked him full in the face. 'Yes. You are doomed, Prince Arjavh.'

'It is a matter of time before you raze our Loos Ptokai.'

This time I avoided his urgent gaze and merely nodded.

'So – you...' He broke off.

I became impatient. Many emotions mingled in me. 'My oath,' I reminded him. 'I must do what I swore I would do, Arjavh.'

'I do not fear to lose my own life...' he began.

'I know what you fear,' I told him.

'Could not the Eldren admit defeat, Erekosë? Could they not acknowledge mankind's victory? Surely, one city...?'

'I swore an oath.' Now sadness filled me.

'But you cannot...' Ermizhad gestured with her slim hand. 'We are your friends, Erekosë. We enjoy each other's company. We – we *are* friends.'

'We are of different races,' I said. 'We are at war.'

'I am not asking for mercy,' Arjavh said.

'I know that,' I replied. 'I do not doubt Eldren courage. I have seen too many examples of it.'

'You abide by an oath given in anger, offered to an abstraction, that leads you to slay those you love and respect. An oath made to strengthen an already faltering resolve. You hated killing. I know you did!' Ermizhad's voice was puzzled. 'Are you tired of killing, Erekosë?'

'I am very tired of killing,' I told her.

161

'Then...?'

'But I began this thing,' I continued. 'Sometimes I wonder if I really do lead my men – or if they push me ahead of them. Perhaps I am wholly their creation. The creation of the will of Humanity. Perhaps I am a kind of patchwork hero that they have manufactured. Perhaps I have no other existence and when my work is done, I will fade as their sense of danger fades.'

'I think not,' said Arjavh soberly.

I shrugged. 'You are not me. You have not had my strange dreams.'

'You still have those dreams?' Ermizhad asked.

'Not recently. Since I began this campaign, they have gone away. They only plague me when I attempt to assert my own individuality. When I do what is required of me, they leave me in peace. I am a ghost, you see. Nothing more.'

Arjavh sighed. 'I do not understand this. I think you are suffering from a terrible self-deception, Erekosë. You could assert your own will – but you are *afraid* to! Instead, you abandon yourself to hate and bloodshed, to this peculiar melancholia of yours. You are depressed because you are *not* doing what you really desire to do. The dreams will come again, Erekosë. Mark my words – the dreams will come again and they will be more terrible than any you have experienced before.'

'Stop!' I shouted. 'Do not spoil this last meeting of ours. I came here because...'

'Because?' Arjavh raised a slim eyebrow.

'Because I needed some civilised company.'

'To see your own kind,' Ermizhad said softly.

I turned on her, rising from the table. 'You are not my own kind! My race is out there, beyond those walls, waiting to vanquish you!'

'We are kin in spirit,' Arjavh said. 'Our bonds are finer and stronger than bonds of blood.'

My face twisted and I buried it in my hands. 'No!'

Arjavh put a hand on my shoulder. 'You are more substantial

than you will allow yourself to be, Erekosë. It would take a great deal of a particular kind of courage if you would pursue the implications of another course of action.'

I let my hands fall to myself. 'You are right,' I told him. 'And I do not have that courage. I am just a sword. A force, like a whirlwind. There is nothing else to me – nothing I would allow. Nothing I am allowed…'

Ermizhad interrupted fiercely. 'For your own sake, you must allow that other self to rule. Forget your oath to Iolinda. You do not love her. You have nothing in common with the bloodthirsty rabble that follows you. You are a greater man than any you lead – greater than any you fight.'

'Stop it! This is Eldren sophistry. You would save your skins with words, having failed with swords!'

'She is right, Erekosë,' Arjavh said. 'It is not for *our* lives that we argue. It is for *your* spirit.'

I slumped down into my seat. 'I sought to avoid confusion,' I said, 'by taking a simple course of action. It is true that I feel no kinship with those I lead – or those who thrust me before them – but undeniably they *are* my kin. My duty…'

'Let them fare how they will,' Ermizhad said. 'Your duty is not to them. It is to yourself.'

I sipped some wine. Then I said quietly: 'I am afraid.'

Arjavh shook his head. 'You are brave. It is not your fault.'

'Who knows?' I said. 'Perhaps at some stage in one of my incarnations I committed an enormous crime. And now I am paying the price.'

'That is self-pitying speculation,' Arjavh reminded me. 'It is not – it is not – manly, Erekosë.'

I inhaled deeply. 'I suppose not.' Then I looked at him. 'But if Time is cyclic – in some form, at least – it could be that I have not yet committed that crime.'

'It is idle to speak of "crime" in this way,' Ermizhad said impatiently. 'What does your heart tell you to do?'

'My heart? I have not listened to it for many months.'

163

'Listen to it now!' she said.

I shook my head. 'I have forgotten how to listen to it, Ermizhad. I must finish what I set out to do. What I was called here to do.'

'Are you sure it was King Rigenos who called you?'

'Who else?'

Arjavh smiled. 'This, too, is idle speculation. You must do what you must do, Erekosë. I will plead for my people no longer.'

'Thank you for that,' I said. I rose, staggered slightly and screwed up my eyes. 'Gods! I am so *weary*!'

'Rest here tonight,' Ermizhad said quietly. 'Rest with me.'

I looked at her.

'With me,' she said.

Arjavh began to speak, changed his mind and left the room.

I realised then that I wanted nothing else but to do as Ermizhad suggested. Yet I shook my head. 'It would be weakness.'

'No,' she said. 'It would give you strength. It would enable you to make a clearer decision.'

'I have made my decision. Besides, my oath to Iolinda…'

'You swore no oath of faithfulness.'

I spread my hands. 'I cannot remember.'

She moved towards me and stroked my face. 'Perhaps it would end something,' she suggested. 'Perhaps it would restore your love for Iolinda.'

Now physical pain seemed to seize me. I even wondered for a moment if they had poisoned me. 'No.'

'It would help,' she said. 'I know it would help. How, I am not sure. I do not even know if it suits my own desires, but…'

'I *cannot* weaken now, Ermizhad.'

'Erekosë, it would *not* be weakness!'

'Still…'

She turned away from me and said in a soft, strange tone, 'Then rest here anyway. Sleep in a good bed so that you will be fit for tomorrow's fighting. I love you, Erekosë. I love you more than I love anything. I will aid you in whatever course of action you decide upon.'

'I have already decided,' I reminded her. 'And you cannot aid me there.' I felt dizzy. I did not want to return to my own camp in that condition, for they would be sure I had been drugged and would lose all confidence in me. Better to stay the night and greet my troops refreshed. 'Very well, I will stay here tonight,' I said. 'Alone.'

'As you wish, Erekosë.' She moved towards the door. 'A servant will come to show you where to sleep.'

'I'll sleep in this room,' I told her. 'Have someone bring in a bed.'

'As you wish.'

'It will be good to sleep in a real bed,' I said. 'My thoughts will be sharper in the morning.'

'I hope so. Goodnight, Erekosë.'

Had they known that the dreams would return that night? Was I the victim of immense and subtle cunning such as only the unhuman Eldren possessed?

I lay on my bed in the Eldren fortress city and I dreamed.

But this was not a dream in which I sought to discover my true name. I had no name in this dream. I did not want a name.

I watched the world turning and I saw its inhabitants running about its surface like ants in a hill, like beetles in a dung heap. I saw them fighting and destroying, making peace and building – only to drag those buildings down again in another inevitable war. And it seemed to me that these creatures had evolved only so far from the beast state and that some quirk of destiny had doomed them to repeat, over and over again, the same mistakes. And I realised that there was no hope for them – these imperfect creatures that were halfway from the animals, halfway from the gods – that it was their fate, like mine, to struggle for ever and forever fail to be fulfilled. The paradoxes that existed in me existed in the whole race. The problems for which I could find no solution in fact had no solution. There was no point in seeking an answer; one could only accept what existed or else reject it, as one pleased. It would always be the same. Oh, there was much to love them for and nothing at all to hate them for. How could they be hated, when their errors resulted from the quirk of fate that had made them the half-creatures that they were – half-blind, half-deaf, half-dumb?

I woke up and felt very calm. And then, gradually, a sense of terror possessed me as the implications of my thoughts began to dawn on me.

Had the Eldren sent this dream – with their sorcery?

I did not think so. This dream was the dream that the other dreams had sought to hide from me. I was sure of it. This was the stark truth.

And the stark truth horrified me.

It was not my fate to wage eternal war – it was the fate of my entire race. As part of that race – as its representative, in fact – I, too, must wage eternal war.

And that is what I wished to avoid. I could not bear the thought of fighting for ever, wherever I was required. And yet whatever I did to try to end the cycle would be hopeless. There was only one thing I could do.

I buried the thought.

But what else?

Try for peace? See if it would work? Let the Eldren live?

Arjavh had expressed impatience with idle speculation. But this, too, was idle speculation. The human race was sworn to destroy the Eldren. This done, of course, it would then turn upon itself again and begin the perpetual squabbling, the constant warring that its peculiar destiny decreed for it.

And yet – should I not, at least, attempt to make the compromise?

Or should I continue with my original ambition, destroy the Eldren, let the race resume its fratricidal sport? In a way it seemed to me that, while some Eldren lived, the race might hold together. If the common enemy remained, at least some sort of unity would exist in the Human Kingdoms. It seemed critical to me then that some Eldren be spared – for the sake of Humanity.

I suddenly realised that there was no contradiction in my loyalties at all. What I had thought was contradictory was, in fact, two halves of a whole. The dream had merely helped me unite them and see everything clearly.

Perhaps this was a complex piece of rationalisation. I shall never know. I feel that I was right, though it is possible that subsequent events proved me wrong. At least I tried.

I sat up in my bed as a servant came in with water for me to wash and my own clothes freshly laundered. I washed, dressed myself and when a knock came at the door I called out for the person to enter.

It was Ermizhad. She brought me my breakfast and set it on the table. I thanked her and she looked at me oddly.

'You seem to have changed since last night,' she said. 'You seem more at one with yourself.'

'I think I am,' I told her as I ate. 'I had another dream last night.'

'Was it as terrifying as the others?'

'More terrifying in certain aspects,' I said. 'But it did not raise problems, this time. It offered me a solution.'

'You feel you can fight better.'

'If you like. I think it would be in the interest of my race if we made peace with the Eldren. Or, at least, declared a permanent truce.'

'You have realised at last that we offer you no danger.'

'On the contrary, it is the very danger you offer that makes *your* survival necessary to my race.' I smiled, remembering an old aphorism from somewhere. 'If you did not exist, it would be necessary to invent you.'

A look of intelligence brightened her face. She smiled, too. 'I think I understand you.'

'Therefore, I intend to present this conclusion to Queen Iolinda,' I said. 'I hope to persuade her that it is in our interest to end this war against the Eldren.'

'And your terms?'

'I see no need to make terms with you,' I said. 'We will merely stop fighting and go away.'

She laughed. 'Will it be so easy?'

I looked squarely at her, deliberated for a moment, and then I shook my head. 'Perhaps not. But I must try.'

'You have become very rational suddenly, Erekosë. I am glad. Your sleep here did do you some good, then.'

'And the Eldren, too, perhaps.'

She smiled again. 'Perhaps.'

'I will return to Necranal as soon as possible and speak with Iolinda.'

'And if she agrees, you will marry her?'

I felt weak, then. At last I said: 'I must do that. Everything would be negated if I did not. You understand?'

'Entirely,' she said and there were tears in her eyes as she smiled.

Arjavh came in a few minutes later and I told him what I intended to do. He received the news rather more sceptically than Ermizhad.

'You do not think I mean what I say?' I asked him.

He shrugged. 'I believe you completely, Erekosë. But I do not think the Eldren will survive.'

'What is it? Some disease? Something in you that…?'

He laughed shortly. 'No, no. I think you will propose a truce and that the people will not let you make it. Your race will only be satisfied when every Eldren has perished. You said that it is their destiny always to fight. Could it not be that secretly they resent the Eldren because the presence of the Eldren means that they cannot go about their normal activities – I mean by that their fighting amongst themselves? Could this be nothing more than a pause before they wipe us out? And if they do not wipe us out now, they will do it very soon, whether you lead them or no.'

'Still, I must try,' I said.

'Try by all means. But they'll hold you to your vow, I'm sure.'

'Iolinda is intelligent. If she listens to my arguments…'

'She is one of them. I doubt if she will listen. Intelligence has little to do with it. Last night when I pleaded with you, I was not myself – I panicked. I know, really, that there can be no peace.'

'I must try.'

'I hope you succeed.'

Perhaps I had been beguiled by the charms of the Eldren, but I did not think so. I would do my best to bring peace to the wasted land of Mernadin, though it meant I could never see my Eldren friends again – never see Ermizhad.

I put the thought from my head and resolved to dwell upon it no longer.

Then a servant entered the room. My herald, accompanied by several marshals, including Count Roldero, had presented himself outside the gates of Loos Ptokai, half-certain that I had been murdered by the Eldren.

'Only sight of you will reassure them,' Arjavh murmured. I agreed and left the room.

I heard the herald calling as I approached the city wall. 'We fear that you have been guilty of great treachery. Let us see our master – or his corpse.' He paused. 'Then we shall know what to do.'

Arjavh and I mounted the steps to the battlements and I saw relief in the herald's eyes as he noted I was unharmed.

'I have been talking with Prince Arjavh,' I said. 'And I have been thinking deeply. Our men are weary beyond endurance and the Eldren are now only a few, with just this city in their possession. We could take Loos Ptokai, but I see no point to it. Let us be generous victors, my marshals. Let us declare a truce.'

'A truce, Lord Erekosë!' Count Roldero's eyes widened. 'Would you rob us of our ultimate prize? Our final, fierce fulfilment? Our greatest triumph? *Peace!*'

'Yes,' I said, 'peace. Now go back. Tell our warriors I am safe.'

'We can take this city easily, Erekosë,' Roldero shouted. 'There's no need to talk of peace. We can destroy the Eldren once and for all. Have you succumbed to their cursed enchantments again? Have they beguiled you with their smooth words?'

'No,' I said, 'it was I who suggested it.'

Roldero swung his horse around in disgust.

'Peace!' he spat as he and his comrades headed back to the camp. 'Our Champion's gone mad!'

Arjavh rubbed his lips with his finger. 'Already, I see, there is trouble.'

'They fear me,' I told him, 'and they'll obey me. They'll obey me – for a while, at least.'

'Let us hope so,' he said.

Chapter Twenty-Four
The Parting

T HIS TIME THERE were no cheering crowds in Necranal to welcome me, for news of my mission had gone ahead of me. The people could hardly believe it but where they did believe it, they disapproved. I had shown weakness, in their eyes.

I had not seen Iolinda, of course, since she had become queen. She had a haughty look now as she strode about her throne room, awaiting me.

Privately I was a little amused. I felt like the man who, as an old rejected suitor, returns to see the object of his passion married and become a shrew. I was, therefore, somewhat relieved.

It was a small relief.

'Well, Erekosë,' she said. 'I know why you are here – why you have forsaken your troops, gone against your word to me that you would destroy every Eldren. Katorn has told me.'

'Katorn is here?'

'He came here as soon as he heard your pronouncement from the battlements of Loos Ptokai, where you stood with your Eldren friends.'

'Iolinda,' I said urgently. 'I am convinced that the Eldren are weary of war, that they never intended to threaten the Two Continents at all. They want only peace.'

'Peace we shall have. When the Eldren race has perished.'

'Iolinda, if you love me, you will listen to me, at least.'

'If *I* love *you*? And what of the Lord Erekosë? Does he still love his queen?'

I opened my mouth, but I could not speak.

And suddenly there were tears in her eyes. 'Oh, Erekosë.' Her tone softened. 'Can it be true?'

'No,' I said thickly. 'I still love you, Iolinda. We are to be married.'

But she knew. She had suspected; but now she knew. However, if peace could result from my action, I was still prepared to pretend, to lie, to declare my passion for her, to marry her.

'I still want to marry you, Iolinda,' I said.

'No,' she said. 'No. You do not.'

'I will,' I said desperately. 'If peace with the Eldren comes about...'

Again her wide eyes blazed. 'You insult me, my lord. Not on those terms, Erekosë. Never. You are guilty of high treason against us. The people already speak of you as a traitor.'

'But I conquered a continent for them. I took Mernadin.'

'All but Loos Ptokai – where your wanton Eldren bitch waits for you.'

'Iolinda! That is not true!'

But it was almost true.

'You are unfair...' I began.

'And you are a traitor! Guards!'

As if they had been prepared for this, a dozen of the Imperial Guards rushed in, led by their captain, Lord Katorn. There was a hint of triumph in his eyes and then I knew for certain that he had always hated me because he desired Iolinda.

And I knew, whether I drew my sword or not, he would slay me where I stood.

So I drew my sword. The sword Kanajana. It glowed and the glow was reflected in Katorn's black eyes.

'Take him, Katorn!' cried Iolinda. And her voice was a scream of agony. I had betrayed her. I had failed to be the strength she needed so desperately. 'Take him. Alive or dead. He is a traitor to his kind!'

I was a traitor to her. That was what she really meant. That was why I must die.

But I still hoped to save something. 'It is untrue...' I began. But Katorn was already cautiously advancing, his men spreading out behind him. I backed to a wall, near a window. The throne room was on the first storey of the palace. Outside were the private gardens of the queen. 'Think, Iolinda,' I said. 'Retract your command. You are driven by jealousy. I'm no traitor.'

'*Slay him, Katorn!*'

But I slew Katorn. As he came rushing at me, my sword flicked across his writhing, hate-filled face. He screamed, staggered, his hands rushed up to his head and then he toppled in his golden armour, toppled and fell with a crash to the flagstones.

He was the first human I was to slay.

The other guards came on, but more warily. I fought off their blades, slew a couple more, drove the others back, glimpsed Queen Iolinda watching me, her eyes full of tears, and leaped to the sill of the window.

'Goodbye, Queen. You have lost your champion now.'

I jumped.

I landed in a rosebush that ripped at my skin, broke free and ran towards the gate of the garden, the guards behind me.

I tore the gate open and rushed down the hill and into the twisting streets of Necranal, with the guards in pursuit, their ranks joined by a howling pack of citizens who had no idea why I was wanted or even who I was. They chased me for the sheer pleasure of the hunt. My situation reflected more than ever the perpetual paradox of my life since I had obeyed Humanity's summons. Not long since I had led them. I had been the most powerful man in the world. And now, suddenly, I was a fugitive, running through the streets like a common pickpocket.

So it was thus that things turned. Iolinda's pain and jealousy had clouded her mind. And soon her decision would be the cause of more bloodshed than even she had demanded.

I ran, blindly at first, and then towards the river. My crew, I hoped, would still be loyal to me. If they were, then there was a faint chance of escape. I gained the ship just before my pursuers. I leaped aboard screaming:

'Prepare to sail!'

Only half the crew was aboard. The rest was on shore, in the taverns, but those remaining hurriedly shipped out the oars while we held the guards and the citizens at bay.

Then we shoved off and began our hasty flight down the Droonaa River.

It was some time before they managed to commandeer a ship for pursuit and by that time we were safely outdistancing them. My crew asked no questions. They were used to my silences, my actions which sometimes seemed peculiar. But, a week after we were on course over the sea, bound for Mernadin, I told them briefly that I was now an outlaw.

'Why, Lord Erekosë?' asked my captain. 'It seems unjust.'

'It is unjust, I think. Call it the queen's malice. I suspect Katorn spoke against me, making her hate me.'

They were satisfied with the explanation and, when we put in at a small cove near the Plains of Melting Ice, I bade them farewell, mounted my horse and rode swiftly for Loos Ptokai, knowing not what I should do when I got there. Knowing only that I must let Arjavh know the turn events had taken.

He had been right. Humanity would not let me show mercy.

My crew bid me farewell with a certain amount of affection. They did not know – and neither did I – that they were soon to be killed because of me.

Now I crept into Loos Ptokai. I sneaked through the great siege camp that we had constructed there and, at night, entered the city of the Eldren.

Arjavh rose from his bed when he heard I had returned.

'Well, Erekosë?' He looked searchingly at me. Then he said: 'You were not successful, were you? You have been riding hard and you have been fighting. What happened?'

I told him.

He sighed. 'Well, our advice was foolish. Now you will die when we die.'

'I would rather that, I think,' I said.

*

Two months passed. Two ominous months in Loos Ptokai. Humanity did not attack the city immediately and it soon emerged that they were awaiting orders from Queen Iolinda. She, it appeared, had refused to make a decision.

The inaction was oppressive in itself.

I fretted often at the battlements, looking out over the great camp and wishing that the thing would start and be finished. Only Ermizhad eased my unhappiness. We openly acknowledged our love now.

And because I loved her, I began to want to save her.

I wanted to save her and I wanted to save myself and I wanted to save all the Eldren in Loos Ptokai, for I wanted to stay with Ermizhad for ever. I did not want to be destroyed.

Desperately I tried to think of ways in which we could defeat that great force, but every plan I made was a wild one and could not work.

And then, one day, I remembered a conversation I had had with Arjavh on the plateau after he had defeated me in battle.

I went looking for him and found him in his study. He was reading from one of the beautifully decorated Eldren scrolls.

'Erekosë? Are they beginning their attack?'

'No, Arjavh. But I recall that you told me once about some ancient weapons your race had – that you still have.'

'What?'

'The old terrible weapons,' I said. 'The ones you swore never to use again because they could destroy so much!'

He shook his head. 'Not those.'

'Use them this once, Arjavh,' I begged him. 'Make a show of strength, that is all. They will be ready to discuss peace then.'

He rolled up his scroll. 'No. They will never discuss peace with us. They would rather die. I do not think that even this situation merits the breaking of that ancient vow.'

'Arjavh,' I said. 'I respect the reasons for refusing to use the weapons. But I have grown to love the Eldren. I have already broken one vow. Let me break another – for you.'

He still shook his head.

'Just agree to this, then,' I said. 'If the time comes when I feel we could use them, will you let me decide – take the decision out of your hands, make it my responsibility?'

He looked searchingly at me. The orbless eyes seemed to pierce me.

'Perhaps,' he said.

'Arjavh – will you?'

'We Eldren have never been motivated as much by self-interest as you humans – and never to the extent of destroying another race, Erekosë. Do not confuse our values with those of mankind.'

'I am not,' I replied. 'That is my reason for asking you this. I could not bear to see your noble race perish at the hands of those beasts beyond our walls!'

Arjavh stood up and replaced the scroll in the shelves. 'Iolinda spoke the truth,' he said quietly. 'You are a traitor to your own race.'

'"Race" is a meaningless term. It was you and Ermizhad who told me to be an individual. I have chosen my loyalties.'

He pursed his lips. 'Well…'

'I seek only to stop them continuing in their folly,' I said.

He clenched his thin, pale hands together.

'Arjavh. I asked you because of the love I have for Ermizhad and the love she has for me. Because of the great friendship you have given me. For all Eldren left alive, I beg you to let me take the decision if it becomes necessary.'

'For Ermizhad?' He raised his slanting eyebrows. 'For you? For me? For my people? Not for revenge?'

'No,' I said quietly. 'I do not think so.'

'Very well. I leave the decision to you. I suppose that is fair. I do not want to die. But remember – do not act as unwisely as others of your kind.'

'I will not,' I promised.

I think I kept that particular promise.

Chapter Twenty-Five

The Attack

A ND THE DAYS continued to pass. Gradually the air began to chill; night came sooner. Winter threatened. If winter arrived before Count Roldero, we would be safe until spring, for the invaders would be fools to attempt a heavy siege.

They realised this, too, and it seemed Iolinda must have come to a decision. She gave them permission to attack Loos Ptokai.

After much bickering among themselves, I learned, the marshals elected one of themselves, the most experienced, to act as their war champion.

They elected Count Roldero.

The siege commenced in earnest.

Their massive siege engines were brought forward, including the giant cannon known as the Firedrakes – great black things of iron, decorated with fierce reliefs.

Roldero rode up and his herald announced his presence. I went to speak with him from the battlements.

'Greetings, Erekosë the Traitor!' he called. 'We have decided to punish you – and all the Eldren within these walls. We would have slaughtered the Eldren cleanly, but now we intend to put to slow death all those we capture.'

I was saddened.

'Roldero, Roldero,' I begged. 'We were friends once. You were perhaps the only true friend I had. We drank together and fought together, made jokes together. We were comrades, Roldero. Good comrades.'

His horse fidgeted beneath him, pawing at the earth.

'That was an age ago,' he said without looking up at me.

'Little more than a year, Roldero.'

'But we are not those two friends any longer, Erekosë.' He looked up, shielding his eyes with a gauntleted hand. I saw that his face had grown old and it bore many new scars. Doubtless I looked as changed as he. 'We are different men,' Roldero said, and wrenching at his reins drove his horse away, digging his long spurs savagely into its flanks. Now there was nothing we could do but fight.

The Firedrakes boomed and their solid shot slammed against the walls. Blazing fireballs from captured Eldren artillery (we had become less fastidious as the war went on) screamed over the walls and into the streets. These were followed by thousands of arrows that came in a black shower, blotting out the light.

And then a million men rushed against our handful of defenders.

We replied with what cannon we had, but we relied mainly on archers to meet that first wave, for we were short of shot.

And we repelled them. After ten hours of fighting they fell back.

Then, next day and the day after, they continued to attack. But Loos Ptokai, the ancient capital of Mernadin, held firm.

Battalion upon battalion of yelling warriors mounted the siege towers and we again replied with arrows, with molten metal and, economically, with the fire-spewing cannon of the Eldren. We fought bravely, Arjavh and I leading the defenders and, whenever they sighted me, the warriors of Humanity screamed for vengeance and died striving for the privilege of slaying me.

We fought side by side, like brothers, Arjavh and I, but our Eldren warriors were tiring and, after a week of constant barrage, we began to realise that we could not much longer hold back that tide of steel.

That night we sat together after Ermizhad had gone to bed. We massaged our aching muscles and we spoke little.

Then I said: 'We shall all be dead soon, Arjavh. You and I. Ermizhad. The rest of your folk.'

He continued to dig his fingers into his shoulder, kneading it to loosen it. 'Yes,' he said. 'Soon.'

I wanted him to raise the subject that was on the tip of my tongue, but he would not.

The next day, scenting our defeat, the warriors of Humanity came at us with greater vigour than ever. The Firedrakes were brought in closer and began steadily to bombard the main gates.

I saw Roldero, mounted on his great black horse, directing the operation and there was something about his stance that made me realise that he was sure he would break our defences that day.

I turned to Arjavh, who stood beside me on the wall, and I was about to speak when several of the Firedrakes boomed in unison. The black metal shook, the shot screamed from their snouts, hit the main gates, which were of metal, and split the left one down the middle. It did not fall, but it was so badly weakened that one more cannonade would bring it completely down.

'Arjavh!' I yelled. 'We must break out the old weapons. We must arm the Eldren!'

His face was pale, but he shook his head.

'Arjavh! We must! Another hour and we'll be driven off these battlements! Another three and we'll be overwhelmed entirely!' He looked to where Roldero was directing the cannoneers and this time he did not remonstrate. He nodded. 'Very well. I agreed that you would decide. Come.'

He led me down the steps.

I only hoped he had not overestimated their power.

Arjavh led me to the vaults that lay at the core of the city. We moved along bare corridors of polished black marble, lighted by small bulbs which burned with a greenish glow. We came to a door of dark metal and he pressed a stud beside it. The door moved open and we entered an elevator which bore us yet farther downwards.

I was again astonished at the Eldren. They had deliberately given up all these marvels to satisfy their ideals of justice and honour.

Then we stepped into a great hall full of weirdly wrought

machines that looked as if they had just been manufactured. They stretched for nearly half a mile ahead of us.

'These are the weapons,' said Arjavh bleakly.

Around the high walls were arranged handguns of various kinds; there were rifles and objects that looked to John Daker's eye like anti-tank weapons. There were squat war machines on caterpillar treads, with glass cabins and couches for a single man to lie flat upon and operate the controls. I was surprised that there were no flying machines of any kind – or none that I recognised as such. I mentioned this to Arjavh.

'Flying machines! It would be interesting if such things could be invented. But I do not think it is possible. We have never, in all our history, been able to develop a machine that will safely stay in the air for any length of time.'

I was amazed at this odd gap in their technology, but I commented on it no further.

'Now you have seen these fierce things,' he said, 'do you still feel you should use them?'

He doubtless thought such weapons were not familiar to me. They were not so very different to the war machines John Daker had known. And, in my dreams, I had seen much stranger weapons.

'Let us ready them,' I said to him.

We returned to the surface and there instructed our warriors to transport the weapons to the surface.

Roldero had smashed in one of our gates now and we had had to bring up cannon to defend it, but the warriors of Humanity were beginning to press in and some hand-to-hand fighting was going on at the approach to the gates.

Night was falling. I hoped that, in spite of their gain, the human army would retreat at dark and give us the time we needed. Through the gap in the gate I saw Roldero urging his men in. Doubtless he hoped to consolidate his advantage before the twilight ended.

I ordered more men to the breach.

Already I was beginning to doubt my own decision.

Perhaps Arjavh was right and it was criminal to let the power of the ancient weapons loose. But then, I thought, what does it matter? Better destroy them and half the planet than let them destroy the beauty that was the Eldren.

I was forced to smile at this reaction in myself. Arjavh would not have approved of it. Such a thought was alien to him.

I saw Roldero bring in more men to counter our forces and I swung into the saddle of a nearby horse, spurring it towards the crucial breach.

I drew my poison sword, Kanajana, and I voiced my battle-cry – the battle-cry that only a short while ago had urged these warriors I attacked into battle against those I now led. They heard it and, as I suspected, were disconcerted.

I leaped my horse over the heads of my own men and confronted Roldero. He looked at me in astonishment and pulled his horse up short.

'Would you fight me, Roldero?' I said.

He shrugged. 'Aye. I'll fight you, traitor.'

And he rushed at me with his reins looped over his arm and both hands around the hilt of his great sword. It whistled over my head as I ducked.

Everywhere about us, beneath the broken walls of Loos Ptokai, human and Eldren fought desperately in the fading light.

Roldero was tired, more tired than I was, but he battled valiantly on and I could not get through his guard. His sword caught me a blow on my helmet and I reeled and struck back and caught *him* on the helmet. My helmet stayed on, but his was half-pulled off. He wrenched it off all the way and flung it aside. His hair had turned completely white since I had last seen him bareheaded.

His face was flushed and his eyes bright, his lips drawn back over his teeth. He tried to stab his sword through my visor, but I ducked under the blow and he fell forward in his saddle and I brought up my sword and drove it down into his breastbone.

He groaned and then his face lost all its anger and he gasped: 'Now we can be friends again, Erekosë...' and he died.

I looked down at him as he collapsed over the neck of his horse. I remembered his kindness, the wine he had brought me to help me sleep, the advice he had tried to give me. And I remembered him pushing the dead king from his saddle. Yet, Count Roldero was a good man, a good man forced by history to do evil. By his own rule he had been condemned.

His black horse turned and began to canter back towards the count's distant pavilion.

I raised my sword in salute and then shouted to the humans who fought on. 'Look, warriors of Humanity! Look! Your war champion is defeated!'

The sun was setting.

The warriors began to withdraw, looking at me in hatred as I laughed at them, but not daring to attack me while the bloody sword Kanajana was in my hand.

One of them did call back, however.

'We are not leaderless, Erekosë, if that is what you think. We have the queen to send us into battle. She has come to be witness to your destruction tomorrow!'

Iolinda was with the besiegers!

I thought swiftly and then yelled: 'Tell your mistress to come tomorrow to our walls. Come at dawn to parley!'

Through the night we worked to reinforce the gate and to position the new-found weapons. They were raised wherever they would fit and the Eldren soldiers were armed with the hand weapons.

I wondered if Iolinda would get the message and, if she did get it, whether she would deign to come.

She came. She came with her remaining marshals in all their proud panoply of war. That panoply seemed so insignificant now, against the power of the ancient Eldren weapons.

We had set one of the new cannon pointing up at the sky so that we could demonstrate its fearful potential.

Iolinda's voice drifted up to us.

'Greetings, Eldren – and greetings to your human lapdog. Is he a well-trained pet now?'

'Greetings, Iolinda,' I said, showing my face. 'You begin to show your father's penchant for poor insults and obvious irony. Let's waste no further time.'

'I am already wasting time,' she said. 'We are going to destroy you all today.'

'Perhaps not,' I said. 'For we offer you a truce – and peace.'

Iolinda laughed aloud. '*You* offer us peace, traitor! You should be begging for peace – though you'll get none!'

'I warn you, Iolinda,' I shouted desperately. 'I warn you all. We have fresh weapons – weapons which once came near to destroying this whole Earth! Watch!'

I gave the order to fire the giant cannon.

An Eldren warrior depressed a stud on the controls.

There came a humming from the cannon and all at once a tremendous blinding bolt of golden energy gouted from its snout. The heat alone blistered our skins and we fell back, shielding our eyes.

Horses shrieked and reared. The marshals' faces were grey and their mouths gaped. They fought to control their mounts. Only Iolinda sat firmly in her saddle, apparently calm.

'That is what we offer you if you will not have peace,' I shouted. 'We have a dozen like it and there are others that are different, but as powerful, and we have hand cannon which can kill a hundred men at a sweep. What say you now?'

Iolinda raised her face and stared directly up at me.

'We fight,' she said.

'Iolinda,' I pleaded. 'For our old love, for your own sake – do not fight. We will not harm you. You can go home, all of you, and live in security for the rest of your lives. I mean it.'

'Security!' She laughed bitterly. 'Security, while such weapons as these exist!'

'You must believe me, Iolinda!'

'No,' she said. 'Humanity will fight to the end and, because the Good One favours us, doubtless we will win. We are pledged to

183

wage war on sorcery and there was never greater sorcery than what we have seen today.'

'It is not sorcery. It is science. It is only like your cannon, but more powerful.'

'Sorcery!' Everyone was murmuring it now. They were like savages, these fools.

'If we continue to fight,' I said, 'it will be a fight to the finish. The Eldren would prefer to let you go, once this battle is won. But if we win, I intend to clean the planet of your kind, just as you swore you would do to the Eldren. Take the chance. A peace! Be sane.'

'We will die by sorcery,' she said, 'if we have to. But we will die fighting it.'

I was too weary to continue. 'Then let us finish this business,' I told her.

Iolinda wheeled her horse away and, with her marshals in her wake, galloped back to order the attack.

I did not see Iolinda perish. There were so many that perished that day.

They came and we met them. They were helpless against our weapons. Energy spouted from the guns and seared into their ranks. How quickly they fell and how tragically they died. We all felt sorrow as we let loose the howling waves of force which swept across them and destroyed them, turning proud men and beasts to blackened rubble.

We did as they had predicted we would do. We destroyed them all.

I pitied them as they came on, the cream of Humanity's men-folk. Each wave was burned down as soon as it came within two hundred yards of our walls. We begged them to retreat. They came again. I began to guess that they wished to die. They sought rest in death.

It took two hours to destroy a million warriors.

When the extermination was over, I was filled with a strange emotion which I could not then and cannot now define. It was a mixture of grief, relief and triumph. I mourned for Iolinda. She was somewhere there in the heap of blackened bone and smouldering flesh – one piece of ruined meat amongst many, her beauty gone in the same instant as her life.

And it was then that I made my final decision. Or did I, indeed, make it at all? Was it not what I had been brought here to do?

Or was it the crime I had mentioned earlier? Was this the crime I committed that doomed me to be what I was?

Was I right?

In spite of Arjavh's constant antagonism to my plan, I ordered the machines out of Loos Ptokai and, mounted in one of them, led them overland.

This is what I did:

Two months before, I had been responsible for winning the cities of Mernadin for Humanity. Now I reclaimed them in the name of the Eldren.

I reclaimed them in a terrible way. I destroyed every human being occupying them.

A week and we were at Paphanaal, where the fleets of mankind lay at anchor in the great harbour.

I destroyed those fleets as I destroyed the garrison – men, women and children perished. None was spared.

And then, for many of the machines were amphibious, I led the Eldren across the sea to the Two Continents, though Arjavh and Ermizhad were not with me.

These cities fell: Noonos of the jewel-studded towers fell. Tarkar fell. The wondrous cities of the wheatlands, Stalaco, Calodemia, Mooros and Ninadoon, all fell. Wedmah, Shilaal, Sinana and others fell, crumbling in an inferno of gouting energy. They fell in a few moments.

In Necranal, the pastel-coloured city of the mountain, five million citizens died and all that was left of Necranal was the scorched, smoking mountain itself.

But I was thorough. Not merely the great cities were destroyed.

Villages were destroyed. Hamlets were destroyed. Towns and farms were destroyed.

I found some people hiding in caves. The caves were destroyed.

I destroyed forests where they might flee. I destroyed the very stones they might creep under.

I would doubtless have destroyed every blade of grass if Arjavh had not come hurrying over the ocean to stop me.

He was horrified at what I had done. He begged me to stop.

I stopped.

There was no more killing to do.

We made our way back to the coast and we paused to look at the smouldering mountainside that had been Necranal.

'For one woman's wrath,' said Prince Arjavh, 'and another's love, you did this?'

I shrugged. 'I do not know. I think I did it for the only kind of peace that will last. I know my race too well. This Earth would have been forever rent by strife of some kind. I had to decide who best deserved to live. If they had destroyed the Eldren, they would have soon turned on each other, as you know. And they fight for such empty things, too. For power over their fellows, for a bauble, for an extra acre of land that they will not till, for possession of a woman who doesn't want them.'

'You decided that! You took this vast responsibility onto your own shoulders? You judged them and executed them according to your own interpretation of justice?' Arjavh said quietly. 'Really, Erekosë, I do not think you know yet what you have done.'

I sighed. 'But it is done,' I said.

'Yes.' His eyes were full of a profound pity for me. He gripped my arm. 'Come, friend. Back to Mernadin. Leave this stink behind. Ermizhad awaits you.'

I was an empty man, then, bereft of emotion. I followed him towards the river. It moved sluggishly now. It was choked with black dust, with burned flesh.

'I think I did right,' I said. 'It was not my will, you know, but something else. I think it might have been my fate from the beginning. I think it was another will than mine which dragged me here – not Rigenos. Rigenos, like me, was a puppet – a tool used, as I was used. It was preordained that Humanity should die on this planet.'

'It is better that you think that,' he said. 'Come now. Let us go home.'

Epilogue

*T*HE SCARS OF *that destruction have healed now, as I end my chronicle. I returned to Loos Ptokai to wed Ermizhad, to have the Eldren secret of immortality conferred upon me, to brood for a year or two until my brain cleared.*

It is clear now. I feel no guilt for what I did. I feel more certain than ever that it was not my decision.

Perhaps that is madness? Perhaps I have rationalised my guilt? If so, I am at one with my madness, it does not tear me in two as my dreams used to. I have those dreams rarely these days.

So we are here, the three of us – Ermizhad, Arjavh and I. Arjavh is undisputed ruler of the Earth, an Eldren Earth, and we rule with him.

We cleansed this Earth of humankind. I am its last representative. And in so doing I feel that we knitted this planet back into the pattern, allowed it to drift, at last, harmoniously with a harmonious universe. For the universe is old, perhaps even older than I, and it could not tolerate the humans who broke its peace.

Did I do right?

You must judge for yourself, wherever you are.

For me, it is too late to ask that question. I have sufficient control nowadays never to ask it. The only way in which I could answer it would involve destroying my own sanity.

One thing puzzles me. If, indeed, Time is cyclic, in some manner, and the universe we know will be born again to turn another long cycle, then Humanity will one day arise again, somehow, on this Earth and my adopted people will disappear from the Earth, or seem to.

And if you are human who reads this, perhaps you know. Perhaps my question seems naïve and you are at this moment laughing at me. But I have no answer. I can imagine none.

I am not to be the father of your race, human, for Ermizhad and I cannot produce children.

Then how shall you come again to disrupt the harmony of the universe?

And will I be here to receive you? Will I become your hero again or will I die with the Eldren fighting you?

Or will I die before then and be the leader who brings disrupting Humanity to Earth? I cannot say.

Which of the names will I have next time you call?

Now Earth is peaceful. The silent air carries only the sounds of quiet laughter, the murmur of conversation, the small noises of small animals. We and Earth are at peace.

But how long can it last?

Oh, how long can it last?

Phoenix in Obsidian

Prologue

A BRIGHT PLAIN *without horizons. The plain is the colour of raw, red gold. The sky is a faded purple. Two figures stand on the plain: a man and a woman. The man, dressed in dented armour, is tall with weary angular features. The woman is beautiful – dark-haired and delicate, clad in a gown of blue silk. He is* ISARDA OF TANELORN. THE WOMAN *is nameless.*

THE WOMAN
What are Time and Space but clay for the hand that holds the Cosmic Balance? This Age is moulded – that one squeezed from existence. All is flux. Lords of Law and Chaos struggle in eternal battle and neither ever completely wins or loses. The Balance tilts this way and that. Time upon Time the Hand destroys its creations and begins anew. And the Earth is forever changing. The Eternal War is the only constant in Earth's many histories, taking a multitude of forms and names.

ISARDA OF TANELORN
And those who are involved in this struggle? Can they ever realise the true nature of their strivings?

WOMAN
Rarely.

ISARDA
And will the world at length be granted rest from this state of flux?

WOMAN

We shall never know, for we shall never come face to face with the One who guides the Hand.

ISARDA

(*He spreads his arms.*) But surely some things are constant...

WOMAN

Even the meandering river of Time can be dammed or rechannelled at the will of the Cosmic Hand. We are as uncertain of the shape of the future as we are of the validity of our reported history. Perhaps we only exist for this instant of Time? Perhaps we are immortal and will exist for ever? Nothing is known for certain, Isarda. All knowledge is illusion – purpose is a meaningless word, a mere sound, a reassuring fragment of melody in a cacophony of clashing chords. All is flux – matter is like these jewels. (*She throws a handful of gleaming gems upon the golden surface; they scatter. When the last jewel has ceased to move, she looks up at him.*) Sometimes they fall into a rough pattern, usually they do not. So at this moment, a pattern has been formed – you and I stand here speaking. But at any moment that which constitutes our beings may be scattered again.

ISARDA

Not if we resist. Legends speak of those who forced Chaos into shape by effort of will. Aubec's hand formed your land and, indirectly, you.

WOMAN

(*Wistfully.*) Perhaps there are such people. But they go directly against the will of the One who formed them.

ISARDA

(*After a pause.*) And what if they do exist? What would become of them?

WOMAN

I do not know. But I do not envy them.

ISARDA

(*He looks away across the golden plain. He speaks softly.*) Nor I.

WOMAN

They say your city Tanelorn is eternal. They say that because of a Hero's will she has existed through every transformation of the Earth. They say that even the most haunted of folk find peace there.

ISARDA

It is also said that they must first have a will for peace before they can find Tanelorn.

WOMAN

(*Bowing her head.*) And few have that.

> – The Chronicle of the Black Sword
> (Vol. 1008 Scr. 14: *Isarda's Reckoning*)

Book One

Premonitions

But yesternight I pray'd aloud
In anguish and in agony,
Up-starting from the fiendish crowd
Of shapes and thoughts that tortured me:
A lurid light, a trampling throng,
Sense of intolerable wrong,
And whom I scorned, those only strong!
Thirst of revenge, the powerless will
Still baffled, and yet burning still!
Desire with loathing strangely mixed
On wild or hateful objects fixed.
Fantastic passions! Maddening brawl!
And shame and terror over all!
Deeds to be hid which were not hid,
Which all confused I could not know
Whether I suffered, or I did:
For all seem'd guilt, remorse or woe,
My own or others still the same
Life-stifling fear, soul-stifling shame.

– S.T. Coleridge,
'The Pains of Sleep'

Chapter One
Of an Earth Reborn

I KNOW GRIEF and I know love and I think I know what death may be, though it is said I am immortal. I have been told I have a destiny, but what that is, save forever to be moved by the tides of chance, to perform miserable deeds, I do not know.

I was called John Daker and perhaps many other names. Then I was called Erekosë, the Eternal Champion, and I slew the human race because it had betrayed what I considered to be my ideals, because I loved a woman of another race, a race I thought nobler and which was called the Eldren. The woman was called Ermizhad and she could never bear me children.

And, having slain my race, I was happy.

With Ermizhad and her brother Arjavh I ruled the Eldren, that graceful people which had existed on Earth well before mankind had come to disrupt its harmony.

The dreams, which had beset my sleeping hours when I had first come to this world, were now rare and hardly remembered at all on waking. Once they had terrified me, made me think that I must be insane. I had experienced fragments of a million incarnations, always as some sort of warrior; I had not known which identity was my 'true' one. Torn by divided loyalties, by the stresses in my own brain, I had been mad for a while, of this I was now sure.

But I was mad no longer and I committed myself to restoring the beauty I had destroyed in my warrings – first as the Champion of one side, then of the other – over the Earth.

Where armies had marched we planted shrubs and flowers. Where cities had been we made forests grow. And the Earth became gentle, calm and beautiful.

And my love for Ermizhad did not wane.

It grew. It developed so that I loved each new facet I discovered in her character.

The Earth became harmonious. And Erekosë, the Eternal Champion, and Ermizhad, Paramount Princess of the Eldren, reflected that harmony.

The great, terrifying weapons which we had used to overcome mankind were sealed away, and we swore that we should never use them again.

The Eldren cities, razed by the Marshals of Humanity when I had led them, were restored, and soon Eldren children sang in their streets, flowering shrubs bloomed on their balconies and terraces. Green turf grew over the scars cut with the swords of mankind's paladins. And the Eldren forgot the men who had once sought to destroy their race.

Only I remembered, for mankind had called me to lead them against the Eldren. Instead I had betrayed mankind – every man, woman and child had died because of me. The Droonaa River had flowed with their blood. Now it flowed with sweet water. But the water could not wash away the guilt that would sometimes consume me.

And yet I was happy. It seemed to me that I had never known such peace of soul, such tranquillity of mind.

Ermizhad and I would wander about the walls and terraces of Loos Ptokai, the Eldren capital, and we never tired of each other's company. Sometimes we would discuss a fine point of philosophy, at other times we were content to sit in silence, breathing in the rich and delicate scents of a garden.

And when the mood took us, we would embark upon a slender Eldren ship and sail about the world to witness its wonders – the Plains of Melting Ice, the Mountains of Sorrow, the mighty forests and gentle hills, the rolling plains of the two continents once inhabited by mankind, Necralala and Zavara. But then, sometimes, a mood of melancholy would sweep over me and we would set sail again for the third continent, the southern continent called Mernadin, where the Eldren had lived since ancient times.

It was at these times that Ermizhad would comfort me, sooth-ing away my memories and my shame.

'You know that I believe all this was preordained,' she would say. Her cool, soft hands would stroke my brow. 'Mankind's pur-pose was to destroy our race. This ambition destroyed them. You were merely the instrument of their destruction.'

'And yet,' I would reply, 'have I no free will? Was the only solu-tion the genocide I committed? I had hoped that mankind and the Eldren could live in peace...'

'And you tried to bring such a thing to pass. But they would have none of it. They tried to destroy you as they tried to destroy the Eldren. They almost succeeded. Do not forget that, Erekosë. They almost succeeded.'

'Sometimes,' I would confide, 'I wish that I were back in the world of John Daker. I once thought that world overly compli-cated and stifling. But now I realise that every world contains the same factors I hated, if in a different form. The Cycles of Time may change, Ermizhad, but the human condition does not. It was that condition I hoped to change. I failed. Perhaps that is my destiny – to strive to change the very nature of humanity – and fail...'

But Ermizhad was not human and, while she could sympathise and guess at what I meant, she could not understand. It was the one thing she could not understand.

'Your kind had many virtues,' she would say. Then she would pause and frown and be unable to complete her statement.

'Aye, but their very virtues became their vices. It was ever thus with mankind. A young man hating poverty and squalor would seek to change it by destroying something that was beautiful. See-ing people dying in misery, he would kill others. Seeing starvation, he would burn crops. Hating tyranny, he would give himself body and soul to that great tyrant War. Hating disorder, he would invent devices that brought further chaos. Loving peace, he would repress learning, outlaw art, cause conflict. The history of the human race was one prolonged tragedy, Ermizhad.'

And Ermizhad would kiss me lightly. 'And now the tragedy is ended.'

'So it seems, for the Eldren know how to live in tranquillity and retain their vitality. Yet sometimes I feel that the tragedy is still being played – perhaps played a thousand times in different guises. And the tragedy requires its principal actors. Perhaps I am one such. Perhaps I shall be called again to play my rôle. Perhaps my life with you is merely a pause between scenes...'

And to this statement she could offer no reply, save to take me in her arms and bring me the comfort of her sweet lips.

Gaily coloured birds and graceful beasts played where mankind had once raised its cities and beaten its battle-drums, but within those newborn forests and on the grass of those fresh-healed hills there were ghosts. The ghosts of Iolinda, who had loved me, of her father, the weak king Rigenos, who had sought my help, of Count Roldero, kindly Grand Marshal of Humanity, of all the others who had died because of me.

Yet it had been no choice of my own to come to this world, to take up the sword of Erekosë, the Eternal Champion, to put on Erekosë's armour, to ride at the head of a bright army as mankind's chief paladin, to learn that the Eldren were not the Hounds of Evil which King Rigenos had described, that they were, in fact, the victims of mankind's insensate hatred...

No choice of my own...

At root, that was the phrase most often haunting my moods of melancholy.

Yet those moods came more rarely as the years rolled by and Ermizhad and I did not age and continued to feel the same passion we had felt at our first meeting.

They were years of laughter, fine conversation, ecstasy, beauty, affection. One year blended into another until a hundred or so had passed.

Then the Ghost Worlds – those strange worlds which shifted through Time and Space at an angle to the rest of the universe we knew – came again in conjunction with the Earth.

Chapter Two
Of a Growing Doom

Ermizhad's brother was Prince Arjavh. Handsome, in the manner of the slender Eldren, with a pointed golden face and slanting eyes that were milky and blue-flecked, Arjavh had as much affection for me as I had for him. His wit and his wisdom had often inspired me and he was forever laughing.

So it was that I was surprised one day to visit him in his laboratory and find him frowning.

He looked up from his sheets of calculations and tried to alter his expression, but I could tell he was concerned – perhaps about some discovery he had made in his researches.

'What is it, Arjavh?' I asked lightly. 'Those look to me like astronomical charts. Is a comet on course for Loos Ptokai? Must we all evacuate the city?'

He smiled and shook his head. 'Nothing so simple. Perhaps not as dramatic, either. I am not sure there is anything to fear, but we would do well to be prepared, for it seems the Ghost Worlds are about to touch ours again.'

'But the Ghost Worlds offer the Eldren no harm, surely. You have summoned allies from them in the past.'

'True. Yet the last time the Ghost Worlds were in conjunction with Earth – that was the time you came here. Possibly it was coincidental. Possibly you are from one of the Ghost Worlds and that is how it was in Rigenos's power to call you.'

I frowned. 'I understand your concern. It is for me.'

Arjavh nodded his head and said nothing.

'Some say Humanity came originally from the Ghost Worlds, do they not?' I gave him a direct look.

'Aye.'

'Have you any specific fears on my behalf?' I asked him.

He sighed. 'No. Though the Eldren invented a means of bridg-ing the dimensions between our Earth and the Ghost Worlds, we never explored them. Our visits could, of necessity, only be brief and our contact was with those dwellers in the Ghost Worlds who were kin to the Eldren.'

'Do you fear that I will be recalled to the world I left?' I became tense. I could not bear the thought of being parted from Ermizhad, from the tranquil world of the Eldren.

'I do not know, Erekosë.'

Was I to become John Daker again?

Though I only dimly remembered my life in that era I for some reason called the Twentieth Century, I knew that I had not felt at ease there, that there had been within me an intense dissatisfac-tion with my life and circumstances. My naturally passionate and romantic disposition (which I did not regard as a virtue, for it had led me to commit the deeds I have already recounted) had been repressed by my surroundings, by my society and by the work I had done to make a living. I had felt more out of place there, among my own kind, than I did living here with an alien race. I felt that it might be better to kill myself, rather than return to John Daker's world, perhaps without even the memory of this one.

On the other hand, the Ghost Worlds might be nothing to do with me. They might belong to a universe which had never been inhabited by men (though the Eldren researches did not suggest this).

'Is there nothing else we can discover?' I asked Prince Arjavh.

'I am continuing my investigations. It is all I can do.'

Gloomily, I left his laboratory and returned to the chambers where Ermizhad awaited me. We had planned to ride out over the familiar fields surrounding Loos Ptokai, but now I told her that I did not feel like riding.

Noting my mood, she said: 'Are you remembering what passed a century ago, Erekosë?'

I shook my head. Then I told her what Arjavh had said.

She, too, became thoughtful. 'It was probably a coincidence,' she said. But there was little conviction in her tone. There was a trace of fear in her eyes when she looked up at me.

I took her in my arms.

'I should die, I think, if you were taken from me, Erekosë,' she said.

My lips were dry, my throat tight. 'If I were taken,' I told her, 'I would spend eternity in finding you again. And I would find you again, Ermizhad.'

When she spoke next, it was almost in astonishment. 'Is your love for me that strong, Erekosë?'

'It is stronger, Ermizhad.'

She drew away from me, holding my hands in hers. Those hands, hers and mine, were trembling. She tried to smile, to banish the premonitions filling her, but she could not.

'Why, then,' she said, 'there is nothing at all to fear!'

But that night, as I slept beside her, the dreams which I had experienced as John Daker, which had plagued me in my first year on this new world, began to creep back into the caverns of my mind.

First there were no images. Only names. A long list of names chanted in a booming voice that seemed to have a trace of mockery in it.

Corum Jhaelen Irsei. Konrad Arflane. Von Bek. Urlik Skarsol. Aubec of Kaneloon. Shaleen. Artos. Alerik. Erekosë...

I tried to stop the voice there. I tried to shout, to say that I was Erekosë – only Erekosë. But I could not speak.

The roll continued:

Ryan. Hawkmoon. Powys. Cornell. Brian. Umpata. Sojan. Klan. Clovis Marca. Pournachas. Oshbek-Uy. Ulysses. Ilanth. Renark.

My own voice came now:

'NO! I AM ONLY EREKOSË.'

'Champion Eternal. Fate's Soldier.'

'NO!'

Elric. Mejink-La-Kos. Cornelius.
'NO! NO! I AM WEARY. I CAN WAR NO MORE!'
The sword. The armour. The battle banners. Fire. Death. Ruin.
'NO!'

'Erekosë!'
'YES! YES!'
I was screaming. I was sweating. I was sitting upright in the bed. And it was Ermizhad's voice that was calling my name now. Panting, I fell back onto the pillows, into her arms.

'The dreams have returned.'

I lay my head upon her breast and I wept.

'This means nothing,' she said. 'It was only a nightmare. You fear that you will be recalled and your own mind gives substance to that fear. That is all.'

'Is it, Ermizhad?'

She stroked my head.

I looked up and saw her face through the darkness. It was strained. There were tears in her blue-flecked eyes.

'Is it?'

'Yes, my love. Yes.'

But I knew that the same sense of doom that lay upon my heart now lay upon hers.

We slept no more that night.

Chapter Three
Of a Visitation

NEXT MORNING I went straight to Prince Arjavh's laboratory and told him of the voice that had come to me in my sleep.

It was plain that he was distressed and plain also that he felt impotent to help me.

'If the voice was a mere nightmare – and I agree that it might be – then I could give you a potion to ensure dreamless sleep,' he said.

'And if not?'

'There is no way I can protect you.'

'Then the voice could be calling from the Ghost Worlds?'

'Even that is not certain. It could be that the information I gave you yesterday merely triggered some empathetic impulse in your own brain – which allowed this "voice" to make contact with you again. Perhaps the tranquillity you have known here made it impossible for you to be reached. Now that your brain is again in torment, then whatever it is that seeks to speak to you might now be able to do so.'

'These suppositions do not ease my mind,' I said bitterly.

'I know they do not, Erekosë. Would that you had never come to my laboratory, and learned of the Ghost Worlds. I should have kept this from you.

'It would have made no difference, Arjavh.'

'Who knows?'

I stretched out my hand. 'Give me the potion of which you spoke. At least we'll be able to put the theory to the test – that my own brain conjures this mocking voice.'

He went to a chest of glowing crystal and opened the lid, taking a small leather bag from it.

'Pour this powder into a goblet of wine tonight and drink all down.'

'Thank you,' I said as I took the bag.

He paused before he spoke again. 'Erekosë, if you are called from us, we shall waste no time in trying to find you. You are loved by all the Eldren and we would not lose you. If, somewhere in those unimaginable regions of Time and Space, you can be found – we shall find you.'

I was a little comforted by this assurance. Yet the speech was too much like a leave-taking for me to like it greatly. It was as if Arjavh had already accepted that I would be going.

Ermizhad and I spent the rest of that day walking hand in hand among the bowers of the palace garden. We spoke little, but gripped each other tightly and hardly dared look into each other's eyes for fear of the grief which would be mirrored there.

From hidden galleries came the intricate melodies of the great Eldren composers, played by musicians placed there by Prince Arjavh. The music was sweet, monumental, harmonious. To some degree it eased the dread that filled my brain.

A golden sun, huge and warm, hung in a pale blue sky. It shone its rays on delicately scented flowers in a multitude of hues, on vines and trees, on the white walls of the gardens.

We climbed the walls and looked out over the gentle hills and plains of the southern continent. A herd of deer was grazing. Birds sailed lazily in the sky.

I could not leave all this beauty to return to the noise and the filth of the world I had left, to the sad existence of John Daker.

Evening came and the air was filled with birdsong and the heavier perfume of the flowers. Slowly we walked back to the palace. Tightly we held each other's hands.

Like a condemned man, I mounted the steps that led to our chambers. Disrobing myself, I wondered if I should ever wear such clothes again. Lying down upon the bed while Ermizhad prepared the sleeping draught, I prayed that I should not rise next morning in the apartment in the city where John Daker had lived.

I stared up at the fluted ceiling of the chamber, looked around at the bright wall hangings, the vases of flowers, the finely wrought furnishings, and I attempted to fix all this in my mind, just as I had already fixed Ermizhad's face.

She brought me the drink. I looked deep into her tear-filled eyes and drank.

It was a parting. A parting we dare not admit.

Almost immediately I sank into a heavy slumber and it seemed to me at that moment that perhaps Ermizhad and Arjavh had been right and that the voice was simply a manifestation of my unease.

I do not know at what hour I was disturbed in that deep, drugged sleep. I was barely conscious. My brain seemed swaddled in fold upon fold of dark velvet, but muffled, and as if from far off, I faintly heard the voice again.

I could make out no words this time and I believe I smiled to myself, feeling relief that the drug was guarding me from that which sought to call me away. The voice became more urgent, but I could ignore it. I stirred and reached out for Ermizhad, throwing one arm across her slumbering body.

Still the voice called. Still I ignored it. Now I felt that if I could last this night, the voice would cease its attempt to recall me. I would know that I could not be drawn away so easily from the world where I had found love and tranquillity.

The voice faded and I slept on, with Ermizhad in my arms, with hope in my heart.

The voice returned some time later, but still I could ignore it.

Then the voice apparently ceased altogether and I sank again into my heavy sleep.

I think it must have been an hour or two before dawn that I heard a noise not within my head but in the room. Thinking that Ermizhad must have arisen, I opened my eyes. It was dark. I saw nothing. But Ermizhad was beside me. Then I heard the noise again. It was like the slap of a scabbarded sword against an armoured leg. I sat upright. My eyes were clogged with sleep, my head felt muzzy under the effects of the drug. I peered drowsily about the room.

And then I saw the figure who stood there.

'Who are you?' I asked, rather querulously. Maybe it was some servant? In Loos Ptokai there were no thieves, no threats of assassination.

The figure did not answer. It seemed to be staring at me. Gradually I distinguished more details and then I knew that this was no Eldren.

The figure had a barbaric appearance, though its apparel was rich and finely made. It wore a huge, grotesque helmet which completely framed a heavily bearded face. On its broad chest was a metal breastplate, as intricately ornamented as the helm. Over this was a thick, sleeveless coat of what appeared to be sheepskin. On his legs were breeches of lacquered hide, black and with sinuous designs picked out in gold and silver. Greaves on his legs matched the breastplate and his feet were encased in boots of the same shaggy, white pelt as his long coat. On his hip was a sword.

The figure did not move, but continued to regard me from the shadow cast by the peak of the grotesque helmet. The eyes were visible now. They burned. They were urgent.

This was no human of this world, no follower of King Rigenos who had somehow escaped the vengeance I had brought. A faint recollection came and went. But the garb was not that of any period of history I could remember from my life as John Daker.

Was this a visitor from the Ghost Worlds?

If so, his appearance was very different from that of the other Ghost Worlds dwellers who had once helped Ermizhad when she was a prisoner of King Rigenos.

I repeated my question.

'Who are you?'

The figure tried to speak but plainly could not.

He raised both hands to his head. He removed his helmet. He

brushed back black, long hair from his face. He moved nearer to the window.

The face was familiar.

It was my own.

I shrank back in the bed. Never before had I felt such complete terror. I do not think I have felt it since.

'What do you want?' I screamed. 'What do you want?'

In some other part of my churning brain I seem to remember wondering why Ermizhad did not awake but continued to sleep peacefully at my side.

The figure's mouth moved as if he was speaking, but I heard no words.

Was this a nightmare induced by the drug? If so, I think I should have preferred the voice.

'Get out of here! Begone!'

The visitation made several gestures which I could not interpret. Again its mouth moved, but no words reached me.

Screaming, I leapt from the bed and rushed at the figure which bore my face. But it moved away, a puzzled expression on its features.

There were no swords now in the Eldren palace, or I would have found one and used it against the figure. I think I had some mindless scheme to grasp his sword and use it against him.

'Begone! Begone!'

Then I tripped, fell scrabbling on the flagstones of the bed-chamber, shaking still with terror, screaming at the apparition which continued to look down at me. I rose again, tottered and was falling, falling, falling...

And as I fell, the voice filled my ears once again. It was full of triumphant joy.

'URLIK,' it cried. 'URLIK SKARSOL! URLIK! URLIK! ICE-HERO, COME TO US!'

'I WILL NOT!'

But now I did not deny that the name was mine. I tried to refuse the one or ones who called it. As I whirled and tumbled through the corridors of eternity, I sought to fling myself back – back to Ermizhad and the world of the Eldren.

'URLIK SKARSOL! COUNT OF THE WHITE WASTES! LORD OF THE FROZEN KEEP! PRINCE OF THE SOUTHERN ICE! MASTER OF THE COLD SWORD! HE WILL COME IN FURS AND METAL, HIS CHARIOT DRAWN BY BEARS, HIS BLACK BEARD BRISTLING, TO CLAIM HIS BLADE, TO AID HIS FOLK!'

'I WILL GIVE YOU NO AID! I DESIRE NO BLADE! LET ME SLEEP! I BEG YOU – LET ME SLEEP!'

'AWAKE, URLIK SKARSOL. THE PROPHECY DEMANDS IT!'

Now fragments of a vision came to me. I saw cities carved from cliffs of volcanic rock – obsidian and moody, built on the shores of sluggish seas, beneath dark, livid skies. I saw a sea that was like grey marble veined with black and I realised it was a sea on which floated great ice-floes.

The vision filled me with grief – not because it was strange and unfamiliar, but because it was familiar.

I knew for certain then that, weary with war, I had been called to fight yet another fight...

Book Two

The Champion's Road

The Warriors are in Silver,
The Citizens in Silk.
In Brazen Car the Champion rides,
A Hero clad in Grief,

— The Chronicle of the Black Sword

Chapter One

The Ice Wastes

I WAS STILL travelling, but it was no longer as if I had been tugged down into a maelstrom. I was moving slowly forward, though I was not moving my legs.

My vision cleared. The scene before me was concrete enough, though scarcely reassuring. I clung to a wisp of hope that I was still dreaming, but everything in me told me that this was not so. Just as John Daker had been called against his will to the world of the Eldren, so had Erekosë been called to this world.

And I knew my name. It had been repeated often enough. But I knew it as if it had always been mine. I was Urlik Skarsol of the South Ice.

The scene before me confirmed it, for I stared across a world of ice. It came to me that I had seen other ice plains in other incarnations, but this one I recognised for what it was. I was travelling over a dying planet. And in the sky above me was a small, dim red sun – a dying sun. That the world was Earth, I was certain, but it was an Earth at the end of its cycle. John Daker would have seen it as being in his distant future, but I had long since ceased to make easy definitions of 'past' and 'future'. If Time were my enemy, then she was an enemy without face or form; an enemy I could not see; an enemy I could not fight.

I was travelling in a chariot which seemed fashioned of silver and bronze, its heavy decoration reminiscent of the decoration I had seen on the armour of my voiceless visitor. Its four great iron-shod wheels had been bolted to skis apparently made of polished ebony. In the shafts at the front were the four creatures which dragged the chariot over the ice. The creatures were larger, longer-legged variations of the polar bears which had existed on

John Daker's world. They loped at a regular and surprisingly rapid speed. I stood upright in the chariot, holding their reins. Before me was a chest designed to fit the space. It seemed made of some hard wood overlaid with silver, its corners strengthened with strips of iron. It had a great iron lock and handle at the centre of the lid and the whole chest was decorated in black, brown and blue enamelwork depicting dragons, warriors, trees and flowers, all flowing and intertwining. There were strange, flowing runes picked out around the lock and I was surprised that I could read them easily: *This is the chest of Count Urlik Skarsol, Lord of the Frozen Keep.* On the right of the chest three heavy rings had been soldered to the side of the chariot and through the rings was placed the silver- and brass-shod haft of a lance which must have been at least seven feet long, ending in a huge, cruelly barbed head of gleaming iron. On the other side of the chest was a weapon whose haft was the twin to the spear's, but whose head was that of a great, broad-bladed axe, as beautifully decorated as the trunk, with delicately engraved designs. I felt at my belt. There was no sword there, only a pouch and, on my right hip, a key. I unhooked the key from my belt and looked at it curiously. I bent and inserted it with some difficulty (for the chariot had a tendency to lurch on the rough ice) and opened the trunk, expecting to find a sword there.

But there was no sword, only provisions, spare clothing and the like – the things a man would take with him if he were making a long journey.

I smiled despairingly. I had made a very long journey. I closed the chest and locked it, replacing the key on my belt.

And then I noticed what I was wearing. I had a heavily decorated iron breastplate, a huge coat of thick, coarse wool, a leather jerkin, breeches of lacquered leather, greaves of the same design as the breastplate, boots apparently of the same sheepskin-like stuff as the coat. I reached up to my head and touched metal. I ran my fingers over the serpentine designs which had been raised on the helmet.

With a growing sense of terror I moved my hands to my face. Its contours were familiar enough, but there was now a thick moustache on my upper lip, a great crop of black whiskers on my chin.

I had seen a hand-mirror in the chest. I seized the key, unlocked the bolt, flung back the lid, rummaged until I found the mirror which was of highly polished silver and not glass. I hesitated for a moment and then forced my hand to raise the mirror to my face.

I saw the face and helmet of my visitor – of the apparition which had come to me in the night.

I was now that apparition.

With a moan, with a sense of foreboding in my heart which I was unable to vocalise, I dropped the mirror back into the chest and slammed the lid shut. My hand went out to grip the haft of the tall lance and I clung to it, thought I must snap it with the force I applied.

And here I was on the pale ice beneath a darkling sky, alone and in torment, cut off from the one woman who had brought me tranquillity of spirit, the one world where I had felt free and at peace. I felt as a man must feel who has been in the grip of uncontrollable madness, thinks he is cured and then finds himself once again seized by the horrible insanity of which he thought himself purged.

I opened my mouth and I cried out against the ice. The breath steamed from my lips and boiled in the air like ectoplasm, writhed as if imitating the agony of spirit that was within me. I shook my fist at the dim, red, faraway globe that was this world's sun.

And all the while the white bears loped on, dragging me and my chariot to an unknown destination.

'Ermizhad!' I cried. 'Ermizhad!'

I wondered if somewhere she would hear me, call me as that other voice had called me.

'Ermizhad!'

But the dark sky was silent, the gloomy ice was still, the sun looked down like the eye of an old, old, senile man, uncomprehending.

On and on ran the tireless bears; on, across the perpetual ice; on, through perpetual twilight. On and on, while I wept and moaned and shrieked and at last was quiet, standing in my lurching chariot as if I, too, were made of ice.

I knew that, for the moment, I must accept my fate, discover where the bears were taking me, hope that when I reached my destination I would be able to discover a means of going back to the Eldren world, of finding my Ermizhad again.

I knew the hope was a faint one, but I clung to it as I had clung to the shaft of the spear. It was all I had. But where she was in the universe – in a host of alternate universes if the Eldren theories were right – I had no idea. Neither did I know where this world was. While it might be one of the Ghost Worlds and therefore possible for Eldren expeditions to reach, it could as easily be some other Earth, sundered by aeons from the world I had grown to love and to think of as my own.

But now I was again the Eternal Champion, summoned, no doubt, to fight in some cause with which I had scant sympathy, by a people who could easily be as wretched and self-deceiving as those who had been ruled by King Rigenos.

Why should I be singled out for this everlasting task? Why was I to be allowed no permanent peace?

Again my thoughts turned to the possibility that I had been responsible, in some incarnation, of a cosmic crime, so terrible that it was my fate to be swept back and forth across eternity. But what that crime could be that it deserved so frightful a punishment, I could not guess.

It seemed to grow colder. I reached into the chest and knew I should find gauntlets there. I drew the gloves onto my hands, wrapped the heavy coat more tightly about me, sat down on the chest, still holding the reins, and sank into a doze which I hoped would heal, at least a little, my wounded brain.

And still we drove over ice. Thousands of miles of ice. Had this world grown so old and cold that now there was nothing but ice from pole to pole?

Soon, I hoped, I would find out.

Chapter Two
The Obsidian City

A CROSS THE TIMELESS ice, beneath the waning sun, I moved in my chariot of bronze and silver. The long-limbed white bears only rarely slowed and never stopped. It was as if they, like me, were possessed of some force they could not control. Rusty clouds crossed the sky occasionally – slow ships on a livid sea – but there was nothing to mark the passing of the hours for the sun itself was frozen in the sky and the faint stars which gleamed behind it were arranged in constellations which were only vaguely familiar. It came to me then that the globe itself had apparently ceased to spin or, if it moved at all, moved so gradually as not to be apparent to a man without the necessary measuring instruments.

I reflected bitterly that the landscape certainly matched my mood, probably even exacerbated it.

Then, through the gloom, I thought I saw something which relieved the monotony of ice which hitherto had lain on all sides. Perhaps it was nothing more than a band of low cloud, but I kept my gaze fixed hopefully upon it and, as the bears drew closer, saw that these were the dark shapes of mountains apparently rising out of the ice plain. Were they mountains of ice and nothing more? Or were they of rock, indicating that not all the planet was covered by ice?

I had never seen such jagged crags. Despondently I concluded that they must be made of ice shaped by wind and time into such peculiar serrations.

But then, as we drew yet closer, I remembered the vision I had had when I was dragged away from Ermizhad's side. Now it seemed these were, indeed, rocks – volcanic rocks with a glassy lustre. Colours became apparent – deep greens and browns and blacks.

I shouted to the bears and jerked the reins to make them go faster.

And I discovered that I knew their names.

'Ho, Snarler! Ho, Render! Ho, Growler! Ho, Longclaw! Faster!'

They leaned in their harness and their speed increased. The chariot lurched and jogged and skipped over the rough ice.

'Faster!'

I had been right. Now I could see that the ice gave way to rock that was, if anything, smoother than glass. The ice thinned and then the chariot was bumping onto the rock that formed the foot-hills of the mountain range which now flung its spikey peaks into a mass of low, rust-coloured clouds, where they were lost to my view.

These were high and gloomy peaks. They dominated me, seemed to threaten me, and they were certainly no comfort to the eye. But they offered me some hope, particularly as I made out what could be a pass between two tall cliffs.

The range seemed principally a mixture of basalt and obsidian and on both sides of me now were huge boulders between which passed a natural causeway down which I drove my straining bears. I could see the strangely coloured clouds clinging to the upper slopes of the cliffs, almost as smoke clings to oil.

And now, as I discerned more detail, I could only gasp at the wonder of the cliffs. That they were volcanic in origin there was no doubt, for the spikey upper peaks were plainly of pumice, while the lower flanks were either of black, green or purple obsid-ian, smooth and shiny, or basalt which had formed into something not unlike the delicately fluted columns of fine Gothic architec-ture. They could almost have been built by some intelligence possessed of gigantic size. Elsewhere the basalt was red and deep blue and cellular in appearance, almost like coral. In other places the same rock was a more familiar coal black and dark grey. And at still more levels there were veins of iridescent rock that caught what little light there was and were as richly coloured as the feathers of a peacock.

I guessed that this region must have resisted the march of the ice because it had been the last volcanically active region on the planet.

Now I had entered the pass. It was narrow and the cliffs seemed as if they were about to crush me. Some parts of them were pitted with caves which my fancy saw as malicious eyes staring down at me. I kept a firm grip on my lance as I drove. For all my imaginings, there was always the chance that there were real dangers here from beasts which might inhabit the caves.

The pass wound around the bases of many mountains, all of the same strange formations and colours. The ground became less level and the bears had great difficulty pulling the chariot. At last, though I had no inclination to stop in that gloomy pass, I drew rein and dismounted from the chariot, inspecting the runners and the bolts attaching them to the wheels. I knew instinctively that I had the appropriate tools in my chest and I opened the lid and eventually discovered them in a box of the same design and manufacture as the chest itself.

With some effort I unbolted the runners and slid them into lugs along the side of the chariot.

Just as I had discovered, as Erekosë, that I had an instinctive skill with weapons and horses, that I knew every piece of armour as if I had always worn it, now I found that the workings of this chariot were completely familiar to me.

With the wheels free, the chariot moved much faster, though it was even more difficult to keep my balance than before.

Many hours must have passed before I rounded a curve in the pass and saw that I had come to the other side of the mountain range.

Smooth rock sloped down to a crystalline beach. And against the beach moved the sluggish tide of an almost viscous sea.

Elsewhere the mountains entered the sea itself and I could see jagged peaks jutting out of the water which must have contained a much greater quantity of salt than even the Dead Sea of John

Daker's world. The low, brown clouds seemed to meet the sea only a short distance out. The dark crystals of the beach were devoid of plant life and here even the faint light from the small, red sun barely pierced the darkness.

It was as if I had come to the edge of the world at the end of time.

I could not believe that anything lived here – whether man, plant or beast.

But now the bears had reached the beach and the wheels crunched on the crystal and the creatures did not stop, but turned sharply towards the east, dragging me and the chariot along the shore of that dark and morbid ocean.

Though it was warmer here than it had been on the ice, I shuddered. Again my imagination took an unpleasant turn as I guessed at what kind of monsters might dwell beneath the surface of the twilit sea, what kind of people could bear to live beside it.

I was soon to have my answer – or, at least, part of it – when through the gloom I heard the sound of human voices and soon saw those who had uttered them.

They rode huge animals which moved not on legs but on strong, muscular flippers and whose bodies sloped sharply back to end in wide tails which balanced them. In some astonishment I realised that these riding beasts had been, at some earlier period of their evolution, sea-lions. They still had the doglike, whiskered faces, the huge, staring eyes. The saddles on their backs had been built up so that the rider sat almost level. Each rider held a rod of some kind which issued a faint glow in the darkness.

But were the riders human? Their bodies, encased in ornate armour, were bulbous and, in comparison, their arms and legs were sticklike, their heads – also enclosed in helmets – tiny. They had swords, lances and axes at their hips or in sheaths attached to their saddles. From within their visors their voices boomed and were echoed by the lowering cliffs, but I could distinguish no words.

They rode their seal-beasts skilfully along the shores of the salt-thick sea until they were only a few yards from me. Then they stopped.

In turn, I stopped my chariot.

A silence fell. I placed my hand upon the shaft of my tall spear while my bears moved restlessly in their harness.

I inspected the riders more closely. They were somewhat frog-like in appearance, if the armour actually displayed the basic shapes of their bodies. The accoutrements and armour were so ornate and, to my taste, overworked, that it was almost impossible to pick out individual designs. Most of the suits were of a reddish gold in colour, though glowing greens and yellows became apparent in the light from their dim torches.

After some moments in which they made no further effort to communicate with me I decided to speak.

'Are you those who called me?' I asked.

Visors turned, gestures were made, but they did not reply.

'What people are you?' I said. 'Do you recognise me?'

This time a few words passed between the riders but they still did not speak directly to me. They urged their beasts into a wide semicircle and then surrounded me. I kept my hand firmly on the shaft of my lance.

'I am Urlik Skarsol,' I said. 'Did you not summon me?'

Now one spoke, his voice muffled in his helm. 'We did not summon you, Urlik Skarsol. But we know your name and bid you be our guest in Rowernarc.' He gestured with his torch in the direction from which they had come. 'We are Bishop Belphig's men. He would wish us to make you welcome.'

'I accept your hospitality.'

There had been respect in the speaker's voice after he had heard my name, but I was surprised that he had not been expecting me. Why had the bears brought me here? Where else was there to go, save beyond the sea? And it seemed to me that beyond the sea lay nothing but limbo. I could imagine those sluggish waters dripping over the edge of the world into the total blackness of the cosmic void.

I allowed them to escort me along the beach until it curved into a bay, at the end of which was a steep, high cliff up which climbed a number of paths, evidently cut by men. These paths led to the mouths of archways as heavily ornamented as the armour worn by the riders. High above, the most distant archways were half hidden by the thick, brown clouds clinging to the rock.

This was not merely a village of cliff-dwellers. Judging by the sophistication of the ornament, it was a great city, carved from the gleaming obsidian.

'That is Rowernarc,' said the rider nearest me. 'Rowernarc – the Obsidian City.'

Chapter Three
The Lord Spiritual

THE PATHS UP to the yawning gateways in the cliff face were wide enough to take my chariot. Somewhat reluctantly the bears began to climb.

The froglike riders led the way, ascending higher and higher along the obsidian causeways, passing several baroque arches festooned with gargoyles which, while being of exquisite workmanship, were the products of dark and morbid brains.

I looked towards the gloomy bay, at the low, brown clouds, at the heavy, unnatural sea, and it seemed for a moment that all this world was enclosed in one murky cave – in one cold hell.

And if the landscape reminded me of Hell, then subsequent events were soon to confirm my impression.

Eventually we reached an archway of particularly heavy decoration – all carved from the multicoloured living obsidian – and the strange seal-beasts turned and stopped and thwacked their fore-fins on the ground in a complicated rhythm.

Within the shadow of the arch I could now detect a barrier. It seemed to be a door – but a door that was made of solid porphyritic rock from which all kinds of strange beasts and half-human creatures had been carved. Whether these representations, too, were the inventions of near-crazed minds or whether they were taken from types actually to be found in this world, I could not tell. But some of the designs were loathsome and I avoided looking at them as much as possible.

In answer to the strange signal of the seals, this door began to scrape backwards – the whole block moving into the cavern behind it – to allow us passage around it. My chariot wheel caught on one edge and I was forced to manoeuvre for a moment before I could pass into the chamber.

This chamber was poorly lit by the same staffs of faint artificial light which the riders had carried. The staffs reminded me of battery-operated electric torches which needed recharging. Somehow I thought that these could not be recharged. I had the feeling that as the artificial brands died, so a little more light vanished from this world. It would not be long, I thought, before all the brands were extinguished.

The froglike riders were dismounting, handing their beasts over to grooms who, to my relief, looked ordinarily human, though pale and somewhat scrawny. These grooms were dressed in smocks bearing a complicated piece of embroidered insignia which again was so complex as to have no indication to me what it was meant to represent. I suddenly had an insight into the lives of these people. Living in their rock cities on a dying planet, surrounded by bleak ice and gloomy seas, they whiled away their days at various crafts, adding embellishment upon complicated embellishment, producing work which was so introverted that it doubtless lost its meaning even to them. It was the art of a decaying race and yet, ironically, it would outlast them by centuries, perhaps for ever when the atmosphere eventually disappeared.

I felt a reluctance to deliver my chariot and its weapons over to the grooms, but there was little else I could do. Seal-beasts and chariot were led off down a dark, echoing passage and the armoured creatures once again turned to regard me.

One of them stretched, then lifted off his ornate helm to reveal a white, human face with pale, cold eyes – weary eyes, it seemed to me. He began to unbuckle the straps of his armour and it was drawn away to show the thick padding beneath. When the padding was pulled off, I saw that the body, also, was of perfectly normal proportions. The others stripped off their armour and handed it to those waiting to receive it. As a gesture, I took off my own helmet and held it crooked in my left arm.

The men were all pale, all with the same strange eyes which

were not so much unfriendly as introspective. They wore loose tabards which had every inch covered in dark-hued embroidery, trousers of similar material which were baggy and tucked into boots of painted leather.

'Well,' sighed the man who had first removed his armour, 'here we are in Haradeik.' He signed to a servant. 'Seek our master. Tell him Morgeg is here with his patrol. Tell him we have brought a visitor – Urlik Skarsol of the Frozen Keep. Ask him if he would grant us an audience.'

I frowned at Morgeg. 'So you know of Urlik Skarsol. You know that I hail from the Frozen Keep.'

A tiny, puzzled smile came to Morgeg's mouth. 'All know of Urlik Skarsol. But I have heard of no man who has ever met him.'

'And you called this city Rowernarc when we arrived, but now you call it Haradeik.'

'Rowernarc is the city. Haradeik is the name of our particular warren – the province of our master, Bishop Belphig.'

'And who is this bishop?'

'Why, he is one of our two rulers. He is Lord Spiritual of Rowernarc.'

Morgeg spoke in a low, sad tone which I guessed was habitual rather than reflecting a particular mood of his at this moment. Everything he said sounded offhanded. Nothing seemed to matter to him. Nothing seemed to interest him. He seemed almost as dead as the murky, twilight world outside the cavern city.

Quite soon the messenger returned.

'Bishop Belphig grants an audience,' he told Morgeg.

By this time the others had gone about their business and only Morgeg and I remained in the antechamber. Morgeg led me along a poorly lit passage, every inch of which was decorated – even the floor was of crystalline mosaic, and harpies, chimerae and musimonii glared down at me from the low ceiling. Another antechamber, another great door, slightly smaller than the outer one, which withdrew to allow us entrance. And we were in a large hall.

It was a hall with a high arched ceiling coming almost to a

point at the top. At the end of it was a dais hung with draperies. On each side of the dais was a glowing brazier, tended by servants, which issued ruddy light and sent smoke curling towards the ceiling where, presumably, it found egress, for there was only a hint of smoke in the air I breathed. As if preserved in volcanic glass, stone monsters writhed and crouched on walls and ceiling, leering, baring unlikely fangs, laughing at some obscene joke, roaring, threatening, twisting in some secret agony. Many bore resemblances to the heraldic monsters of John Daker's world. Here were cockfish, opinicus, mantigoras, satyrs, man-lions, melusines, camelopards, wyverns, cockatrices, dragons, griffins, unicorns, amphisboenae, enfields, bagwyns, salamanders – every combination of man, beast, fish and fowl – all of huge size, rending each other, crawling over each other's backs, copulating, tangling tails, defecating, dying, being born…

This, surely, was a chamber of Hell.

I looked towards the dais. Behind draperies, in some sort of throne, a figure lounged. I approached the dais, half expecting the figure to be possessed of a spiked tail and a pair of horns.

A foot or two from the dais Morgeg stopped and bowed. I did likewise. The drapes were drawn back by servants and there sat a man very different from what I had expected – very different from the pale, sad-eyed Morgeg.

The voice was deep, sensuous, jovial. 'Greetings, Count Urlik. We are honoured you should decide to pay a visit to this rat's nest we call Rowernarc, you who are of the free and open icelands.'

Bishop Belphig was fat, dressed in rich robes, a circlet around his long, blond hair, keeping it from his eyes. His lips were very red and his eyebrows very black. With a sudden shock I realised that he was using cosmetics. Beneath them doubtless he, too, was as pale as Morgeg and the rest. Perhaps the hair was dyed. Certainly the cheeks were rouged, the eyelashes false, the lips painted.

'Greetings, Bishop Belphig,' I replied. 'I thank the Lord Spiritual of Rowernarc for his hospitality and would beg a word or two with him in private.'

'Aha! You have some message for me, dear count! Of course. Morgeg – the rest of you – leave us for a while. But stay within earshot if I should want to call you suddenly.'

I smiled slightly. Bishop Belphig did not want to risk the fact that I might be an assassin.

When they had gone Belphig waved a beringed hand in an expansive gesture. 'Well, good count? What is your message?'

'I have no message,' I said. 'I have only a question. Perhaps several questions.'

'Then ask them, sir! Please, ask them!'

'First, I would know why my name is familiar to you all. Secondly, I would ask if it was you, who must have certain mystical knowledge, who summoned me here. The other questions depend on your answers to the first two.'

'Why, dear count, your name is known to all! You are a legend, you are a fabulous hero. You must know this!'

'Presume that I have awakened just recently from a deep sleep. Presume that most of my memories are gone. Tell me of the legend.'

Bishop Belphig frowned and he put fat, jewelled fingers to fat, carmine lips. His voice was more subdued, more contemplative when next he spoke. 'Very well, I will presume that. There are said to have been four Ice Lords – of North, South, East and West – but all died save the Lord of the South Ice, who was frozen in his great keep by a sorceress until he should be called for – summoned when his people were in great danger. All this took place in antiquity, only a century or two after the ice had destroyed the famous cities of the world – Barbart, Lanjis Liho, Korodune and the rest.'

The names were faintly familiar but no memories were awakened within me by the remainder of the bishop's story.

'Is there any more of the legend?' I asked.

'That is the substance of it. I can probably find a book or two containing some sort of amplification.'

'And it was not you who called me?'

'Why should I summon, you? To tell you the truth, Count Urlik, I did not believe the legend.'

'And you believe it now? You do not think me an imposter?'

'Why should you be an imposter? And if you are, why should I not humour you if it suits you to say you are Count Urlik.' He smiled. 'There is precious little that is new in Rowernarc. We welcome diversion.'

I returned his smile. 'A pleasantly sophisticated view, Bishop Belphig. However, I remain puzzled. Not long since, I found myself on the ice, travelling here. My accoutrements and my name were familiar, but all else was strange. I am a creature, my lord, with little volition of his own. I am a hero, you see, and am called whenever I am needed. I will not bore you with the details of my tragedy, save to say that I would not be here unless I was needed to take part in a struggle. If you did not call me, then perhaps you know who did.'

Belphig drew his painted brows together in a frown. Then he raised them and gave me a quizzical look. 'I fear I can offer no suggestion at present, Count Urlik. The only threat facing Rowernarc is the inevitable one. In a century or two the ice will creep over our mountain barrier and extinguish us. In the meantime, we while away the hours as best we can. You are welcome to join us here, if the Lord Temporal agrees, and you must promise to recount your whole story to us, no matter how incredible you think it is. In return, we can offer you such entertainments as we have. These may be stimulating if they are new to you.'

'Has Rowernarc, then, no enemies?'

'None powerful enough to form a threat. There are a few bands of outlaws, some pirates – the kind of garbage that collects around any city – but they are all.'

I shook my head in puzzlement. 'Perhaps there are internal factions at Rowernarc – groups who wish, say, to overthrow you and the Lord Temporal?'

Bishop Belphig laughed. 'Really, my dear count, you seem to desire strife above all else! I assure you that there are no issues in

Rowernarc on which anyone would care to spend much time. Boredom is our only enemy and now that you are here that enemy has been put to flight!'

'Then I thank you for your offer of hospitality,' I said. 'I will accept it. Presumably you have libraries in Rowernarc – and scholars.'

'We are all scholars in Rowernarc. Yes, we have libraries, many of which you may use.'

At least, I thought, I would be able here to spend the best part of my time seeking to find a means of returning to Ermizhad and the lovely world of the Eldren (to which this world was in hateful contrast). Yet I could not believe that I had been called here for nothing, unless it was to a life of exile in which, as an Immortal, I would be forced to witness the eventual death of the Earth.

'However,' continued Bishop Belphig, 'I cannot alone make this decision. We must also consult my fellow ruler, the Lord Temporal. I am sure he will agree to your requests and make you welcome. Apartments must be found for you, and slaves and the like. These activities will also help relieve the ennui which besets Rowernarc.'

'I desire no slaves,' I said.

Bishop Belphig chuckled. 'Wait until you see them before you make your decision.' Then he paused and gave me an amused look from his made-up eyes. 'But perhaps you are of a period where the holding of slaves is frowned upon, eh? I have read that history has had such periods. But in Rowernarc slaves are not held by force. Only those who wish to be slaves are such. If they choose to be something else, why, then, they can be whatever they desire. This is Rowernarc, Count Urlik, where all men and women are free to follow any inclination they choose.'

'And you chose to be Lord Spiritual here?'

Again the bishop smiled. 'In a sense. The title is an hereditary one, but many born to this rank have preferred other occupations. My brother, for instance, is a common sailor.'

'You sail those salt-thick seas?' I was astonished.

'Again – in a sense. If you know not the customs of Rowernarc, I believe you will find many of them interesting.'

'I am sure I will,' I said. And I thought privately that some of those customs I should not find to my taste at all. Here, I thought, I had found the human race in its final stages of decadence – perverse, insouciant, without ambition. And I could not blame them. After all, they had no future.

And there was something, too, in me which reflected Bishop Belphig's cynicism. For had not I little to live for, also?

The bishop raised his voice. 'Slaves! Morgeg! You may return.'

They trooped back into the murky chamber, Morgeg at their head.

'Morgeg,' said the bishop, 'perhaps you will send a messenger to find the Lord Temporal. Ask him if he will grant an audience to Count Urlik Skarsol. Tell him I have offered the count our hospitality, if he should agree.'

Morgeg bowed and left the chamber.

'And now, while we wait, you must dine with me, my lord,' Bishop Belphig said to me. 'We grow fruits and vegetables in our garden caverns and the sea provides us with meat. My cook is the best in all Rowernarc. Will you eat?'

'Gladly,' I said, for I had realised that I was famished.

Chapter Four
The Lord Temporal

T HE MEAL, THOUGH somewhat rich and overspiced for my taste, was delicious. When it was over, Morgeg came back to say that the Lord Temporal had been given the message.

'It was some time before we could find him,' Morgeg said, offering Belphig a significant look. 'But he will give an audience to our guest now, if our guest desires.' He looked at me with his pale, cold eyes.

'Have you had enough to eat and drink, Count Urlik?' Bishop Belphig asked. 'Is there anything else you desire?' He wiped his red lips with a brocade napkin, removed a sauce stain from his jowl.

'I thank you for your generosity,' I said rising. I had drunk more salty wine than I should have liked, but it helped dampen the morbid thoughts of Ermizhad which still plagued me – would plague me for ever, until I found her again.

I followed Morgeg from the grotesque chamber. As I reached the door I looked back, thinking to thank Bishop Belphig again.

He had smeared some of the sauce over the body of a young boy slave. As I watched, he bent to lick at the stuff he had put there.

I turned quickly and increased my stride as Morgeg led me back the way we had come.

'The Lord Temporal's province is called Dhötgard and lies above this one. We must go to the outer causeway again.'

'Are there no passages connecting the various levels?' I asked.

Morgeg shrugged. 'Aye, I believe so. But this way is easier than searching for the doors and then trying to get them open.'

'You mean you do not use many of the passages?'

Morgeg nodded. 'There are fewer of us now than there were even fifty years ago. Children are rare in Rowernarc these days.' He spoke carelessly and once again I had the impression that I spoke to a corpse brought back from the dead.

Through the great main door of Haradeik we passed and into the cold air of the causeway that hung above the dark bay where the sluggish sea spread pale salt on the black crystals of the beach. It seemed an even gloomier landscape than it had seemed before, with the clouds bringing the horizon so close and the jagged crags on all other sides. I felt a sense of claustrophobia as we walked up the causeway until we came to an archway which was little different in style from the one we had just left.

Morgeg cupped his hands together and shouted through them. 'Lord Urlik Skarsol comes to seek audience with the Lord Temporal!'

His voice found a muffled echo in the mountains. I looked up, trying to see the sky, trying to make out the sun behind the clouds, but I could not.

There was a grating noise as the door slid in just sufficiently for us to squeeze past and find ourselves in an antechamber with smooth walls and even less light than that which had barely illuminated Haradeik. A servant in a plain white tabard was waiting for us. He rang a silver hand-bell and the door moved back. The machinery operating these doors must have been very sophisticated, for I could see no evidence of pulleys and chains.

The passage we moved down was the twin to the one in Bishop Belphig's 'province' save that here there were no bas-reliefs. Instead there were paintings, but the light was so poor and the paint so old that I could scarcely make out any details. We turned into a similar passage, our footsteps sounding loudly on the carpet-covered floor. Another passage and then we reached an archway which was not blocked by a door. Instead, a curtain of plain, soft leather had been hung across it. I felt that such simplicity was incongruous in Rowernarc, but I was even more surprised when the servant parted the curtain and led us into a chamber whose walls were completely bare, save that they had been covered with a surface of white paint. Huge lamps brightly lit the room. These lamps were probably oil-burning, for a faint smell issued from them. In the middle of the room was a desk and two benches. Save for ourselves, there were no other occupants.

Morgeg looked around at the room and his expression was one of discomfort.

'I will leave you here, Count Urlik. Doubtless the Lord Temporal will emerge soon.'

When Morgeg had left, the servant indicated that I sit on one of the benches. I did so, placing my helm beside me. Like the room, the desk was bare, apart from two scrolls placed neatly near the end. There was nothing for me to do but look at the white walls, the silent servant who had taken up a position by the arch curtain, the almost bare desk.

I must have sat there for an hour before the curtain parted and a tall figure entered. I rose to my feet, hardly able to restrain the expression of astonishment which tried to come over my face. The figure signed for me to sit down again. He had an abstracted look as he walked to the desk and sat behind it.

'I am Shanosfane,' he said.

His skin was a flat, coal black and his features were fine-boned and ascetic. I reflected, ironically, that somehow the rôles of Shanosfane and Belphig had become muddled – that Belphig should have been the Temporal Lord and Shanosfane the Spiritual Lord.

Shanosfane wore loose, white robes. The only decoration was a fibula at his left shoulder which bore a device I took to be the sign of his rank. He rested his long-fingered hands on the desk and regarded me with a distant expression which nonetheless betrayed a great intelligence.

'I am Urlik,' I replied, thinking it best to speak as simply.

He nodded, peering at the desk and tracing a triangle upon it with his finger. 'Belphig said you wished to stay here.' His voice was deep, resonant, far away.

'He told me there were books I might consult.'

'There are many books here, though most are of a whimsical kind. The pursuit of true knowledge no longer interests the folk of Rowernarc, Lord Urlik. Did Bishop Belphig tell you that?'

'He merely said I should find books here. Also he told me that all men were scholars in Rowernarc.'

A gleam of irony came into Shanosfane's dark eyes. 'Scholars? Aye. Scholars in the art of the perverse.'

'You seem to disapprove of your own people, my lord.'

'How can I disapprove of the damned, Count Urlik? And we are all damned – they and I. It has been our misfortune to be born at the end of time…'

I spoke feelingly. 'It is no misfortune if death is all you have to face.'

With curiosity he looked up. 'You do not fear death, then?'

I shrugged. 'I do not know death. I am immortal.'

'Then you are really from the Frozen Keep?'

'I do not know my origins. I have been many heroes. I have seen many ages of the Earth.'

'Indeed?' His interest grew and I could tell it was a purely intellectual interest. There was no empathy here, save possibly of minds. There was no emotion. 'Then you are a traveller in Time?'

'I am, in a sense, though not, I think, the sense you mean.'

'Some several centuries – or perhaps millennia – ago there was a race of folk lived on the Earth. I heard they learnt the art of time travel and left this world, for they knew it was dying. But doubtless it is a legend. But then, so are you a legend, Count Urlik. And you exist.'

'You believe that I am no imposter, then?'

'I think that is what I believe. In what sense do you travel in Time?'

'I am drawn wherever I am called. Past, present and future have no meaning for me. Ideas of cyclical Time have little meaning, for I believe there are many universes, many alternative destinies. The history of this planet might never have included me, in any of my incarnations. And yet it might have included them all.'

'Strange...' Shanosfane spoke musingly, raising a delicate black hand to his fine brow. 'For our universe is so confined and clearly marked, while yours is vast, chaotic. If – forgive me – you are not insane, then some theories of mine are confirmed. Interesting...'

'It is my intention,' I continued, 'to seek the means of returning to one of these worlds, if it still exists, and using everything in my power to remain there.'

'It does not excite you to move from world to world, from Time to Time?'

'Not for eternity, Lord Shanosfane. Not when, on one of those worlds, is a being for whom I have an abiding love and who shares that love.'

'How found you that world?'

I began to speak. Soon I discovered that I was telling him my whole story, everything that had happened to me since John Daker had been called by King Rigenos to aid the forces of Humanity against the Eldren, every fragment of my recollections of other incarnations, everything that had befallen me until the Rowernarc patrol had met me on the beach. He listened with great attention, staring up at the ceiling as I spoke, never interrupting me, until I had finished.

He said nothing for a while, but then signed to his patient servant. 'Bring water and some rice.' For a few moments more he considered my story. I thought he must surely believe me a madman now.

'You say you were called to come here,' he said eventually. 'Yet we did not call you. It is unlikely that, whatever the danger, we should place much faith in a legend of the sort that has existed throughout history if my reading is accurate on the matter.'

'Are there any others who might have summoned me?'

'Yes.'

'Bishop Belphig said this was unlikely.'

'Belphig shapes his thoughts to fit his moods. There are communities beyond Rowernarc, there are cities beyond the sea. At least, there were, before the Silver Warriors came.'

'Belphig mentioned nothing of the Silver Warriors.'

'Perhaps he forgot. It has been some while since we last heard of them.'

'Who are they?'

'Oh, ravagers of some description. Their motives are obscure.'

'Where do they come from?'

'They come from Moon, I think.'

'From the sky? Where is Moon?'

'On the other side of the world, they say. The few references I have seen do mention that it was once in the sky, but no longer.'

'These Silver Warriors – are they human?'

'Not according to the accounts I received.'

'And do they offer you harm, Lord Shanosfane? Will they try to invade Rowernarc?'

'Perhaps. I think they want the planet for themselves.'

I looked at him feeling somewhat shocked by his lack of interest.

'You do not care if they destroy you?'

'Let them have the planet. What use is it to us? Our race will soon be overwhelmed by the ice that creeps a little closer each year as the sun fades. These people seem better adapted to live in the world than we are.'

Though I could understand his argument, I had never encountered such complete disinterest before. I admired it, but I felt little true sympathy with it. It was my destiny to struggle – though for what cause I had no clear idea – and even while I hated the fact that I must do battle through eternity (or so it seemed) my instincts were still those of a warrior.

While I tried to think of an answer, the black Lord Temporal rose. 'Well, we will talk again. You may live in Rowernarc until you desire to leave.'

And with that he left the room.

As he left, the servant entered with the tray of rice and water. He turned and, holding the tray, followed behind his master.

Now that I had met both the Lord Spiritual and the Lord Temporal of Rowernarc I was even more confused than when I had first arrived here. Why had Belphig not told me of the alien Silver Warriors? Was I destined to fight them or – another thought came – were the folk of Rowernarc the enemy I had been called to war against?

Chapter Five
The Black Sword

AND SO, UNHAPPY, torn by my longing for Ermizhad, by my great sense of loss, I settled in the Obsidian City of Rowernarc, there to brood, to pore over ancient books in strange scripts, to seek some solution to my tragic dilemma and yet feel my despair increasing with every day that passed.

To be accurate, there were no days and nights in the Obsidian City. People slept, awakened and ate when they felt like it and their other appetites were followed in the same spirit, for all that those appetites were jaded and novelty did not exist.

I had been given my own apartments on the level below Haradeik, Bishop Belphig's province. Though they were not quite as baroque as the bishop's apartments, I would have preferred the simplicity which Shanosfane's had. I learned, however, that Shanosfane himself had ordered most decoration removed from Dhötgard when he had assumed his position on the death of his father. The apartments were more than comfortable – the most committed sybarite would have found them luxurious – but for the first weeks of my stay I was plagued with visitors.

It was a seducer's dream, but for me, with my love for Ermizhad unwaning, it was a nightmare.

Woman after woman would present herself in my bedchamber, offering me more exotic delights than even Faust had known. As politely as I could – and much to their astonishment – I refused them all. Men, too, came with similar promises and, because the customs of Rowernarc were such that these advances were not considered shameful, I refused them with equal politeness.

And then Bishop Belphig would arrive with presents – young slaves as covered in cosmetics as he was – rich foodstuffs for which

I had no appetite – books of erotic verse which did not interest me – suggestions of acts which might be committed upon my person which disgusted me. Since I owed my roof and the possibility of research to Belphig, I retained my patience with him and judged that he only meant well, though I found both his tastes and his appearance sinister.

On my visits to the various libraries situated on different levels of the Obsidian City I witnessed sights which I would not have believed existed outside the pages of Dante's *Inferno*. Orgies were unceasing. I would stumble upon them wherever I went. In some of the libraries I visited I found them. And they were never orgies of plain fornication.

Torture was common and witnessed by whoever chose to be a spectator. That the victims were willing did not make the sights any easier for me to bear. Even murder itself was not outlawed, for the murdered man or woman desired death as much as the murderer desired to kill.

These pale people with no future, no hope, nothing to prepare for save death, spent their days in experimenting with pain quite as much as they experimented with pleasure.

Rowernarc was a city gone mad. A dreadful neurosis had settled upon it and it seemed pitiful to me that these people, so sophisticated and talented, should waste their final years in such ultimately self-destructive pursuits.

The grotesque galleries and halls and passages would ring to the sound of screams – high-pitched screams of laughter, ululating screams of terror – with moans, with grunts and bellowings.

Through all this I would stride, sometimes tripping over a prone, drugged body in the gloom, sometimes having to disentangle myself from the arms of a naked girl barely out of puberty.

Even the books I found were frustrating. Lord Shanosfane had warned me in his own way. Most of the books were examples of completely decadent prose, so convoluted as to be nearly meaningless. Not only works of fiction, but all the works of fact, were written in this manner. My brain would spin as I attempted to make sense of it all – and failed.

At other times, when I had given up trying to interpret these decadent texts, I would pass through a gallery and see Lord Shanosfane wandering across a hall, his ascetic face frozen in abstracted thought, while all around him his subjects sported, sometimes leering and gesturing at him obscenely. Occasionally he would look up, put his head to one side, regard them with a slight frown and then walk on.

The first few times I saw him I hailed him, but he ignored me as he would have ignored anyone else. I wondered what ideas were forming and re-forming in that strange, cool brain. I felt sure that if he would grant me another audience I would learn much more from him than I had managed to learn from the texts I studied, but since the first day I had arrived at Rowernarc he had not agreed to see me.

My sojourn in Rowernarc was so much like a dream itself that perhaps that was the reason why my slumber was dreamless for the first fifty nights of my stay there. But on what I reckon to be the fifty-first night, those familiar visions returned.

They had terrified me as I lay in Ermizhad's arms. Now I almost welcomed them…

I stood on a hill and spoke with a faceless knight in black-and-yellow armour. A pale flag without insignia fluttered on a staff erected between us.

Below us, in the valley, towns and cities were burning. Red fires sprouted everywhere. Black smoke cruised above the scenes of carnage from time to time revealed.

It seemed to me that the whole human race fought in that valley – every human being who had ever drawn breath was there, save me.

I saw great armies marching back and forth. I saw ravens and vultures feasting on battlefields. I heard the distant sounds of drums and guns and trumpets.

'You are Count Urlik Skarsol of the Frozen Keep,' said the faceless knight.

'I am Erekosë, adopted Prince of the Eldren,' I replied firmly;
The faceless knight laughed. 'No longer, warrior. No longer.'

'Why am I made to suffer so, Sir Knight in Black and Yellow?'

'You need not suffer – not if you accept your fate. After all, you cannot die. True you may seem to perish, but your incarnations are infinite.'

'That knowledge is what causes the suffering! If I could not remember previous incarnations, then I would believe each life to be my only one.'

'Some people would give much for such knowledge.'

'The knowledge is only partial. I know my fate, but I do not know how I earned it. I do not understand the structure of the universe through which I am flung, seemingly at random.'

'It is a random universe. It has no permanent structure.'

'At least you have told me that.'

'I will answer any question you put to me. Why should I lie?'

'Then that is my first question: Why should you lie?'

'You are over-cunning, Sir Champion. I should lie if I wished to deceive you.'

'Do you lie?'

'The answer is…'

The Knight in Black and Yellow faded. The armies were marching around and around the hills, up and down them, in all directions across the valley. They were singing many different songs, but one song reached my ears.

> 'All Empires fall,
> All ages die,
> All strife shall be in vain.
> All kings go down,
> All hope must fail,
> But Tanelorn remains –
>   Our Tanelorn remains…'

A simple soldier's chant, but it meant something to me – something important. Had I once belonged to this place Tanelorn? Or had I sought to find it?

I could not distinguish which of the armies was singing the song. But it was already fading away.

> '*All words must die,*
> *Fade into night,*
> *But Tanelorn remains –*
>   *Our Tanelorn remains...*'

Tanelorn.

The sense of loss I had felt when parted from Ermizhad came to me then – and I associated it with Tanelorn.

It seemed to me that if I could find Tanelorn, I would find the key to my destiny, find a means of ending my misery and my doom...

Now another figure stood on the other side of the plain flag and still the armies marched below us, still the towns and cities burned.

I looked at the figure.

'Ermizhad!'

Ermizhad smiled sadly. 'I am not Ermizhad! Just as you have one spirit and many forms, so has Ermizhad one form but many spirits!'

'There is only one Ermizhad!'

'Aye – but many who resemble her.'

'Who are you?'

'I am myself.'

I turned away. I knew that she spoke truth and was not Ermizhad, but I could not bear to look on Ermizhad's face; I was tired of riddles.

Then I said to her: 'Do you know of Tanelorn?'

'Many know of Tanelorn. Many have sought her. She is an old city. She has lasted through eternity.'

'How may I reach Tanelorn?'

'Only you may answer that question, Champion.'

'Where lies Tanelorn? On Urlik's world?'

'Tanelorn exists in many Realms, on many Planes, in many Worlds, for Tanelorn is eternal. Sometimes hidden, sometimes there for all to visit – though most do not realise the nature of the city – Tanelorn shelters many Heroes.'

'Will I find Ermizhad if I find Tanelorn?'

'*You will find what you truly desire to find. But first you must take up the Black Sword again.*'

'*Again? Have I borne a black sword before?*'

'*Many times.*'

'*And where shall I find the sword?*'

'*You will know it. You will always know the Black Sword for to bear it is your destiny and your tragedy.*'

And then she, too, was gone.

But the armies continued to march and the valley continued to burn and over my head the standard without insignia still flew.

Then, where she had been, something inhuman materialised, turned into a smoky substance, formed itself in to a different shape.

And I did recognise that shape. It was the Black Sword. A huge, black broadsword carved with runes of terrifying import.

I backed away.

'*NO! I WILL NEVER AGAIN WIELD THE BLACK SWORD!*'

And a sardonic voice, full of evil and wisdom, seemed to issue from the blade itself.

'*THEN YE SHALL NEVER KNOW PEACE!*'

'*BEGONE!*'

'*I AM THINE – ONLY THINE. THOU ART THE ONLY MORTAL WHO CAN BEAR ME!*'

'*I REFUSE YOU!*'

'*THEN CONTINUE TO SUFFER!*'

I awoke shouting. I was sweating. My throat and mouth were parched.

The Black Sword. I knew the name now. I knew that it was somehow tied up with my destiny.

But the rest – had it been merely a nightmare? Or had it offered me information in a symbolic form? I had no means of telling.

In the darkness I flung out an arm and touched warm flesh.

I was back with Ermizhad again!

I took that naked body to me. I bent to kiss the lips.

Lips raised themselves to mine. Lascivious lips that were hot and coarse. The body writhed against me. A woman began to whisper obscenities into my ear.

I leapt back with an oath. Rage and disappointment consumed me. It was not Ermizhad. It was one of the women of Rowernarc who had slipped into my bed while I lay experiencing my dreadful dreams.

Despair swept through me, wave upon wave. I sobbed. The woman laughed.

And then something filled me – some emotion that seemed alien to me and yet which possessed me.

Fiercely I flung myself on the girl.

'Very well,' I promised, 'if you will have such pleasures – then have them all!'

And in the morning I lay in my disordered bed exhausted while the woman clambered from it and staggered away, a strange expression upon her features. I do not think pleasures were what she had experienced. I know that I had not. I felt only disgusted with myself for what I had done.

All the while one image remained in my brain. It was to rid myself of that image, I think, that I had taken the girl as I had. Perhaps the image had driven me to do what I had done. I do not know. I did know, however, that I would do it again if it would burn the image of the Black Sword from my mind for only a few moments.

There were no dreams the next night, but the old fear had returned. And when the girl I had ravaged the night before came to my room simpering I almost dismissed her before I learned that she came with a message from Bishop Belphig whose slave she apparently was.

'My master says that a change of scenery might improve your temper. Tomorrow he embarks on a great Sea Hunt and asks if you would care to join him.'

I flung down the book I was trying to interpret. 'Aye,' I said. 'I'll come. It sounds a healthier way of wasting time than puzzling over these damned books.'

'Will you take me with you, Lord Urlik?'

The heated expression on her face, the moist lips, the way she held herself, all made me shudder.

But I shrugged my shoulders.

'Why not?'

She chuckled. 'And shall I bring a tasty friend?'

'Do what you wish.'

But when she had gone I flung myself down to my knees on that hard, obsidian floor and I buried my head in my arms and I wept.

'Ermizhad! Oh, Ermizhad!'

Chapter Six
The Great Salt Sea

I JOINED BISHOP Belphig on the outer causeway the next morning. Even in the light of that perpetual dusk I could see better
the face the cosmetics sought to hide. There were the jowls, the
pouched eyes, the downcurved, self-indulgent mouth, the lines of
depravity, all smeared about with colours and creams, serving
only to make his appearance that much more hideous.

The Lord Spiritual's entourage was with him – painted boys
and girls giggling and simpering, carrying pieces of luggage, shivering in the dull coolness of the outer air.

The bishop put a fat arm through one of mine and led me
ahead of the crowd, down towards the bay where the strange ship
waited.

I suffered this gesture and looked back to see if my weapons
were being brought. They were. Slaves staggered along with my
long, silver-shod spear and battle-axe. Why I had decided to bring
these weapons I do not know, but the bishop plainly did not think
my decision incongruous though I was not at all sure he was
pleased about it, either.

For all its decadence and despair, I did not find Rowernarc itself
menacing. The people offered me no harm and, once aware that I
did not wish to join in their sports, tended for the most part to
leave me to my own devices. They were neutral. Lord Shanosfane, too, had an air of neutrality. But I did not get this impression
of Bishop Belphig. There was, indeed, something sinister about
him and I was beginning to feel that he was perhaps the sole
member of that peculiar community who possessed some sort of
motive, however perverse; some ambition beyond the need to
find new ways of whiling away the days.

Yet for all appearances Bishop Belphig was the most dedicated of all sybarites and it was my possibly puritanical eye that saw menace in him. I reminded myself that he was the sole inhabitant of Rowernarc who had displayed any sort of deviousness.

'Well, my dear Lord Urlik, what do you think of our craft?' Belphig gestured towards the ship with a fat, beringed finger. He was dressed in the bulbous armour I had originally seen worn by the riders on the beach, but his helm was being carried by a slave. A brocade cloak flowed from his shoulders.

'I have never seen an odder craft,' I replied frankly.

We were approaching the shore and I could see the craft quite clearly. She was quite close to the beach on which stood a number of figures whom I guessed were part of her crew. She was about forty feet in length and very high. As ornately decorated as anything else of Rowernarc, plated with reliefs of silver, bronze and gold, she had a kind of pyramidal superstructure on which were situated various terraces – a succession of narrow decks. At the top was a square deck from which several banners flew. The hull was raised above the level of the ocean on struts connected to a broad, flat, slightly curved sheet of highly polished material resembling something very like fibreglass and resting on the water. She had no masts but on each side were arranged wheels of broad-bladed paddles. Unlike the blades of a paddle-steamer, these were not contained within an outer wheel but were naked. But even the large paddles did not seem strong enough to push the craft through the water.

'You must have very powerful engines,' I commented.

'Engines?' Belphig chuckled. 'She has no engines.'

'Then...'

'Wait until we are aboard.'

The group of people waiting on the beach had two litters ready. Plainly these were meant for us. Belphig and I crunched across the crystal until we reached them. Then the bishop entered one and, somewhat reluctantly, I climbed into the other. The alternative, I guessed, was to wade through that murky, viscous water and merely the sight of it filled me with distaste. A grey scum floated at the edges where it touched the beach and the smell of decay and ordure reached my nostrils. I guessed that this was the place into which Rowernarc's waste found its way.

The litters were lifted up and the slaves began to wade through the water that appeared to have the consistency of porridge and which had oily black weed growing on its surface.

A flight of collapsible steps had been lowered down the side of the ship and Belphig led the way up them, puffing and complaining until we were aboard and entering a doorway at the base of the pyramid.

Up we went again until we at last reached the top deck and stood on it, watching the rest of the crew and entourage assembling themselves on the various lower galleries. The prow of the ship was raised and curved and had a high gallery of its own which was protected by a rail of rococo iron. From this gallery what appeared to be long ropes went over the side and into the water. They were secured to stanchions and I took them to be anchor ropes.

Looking over the ship I had the peculiar impression that we were aboard a gigantic cart rather than a seagoing vessel, for the paddle-wheels were arranged on spokes, in pairs, with nothing, apparently, to drive them.

The slave arrived with my spear and axe and handed them to me. I thanked him and fixed them into lugs which were arranged for this purpose around the inside of the rail.

Belphig looked up at the sky, as an ordinary sailor might look to see the lie of the weather. I could see no change in the thick, brown cloud layers, the jagged mountain peaks or the sluggish sea. The sun was again invisible and its faint light was further diffused by the clouds. I drew my heavy coat about me and waited impatiently for Bishop Belphig to give the order to sail.

I was already regretting my decision to accompany the Lord Spiritual on this venture. I had no idea what we were to hunt or in what manner. My sense of discomfort was increasing as some instinct warned me that the bishop had invited me on this hunt for more specific reasons than the relief of my boredom.

Morgeg, the bishop's captain, climbed the central stairway to the top deck and presented himself to his master.

'We are ready to roll, Lord Bishop.'

'Good.' Belphig put a pale hand on my arm in a confiding gesture. 'Now you will see our "engines", Count Urlik.' He smiled secretly at Morgeg. 'Give the order, Sir Morgeg.'

Morgeg leaned over the rail and addressed the armoured men who had now taken up positions in the prow gallery. They were strapped into seats and had the ropes that I thought anchor ropes around their arms. There were whips in their hands, long harpoons at their sides. 'Prepare!' shouted Morgeg through cupped hands. The armoured men stiffened and drew back the arms holding the whips. 'Begin!'

As one, the whips snapped out and cracked the surface of the water. Three times they did this and then I saw a disturbance just ahead of the prow and gasped as something began to emerge from below.

Then four huge, gnarled heads broke from the depths. The heads turned to glare at the whipmen in the prow. Strange, barking noises came from the sinuous throats. Monstrous, serpentine bodies threshed in the water. The beasts had flat heads from the mouths of which long, straight tusks protruded. A harness was attached to these heads and with tugs the whipmen forced them to turn until they were looking out to sea.

Again the whips cracked and the beasts began to move.

With a lurch the ship was off, its paddles not cutting *through* the water but supporting the ship *on* the water, as wheels support a chariot.

And that was what the ship was – a huge chariot designed to roll over the surface, pulled by these ugly monsters that seemed to me to be a cross between sea-serpents of legend, sea-lions of John Daker's world, with a trace of sabre-tooth tiger for good measure!

Out into that nightmare ocean swam the nightmare beasts, pulling our impossible craft behind them.

The whips cracked louder and the drivers sang out to the beasts who swam faster. The wheels rolled rapidly and soon Rowernarc's terrible shore disappeared in murky brown cloud.

We were alone on that nameless, hellish sea.

Bishop Belphig had become animated. He had placed his helm on his head and had opened the visor. In its nest of steel his face looked even more depraved.

'Well, Count Urlik. What do you think of our engines?'

'I have never seen such beasts. I could never have imagined them. How do you manage to train them?'

'Oh, they were bred for this work – they are domestic animals. Once Rowernarc had many scientists. They built our city, channelling our heat from the fires that still flickered in the bowels of the planet. They designed and built our ships. They bred our various beasts of burden. But that, of course, was a thousand years ago. We have no need of such scientists now…'

I thought it a slightly odd statement, though I said nothing. Instead, I asked: 'And what do we hunt, my lord bishop?'

Belphig drew a deep, excited breath. 'Nothing less than the sea-stag himself. It is dangerous work. We might all perish.'

'The thought of dying in this dreadful ocean does not commend itself,' I said.

He chuckled. 'Aye, a foul death. Perhaps the worst death this world can offer. But that is where the thrill lies, does it not?'

'For you, perhaps.'

'Ah, come now, Count Urlik. I thought you were beginning to enjoy our ways.'

'You know that I am grateful for your hospitality. Without it I suppose I would have perished. But "enjoy" is not the word I would have chosen.'

He licked his lips, his pale eyes bright and lascivious. 'But the slave girl I sent…?'

I drew a heavy breath of that cold, salt-clogged air. 'I had had a nightmare shortly before I discovered her in my bed. It seemed to me that she was merely part of that nightmare.'

Belphig laughed and clapped me on the back. 'Oho, you lusty dog! No need to be shy in Rowernarc. The girl told me all!'

I turned away and put my two hands on the rail, staring over the dark waters. A rime of salt had formed on my face and beard, scouring my flesh. I welcomed it.

The sea-beasts strained and threshed and barked, the wheels of the ship slapped the surface of the salt-thick water, Bishop Belphig chuckled and exchanged glances with the dead-faced Morgeg. Sometimes the brown clouds broke and I saw the contracted sphere of the dull, red sun like a jewel hanging from a cavern roof. Sometimes the clouds gathered so close that they blotted out all the light and we moved through pitch-darkness broken only by the faint illumination of our artificial torches. A faint wind came and ruffled my coat, stirred the limp banners on their masts, but scarcely brought a ripple to the viscous ocean.

Within me my torment seethed. My lips formed the syllables of Ermizhad's name but then refused to move as if to utter that name, even under my breath, was to taint it.

Onward the ship rolled. Its crew, the slaves of despair, moved about upon its decks or sat listlessly against its rails.

And all the time Bishop Belphig's fat jowls shook as his obscene laughter bubbled through the air.

I began to think that I did not in the least care now if I perished in the waters of that great salt sea.

Chapter Seven
The Bell and the Chalice

Later Belphig retired to his cabin with his slaves and the girl who had brought me the message came on deck and put her warm hand on my cold one.

'Master? Do you not want me?'

'Give yourself to Morgeg or whoever else desires you,' I said hollowly, 'and I beg you forget that other time.'

'But, master, you told me I could bring someone else, also… I thought you had learned to take pleasure in our ways…'

'I take no pleasure in your ways. Please go.'

She left me alone on the deck. I rubbed at my weary eyes. They were encrusted with salt. After a few moments I, too, went below, sought my cabin, locked the door and ignored the shut-bunk with its profusion of furs and silks in favour of the hammock, doubtless slung there for a servant's use.

Rocked in the hammock, I was soon asleep.

Dreams came, but they were faint dreams. A few scenes. A few words. But the only words that made me shiver were the words which forced me to wake myself:

BLACK SWORD
BLACK SWORD
BLACK SWORD
THE BLACK SWORD IS THE CHAMPION'S SWORD
THE WORD OF THE SWORD IS THE CHAMPION'S LAW
BLACK SWORD
BLACK SWORD
BLACK SWORD

*THE BLADE OF THE SWORD HAS THE BLOOD OF THE
   SUN
THE HILT OF THE SWORD AND THE HAND ARE AS
   ONE
BLACK SWORD
BLACK SWORD
BLACK SWORD
THE RUNES ON THE SWORD ARE THE WORMS THAT
   ARE WISE
THE NAME OF THE SWORD IS THE SAME AS THE
   SCYTHE
BLACK SWORD
BLACK SWORD
BLACK...*

The rhythm continued to drum in my skull. I shook my head and
half fell from my hammock. Outside the cabin I heard hasty footsteps. Now they sounded above my head. I went to a washstand,
splashed water over my hands and face, opened the door and
climbed the intricately carved companionway to the top deck.

Morgeg and another man stood there. They were leaning over
the rail, their ears cocked to the wind. Below, in the prow, the drivers continued to lash the sea-beasts on.

Morgeg stepped back from the rail when he saw me. There was
a trace of concern in his pale eyes.

'What is it?' I asked.

He shrugged his shoulders. 'We thought we heard something.
A sound we have not heard before in these waters.'

I listened for a while with some concentration but all I could
hear was the crack of the drivers' whips, the slap of the wheels on
the water.

Then I heard it. A faint booming ahead of us. I peered into the
murky brown fog. The booming came more strongly now.

'It's a bell!' I said.

Morgeg frowned.

'A bell! Perhaps there are rocks ahead and they are warning us off.'

Morgeg jerked his thumb at the sea-beasts. 'The *slevahs* would sense rocks if they were near and turn aside.'

The sound of the tolling bell increased. It must have come from a huge bell, for it was deep and the ship vibrated with the noise.

Even the sea-beasts were disturbed by it. They tried to turn away, but the drivers' whips kept them on course.

Still the tolling grew in intensity until it seemed to surround us. Bishop Belphig appeared on deck. He was not wearing his armour, but some kind of nightshirt by the look of it. Over this he had thrown a huge fur. His cosmetics were smeared and only half applied. Doubtless the bell had disturbed him in the middle of his revels. There was fear on his face.

'Do you know what that bell is?' I asked him.

'No. No.'

But I thought that he did know – or that he guessed what it was. And he was afraid of the bell.

Morgeg said: 'Bladrak's –'

'Silence!' Belphig snapped. 'How could it be?'

'What is Bladrak?' I said.

'Nothing,' Morgeg murmured, his eyes on the bishop.

I did not pursue the subject, but the sense of menace I had felt when first boarding the craft now increased.

The tolling was so loud now that it hurt my ears to hear it.

'Turn the ship about,' Belphig said. 'Give the order, Morgeg. Hurry!'

His evident fear I found almost amusing after the bland impression of self-assurance he had given me earlier.

'Are we going back to Rowernarc?' I asked him.

'Yes, we'll…' He frowned, his eyes flashing first to me, then to Morgeg, then to the rail. He tried to smile. 'No, I think not.'

'Why have you changed your mind?' I asked.

'Be quiet, curse you!' Immediately he controlled himself. 'Forgive me, Count Urlik. This dreadful noise. My nerves...' And he disappeared down the companionway.

Still the bell boomed, but the drivers were turning the *slevahs* now. They reared and threshed in the water, dragging the ship full about.

The drivers lashed them again and their speed increased.

The booming continued, but it was just a little fainter now.

Spray rose with the speed and force with which the wheels slapped the sea's surface. The huge sea-chariot rocked and jolted and I clung hard to the rail.

The tolling of the bell subsided.

Soon silence sat upon the sea once again.

Bishop Belphig re-emerged, clad in his armour, wearing his cloak. His cosmetics had been properly applied, but I saw that the face beneath them was paler than usual. He bowed to me, nodded to Morgeg. He tried to smile.

'I am sorry that I lost my head for a moment, Count Urlik. I had but recently awakened. I was disorientated. That sound was terrifying, was it not?'

'More terrifying, I suspect, to you than to me, Bishop Belphig. I thought you recognised it.'

'No.'

'And so did Morgeg – he uttered a name – Bladrak...'

'A legend of the sea.' Belphig waved his fat hand dismissively. 'Um – concerning a monster, Bladrak, with a voice like a huge bell. Naturally Morgeg, who is of a superstitious turn of mind, thought that Bladrak had come to... er, gobble us up.' His titter was high-pitched, his tone completely unconvincing.

However, as the man's guest I could scarcely push my questioning any farther. I had to accept what was, to me, evidently a hastily invented lie. I returned to my cabin as Belphig instructed Morgeg in a fresh course. And in my cabin I again found the girl I had dismissed. She was lying in the bed, smiling at me, completely naked.

I returned her smile and climbed into my hammock.

But I was soon to be disturbed again.

Almost as soon as I had closed my eyes I heard a shout from above. Again I leapt from the hammock and rushed up onto the top deck. This time I heard no bells, but Morgeg and Belphig were calling down to a sailor on a lower deck. I heard the sailor's voice.

'I swear I saw it! A light to port!'

'We are miles from the nearest land,' Morgeg argued.

'Then perhaps, sir, it was a ship.'

'Is this another legend coming true?' I asked Belphig. He started when he heard me and straightened up.

'I really cannot understand it all, Count Urlik. I think the sailor is imagining things. Once you get one unexplained event at sea, others quickly follow, eh?'

I nodded. There was truth in that. But then I saw a light. I pointed. 'It must be another ship.'

'The light is too bright for a ship.'

I then found an opportunity to put a question to him which had been on my mind since my meeting with Lord Shanosfane. 'What if it is the Silver Warriors?'

Belphig darted me a penetrating look. 'What do you know of the Silver Warriors?'

'Very little. Their race is not the same as yours. They have conquered most of the farther shore of this sea. They are thought to come from a land called Moon on the other side of the world.'

He relaxed. 'And who told you all this?'

'My Lord Shanosfane of Dhötgard – the Lord Temporal.'

'He knows little of the events in the world,' Bishop Belphig said. 'He is more interested in abstracted speculation. The Silver Warriors are not a great threat. They have harried one or two cities of the farther shore, that is true, but I believe they have disappeared again now.'

'Why did you not tell me of them when I asked if you had any enemies or potential enemies?'

'What? Enemies?' Belphig laughed. 'I do not consider warriors from the other side of the world, who have never offered us threat, *enemies!*'

'Not even potential *enemies*?'

'Not even that. How could they attack us? Rowernarc is impregnable.'

The hoarse voice of the sailor came again. 'There! There it is!'

He was right.

And also I seemed to hear a voice calling over the ocean. A lost voice, an ethereal voice.

'Some mariner in trouble perhaps?' I suggested.

Bishop Belphig assumed an impatient expression. 'Most unlikely.'

Both light and voice were coming closer. I made out a word. It was a very definite word.

'BEWARE!' cried the voice. 'BEWARE.'

Belphig sniffed. 'A pirate's trick, maybe. Best ready the warriors, Morgeg.'

Morgeg went below.

And then the source of the light was much closer and a peculiar screaming began. A wail.

It was a huge golden cup, suspended against the darkness. A great chalice. Both the bright light and the wailing came from it.

Belphig staggered back, shielding his eyes. Doubtless he had never seen such brightness in his whole life.

A voice spoke once again.

'URLIK SKARSOL, IF YOU WOULD RID THIS WORLD OF ITS TROUBLES AND FIND A SOLUTION TO YOUR OWN — YOU MUST TAKE UP THE BLACK SWORD AGAIN.'

The voice of my dreams had entered the realm of reality. Now it was my turn to be terrified.

'No!' I shouted. 'I will never wield the Black Sword. I swore I would not!'

Though I spoke the words, they did not come from my conscious brain, for I still had no idea what the Black Sword was and why I refused to use it. These words were spoken by all the warriors I had been and all the warriors I was to become.

'YOU MUST!'

'I will not!'

'IF YOU DO NOT, THIS WORLD WILL PERISH.'

'It is already doomed!'

'NOT SO!'

'Who are you?' I could not believe that this was a supernatural manifestation. Everything I had experienced so far had had some kind of understandable explanation – but not this screaming chalice – not this voice that boomed from the heavens like the voice of god. I tried to peer at the great golden cup, see what held it, but apparently nothing did hold it.

'Who are you?' I shouted again.

Bishop Belphig's unhealthy face was wreathed in light. It writhed in terror.

'I AM THE VOICE OF THE CHALICE. YOU MUST TAKE UP THE BLACK SWORD.'

'I will not!'

'BECAUSE YOU WOULD NOT LISTEN FROM WITHIN, I HAVE COME TO YOU IN THIS FORM TO IMPRESS UPON YOU THAT YOU MUST TAKE UP THE BLACK SWORD –'

'I will not! I swore I would not!'

'– AND WHEN YOU HAVE TAKEN UP THE SWORD, THEN YOU MAY FILL THE CHALICE! ANOTHER CHANCE WILL NOT COME, ETERNAL CHAMPION.'

I clapped my hands to my ears, closing my eyes tight shut.

I felt the light fade.

I opened my eyes.

The screaming chalice had disappeared. There was only gloom again.

Belphig was shaking with fear. It was plain, when he looked at me, that he associated me with the source of his terror.

I said grimly: 'That was no doing of mine, I assure you.'

Belphig cleared his throat several times before he spoke. 'I have heard of men able to create illusions, Count Urlik, but never illusions so powerful. I am impressed, but I hope you will not see fit to use your power again on this voyage. Merely because I could not answer your questions concerning that bell does not mean that you can –'

'If that were an illusion, Bishop Belphig, it was no creation of mine.'

Belphig began to speak, then changed his mind. Shuddering, he went below.

Chapter Eight

The Sea-Stag's Lair

I STAYED ON the deck for a long time, peering into the twilight, wondering if I would see something that would give me a clue as to the origin of that strange visitation. Save for the experience in my bedroom on the Eldren Earth, when I had seen myself as I now was, this was the first time that my dreams had come in waking hours.

And it had been no dream, of course, because Bishop Belphig had witnessed it – as had many members of his crew and entourage. On the lower terraces they were murmuring among themselves, looking up at me in some trepidation, doubtless hoping I would bring no further manifestations of that sort upon them.

But if the screaming chalice had been connected with me, the unseen bell had been connected in some way with Bishop Belphig.

And why was Belphig continuing with the hunt, when any sensible person would have returned to the safety of the Obsidian City? Perhaps he had arranged a rendezvous with someone in these waters? But with whom? One of the pirates he had mentioned? Perhaps even the Silver Warriors?

But these were minor matters of speculation compared with the latest event. What was the Black Sword? Why did something within me refuse it, even though I did not know what it was. Certainly the name had a peculiar sort of familiarity and it was also plain that I did not wish to think about it – that was why I had taken the girl that night. It seemed I was ready to do anything to forget the sword, to escape from it.

*

At length, weary and full of confusion, I returned to my quarters and fell into my hammock.

But I could not sleep. I did not want to sleep, for fear the dreams would return.

I remembered the words: *If you would rid this world of its troubles and find a solution to your own, you must take up the Black Sword again.*

And the monotonous chant came back to me: *Black Sword. Black Sword. Black Sword. The Black Sword is the Champion's Sword – the Word of the Sword is the Champion's Law...*

In some previous incarnation – whether in the past or the future, for Time in my own context was a meaningless word – I must have rid myself of the Black Sword. And in parting with it I had, say, committed a crime (or at least had offended someone or something which desired that I retain the sword) for which I was now being punished by being moved hither and yon through Time and Space. Or perhaps, as my dream had suggested, the punishment was that I be *aware* of my incarnations and thus know my true tragedy. A subtle punishment if that were so.

Although I desired nothing more than rest and a chance to be reunited with Ermizhad, something in me still refused to pay the price, which was my agreement that I would take up the Black Sword again.

The Blade of the Sword has the Blood of the Sun – The Hilt of the Sword and the Hand are as One...

A rather more cryptic statement. I had no idea what the first part meant. Presumably the second part simply meant that my own fate and that of the sword were intertwined.

The Runes on the Sword are the Worms that are wise – The Name of the Sword is the same as the Scythe.

Here the first part was easier to understand than the second. It merely meant that some kind of wisdom was written on the blade. And it was just possible that the Scythe referred to was nothing more than the same scythe that Death was said to wield.

But I still knew no more than I had known before. It seemed

that I must decide to take up the sword again without being told why I had originally decided to put it down...

There was a knock on the cabin door. Thinking it was the girl again, I cried out: 'I do not wish to be disturbed.'

'It is Morgeg,' replied the one who had knocked. 'Bishop Belphig instructed me to tell you that the sea-stag has been sighted. The hunt is about to begin.'

'I will come in a moment.'

I heard Morgeg's footfalls fade. I put my helm on my head, took up my axe and my spear and went to the door.

Perhaps the excitement of the hunt would drive some of my confusion away.

Belphig seemed to have regained all his old bland confidence. He was in full armour, his visor raised, and Morgeg now wore armour, too.

'Well, Count Urlik, we shall soon have the diversion we actually sought when we originally set out, eh?' He slapped the rail with his gauntleted hand.

The wheels of the ship were moving comparatively slowly over the viscous ocean and the sea-beasts pulling the gigantic sea-chariot were swimming at an almost leisurely rate.

'The sea-stag's horns broke the surface a while ago,' Morgeg said. 'The beast must be quite near. It has no gills and must eventually surface again. That is when we must be ready to strike.' He indicated the warriors lining the rails above the ship's hull. They all held long, heavy harpoons, each with up to ten cruel barbs.

'Is the beast likely to attack?' I asked.

'Have no fear,' Bishop Belphig said. 'We are safe enough up here.

'I came for the excitement,' I told him. 'I would experience it.'

He shrugged. 'Very well. Morgeg, will you escort Count Urlik to the lower deck.'

Spear and axe in hand I followed Morgeg down the several companionways to the lower deck and emerged to discover that the sea-chariot's wheels had stopped almost completely.

Morgeg craned his neck and peered into the gloom. 'Ah,' he said. And he pointed.

I had the impression of antlers very much like those of the stags I had seen on John Daker's world. I had no means, however, of judging their size.

I wondered if this were some land beast that had taken to the sea just as the seals had returned to the land. Or perhaps it was another hybrid, bred centuries before by Rowernarc's scientists.

The atmosphere on the great chariot was tense. The antlers seemed to be coming closer, as if to inspect the strangers who had intruded into its province.

I moved nearer to the rail, a warrior making room for me.

Morgeg murmured, 'I will return to my master's side.' And he left me.

I heard a snort – a gigantic snort. This beast was plainly larger than an ordinary stag!

Now I could see red eyes glaring at us. A huge, bovine face emerged from the twilight, its nostrils dilating and contracting. It snorted again and this time I felt its breath strike my face.

In silence, the harpooners prepared for its charge.

I looked up at the prow, noticing that the *slevahs* had submerged, as if they wanted no part of this madness...

The sea-stag bellowed, raising its massive body from the viscous waters. The thick, saline liquid ran in streamers down its coarse, oily pelt and I saw that its muscular forelegs were, in fact, flippers terminating in a clublike appendage that only barely recalled the hoof of a true stag. These flippers it now thrashed in the air, then sank down into the sea again, re-emerging a moment later with lowered head to charge our chariot.

From the top deck Morgeg's voice came:

'Let fly with the first harpoons!'

A third of the warriors flung back their arms and hurled their heavy lances at the advancing beast. The horns were almost fifteen feet long, with an even longer span.

Some of the harpoons flew past the sea-stag and lay for a

moment on the surface of the water before sinking, others buried themselves in the body of the stag. But none struck the head and while it screamed with pain, it paused only for a moment before continuing its charge.

'Let fly with the second harpoons!'

The second wave of lances flew out. Two struck the horns and clattered harmlessly off them. Two struck the body but were shaken out by a twist of the animal's shoulders. The horns struck the chariot and sharp bone met metal with an awful clangour. The ship rocked, threatened to topple, righted itself on its flat, lower hull. One of the horns swept along the rail and, shrieking, several harpooners were hurled overboard, their armour gashed. I leaned over to see if they could be helped, but they were already sinking, as a man sinks in quicksand, some holding up their arms pleadingly, though their eyes spoke of the hopelessness of help.

This was a brutal, disgusting business, particularly since the instigator of the hunt was at the top of the ship in a relatively safe position.

Now the dripping head loomed over us and we staggered back as it opened its mouth to show teeth half the size of a large man's height, a red, curling tongue.

Dwarfed by the monster, I took up my stance on the swaying deck, drew back the arm holding my own spear and flung it into that open mouth. Its point entered the flesh of the gullet and the mouth instantly closed as, in agony, the beast backed off, moving its jaw from side to side as it tried to rid itself of the thing inside it.

One of the harpooners clapped me on the back as we saw dark blood begin to run from the sea-stag's snout.

From far above came the bland voice of Bishop Belphig. 'Well done, Sir Champion!'

At that moment I would rather the spear had entered Belphig's heart than the gullet of the monster whose territory we had invaded.

I grabbed up a harpoon from where it had been dropped by one of the men who had been swept overboard. I aimed again for the head, but the point struck the base of the left horn and dropped harmlessly into the sea.

The monster coughed and bits of the shaft of my spear were spewed out, some of them striking the ship's superstructure.

Then it charged again.

This time, as if encouraged by my partial success, one of the harpooners managed to drive his weapon into the sea-stag's flesh just below the right eye. A terrible scream came from the injured throat and, admitting defeat, the beast turned and began to swim away.

I drew a sigh of relief, but I had not reckoned with Bishop Belphig's bloodlust.

'Pursue it – quickly. It is making for its lair!' he cried.

The drivers lashed the sea-beasts to the surface, jerked on the ropes that were their reins and, using the whips, turned them in pursuit of the disappearing stag.

'This is insanity! Let the thing go!' I shouted.

'What – and return to Rowernarc without a trophy!' screamed back the bishop. 'Give chase, whipmen. Give chase!'

The wheels began to whirl over the water again as we pursued our wounded quarry.

One of the harpooners gave me a sardonic look. 'They say our Lord Spiritual prefers slaughter to fornication.' He rubbed at his face. Blood spat by the stag had covered him.

'I do not know if he understands the difference any longer,' I said. 'Where is the monster heading?'

'Sea-stags make their lairs in caves. There is probably a small island nearby. Our friend will head for that.'

'Have they no herds?'

'At certain times. But this is not their herding season. That is why it is relatively safe to hunt them. A herd, even mainly of cows, would quickly finish us.'

Two of the wheels on our side of the ship had been badly battered and the sea-chariot lurched unevenly as it sped over the ocean. The *slevahs* must have been even more powerful than the sea-stag to be able to cut through those thick waters and draw the heavy craft behind them.

The horns of the stag were still in sight through the gloom and, just ahead of that, the outline of a spike of obsidian rock, doubtless of the same range as the mountain from which Rowernarc had been carved.

'There!' The harpooner pointed. Grimly he hefted his barbed lance.

I bent and took the remaining harpoon off the deck.

Morgeg's distant voice shouted: 'Prepare!'

The stag had disappeared, but the tiny island of glassy rock could clearly be seen. The sea-chariot slewed round as the sea-beasts avoided dashing themselves onto the rock. We saw the black mouth of a cave.

We had found the monster's lair.

From within the cave came an almost pathetic snort of pain.

And then came the astonishing order from above.

'Prepare to disembark!'

Belphig meant his men to enter the cave armed only with their harpoons!

Chapter Nine

The Slaughtering in the Cave

A ND SO WE disembarked.

All save Belphig, his entourage and the whipmen in the prow, began to wade through the clinging shallows and gain a slippery foothold on the rock. I had my battle-axe crooked in one arm, the barbed harpoon held at my side in the other hand. Belphig watched and waved from the top deck.

'Good luck, Count Urlik. If you kill the stag it will be another great deed to add to your long list...'

I thought the whole nature of the hunt was useless and cruel, but I felt I must go with the others to finish what we had begun – either to kill the monster or be killed by it.

With some difficulty we clambered around the rock until we had reached the mouth of the cave. A terrible stench was issuing from it, as if the beast had already begun to rot.

The man who had spoken earlier now said: 'That's the stink of its dung. The sea-stag is not a clean beast.'

Now I felt even more reluctant to enter the cave.

Another bellow came, as the stag scented us.

The harpooners hung back nervously. No man wished to be the first into the lair.

At last, dry-mouthed but desperate, I elbowed my way forward, took a good grip on my harpoon and stepped into the black maw.

The stench was nauseating and I felt I would choke on it. There was a heavy movement and I thought I saw the outline of one of the stag's great antlers. A rapid snorting came from the thing's nostrils then. I heard its gigantic flippers thud on the floor. I had the impression of a long, sinuous body ending in a wide, flat tail.

The rest of the men were following me. From one of them I took a brand and touched the stud in its handle. Faint light illuminated the cavern.

The shadow of the sea-stag was what I saw first and then I saw the beast himself, on my right, pressed against the wall, blood pouring from its wounds, its massive body looking even larger on land than it had in the sea.

It hauled itself about on its giant flippers. It lowered its head menacingly but it did not charge. It was warning us away. It was giving us the chance to leave without a fight.

I was tempted to recall the men – lead them from the cave – but I had no authority over them. Bishop Belphig was their master and he would punish them if they did not obey him.

So, knowing that this would incense the beast, I hurled my harpoon at its left eye.

It turned its head just as the lance left my hand and the weapon grazed its snout.

It charged.

There was confusion then. Men screamed, tried to dodge, tried to get a clear cast at it, backed away, were impaled on its antlers.

When it raised its head three men hung on its horns, their bodies completely pierced. Two were dead. One was dying. Small moans came from his lips.

There was nothing I could do to save him. The stag shook its great head, trying to dislodge the corpses, but they remained where they were.

An idea began to form in my mind.

But then the stag lowered its head and charged again. I jumped aside, striking out with my long-hafted battle-axe and cutting a deep groove in its left shoulder. It turned towards me, its teeth snapping, its red eyes glaring in a mixture of anguish and surprise. I struck it another blow and it withdrew its bleeding snout. Again it shook its horns and now one of the torn bodies fell limply to the filthy floor of the cave. The stag nudged at it awkwardly with a flipper.

I looked for the remaining harpooners. They were huddled near the cave entrance.

The stag was now between me and the others. The cave was lit still by two brands which had fallen to the floor. I retreated into the shadows. The stag saw the others, lowered its head again and charged.

I was knocked flat by its huge fish tail as it moved past.

The beast bellowed as the harpooners scattered. I heard their cries as they were caught on its horns, as they plunged into the thick waters, seeking to escape.

And now I was alone in the cave.

The sea-stag began to scrape its horns on the edges of the cave mouth, scraping off human flesh.

I decided that I was as good as dead. How could I defeat such a monster alone? Its body blocked the entrance – my only chance of escape. Sooner or later it would remember I was there, or possibly scent me.

I kept as still as possible. The stink of ordure clogged my mouth and nostrils. I had no harpoon with which to defend myself, only the axe – an unsuitable weapon for dealing with a giant sea-stag...

Once again the beast opened its bovine snout and sent up a huge bellowing. Then the noise dropped as it moaned to itself.

Would it decide to enter the sea again? To heal its wounds in the salt?

I waited tensely for it to decide. But then there was another rattle of harpoons against rock and antlers and the monster screamed and backed into the cave.

Again I was forced to dodge its tail.

I prayed that the harpooners would return – at least long enough to give me the chance to get past the stag to a safer position.

The stag snorted, dragging its whalelike body first one way and then another across the floor of the cave, as it, too, expected the arrival of the warriors.

But nothing happened.

Did they think me dead?

Were they abandoning the chase?

I listened for shouts, but heard nothing.

Another bellow. Another movement of the unnatural body.

I began to edge along the wall of the cave, moving as softly as possible.

I was halfway to the cave-mouth when my foot struck a yielding object. It was the corpse of one of the harpooners. I lifted my leg to step over the thing but my foot then caught on a piece of loose armour and sent it clattering across the obsidian floor.

The beast snorted and turned its baleful eyes to regard me.

I stood stock-still, hoping it would not realise that I lived.

It shook its horns again and dragged its body round. My mouth and throat were dry.

It raised its muzzle and bellowed, its lips curling back from its huge teeth. Blood now encrusted those lips and it was plainly half blind in one eye.

Then, horrifyingly, it raised its body up and its strange flippers, with their clublike appendages, thrashed at the air, fell back to the ground, shook the floor of the cavern.

The antlers were lowered.

The stag charged.

I saw the huge horns bearing down on me and I had seen how they could impale a man. I flung my body flat against the wall and to one side. The antlers crashed within inches of my right shoulder and the stag's massive forehead – as wide as my body was long – was a foot from my face.

The idea I had had earlier came back to me. I believed there was only one chance of defeating the monster.

I jumped.

I leapt towards that forehead, grabbed the oily pelt, literally ran up its snout and then wrapped my legs and one arm around the branches of the left antler.

The beast was puzzled. I do not think it realised I was there.

I raised the axe.

The stag looked about the cavern for me, still snorting.

I brought the axe down.

It bit deep into his skull. He roared and screamed and shook his head rapidly from side to side. But I had expected this and I clung to the branches as tenaciously as was possible, striking again at the exact place I had struck before.

I split the bone. A little blood came. But all this served to do was to make the stag's movements more frantic. Its body sliding behind it, it waddled on its flippers, moving rapidly about the cave, scraping its antlers on roof and walls, trying to dislodge me.

But I hung on.

And I struck again.

This time pieces of bone flew into the air and a stream of blood poured from the skull.

Another fearsome bellow which became a scream of rage and terror.

Another blow.

The axe haft snapped with the force of my striking and I was left holding nothing but a piece of broken pole.

But the blade had buried itself in the brain.

The bulk of the stag crashed to the floor as the strength went out of the flippers.

It moaned pathetically. It tried to rise.

With a spluttering noise the last mixture of breath and blood left its body.

The head fell to one side and I fell with it, leaping free just as the antlers reached the floor.

The sea-stag was dead. I had killed it single-handed.

I tried to tug the broken haft of the axe out of the beast's head, but it was buried too deep. I left my axe there and stumbled, half dazed, from the mouth of the cave.

'It is over,' I said. 'Your quarry is vanquished.'

I felt no pride in my accomplishment. I looked towards the ship.

But no ship was there.

Bishop Belphig's sea-chariot had rolled away, presumably back to Rowernarc – doubtless because they thought me dead.

'Belphig!' I shouted, hoping my voice would carry over the waters where my eye could not see. 'Morgeg! I am alive! I have killed the stag!'

But there was no reply.

I looked at the low, brown clouds. At the murky, moody ocean.

I had been abandoned in the middle of a nightmare sea through which, as Belphig had said, no ships passed. I was alone save for the corpses of the harpooners, the carcass of the sea-stag.

Panic seized me.

'BELPHIG! COME BACK!'

A slight echo. Nothing more.

'I AM ALIVE!'

And the echo seemed stronger this time and it seemed sardonic.

I could not stay alive for long on that bleak sliver of rock which was less than fifty yards across. I stumbled up the sides, climbing as high as I could. But what point was there in that when the twilight sea had no horizon that was not obscured on all sides by the brown cloud banks?

I sat down on a small ledge, the only reasonably flat surface on the entire rock.

I was trembling. I was afraid.

The air seemed to grow colder and I drew my coat about me but it would not keep out the chill that grasped my bones, my liver, my heart.

An Immortal I might be. A phoenix forever reborn. A wanderer in eternity.

But if I was to die here, that dying would seem to take an eternity. If I were a phoenix, then I was a phoenix trapped in obsidian as a fly is trapped in amber.

At that thought all my courage went out of me and I contemplated my fate with nothing but despair.

Book Three

Visions and Revelations

Destiny's Champion,
Fate's fool.
Eternity's Soldier,
Time's Tool.

– The Chronicle of the Black Sword

Chapter One
The Laughing Dwarf

T HE FIGHT WITH the sea-stag had so exhausted me that, after a while, I fell asleep with my back against the rock and my legs stretched before me on the ledge.

When I awoke it was with some of my courage returned, though I could see no easy solution to my plight.

From the mouth of the cave below, the stench had increased as the stag's flesh began to rot. There was also an unpleasant slithering sound. Peering over the edge I saw that small snakelike creatures were wriggling into the cave in their thousands. Doubtless these were the carrion eaters of the sea. Hundreds of black bodies were tangled together as they moved up the rock to where the sea-stag lay.

Any thought I might have entertained of using the stag's carcass as meat to sustain me disappeared completely. I hoped the disgusting creatures would finish their meal quickly and leave. At least there were harpoons in the cave. As soon as I could reach them I would gather them up. They would be useful for defence against any other monster that might lurk in these waters and there might also be fish of some kind in the shallows, though I rather doubted It.

It occurred to me that Bishop Belphig might have planned to maroon me all along, simply because my questions were embarrassing him.

Had he planned the hunt with that in mind? If so, by going with the men into the sea-stag's lair, I had played completely into his hands.

For want of anything else to do, I made a circuit of the island. It did not take long. My first impression had been the right one. Nothing grew here. There was no drinkable water. The people of

Rowernarc got their water from melting ice, but there was no ice on that jagged spur of obsidian.

The writhing carrion creatures were still entering the cavern which was now filled with a slithering and hissing as they fought over the carcass.

Momentarily a rent appeared in the bank of clouds overhead and the faint rays of the dying sun were reflected on the black waters.

I returned to my ledge. There was nothing to do until the carrion eaters had finished their meal.

Hope of finding Ermizhad had waned, for it was unlikely I could ever return to Rowernarc. And if I died I might find myself in an incarnation worse than this one. I might not even remember Ermizhad, just as I could now not remember why the Black Sword was such an important factor in my destiny.

I remembered Ermizhad's lovely face. I recalled the beauty of the planet to which I had brought tranquillity at the cost of genocide.

I began to doze again and soon I was no longer alone, for the familiar visions and voices returned. I fought to drive them from my brain, keeping my eyes open and staring into the gloom. But soon the visions imposed themselves against the clouds and the sea, the words seemed to come from all sides.

'Leave me in peace,' I begged. 'Let me die in peace!'

The slithering and hissing from the cavern of death mingled with the whispers and the echoes of the ghostly voices.

'Leave me alone!'

I was like a child, frightened by the things it imagines in the dark. My voice was the impotent pleading of a child.

'Please leave me alone!'

I heard laughter. It was low, sardonic laughter and it seemed to come from above. I looked up.

Once again a dream seemed to have assumed physical reality, for I saw the figure quite clearly. It was climbing down the rock towards me.

It was a dwarf with bandy legs and a light beard. Its face was young and its eyes bright with humour.

'Greetings,' it said.

'Greetings,' I replied. 'Now vanish, I beg you.'

'But I have come to pass the time with you.'

'You are a creature of my imagination.'

'I resent that. Besides, you must have an unpleasant imagination if you can create so poor a thing as myself. I am Jermays the Crooked. Do you not remember me?'

'Why should I remember you?'

'Oh, we have met once or twice before. Like you, I have no existence in time as most people understand it – as you once understood it, if my memory serves. I have been of assistance to you in the past.'

'Mock me not, phantom.'

'Sir Champion, I am not a phantom. At least, not much of one. True I live for the most part in the shadow worlds, the worlds which have little true substance. A trick played on me by the gods that made me the crooked thing I am.'

'Gods?'

Jermays winked. 'Those who claim to be gods. Though they're as much slaves of fate as we are. Gods – powers – superior entities – they are called many things. And we, I suppose, are demigods – the tools of the gods.'

'I have no time for mystical speculation of that kind.'

'My dear Champion, at this moment you have time for anything. Are you hungry?'

'You know that I am.'

The dwarf reached into his green jerkin and pulled out half a loaf of bread. He handed it to me. It seemed substantial enough. I bit it. It seemed quite real. I ate it and I felt my stomach filled.

'I thank you,' I said. 'If I am to go mad, then this seems the best way.'

Jermays sat beside me on the ledge, resting the spear he carried against the rock. He smiled. 'You are certain my face is not familiar?'

'I have never seen you before.'

'Strange. But then perhaps our temporal identities are in different phases and you have not yet met me, though I have met you.'

'Quite possible.'

Jermays had a wineskin hanging on his belt. He unhooked it, took a swig and handed it to me.

The wine was good. I drank sparely and gave him back the skin.

'I see you do not have your sword with you,' he commented.

I gave him a searching look, but there seemed no irony in his voice. 'I have lost it,' I said.

He laughed heartily. 'Lost it! Lost that black blade! Oh! ho! ho! ho! You are making fun of me, Sir Champion.'

I frowned impatiently. 'It is true. What do you know of the Black Sword?'

'What all know. It is a sword that has possessed many names, as you have possessed many names. It has appeared in different guises, just as your physical appearance is not always the same. They say it was forged by the Forces of Darkness for the one destined to be their champion, but that is a rather unsophisticated view, wouldn't you agree?'

'I would.'

'The Black Sword is said to exist on many planes and it is also said to have a twin. Once when I knew you you were called Elric and the blade was called *Stormbringer* – its twin *Mournblade*. However, some say that the duality is an illusion, that there is only one Black Sword and that it existed before the gods, before Creation.'

'These are legends,' I said. 'They do not explain the nature of the thing at all. I have been told it is my destiny to bear it, yet I refuse. Does that mean aught to you?'

'It means that you must be an unhappy man. The Champion and the Sword are One. If man betrays blade or blade betrays man, then a great crime is committed.'

'Why is this so?'

Jermays shrugged and smiled. 'I know not. The gods know not. It has always been. Believe me, Sir Champion, it is the same as asking what created the universes through which you and I move so freely.'

'Is there any means of staying on one plane, on one world?'

Jermays pursed his lips. 'I have never considered the problem. It suits me to travel as I do.' He grinned. 'But, then, I am not a Hero.'

'Have you heard of a place called Tanelorn?'

'Aye. You might call it a veteran's town.' He rubbed his long nose and winked. 'It's said to be in the domain of the Grey Lords, those who serve neither Law nor Chaos...'

A faint memory stirred. 'What do you mean by Law and Chaos?'

'Some call them Light and Darkness. Again there are disputes among philosophers and the like as to what defines them. Others believe that they are one – part of the same force. On different worlds, in different times, they believe different things. And what they believe, I suppose, is true.'

'But where is Tanelorn?'

'Where? A strange question for you to ask. Tanelorn is always there.'

I rose impatiently. 'Are you part of my torment, Master Jermays? You further complicate the riddles.'

'Untrue, Sir Champion. But you ask impossible questions of me. Perhaps a wiser being could tell you more, but I cannot. I am not a philosopher or a hero – I am just Jermays the Crooked.' His smile wavered and I saw sadness in his eyes.

'I am sorry,' I said. I sighed. 'But I feel there is no solution to my dilemma. How did you get to this place?'

'A gap in the fabric of another world. I do not know how I go from plane to plane, but I do and there it is.'

'Can you leave?'

'I will, when it is time to leave. But I do not know when that will be.'

'I see.' I peered out at the gloomy sea.

Jermays wrinkled his nose. 'I have seen few places as unpleasant as this. I can see why you should want to leave. Perhaps if you took up the Black Sword again...?'

'No!'

He was startled. 'Forgive me. I did not comprehend that you were so adamant about the matter.'

I spread my hands. 'Something spoke from within me. Something that refuses – at all costs – to accept the Black Sword.'

'Then you...'

Jermays was gone.

Again I was alone. Again I wondered if he had been an illusion, if my whole experience here was an illusion, if this entire thing were not some event taking place in the sleeping or insane brain of John Daker...

The air before me suddenly shivered and became bright. It was as if I looked through a window into another world. I moved towards the window but it always remained the same distance from me.

I peered through the window and I saw Ermizhad. She looked back at me.

'Erekosë?'

'Ermizhad. I will return to you.'

'You cannot, Erekosë, until you have taken up the Black Sword again...'

And the window closed and I saw only the dark sea again.

I roared my rage to the lowering sky.

'Whoever you are who has done this thing to me – I will have my vengeance on you!'

My words were absorbed by stark silence.

I knelt upon the ledge and sobbed.

'CHAMPION!'

A bell tolled. The voice called.

'CHAMPION!'

I stared about and saw nothing.
'CHAMPION!'

Now a whisper: *'Black Sword. Black Sword. Black Sword.'*
'No!'
'You avoid the destiny for which you were created. Take up the Black Sword again, Champion. Take it up and know glory!'
'I know only misery and guilt. I will not wield the Sword.'
'You will.'

The statement was a positive one. It had no threat in it, only certainty.

The slithering carrion eaters had retreated to the sea. I made my way down to the cave and discovered the bones of the mighty sea-stag, the skeletons of my companions. The huge skull with its proud antlers regarded me as if in accusation. Quickly I found the harpoons, wrenched my broken axe from the skull and retreated back to my ledge.

I frowned, remembering the sword of Erekosë. That strange, poisoned blade had seemed powerful enough. I had had little reluctance to wield it. But perhaps that sword had been, as Jermays had hinted, merely an aspect of the Black Sword. I shrugged the thought off.

On my ledge, I arranged my weapons about me and waited for another vision.

Sure enough, it came.

It was a large raft, fashioned rather like a huge sleigh and reminiscent, in ornament, of the sea-chariot that had brought me here. But this was not drawn by sea-beasts. Instead it was pulled over the waters by birds that were like overgrown herons covered not by feathers but with dull, gleaming scales.

There was a group of men aboard the sleigh, dressed in heavy furs and mail armour, carrying swords and spears.

'Go away!' I shouted. 'Leave me in peace!'

They did not heed me, but turned their weird craft towards the rock.

I picked up the battle-axe by its broken haft. This time, I decided, hallucination or not, I would drive my tormentors away or perish in the attempt.

Now someone was calling to me and the voice seemed familiar. I knew I had heard it in one of my dreams.

'Count Urlik! Count Urlik – is that you?'

The speaker had thrown back his fur hood to reveal a shock of red hair, a young, handsome face.

'Begone!' I cried. 'I will listen to no more riddles!'

The face seemed puzzled.

The scaly herons turned in the sky and the baroque sleigh bounced closer. I stood on my ledge, my battle-axe held threateningly in my hand.

'Begone!'

But the herons were over my head. They settled on the top of the crag and folded their leathery wings. From the sleigh the red-haired man jumped, the others following. His arms were spread wide. His face held a grin of relief.

'Count Urlik. We have found you at last. We expected you at the Scarlet Fjord many days since!'

I did not lower my guard.

'Who are you?' I said.

'Why I am Bladrak Morningspear. I am the Hound of the Scarlet Fjord!'

Still I was wary.

'And why are you here?'

He put his hands on his hips and laughed uncertainly. His fur robe fell away to reveal muscular arms on which barbaric golden bracelets were twined.

'We have been seeking you, my lord. Did you not hear the bell?'

'I heard a bell, aye.'

'It was the Bell of Urlik. The Lady of the Chalice told us it would bring you to us to help in our war against the Silver Warriors.'

I slightly relaxed my grip on the broken haft. Then these people really were of this world. But why had Belphig feared them? Now, at least, it seemed, I would find an answer to some of the mysteries.

'Will you return with us, my lord, to the Scarlet Fjord? Will you come aboard our boat?'

Warily, I left the ledge and approached him.

I do not know how many days or hours I had been on the sea-stag's island, but I suppose I made a peculiar appearance. My eyes were wild and wary, like those of a madman, and I clung to a broken axe as if it were the only thing in the world I trusted.

Bladrak was puzzled but he kept his good humour. He spread one hand out to indicate the boat. 'We are relieved to see you, Count Urlik of the Frozen Keep. It is almost too late. We hear the Silver Warriors plan a massive attack on the southern shore.'

'Rowernarc?'

'Aye, Rowernarc and the other settlements.'

'Are you enemies of Rowernarc?'

He smiled. 'Well, we are not allies. But let us make haste to return. I will tell you more when we are safe in port. These are dangerous waters.'

I nodded. 'I have discovered that.'

Some of the men had been inspecting the cave. They came out, lugging the massive skull of the slain sea-stag.

'Look, Bladrak,' one called. 'It has been killed by an axe.

Bladrak raised his eyebrows and looked at me. 'Your axe?'

I nodded. 'I had nothing against the poor beast. It was really Belphig's quarry.'

Bladrak threw back his head and laughed. 'Look, friends,' he called, pointing at me, 'there is proof we have our Hero!'

Still somewhat dazed I entered the boat and took my place on one of the benches bolted to the bottom. Bladrak sat beside me. 'Let's be away,' he said.

The men who had found the sea-stag's skull hastily dumped it in the back of the boat and clambered aboard. Some of them jerked on the herons' reins and they took to the air again.

Suddenly the boat lunged forward and was flying across the dark sea.

Bladrak looked back. The giant skull had been placed so that it covered a long, slender box which was, in contrast to everything else aboard, completely without ornament. 'Be careful of the box,' he said.

'The bell you sounded,' I said. 'Did it toll just recently?'

'Aye – we tried again, since you had not come. Then the Lady of the Chalice said that you were somewhere on the Great Salt Sea and so we went looking for you.'

'When did you first summon me?'

'Some sixty days ago.'

'I went to Rowernarc,' I said.

'And Belphig captured you?'

'Perhaps. Yes, I suspect that is what he did. Though I did not know it at the time. What do you know of Belphig, Sir Bladrak?'

'Little enough. He has always been an enemy of the free sailors.'

'Are you those whom he called pirates?'

'Oh, doubtless, aye. Traditionally we have lived by raiding the ships and cities of the softer folk along the coast. But now we give our full attention to the Silver Warriors. With you to aid us we stand some chance of beating them, though time is very short.'

'I hope you do not rely too much on me, Bladrak Morning-spear. I have no supernatural powers, I assure you.'

He laughed. 'You are very modest for a hero. But I know what you mean – you are without weapons. All that has been dealt with by the Lady of the Chalice.' He flung his hand backward to indi-cate the slender box in the stern. 'See, my lord, we have brought your sword for you!'

Chapter Two
The Scarlet Fjord

A T BLADRAK'S WORDS a great sense of dread filled me. I stared at him in horror, hardly able to comprehend what had happened.

I had been manipulated into this situation and Bladrak had been an unknowing agent of this trick.

Bladrak was taken aback. 'What is it, my lord? Have we done wrong? Have we done something that will bring doom upon you?'

My voice was hoarse and I hardly knew the words I spoke for, consciously, I still had no idea of the Black Sword's nature. 'Doom on us all, Bladrak Morningspear, in some form or other. Aye, and perhaps the accomplishment of what you desire. Do you know the price?'

'Price?'

My face twisted. I flung my hands to cover it.

'What price is that, Count Urlik?'

I cleared my throat but still did not look at him. 'I do not know, Bladrak. That, in time, we shall both discover. As for now, I wish that sword kept away from me. I do not want the box opened.'

'We will do all you desire, Count Urlik. But you will lead us, will you not, against the Silver Warriors?'

I nodded. 'If that was why I was called, that is what I will do.'

'Without the sword?'

'Without the sword.'

I said nothing further on our journey to Bladrak's home, but sometimes, involuntarily, my eyes strayed to the black box which lay beneath the staring skull of the slain sea-stag. Then I would twist my head away and my melancholy would suffuse my brain.

Then, at last, tall cliffs loomed out of the clouds. Massive, black, they were even more unwelcoming than the obsidian crags of Rowernarc.

Hanging over a part of this range I detected a rosy glow and I stared at it in curiosity.

'What is that?' I asked Bladrak.

He smiled. 'The Scarlet Fjord. We are about to enter it.'

We were very close to the cliffs, but we did not alter course. The herons flew directly towards them. Then I saw why. There was a gap between two and deep water filled it. This must be the entrance to the fjord. One of Bladrak's men raised a huge, curling horn to his lips and blew a wild blast upon it. From above came an answering blast and, looking up, I saw that there were battlements carved on both sides of the narrow opening and at the battlements stood warriors.

It was so dark between the cliffs that I thought we must surely be dashed to pieces, but the herons guided us around a bend and then I blinked in wonder. The water was scarlet. The air was scarlet. The rock shone with a deep, ruby colour, and the fjord was full of warmth.

The warm, red light issued from the mouths of a thousand caves which honeycombed the eastern wall of the fjord.

'What are those fires?' I asked.

Bladrak shook his head. 'None know. They have been there for ever. Some believe them to be volcanic, others say that ancient scientists invented a peculiar kind of fire which fed on rock and air alone, but when they had invented it they had no use for it. They could not put it out, so they buried it. And the Scarlet Fjord was born.'

I could not keep my gaze off the wonder of those burning cliffs. Everything was bathed in the same red light. I felt truly warmed for the first time since I had arrived.

Bladrak indicated the western and southern walls of the fjord. 'That is where we live.'

Carved where the cliffs met the water were long quays. At

these quays were tied many boats of a similar design to that in which we sailed. Above the quays were ramps and steps and terraces. Plain, square doorways had been cut from the rock and outside them now stood hosts of men, women and children, all dressed in simple, plain-coloured smocks, tabards and dresses.

When they saw us head for the southern quay they began to cheer. Then they began to chant.

It was one word they chanted.

'Urlik! Urlik! Urlik!'

Bladrak raised his arms to them, begging for silence, his grin widening as they only reluctantly subsided.

'Friends of the Scarlet Fjord! Free folk of the South! Bladrak has returned with Count Urlik who will save us. Look!' He pointed dramatically first at the sea-stag's skull and then at my broken axe. 'With that axe alone he killed the Bellyripper. Thus will we destroy the Silver Warriors who enslave our brothers of the North!'

And this time the cheer, to my embarrassment, was even louder. I resolved to tell Bladrak as soon as possible that I had not been solely responsible for slaying the stag.

The boat was berthed and we stepped onto the quay. Rosy-cheeked women approached us and embraced Bladrak, curtseyed to me.

I could not help but notice the contrast between these folk and the neurasthenic people of Rowernarc, with their pale skins and their unhealthy appetites. Perhaps it was that the folk of Rowernarc were overcivilised and could only think of the future, while the dwellers of the Scarlet Fjord lived in the present, concerning themselves with immediate problems.

And the immediate problem of these people was plainly the threat of the Silver Warriors.

At least, I told myself, I would not now be dealing with the evasions of a Bishop Belphig. Bladrak would tell me everything he knew.

The so-called Hound of the Scarlet Fjord led me into his apartments. They were comfortably furnished and lit by lamps that also shone with a rosy glow. The decoration of the furniture and wall hangings more closely resembled those that I had seen on my chariot and my weapons when I had found myself on the frozen plain.

I sat down thankfully in a chair carved from solid amber and surprisingly comfortable. Many of the furnishings were in amber and the table itself was carved from a solid block of quartz.

I could not help reflecting on the irony that if Man's history had begun with the Stone Age it was about to end with a Stone Age, also.

The food was simple but tasty and I learned from Bladrak that this, like that of Rowernarc, was grown in special gardens in the deepest caves.

When we had eaten, we sat with our wine-cups and said nothing for a while.

Then I spoke.

'Bladrak. You must assume that my memory is poor and answer even the simplest questions I ask you. I have endured much of late and it has made me forgetful.'

'I understand,' he said. 'What do you wish to know?'

'First, exactly how I was summoned.'

'You know that you slept in the Frozen Keep, far away on the South Ice?'

'I know that I found myself on the South Ice, riding in a chariot towards the coast.'

'Aye – heading for the Scarlet Fjord. But as you came along the coast you were diverted at Rowernarc.'

'That explains much,' I said, 'for I could find no-one there who admitted to summoning me. Indeed, some, like Belphig, seemed to resent me.'

'Aye, and they held you there until they could maroon you on the island we found you on.'

'Perhaps that was their intention. I am not sure. But why Belphig should wish to do such a thing is hard to say.'

'The brains of the folk of Rowernarc are –' Bladrak gestured at his head with his finger – 'addled – askew – I know not – something...'

'But Belphig must have known of the bell, for when it sounded a second time he turned the ship about and your name was mentioned. That means that he knew you were summoning me. And they did not tell me. Why did the bell sound over the sea? And why did I not hear a bell the first time, only a voice.'

Bladrak looked at his beaker. 'They say the bell speaks with a human voice across the planes of the universe, but only sounds like a bell on this plane. I do not know if that is true, for I have only heard it ring in the ordinary way.'

'Where is the bell?'

'I know not. We pray, the bell rings. The Lady of the Chalice told us that.'

'Who is the Lady of the Chalice? Does she appear with a gigantic golden cup which screams?'

'Nay...' Bladrak gave me a sideways look. 'That is just her name. She came to us when the danger of the Silver Warriors grew great. She said there was a hero who would help us. She said he was Urlik Skarsol, Count of the White Wastes, Lord of the Frozen Keep, Prince of the Southern Ice, Master of the Cold Sword...'

'The *Cold* Sword? Not the Black Sword?'

'The Cold Sword.'

'Continue.'

'The Lady of the Chalice said that if we called the hero urgently enough it would sound Urlik's Bell which would summon him. He would come to our aid, he would take up the Cold Sword and the blood of the Silver Warriors would fill the Chalice and feed the Sun.'

I sighed. I supposed that the Cold Sword was the local name for the Black Sword. Jermays had said the sword had many names on many worlds. But something within me was still resolute.

'We shall have to manage against the Silver Warriors without the sword,' I said firmly. 'Now tell me who these warriors are.'

'They came from nowhere a year or so since. It is believed that they are Moonites whose own home grew too cold to support them. They have a cruel queen it is said, but none has ever seen her. They are virtually invulnerable to ordinary weapons and therefore well-nigh invincible in battle. They easily took the cities of the Northern coast, one after the other. Most of the people there, like those of Rowernarc, are too self-absorbed to know what happens to them. But the Silver Warriors have enslaved them and put them to death and made them brainless, inhuman creatures. We are the free sailors, we lived off the soft citizens, but now we rescue those we can and bring them here. For some while that is what we have been doing. But now all the signs show that the Silver Warriors are planning to attack the Southern coasts. In a direct fight we could not possibly defeat them. Soon the whole race will be enslaved.'

'Are these warriors of flesh and blood?' I asked, for I had the notion that they might be robots or androids of some kind.

'Aye, they are of flesh and blood. They are tall and thin and arrogant and speak rarely and wear that strange silver armour. Their faces, too, are silver, as are their hands. We have seen no other parts of their bodies.'

'You have never captured one?'

'Never. Their armour burns us when we touch it.'

I frowned.

'And what do you want me to do?' I asked.

'Lead us. Be our Hero.'

'But you seem well equipped to lead your folk.'

'I am. But we are dealing here with something beyond our usual experience. You are a Hero – you can anticipate more things than can we.'

'I hope you are right,' I said. 'I hope you are right, Sir Bladrak of the Scarlet Fjord.'

Chapter Three
The Raid on Nalanarc

B LADRAK INFORMED ME that an expedition against the Silver Warriors was already planned for the next day. The ships had been prepared for it and he had been awaiting my arrival before setting off against the island of Nalanarc which lay a few miles distant from the north-western coast. The object of the raid was not to kill the Silver Warriors, but to rescue the prisoners they had on the island. Bladrak was not sure what the prisoners were being used for, but he suspected they were engaged in making ships and weapons for the attack the Silver Warriors planned on the Southern coast shortly.

'How do you know they plan this attack?' I asked.

'We got the news from some of the slaves we rescued. Besides, it's been obvious to anyone who's been near 'em that they're planning the attack on the South. What would you do if you were a conqueror and were constantly raided from one particular area?'

'Set out to eliminate the source of my irritation,' I said.

When the great fleet sailed I sailed with it.

We left the waving, cheering women behind in the Scarlet Fjord, passed between the cliffs and were soon on the open sea.

Initially there was some confusion as the herons crossed some of their lines and had to be untangled, but this did not last long and soon we were heading north.

Bladrak was singing some obscure, symbolic chant that I doubt even he knew the meaning of. He seemed full of high spirits though I discovered he had made no specific plans for the raid, save to get there somehow and get the slaves off somehow.

I outlined a plan to him and he listened with keen interest. 'Very well,' he said, 'we'll try it.'

It was a simple enough plan and, not knowing the Silver Warriors, I had no idea if it would work or not.

We sped over the waters for some time, the runners of the sleds skipping over the thick surface.

Through the murk we passed until a large island could be seen ahead.

Now Bladrak shouted to his leading craft. 'Go in quickly, loose your weapons and then retreat. Wait for their own boats to follow and then lead them a dance while we get the slaves aboard in the confusion.'

That was my plan. I prayed it was a good one.

The leading craft acknowledged Bladrak's orders and sped ahead while the others slowed and waited in a bank of brown cloud.

Soon we heard a distant commotion, then we saw the ships of the Scarlet Fjord scudding away from the island. They were pursued by larger, heavier craft which seemed to be the first ships that actually moved through the waters, but I could not see, from that distance, what powered them.

Now we moved in.

The island of Nalanarc grew larger and larger and I could see through the twilight that there were buildings actually raised on parts of the place. Perhaps the Silver Warriors did not build habitually in the living stone as did Bladrak's and Rowernarc's people.

The buildings were square, squat, dimly lit from within. They were built down a hill with a large building centrally placed at the top. At the bottom of the hill were the familiar openings to caverns.

'That is where the slaves are,' Bladrak told me. 'They are worked in those caverns building ships and weapons until they die, then a new batch replaces them. Men and women of all ages are there. They are hardly fed anything. There are always plenty more, you see. I do not think the Silver Warriors mean our folk to live once the world is theirs.'

While I was prepared to believe Bladrak, I had once before been told by those who had summoned me that the people they fought were unremittingly evil. I had discovered that the Eldren were in fact the victims. I wanted to see for myself what the Silver Warriors were doing.

The herons drew our boats up onto the island's beach and we piled out, heading for the caverns at the base of the hill.

It was plain that almost all the Silver Warriors had gone in pursuit of the few ships we had sent in ahead. I guessed it would not be a tactic we could use twice.

Into the caves we ran and I had my first sight of the warriors.

They were on average a good seven feet high, but extremely thin, with long arms and legs and narrow heads. Their skin was actually white, but with a faint silver sheen. Their armour covered their bodies, apparently without joins, and their heads were encased in tight-fitting helmets.

They were armed with long, double-bladed halberds. When they saw us, they came rushing at us with them. But they seemed somewhat clumsy with the halberds and I guessed they might be used to some other kind of weapon.

We had armed ourselves with what Bladrak had assured me were the only useful tools against the Silver Warriors whose armour could not be pierced and would burn whoever tried to handle it.

These weapons were wide-meshed nets which we flung at them as they approached. The nets clung to their bodies and tripped them and they could not free themselves.

I looked about the cavern workshops and was horrified by the condition of the naked men, women and children who had been set to labouring here.

'Get these people out as quickly as you can,' I said.

One Silver Warrior had not been entangled by a net. He came running at me with his halberd. I knocked it aside with my restored battle-axe and, heedless of the warning Bladrak had given me, chopped at his body.

A horrible jolt ran up my arms and sent me staggering. But the Silver Warrior had been toppled too.

I was incredulous. I knew I had received nothing less than an electric shock.

Now Bladrak and his men were herding the dazed slaves out of the caves towards the ships.

I looked up at the larger building on the top of the hill. I saw a glint of silver and I saw a shape that was familiar framed against a window.

It was someone wearing the bulbous armour of Rowernarc.

Filled with curiosity and careless of the potential danger, I dodged behind one of the square, featureless buildings and then began to creep closer up the hill.

The figure was probably unaware that he could be seen so easily from below. He was gesturing angrily as he watched Bladrak's men helping the wretched slaves aboard their ships.

I heard a voice.

I could not make out the words, but the tone was more than familiar to me.

I crept closer, anxious to have confirmed by my eyes what had already been confirmed by my ears.

I saw the face now.

It was Bishop Belphig, of course. Every suspicion I had had about him was proved right.

'Have you no understanding?' he was crying. 'That pirate Bladrak will not only make off with most of your labour force – he will turn half of those into soldiers to fight against you.'

I heard a murmured reply, then a group of Silver Warriors came running down the hill, saw me – and charged with their halberds.

I turned and fled, just as Bladrak's boat was leaving.

'We thought we had lost you, Sir Champion,' he grinned. 'What were you doing up there?'

'I was listening to a conversation.'

Halberds fell into the water on either side of us but we were soon out of range.

Bladrak said: 'It will take them time to bring up their heavier weapons. We did well. Not a man wounded, even – and a satisfactory cargo.' He gestured towards the boats crammed with rescued slaves. Then what I had said registered with him.

'Conversation? What did you learn?'

'I learned that Rowernarc has a leader who would bring about her ruin,' I said.

'Belphig?'

'Aye. He's up there, doubtless with the leader of the Silver Warriors on the island. Now I know his main reason for his "hunt". He wished to rid himself of me, for fear I should aid you against his allies – and he needed to make a secret rendezvous with the Silver Warriors.'

Bladrak shrugged. 'I always suspected him of something of the sort. They have no values, those folk in Rowernarc.'

'Save, perhaps, their Lord Temporal – Shanosfane. And no human being deserves the fate of these wretches.' I jerked my thumb at the thin, dirty bodies of the Silver Warriors' ex-slaves.

'What would you do about it, Count Urlik?'

'I must think, Sir Bladrak.'

He gave me a long, hard look and said softly: 'Are you sure it is not yet time to use your sword?'

I avoided his eye and stared out to sea. 'I have not said I intend to use the sword at any time.'

'Then I do not think we shall live long,' he said.

Chapter Four
The Lady of the Chalice

A<small>ND THUS WE</small> came back to the Scarlet Fjord. The freed slaves looked around them in wonder as our boats tied up at quays bathed in rosy light from the honeycombed cliff on the far side of the fjord.

'Best mount extra guards from now on,' Bladrak told one of his lieutenants. Absently, he twisted one of the golden bracelets on his arm. 'Belphig knows us and he knows the Scarlet Fjord. They'll try reprisals.'

Weary from our expedition we went inside and pleasant women brought us meat and wine. There was plenty of extra room in the city of the Scarlet Fjord and the freed slaves would find themselves well provided for. Bladrak was frowning, though, as he sat opposite me and looked across the quartz table.

'Are you still thinking of the Black Sword?' I asked him.

He shook his head. 'No. That's for you to think about. I was considering the implications of Belphig's perfidy. From time to time we have the odd man or woman in the Scarlet Fjord who decides that Rowernarc offers pursuits more to their taste. We allow them to leave, of course, and – they go...'

'You mean that Belphig may be aware of many of your plans?' I said.

'You mentioned that he was unnerved by the sound of Urlik's Bell. Plainly he knows everything about you, about the Lady of the Chalice and so on. Equally plainly, he sought to soften you up in Rowernarc – in the hope he could bring you over to his side. When that failed...'

'He marooned me. But now he must know I sail with you.'

'Aye. And he will pass on all his information to his alien masters. What do you think they will do then?'

'They will try to strike before we grow any stronger.'

'Aye. But will they strike at the Scarlet Fjord first – or will they take Rowernarc and the cities further up the coast?'

'It will be easier for them to take the cities, I suspect,' I replied. 'Then they can concentrate their full power upon the Scarlet Fjord.'

'That's my guess, also.'

'The question now is – do we remain here, building up our strength for a siege, or do we go to the aid of Rowernarc and the rest?'

'It's a difficult problem.' Bladrak stood up, running his fingers through his red hair. 'I would like to consult one who could offer us wisdom on the matter.'

'You have philosophers here? Or strategists?'

'Not exactly. We have the Lady of the Chalice.'

'She dwells in the Scarlet Fjord? I did not realise…'

He smiled and shook his head. 'She may come to the Scarlet Fjord, however.'

'I should like to meet this woman. After all, she seems responsible for my fate.'

'Then come with me,' Bladrak said, and he led me through an inner door and into a long passage which sloped sharply downward.

Soon a strong saline smell reached my nostrils and I noticed that the walls were damp. I guessed that we were actually under the fjord itself.

The passage widened into a chamber. From the roof grew long stalactites in milky blues, yellows and greens. A soft radiance issued from the stalactites themselves and cast our gigantic shadows on the rough igneous rock of the cavern's walls. In the centre of the chamber an area of basalt had been smoothed and levelled and into it had been placed a small staff of about half a man's height. The staff was a deep, lustreless black with mottlings of dark blue. The cavern contained no other artefact.

'What is the staff for?' I asked.

Bladrak shook his head. 'I do not know. It has always been here. It was here long before my ancestors came to the Scarlet Fjord.'

'Has it any connection with the Lady of the Chalice?'

'I think it might have, for it is here that she appears to us.' He looked about him, half nervously I thought. 'Lady?'

It was all he said. Then a distant, high-pitched, oscillating whine came from all around us in the air. The stalactites vibrated and I prayed they would not be brought down on our heads by the sound. The short staff imbedded in the basalt seemed to change colour slightly, but that might have been something cast by one of the vibrating stalactites. The whine increased until it began to sound like a human scream and I recognised it with some trepidation. I blinked my eyes. I thought I saw the outline of the huge golden chalice again. I turned to say something to Bladrak and then looked back in astonishment.

A woman stood there. She was wreathed in golden light. Her dress and her hair were of gold and on her hands she wore gloves.

Her face was covered by a golden veil.

Bladrak kneeled. 'Lady, we need your help again.'

'My help?' came a sweet voice. 'When your great hero Urlik has joined you at last?'

'I have no power of prophecy, my lady,' I replied. 'Bladrak believes that you might have.'

'My own powers are limited and I am not permitted to reveal all I see, even then. What do you wish to know, Sir Champion?'

'Let Bladrak tell you.'

Bladrak climbed to his feet. Quickly he outlined the problem. Should we go to the aid of Rowernarc and the other cities? Or should we wait until the Silver Warriors attacked us?

The Lady of the Chalice seemed to deliberate. 'The fewer killed in this struggle the better I shall like it,' she said. 'It would seem to me that the sooner it is over the more folk will be saved.'

Bladrak gestured with his hands. 'But Rowernarc has brought this on herself. Who is to say how many warriors are on Belphig's side? Perhaps the city will fall without bloodshed...'

'There would be bloodshed soon enough,' said the Lady of the Chalice. 'Belphig would destroy all he did not trust.'

'Likely, aye...' mused Bladrak Morningspear. He glanced at me.

'Is there a way of killing the Silver Warriors?' I asked the mysterious woman. 'At the moment we are badly handicapped.'

'They cannot be killed,' she said. 'Not by your weapons, at least.'

Bladrak shrugged. 'Then I will risk many men in trying to save the worthless citizens of Rowernarc. I am not sure they would like to die for that cause, Lady.'

'Surely some are not worthless,' said she. 'What of Lord Shanosfane? He would be in great danger if Belphig gained complete power over Rowernarc.'

I admitted that Shanosfane was in danger and I agreed that the strange, abstracted Lord Temporal was worth saving from Belphig.

Then she asked, rather strangely: 'Would you say that Lord Shanosfane was a good man?'

'Aye,' I replied. 'Eminently good.'

'I think, then, that you will need him in the near future,' she said.

'Perhaps we can get to Rowernarc before Belphig finishes his business on Nalanarc?' I suggested. 'We could get the populace away before the Silver Warriors attacked.'

'Belphig's business on Nalanarc was finished for him,' Bladrak pointed out. 'And now that we know he is allied to the Silver Warriors, he will waste no time in attacking.'

'True.'

'But only the Black Sword will defeat Belphig,' said the veiled woman, 'and now you possess it, Lord Urlik.'

'I will not use it,' I said.

'You will use it.' The air pulsed. She vanished.

I recognised the statement. It had no threat in it, only certainty. I had heard it before while marooned on the sea-stag's island.

I rubbed my face with my hands. 'I would be grateful if I was allowed to work out my own destiny for once,' I said. 'For good or ill.'

'Come.' Bladrak began to leave the cavern.

I followed him, lost in my own thoughts. Everything was conspiring to force me into a pattern of behaviour which all my instincts rejected. But perhaps my instincts were wrong...

We returned to Bladrak's apartments in time to receive a messenger who had just arrived.

'My lords, the Silver Warriors' fleet has left harbour and is sailing directly south.'

'Bound for...?' Bladrak queried.

'For Rowernarc, I think.'

Bladrak snorted. 'We've been wasting time, I see. We'll never reach Rowernarc before they do. Also it could be a trick to divert us. For all I know their real ambition is to draw us off while another fleet attacks the Scarlet Fjord.' He looked sardonically at me. 'We are still in a quandary, Count Urlik.'

'The Lady of the Chalice seemed to indicate that it would be to our advantage if Shanosfane were saved,' I said. 'We must think of him, at least.'

'Risk a fleet for one man of Rowernarc?' Bladrak laughed, 'No, Sir Champion!'

'Then I must go alone,' I said.

'You'll achieve nothing – save to lose us our Hero.'

'Your Hero, Sir Bladrak,' I pointed out, 'has done precious little for you so far.'

'Your rôle will be clear soon.'

'It is clear now. I have a great respect for Lord Shanosfane. I cannot bear to think of him being butchered by Belphig.'

'I understand – but you cannot risk so much, Count Urlik.'

'I could afford to,' I said, 'if I had an ally.'

'An ally? I could not desert my folk to embark upon an –'

'I speak not of you, Bladrak. I appreciate that you must stay with your people. I did not mean a human ally.'

He looked at me in astonishment. 'Supernatural? What?'

In me now was a mixture of melancholy and relief. There was but one course open to me. I took it. I at once felt that I was giving in and making a courageous decision.

'The Black Sword,' I said.

Bladrak, too, looked as if he had had a weight removed from his shoulders. He grinned and clapped me on the back. 'Aye. It would seem a shame not to blood it now that you have it.'

'Bring it to me,' I told him.

Chapter Five
The Waking of the Sword

T HEY BROUGHT THE ebony case and they laid it on the table carved from quartz while conflicting emotions fought within me until I was so dizzy I could scarcely see the thing.

I put my hands upon the case. It felt warm. There seemed to be a faint pulse coming from within it, like the beating of a heart.

I looked at Bladrak who was staring at me, grim-faced. I took hold of the clasp and tried to raise it.

It was tightly locked.

'It will not open,' I said. I was almost glad. 'I cannot move it. Perhaps, after all, it was not meant...'

And then, inside my head, loudly came the chant again:

BLACK SWORD
BLACK SWORD
BLACK SWORD
THE BLACK SWORD IS THE CHAMPION'S SWORD
THE WORD OF THE SWORD IS THE CHAMPION'S LAW
BLACK SWORD
BLACK SWORD
BLACK SWORD
THE BLADE OF THE SWORD HAS THE BLOOD OF THE SUN
THE HILT OF THE SWORD AND THE HAND ARE AS ONE
BLACK SWORD
BLACK SWORD
BLACK SWORD

THE RUNES ON THE SWORD ARE THE WORMS THAT
  ARE WISE
THE NAME OF THE SWORD IS THE SAME AS THE
  SCYTHE
BLACK SWORD
BLACK SWORD
BLACK SWORD
THE DEATH OF THE SWORD IS THE DEATH OF ALL
  LIFE
IF THE BLACK SWORD IS WAKENED IT MUST TAKE
  ITS BLACK FIEF
BLACK SWORD
BLACK SWORD
BLACK SWORD

Now I wavered in my resolve at the last phrase. A huge sense of doom pressed upon me. I staggered back, my lips writhing, my whole soul in agony.

'No…'

Bladrak leapt forward and supported me.

My voice was strangled. 'Bladrak – you must leave here.'

'Why, Lord Urlik, you seem to need…'

'Leave here!'

'But I would help you…'

'You will perish if you stay.'

'How do you know that?'

'I am not sure – but I do know it. I speak truly, Bladrak. *Leave – for pity's sake!*'

Bladrak hesitated for another moment and then ran from the room, locking the door behind him.

I was alone with the case that held the Black Sword and the voice continued to chant in my head:

BLACK SWORD
BLACK SWORD

BLACK SWORD
AROUSE THE BLACK BLADE AND THE PATTERN IS
  MADE
THE DEED WILL BE DONE AND THE PRICE WILL BE
  PAID
BLACK SWORD
BLACK SWORD
BLACK SWORD

'Very well!' I screamed. 'I will do it. I will take up the Black Sword again. I will pay the price!'

The chanting ceased.

There was a terrible stillness in the room.

I heard my own breath rasping as my eyes fixed on the case on the table and were held by it.

In a low voice I said at last:

'Come to me, Black Sword. We shall be as one again.'

The lid of the case sprang open. A wild, triumphant howling filled the air – an almost human voice which awakened a thousand memories within me.

I was Elric of Melniboné and I defied the Lords of Chaos with my rune-sword Stormbringer in my hands and a wild joy in my heart...

I was Dorian Hawkmoon and I fought against the Beast Lords of the Dark Empire and my sword was called the Sword of the Dawn...

I was Roland dying at Roncesvalles with the magic blade Durandana slaying half a hundred Saracens...

I was Jeremiah Cornelius. No sword now but a needle gun shooting darts as I was chased through a city by a surging, insane mob...

I was Prince Corum in the Scarlet Robe, seeking vengeance at the Court of the Gods...

I was Artos the Celt, riding with my burning blade uplifted against the invaders of my kingdom's shores...

And I was all of these and more than these and sometimes my weapon

was a sword, at others it was a spear, at others a gun… But always I bore
a weapon that was the Black Sword or a part of that strange blade.
    Always a weapon – always the warrior.
    I was the Eternal Champion and that was my glory and my doom…

And a strange mood of reconciliation came over me then and I
was proud of my destiny.
    Yet why had I denied it?

I recalled a billowing cloud of brightness. I remembered grief. I remem-
bered sealing the sword in its case and swearing I would not bear it
again. I remembered a voice and a prophecy…
    'In refusing one doom, ye shall know another – a greater…'
    'No doom can be greater,' I shouted.
    Then I was John Daker – unhappy, unfulfilled, before the voice called
across the aeons for him to become Erekosë.
    The crime I had committed was in refusing the Black Sword.
    But why had I refused it? Why had I tried to rid myself of it?
    It seemed to me that that had not been the first time I had tried to part
my own destiny from that of the Black Sword…
    'Why?' I murmured. 'Why?'

'Why?'
    Then from the case a strange, black radiance spilled and I was
drawn towards it until I stared down upon that familiar sight.
    It was a heavy, black broadsword. Carved into its blade and hilt
were runes which I could not read. Its pommel was a sphere of
gleaming black metal. It was more than five feet long in its blade
and its hilt was more than large enough to accommodate two
hands.
    My own hands reached involuntarily towards it now.
    They touched the hilt and the sword seemed to rise and settle
comfortably in my grip, purring as a cat might purr.
    I shuddered and yet I was filled with joy.
    But now I understood what was meant by the term 'unholy joy'.

With this sword in my hands I ceased to be a man and became a demon.

I laughed. My laughter was gigantic and shook the room. I swung the sword about and it shrieked its wild music. I raised it and I brought it down upon the table of quartz.

The table split completely in twain. Chips of quartz flew everywhere.

'This is the Whole Sword!' I cried. 'This is the Cold Sword! This is the Black Sword and soon it must feed!'

In the recesses of my brain I understood that it was rare for me to hold the actual blade. Usually I had a weapon which drew its power from the Black Sword, which was a manifestation of the Black Sword.

Because I had sought to challenge Destiny, Destiny had taken vengeance. What followed could only be accomplished with the whole power of the Black Sword, but I still did not know what it was to be.

One of Bladrak's girls entered the room through another door. Her face was horrified as she saw me.

'My master sent me to ask if –' She screamed.

The Black Sword twisted in my hand and plunged towards her, almost dragging me with it. It buried itself in her body, passing completely through to the other side. She danced in a dreadful jig of death as, with her remaining life, she sought to drag herself off the blade.

'It is cold – aaah, how it is cold!' she sighed.

And then she died.

The sword was wrenched from her. Blood seemed to increase its dark radiance. It howled again.

'No!' I shouted. 'That should not have been! Only my enemies are to be slain!'

And I thought something like a chuckle escaped the sated sword as Bladrak rushed in to see what had happened, looked at me, looked at the sword, looked at the dead girl and groaned in terror.

He rushed to the case. There was a sheath in there and he flung it at me. 'Sheathe the thing, Urlik! Sheathe it, I beg you!'

Silently I accepted the sheath. Almost without my raising it the Black Sword slid into the scabbard.

Bladrak looked at the poor, dead woman, at the shattered table. Then he looked at my face and an expression of anguish covered his features.

'Now I know why you did not wish to wield the blade,' he said softly.

I could not speak. I attached the great scabbard to my belt and the Black Sword hung at my side at an angle.

Then I said: 'You all wished me to arouse the blade and use it. Now, I think, we begin to understand the consequences. The Black Sword must be fed. It will feed on friends if it cannot feed on enemies...'

Bladrak turned his eyes away.

'Is a boat ready?' I asked him.

He nodded.

I left that ruined room of death.

Chapter Six
The Black Blade's Fief

T HEY HAD GIVEN me a boat and a steersman.

The boat was a small one, with high, curving sides, plated with red gold and bronze. The steersman sat in front of me, controlling the leather-winged herons which flew low through the twilight air.

The Scarlet Fjord was soon no more than a glow hanging above the distant cliffs, then that vanished and brown cloud enclosed our gloomy world.

For a long while we sped over the black and sluggish sea until the jagged obsidian cliffs came in sight. Then we saw the bay overlooked by Rowernarc – and in the bay were crammed the besieging ships of the Silver Warriors.

Belphig had not wasted time. It was possible that I had arrived too late.

The craft of the invaders were very large and similar in design to Belphig's sea-chariot, but apparently with no *slevahs* to tow them.

We stayed out of sight and the steersman brought the boat to a halt on the crystalline beach quite close to the spot where Belphig's men had first encountered me.

Telling the steersman to await my return, I began to move cautiously along the shore in the direction of the Obsidian City.

Keeping to the cover of the rocks, I was able to round the corner of the bay and see exactly what I faced.

Plainly Rowernarc had capitulated without a battle. Prisoners were being herded down the ramps towards the ships.

Handling their halberds as awkwardly as ever, the slim Silver Warriors were dotted everywhere on the causeways.

Belphig himself was not in sight, but halfway up the cliff I saw my chariot, its bears in their harness, being trundled down to the beach. Doubtless this was part of their booty.

Shanosfane was not among the prisoners. I guessed that Belphig had had him confined to his 'province' of Dhötgard for the moment – if the Lord Spiritual had not already killed the Lord Temporal.

But how was I to reach Dhötgard when every level was crowded with the alien invaders?

Even with the aid of the Black Sword I would surely be swamped by weight of numbers if I tried to cut my way up to Dhötgard. And if I reached the place, how would I return?

Then a thought came to me as I watched my bears being urged towards the sea where a series of planks had been placed between the shallows and the nearest ship.

Deliberating no further I leapt up, drew my sword and ran for the chariot.

I had almost reached it before I was seen. A Silver Warrior shouted in a high, fluting voice, flinging his halberd at me. I knocked it aside with the sword, which, for all its weight, handled as easily as a fencing foil. I sprang into the chariot and gathered up the reins, turning the bears back towards the Obsidian City.

'Ho, Render! Ho, Growler!'

As if their spirits had risen at my sudden appearance, the bears reared in their harness and wheeled about.

'Ho, Longclaw! Ho, Snarler!'

The wheels of the chariot scraped round in the crystal rock and then we were driving straight for the causeway.

I ducked as more halberds were thrown, but they were poor throwing weapons at the best of times and the Silver Warriors' lack of skill with them did not help. Slaves and soldiers scattered and we had reached the first level in no time.

Now the Black Sword was crooning again. An evil song, a mocking song.

As I raced past them, I slashed at warriors who tried to stick me with their weapons and now when I struck their armour it was they who yelled, not me…

Up and up we charged and I felt an old, familiar battle-joy returning. The Black Sword cut off heads and limbs and bright blood streamed the length of its blade, dappling the sides of the chariots and the white pelts of the bears.

'On, Render! On, Longclaw!'

We were almost at the level of Dhötgard. Everywhere men were shouting and running in all directions.

'On, Snarler! On, Growler!'

Even faster ran my mighty bears until we came to the great door which protected Dhötgard. It had been drawn right back. I guessed that some spy in Shanosfane's household had been paid to do this. But it suited me now for I was able to drive the chariot right into the palace and continue at breakneck speed through the very passages themselves.

At last I reached the plain chamber where I had first met Shanosfane. I brushed aside the curtain and there he was.

He looked a little thinner, there was some hurt in his eyes, but he looked up from a manuscript as if he had been disturbed only for a moment when the Silver Warriors had arrived in Rowernarc.

'My Lord Urlik?'

'I have come to rescue you, Lord Shanosfane.'

His black features showed mild surprise.

'Belphig will kill you now that he has helped betray Rowernarc.'

'Why should Belphig kill me?'

'You threaten his rule.'

'Rule?'

'Lord Shanosfane, if you remain here you are doomed. There will be no more reading. No more study.'

'I do it only to pass the time…'

'Do you not fear death?'

'No.

'Well, then…' I sheathed my sword, ran forward and knocked him sharply on the back of the neck. He slumped onto the desk. I flung him over my shoulder and ran for the exit. My bears were snarling as Silver Warriors rushed towards us. I dumped Shanosfane in the chariot and leapt at the warriors.

Plainly they were used to weapons that could not harm them. The Black Sword whined and howled and it sheered through their strange armour to reveal that they were, indeed, very much like men. Their blood spilled as easily. Their innards spewed from the cuts the blade made. Their silver-flecked faces showed their pain.

I got back into the chariot, flicked the reins, turning it in the narrow passage and then gathering speed as we made for the main door.

Then I saw Belphig. He yelped as he saw our headlong approach and he flattened himself against the wall. I leaned out, trying to reach him with the sword, but he was too far distant.

We went around the door block and out onto the causeway again, going down much faster than we had come up.

This time our path was not blocked by Silver Warriors. They had learned to be wary. But they still flung their halberds at a safe distance and two nicked slight wounds in my left arm and my right cheek.

I was laughing at them again, holding my huge sword aloft. More powerful than the sword of Erekosë (which had been one of its partial manifestations) it thrummed out its evil song of death as my bears bore us towards the beach.

There was cheering now, from some quarters, as the prisoners saw me re-emerge. I shouted to them.

'Fight, men of Rowernarc! Fight! Turn on the Silver Warriors! Slay them if you can!'

Downward the chariot rumbled.

'Kill them or you will die!'

Some of the prisoners picked up halberds and began to fling them at their vanquishers. The Silver Warriors were again startled, not knowing how to react.

'Now flee!' I cried. 'Make for the depths of the mountains and then head along the coast for the Scarlet Fjord. You will be welcome there – and safe. The Black Sword will defend you!'

I hardly knew what I was shouting, but it had a surprising effect on the spiritless people of Rowernarc. While the Silver Warriors were confused, they began to run. They still had time to be soldiers, I thought. And soldiers the survivors would become – for now they knew what their fate would be if they did not fight.

Laughing in my crazy battle-joy I drove the chariot down the cliff and its wheels bounced over the crystal.

'Shanosfane is safe!' I called to those who listened. 'Your leader is with me.' As best I could I raised his prone body. 'He is alive but unconscious!' I saw one of his eyelids flutter. He would not be unconscious for long.

Belphig and a party of Silver Warriors were still in pursuit. From one of the entrances now came Morgeg and his men on their seal-beasts and I knew I had to fear these more than the clumsy aliens.

Across the beach they crashed in pursuit. A spear grazed the shoulder of one of my bears. The powerful animals were labouring somewhat now, for I had driven them hard.

And then, halfway to where I had left the boat, the chariot wheel hit a rock and Shanosfane and I were flung onto the ground as the bears raced on, dragging the chariot behind them. It bounced, hit another rock, righted itself and, riderless, disappeared into the gloom.

I put Shanosfane over my shoulder again and began to run; but the thump of the seal-beasts' fins came close behind. I saw the boat ahead. I turned to look at Morgeg and the others. They would reach me before I could get to the boat.

Shanosfane was moaning, rubbing his head. I put him down.

'See that boat, Lord Shanosfane. It will take you to safety. Get to it as quickly as you can.'

I took the Black Sword in both hands as the dazed Shanosfane staggered away.

Then I prepared to stand my ground.

Morgeg and six other riders, all armed with axes, charged at me. I whirled the huge sword around my head and sheered half through the necks of two of the seals. They bellowed as the blood pumped from their veins. They tried to come on, but collapsed and threw their riders from their saddles. I killed one of the riders at once, lunging the Black Sword through steel and padding straight into his heart. I brought the blade round and killed a man who was still mounted. He jerked in his saddle and then toppled out.

The other man on foot came at me crablike with his battle-axe circling his head. I chopped at the haft of the axe and the blade went spinning through the air to strike a rider directly in the face and knock him from his saddle. I drove my sword through the weaponless warrior's gorget.

Now Morgeg fought to control his frightened mount. He glared at me in hatred.

'You are tenacious, Count Urlik,' he said.

'It seems so.' I feinted at him.

There was only one rider left alive save Morgeg. I lowered my sword and spoke to the man. 'Would you leave while I kill Morgeg? Or will you stay and be slain with him?'

The man's pale face twitched, his mouth dropped open, he tried to say something, failed and wheeled his seal-beast about, heading back to Rowernarc.

Morgeg said quietly, 'I think I should like to return, also.'

'You cannot,' I said simply. 'I have to repay you for marooning me on that island.'

'I thought you were dead.'

'You did not check.'

'I thought the sea-stag killed you.'

'I killed the sea-stag.'

He licked his lips. 'In that case, I should definitely like to return to Rowernarc.'

I lowered the Black Sword. 'You may do so if you tell me one thing. Who leads you?'

'Why, Belphig leads us!'

'No. I mean who is the leader of the Silver Warr –'

Morgeg thought he had seen a chance. He swung his axe down on me.

But I blocked the blow with the flat of the sword. I turned my own weapon and the axe flew from his hand. The sword could not be stopped as it went to his groin and the point drove deeply in.

'Cold...' murmured Morgeg as his eyes closed. 'So cold...'

The corpse fell backwards in the saddle and the seal-beast reared and turned, charging towards the bay.

I saw Belphig at the head of a group of Silver Warriors. There were a score of them and I wondered if even the Black Sword could deal with so many.

I heard a shout from seaward. I heard the noise of wings beating overhead.

'Lord Urlik! Now!'

It was the steersman's voice. He had bundled Shanosfane aboard and had come along the coast to find me.

I sheathed the Black Sword and plunged knee-deep into the water. The stuff clung to my legs, hampering me. Belphig and his men were almost upon us. Behind him, in the way, everything was still in confusion.

I grasped the smooth side of the boat and hauled myself in, gasping. Immediately the steersman turned the herons and we were heading out to sea.

Belphig and the Silver Warriors came to a stop at the edge of the water and were soon swallowed in the gloom.

We raced back for the Scarlet Fjord.

Bladrak Morningspear had an unusually grim expression on his face as he sat in an amber chair and looked across the room at Shanosfane and myself.

We were in another room of his apartments, as far away from the chamber of death as possible. I had taken off the scabbarded Black Sword and leaned the thing against the wall.

'Well,' said Bladrak quietly, 'the Black Sword has earned its price, it seems. You must have killed many Silver Warriors as well as those riders of Belphig's – and perhaps you showed the folk of Rowernarc that there was some point in defending themselves.'

I nodded.

'And you, my Lord Shanosfane, are you pleased that you have avoided death?'

Bladrak spoke almost sardonically.

Shanosfane looked at him from those deep, detached eyes. 'I am not sure what difference there is between life and death, Sir Bladrak.'

Bladrak's expression seemed to indicate that he had made a point. He got up and began to pace about.

I said to Shanosfane: 'Do you know who rules the Silver Warriors?'

Shanosfane looked slightly surprised. 'Why, Belphig, of course...'

'He means that he wants to know who commands Belphig,' Bladrak said. 'Who is supreme ruler of the Silver Warriors?'

'Why, Belphig. Bishop Belphig. He is their supreme ruler.'

'But he is not of their race!' I exclaimed.

'He has their queen prisoner.' Shanosfane's gaze wandered around the room and then fixed curiously on the Black Sword. 'They are not really warriors, those people. They are peaceful. They have never known war. But Belphig makes them do his will – for if they do not, he will destroy their queen, whom they love above life.'

I was astonished and I could see that Bladrak was equally surprised. 'So that is why they are such poor halberdiers,' I murmured.

'They know how to build engines to make ships move through the water,' Shanosfane said. 'They have several such mechanical skills. Belphig told me all this.'

'But why is he enslaving our people?' Bladrak demanded. 'What use is there in it?'

Shanosfane looked calmly at Bladrak. 'I do not know. What use is there in any activity? Perhaps Belphig's plan is as good as any other.'

'You have no idea of his ultimate ambitions?' I said.

'I told you. None at all. I did not think to enquire.'

'Do you not care that your people are being enslaved – killed!' Bladrak shouted. 'Does not that touch you anywhere in that cold soul of yours?'

'They were slaves already,' Shanosfane said reasonably. 'And they were dying. How much longer do you think our race could have lived like that?'

Bladrak turned his back on the Lord Temporal.

'Lord Urlik, you wasted your time,' he said.

'Because Lord Shanosfane does not think as we do,' I replied, 'it does not follow that he was not worth saving.'

'I was not worth saving.' A peculiar look came into Shanosfane's eyes. 'I do not think I have been saved. Who told you to rescue me?'

'We decided to do it ourselves,' I replied. And then I paused. 'No, perhaps not – perhaps it was the Lady of the Chalice who suggested it.'

Shanosfane returned his attention to the Black Sword.

'I think I would like it if you could leave me alone,' he said. 'I would meditate.'

Bladrak and I went to the door and walked out into the corridor.

'Well, perhaps he was worth saving after all,' Bladrak admitted reluctantly. 'He gave us information we should not have had otherwise. But I have no liking for the fellow and cannot see why you admire him. He is nothing but a –'

We stopped in our tracks as a blood-curdling scream came from the room we had just left. We looked at each other, sharing a certain knowledge.

We ran back towards the door.

But the Black Sword had done its work. Shanosfane lay spread-eagled on the floor with the blade waving from the middle of his chest like an obscene plant. Whether the sword had attacked him or whether he had managed to kill himself with it we would never know.

Shanosfane was not dead. His lips were moving.

I bent to listen to the words he whispered. 'I had not realised it would be so – so chill…'

Those incredibly intelligent eyes closed and he spoke no more.

I tugged the Black Sword from his body and put it back in its sheath.

Bladrak was pale. 'Was that why the Lady of the Chalice made you bring him here?' he said.

I did not understand him at first. 'What do you mean?'

'Did the sword need the life of a good man – an especially good man – as its price for helping us? The Black Sword's reward – the soul of the Black King?'

I remembered the words of the chant: *If the Black Sword is wakened, it must take its Black Fief…*

I clenched my hands together as I looked down at the corpse of the scholar king.

'Oh, Bladrak,' I said, 'I am afraid of our future.'

And a coldness, colder than the coldest ice, filled the room.

Book Four

The Blood of the Sun

A knife, a cup and a man shall be
The means by which the world's set free.

– The Chronicle of the Black Sword

Chapter One

Siege of the Scarlet Fjord

DEPRESSION SETTLED OVER us and even the fires of the
Scarlet Fjord seemed to fade.

We lived in the shadow of the Black Sword and now I had an
inkling of the reasons why I had wanted to rid myself of it.

One could not master the sword. It demanded lives as some
greedy Moloch – some fierce, barbaric god of ancient times –
demanded sacrifice. And, what was worse, it often chose its own
sacrifices from among the friends of the man who bore it.

A jealous sword, indeed.

I know that Bladrak did not blame me for what had taken place. In
fact he claimed that the fault was shared between himself and the
Lady of the Chalice – for they had encouraged me, against my
will, to awaken the Black Sword and use it.

'It has already aided us,' I pointed out. 'Without it, I should not
have survived in Rowernarc and we should not have learned from
Shanosfane the truth of Belphig's status and the nature of his hold
over the Silver Warriors.'

'It has been well paid for its work…' Bladrak growled.

'If we knew where Belphig hid this queen,' I said, 'then we
could free her. The Silver Warriors would refuse to serve Belphig
and the threat would be over.'

'But we know not where, in the whole world, she is!'

'If the Lady of the Chalice were to be asked…' I began, but
Bladrak silenced me.

'I am not sure that the Lady works entirely in our interest,' he
said. 'I think she uses us in some larger scheme of her own.'

'Aye – you could be right.'

*

Now we walked along the quays, staring down at the red-stained water, at the many boats we were preparing for our war against the Silver Warriors. The knowledge that the slender, awkward aliens fought us only because they had been forced to do so by Belphig took some of the savagery out of our feelings and our work had slowed accordingly.

Unable to hate the Silver Warriors, it was harder for us to contemplate killing them. But we should have to kill them or see the whole of humanity slain or enslaved.

I looked across the fjord to the mysterious source of its heat and light – the honeycomb cliff from which the scarlet radiance issued.

There was a power there but I could not begin to guess at its nature. Something created millennia before which continued to burn at the same constant temperature while the rest of the world grew cold. Once, I thought, the Scarlet Fjord had been something other than a camp for the outlaws who chose not to live in the soft decadence of cities like Rowernarc. Was the Lady of the Chalice the last descendant of the scientists who had dwelt here? Perhaps Shanosfane could have told us. Perhaps that was why the Black Sword had killed him, because we were meant to remain in ignorance…

Suddenly Bladrak put a hand on my shoulder. He cocked his head and listened.

I heard it then. The sound of a horn. It blew louder.

'The guards,' said Bladrak. 'Come, Lord Urlik, let's see why they sound the alarm.' He leapt into a boat which had already been harnessed to a pair of the heronlike flying creatures. They were asleep on the perches built along the quayside. He shook their reins and awakened them as I joined him. The birds squawked and took to the air. We headed towards the narrow opening of the fjord.

Between the tall, black cliffs we moved until the open sea was in sight. And then we saw the reason for the guards' alarum.

It was Belphig's fleet.

There were between five hundred and a thousand great ships massing there and the air was full of the drone of their engines. Low, sluggish waves rocked our craft as their wash reached us.

'Belphig brings all his strength against us!' Bladrak rasped. 'Our boats could never hope to beat those huge craft…'

'But in one thing their size is against them,' I pointed out. 'They can only enter the fjord one at a time. If we mass our warriors on the cliffs above the opening, we might be able to attack them when they try to enter the approach to the Scarlet Fjord.'

He brightened a little. 'Aye. It might work. Let's get back.'

We were waiting in the heights when the first of the great craft, with its strange pyramidal arrangement of decks, nosed its way between the cliffs. We had arranged boulders on the ledges in readiness.

The ship came directly beneath us and I drew the Black Sword and shouted: 'Now!'

The boulders were levered over the ledges and crashed into the decks. Several crunched straight through, while others smashed down the terraces, taking timbers and warriors with them.

A mighty cheer went up from the warriors of the Scarlet Fjord as the ship keeled over and the soldiers in their silver armour were toppled into the viscous sea which sucked them down as they struggled and screamed in their strange high-pitched voices.

As I watched them die, I thought that these poor creatures were as much victims of Belphig's perfidy as were we. Yet what else could we do but kill them? They fought so that a queen they loved more than life would not perish. We fought for our freedom. What Belphig himself fought for I was yet to learn.

Another ship tried to enter the gulf and again we showered down our boulders. This ship split in twain, both ends rising steeply out of the water like the slowly closing snout of some sea-monster, sandwiching those who had survived and crushing them before there was a burst of white hotness from the centre and the waters bubbled and steam struck our faces. I realised that we had destroyed one of the engines. They seemed unstable things. Perhaps we had found another weakness of the Silver Warriors.

After two more attempts, the ships withdrew, surrounding the entrance to the fjord in a semicircle many craft deep.

The siege of the Scarlet Fjord had begun in earnest.

Bladrak and I conferred in his apartments again. His spirits had lifted with our victories but now, as the implications dawned on him, he began to frown.

'You are afraid that we cannot sustain a long siege,' I said.

He nodded. 'We grow much of what we need in our cavern gardens, but the slaves we have rescued have tripled our numbers and the gardens cannot support so many. Our raids brought us the extra food we needed, but with Belphig's ships blocking the fjord we can do no more raiding.'

'How long do you think we can last?'

He shrugged his shoulders. 'Twenty days or so. We have no stores. They all went to feed the newcomers. Crops continue to grow, but not fast enough. Belphig probably knows this.'

'I am sure he does and is counting on it.'

'What are we to do, Lord Urlik? Go and do battle? At least we will die swiftly…'

'That is the last resort. Is there no other way out of the fjord?'

'Not by sea. And the path across the mountains leads only to the ice wastes. We should perish there as quickly as we'd perish here.'

'How long does it take to reach the ice?'

'On foot? Eight days, I think. I have never made the journey.'

'So even if a foraging party was sent out it could not expect to find food and return in time.'

'Exactly.'

I rubbed at my beard, thinking deeply. Eventually I said: 'Then there is only one thing to do at this point.'

'What is that?'

'We must seek the advice of the Lady of the Chalice. Whatever her motives, she seems to want Belphig defeated. She must aid us, if she can.'

'Very well,' said Bladrak. 'Let us go now to the cavern where the dark staff is.'

'Lady?'

Bladrak looked around him, his face shadowed in the soft, weird glow from the stalactites.

The strong smell of salt was in my nostrils. While Bladrak called the Lady of the Chalice, I inspected the short staff that was imbedded in the basalt of the floor. I touched it and withdrew my fingers with a gasp, for it had burned them. Then I realised that it was not extreme heat that had caused the pain – but extreme cold.

'Lady?'

The thin whine came and it grew to an oscillating shriek. I turned, caught a glimpse of an outline of a great chalice, saw it fade as the shriek died, and then the Lady of the Chalice, clad in golden radiance, her face, as before, completely veiled, stood before us.

'Belphig has almost vanquished you,' she said. 'You should have used the Black Sword sooner.'

'And slain more friends?' I asked.

'You are too sentimental for a great Champion,' she said. 'The issues for which you fight are vast in scope and implication.'

'I am tired of great issues, madam.'

'Then why did Bladrak summon me?'

'Because there was nothing else to do. We are boxed up and will eventually die. The only solution I can see is to rescue the Queen of the Silver Warriors whom Belphig has captured. If she is freed, then Belphig will lose his main strength.'

'That is true.'

'But we know not where to seek this queen,' Bladrak said.

'Ask me a direct question,' the Lady of the Chalice told him.

'Where is the Queen of the Silver Warriors?' I asked. 'Do you know?'

'Aye – I know. She is at Moon, a thousand miles from here across the ice. She is guarded both by Belphig's men and by enchantments of Belphig's arrangement. She cannot leave her apartments and neither can she be visited, save by Belphig himself.'

'So she cannot be rescued.'

'She can be by one man – by you, Urlik, with the aid of the Black Sword.'

I looked at her sharply. 'This is why you helped Bladrak summon me. This is why you brought the sword here and made me use it. For reasons of your own you wish the Silver Queen freed.'

'A simple judgement, Count Urlik. But it will benefit us all if she is freed, I agree.'

'I could not cross a thousand miles of ice on foot. Even if I had not lost my bear chariot, I would not be able to get there in time to free the queen and save the Scarlet Fjord.'

'There is one way,' said the Lady of the Chalice. 'A dangerous way.'

'By using a boat as a sled and having the herons drag it?' I said. 'They would not last that long and I suspect that the boats are not sturdy enough to –'

'I do not mean that.'

'Then explain quickly, Lady,' I said grimly.

'The people who created the Scarlet Fjord were engineers who experimented with many devices. Many were unsuccessful. Many were partially successful. When they went away from here having found a means of travelling through Time, they left some of their inventions behind them. One of these was sealed in a cave in a mountain on the far side of this range, near the ice wastes. It was an air-chariot, flying under its own power, but it was abandoned because of one defect. The engine used radiated a substance which enfeebled the pilot, blinded him and eventually killed him.'

'And you want me to use such a craft to go to Moon?' I laughed. 'And die before I reach the place? What would be accomplished by that?'

'Nothing. I do not know how long the radiation takes to kill. It could be that you would get to Moon before that happened.'

'Are there any permanent effects of these rays should I survive?'

'None that I know of.'

'Where exactly is this craft hidden?'

'There is a pass that leads through the mountains to the ice. At the end of the pass is a mountain that stands alone. Steps are carved into the mountain and at the top of the steps is a sealed door. You must break the door and enter. There you will find the air-chariot.'

I frowned. I still distrusted the Lady of the Chalice. She, after all, had been the immediate cause of my separation from Ermizhad and my subsequent agony of mind.

'I will do this thing, Lady,' I said, 'if you will promise me something.'

'What is that?'

'That you will reveal all that you know of my fate and my place in this universe.'

'If you are successful I promise I shall tell you all I know.'

'Then I leave at once for Moon.'

Chapter Two
The City Called Moon

AND SO I left the Scarlet Fjord, climbing up into the black, igneous cliffs that brooded eternally beneath the dark, twilight sky. I had a map with me, some provisions and my sword. My bulky furs keeping out the worst of the cold, I moved through the mountains as rapidly as was possible.

I slept little, with the result that I could barely keep my eyes open and the whorls of obsidian, the frozen cascades of basalt, the oddly shaped pumice visible in all directions took on the appearance of leering faces, of menacing figures of giants and monsters, until I felt surrounded by the creatures of nightmare and I gripped my sword tighter but continued, doggedly, to move on. And at last I saw the ice plains ahead and the clouds thinned out to reveal the red sphere of the sun, the faint stars gleaming behind it.

I welcomed that sight. If I had thought the ice gloomy and bleak when I first found myself in this world, it had been nothing compared with the mood of the mountains which surrounded Earth's last, dark sea. I trudged over the smooth, glassy rock of the pass and I saw the mountain ahead of me.

As the Lady of the Chalice had said, it stood alone, directly before me, on the edge of the ice plain.

I staggered as sleep tried to overcome me. I forced my feet to plod the last half-mile to the base of the mountain where ancient steps had been carved. And on the first of those steps I succumbed to sleep, not knowing for what new task my energies would be needed.

I awoke only barely refreshed and began to climb the steps until I came at length to what had evidently once been the mouth of a natural cave. But that cave mouth had been sealed with molten rock. The length and breadth was filled with a flow of red-and-yellow obsidian.

I had expected to find a door which I should be able to force, but there was no means of opening this!

I turned and looked back over the mountains. The brown clouds clung to them, increasing their enigmatic appearance. They seemed to share the joke which the Lady of the Chalice had played upon me.

'Damn you!' I yelled.

'Damn you,' they replied. 'Damn you.' And those echoes damned me a hundred times before they died.

Snarling with frustrated anger I drew the Black Sword. Its black radiance spilled out against the obsidian flow. Fiercely I attacked that which sealed the cavern's entrance. The blade bit deep into the rock and pieces of it flew in all directions.

Astonished, I struck again. And again a huge piece of the glassy stone fell away as if blasted.

Again the Black Sword crashed against the rock. And this time, with a rumble, it collapsed completely, revealing a dark chamber. I stepped over the rubble, sheathing the sword. I peered about me, but could see nothing. From my belt I took the torch Bladrak had given me just before I left. I depressed the stud in the handle and a faint light blossomed.

There was the machine the Lady of the Chalice had told me I should find...

But she had not told me I should also find the pilot.

He sat in the air-chariot and he stared at me in silence, grinning as if in anticipation of my fate. He was long and thin and dressed in the silver armour of those who now served Belphig. He lounged awkwardly in the seat and I guessed he had lounged in the same attitude for centuries, for it was a fleshless skull that grinned at me and fleshless hands that gripped the side of the chariot. I guessed that he had been left there as a warning, perhaps, of the lethal rays of the chariot's engine. With an oath I knocked the skull from the neck and dragged the bones out of the car, hurling them across the cavern floor.

The Lady of the Chalice had told me that I should find the controls simple enough. She had been right. There were no instruments as such that I recognised, merely a crystal rod rising from the floor. By squeezing the rod in my hand I could activate the engine. By pushing the rod forward I could move ahead, by pushing it back I could slow my speed and stop, by pulling it back at an angle I could gain height and by pushing it forward at an angle I could lose height. Similarly the crystal rod could be moved from side to side.

I was anxious to leave the former pilot behind. I got into the chariot and squeezed the rod. Immediately the whole chariot began to glow with a pink luminosity so that it resembled flesh. A throb came from below my feet and I guessed that the engine was there. I licked my dry lips and pushed the lever very slightly forward. The air-chariot began to move towards the entrance of the cave. I took it into the air a few feet to avoid the rubble and then we were in the open air again and I discovered that quite small movements of my hand would control the craft. I inspected my map and took a bearing from the compass imbedded in the top of the lever, then I increased speed and headed for the city called Moon.

The obsidian mountains had disappeared and now there was only ice – seemingly infinite ice that streamed past me as I flew. Occasionally the flat plain was broken by frozen drifts and spires but for the most part nothing relieved that cold, desolate landscape.

I began to doubt that the Lady of the Chalice had been right when she had mentioned the engine's poisonous radiations, but soon I realised that my vision had dimmed slightly, that I felt lethargic and my bones ached.

I was driving the air-chariot at its maximum speed, but there was no clear means of judging how fast that was. The cold air bit at my flesh and frost rimed my beard and my thick coat was blown about as the white breath was whipped from my mouth.

The discomfort increased. It also seemed to me that I was leaving the sun far behind, that the world was growing darker.

Soon the sun was close to the horizon and the stars blazed more brightly in the sky. But by this time I had fallen back against the support of my seat and nausea shook my body.

I was dying, I was sure. At one stage I was forced to slow my speed and vomit over the side of the craft. I wanted to stop altogether, to get away from the source of my discomfort, but I knew that to leave the aircraft would be to ensure my death. I increased speed again.

And then I saw it ahead. It was a huge white mountain, pitted with great craters, rising out of the ice. I recognised it, of course, for it was the moon itself. How many thousands of years had passed since it had crashed into the Earth? A dim memory came back to me. I was sure I had witnessed this sight before. A name, an impression of despair. What was the name?

It had gone.

With the last of my strength I brought the air-chariot to a skidding halt on the ice and pulled my aching body from it.

Then I began to crawl across the ice towards the towering mountain that had once been Earth's satellite.

The farther from the air-chariot I crawled the more my strength began to return. By the time I had reached the curved side of the mountain I felt greatly recovered. I could see now that even the mountain was covered with a thin layer of ice in some parts, but not enough to obscure its outlines. Above me I could see a light gleaming and wondered if this was an entrance to the city the Silver Warriors had been forced to desert when they joined Belphig in his war against us. There was nothing for it but to begin to climb. The ice and the rock were rough enough to make climbing fairly easy but I was forced to rest several times and had by no means regained my full strength when I neared the top and saw fierce light suddenly burst out from the centre of a crater and a dozen riders, mounted on seal-beasts, framed against it.

I had been seen. Perhaps Belphig had even been prepared for my coming.

I slid down the walls of the crater, put my back against the rock, drew out the Black Sword in both hands and awaited the riders.

They charged me with the long, barbed harpoons I had last seen when we had hunted the sea-stag. One of them would rip me from chin to stomach if it pierced my armour.

But the Black Sword itself seemed to be lending me energy. With a single movement I swung it so that I sheared through the head of every harpoon. They clattered to the rock and the useless shafts thudded into the stone as the astonished riders pulled their beasts up short. I plunged the blade into the throat of the nearest seal-beast and it coughed and collapsed, tumbling its rider forward so that I could bring the sword crashing down to shear into his back as he fell.

The laughter began to bubble from my lips now.

I jeered at them as I slew them. They milled in confusion, drawing axes and swords from their scabbards, shouting to each other. An axe struck my mailed shoulder but did not cut through the links. I killed my antagonist with a stroke that cut his face in half and the impetus of my swing clove the body of the man beside him.

They tried to press in, to hamper my movements so that they could cut me down. But the Black Sword would not let them. It moved so rapidly that it opened their ranks every time they managed to close them. A hand, still clutching a sword, flew away into the shadows. A head dropped to the ground. A body spilled entrails over the high saddle. Everywhere the Black Sword swept it left red ruin in its wake.

And at last they were all dead, save for a few seal-beasts that lumbered back towards the source of the bright light.

I followed them, still laughing.

Instead of exhausting me, the slaughter seemed to have filled me with extra power. I felt light-headed and light-footed, too.

I raced after the seal-beasts, blinking in the light, and saw them moving down a long metal ramp which curved into the bowels of the fallen sphere.

More cautiously now I began to move down the ramp. I was just in time, for two doors began to move across the opening and met. I prayed that I had not entered a trap.

Down and down I went until I could see a floor below me. It seemed made of molten silver and it rippled like water, but as I reached it and set a wary foot upon it it felt solid enough.

From out of a doorway in the far wall three more men came running. They, too, were dressed in the bulbous armour of Rowernarc, but they carried the double-bladed halberds I had until now only seen in the hands of the Silver Warriors.

These men were more skilled with the weapons. They spread out and began to swing the things around their heads. I watched them all warily, seeking an opening.

Then one released his and it whistled through the air at me. I flung up my sword to block it and just managed to hurl it aside as the next halberd flew – and then the next. I dodged one and was caught a glancing blow by the other. I was flung to the ground, the Black Sword leaving my hand and skidding across that floor of rippling silver.

Weaponless I rose to my feet as Belphig's men drew their swords. They were grinning. They knew I was doomed.

I looked for the sword but it was too far away to reach in time. I backed away from the warriors and my foot struck something. I glanced down. It was the haft of one of the fallen halberds. They saw it at the same time and began to run towards me. I picked up the halberd, knocked one swordsman in the face with the butt and rammed the spike into another's throat. Then I burst through them and ran for the sword.

But they closed with me before I could reach it. I turned again, blocking a thrust with the shaft and then reversing the movement to bring the axe blade down onto the helm of the second man. He staggered, dazed, and I skidded across the floor to the sword.

It settled into my hands and began to moan like a savage hound that needs to kill.

I let it kill. I split my first assailant from skull to midriff and I chopped the body of the second man in two.

Then I shuddered as the battle-fever began to leave me. Sheathing the sword again I ran towards the entrance through which the warriors had come.

I was in a long, twisting corridor. It was more like a tube, for it was completely round and the floor curved steeply upwards on both sides. Down this I ran and emerged at length into a spherical chamber. I had a feeling that these passages had not originally been used by human beings but had possibly carried traffic or liquids of some kind. Steps led up to the domed roof of the chamber. I climbed them and emerged in a circular room which had a roof like frosted glass. I peered through the glass and realised that it formed the floor of the chamber above me. But I could see no means of reaching that chamber. Then I thought I saw something move in the room above. I drew my sword.

An opening suddenly appeared in the smooth ceiling. A perfectly round opening in the exact centre of the circle. Then a kind of clear tube descended until it was only a few feet above the floor of the lower chamber. There were handholds on the inside of the tube.

Still wary, I approached the tube and began to climb, the Black Sword balanced in my right hand. I poked my head over the top and there was a sparsely furnished room of great size. Walls and floor were of the same rippling silver. A white bed was there and various chairs and objects whose use I could not guess. And standing near the bed was a woman whose skin was silver, whose eyes were deep black and whose dress was blood-red. Her hair was nearly white and her beauty was ethereal. She smiled at me and she moved her lips, but I could not hear her.

I advanced across the transparent floor towards her and suddenly my face struck something cold and hard and I recoiled. I put out my hand and felt smoothness. I was separated from the Silver Queen by an invisible wall.

She gestured, trying to tell me something, but I could not understand her.

What kind of enchantment had Belphig put upon her? His scientific powers were either much greater than he had led me to suspect or else, more likely, he had borrowed them from the Silver Warriors whose ancestors, I now guessed, were the same scientists who had originally occupied the place I knew as the Scarlet Fjord.

Desperation now consumed me. I took the Black Sword and I struck a mighty blow against the invisible wall.

A dreadful shrieking filled the air. A shock ran the length of my body and I was hurled backward. My senses swam. I had grown to rely too much on the power of the Black Sword, I thought, as I collapsed into oblivion.

Chapter Three

The Phoenix and the Queen

THERE WAS A chanting in my ears:

BLACK SWORD
BLACK SWORD
BLACK SWORD
THE BLADE OF THE SWORD HAS THE BLOOD OF
THE SUN...

I opened my eyes and saw the stars in the dark sky. I turned my head, realising that I was in the air-chariot again.

At the wheel sat a man in silver armour.

This must be a dream. I was dreaming that the skeleton was piloting the chariot.

If not, then I was a prisoner of the Silver Warriors. I straightened my back and felt the pommel of my sword. I was not tied and I had not been disarmed.

The pilot in silver armour turned his head – and I saw that it was no man at all but the woman I had seen just before I lost consciousness. She had a sardonic look in her black eyes.

'I thank you for your valour in saving me,' she said.

I knew the voice.

'Your sword shattered the barrier. Now we return to the Scarlet Fjord so that I may tell my warriors I am free and they need do Belphig's work no longer.'

'You are the Lady of the Chalice,' I said incredulously.

'That is what Bladrak's people called me.'

'Then all my fighting was in vain. You were already free!'

She smiled. 'No. What you saw was only a manifestation. I

could not have appeared anywhere else but in that chamber – the chamber of the staff. Belphig did not realise that I had a means of communicating with his enemies.'

'But I saw the chalice at sea!'

'The image of the chalice could be projected to a few other places, true, but I could not transfer my own image there.'

I looked at her with deep suspicion. 'And how came you by the Black Sword?'

'The folk of Moon have much wisdom, Sir Champion. We were great once. There was a prophecy that you would come again, awakening from your Frozen Keep. It seemed nothing but a legend, but I studied it for I needed to hope. I discovered a great deal.'

'And you promised to tell me everything you learned.'

'Aye, I did.'

'First, you could inform me what Belphig's ambition is.'

'Belphig is a fool – though cunning. He knew of Moon and he found it eventually, having trekked for weeks across the ice with his men. Having forgotten that war existed, we trusted him. He learned many of our secrets and then, one day, imprisoned me as you found me. He then forced the Silver Warriors to serve him, as you know.'

'But why?'

The Silver Queen swayed in her seat and I realised that the rays from the craft's engine were affecting us both.

'He – he had a scheme but it needed more labour than the warriors themselves could supply. Ultimately he desired to build a vessel that would travel through space. He wished to find a new sun that had not grown old. It was a stupid scheme. We have the knowledge for building such a ship, but we do not know how to power it or how long it would take to travel to another sun. Belphig would believe none of this. He felt that if he tortured me and my people long enough we would eventually reveal everything to him. He is insane.'

'Aye,' I said, 'and his insanity has caused much grief on this already grieving planet.'

She moaned. 'My eyes – I cannot see…'

I hauled her out of the seat and climbed in myself, grasping the crystal rod and keeping the craft on course.

'So you conjured up the Black Sword,' I said. 'And the chalice of gold. And did you send those dreams to plague me?'

'I – I sent no – dreams…'

'I thought not. I do not believe you understand everything you have been doing, my lady. You used the legend and you used me. But I believe that the Black Sword – or whatever power controls it – has used us both. Do you know of Tanelorn?'

'I know where it is said to be.'

'Where is that?'

'At the centre of what we call the "multiverse" – the infinite matrices – universe upon universe, each divided from the other. But there is a centre, it is said – a hub about which these universes revolve. The hub is a planet, some think, and that planet is mirrored in many of the other worlds. This Earth is one version. The Earth you came from is another – and so on. And Tanelorn is mirrored elsewhere – but with one difference, it does not change. It does not decay as the other worlds decay. Tanelorn, like you, Sir Hero, is eternal.'

'And how may I find Tanelorn and the powers who rule there?'

'I know not. You must seek that information elsewhere.'

'I may never find it.'

The conversation had exhausted her and I, too, was seriously feeling the effects of the poison radiation. I was bitterly disappointed for, though I had discovered something more, I still had not all the information I had hoped for.

'Tell me what the chalice is,' I said weakly. But she had fainted. Unless we reached the Scarlet Fjord soon, there would be little point in seeking more information.

Then, at last, I saw the mountains ahead and I pulled back the lever to increase the aircraft's height for I intended to fly all the way to the Scarlet Fjord and that was still a good distance away on the other side of the range.

We passed into a bank of thick, brown cloud and I felt salty moisture on my face. I could see only a short distance ahead and I prayed I had taken the vessel up high enough to avoid the highest crags. If not, then we should crash and be killed instantly.

I fought to keep my vision clear and rid my head of dizziness, my body of its ache. If I lost control of the craft we were bound to go into the side of a mountain.

Then came a break in the cloud.

I saw the dark, brooding sea below me.

We had overshot the fjord.

Quickly I turned the craft and decreased height.

Within moments I saw the bishop's great fleet below.

I fought against the nausea and the dizziness engulfing me. I circled down and saw that Belphig stood on the top deck of the largest ship. He was talking to two tall Silver Warriors but looked up in astonishment when he saw my craft.

'Urlik!' he screamed. Then he laughed. 'Do you think you can save your friends with that little flying boat? A third of them are dead of starvation already. The rest are too weak to resist us. We are just about to sail into the fjord. Bladrak was the last to resist. Now the world is mine.'

I turned and tried to revive the Silver Queen. She moaned and stirred but I could not arouse her. I lifted her upright as best I could in my own weakened condition and I showed her to Belphig.

Then the air-chariot began to lose height as I could control it no longer.

In a moment, I knew, I would be swallowed by that salt-thick sea.

But now a new sound came to my ears and I forced my head around to see Bladrak's boats emerging from the gap between the cliffs.

Despairing of my help, Bladrak had decided to die fighting.

I tried to call out, to tell him there was no need, but the boat had hit the water and was skidding over the surface towards the looming shape of one of the ships of Belphig's fleet.

I managed to turn the craft a little, but we smashed into a paddle with a mighty crash, the air-chariot overturned and the Silver Queen and myself were plunged into the thick water.

There were other sounds of confusion. I heard a shout and saw something drop from the side of the ship. Then the water entered my mouth and I knew I was drowning.

A moment later something seized me and dragged me from the ocean. I gasped. I was in the hands of one of the Silver Warriors. But he was smiling at me – he was virtually grinning. He pointed. Nearby the Silver Queen was reviving. He knew I had rescued her.

We were on a raft that must have been flung overboard the moment we were struck. And now they were hauling the raft up the side of the ship. From high above a querulous voice was screaming.

We had crashed into Belphig's flagship.

I let the Silver Warriors help me to my feet when we reached the deck.

I looked up.

Belphig looked down.

He knew he was beaten, that the men from Moon would no longer follow him.

And he laughed.

I found myself laughing back.

I drew my Black Sword, still laughing. He drew his own sword and chuckled. I ducked my head and entered the door and began to climb the staircase that wound through the levels of the deck until I emerged on the top one and faced him.

He knew he was going to die. The thought had turned him quite mad.

I could not kill him then. I had killed too much. He was harmless now. I would spare him.

But the Black Sword thought otherwise. As I made to sheathe the blade it turned in my hand, flung my arm back.

Belphig screamed and raised his sword to defend himself from the imminent blow. I tried to stop the Black Sword from falling.

But fall it did.

It was inevitable.

It sheared through Belphig's sword, then it paused as the bishop wept and stared at it. Then, my hands still round its hilt, it drew itself back and plunged itself deep into his fat, painted body.

Belphig shivered and his carmined lips fluttered. A strange intelligence entered his eyes. He screwed up his decorated eyes and tears fell down his rouged cheeks.

I think he died then. I hoped that he had.

Aboard the big ships the Silver Warriors were handing out food to the men who had sailed from the Scarlet Fjord expecting to be killed.

From below the Silver Queen called to me and I saw that she had Bladrak aboard. He was thin, but he still had his swagger as he hailed me.

'You have saved us all, Sir Champion.'

I smiled bitterly. 'All but myself,' I said. I climbed back down the staircase until I stood on the lowest deck. The Silver Queen was talking with her men whose faces were full of joy now that she was safe.

She turned to me. 'You have earned the undying loyalty of my people,' she said.

I was unimpressed. I was weary. And, oh, how I needed my Ermizhad.

I had thought that if I followed my fate, if I took up the Black Sword, then at least I would have a chance of being reunited with her.

But it seemed this was not to be.

And still I did not understand all of the prophecy concerning the Black Sword.

The Blade of the Sword has the Blood of the Sun...

★

Bladrak clapped me on the back. 'We are going to feast, Count Urlik. We are going to celebrate. The Silver Warriors and their lovely queen are to be our guests in the Scarlet Fjord!'

I looked hard at the Silver Queen. 'What has the chalice to do with me?' I said firmly, not replying to Bladrak.

'I am not sure...'

'You must tell me what you do know,' I said, 'or I will kill you with the Black Sword. You have unleashed forces you do not understand. You have tampered with destinies. You have brought great grief upon me, O Queen in Silver. And still, I think, you do not understand. You sought to save a few lives on a dying planet by scheming to call the Eternal Champion. It suited those forces of destiny which control me to help you in your scheme. But I do not thank you for it – not with this hellsword hanging from me – this thing I thought myself rid of!'

She stepped back, the smile fading, and Bladrak looked grim.

'You have used me,' I said, 'and now you celebrate. But what of me? What have I to celebrate? Where am I to go now?'

And then I stopped, angered at my own self-pity. I turned away, for I was weeping.

The Scarlet Fjord rang with merriment. Women danced along the quays, men roared out songs. Even the Silver Warriors seemed lusty in comparison with their former demeanour.

But I stood on the deck of the great sea-chariot and I talked with the Silver Queen.

We were alone. Bladrak and the rest were joining in the merrymaking.

'What is the golden chalice?' I said. 'What do you mean by using it to such a petty end?'

'I do not think the end petty.'

'How did you gain the power to use the chalice?'

'There were dreams,' she said, 'and voices in the dreams. Much of what I did was in a trance.'

I looked at her with sympathy then. I had known the kind of dreams she described.

'You were told to call the chalice as you were told to call the Black Sword?'

'Aye.'

'And you do not know what the chalice is or why it makes that sound?'

'The legend said that the chalice is meant to hold the blood of the sun. When that blood is poured into it, the chalice will take it to the sun and the sun will come to life again.'

'Superstition,' I said. 'A folktale.'

'Possibly.' She was subdued. I had shamed her. Now I felt sorry for my outburst.

'Why does the chalice scream?'

'It calls for the blood,' she murmured.

'And where is that blood?' Suddenly I looked down at my sword and grasped the hilt. 'The Blade of the Sword has the Blood of the Sun!' I frowned. 'Can you summon the chalice again?'

'Aye – but not here.'

'Where?'

'Out there,' she said, pointing beyond the mountains.

'On the ice. Will you come with me to the ice – now?'

'I owe you that,' she said.

Chapter Four

The Knife and the Cup

THE SILVER QUEEN and the Eternal Champion were two weeks departed from the Scarlet Fjord. They had gone in a boat which had taken them to deserted Rowernarc. They had sought the chariot in which the Eternal Champion had come to Rowernarc. They found it. They fed the beasts that pulled the chariot and then they climbed into it and were borne through the mountains, out to the plains of the South Ice.

Now the Silver Queen and the Eternal Champion stood surrounded on all sides by ice and a wind came up. It blew our cloaks about our bodies as we stared up at the small red sun.

'You affected many destinies when you chose to summon me,' I said.

She shivered. 'I know,' she said.

'And now we must fulfil the whole prophecy,' I said. 'The whole of it.'

'If that will free you, Champion.'

'It might bring me an inch nearer to that which I desire,' I told her. 'No more. We deal in cosmic matters, Silver Queen.'

'Are we only pawns, Sir Champion? Can we control nothing of that destiny?'

'Precious little, Queen.'

She sighed and spread her arms, turning her face to the brooding sky. 'I summon the Screaming Chalice!' she cried.

I unsheathed the Black Sword and I stood with it point first in the ice, my two hands gripping the two halves of the crosspiece.

The Black Sword began to tremble and it began to sing.

'I summon the Screaming Chalice!' the Queen of Moon cried again.

The Black Sword shuddered in my grasp.

Now tears fell down the Silver Queen's silver cheeks and she fell to her knees on the ice.

The wind blew stronger. It came from nowhere. It was not a natural wind.

For the third time she called: 'I summon the Screaming Chalice!'

I raised the Black Sword – or it dragged my hands behind it – and almost tenderly I plunged the blade into her back as she lay spreadeagled on the ice. I had slain her in this manner so that I should not see her face.

Her body writhed. She groaned and then she screamed and her voice blended with the moan of the wind, with the howling of the sword, with my cries of anguish and then, at last, with the shrill whine that grew so that it drowned all other sound.

And the Screaming Chalice stood upon the ice, blinding me with its radiance. I flung one hand over my eyes and felt the Black Sword leave my grasp.

When I looked again I saw that the huge sword was hovering over the chalice.

And from it poured blood.

Blood ran down the black blade and flooded into the chalice, and when the chalice was full the Black Sword fell to the ice.

And it seemed to me then – although I could not swear this happened – that a huge hand reached down from the faded sky and picked up the chalice and drew it higher and higher into the air until it vanished.

And then I saw a crimson aura spring around the sun. It flickered and was hardly visible at first, but then it grew brighter and the twilight turned into late afternoon and I knew that soon it would be morning again.

Do not ask me how this came to pass – how Time itself was turned back. I have been many heroes on many worlds, but I do not believe I have ever witnessed another event as strange and terrifying as that which took place on the South Ice after the Black Sword slew the Silver Queen.

The prophecy was complete. It had been my fate to bring death to this dying world – and now life.

I thought of the Black Sword differently then. It had done much that was evil in my eyes, but perhaps the evil had been to accomplish a greater good.

I walked to where it had fallen. I stooped to pick it up.

But the sword had gone. Only its shadow was left on the ice.

I removed the scabbard from my belt and put it near that shadow. I walked back to where I had left my chariot and I climbed into it.

I looked at the corpse of the Silver Queen, stretched where I had slain her. To save her people she had conjured up cosmic forces of indescribable power. And those forces had brought about her death.

'Would that they had brought about mine,' I murmured as the chariot's wheels began to move forward on its skis.

I did not expect to be much longer on the South Ice. Soon, I knew, I would be called again. And when I was called I would try once more to find my way back to Ermizhad, my Eldren princess. I would look for Tanelorn – eternal Tanelorn – and one day, perhaps, I would know peace again.

The Dragon in the Sword

For Minerva, the noblest Roman

Rose of all Roses, Rose of all the World!
You, too, have come where the dim tides are hurled
Upon the wharves of sorrow, and heard ring
The bell that calls us on; the sweet far thing.
Beauty grown sad with its eternity
Made you of us, and of the dim grey sea.
Our long ships loose thought-woven sails and wait,
For God has bid them share an equal fate;
And when at last defeated in His wars,
They have gone down under the same white stars,
He shall no longer hear the little cry
Of our sad hearts, that may not live nor die.

– W.B. Yeats,
'The Rose of War'

Prologue

I AM JOHN Daker, the victim of the whole world's dreams. I am Erekosë, Champion of Humanity, who slew the human race. I am Urlik Skarsol, Lord of the Frozen Keep, who bore the Black Sword. I am Ilian of Garathorm, Elric Womanslayer, Hawkmoon, Corum and so many others – man, woman or androgyne. I have been them all. And all are warriors in the perpetual War of the Balance, seeking to maintain justice in a universe always threatened by encroaching Chaos, to impose Time upon an existence without beginning or end. Yet even this is not my true doom.

My true doom is to remember, however dimly, each separate incarnation, every moment of an infinity of lives, a multiplicity of ages and worlds, concurrent and sequential.

Time is at once an agony of the Present, a long torment of the Past and the terrible prospect of countless Futures. Time is also a complex of subtly intersecting realities, of unguessable consequences and undiscoverable causes, of profound tensions and dependencies.

I still do not truly know why I was chosen for this fate or how I came to close the circle which, if it did not release me, at least promised to limit my pain.

All I do know is that it is my fate to fight for ever and to possess peace but briefly, for I am the Champion Eternal, at once a defender of justice and its destroyer. In me, all humanity is at war. In me male and female combine, in me they struggle; in me so many races aspire to make reality of their myths and their dreams…

Yet I am no more or less a human creature than any of my fellows. I can be possessed as easily by love as by despair, by fear as by hatred.

I was and am John Daker and I came at last to find a certain peace, the appearance of conclusion. This is my attempt to put down my final story...

I have described how I was called by King Rigenos to fight against the Eldren and how I fell in love and came to commit a terrible sin. I have told what befell me when (I believed as punishment for my crime) I was called to Rowernarc, how I was induced to wield the Black Sword against my will, how I encountered the Silver Queen and what we did together on the South Ice plains. I believe, too, I have set down somewhere other adventures of mine (or they have been set down by others to whom I recounted them); I have told a little of how I came to voyage on a dark ship captained by a blind man. I am not sure, however, if I ever described how I came to leave the world of the South Ice or my identity as Urlik Skarsol, so I shall begin my story with my final recollections of the dying planet whose lands were slowly falling to the conquest of cold and whose sluggish seas were so thick with salt they could virtually sustain the weight of a grown man. Having succeeded in that world at redressing at least to some degree my earlier sins, I had hoped I might now be united again with my one and only love, the beautiful Eldren princess, Ermizhad.

Although a hero to those whom I had helped, I grew more and more lonely. Increasingly, too, I was subject to fits of almost suicidal melancholy. Sometimes I would fall into senseless raging against my fate, against whatever and whoever separated me from the woman whose face and presence filled my hours, waking and sleeping. Ermizhad! Ermizhad! Had anyone ever loved so thoroughly? So constantly?

In my chariot of silver and bronze, drawn by great white bears, I ranged the South Ice, forever restless, full of my memories, praying to be restored to Ermizhad, aching with longing for her. I slept little. From time to time I would return to the Scarlet Fjord, where there were many who were glad to be my friends and auditors, but I found the ordinary business of people's lives almost irritating. Hating to appear churlish, I avoided their hospitality and companionship whenever possible. I would confine myself to my chambers and there, half asleep, perpetually exhausted, I would seek to place my soul in limbo, to depart from my body, to quest through the astral plane (as I thought of it) for my lost love. But there were so many planes of existence – an infinite number of worlds in the multiverse, as I knew already, a vast variety of possible chronologies and geographies. How was it possible to quest through all of these and find my Ermizhad?

I had been told I might discover her in Tanelorn. But where was Tanelorn? I knew from my memories of other existences that the city took many forms and was forever elusive, even to one skilled in moving between the multitudinous layers of the Million Spheres. What chance had I, bound to a single body, a single earthly plane, of finding Tanelorn? If yearning were enough, then certainly I should have discovered the city a dozen times already.

Exhaustion gradually took its toll on me. Some thought I might die of it, others that I might go mad from it. I assured them my will was too strong for that. I agreed, however, to accept their medicines and these at last sent me into deep sleep where, almost to my joy, I began to experience the strangest dreams.

At first I seemed to be adrift in a formless ocean of colour and light which swirled in every direction. Gradually I realised that what I witnessed was something of the entire multiverse. To a degree at least I was perceiving every individual layer, every period, at once. Therefore my senses were incapable of selecting any particular detail from this astonishing vision.

Then I became aware that I was falling, very slowly, through all these ages and realms of reality, through whole worlds, cities, groups of men and women, forests, mountains, oceans, until I saw ahead of me a small flat island of green which offered a reassuring appearance of solidity. As my feet touched it I smelled fresh grass, saw little clumps of turf, some wild flowers. Everything looked wonderfully simple, though it existed in that churning chaos of pure colour, of tides of light which constantly changed in intensity. Upon this fragment of reality another figure stood. It was armoured all of a piece, in chequered yellow and black, from crown to heel, and its face was visored so that I could see nothing of the creature within.

I knew him already, however, for we had met before. I knew him as the Knight in Black and Yellow. I greeted him, but he did not answer. I wondered if he had frozen to death within his armour. Between us there fluttered a pale flag, bereft of insignia. It might have been a truce flag save that he and I were not enemies. He was a huge man, taller even than myself. When we had last met we had stood together on a hill and watched the armies of humanity fighting back and forth across the valleys. Now we watched nothing. I wanted him to raise his helm and reveal his face. He would not. I wanted him to speak to me. He would not. I wanted him to reassure me that he was not dead. He offered no such reassurance.

This dream was repeated many times. Night after night I begged him to reveal himself, made the identical demands I had always made and received no response.

Then one night there came at last a change. Before I could begin my ritual of requests the Knight in Black and Yellow spoke to me...

— *I have told you before. I will answer any question you put to me.* It was as if he continued a conversation whose beginning I had forgotten.

— *How can I rejoin Ermizhad?*

— *By taking passage on the Dark Ship.*

— *Where shall I find the Dark Ship?*

— *The ship will come to you.*

— *How long must I wait?*

— *Longer than you wish. You must curb your impatience.*

— *That is an insubstantial answer.*

— *I promise you it is the only one I can offer.*

— *What is your name?*

— *Like you, I am endowed with a great many names. I am the Knight*

in Black and Yellow. I am the Warrior Who Cannot Fight. I am some-
times called The Black Flag.

— *Let me see your face.*

— *No.*

— *Why so?*

— *Ah, now, this is delicate. I think it is because the time has not*
come. If I showed you too much it would affect too many other chronolo-
gies. You must know that Chaos threatens everything in all the realms of
the multiverse. The Balance tilts too heavily in its favour. Law must be
supported. We must be careful to do no further harm. You shall hear my
name soon, I am certain of that. Soon, that is, in terms of your own time
span. In terms of mine ten thousand years could pass...

— *Can you help me return to Ermizhad?*

— *I have already explained that you must wait for the ship.*

— *When shall I have peace of mind?*

— *When all your tasks are done. Or before there are tasks for you to do.*

— *You are cruel, Knight in Black and Yellow, to answer me so vaguely.*

— *I assure you, John Daker, I have no clearer answers. You are not the*
only one to accuse me of cruelty...

He gestured and now I could see a cliff. On it, lined at the very
edge, some on foot, some on mounts (not all by any means ordinary horses), were rank upon rank of fighters in battered armour. I
was close enough, somehow, to observe their faces. They had
blank eyes which had become used to too much agony. They
could not see us, yet it seemed to me they prayed to us – or at least
to the Knight in Black and Yellow.

I cried out to them: *Who are you?*

And they answered me, lifting their heads to chant a frightful
litany. *We are the lost. We are the last. We are the unkind. We are the*
Warriors at the Edge of Time. We are the ravaged, we are the despairing,
we are the betrayed. We are the veterans of a thousand psychic wars.

It was as if I had given them a signal, an opportunity to express
their terrors, their longings and their agony of centuries. They
chanted in a single cold, melancholy voice. I felt that they had
been standing on the cliff's edge for eternity, speaking only when

asked my question. Their chant did not pause but grew steadily louder...

We are the Warriors at the Edge of Time. Where is our joy? Where is our sorrow? Where is our fear? We are the deaf, the dumb, the blind. We are the undying. It is so cold at the Edge of Time. Where are our mothers and our fathers? Where are our children? It is too cold at the Edge of Time! We are the unborn, the unknown, the undying. It is too cold at the Edge of Time! We are tired. We are so tired. We are tired at the Edge of Time...

Their pain was so intense I tried to cover my ears. — *No!* I screamed. — *No! You must not call to me. You must go away!*

And then there was silence. They were gone.

I turned to speak to the Knight in Black and Yellow, but he, too, had vanished. Had he been one of those warriors? Did he lead them, perhaps? Or, I wondered, were they all aspects of a single being – myself?

Not only could I not answer any of these questions, I did not really wish to have the answers.

I am not sure if it was at that point, or at some later time, in another dream, that I found myself standing upon a rocky beach looking out into an ocean shrouded in thick mist.

At first I saw nothing in the mist, then gradually I perceived a dark outline, a ship heaving at anchor close to the shore.

I knew this was the Dark Ship.

Aboard this ship, dotted here and there, orange light glowed. It was a warm, reassuring light. Also I thought I heard deep voices calling from the deck to the yards and back again. I believe I hailed the ship and that she responded, for soon – perhaps brought there in a longboat – I was standing on her main deck, confronting a tall, gaunt man in a soft leather sea-coat which reached below his knees. He touched my shoulder as if in greeting.

My other recollection is that the ship was carved, every inch of her, with peculiar designs, many geometrical, many representing bizarre creatures, entire stories or incidents from all manner of unguessable histories.

— *You'll sail with us again*, the Captain said.

— *Again*, I agreed, though I could not recall, just then, when I had sailed with him before.

Thereafter I left the ship several times, in several different guises, and pursued all manner of adventures. One came to memory sharper than the others and I even remembered my name. It was Clen of Clen Gar. I remembered some kind of war between Heaven and Hell. I remembered deceit and treachery and some kind of victory. Then I was aboard the ship again.

— *Ermizhad! Tanelorn! Do we sail there?*

The Captain put the tips of his long fingers to my face and touched my tears. — *Not yet.*

— *Then I'll spend no more time aboard this vessel...* I grew angry. I warned the Captain he could not hold me prisoner. I would not be bound to his ship. I would determine my own destiny in my own way.

He did not resist my leaving, though he seemed sad to see me depart.

And I was awake again, in my bed, in my chambers at the Scarlet Fjord. I had a fever, I believe. I was surrounded by servants who had come at my shouting. Through them pushed handsome, red-headed Bladrak Morningspear, who had once saved my life. He was concerned. I remember screaming at him to help me, to take his knife and release me from my body.

— *Kill me, Bladrak, if you value our comradeship!*

But he would not. Long nights came and went. In some of them I thought I was upon the ship again. At other times I felt I was being called. Ermizhad? Was it she who called? I sensed a woman present...

But when I next set eyes upon a fresh visitation it was a sharp-faced dwarf I saw. He was dancing and capering, apparently oblivious of me, humming to himself. I thought I recognised him, but could not remember his name. — *Who are you? Are you sent by the blind captain? Or do you come from the Knight in Black and Yellow?*

I seemed to have surprised the dwarf who turned sardonic features on me for the first time, pushed back his cap and grinned. — *Who am I? I had not meant to have you at a disadvantage. We were old friends, you and I, John Daker.*

— *You know me by that old name? As John Daker?*

— *I know you by all your names. But you shall be only two of those names more than once. Is that a riddle?*

— *It is. Must I now find the answer?*

— *If you feel you need one. You ask many questions, John Daker.*

— *I would prefer it if you called me Erekosë.*

— *You'll have your wish again. Now, there's a straight answer for you, after all! I'm not such a bad dwarf, am I?*

— *I remember! You're called Jermays the Crooked. You are like me – the incarnation of many aspects of the same creature. We met at the sea-stag's cave.*

I recalled our conversation. Had he been the first to tell me of the Black Sword?

— *We were old friends, Sir Champion, but you failed to remember me then, just as you fail to remember me now. Perhaps you have too much to remember, eh? You have not offended me. I note you appear to have lost your sword...*

— *I shall never bear it again. It was a terrible blade. I have no further use for it. Or for any sword like it. I recall you said there were two of them...*

— *I said that there were sometimes two. That perhaps it was an illusion; that there was in fact only one. I am not sure. You bore the one you shall call (or have called) Stormbringer. Now, I suppose, you seek Mournblade.*

— *You spoke of some destiny attached to the blades. You suggested my destiny was linked with theirs...*

— *Ah, did I now? Well, your memory's improving. Good, good. It will be of some help to you I am sure. Or perhaps not. Do you already know that each of these swords is a vessel for something else? They were forged, I understand, to be filled, to be inhabited. To possess, if you like, a soul. You're baffled, I can see. Unfortunately I'm fairly mystified myself. I get* intimations, of course. Intimations of our various fates. And those are frequently mixed up. I'll confuse you and very likely myself also if I continue in this vein! I can already see you are unwell. Is it merely a touch of physical sickness or does it extend to your brain?

— Can you help me find Ermizhad, Jermays? Can you tell me where lies Tanelorn? That is all I wish to know. The rest of it I do not care for at all. I want no more talk of destiny, of swords, of ships and strange countries. Where is Tanelorn?

— The ship sails there, does it not? I understand that Tanelorn is her final destination. There are so many cities called Tanelorn and the ship carries a cargo of so many identities. Yet all are the same or some aspect of the same personality. Too much for me, Sir Champion. You must go back aboard.

— I do not wish to return to the Dark Ship.

— You disembarked too soon.

— I did not know where the ship was bearing me. I was afraid I would lose direction and never discover Ermizhad again.

— So that was why you left! Did you think you had found your goal? That there was any other way of finding it?

— Did I disembark against the Captain's will? Am I being punished for that?

— It's unlikely. The Captain's no great punisher. He is not an arbiter. Rather he is a translator, I would say. But all that's for you to ascertain for yourself once you return to the ship.

— I do not want to be aboard that Dark Ship again.

I wiped a mixture of tears and perspiration from my eyes and it was as if I had wiped Jermays from my vision, for he had gone.

I rose and clad myself, yelling for my old armour. I made them put it on me, though I could scarcely hold myself steady on my feet. Then I ordered a great sea-sled harnessed with the mighty herons trained to pull it across those salty, undulating plains, those dying oceans. I snarled at those who would follow me. I ordered them to go back to the Scarlet Fjord. I refused their friendship. I sped from the sight of all humankind, into the brine-heavy night, my head lifted back as I howled like a dog and I cried for my

Ermizhad. There was no response. I had hardly expected any. So I called instead to the Captain of the Dark Ship. I called to every god and goddess I could name. And lastly I called to myself – to John Daker, Erekosë, Urlik, Clen, Elric, Hawkmoon, Corum and all the others. I called lastly to the Black Sword itself, but I was received by a most terrible, unkind silence.

I looked into the faded light of dawn and thought I saw a great cliff lined with gaunt warriors. It was those same warriors who had stood upon the edge of that cliff for an eternity, each one with my face. But I had seen nothing but clouds, thick as the ocean on which I sailed.

— *Ermizhad! Where are you? Who or what will take me to you?*

I heard a sly, unpleasant wind whispering near the horizon. I heard the flap of my herons' wings. I heard my sea-sled thump upon the surface of the waves. And I heard my own voice saying that there was only one thing I could do, since no power would come to my aid. It was, of course, the reason I had come out here alone. Why I had clad myself in the full battle armour of Urlik Skarsol, Lord of the Frozen Keep. — *You must throw yourself in to the sea*, I said. — *You must let yourself sink. You must drown. In dying, you will surely find a fresh incarnation. Perhaps you will even be taken back to Erekosë and be reunited with your Ermizhad. After all, it will be an act of faith even the gods cannot ignore. Perhaps it is what they are waiting for? To see how brave you are prepared to be. And to see how truly you love her.* And with that I let go the reins of those massive birds and prepared to dive into the horrible and viscous ocean.

But now the Knight in Black and Yellow stood upon the platform beside me and he had put a steel glove upon my shoulder. And in his other hand he bore the Blank Standard. And this time he lifted his visor so that I might see his face.

That face was a memory of greatness. It displayed enormous and ancient wisdom. It was a face which had seen far more than I would wish to see in all my incarnations. The bone structure was ascetic and fine, the huge eyes penetrating and authoritative. His flesh was the colour of polished jet and his voice was deep, full of the power of approaching thunder.

— *It would not be bravery, Champion. It would be at best folly. You think you seek for something, but yours would be an act of someone merely wishing to escape torment. There are aspects of the Champion far less tolerable than your present one. And, besides, I can tell you that this particular ordeal will not last for very much longer. I would have come to you sooner, but I had business elsewhere.*

— *With whom?*

— *Oh, with you, of course. But that is a tale being told in some other world and perhaps in your future, for the Million Spheres roll through Time and Space at many differing speeds and where or when they intersect is frequently surprising, even to me. But I can assure you this is a poor time to be doing away with your life – or this body, even. I could not speak for the consequences, though I believe they would not be pleasant. A great and momentous adventure lies ahead of you. If you fulfil your duty as Champion in the most effective way, it could result in your partial release from this doom. It could produce a beginning and an ending of enormous import. Let them call you. Surely you have heard them?*

— *I have distinguished nothing from the voices I have heard. It cannot be those warriors who call…*

— *What they call for is release from their particular doom. No, these are others who call, as you have been called before. Have you heard no name? A name new to you?*

— *I think not.*

— *This means you should return to the Dark Ship. It is all I can think. I am deeply puzzled…*

— *If you are puzzled, Sir Knight, then I am truly confounded! I have no wish to give myself up to that man and his ship. It increases my sense of impotence. Moreover, I remain in the same flesh. In this flesh, surely I cannot find Ermizhad. I must be either Erekosë or John Daker again.*

— *Perhaps your new guise was not ready. The checks and balances involved in this are extremely delicate. But I do know you must somehow return to that ship…*

— *Can you offer me no more than that? Can you offer me hope that if I do board the Dark Ship again I shall find my Ermizhad?*

— *Forgive me, Sir Champion.* The black giant's hand remained on my shoulder. — *I am not entirely omniscient. Who can be when the very structure of Time and Space is in flux?*

— *What are you telling me?*

— *I can tell you no more than I perceive myself. Let the ship take you, that is all I can say. Through this medium, I know, you will be transported to those who most require your help and whose help in turn could gain for you some form of release from your present torment. Also you will be united in such a way to promise further unity. This much I can sense...*

— *But where shall I look for this ship?*

— *If you are willing, the ship will come to you. It will find you, fear not.* Then the Knight in Black and Yellow whistled suddenly and from out of the orange mist there now galloped a great stallion, its hoofs striking the water but not penetrating the surface. This beast the Knight in Black and Yellow mounted. Its coat was as black as his skin and I marvelled at how it could stand on those waves without sinking an inch. Indeed, I was so astonished by this apparition that I forgot to ask the rider any further questions. I could only stand and watch as he raised the Blank Standard by way of salute to me then turned the battlehorse towards the clouds and rode rapidly away.

I remained mystified, yet the Knight in Black and Yellow had brought me a form of hope and had stopped me from continuing in my madness. I would not kill myself, after all, though I did not relish a further passage aboard the Dark Ship, either. Instead, I thought, I would lie down upon my sea-sled while the herons bore me wherever they chose (perhaps back to the Scarlet Fjord, for they must soon reach the limit of their endurance, or perhaps they would come to perch upon the sled with me before continuing their journey out across the ocean. Sooner or later, I knew, they would turn homeward). I had wanted to ask the Knight's name. Sometimes names brought with them reawakened memories, intimations of my future, incidents from my past.

I slept and as I slept the dreams returned. I heard distant voices and I knew it was the warriors who chanted; the Warriors of the Edge. — *Who are you?* I begged. I was growing tired of my own questions. There were too many mysteries. But then the chanting of the warriors began to change in tone until at last I heard a single name: *SHARADIM! SHARADIM!*

The word was meaningless to me. It was not my name, I knew. It had never been my name. Nor would it ever be my name. Was I the victim of some dreadful cosmic error?

— *SHARADIM! SHARADIM! THE DRAGON IS IN THE SWORD! SHARADIM! SHARADIM! COME TO US, WE BEG! SHARADIM! SHARADIM! THE DRAGON MUST BE RELEASED!*

— *But I am not Sharadim.* I spoke aloud. — *I cannot help you.*

— *PRINCESS SHARADIM, YOU MUST NOT REFUSE US!*

— *I am neither a princess nor your Sharadim. I wait to be called, it is true. But it is another you need...*

Could there be another poor soul, I wondered, who was doomed as I was doomed? Were there many such as I?

— *A DRAGON FREED IS A RACE RELEASED! LET US REMAIN IN EXILE NO LONGER, SHARADIM! LISTEN, THE FIREDRAKE ROARS WITHIN THE BLADE. SHE, TOO, WOULD BE REUNITED WITH HER KING. SET US ALL FREE, SHARADIM! SET US ALL FREE! ONLY THOSE OF YOUR BLOOD MAY TAKE THE SWORD AND DO WHAT MUST BE DONE!*

This had a familiar ring to me, yet I knew in my bones I was not Sharadim. As John Daker would have thought, I was like a radio tuner receiving messages on the wrong band. And this was all the more ironic since I currently longed to be drawn from my body and into another, preferably into the body of Erekosë, reunited with his Ermizhad.

Yet I could not dismiss them. The chanting grew louder and now I even thought I could see shadowy figures – female figures – forming a circle around me. But I was still on the sled. I could feel its uneven surface beneath my hands as I slept. Nonetheless the circle continued to move slowly around me, first clockwise, then anticlockwise. And this was an outer circle. The inner circle surrounding me was made of pale flame which almost blinded me.

— *I cannot come! I am not the one you seek! You must look elsewhere! I am needed in another place...*

— SET THE FIREDRAKE FREE! SET THE FIREDRAKE FREE! SHARADIM! SHARADIM! SET HER FREE, SHARADIM!

— *No! It is I whom you must free! Please believe me, whoever you are, that I am not whom you seek! Let me go! Let me go!*

— SHARADIM! SHARADIM! SET THE FIREDRAKE FREE!

Their voices seemed almost as desperate as my own. But however much I called to them they could not hear me above their own chanting. I felt kinship with them. I would have spoken to them and tried to give them the little information I possessed, but my voice continued to be unheard.

For all this, I seemed to recall an earlier conversation. Had I once been told about a dragon in a sword? Was it a conversation with the Knight in Black and Yellow? Or with Jermays the Crooked? Or had the Captain told me that I had been elected to seek such a blade and was that why I decided to leave his ship? I could not remember. All those dreams ran together, just as most of my earlier incarnations were frequently indistinguishable one from the other, rising unbidden to my mind, as débris will rise suddenly to the surface of a lake and sink again as mysteriously.

Now a voice cried ELRIC! Now ASQUIOL! Another group chanted for Corum. Still others wanted Hawkmoon, Rashono, Malan'ni. I screamed for them to stop. None called for Erekosë. None called for me! Yet I knew I was all of these. All of these and many, many more.

But I was not Sharadim.

I began to run from those voices. I begged for release. All I wanted was Ermizhad. My feet sank a little into the saline crust of the ocean. I thought I would drown, after all, for I had left the sled. I was wading through water up to my thighs, holding my sword above my head. And before me, dark against the mist, was a tall ship with high castles fore and aft, with a good, thick central mast on which was furled a heavy sail, with woodwork all minutely carved and a massive, curving prow, with large wheels on both high decks, for steering. And I cried out:

— *Captain! Captain! It is I! It is Erekosë returned! I am here to complete my task. I will do what you wish me to do!*

— *Aha, Sir Champion. I had hoped to find you here. Come aboard, come aboard and be welcome. There are no other passengers, as yet. There's much for you to do, however...*

And I knew the Captain addressed me and that I had left the world of Rowernarc, the South Ice and the Scarlet Fjord, left them behind for ever. It would be assumed I had ridden out over the ocean and encountered a sea-stag or had drowned. I regretted only the character of my parting from Bladrak Morningspear, who had been a good comrade.

— *Will my voyage be a long one, Captain?* I climbed the ladder which had been lowered for me and I realised that I was clad only in a simple kilt of soft leather, in sandals and with a wide baldrick across my chest. I looked into the eyes of the smiling captain who reached out a muscular hand and helped me to clamber over the side. He was dressed in the same simple clothes as before, including his long calfskin sea-coat.

— *Nay, Sir Champion. I think you'll find this particular part of it short enough. There is some business between Law and Chaos and the ambitions of the Archduke Balarizaaf, whoever he may be!*

— *You do not know our destination?* I followed him to his own small cabin under the quarter-deck where a meal had been laid out on his table for just the two of us. It smelled excellent. He gestured to me to sit across from him.

He said: — *I think it could be to the Maaschanheem. Do you know that realm?*

— *I do not.*

— *Then you'll soon be familiar with it. But perhaps I should not speak. I can sometimes be an erratic compass. Still, destination's the least of our problems. Eat, for you'll soon be disembarking again. The food will sustain you in your task.*

He joined me at the meal. The food was wholesome and filling, but it was the wine which did me most good. Fiery stuff, it instilled in me purpose and energy. — *Perhaps you can tell me something of this Maaschanheem, Captain?*

— *It is a world not far removed from the one you knew as John Daker. Far closer, in fact, than any you've journeyed to so far. The people of Daker's world who understand such things say it is one of the realms of their Middle Marches, for frequently their world intersects with it, though only certain adepts can pass from one place to the other. Yet that Earth is not truly part of the system to which Maaschanheem belongs. There are six realms within that system and they are called by those who inhabit them the Realms of the Wheel.*

— *Six planets?*

— *No, Sir Champion. Six realms. Six cosmic planes which move around a central hub, revolving independently and swinging upon an axis, presenting different facets to each other at different points in their movement while, at the same time, each also goes around a more familiar sun, such as the sun you are used to seeing in your own sky. John Daker's sky. For the Million Spheres are all aspects of one planet, which Daker called Earth, just as you are a single aspect of an infinity of heroes. Some call this the multiverse, as you know already. Spheres within spheres, surface sliding into surface, realm into realm, sometimes meeting and forming gateways one between the other. And sometimes they never meet. Then, of course, it is difficult to cross, unless you sail between the realms in a ship like ours.*

— *You paint a gloomy picture, Sir Captain, for one like me who seeks an object in all this multiplicity of existences.*

— *You should be joyful, Champion. Were it not for all this variety you could not live at all. If there were only one aspect of your Earth, one aspect of yourself, one aspect of Law and another of Chaos, it would have vanished almost as soon as it was created. The Million Spheres offer infinite variety and possibility.*

— *Which Law would curtail?*

— *Aye, or Chaos leave utterly unchecked. That is why you fight for the Cosmic Balance. To maintain a true equilibrium between the two so that humanity might flourish and explore all its potential. You have a great responsibility, Sir Champion, in whatever guise you take.*

— *And the guise I take next? Can it be that of a woman? Of a certain Princess Sharadim?*

The Captain shook his head. — *I do not think so. You'll discover your name soon enough. And if you are successful in this adventure you must promise to return to me when I come for you. Will you promise?*

— *Why should I?*

— *Because it is likely to be to your advantage, believe me.*

— *And if I do not return to you?*

— *I cannot say.*

— *Then I shall not promise. I am of a mind to demand more specific answers to my questions at present, Sir Captain. All I can tell you is that it is very likely I shall seek out your ship again.*

— *Seek us out? You have a better chance of finding Tanelorn unaided.* The Captain seemed amused. — *We are not sought. We find.* He then became honestly concerned, shaking his head from side to side. He brought the conversation to a polite but abrupt end. — *It is late now. You must sleep and restore yourself further.*

He led me to one of the large cabins at the aft of the ship. The place was fitted to take many more men than I, but I was alone in it. I picked myself a bunk, washed myself in the water provided and lay down to sleep. I reflected ironically that I could be sleeping within a dream, within a dream, within another dream. How many layers of reality did I currently perceive, let alone those of which the Captain had spoken?

Again as I drifted into slumber I heard that same chanting, those same women, and I tried again to tell them they attempted to summon the wrong person. I knew this now for certain. I had had it confirmed by the Captain himself.

— *I am not your Princess Sharadim!*

— *SHARADIM! RELEASE THE DRAGON! SHARADIM! TAKE UP THE BLADE! SHARADIM, SHE SLEEPS IMPRISONED, WITHIN THE STEEL THAT CHAOS MADE! SHARADIM,*

COME TO US AT THE MASSING! PRINCESS SHARADIM, ONLY YOU CAN HOLD THE SWORD. COME TO US, PRINCESS SHARADIM! WE SHALL WAIT FOR YOU THERE!

— *I am not Sharadim!*

But the voices were fading, their chant to be replaced by another.

— *We are the tired, we are the sad, we are the unseeing. We are the Warriors at the Edge of Time. We are tired, so tired. We're tired of making love...* Fleetingly I saw again the warriors who waited at the Edge. I tried to speak to them, but they had already faded. I was yelling. I was awake and the Captain stood over me.

— *John Daker, it is time for you to leave us again.*

Outside it was as dark and as misty as always. Overhead the sail was swollen like the belly of a starving child. Then, all of a sudden, it grew empty and flapped against the mast. There was a sense that the ship rode again at anchor.

The Captain pointed to the rail and I followed his blind gaze, looking down to where another man was standing – a man who was identical to the Captain, save that he could see. He signed for me to clamber down the ladder and join him in the boat. Now I wore no kilt and bore no sword. I was stark naked. — *Let me find some clothes. A weapon.*

At my side the Captain shook his head. — *All that you need will be waiting for you, John Daker. A body, a name, a weapon... Remember one thing. It will go best for you if you return to us when we come for you.*

— *I would rather pretend, at least for now, to have some mastery over my own fate*, I told him.

And as I climbed down the ladder and entered the longboat I thought I heard the Captain's gentle laughter. It did not mock me. It was not sardonic. But nonetheless it was a comment on my final statement.

The longboat took me out of mist and into a cold dawn. Grey light illuminated streaks of grey cloud. Large white birds flapped over what looked to be a vast fenland, glittering with grey water, with grey tufts of reeds. And standing nearby, on a hummock of land, I saw a figure. It was like a statue, it was so still and stiff. Yet in my heart I knew it was made neither of iron nor of stone. The figure, I knew, was made of flesh. I could guess something of its features…

I could already see that it was clothed in dark, tight-fitting leather, with a heavy leather cape pushed back from its shoulders, a sturdy conical cap upon its head. There was a long-hafted pike in its hand on which it seemed to lean and it bore other weapons whose details were harder to determine.

Yet even as our longboat approached this rigid figure I saw another in the distance. This was a man who seemed inappropriately dressed for the world he traversed. He was weary and had the air of one pursued. He wore what seemed to be the remains of a twentieth-century suit of clothes. He was weather-beaten, with pale blue eyes staring from features affected by something more than just the wind and the sun. He was probably not more than thirty-five years old. His head was bare, revealing light blond hair and he seemed tall and sturdily built, though somewhat thin. By the look of him he was close to collapse as he waved at the statue and shouted something I could not hear. By what was evidently an effort of will he continued to plod and to stumble across the chilly marshland waste.

The Captain's twin gestured for me to get out of the longboat. I was a little reluctant. As I put one naked foot onto the yielding peat he said:

— *John Daker, let me wish you something other than luck. Let me wish instead that, when the time comes, you will be able to call upon your resources of courage and sanity when you most need them! Farewell! I trust you will wish to sail with us again…*

Not one whit improved in spirit by this, I stepped with greater alacrity from the longboat. — *For my part, I hope never to see you or your ship again…*

But the boat, the oarsman and the frozen figure had all vanished. I turned a stiff neck to look for them, aware that I felt suddenly warmer. I realised immediately why the figure had disappeared, at least. It was because I now inhabited and animated him. Yet still I did not know my name or what my purpose was in this new realm.

The other man was still wading towards me, still shouting for my attention. I raised my heavy pike in greeting.

I felt the sharp pang of fear. I had a premonition that in this fresh incarnation I stood to lose everything I had ever possessed; everything I had ever desired...

Book One

He slept aloft on a sarsen stone
Dreaming to, dreaming fro,
And the more he dreamt was the more alone
And the future seemed behind him;

But waking stiff and scrambling down
At the first light, the cramped light,
The wood below him seemed to frown
And the past deployed before him;

For his long-lost dragon lurked ahead,
Not to be dodged and never napping,
And he knew in his bones he was all but dead,
Yet that death was half the story.

– Louis MacNeice,
'The Burnt Bridge'

Chapter One

THE MAN CALLED himself Ulric von Bek and he had come out of a camp in Germany called Sachsenburg. His crime had been that he was a Christian and had spoken against the Nazis. He had been released (thanks to well-meaning friends) in 1937. In 1939, when his attempt to kill Adolf Hitler had failed, he had escaped the Gestapo by entering the realm we now both occupied. I called it Maaschanheem but he called it simply the Middle Marches. He was surprised that I should be so familiar with the world he had left behind him. 'You look more like a warrior from the *Nibelungenlied*!' he said. 'And you speak this oddly archaic German which seems to be the language hereabouts. Yet you say you were from England originally?'

I saw no point in telling him too much of my life as John Daker, nor in mentioning that I had been born into a world where Hitler was defeated. I had long learned that such revelations frequently had disastrous consequences. He was here not merely to escape but also to find a means of destroying the monster who had taken possession of his country's soul. Anything I said might divert him from our destiny. For all I knew, von Bek might have been responsible for defeating Hitler! I explained as much of my own circumstances as I thought politic and even this was enough to leave him open-mouthed.

'The fact remains,' I told him, 'that neither you nor I is any better equipped to deal with this world. At least you have the advantage of knowing your own name!'

'You have no memory at all of Maaschanheem?'

'None. The only thing I seem to have is my usual facility to speak whatever language prevails on whatever plane I find myself. You said you had a map?'

'A family heirloom which I lost in that fight I told you of, with the little armoured boys who tried to drag me off. It was not very specific. It had been drawn up, I would guess, some time in the fifteenth century. It enabled me to reach this place and I had hoped it would enable me to leave when my reasons for being here were over, but now I fear I'm stuck here for good unless I find someone to aid me in leaving.'

'The place is populated, at least. You have already encountered some of the inhabitants. There may be those who can help you.'

We made a peculiar pair. I was dressed in clothing which seemed appropriate for the terrain, with tall boots to my thighs, a kind of long-handled brass hook at my belt (like a heavy salmon gaff), a curved knife with a serrated blade and a pouch containing some edible dried meat, some coins, a block of ink, a writing stick and a few rather grubby pieces of rag paper. It gave me no real clue as to my trade but at least I did not have the misfortune to be dressed in a ragged grey flannel suit, a rather loud fairisle pullover and a collarless shirt. I offered von Bek my cloak but he refused for the moment. He said he had become used to the rather melancholy weather of this place.

We were in a strange sort of world. The grey clouds very occasionally parted and let down some thin sunshine which illuminated shallow waters in every direction. The world seemed to consist of long strips of low-lying land divided by swamps and creeks. Hardly any tall trees grew there. Only a few shrubs offered cover to the oddly coloured waterbirds and bizarre little animals we occasionally sighted. We sat together on a mound of grass staring around us and chewing on the dried meat I had found. Von Bek (he added with some embarrassment that he was a count in Germany) was ravenous and it was obvious he could scarcely contain himself from devouring the food before he had properly chewed it. We agreed that we might as well stick together, since we were both in similar circumstances. He pointed out that his purpose here was to find a means of destroying Hitler and that this would always be paramount with him. I said that I too was determined to accomplish a particular task but that so long as my self-interest was not directly challenged I would be more than happy to count him as an ally.

It was at this point that von Bek's eyes narrowed and he pointed behind me. Turning, I saw in the far distance what looked like a building of some description. I was certain I had not seen it there before, but assumed it had been hidden in mist. It was too far away to make out details. 'Nonetheless,' I said, 'we'd be well advised to head in that direction.'

Count von Bek agreed enthusiastically. 'Nothing ventured, nothing gained,' he said. He had improved physically and mentally, thanks to food and rest, and seemed a cheerful, stoical individual. What we used to call 'the best type of German' when I was at school all those aeons ago.

It was long, slow going through that marshland. We had constantly to stop, to test the ground ahead with my pike or the gaff which von Bek now held, to look for means of crossing from one clump of solid earth to the next, to rescue one another from plunging waist-deep into deceptive patches of water, from falling into the sharp fronds of reeds which were in the main the tallest plants in the region. And sometimes we could see the building ahead of us, sometimes it seemed to vanish. Sometimes too it had the appearance of a good-sized town or a large castle. 'A definitely medieval appearance, I think,' said von Bek. 'Why, I wonder, am I reminded of Nuremberg?'

'Well,' I said, 'let's hope the occupants are not similar to those currently in residence in your world!'

Again he showed a little surprise at my detailed knowledge of his world and I made a private resolution to make as few references as possible to Nazi Germany and the twentieth century which we had in common.

As I helped von Bek through one particularly foul section of the mire he said to me: 'Is it possible we were meant to meet here? That our destinies are somehow linked?'

'Forgive me if I seem dismissive,' I said, 'but I have heard too much of destinies and cosmic plans. I am sick of them. All I want is to find the woman I love and remain with her where we shall be undisturbed!'

He seemed sympathetic to this. 'I must admit all this talk of dooms and destinies has a somewhat Wagnerian ring to it – and reminds me a little too much of the Nazis' debasement of our myths and legends to justify their own ghastly crimes.'

'I've experienced many justifications for acts of the grossest cruelty and savagery,' I agreed. 'And most of them have a high-sounding or sentimental character to them, whether it be one person flogging another as in de Sade or a national leader urging his people on to kill and be killed.'

It seemed to me that the air was growing colder and there was a hint of rain. This time I insisted that von Bek take my cloak and he at last agreed. I leaned my pike upon a hillock, close to a bed of par-ticularly tall reeds, and he placed his fishing gaff on the ground so that he could settle the leather garment better about his shoulders.

'Is the sky darkening?' he wondered, looking up. 'I have diffi-culty telling time here. I've been here for two full nights but have yet to work out how long the days are.'

I had a feeling that twilight was approaching and was about to suggest we have another look in my pouch to see if I possessed any means of making a fire when something struck my shoulder a heavy blow and sent me face forward onto the ground.

I was on one knee and turning, trying to reach my pike which, apart from the short knife, was my only weapon, when about a dozen weirdly armoured warriors rose up out of the reed bed and moved rapidly towards us.

One of them had cast a club and it had been that which had thrown me down. Von Bek was yelling, stooping to reach for his gaff, when a second club caught him on the side of the head.

'Stop!' I cried to the men. 'Why don't you parley? We are not your enemies!'

'That's your delusion, my friend,' one of them growled while the others uttered unpleasant laughs in response.

Von Bek was rolling on his side, clutching his face. It was livid from where the club had hit him.

'Will you kill us without challenging us?' he shouted.

'We'll kill you any way we choose. Marsh vermin are fair game for anyone and you know it.'

Their armour was a mixture of metal and leather plates, painted light green and grey to merge with the landscape. Even their weapons had the same colouring and they had smeared mud on their exposed skin to further disguise themselves. Their appearance was barbaric enough, but worst of all was the noxious smell which came off them – a mixture of human stink, animal ordure and the filth of the swamps. This alone might have been enough to knock a victim off his feet!

I did not know what marsh vermin were, but I knew that we had little chance of surviving the attack as, with raised clubs and swords, they advanced, chuckling, towards us.

I tried to reach my pike but I had been knocked too far away from it. Even as I scrambled across the wet and yielding grass I knew that another club or a sword would find me before I could get to my weapon.

And von Bek was in an even worse position than I was.

All I could think of to do was to shout at him.

'Run, man! Run, von Bek! There's no sense in us both dying!'

It was growing darker by the moment. There was a slight chance that my companion could escape into the night.

As for myself, I threw up my arms instinctively as a mass of weapons was lifted to dispatch me.

Chapter Two

T HE FIRST BLOW landed on my arm and came close to breaking it. I waited for the second and the third. One was bound
to make me unconscious and that was all I could hope for – a
swift and painless death.

Then I heard an unfamiliar sound which, at the same time, I
recognised. A sharp report swiftly followed by two more. My closest assailants had fallen, evidently stone dead. Without pausing to
question my good fortune I seized first one sword and then
another. They were awkward, heavy blades of the sort favoured
by butchers rather than fencers, but they were all I wanted. I now
had a chance at life!

I backed to where I had last seen von Bek and from the corner
of my eye saw him rising from a kneeling position, a smoking
automatic pistol held in both hands.

It had been a long while since I had seen or heard such a
weapon. I felt a certain grim amusement when I realised that
von Bek had not come completely unarmed from his realm to
the Maaschanheem. He had possessed the presence of mind to
bring with him something of considerable use in such a world
as this!

'Give me a blade!' shouted my companion. 'I've no more than
two shots left and I prefer to save those.'

Scarcely glancing at him I tossed him one of my swords and
together we advanced on our enemies who were already badly
demoralised from the unexpected shots. Plainly they had never
experienced pistol-fire before.

The leader snarled and flung another club at me, but I dodged
it. The rest followed suit so that we received a barrage of those
crude weapons which we either avoided or deflected. Then we

were face to face with our attackers, who seemed to have little further stomach for fighting.

I had killed two scarcely before I thought about it. I had had an eternity of such contests and knew that one must kill in them or risk losing one's own life. By the third man, I had recovered my senses enough to knock the sword from his hand. Meanwhile, von Bek, plainly an expert with the sabre, like so many of his class, had dealt with another couple until only four or five of the fellows remained.

At this the leader roared for us to stop.

'I take it back! You're no marsh vermin, after all. We were wrong to attack you without parleying. Hold your swords, gentlemen, and we'll talk. The gods know I'm not one who refuses to admit a mistake.'

Warily, we put up our blades, ready for any likely treachery from him and his men.

They made a great play, however, of sheathing their weapons and of helping their surviving comrades to their feet. The dead they automatically stripped of their purses and remaining weapons. But their leader growled at them to stop. 'We'll unshell 'em when this business is dealt with to everyone's satisfaction. Look, home's close enough now.'

I stared in the direction he had indicated to them and saw to my utter astonishment that the building – or two – von Bek and I had been making for was now considerably nearer. I could see the smoke from its chimneys, the flags on its turrets, lights flickering here and there.

'Now, gentlemen,' says the leader. 'What's to be done? You've killed a good few of ours, so I'd say we're at least even on the score, given that we attacked you but that you have no serious injuries. Also you have two of our swords, which are of fair value. Would you go on your way and no more said on the matter?'

'Is this world so lawless you can attack another human creature at will and not suffer further consequences?' von Bek asked. 'If so, it's no better than the one I've recently departed!'

I saw no great point in continuing this kind of argument. I had learned that men such as these, whatever sort of world they lived in, had neither stomach for nor understanding of a fine moral point. It seemed to me that they had characterised us as some kind of outlaw and that, upon finding us to be otherwise, were showing more, if grudging, respect. My own idea was that we should take our chances in their town and see what services we could offer its rulers.

The substance of this I whispered to von Bek who seemed reluctant to let the matter go. It was obvious that he was a man of considerable principle (it took such people to stand against the terror instilled by Hitler) and I respected him for it. But I begged him to judge these people later, when we knew a little more about them. 'They are fairly primitive, it seems to me. We should not expect too much of them. Also, they could be our only means of discovering more of this world and, if necessary, escaping it.'

Rather like a grumbling wolfhound which desires only to protect its owners (or in this case an ideal), von Bek desisted. 'But I think we should keep the swords,' he said.

It was growing steadily darker. Our attackers appeared to become more nervous. 'If there's more parleying to be done,' said the leader, 'maybe you'd care to do it as our guests. We'll offer you no more harm tonight, I promise. You have a Boarding Promise on that.'

This seemed to mean a great deal to him and I was prepared to accept his word. Thinking we hesitated he pulled off his grey-green helmet and put this over his heart.

'Do you know, gentlemen,' said he, 'that I be called Mopher Gorb, Binkeeper to Armiad-naam-Sliforg-ig-Vortan.' This giving of names also seemed to have significance.

'Who is this Armiad?' I asked and saw a look of considerable surprise cross his ugly features.

'Why, he's Baron Captain of our home hull, which is called the *Frowning Shield*, accountant to our anchorage, The Clutching Hand. You have heard of these, if not of Armiad. He succeeded Baron Captain Nedau-naam-Sliforg-ig-Vortan...'

With a cry, von Bek held up his hand. 'Enough. All these names give me a headache. I agree that we should accept your hospitality and I thank you for it.'

Mopher Gorb, however, made no move. He waited expectantly for something. Then I realised what I must do. I removed my own conical helmet and placed it over my heart. 'I am John Daker called Erekosë, sometime Champion of King Rigenos, late of the Frozen Keep and the Scarlet Fjord and this is my sword-brother Count Ulric von Bek, late of Bek in the principality of Saxony in the land of the Germans…' I continued a little further in this vein until he seemed satisfied that enough names and titles had been uttered, even if he failed to understand a word of them. Plainly the offering of names and titles was a sign that you meant to keep your word.

By this time von Bek, less versed in these matters and less flexible than myself, was close to laughing, so much so that he refused to meet my eye.

While this had been going on, the 'home hull' had been growing in size. It now became apparent that its monstrous bulk was on the move. It was not so much an ordinary city or castle as a lumbering ship of some kind, unbelievably big (though I suppose a deal smaller than some of our transatlantic liners) and powered by some form of engine which was responsible for the smoke I had mistaken for ordinary signs of domestic life. Yet I might have been forgiven for thinking it a medieval stronghold from a distance. The chimneys seemed to be positioned at random here and there. The turrets, towers, spires and crenellations had the appearance of stone, though more likely were of wood and lath, and what I had thought were flagposts were actually tall masts from which were hung yards, a certain amount of canvas, a wealth of rigging, like the work of a mad spider, and a rich variety of rather dirty banners. The smoke from the funnels was yellowish grey and occasionally bore with it a sudden gouting of hot cinders which presumably did not much threaten the decks below but which surely must cover them with ash from top to bottom. I wondered how the people could bear to live in such filth.

As the massive, bellowing vessel made its slow progress through the shallow waters of the marsh I knew that the smell of our attackers was characteristic of their ship. Even from that distance I could smell a thousand hideous stinks, including the cloying smoke. The furnaces feeding those chimneys must burn every sort of offal and waste, I thought.

Von Bek looked at me and was for refusing Mopher Gorb's hospitality, but I knew it was too late. I wished to find out more of this world, not insult its inhabitants so thoroughly that they would feel honour-bound to hunt us down. He said something to me which I could not hear above the shouting and booming of the ship which now towered above us, framed against the grey twilight clouds.

I shook my head. He shrugged and drew a neatly folded silk handkerchief from a pocket. He placed this fastidiously to his mouth and pretended, as far as I could tell, that he had a cold.

All around the gigantic hull, which was a patchwork of metal and timber, repaired and rebuilt a hundred times over, the muddy waters of the swamp were churning and flying in every direction, covering us with spray, a few clumps of turf and not a little mud. It was almost a relief when a kind of drawbridge was lowered from close to the vessel's bottom, near its great curving back, and Mopher Gorb stepped forward to shout reassurance to someone within.

'They are not marsh vermin. They are honoured guests. I believe they are from another realm and go to the Massing. We have exchanged names. Let us embark in peace!'

Some tiny part of my brain was suddenly alerted. There was one familiar word in all this which I could not quite identify.

Mopher had referred to 'the Massing'. Where had I heard that expression used? In what dream? In what previous incarnation? Or had it been a premonition? For it was the doom of the Eternal Champion to remember the future as well as the past. Time and Consequences are not the same thing to the likes of us.

No amount of effort brought me further illumination and I deliberately dismissed the problem as we followed Mopher Gorb,

Binkeeper of the *Frowning Shield* (evidently the name of this ship), into the dark, stinking bowels of his home hull.

As we walked up the gangplank the smell was so bad that I was close to vomiting, but I controlled myself. There were lights burning within the vessel. Below our feet were slats and through the gaps in these I could see further down into the ship where naked people ran to and fro tending to what I assumed were the rollers on which the great vessel moved. I could make out a series of catwalks, some of metal, some of wood and some which were mere ropes stretched between other gangways. I heard cries and shouts above the slow rumble of the rollers and assumed these men and women must be oiling and cleaning the machinery as it turned. Then we had advanced up another flight of wooden steps and were standing in a large hall full of weapons and armour and tended by a sweating individual of some six and a half feet tall and so fat it seemed a miracle he could move at all.

'You've exchanged names and so are welcome on board the *Frowning Shield*, gentlemen. I am called Drejit Uphi, Chief Weapon Master of our hull. I see you are bearing two of our blades and would be obliged for their return. You, too, Mopher. And the rest. All blades called in. And all armour returned, too. What of the rest? Must we send heifers to unshell 'em?'

Mopher seemed shamefaced. 'Aye. We attacked these guests, thinking they were marsh vermin. They convinced us to the contrary. Umift, Ior, Wetch, Gobshot, Pnatt and Strote need stripping. They're all fuel now.'

This reference to fuel gave me some notion of why the smoke from the chimneys was particularly hideous and why everything aboard seemed covered in a slightly sticky, oily film.

Drejit Uphi shrugged. 'My congratulations, sirs. You are good fighters. These warriors were seasoned and clever.' He spoke as politely as he could but it was plain he was strongly displeased, both with Mopher and with us.

They did not think to take von Bek's pistol and so I felt a little more secure as, when Mopher had stripped off his armour to reveal dirty cotton jerkin and breeches, we followed the Binkeeper into the upper levels of the city-ship.

The whole hull was crowded, very much like a medieval town, with people in every alley, gangway and boardwalk, carrying burdens, calling to each other, bartering, gossiping and arguing. They were all dirty, all very pale and somewhat sickly-looking and, of course, no piece of clothing was free of the ash which fell everywhere and clogged throats as thoroughly as it covered our skins. By the time we had come out into the open night air again and were crossing a long bridge over what on land I might have thought to be a market square we were both of us wheezing and had streaming noses and eyes. Mopher recognised what was happening to us and laughed. 'Sooner or later your body gets used to it,' he said. 'Look at me! You'd hardly guess I had half the ship's carrion in my lungs by now!'

And he laughed again.

I clung to the rail of the bridge as it swayed in the wind and shivered from the motion of the ship which was still on the move. Overhead in the yards I saw figures constantly at work while others swarmed up and down the rigging, all illuminated by sudden gouts of fiery ash from the chimneys. The larger pieces, I now saw, were caught in wire nets surrounding the chimneys and either gathered around the sides at the top or fell back in again.

Von Bek shook his head. 'Squalid and ramshackle though the whole thing is, it's a miracle of crazed engineering. One must suppose it's steam which powers all this.'

Mopher had overheard him. 'The Folfeg are famous for their scientific devices,' he said. 'My grandfather was a Folfeg, of The Wounded Crayfish anchorage. He it was made the boilers of the great *Glowing Mosslizard*, who sought to follow Ilabarn Kreym over the Edge. The hull returned, as all of the Maaschanheem know, without a single crew member left alive – yet her engines had not failed. Those engines brought her back to The Wounded Crayfish. In the days of the Wars between the Hulls she conquered fourteen rival anchorages, including The Torn Banner,

The Drifting Fern, The Lobster Set Free, The Hunting Shark and The Broken Pike, and all those hulls besides.'

Von Bek was more curious than I was. 'How do you name your anchorages?' he asked. 'I take it these are the strips of firm land between which your hulls sail.'

Again the Binkeeper was confused. 'Just so, sir. The anchorages are named for what they most closely resemble upon the map. How the land is shaped, sir.'

'Of course,' said von Bek, replacing his handkerchief over his mouth so that his voice was muffled. 'Forgive my naïveté.'

'You may ask us any question here,' said Mopher trying to remove the frown from his hairy features, 'for we have exchanged names and only what is Sacred may not be communicated to you.'

Now we had come to the end of the bridge and reached a portcullis, all iron lattice through which we could see a shadowy hall in which lanterns gleamed. At Mopher's shout the massive gate was raised and we passed through. The hall was more elaborately decorated and moreover I now realised that the portcullis was covered in fine gauze. Very little of the ash had actually permeated this part of the ship.

Now a trumpet sounded (a somewhat unpleasant squawk) and from a dimly lit gallery above our heads a voice cried:

'Hail to our honoured guests. Let them feast tonight with the Baron Captain and keep passage with us until the Massing.'

We could see little of the speaker, but apparently he was simply a herald. Now down a wide open staircase on the other side of the hall bustled a short, stocky individual with the face of a prize-fighter and the demeanour of an aggressive man who seeks to control a normally short temper.

He held a skull-cap across a chest covered in the most elaborate red, gold and blue brocade and on his thick legs were flaring breeches weighted at the bottoms with heavy balls of differently coloured felt. On his head was one of the strangest hats I had ever seen in all my rangings through the multiverse, and it was no wonder he did not choose to use this for the ritualistic covering of the heart. The hat was at least a yard high, very much like an old-fashioned stovepipe but with a narrower brim. I guessed that it was stiffened from inside, yet nonetheless it tended to lean wildly in more than one direction and it was coloured a garish mustard yellow so bright I feared it would blind me.

The owner of this costume plainly felt it to be not only perfectly congruous but rather impressive. As he reached the bottom of the stairs he paused, made a small gesture to acknowledge us, then turned to Mopher Gorb. 'You're dismissed, Binkeeper. And as I'm sure you'll be aware you'll be responsible for stocking no more bins this tour. It was poor judgement to mistake our guests for marsh vermin. And you lost good hands as a result.'

Mopher Gorb bowed low. 'I accept this, Baron Captain.'

The ship suddenly shuddered and seemed to moan and complain deep within itself. For a few moments we all clutched for whatever support was available until the motion calmed. Then Mopher Gorb continued. 'I give over my bins to the one who would succeed me and pray that they catch good vermin for our boilers.'

Although only dimly aware of what he meant I found myself again close to vomiting.

Mopher Gorb slunk back through the portcullis which was wound down rapidly behind him and the Baron Captain strutted towards us, his great hat nodding on his head.

'I am Armiad-naam-Sliforg-ig-Vortan, Baron Captain of this hull, accountant to The Clutching Hand. I am deeply honoured to welcome you and your friend.' He was addressing me directly, a somewhat unpleasantly placatory note in his voice. I was evidently surprised by his response and he smiled. 'Know you, sir, that the names you gave my Binkeeper were but a few of your titles, as I understand, for you would not demean yourself to offer your true name and rank to such as he. However, as a Baron Captain I am permitted, am I not, to address you by the name known best by us, at least, in this our Maaschanheem.'

'You know my name, Baron Captain?'

'Oh, of course, your highness. I recognise your face from our own literature. All have read of your exploits against the Tynur raiders. Your quest for the Old Hound and her child. The mystery you solved concerning the Wild City. And many, many more. You are quite as much a hero amongst the Maaschanheemers, your highness, as you are amongst your own Draachenheemers. I cannot tell you how deeply glad I am to be able to entertain you, without any wish for publicity for this hull or myself. I would like this clear that we are only too honoured to have you aboard.'

I could barely control my smile at this unpleasant little man's awkward and somewhat disgusting attempts at good manners. I decided to take a haughty tone, since he expected it of me.

'Then how, sir, do you call me?'

'Oh, your highness!' he simpered. 'But you are Prince Flamadin, Chosen Lord of the Valadek, and a hero throughout the Six Realms of the Wheel!'

It seemed I had learned my name at last. And once again, I feared, more was expected of me than I cared or desired.

Von Bek was sardonic. 'You hid this great secret from me, also, Prince Flamadin.'

I had already explained to him my circumstances. I glared at him.

'Now, good gentlemen, you must be my guests at a feast I have had prepared for you,' said Baron Captain Armiad, pointing with his skull-cap to the far end of the hall, one wall of which was slowly rising up to reveal a brilliantly lit room in which was set a great oaken table already covered in a variety of hideous-looking food.

Again I avoided von Bek's eye and prayed that it would be possible, somehow, to find at least a morsel or two that was to some degree palatable.

'I understand, good gentlemen,' said Armiad as he led the way to our seats, 'that you have chosen to take passage on our hull and that you journey to the Massing.'

Since I was more than curious to discover the nature of this Massing I nodded gravely.

'I must take it that you are upon a fresh adventure,' said Armiad. His huge hat waved dangerously as he seated himself beside me. Although not quite as obnoxious, his smell was not greatly different from his hirelings.

I knew that this was a man who not only disdained good manners as a rule but was scarcely familiar with the ordinary rituals involved. Moreover I believed that, if he did not think it served his purposes much better to entertain us as guests, he would as cheerfully have slit out throats and fed our corpses to his bins and boilers. I felt relieved that he had recognised me for this Prince Flamadin (or had mistaken me for him!) and resolved to accept as little of his hospitality as possible.

As we ate I asked him how long he thought it would take before we reached the Massing.

'Another two days, no more. Why, good sir, are you anxious to be there before all are assembled? If so, we can increase speed. A simple matter of mechanical adjustments and fuel consumption...'

I shook my head hastily. 'Two days is excellent. And does everyone attend this Massing?'

'Representatives of all Six Realms, as you know, your highness. I cannot speak, of course, for any unusual visitors to our Massing. We have held it, as you know, in the Maaschanheem whether the Realms come together or not. Every year, since the Armistice, when the Wars between the Hulls were finally resolved. There will be many coming, all under truce, naturally. Even marsh vermin, those horrid renegades without hull or anchorage, could come and not go to the bins. Yes, there will be a fine company, all in all, your highness. And I shall make sure you have a vantage place amongst the most privileged hulls. None would dare refuse you. The *Frowning Shield* is yours!'

'I am greatly obliged to you, Baron Captain.'

Servants came and went, putting dreadful dishes under our noses and these, it seemed, it was politic to refuse for none seemed angered. I noted that, like me, von Bek was making do with a salad of relatively tasty marsh-plants.

Von Bek spoke for the first time. 'Forgive me, Baron Captain. As his highness has no doubt indicated, I have a condition which has robbed me of much of my memory. What other realms than this one do you speak of?'

I admired his directness and his method of explaining himself so that I should not be embarrassed.

'As his highness knows,' said Armiad with barely restrained impatience, 'we are Six Realms, the Realms of the Wheel. There is Maaschanheem, which is this Realm. There is Draachenheem, which is where Prince Flamadin rules (when not adventuring elsewhere!),' a nod to me, 'and Gheestenheem, Realm of the Cannibal Ghost Women. The other three Realms are Barganheem, claimed by the mysterious Ursine Princes, Fluugensheem, whose people are guarded by the Flying Island, and Rootsenheem, whose warriors have skins of glowing blood. There is also, of course, the Realm of the Centre itself, but none comes from there nor ventures there. We call it Alptroomensheem, Realm of the Nightmare Marches. Are you fully reminded now, Count von Bek?'

'Thoroughly, Baron Captain. I thank you for your trouble. I have a poor memory for names at the best of times, I fear.'

In some relief, or so it seemed to me, the Baron Captain turned his pugnacious, barely polite eyes towards me again. 'And shall your betrothed meet us at the Massing, your highness? Or does the Princess Sharadim remain to guard the Realm while you go adventuring?'

'Aha,' I said, taken aback and unable to disguise my shock. 'The Princess Sharadim. I cannot say as yet.'

And somewhere, even now, in the back of my mind I could hear that desperate chanting.

SHARADIM! SHARADIM! THE FIREDRAKE
MUST BE FREED!

It was at that point that I claimed weariness and begged Baron Captain Armiad that I be shown to my bed.

Once in my quarters I was joined by von Bek, whose rooms were next to mine. 'You seem unwell, Herr Daker,' he said. 'Are you afraid you'll be found out in your deception and that the real prince will turn up at this Massing of theirs?'

'Oh,' I said, 'I've little doubt I'm the real prince, my friend. But what shocks me is that the only name I've heard since I arrived in this world which is in any way familiar is that of the woman to whom I am apparently betrothed!'

Von Bek said: 'That at least should save you embarrassment when you eventually meet her.'

'Perhaps,' I said, but privately I was deeply disturbed and could not be sure why.

That night I scarcely slept at all.

I had come to fear sleep.

Chapter Three

Next morning, I had no difficulty arousing myself. The night had been filled with visions and hallucinations, with the chanting women, the despairing warriors, the voices calling not only Sharadim but calling me also – calling me by a thousand different names.

When von Bek found me, as I was putting the finishing touches to my toilet, he remarked again on how ill I seemed. 'Are these dreams of yours a permanent condition of the life you've described?'

'Not permanent,' I told him, 'but frequent.'

'I do not envy you, Herr Daker.'

Von Bek had been given fresh clothing. He moved awkwardly in the soft leather shirt and trousers and the thicker leather jerkin, the tall boots. 'I look like some robber in a Sturm und Drang play,' he said. He continued to be sardonically amused by his situation and I must admit I was glad of his company. It was a relief, at least, from my doom-filled premonitions and dreams.

'These clothes,' he said, 'are at least fairly clean! And I see they gave you hot water, too. I suppose we should count ourselves fortunate. You were so distressed last night I forgot to thank you for your help.' He held out his hand. 'I should like to offer you my friendship, sir.'

I shook his hand warmly. 'And you are assured of mine,' I told him. 'I'm happy to have such a comrade. I had not expected so much.'

'I've read of many marvels in the Middle Marches,' he continued, 'but nothing so strange as this great lumbering ship. I was up earlier inspecting her machinery. It's crude – steam of course – but it works to achieve its end. You've never seen so many rods and pistons at so many stages of age! The thing must be extremely old and there have been few improvements made, I would guess, in a century or more. Everything is patched and mended, lashed together, crudely welded. The boilers and furnaces themselves are massive. And oddly efficient. It moves a tonnage at least the size of your *Queen Elizabeth* and is only partially supported by water. It depends, of course, more on manpower than an ocean liner, and that could have something to do with it. My engineering background, I must admit, is limited to a year at technical college which my father insisted upon. He was a progressive type!'

'More progressive than mine,' I told him. 'I know nothing at all of such things. I wish I did. Not that I've been called upon to use skills of that sort in the worlds I've known. Magic is more the order of the day. Or what we of the twentieth century called magic.'

'My family,' he said with one of his ironical smiles, 'has some familiarity with magic, also.'

Count von Bek then proceeded to tell me his family history, going back to the seventeenth century. His ancestors, it seemed, had always possessed the means of travelling between different realms and to different worlds where different rules applied. 'There are supposed to be reminiscences in existence,' he added, 'but we've never come across them, save for one which is very likely a partial fake!' It was because of this that he had sought out the aid of one he called 'Satan' in his fight against Hitler. Satan had helped him discover the means through to the Middle Marches and had said that there was some hope he might find there a means of defeating the Chancellor. 'But whether this Satan was the same as was cast from Heaven or whether he is a minor deity, an imprisoned godling of some description, I have never been able to decide. Nonetheless, he helped me.'

I was relieved. Von Bek would not, as I had thought he might, require too much in the way of introduction to what had become familiar facts of life for me. This realm, however, seemed to possess little in the way of supernatural marvels, save that it took the existence of other planes for granted. In that respect, I found it reassuring.

Von Bek, who had, as he said, already partly explored the ship, led me down the creaking wooden corridors of what I suppose I had begun to think of as the Baron Captain's palace and into a small chamber hung with quilted cloth whose workmanship looked too fine to be from this world. Here a wooden table had been prepared. I tasted a piece of salty, powdery cheese, a little hard bread, a sip of what I took to be very thin yogurt, and finally settled for a relatively uncloudy mug of tepid water and the egg of some unknown bird, hard-boiled. Then I followed von Bek through another maze of swaying, narrow gangways, out across a flimsy catwalk stretching between two masts. The thing swayed so violently I grew dizzy and clung hard to the rail. Far below, the people of the ship were going about their business. I saw carts drawn by beasts similar to oxen, heard the cries of women calling from window to window in the ramshackle buildings, saw children playing in the lower rigging while dogs barked at their feet. Everywhere the smoke billowed, obscuring some scenes completely; then, occasionally, the wind would lift everything clear and it was possible to smell clean air from off the vast, glittering marsh through which the *Frowning Shield* ploughed with a kind of cumbersome dignity.

Though flat and predominantly grey-green, the Maaschanheem was magnificent in its way. The clouds hardly ever lifted for very long, yet the light which filtered through them was forever changing, revealing different aspects of the lagoons, marshes and narrow strips of land, the 'anchorages' of this nomad people. Flocks of strangely beautiful birds could be seen drifting on the water, or wading through the reeds, sometimes rising in a great dark mass to wheel in the air and stream away towards the invisible horizon. Unlikely-looking animals would scuttle through the grasses or raise enquiring heads from the water. The most astonishing of these for me was something resembling an otter, yet it was larger than most sea-lions. It was called, we learned, nothing more fanciful than a *vaasarhund*. I was learning that the language which I spoke more fluently than von Bek was of Teutonic origin, somewhere between old German, Dutch and to a lesser degree English and Scandinavian. Now I knew what had been meant when I had been told that this world bore a closer relation to the world I had left as John Daker than most I had visited as the Eternal Champion.

The water hounds were as playful as otters and would follow the ship at a safe distance when it entered deeper water (though it never floated entirely free of the bottom), barking or leaping for scraps which the citizens of the hull would throw to them.

I learned very quickly that morning that the hull itself and the people aboard were not inherently sinister, though the present ruler and his Binkeepers were singularly unsavoury. They had learned to live with the filth from the chimneys and were used to the stink of the place, but they seemed cheerful and friendly enough, once they were assured that we meant them no harm and were not 'marsh vermin' – a general term, we discovered, for any person who either had no home hull, or who was outlawed for a variety of crimes, or who had chosen to live on land. Some of these bands would, indeed, attack hulls when they got the chance, or kidnap individuals from the ships, but it seemed to me that not all were characteristically evil or deserved to be hunted down. We learned that it was Baron Captain Armiad who had instigated the rule that all landspeople should be killed and their corpses consigned to the bins. 'As a result,' one woman told us as she stood scraping a hide, 'no landspeople will trade with the *Frowning Shield* these days. We are forced to forage what we can from the anchorage or depend on what the Binkeepers strip from the marsh vermin.' She shrugged. 'But that's the new way.'

We found that a rapid way of moving about the city was to use the catwalks between the masts. We could thus save ourselves the time of negotiating the winding streets below and not get lost so easily. The masts had permanent ladders with a kind of cage guard running the length of them, so there was less chance of losing one's grip and being flung backwards to the buildings below.

We fell in with a group of young men and women who were evidently nobles of some sort, though not very well dressed and almost as grimy as the commoners. They sought us out as we crossed the roof of a turret, trying to see towards the back of the ship and its monstrous rudders which were used for braking and for turning, frequently gouging deep into the mud. One of them was a bright-eyed young woman of about twenty, dressed in worn leather similar to von Bek's costume. She was the first to introduce herself. 'I'm Bellanda-naam-Folfag-ig-Fornster,' she said, placing her cap across her heart. 'We wanted to congratulate you on your fight with Mopher Gorb and his collectors. They've grown too used to chasing half-starved outcasts. We hope they'll learn a lesson from what happened yesterday, though I'm not sure his kind are capable of learning.'

She introduced her two brothers and their other friends.

'You have the air of students,' said von Bek. 'Is there a college aboard?'

'There is,' she said, 'and we attend it when it is open. But since our new Baron Captain took power there's been little encouragement given to learning. He has a hearty contempt for what he says are the softer pursuits. There's been little encouragement to artists or intellectuals over the past three years, and our hull is virtually ostracised by all. Those who could leave the *Frowning Shield*, who had skills or knowledge to offer other hulls, have already gone. We have nothing but our youth and our eagerness to learn. There's little hope of changing berths, at least for a long time. There have been worse tyrants in the histories of the hulls, worse warmongers, worse fools, but it is not pleasant to know that you're the laughing stock of the entire realm, that no decent person from another ship would ever wish to marry you or even be seen with you. Only at the Massing do we manage to achieve some kind of communication, but that is somewhat formal and too short.'

'And if you left the ship entirely...?' von Bek began.

'Exactly – marsh vermin. We can only hope that the present Baron Captain falls into the rollers or otherwise meets his end as soon as possible! I'm no snob, I hope, but he is the worst sort of *arriviste.*'

'Your titles are not inherited?' I asked.

'Usually they are. But Armiad deposed our old Baron Captain. Armiad was Baron Captain Nedau's steward and came, as frequently happens when a childless ruler grows old, to assume many of the responsibilities of leadership. We were ready to elect a new Baron Captain, from Nedau's immediate family. He is related to my mother, for instance, on the Fornster side. Also Arbrek's uncle,' she indicated a red-headed young man who was so shy his face was glowing to match his hair, 'was a Lord of the Rendeps, who had an ancient Poetry Bond with the then incumbent ruler. Lastly, the Doowrehsi of the Saintly Monicans had closer blood-claims, though of late a recluse, celibate and a scholar. All of these were to be voted for. Then, in his senility (it could have been nothing else), our Baron Captain Nedau called for a Blood Challenge. Now such a ceremony has not taken place since the Wars of the Hulls, all those many years ago. But it is still upon the Lawmast and had to be honoured. Why Nedau should challenge Armiad, we never discovered, but we assumed he had goaded Nedau to it, perhaps through some deep insult, perhaps by threatening to reveal a secret. Whatever the cause, Armiad naturally accepted the Blood Challenge and the two of them fought across the main hanging gangway between the great middle masts. We watched from below, according to a tradition all of us who still live had forgotten, and though the smoke from a chimney obscured the final moments of the fight there was no question that Nedau was stabbed through the heart before he fell a hundred or more feet into the market square. And so, because an old law was never changed, our new Baron Captain is a gross, ignorant tyrant.'

Von Bek said: 'I know something of such tyrants. Is it not unsafe for you to utter such sentiments aloud and in public?'

'Perhaps,' she agreed, 'but I know him for a coward. Moreover, he is concerned because the other Baron Captains will have little or nothing to do with him. They invite him to no celebrations. They do not make visits to our hull. We are scarcely part of the hull-gatherings any more. All we have is the yearly Massing, when all must gather and no contention is allowed. But even here we are offered the very minimum of civility by the other hulls. This *Frowning Shield* has the reputation of being a barbaric craft, worthy of our dimmest past, before the Wars of the Hulls even. All this did Armiad achieve through calling up that old law. Through murdering, we all think, his master. If he were to commit further crimes against his own people – try to silence the relatives, like us, of the old Baron Captain, he would have even less chance of ever being accepted into the ranks of the other noblemen. His efforts to win their approval have been as ludicrous and ill-conceived as his machinations and his plans have been crude. Every time he attempts to win them over – with gifts, with displays of courage, with examples of his firm policies, such as that with the marsh vermin – he drives them further away from him.' Bellanda smiled. 'It is one of our few amusements left aboard the *Frowning Shield*.'

'And you have no way of deposing him?'

'No, Prince Flamadin. For only a Baron Captain can call a Blood Challenge.'

'Cannot the other Baron Captains help you against him?' von Bek wished to know.

'By law they cannot. It is part of the great truce, when the Wars of the Hulls were finally ended. It is forbidden to interfere with the internal business of another city vessel.' This last offered by a stammering Arbrek. 'We're proud of that law. But it is not to the advantage, at present, of the *Frowning Shield*...'

'Now do you understand,' said Bellanda with a small smile, 'why Armiad cultivates you so? We heard he fawns upon you, Prince Flamadin.'

'I must admit it is not the most agreeable experience I have ever had. Why does he do it, when he does not feel obliged to be civil to his own people?'

'He believes us weaker than himself. You are stronger, as he understands such things. But the real reason for his attempts to win your approval are to do with the fact, I'll swear, that he hopes to impress the other Baron Captains at the Massing. If he has the famous Prince Flamadin of the Valadek at his side when we sail in to the Massing Ground, he believes they must surely accept him as one of themselves.'

Von Bek was highly amused. He exploded with laughter. 'And that's the only reason?'

'The chief reason at any rate,' she said, joining in his amusement. 'He's a simple fellow, isn't he?'

'The simpler they are the more dangerous they can be,' I said. 'I wish we could be of help to you, Bellanda, in relieving you of his tyranny.'

'We can only hope some accident will befall him before long,' she said. She spoke openly. Plainly, they did not plan to perpetuate their hull's history of murder.

I was grateful to Bellanda for illuminating me on the matter. I decided to seek her help a little further. 'I gathered from Armiad last night,' I said, 'that I am something of a folk hero amongst at least some of your people. He spoke of adventures which are not wholly familiar to me. Do you know what that means?'

She laughed again. 'You're modest, Prince Flamadin. Or you feign modesty with great charm and skill. Surely you must know that in the Maaschanheem, as well as, I think, in other Realms of the Wheel, your adventures are told by every market tale-spinner. There are books sold throughout the Maaschanheem, not all originating from our book-manufacturing hulls, which purport to describe how you defeated this ogre or rescued that maiden. You cannot say you've never seen them!'

'Here,' said one of the younger men, pushing forward and brandishing a brightly coloured book which reminded me a little of our old Victorian penny dreadfuls or dime novels. 'See! I was going to ask you if you'd sign it, sir.'

Von Bek said softly, 'You told me you were an elected hero in your many incarnations, Herr Daker, but until now I had no proof!'

To my extreme embarrassment he took the book from the boy's hand and inspected it even as he passed it to me. Here was a rough likeness of myself, riding some sort of lizard creature, sword raised high as I did battle with what looked like a cross between the water hounds and large baboons. I had a frightened young woman on the saddle behind me and across the top of this picture, just as in a more familiar pulp magazine, was a title: *PRINCE FLAMADIN, CHAMPION OF THE SIX WORLDS*. Inside, written in lurid prose, was a story, evidently largely fictitious, describing my courageous exploits, my noble sentiments, my extraordinary good looks and so on. I was both baffled and discommoded, yet found myself signing the name – Flamadin – with a flourish before handing the book back. The gesture had been automatic. Perhaps I was, after all, this character. Certainly my responses were familiar ones, just as I could speak the language and read it. I sighed. In all my experience I had never known anything quite so ordinary and so strange at the same time. I was some kind of hero in this world – but a hero whose exploits were thoroughly fictionalised, like those of Jesse James, Buffalo Bill or, to a lesser degree, some of the popular sports and music stars of the twentieth century!

Von Bek hit the nail on the head. 'I had no idea I had been befriended by someone as famous as Old Shatterhand or Sherlock Holmes,' he said.

'Is it all true?' the boy wished to know. 'It's hard to believe you've done so much, sir, and yet still be fairly young!'

'The truth is for you to decide,' I said. 'I dare say there's a fair bit of embellishment, however, in there.'

'Well,' said Bellanda with a broad smile, 'I'm prepared to believe every word. There's idle gossip says your sister is the real power, that you do nothing but lease your name to the sensational writers. But I can now say, since I have met you, Prince Flamadin, that you are every inch a hero!'

'You're very kind,' I replied with a bow. 'But I'm sure my sister deserves a great deal of credit, too.'

'The Princess Sharadim? She refuses to be mentioned in those pages, I hear.'

'Sharadim?' Again that name! Yet only yesterday she had been described as my betrothed.

'Aye…' Bellanda looked puzzled. 'Have I been too bold, Prince Flamadin, in my humour…?'

'No, no. Is Sharadim a common name in my own land…?' I was asking a stupid question. I had baffled her.

'I cannot follow you, sir…'

Von Bek came to my rescue again. 'I had heard that the Princess Sharadim was Prince Flamadin's bride-to-be…'

'So she is, sir,' said Bellanda. 'And the prince's sister. That's a tradition in your realm, is it not?' She grew further confused. 'If I have repeated a piece of stupid gossip or believed too much in these fictions, I really do apologise…'

I recovered myself. 'It is not for you to apologise.' I went towards the edge of the turret and leaned against it. A wind blew up, dispelling the smoke, and freshened my lungs, my skin, helped me cool my mind. 'I am fatigued. Sometimes I forget things…'

'Come,' said von Bek, apologising to the young people, 'I will help you back to your quarters. Rest for an hour. You'll feel better for it.'

I allowed him to lead me away from the thoroughly puzzled group of students.

When we returned to the cabins we found a messenger waiting patiently outside the main door. 'My good gentlemen,' he said, 'the Baron Captain sends his respects. He lunches at your pleasure.'

'Does that mean we should join him as soon as possible?' von Bek asked the man.

'If you are so disposed, sir.'

We went inside and I made my way to my bedroom, sitting

down heavily. 'I apologise, von Bek. These revelations should not affect me so. If it had not been for those dreams – those women calling me Sharadim...'

'I think I can understand,' he said, 'but you should try to pull yourself together. We don't want these people to turn against us. Not just yet, my friend. I believe that amongst the intelligentsia they are curious as to whether you are the hero which the story-books describe. I think there's a rumour that Prince Flamadin is a mere puppet. Did you sense that?'

I nodded. 'Perhaps that's why they call to Sharadim.'

'I'm not sure I follow you.'

'A suggestion that it is she who holds the real power, that her brother – her betrothed – is a mere sham. Perhaps it suits her to have him a kind of living legend, a popular hero. Such relationships are not unheard of in our world, after all.'

'I did not gather as much, but I agree it is a possibility. Does this mean, then, that you and Flamadin of the Valadek are not necessarily of the same character?'

'The shell alters, von Bek. The spirit and the character remain unchanged. It would not be the first time I have been incarnated in the body of a hero who was not all people expected him to be.'

'The other thing I'd be curious about in your shoes, as it were, is how I came to be in this world in the first place. Do you think you'll discover that answer soon?'

'I can be sure of nothing, my friend.' I stood up and straightened my shoulders. 'Let's prepare ourselves for whatever foul experience luncheon is going to bring us.'

As we left for the Baron Captain's hall, von Bek said: 'I wonder if this Princess Sharadim will be at the Massing. I must say I am becoming increasingly curious to meet her. What about you?'

I managed to smile. 'I am dreading such a meeting, my friend. I fear nothing but misery and terror will result from it.'

Von Bek looked hard at my face. 'I think I would be less impressed,' he said, 'if you did not have that exceptionally ghastly grin on your lips.'

Chapter Four

B<small>ARON</small> C<small>APTAIN</small> A<small>RMIAD</small> had a favour to ask me. Since my discussion with the young students, I was not surprised when eventually he came round to asking me if I would do him the honour of accompanying him aboard another hull, just prior to the Massing. 'The hulls come gradually to the Massing Ground, frequently sailing side by side for many miles before the Ground itself is reached. Already the upper lookouts have sighted three other hulls. By their signals they are the *Girl in Green*, the *Certain Scalpel* and the *New Argument*, all from the farthest anchorages. They must have made good time to be so close to the Massing Ground. It is the custom for Baron Captains to make courtesy calls, one upon another, at this time. These calls are only refused in the case of sickness aboard or some other great crisis. I should like to put up flags to the *New Argument*, telling her we wish to pay her a visit. Would you and your friend be curious to see another hull?'

'We'll gladly come,' said I. Not only did I wish to compare the hulls, I wanted to get some idea of how the Baron Captain's peers actually regarded him. From what he said it was not possible to refuse even him. And it was obvious to me that he wished to display his guest to the others so that the word would go round before the Massing. By this means he hoped to win their acceptance or, at very least, increase his prestige.

He was plainly relieved. His little piglike features relaxed. He all but beamed at me. 'Good. Then I'll have the signals set.'

He excused himself a little while later and left us to our own devices. We continued to explore the city ship, again finding ourselves in the company of Bellanda and her friends. These were certainly the most interesting people we had met so far. They took us high up the masts and showed us the smoke from the distant hulls, slowly moving together as they sailed towards the Massing Ground.

A pale-faced boy called Jurgin had a spyglass and knew the flags of all the ships. He called them out as he recognised them: 'There's the *Distant Bargain*, accountant to The Floating Head. And that's the *Girl in Green*, accountant to The Jagged Jug...' I asked him how he could tell so much. He handed me the glass. 'It's simple, your highness. The flags represent what the anchorages look like on the map and the names describe what those representations most resemble. The way we name configurations of stars. The names of the hulls are ancient, in most cases, and are the names of old sailing vessels on which our ancestors first set forth. Only gradually did they grow into the moving cities on which we now live.'

I looked through the glass and eventually made out a banner flying from the tallest mast of the nearest hull. It was a red symbol on a black field. 'I'd guess that's some sort of goblin. A gargoyle.

Jurgin laughed. 'That flag's flown for The Ugly Man anchorage and therefore the hull's the *New Argument* from the farthest north. She's the hull you'll visit this evening, eh?'

I was impressed by his clairvoyance. 'How did you know that? Do you have spies at Court?'

He shook his head, still laughing. 'It's simpler than that, your highness.' He pointed up higher to our own mainmast, where a good score of banners flapped in the light wind. 'That's what our signals say. And the *New Argument* has replied with due courtesy (probably reluctant where our great Baron Captain is concerned) that you are welcome to visit them at the hour before twilight. Which means,' he added with a grin, 'that you'll have no more than an hour of calling, for Armiad hates crossing the marshlands at night. Perhaps he fears the vengeance of all those so-called marsh vermin he's fed to the bins. Doubtless the *New Argument* is equally aware of that fact!'

A few hours later von Bek and myself found ourselves accompanying the Baron Captain Armiad-naam-Sliforg-ig-Vortan, all dressed in his most elaborate (and ludicrous) finery, into a kind of flatboat with small wheels which was poled by about a dozen men (also in somewhat flamboyant livery) and which sometimes floated, sometimes rolled, across the marshes and lagoons towards the *New Argument* which was now quite close to our own *Frowning Shield*. Armiad could barely walk in all his quilted cloak and padded hose, his vast, nodding hat, his grotesquely stuffed doublet. I understand that he had come across the designs in an old picture book and determined that these were the proper and traditional clothes of a true Baron Captain. He had a fair amount of difficulty getting into the barge and had to hold onto his hat with both hands when the wind threatened it. Very slowly the men poled us towards the other hull, while Armiad shouted to them to take care, to be careful not to splash us, to rock the vessel as little as possible.

Dressed in plain garments and without weapons, we had no particular problems of this sort.

The *New Argument* was no less battered and repaired than the *Frowning Shield*, and if anything was somewhat older, but she was altogether in better condition than our hull. The smoke from her chimneys was not the same yellowish oily stuff and the stacks were arranged so that by and large very little ash fell upon the decks themselves. The banners were rather cleaner (though it was impossible for them to be completely fresh) and the paintwork everywhere was brighter. Some care had been taken to maintain the hull and, I suspect, she had been made especially shipshape for the coming Massing. It seemed strange that Armiad could not tell that his own hull could be cleaner, that its condition reflected both his own failure of intelligence, the poor morale of his people and half a dozen other things besides.

We came up to the bulk of the other hull, moving across cold water until we reached a ramp which they lowered for us. With some effort the men poled the craft up the ramp and into the bowels of the *New Argument*. I looked about me with curiosity.

The general appearance of the hull was the same as that which we had left, but there was an orderliness, a smartness about it which made Armiad's vessel seem like an old tramp steamer compared to a navy ship. Moreover, although the men who greeted us were dressed much as those we'd first seen, they were considerably cleaner and plainly had no taste for entertaining the likes of us. Even though von Bek and I had bathed thoroughly and insisted on fresh clothing, we had picked up a film of grime on the way from our quarters to the barge. Also, I was sure, all three of us smelled of the hull, though we had become used to it. It was also plain that the complement of the *New Argument* found Armiad's clothing as ludicrous as did we!

It became very clear to us that it was not mere snobbery which made the other Baron Captains reluctant to have Armiad aboard. However, if they were snobs, Armiad's condition and disposition would have confirmed every prejudice they had.

Although apparently unaware of the impression he gave, Armiad was evidently ill at ease. He blustered at the welcoming party as we were greeted formally and names were offered. He was the very essence of pomposity as he announced those he brought with him as guests of the *New Argument* and he seemed pleased when our hosts recognised my name with evident surprise, even shock.

'Yes, indeed,' he told the group, 'Prince Flamadin and his companion have chosen our hull, the *Frowning Shield*, as their means of travelling to the Massing. They will make our hull their headquarters for the duration. Now, my men, lead us on to your masters. Prince Flamadin is not used to such tardiness.'

Greatly embarrassed by his bad manners and attempting to show our hosts that I did not endorse his remarks, I followed the greeting party up a series of ramps which led to the outer decks. Here, too, a thriving town existed, with twisting streets, flights of stairs, taverns, food shops, even a theatre. Von Bek muttered his approval but Armiad beside him and just behind me said in a loud whisper that he observed signs of decadence everywhere. I had known certain Englishmen who associated cleanliness with decadence and whose opinion would have been confirmed by the additional evidence of thriving arts and crafts on the *New Argument*. I, however, attempted to make conversation with the greeting party, all of whom seemed pleasant enough young men, but they were evidently reluctant to respond to me, even when I praised the appearance and beauty of their hull.

We crossed a series of catwalks to what had the appearance of a large civic building. This possessed none of the fortified appearance of Armiad's palace and we passed through high, pointed arches directly into a kind of courtyard which was surrounded by a pleasant colonnade. From the left side of this colonnade there now emerged another group of men and women, all of them in middle to late years. They wore long robes of rich, dark colours, slouch hats, each of which bore a differently coloured plume, and gloves of brightly dyed leather. Their faces were dimly visible through fine gauze masks which they now removed, placing them over their hearts in a version of the same gesture we had first encountered from Mopher Gorb and his Binmen. I was impressed by their dignified features and surprised, too, that all but two of them, a man and a woman, were brown-skinned. The party greeting us had all been white-skinned.

Their manners were perfect and their greetings elegant, but it was more than plain that they were pleased to see none of us. They clearly did not distinguish between von Bek and myself and Armiad (which I, of course, found wounding to my pride!) and although not directly rude gave the impression of Roman patricians suffering the visit of some coarse barbarian.

'Greetings to you, honoured guests from the *Frowning Shield*. We, the Council to our Baron Captain Denou Praz, Rhyme Brother to the Toirset Larens and our Snowbear Defender, welcome you in his name and beg that you join us for light refreshment at our Greeting Hall.'

'Gladly, gladly,' replied Armiad with an airy wave which he was forced to halt in mid-flight in order to restore his hat to its original position. 'We are more than honoured to be your guests, Prince Flamadin and I.'

THE DRAGON IN THE SWORD

Again their response to my name was not in any sense flattering. But their self-discipline was too great for them to make any open display of distaste. They bowed and led us under the archways, through doors panelled with coloured glass, into a pleasant hall lit with copper lamps, its low ceiling carved with what were evidently stylised versions of scenes from their hull's distant past, largely to do with exploits on ice-floes. I remembered that the *New Argument* was from the North where evidently it sailed far closer to the pole (if indeed this realm possessed a pole as I understood it!).

Rising from a brocaded chair at the end of a table, an old man raised his gauze mask from his face and placed it to his heart. He seemed very frail and his voice was thin when he spoke. 'Baron Captain Armiad, Prince Flamadin, Count Ulric von Bek, I am Baron Captain Denou Praz. Please advance and seat yourselves by me.'

'We've met before once or twice, Brother Denou Praz,' said Armiad in a tone of blustering familiarity. 'Perhaps you remember? At a Hull Conference aboard the *Leopard's Eye* and last year on *My Aunt Jeroldeen*, for our brother Grallerif's funeral.'

'I remember you well, Brother Armiad. Is your hull content?'

'Exceptionally content, thank you. And yours?'

'Thank you, we are in equilibrium, I think.'

It very quickly became obvious that Denou Praz intended to keep the conversation completely formal. Armiad, however, blundered blithely on. 'It is not every day we have a Chosen Prince of the Valadek in our midst.'

'No, indeed,' said Denou Praz unenthusiastically. 'Not, of course, that the good gentleman Flamadin is any longer a Chosen Prince of his people.'

This came as a shock to Armiad. I knew that Denou Praz had spoken pointedly and barely within the bounds of accepted politeness, but I did not know what the significance of his statement was. 'No longer Chosen?'

'Has not the good gentleman told you?' As Denou Praz spoke the other councillors were gathering about the table and seating themselves nearby. Everyone was looking towards me. I shook my head. 'I'm at a loss. Perhaps, Baron Captain Denou Praz, you could explain what you mean.'

'If you do not think it inhospitable?' Denou Praz was, in turn, surprised. I guessed that he had not expected me to respond in that way. But since I was genuinely puzzled I had taken the chance to request illumination from him. 'The news has been in circulation for some time. We have heard of your banishment by Sharadim, your twin, whom you refused to wed. Your giving up of all your duties. Excuse me, good gentleman, but I would not continue for fear of offending the rules of a host...'

'Please do continue, Baron Captain. All this will help explain some of my own mysteries.'

He grew slightly hesitant. It was as if he were no longer absolutely sure of his facts. 'The story is that Princess Sharadim threatened to expose some crime of yours – or some series of deceptions – and that you tried to kill her. Even then, we heard, she was prepared to forgive you if you would agree to take your rightful place beside her as joint Overlord of the Draachenheem. You refused, saying that you wished to continue your adventurings abroad.'

'I behaved like some sort of spoiled popular idol, in other words. And thwarted in my selfish desires I tried to murder my sister?'

'It was the story we had from Draachenheem, good gentleman. A declaration, indeed, signed by Princess Sharadim herself. According to that document you are no longer a Chosen Prince, but an outlaw.'

'An outlaw!' Armiad rose partially from his seat. If he had not suddenly realised where he was he might well have banged his fist on the table. 'An outlaw! You told me nothing of this when you boarded my hull. You said nothing of it when you gave your name to my Binkeeper.'

'The name I gave to your Binkeeper, Baron Captain Armiad, was not that of Flamadin at all. It was you who first used that name.'

'Aha! A cunning deception.'

Denou Praz was horrified at this breach of courtesy. He raised his frail hand. 'Good gentlemen!'

The Council, too, were shocked. One of the women who had first greeted us said hastily: 'We are most apologetic if we have given offence to our guests...'

'Offence,' said Armiad loudly, his ugly face bright red, 'has been given me, but not by you, good councillors, or by you, Brother Denou Praz. My good will, my intelligence, my entire hull have all been insulted by these charlatans. They should have told me the circumstances of their being on our anchorage!'

'It was published widely,' said Denou Praz. 'And it does not seem to me that the good gentleman Flamadin has attempted any deception. After all, he asked that I say what these reports were. If he had known them or had wished to keep them secret, why should he have done that?'

'I beg your pardon, sir,' said I. 'My companion and I had no wish to bring shame on your hull nor to pretend that we were anything more than what we originally said we were.'

'I knew nothing of it!' bellowed Armiad.

'But the journals...' said one of the women gently. 'Hardly one did not have long reports...'

'I allow no such rubbish aboard my hull. It breeds bad morale.'

Now it was obvious to me how a story known throughout the Maaschanheem had failed to reach Armiad's philistine ears.

'You are a cheat!' he flung at me. He glowered, glancing around him from beneath frowning brows as he realised he had won further disapproval from these others. He tried to keep his mouth closed.

'These good gentlemen are your guests, however,' said Denou Praz, combing at his little white goatee with a delicate hand. 'Until the Massing, at least, you are bound to continue extending hospitality to them.'

Armiad let out a sudden breath. Again he was on his feet. 'Is there no contingency in the Law? Can I not say they have given false names?'

'You named the good gentleman Flamadin?' asked an old man from the far end of the table.

'I recognised him. Is that not reasonable?'

'You did not wait for him to declare himself, but named him. That means that he has not gained the sanctuary of your hull through any deliberate deception of you. It seems that self-deception is to blame here...'

'You say it's my fault.'

The councillor was silent. Armiad puffed and blustered again. He glared at me. 'You should have told me you were no longer a Chosen Prince, that you were a criminal, wanted in your own realm. Marsh vermin, indeed!'

'Please, good gentlemen!' Baron Captain Denou Praz raised his thin brown fingers into the air. 'This is not the proper behaviour of hosts or of guests...'

Armiad, desperate for his peers' approval, took a grip on himself. 'You are welcome aboard my hull,' he said to us, 'until the Massing is complete.' He turned to Denou Praz. 'Forgive this breach of etiquette, Brother Denou Praz. If I had known what I brought aboard your hull, believe me I should never...'

The woman councillor broke in. 'These apologies are neither required nor are they within our traditions of courtesy,' she said. 'Names have been exchanged and hospitality extended. That is all. Let us, I beg you, remember that.'

The rest of the meeting was strained, to say the least. Von Bek and I looked at one another without being able to speak while Armiad grunted and grumbled to himself, hardly responding to the formal remarks which Baron Captain Denou Praz and his Council continued to make. Armiad seemed torn. He did not wish to stay at a place where he had lost face so badly, as he saw it. And he did not want to take us back with him. Eventually, however, as he became aware that it was growing dark, he signed for us to rise. He bowed to Denou Praz and made some effort to thank him for his hull's hospitality, to apologise for the tension he had brought. Von Bek and I murmured the briefest and most formal of farewells whereupon Baron Captain Denou Praz said graciously: 'It is not for me to judge men upon what the journals report of their deeds. My guess is that you did not seek the earlier fame which made you a hero in the popular imagination and that you are perhaps made more of a villain now, simply because people saw you for so long as the personification of all that was brave and noble. I hope you will forgive my own breach of poor taste, which made me judge you, good gentleman, before I knew you or understood anything of your circumstances.'

'This apology is unnecessary, Baron Captain. I am obliged to you for your kindness and civility. If I should ever return to your hull, I hope it will be because I have proven myself worthy of treading the boards of the *New Argument*.'

'Damned fancy words,' grumbled Armiad as we were escorted down through the swaying walkways and decks to where our barge stood ready to take us back to the *Frowning Shield*. 'For a man who attempted to murder his own sister! And why? Because she threatened to tell the world the truth about him. You're a sham and a scoundrel. I tell you, you are not welcome aboard our hull for any longer than the Massing. After that it is up to you to take your chances in the anchorages or choose an accountant hull within twenty hours. If a hull will accept you, which I doubt. You're as good as dead, the pair of you.'

The barge rolled down the ramp and out into the shallows. It was close to nightfall and there was a cold wind blowing across the lagoons, making the reeds rustle and sway. Armiad shivered. 'Faster, laggards!' He struck at the nearest man with his fist. 'You two will abuse the hospitality of no other hull. All will know of you by tomorrow, when the Massing begins. You can count yourselves lucky that no blood is permitted to be spilled at the Massing. Not even that of an insect. I would challenge you myself if I thought you worthy of it…'

'A Blood Challenge, my lord baron?' asked von Bek, unable to

417

resist this barb. He had remained amused by the entire affair. 'Would you make a Blood Challenge to Prince Flamadin? I believe that is the prerogative of a Baron Captain, is it not?'

At this, Armiad glared at him so fiercely he might have set the marsh afire. 'Watch your tongue, Count von Bek. I know not of what crimes you are guilty, but doubtless they'll come to light soon enough. You, too, shall pay the penalty of your deception!'

Von Bek murmured to me: 'How true it is when they say there is nothing which makes a man more furious than the discovery that he has deceived himself!'

Armiad had overheard. 'There are conditions to our custom of hospitality, Count von Bek. If you should breach those conditions, I am permitted, under the Law, to exile you or worse. If I had my way, I'd hang you both from the crosstrees. You have to thank those decadent and enfeebled old people of the *New Argument* and their kind for their intercedence. Happily, I respect the Law. As you, evidently, do not.'

I ignored the rest of this. I was thinking deeply. I now had some idea of how Prince Flamadin came to be alone in the Maaschanheem. But why had he refused to marry his twin sister Sharadim, since it was plainly what had been expected of him? And had he tried to murder her? And was he really a sham, to be exposed by her when he proved himself a traitor? No wonder the world had turned against him, if it were true. People hated to worship a hero and then discover him to have ordinary human weaknesses!

Grudgingly Armiad allowed us to return with him to his palace. 'But be careful,' he warned. 'The smallest infringement of the Law is all the excuse I need to evict you...'

We went back to our quarters.

Once in my room, von Bek at last released a great belly laugh. 'The poor Baron Captain thought to gain prestige from you and discovered that he'd lost further face with his peers! Oh, how he'd love to murder us. I shall sleep with my door barred tonight. I should not like to catch a chill and perish...'

I was less amused, largely because I had still more mysteries to consider. I had at least thought myself fortunate in possessing power and prestige in this world. Now that had been taken from me. And if Sharadim was the true strength of the Draachenheem why had I been summoned to inhabit this body?

I had never experienced anything like it. They were calling for Sharadim, my twin (whoever they were!) perhaps because they already knew that she was the real force, that I was merely a sham who had lent his name to a series of sensational fictions. That much was logical enough, and credible. Yet the Knight in Black and Yellow, and the blind captain, both had seemed to think it was crucial for the Eternal Champion to come to this realm.

I did my best not to think too much of all this. Instead I tried to consider our immediate problems. 'Custom allows us to remain here during the Massing. Thereafter, we are outlawed – fair game for Armiad's Binkeepers. Is that the story in brief?'

'It was my understanding,' von Bek agreed. 'He seemed to think nobody would hire us. Not that I have much liking to work my passage on one of these hulls.' Even as he spoke the whole cabin gave a great shudder and we were almost jerked against the far wall. The *Frowning Shield* was on the move again. 'What chance have we, I wonder, of moving to another realm? I understand it is not difficult in the Middle Marches.'

'Our best plan is to wait here and attend the Massing. There we shall have a good idea of who still thinks Prince Flamadin a prize, who does not believe the Sharadim story, who genuinely loathes me.'

'My guess is that you'll find few friends at present. Either you – as Prince Flamadin – were responsible for those crimes or you are the victim of efficient propaganda. I know what it is to be turned into a villain overnight. Hitler and Goebbels are masters at it. But it might be possible at the Massing to prove that you are not guilty of all they say.'

'Where could I begin?'

'That we shall not know until tomorrow. Meanwhile we'd be wise to remain where we are. Have you noticed that I rang for a servant as soon as we came in?'

'And none came. They're normally swift. We are to receive only the minimum of Armiad's hospitality, it seems.'

Neither of us was hungry. We cleaned ourselves as best we could and retired to bed. I knew that I must rest, but the night-mares were particularly potent. The voices still called for Sharadim. I was tormented by them. And then, as I fell deeper and deeper into that particular dream, I began to see clearly the women who called my twin sister. They were tall and astonish-ingly beautiful, both in face and body. They had the fine, slender figures I knew so well, the tapering chins, the high cheekbones and large, slanted almond eyes, the delicate ears and soft hair. Their costumes were different but that was all. The women who formed the circle beyond the pale fire, whose voices filled the darkness, were Eldren women. They were of the race sometimes called Vadhagh, sometimes called Melnibonéan. A race who were close cousins to John Daker's people. As the Eternal Champion I had belonged to both. As Erekosë I had loved such a woman.

And then suddenly as the white flames burned lower and I could see more beyond them I trembled in a mixture of ecstasy and fear, crying out, reaching out – longing to touch that face I had recognised.

— *Ermizhad!* I cried. — *Oh, my darling! I am here. I am here. Pull me through the flames! I am here!*

But the woman, whose arms were linked with those of her sisters, did not hear me. She had her eyes closed. She continued to chant and sway, chant and sway. Now I doubted it was her. Unless it was the Eldren who called me back to them, who called Shara-dim thinking they called me. The fire grew brighter and blinded me. I glimpsed her again. I was almost certain it was my lost love.

I was dragged away from this dream and into another. Now I had no idea what my name was. I saw a red sky in which dragons wheeled. Enormous reptilian flying beasts who appeared to obey a group of people standing upon the blackened ruins of a city. I was not one of these people, but I stood with them. They, too, resembled the Eldren, although their costumes were far more

420

elaborate, somehow almost dandified, though I could not be sure
how I knew so much. But these were Eldren, I was sure, from
another time and place. They seemed distressed. There was a rapport between them and the beasts above which was difficult for
me to understand, although I had an echo of a memory (or a premonition, which is the same thing for such as I). I tried to speak to
one of my companions, but they did not know I was amongst
them. Soon after this, I found myself falling away from them
again and I stood upon a glassy plain without horizon. The plain
changed colour from green to purple to blue and back to green, as
if it had only recently been created and had yet to stabilise. A creature of astonishing beauty, with golden skin and the most benign
eyes I had ever looked into, was speaking to me. But somehow I was
von Bek. The words were completely meaningless to me, for again
they were addressed to the wrong individual. I tried to tell this wonderful creature the truth, but my mouth would not move. I was a
statue, made of the same glassy, shifting substance as the plain.

— *We are the lost, we are the last, we are the unkind. We are the
Warriors at the Edge of Time. We are the cold, the halt, the deaf, the
blind. Fate's frozen forces, veterans of the psychic wars...*

I saw those despairing soldiers again, ranged along the ragged
edge of a great cliff above an unfathomable abyss. Did they
address me, or did they speak whenever they sensed the presence
of an audience of any kind?

I saw a man in black-and-yellow armour, riding a massive black
war-charger across a stretch of wild water. I called out to him but
either he did not hear me or he chose to ignore me. Yet he left a
name behind him on the wind. I heard it. It was Sepiriz...

Then, briefly, I saw Ermizhad's face again. I heard the chanting,
much louder for a few seconds. *SHARADIM! SHARADIM!
SHARADIM! AID US SHARADIM! FREE THE FIREDRAKE!
RELEASE THE DRAGON, SHARADIM, AND SET US FREE!*

— *Ermizhad!*

I opened my eyes and I was shrieking her name into the face of
a concerned and bewildered Ulric von Bek.

'Wake up, man,' he said. 'I think we have reached the Massing Ground. Come and see.'

I shook my head, still deep within my memories of those dreams.

'Are you ill?' he wanted to know. 'Shall I find some sort of doctor? If they have such people aboard this disgusting vessel.'

I drew a series of deep breaths. 'Forgive me. I did not wish to startle you. I had a dream.'

'Of the woman you seek? The one you love?'

'Yes.'

'You cried out her name. I am sorry if I have disturbed you, my friend. I'll leave you alone to recover yourself.'

'No, von Bek. Please stay. Ordinary human company is what I need most at present. You've been on deck already, eh?'

'I find it difficult to sleep because of the movement of the hull. Also the smell. Perhaps I'm too fastidious, but it reminds me just a little of the concentration camp I was sent to.'

I sympathised with him, understanding his distaste for Armiad's ship a little better.

Soon I was dressed and as clean as I could get, following von Bek out to a gallery which ran almost the length of our apartments and which gave a fairly good view to starboard. Through the smoke, the tangled rigging, the banners and chimneys and turrets, I saw that we had effectively beached, prow turned inward, upon an island of firm land which was almost circular in shape, rising to a central point on which was erected a simple stone monolith, similar to some I had seen in Cornwall as John Daker. Almost fifty hulls had already arrived and their massive bulks dwarfed the human figures who milled about them. They continued to make steam, but in a somewhat desultory fashion. Every so often one of the hulls would give off a great hiss and blow smoke high into the air so that I began to be reminded of a company of beached whales, though these were not accidentally arranged. There was an impressive precision to the almost exact distance between each hull.

The hulls formed a semicircle about the island. On the far side was a group of slim, elegant vessels reminiscent of Greek galleys, with shipped oars and relatively little sail on their masts. They were beautifully decorated and richly dressed. I would have taken them for the formal boats of a wealthy nation. There were some five of these. Next to them were six smaller vessels which in their own way were as impressive as the others. These were painted white from stern to prow. Almost everything which could be white was white. Masts, sails, oars – even the single flags flying from each ship were white save for a small dark symbol in the left-hand corner. It seemed to be nothing more than a cross, each end of which was completed by a long barb.

Next came three much bigger, bulkier vessels, apparently also powered by steam, though they resembled nothing I had seen elsewhere. They were primarily wooden, with high castles, ports for guns or oars, a single fat funnel in the stern section and a series of perhaps eight small paddle-wheels on either side. It was almost as if someone had had an idea of a steam ship and attempted to make it, irrespective of whether it worked well or not. But it was obvious that it was not my place to judge. The cumbersome ships were doubtless perfectly functional. Docked beside these were a number of dish-shaped vessels, apparently carved from a single piece of wood (though the tree would have had to have been enormous), gilded and painted and containing only a flagmast on one edge, together with rowlocks all around, through which were placed long wooden oars. These did not seem designed to negotiate anything but the shallowest of inland waters and I guessed that the people who used them had not had to cross an ocean to be here.

Lastly, between the furthest Maaschanheemer hull on our left and the dish-shaped boats, was one great vessel which looked more like a stylised Noah's Ark than anything I had ever seen afloat. It was of wood, with sharply pointed stern and prow; one single huge house on its deck, also of the simplest design, but four storeys high, with windows and doors placed at regular intervals without any attempt at decoration. It was one of the most functional, unimaginative vessels you could find. The only thing which made me curious about it was that the doors seemed a good deal larger than were needed for people of average height. No flags flew from it and von Bek was as incapable as I of guessing who owned it or where it was from.

A few distant figures had landed near their ships, but we could see no details. The people from the white vessels seemed to wear clothing which covered them from head to foot and which was also of an unrelieved whiteness. The people from the very elaborate galleys next to them were, as one might have expected, brightly dressed. The people from the large, open boats had erected tall, angular tents and judging by the smoke from the largest of these were preparing themselves food. There was no sign at all of the occupants of the Ark.

I wished that I might have had Jurgin's spyglass, for I was intensely curious about all the occupants of the so-called Six Realms.

We were speculating on the identities of the people and their ships when a voice from above shouted: 'Enjoy your leisure, good gentlemen! You'll have little enough after the Massing. We'll see if a deposed prince of the Valadek can run as well as the average marsh mouse!'

It was Armiad, red-faced and spitting, clad in some sort of morning robe of purple and cerise, leaning over a balcony above us and to our right and clenching his fists as if he would squeeze the life from out of us if he could.

We bowed to him, wished him a pleasant morning, and went inside. We had decided to risk leaving our quarters now (though we took all we owned with us) and went to look for our young friends in the hope that they would still wish to spend time in our company.

We discovered Bellanda and her companions seated on a flat part of a high foredeck playing some kind of game with coloured counters. They were a little surprised to see us and got up reluctantly from their game.

'You've heard the news, plainly,' I said to Bellanda, whose youthful, pretty face was full of honest embarrassment. 'I have been turned from a hero into a villain, it seems. Would you take my word, for the time being, that I know nothing of the crimes they speak of?'

'You don't have the manner of someone who would easily quit his responsibilities or would try to murder his own sister,' said Bellanda slowly. She looked up at me. 'But you would not have been made into a popular hero if you did not strike people as being honest and upright. It is hard to know a heart from a handsome face, as we say on the *Frowning Shield*. Easier to read the character of an ugly one...' She looked away for a second, but when she looked back her eyes were candid. 'For all that, Prince Flamadin – or is it ex-Prince? – I think we are agreed between us to offer you the benefit of the doubt. We have to trust ourselves. Better than believing either the fictions of the popular prints or the edicts of our good Baron Captain Armiad!' She laughed. 'But why should it matter to you, hero or villain, what our opinion is? We would do you neither harm nor good. We are in a position of almost complete impotence here on the *Frowning Shield*.'

'I think your friendship is what Prince Flamadin desires,' said Ulric von Bek softly. 'For that offers at least a little confirmation that what we value is of positive worth...'

'You're a flatterer, my lord count?' She grinned at my comrade. It was his turn to show a touch of confusion.

Peering up into the crosstrees I saw young Jurgin, using his glass to observe one of the other hulls. After a brief conversation with the others I began to climb the rigging until I was seated beside Jurgin on the yardarm. 'Anything of particular interest?' I asked.

He shook his head. 'I was merely envying the other hulls. We're the filthiest, most unkempt, poorest vessel of all. And we used to be proud of our appearance. What I fail to understand is why Armiad doesn't notice what has happened to our hull since he killed the old Baron Captain. What did he want from that act?'

'The miserable frequently believe that possession of power for its own sake is what has made others more content. They grab such power in many different ways and remain baffled as to why they are just as miserable as they were to begin with. Armiad killed for something he thought would bring him happiness. Now perhaps his only satisfaction is that he can make others as unhappy as himself!'

'A somewhat complicated theory, Prince Flamadin. Are we still to call you that? I saw you with Bellanda and I understood that the others have decided to remain your friends. But since you disinherited yourself...'

'Call me simply Flamadin, if you will. I came up here to ask if I could borrow your glass. I'm particularly curious about the big, plain ship and the people in white. Can you identify them?'

'The big ship is the only vessel of its kind possessed by the Ursine Princes. They will doubtless remain inside until the true Massing begins. The women in white are said to be cannibals. They are not like other human beings. They give birth only to girls, which means they must buy or steal men from other realms, for obvious reasons. We call them the Ghost Women. They are clad entirely in ivory armour, from crown to instep, and one rarely sees their faces. We are taught to be afraid of them and to stay clear of their ships. Sometimes they make forays into other realms for males. They prefer boys and young men. Of course, they'll take nothing at the Massing save what is offered them by way of trade. Your folk are prepared to deal with them and I think Armiad would do so, too, if he was prepared to risk complete ostracism from the other Baron Captains. It is several centuries since any of our hulls traded in slaves.'

'So my own people, the people of the Draachenheem, buy and sell men and women?'

'Did you not know this, prince? We thought it commonly understood. Is it only at a Massing that your folk indulge in such business?'

'You will have to assume that I'm suffering from lapses of

memory, Jurgin. I'm as mystified as you as to the domestic customs of the Draachenheemers.'

'The worst of it is,' said Jurgin handing me his glass, 'that the Ghost Women are said to be cannibals. They are like female spiders who eat the males as soon as their work is done.'

'They're very elegant-looking spiders.' I now had a group of the women in focus. They were conferring amongst themselves. They seemed to be uncomfortable in their ivory armour which, at closer range, I could tell was not simply white but had all the shades from light yellow to brown which ivory possesses when it is used for artefacts. It was covered in fine engraving which reminded me a little of scrimshaw work. It was held together by bone pins and leather toggles and was marvellously articulated so as to enclose the entire body, making the wearers rather resemble elegant insects with unusually marked carapaces. They seemed taller than the average person and had a graceful way of moving in the restricting armour which I thought very attractive. It was hard to believe that people of such beauty could be slave-traders and cannibals.

Two of the women now put helmeted heads together to speak. One of them shook her head impatiently so that the other tried to repeat what she had said and then, in frustration, raised her visor.

I could now see part of the woman's face.

She was both young and unusually beautiful. Her skin was fair and her eyes large and dark. She had the long, triangular face I associated with the Eldren and, as she turned towards me, I almost lost my grip on the spyglass.

I was looking full into the features of one of the women who had plagued my dreams, who had called for my sister Sharadim, who had spoken so desperately of a dragon and a sword...

But what had shocked me so thoroughly was that I had recognised the face.

It was the face of the woman I had searched the aeons to find again; the woman with whom I longed, night and day, to be reunited...

It was the face of my own Ermizhad!

Chapter Five

IT SEEMED TO me that I remained staring at that face for an age. How I did not fall from the rigging I do not know. I was repeating her name over and over. Then, anxiously, I attempted to follow her with the glass as she moved. She smiled at the other woman, seemed to make some slight joke, then reached up her hand to bring her visor down again.

'No!' I did not want her to hide that exquisite face. 'Ermizhad! No! It is I, Erekosë. Cannot you hear me? I have searched for you so long...'

I had the impression of hands trying to help me from the rigging. I tried to fight them off, but there were too many. Slowly I was borne to the deck while enquiring mouths wished to know what was wrong. All I could do was repeat her name and struggle to get free, to follow her. 'Ermizhad!'

I knew in my heart that it was not really my Eldren wife but someone closely resembling her. I knew it, yet I resisted the understanding as thoroughly as I resisted the hands of my astonished companions.

'Daker! Herr Daker! What's wrong? Is it an hallucination?' Count von Bek held my face and stared into my eyes. 'You're acting like a madman!'

I drew a breath. I was panting. I was sweating. I hated them all for holding me as they did. But I forced myself to grow calm. 'I have seen a woman who might be Ermizhad's sister,' I told him. 'The same woman I saw in my dream last night. She must be related. It cannot be her. I am not so crazed that my logic is completely askew. Yet the sight strikes the same chords as if it were really Ermizhad I had seen. I must get to her, von Bek. I must question her.'

Bellanda was shouting from behind me. 'You cannot go. It is

the Law. All our encounters are formal. The true time of the Massing has not yet come. You must wait.'

'I cannot wait,' I told her simply. 'I have already waited too long.' But I let my body relax, felt their grasp grow limp. 'No other creature could believe how many lifetimes I have spent seeking her...'

They became sympathetic. I closed my eyes. Then I opened them a slit. I was looking at a likely route down to the shore.

A moment later I was up, diving from the side of the deck, vaulting the rail, flinging myself towards rigging, then sliding and clambering and dropping down, down to the lowest outside deck. While various workers yelled at me in protest, I pushed through gangs of men hauling on ropes, others who carried barrels down towards the rollers and yet others who bore large pieces of timber sheeting of the kind used for repairs. These I ignored, got to the side and found that ropes had been arranged here so that the hull might be inspected. I swung down one rope, dropped onto a swaying plank, jumped from the plank to a tall ladder and slid down this to the ground. Then I was running over the soft turf of the island towards the boats of the so-called Ghost Women.

I was halfway to their camp, passing the monolith which now raised itself above me, when the pursuers (of whom I'd not been aware) caught up with me. Suddenly I found myself struggling in a huge net while beyond the mesh I saw von Bek, Bellanda, some of the young men and a group of Binkeepers.

'Prince Flamadin!' I heard Bellanda call. 'Armiad seeks any excuse to destroy you. Cross into another camp before the Massing and the penalty can be death!'

'I don't care. I must see Ermizhad. I have seen her – or someone who will know where she is. Let me go. I beg you to let me go!'

Von Bek stepped forward. 'Daker! My friend! These men are commissioned to kill you if necessary. As it happens they have no stomach for Armiad's orders, but they are bound to obey him if you do not pull yourself together.'

'Do you understand what I have seen, von Bek?'

'I think so. But if you wait for the Massing to begin, you can approach this woman in a civilised fashion. It is not long to wait, after all.'

I nodded. I was in danger of losing my mind completely. Also I might bring those who had befriended me into danger. I forced myself to recall the ordinary human decencies.

When next I rose up I was in full charge of my senses. I apologised to everyone. I turned and began to make my way back to our hull. From the ground the grouping of hulls was even more impressive. It was almost as if every great transatlantic liner, including the *Titanic*, congregated here, each one neatly beached with its bow pointing inland, each one bearing on its back a complete and complex medieval town. This sight took my attention away from Ermizhad just a little. I knew that I was experiencing something akin to a continuing hallucination, an extension of my dreams that past night. Yet there was no question but that the woman resembled Ermizhad, down to the shape of her mouth and the subtle colour of her eyes. So the women were Eldren. Yet they were not from the same time, probably not even the same realm, as the one from which I had been wrenched against my will. I resolved to contact those women as soon as I could. They might have some clue, at least, to Ermizhad's whereabouts. And I might also discover why they called for Sharadim.

Von Bek and I had been wise to take all our possessions with us when we left our quarters. When we reached Armiad's portcullis and called to the guard to open it for us there was a silence. This was followed by some kind of mumbled reply to our third request for the gate to be opened.

'Speak up, man!' cried von Bek. 'What's the trouble?'

Finally a guard on the other side yelled that the gate was stuck and that it would be a number of hours before it could be repaired.

Von Bek and I looked hard at one another and smiled. Our suspicions were confirmed. Armiad could not dismiss us from his hull but he could do everything in his power to make life uncomfortable for us.

For my part I was as glad to be out of his company and we made our way back to the part of the ship where our student friends generally congregated. Some of them were there, playing their interminable game with counters, although Bellanda, we learned, had gone to take instruction from a teacher recently dismissed from their school.

With Jurgin's willing assistance, we continued to watch the preparations being made for the Massing. Various stalls, pens, tents and other temporary buildings were being erected. Each group from the Six Realms had brought goods they wished to trade, as well as livestock, publications, new tools. The people of the Draachenheem seemed a little disdainful of the others while the Ghost Women kept themselves thoroughly apart.

One group seemed more used to trading. They had the hardy, simple look of a people who regularly carried on barter in a variety of locations. It was the way in which they set up their stalls, looked at their neighbours, chatted amongst themselves, which characterised them. The only surprise, for me, was their inefficient boats. They must be more used to making overland treks for their normal trading, I thought. These were the people whose realm was called Fluugensheem, who were protected, I remembered being told, by a flying island. They seemed singularly ordinary for folk so exotically named.

There was still no sign of those who had come here in the oddly shaped ark, nor of the occupants of the three bulky paddle-steamers.

'This evening,' Jurgin told me, 'they will begin the first ceremony, when all announce themselves and give up their names. Then you shall see them, every one, including the Ursine Princes.'

He would say no more. When I asked him why the Ursine Princes were so named he would only grin at me. Since my chief interest was in those they called the Ghost Women, I was not greatly upset by his deliberate mystification.

Needless to say von Bek and myself were not amongst those invited to attend the first ceremony, but we watched from the

431

rigging of the *Frowning Shield* as gradually the various peoples of the Six Realms began to assemble about the monolith. This was called, I was told, the Meeting Stone and had been erected several centuries before, when these strange gatherings first began. Until then, Bellanda informed me, all the various realms had regarded the others with superstitious fear and had fought each other at random. Gradually, with familiarity, they had struck upon this means of trading and exchanging information. Every thirteen and a half months, apparently, the Six Realms intersected so that each realm could enter any one of the others. This period was brief – three days or so – but it was enough for everyone to conduct their business, so long as it was agreed that only the most formal rules were applied. No time could be wasted on anything but the agreed activities.

Now the stolid merchants of Fluugensheem came to take their places on one side of the monolith. Next the Ghost Women of Gheestenheem arranged themselves on the other side of the Meeting Stone. They were followed by six Baron Captains of the Maaschanheem, six splendid lordlings of the Draachenheem, and, from the strange steamers, six fur-festooned and bearded Rootsenheemers, wearing great metal gauntlets and metal masks which obscured the top halves of their heads. But it was the last contingent which stunned me.

The Ursine Princes were precisely named. The five great, handsome beasts who marched out of their ark and down the lowered ramp to the ground were not human at all. They were bears, bigger than grizzlies, clad in rippling silks and fine plaids, each wearing upon his shoulders a kind of delicate frame from which, suspended over his head, hung a banner – doubtless the banner of his family.

Von Bek was frowning. 'I am astonished. It is as if I look at the legendary founders of Berlin! You know we have legends… My family has stories concerning intelligent beasts. I had thought they spoke of wolves, but doubtless it is of bears. Have you seen anything like the Ursine Princes in your travels, Daker?'

'Nothing quite like them,' I said. I was greatly impressed by their beauty. Soon they, too, were grouped around the Meeting Stone and we were able to catch a few words of the ceremony. Each person gave his or her name. Each described his or her intention in coming to the Massing. This done, one of the Baron Captains declared: 'Until the morning!'

The response came: 'Until the morning!' Then they all went their separate ways, back to their own ships.

I had strained to hear the Ghost Women announce their names. I had heard nothing which even remotely resembled the sound of 'Ermizhad'.

That night we were guests of the students, sleeping in their already cramped quarters, constantly inhaling ash, besieged by draughts, rolled from side to side by sudden movements of the hull which, although it did not travel, was still subject to peculiar shudderings, like someone in a disturbed sleep. It sometimes seemed to me that the *Frowning Shield* was in tune with my own state of mind.

Again my sleep was constantly interrupted by nightmares. I heard the Ghost Women chanting, still, but no longer in my dreams. I could hear them in their own camp. I longed to go to them but the one time I rose, with the intention of going over the side once more, both von Bek and Jurgin took hold of me and stopped me.

'You must be patient,' von Bek said. 'Remember your promise to us.'

'But they are calling for Sharadim. I need to know what they want.'

'They want her, surely. Not you.' Von Bek's voice was urgent. 'If you left now Armiad and his men would be bound to see you. They'd feel within their rights to kill you. Why risk that when tomorrow you can approach them under the terms of the Massing?'

I agreed that I was being childish. I forced myself to lie down again. I lay there, looking up through the gaps in the roof at the occasional spurt of glowing cinders, the grey, cold sky, trying not to think of Ermizhad or the Ghost Women. I slept a little, but sleep only allowed the voices to sound louder in my ears.

'I am not Sharadim!' I cried out at one point. It was dawn. Around me the students were stirring. Bellanda made her way through the sleeping bodies. 'What is it, Flamadin?'

'I am not Sharadim!' I told her. 'They want me to be my sister. Why is that? They do not call me. They do call me – but they call me by my sister's name. Could Sharadim and Flamadin be the same person?'

'You are twins. But one is male, the other female. You could not be mistaken for her...' Bellanda's voice was a little sluggish with sleep. 'Forgive me. I suppose I'm talking nonsense.'

I put out my hand and touched her. I was apologetic. 'No, Bellanda, it is I who should apologise. I talk nonsense a great deal of the time at present.'

She smiled. 'Then, if you think that, you cannot be completely insane. You say those women were chanting all night for Princess Sharadim? I could not hear them so clearly. It sounded like an incantation. Do they believe Sharadim is a supernatural creature?'

'I cannot say. Until now I have always recognised the name I hear in my dreams. I have responded to it. I was Urlik Skarsol, then I was a variety of other incarnations, then Skarsol again and now Flamadin. The fact is, Bellanda, that I know in my bones they should be calling me!'

But because this sounded like egomaniacal ravings (and might have been) I stopped myself from continuing. I shrugged and lay back in my blanket. 'Later,' I said, 'I shall have the chance to answer them face to face.'

And I slept a little longer, dreaming only pleasantly of my life with Ermizhad when together we had ruled the Eldren.

By the time I awoke again everyone else was already up. I stretched, stumbled to the communal washing stands and tried to clean oily grime from my body.

When I next looked towards the Massing Ground I was surprised and impressed by what I saw.

In some parts little groups of people stood engaged in eager conversations. I saw two bears squatting beside a Ghost Woman displaying charts and all three talking vigorously. Elsewhere the bright awnings of market stalls offered an illusion that this was no more than an ordinary country fair, while the lie was given by a pen in which two awkward and bad-tempered lizards, standing upright on their hind legs and resembling a kind of dinosaur, snapped with red mouths at two Maaschanheemers who were pointing out aspects of the saddles and harness on these beasts and questioning their owner, a tall Draachenheemer. Doubtless the lizards gave that folk its name.

All manner of weird livestock was on display, as well as animals more familiar to me. There were certain goods which I failed completely to identify but which plainly were in great demand.

The noise of all these exchanges was loud but reasonably good-humoured. Many people walked in small groups, neither buying nor selling, but merely enjoying the spectacle.

Over near the great ark, vessel of the Ursine Princes, a less pleasant aspect of the day could be seen. Here were frightened teenage boys, stark naked and chained together, being inspected by Ghost Women. I could scarcely believe that the Eldren had become so corrupt as to be slave-owners and cannibals.

'Are these the people you claim are so much nobler than human beings?' said von Bek. He spoke sardonically, but he was plainly disgusted by the sight. 'I can hardly find help for my own mission here, if such things are commonly permitted.'

Bellanda joined us. 'The Ursine Princes rule a realm where the humans are savages. They kill and eat one another. They buy and sell one another. So the Princes feel it is an ordinary custom amongst humans and do not see why they should not benefit. The boys are well treated – by the bears, at least.'

'And what do the women do with them?'

'Breed from them,' said Bellanda. She shrugged. 'It's no more than a reversal of a situation commonly found amongst our own people.'

'Except that we don't cook and eat our wives,' said von Bek.

Bellanda said nothing.

'For all that,' I said, 'I am now going down there. I intend to approach the Ghost Women and ask them some questions. Surely that is permitted?'

'Permitted to exchange information,' said Bellanda. 'But you must not interrupt a bartering while it is in progress.'

We disembarked from the hull with a crowd of others who were interested in the sights and who casually inspected the variety of goods for sale. With von Bek in my wake, I headed directly for the area near the white ships where the Ghost Women had pitched their tents and enclosures of tightly woven silk. Finding no-one outside, I walked to the largest of the pavilions. The opening was unguarded. I entered. I stopped in some consternation.

Von Bek behind me said: 'My God! A cattle market indeed.'

The place stank of human bodies. Here the slavers had brought their wares to be inspected. One scarred, wide-eyed soul especially impressed me. Some were presumably embarrassed or ashamed by their calling. Others preferred to strike their bargains in relative privacy.

In the gloom of the tent I saw at least a dozen pens, their floors covered with straw, and within the pens were boys and youths, some of whom bore the marks of every kind of cruelty, while others were proud, holding themselves with straight shoulders and glaring into the unseen faces of the Ghost Women who looked them over. Many more were simply passive, as docile as calves.

But what really shocked me was the sight of Baron Captain Armiad, evidently in the process of striking a bargain with one of the ivory-clad women. A ruffian, who was plainly not of the usual hull's complement, held a string of about six boys in a kind of continuous rope halter about their necks. Armiad was pointing out their virtues to the woman, making jokes to her which plainly she neither understood nor cared to hear. Doubtless he had discovered a more lucrative means of ridding himself of some of his surplus population and, since the other Maaschanheemers hated trading in slaves, felt himself safe enough from scrutiny.

He looked up in the middle of a greasy grin, saw von Bek and myself looking at him, and shouted with fury. 'Spies as well as outlaws! So this is how you'd be revenged on me, when I discovered your perfidy!'

I held up my hands, trying to show him that I was not about to interfere with his business. But he was incensed. He knocked the rope from the hand of his hireling. He strode towards me. And he would not stop yelling.

'Keep the damned slaves!' he screamed at the surprised Ghost Woman. 'Have them for your supper tonight, with my compliments. Come, Rooper, we have changed our plans.' He stopped when he reached me. His face was bright red. He glared up into my eyes. 'Flamadin, you renegade. Why did you follow me? Did you hope to blackmail me? To shame me further in front of my fellow Baron Captains? Well, the truth is that I was not selling those lads. I had hoped to free them.'

'I am not interested in your affairs, Armiad,' I said coldly. 'And I am even less interested in your lies.'

'You say I lie?'

I shrugged. 'I am here to speak with the Ghost Women. Please continue with your business. Do whatever you care to do. I have no wish to have anything further to do with you, Baron Captain.'

'You still take a haughty tone for a would-be kin-killer and a disgraced exile.' He lunged at me. I stepped back. From out of his uncharacteristically simple tunic he drew a long knife. Weapons were banned at the Massing, I knew. Even von Bek had left his gun with Bellanda. I reached out to grab his wrist. He dodged back. He stood there panting like a crazed dog. He glared. Then he rushed me again, the knife raised.

By this time there was a cacophony in the Ghost Women's pavilion. Half a dozen age-old laws had been broken at once. I tried to hold him off me, calling to von Bek to help.

My friend, however, had been attacked by Armiad's ruffian and had another knife to contend with.

We found ourselves backing from the great tent, yelling for help and at the same time trying to make Armiad and Rooper see some kind of sense. They were serving themselves badly and attracting unwanted attention.

Suddenly a dozen men and women had fallen on us and dragged Armiad and his henchman back, twisting the knives from their hands.

'I was defending myself,' said Armiad, 'against that villain. These knives were carried by the pair of them, I swear.'

I could not believe that anyone would accept his story, but now a thick-set Draachenheemer spat on the ground at my feet. 'You know me, I think, Flamadin. I was one of those who chose you for our Overlord. But you spurned us. And worse. It is good for you, Flamadin, that no blood may be spilled here. If it were not for that, I'd take a knife to you myself. Traitor! Charlatan!' And he spat again.

Now virtually all the gathered people were staring at me with loathing.

Only the women, their emotions unreadable behind their ivory masks, looked at me in a different way. I had the impression that they had suddenly recognised me and were taking a considerable interest in me.

'When the Massing's done, we'll find you soon enough, Flamadin!' said the Draachenheemer. He strode back into the tent which hid the slave pens.

Armiad was plainly almost as surprised as I had been that people were prepared to believe his story. He gathered his clothing together. He drew himself upright. He snorted and cleared his throat. 'Who else would dare to break our ancient laws?' he asked the crowd in general.

There were some, evidently, who did not believe him. But I think they were outnumbered by those who already hated me and would believe me guilty of a dozen additional crimes, as well as those already published!

THE DRAGON IN THE SWORD

'Armiad,' I said again. 'I assure you I had no intention of meddling in your business. I came to visit the Ghost Women.'

'Who but a slaver pays a visit to the Ghost Women?' he asked of the crowd in general.

A broad-beamed old man made his way through to us. He carried a staff almost twice his height and his ruddy features were stern with the importance of his office. 'No arguments, no fights, no duels. These are our ways. Go you your ways, good gentlemen, and bring no further disgrace upon us.'

The Ghost Women were no longer interested in anyone but me. They were staring hard now. I heard them talking between themselves. I heard the name 'Flamadin' on their lips. I bowed to them. 'I am here as a friend of the Eldren race.'

There was no response. The women remained as impassive as their ivory masks.

'I would speak with you,' I said.

Still there was no response. Two of them turned away.

Armiad was still blustering, accusing me of beginning the whole affair. The old man, who called himself the Mediator, was adamant. It did not matter who had begun the dispute. It must not continue until after the Massing. 'You will both be confined to your hulls under pain of death. That is the Law.'

'But I must speak with the Ghost Women,' I told him. 'It is what I came for. I had no intention of getting into a brawl with that braggart.'

'No further insults!' insisted the Mediator. 'Or there will be further punishment. Return to the *Frowning Shield*, good gentleman. There you must remain until the Massing is done.'

Von Bek murmured, 'You can do nothing now in sight of all these people. You will have to wait until tonight.'

Armiad was giving me an unpleasant grin. I thought he had already planned my demise. I guessed that few now would blame him if he was forced to imprison me and sentence me to death as soon as the Massing was over. His thoughts were so primitive they were not difficult to read.

Reluctantly, however, I walked back towards the hull with Armiad. We were escorted by the Mediator and a mixed group who had evidently been elected by the whole assembly to uphold the Laws. It was not easy to see how I was going to be able to leave the hull and find the Ghost Women.

I looked back over my shoulder. They were standing in a group staring after me, all other dealings forgotten. It was plain that they would be more than interested in a visit from me. But what they wanted of me and what they expected to do with me, I had no idea.

In the hull Armiad let the Mediator's people lead us to our original quarters. He was still grinning. Matters had gone well for him, after all. I did not know how von Bek and I were to be accused or what we would be accused of, but I knew that Armiad already had a plan in mind.

His final words as he stalked away to his own rooms were a gleeful: 'Before long, good gentlemen, you'll be wishing that the Ghost Women had kept you and were stripping the flesh from you before your eyes and eating your parts while the rest of you slowly roasts.'

Von Bek raised an eyebrow. 'Anything would be more enjoyable than your own cuisine, Baron Captain.'

Armiad frowned, failing to understand the reference. Then he glared, almost on principle, and was gone.

A few moments later we heard the outer bars go down over our doors. We could still get to our balcony, but it would be a long and difficult climb to the decks below and there was no certainty that Armiad had not deliberately left that means of escape open to us as a means of trapping us. We would have to plan carefully now and see if there was a less obvious means of escape. It was likely we had a night to ourselves, but we could not be sure.

'I doubt he's as subtle as you think,' said von Bek. He was already casting about for something he could use as a rope.

For my part I needed to think. I sat on the bed, automatically helping him knot the blankets together, while I reviewed the events of the morning.

'The Ghost Women recognised me,' I said.

Von Bek was amused. 'So did most of the entire camp. But you do not seem to have a great many here who approve of you! Your refusal to honour tradition seems a worse crime, to many here, than your attempt to murder your sister! I am familiar with such logic. My own people are often guilty of the same thing. What chance do you think you'll have, even if you get off this hull? Most of the others, with the possible exception of the Ursine Princes and the Ghost Women, would be in full cry after you. Where would we escape to, my friend?'

'I must admit I have thought of the same problem.' I smiled at him. 'I had hoped you might have a solution.'

'Our first task must be to review all possible escape routes,' he said. 'Then we must wait until nightfall. We'll achieve nothing before then.'

'I'm afraid it was not greatly to your advantage,' I said apologetically, 'throwing in your lot with me.'

He laughed. 'I do not believe I had a great deal of choice, my friend. Did you?'

Von Bek had a way of improving my spirits for which I was enormously grateful. Once we had debated all routes to freedom (there was none which seemed very useful), I lay back on my bed and tried to fathom why the Ghost Women had looked at me with such curiosity. Had they, ironically, mistaken me for my twin sister Sharadim?

Night fell eventually. We had decided on our original means of escape, via the balcony and across to the nearest mast, from there down the rigging. We had no weapons of any kind, von Bek having given his pistol to Bellanda. All we could hope for would be to escape our pursuers even if we were seen.

So it was that we found ourselves in the chilly air, seeing a hundred different fires in the distance, hearing the sounds of people of all different races and cultures, some of them not even human, as they celebrated this strange Massing. Von Bek had made a kind of grappling hook from some wooden furniture. The intention was to throw this into the nearest tangle of rigging in the hope that it would hold. He whispered to me to be ready to pay out our home-made rope as soon as he gave the word, then he swung the thing out into space. I heard it hit, hold for a moment, then fall free. Another four or five casts and it seemed to find a good purchase. I let the rope run through my hands until von Bek gave the order to stop. He began to tie the remainder to the gallery rail.

'Now,' he murmured, 'we must trust to luck. Shall I go first?'

I shook my head. Since this affair was a result of my obsessions the least I could do would be to take the chief risk. I clambered to the other side of the balcony, took hold of our rope and began to swing, hand over hand, towards the rigging.

It was at that point that a voice from above shouted triumphantly.

'The thieves are escaping. Capture them, quickly!'

And the whole hull seemed to come alive with men exposing the beams of dark lanterns and training them on von Bek, who was half over the rail, and on me where I hung helplessly, unable to go forward or back.

'We surrender!' cried von Bek lightly, making the best of it. 'We'll go back to our prison.'

And Armiad's answering hiss was full of malicious glee. 'Oh no, you will not, good gentlemen. You must fall to the decks and break a few bones before we recapture you...'

'You're a cold-hearted bastard as well as a mannerless parvenu,' said von Bek. He was loosening the knot holding the rope to the rail. Did he mean to kill me? Then he jumped, grabbed the rope just below me and yelled: 'Hang on, Herr Daker!'

The rope fell free of the rail and we swung with enormous force towards the rigging, striking tarred ropes which cut our faces and hands but also shaking our enemies from their posts nearby. We began to scramble down.

But the whole hull was a-crawl with armed men and even as we set foot on a firm deck two or three sighted us and attacked at a run.

We rushed to the next balustrade and looked down. There was

no way in which we could jump, nothing we could even hope to hang on to.

I heard a peculiar rattle from above and, looking up, saw to my complete astonishment a tall woman in bone-white armour sliding down a rope. She had a sword under her arm, a war-axe dangling from the thong on her wrist. She landed beside us and moved efficiently forward, slicing and carving apparently at the air.

What in fact she did to the Maaschanheemers I was never sure, but they seemed to collapse to the floor in small pieces. She signalled to us to follow her which we did gratefully. Now we could see at least a dozen of the Ghost Women here and there on the ship – and wherever they had gone there were no Maaschanheemers to block our way.

I heard Armiad laughing. It was an unpleasant laugh. He seemed to be choking. 'Farewell, you dogs. You deserve your fate. It is bound to be worse than anything I could conceive!'

The Ghost Women now formed a sort of moving barrier around us as they moved swiftly through the ship, cutting all down before them.

Within moments von Bek and I were over the side and being borne by the women through the camp towards their own tents.

I knew that they had broken all the old laws of the Massing.

What could be so important to them that they were prepared to take such enormous risks? Without the Massing, they would be hard put to find more male slaves for their specific purposes. Their race must surely perish!

I heard von Bek say to me in a voice which shook: 'I think we are their prisoners, my friend, rather than their guests. What on earth can their purpose be with us?'

One of the women said sternly: 'Be silent. Our future and our very existence are now in question. We came to find you, not to fight those others. Now we must leave at once.'

'Leave?' I felt my stomach begin to turn. 'Where are you taking us?'

'To Gheestenheem, of course.

I heard von Bek utter one of his wild laughs. 'Oh, this is too much for me. I've escaped Hitler's torturers only to be someone's Christmas goose. I trust you'll find me tasty, ladies. I am rather leaner than either of us would like at present.'

They had carried us up to one of their slender white ships. Now we were bundled over the side. I could hear oars being unshipped.

'Well, von Bek,' I said to my friend. 'At least we are to solve the mystery of Gheestenheem at first hand!'

I sat upright in the boat. Nobody restrained me as, supporting myself on a wooden seat, I got to my feet and looked out over black water.

Behind us were the fires and huge shadows of the Massing Ground. I was certain I would never see it again.

I turned to address the woman who had led the raid on the hull. 'Why did you risk all you value? You can never attend another Massing, surely? I still do not know if I should be grateful to you or not!'

She was loosening her armour, unstrapping a visor plate. 'You must judge that for yourself,' she said, 'when we reach Gheestenheem.'

She removed her visor.

It was the woman I had seen earlier. As I stared at her beautiful features I remembered a dream I had had once. I had been speaking to Ermizhad. She had told me that she could not be eternally reincarnated, as I was, but that when her spirit came to inhabit another form, the form would always be the same. And she would always love me. I saw no recognition in this face, yet tears came to my eyes as I looked at her.

I said: 'Is it you, Ermizhad?'

The woman regarded me in some surprise.

'My name is Alisaard,' she said. 'Why are you weeping?'

Book Two

Not unremembering we pass our exile from the starry ways:
One timeless hour in time we caught from the long night of
endless days.
With solemn gaiety the stars danced far withdrawn on elfin
heights:
The lilac breathed amid the shade of green and blue and
citron lights,
But yet the close enfolding night seemed on the phantom verge
of things,
For our adoring hearts had turned within from all their
wanderings:
For beauty called to beauty, and there thronged at the
enchanter's will
The vanished hours of love that burn within the Ever-living still.
And sweet eternal faces put the shadows of the earth to rout,
And faint and fragile as a moth your white hand fluttered and
went out.
Oh, who am I who tower beside this goddess of the twilight air?

– 'A.E.' (George Russell),
'Aphrodite'

Chapter One

I REMEMBER LITTLE else of that voyage until dawn of the next day. Here the sun was rising, red, massive and insubstantial, wavering in watery haze and giving a kind of pink and scarlet glaze to the wide waves. There was a wind up, filling the white sail and the sun touched us also so that we were all of the same subtle colourings, blending with the ocean as we drove on towards the east.

Then, gradually, I made out something else ahead. It was as if the sea had thrown up a series of gigantic water-spouts. Then I realised this was not water, but light. Great columns of light plunging down from the sky and illuminating a vast area of water. Behind them were mist, foam and clouds. Within the area surrounded by the columns the water was calm.

Von Bek was in the prow, one hand on a taut rope, the other shielding his eyes. He was excited. There was fresh spray on his skin. He looked as if he had come alive again. I, too, was grateful for the salt water which had washed the oily grime from me.

'What a marvel of Nature!' von Bek exclaimed. 'How do you think it's formed, Daker?'

I shook my head. 'My assumption is always that it is magic.' I began to laugh, realising the irony of my remark.

Shaking out her dark red hair, Alisaard came from below decks. 'Ah,' she said seriously, 'you have seen the Entrance.'

'Entrance?' said von Bek. 'To what?'

'To Gheestenheem, of course.' She plainly found his naïveté charming. I felt an uncalled-for pang of jealousy. Why should this woman not favour whom she chose? She was not my Ermizhad. But it was hard to bear that in mind, the resemblance was so strong. She turned to me. 'Did you sleep? Or did you weep all night, Prince Flamadin?' Her tone was one of amused sympathy. I found that I could not easily believe these women to be cruel slave-owners and cannibals. Nonetheless I felt I had to bear in mind my own experience, that often the most urbane, civilised and humane cultures have at least one aspect to them which, though ordinary in their eyes, may seem perfectly hideous to others. For all that, these women had the grace I associated with my own Eldren.

'Do you call yourselves "Ghost Women"?' I asked her, as much to have her attention as anything.

'No. But we've long since discovered that our best weapon of defence lies in turning the humans' superstitions to our advantage. The armour has a number of practical functions, especially when we are in the vicinity of those smoky hulls, but it also maintains a kind of mystery, frightens those who would offer us all kinds of insult and aggression.'

'Then what do you call yourselves?' I asked, scarcely wanting to hear her answer.

'We are women of the Eldren race,' she said.

'And your people dwell in Gheestenheem?' My heart had begun to pound.

'The women,' she said. 'They dwell in Gheestenheem.'

'Only the women? You have no men?'

'We have men, but we are separated from them. There was an exodus. The Eldren were driven from their original realm by human barbarians who called themselves the Mabden. We sought refuge elsewhere, but in seeking it we were parted. Thus we have perpetuated ourselves for many centuries by means of human males. We, however, may only bear girl children from such a union. It maintains our blood, but it is a distasteful process to us.'

'What becomes of the males when they've served your purpose?'

She laughed, flinging back her fine head so that the sun seemed to set her hair on fire. 'You think we intend to fatten you for a feast, Prince Flamadin? You'll have an answer to your question when we get to Gheestenheem!'

'Why did you risk so much in order to rescue us?'

'We had not intended to rescue you at all. We did not know you were in danger. We wanted to talk to you. Then, when we saw what was happening, we decided to help you.'

'So you came to capture me?'

'To talk. Would you rather we returned you to that smelly hull?'

I was quick to deny any desire to see the *Frowning Shield* ever again. 'When do you intend to offer me an explanation?'

'When Gheestenheem is reached,' she said. 'Look!'

The columns were high overhead now, though our ship had not yet reached them. The white ship was ablaze with reflected light. At first I had thought the columns white, too, like marble, but in fact they were alive with all the colours of the rainbow.

In the stern, the helmswomen leaned hard on their steering oars, moving the ship carefully between the columns.

'It's dangerous to touch them,' Alisaard explained. 'They could burn a ship like ours to ashes in seconds.'

Now I was half-blinded by the dazzling light. I received an impression of massive waves rising up around the base of the columns, of the ship being swept upwards, of us being hurled towards first one pillar of light and then another. But our crew were experienced. Suddenly we were through and bobbing gently on calm water in total silence. I looked upwards. It was as if I was in a massive tunnel which extended into infinity. I could see no end to it. There was an atmosphere of tranquillity within it, however, which dispelled any terror I might have felt on entering it.

Von Bek was astounded. 'It's magnificent! Is this really magic?'

Alisaard said: 'Are you as superstitious as those others, Count von Bek? I had assumed otherwise.'

'This goes beyond any training I had in science,' he told her with a smile. 'What else could this be but magic?'

'We think of it as a perfectly natural phenomenon. It occurs whenever the dimensions of our realms intersect with another. A kind of vortex is formed. Through this, if one has sufficient reason or curiosity or courage, it is possible to reach the Realms of the Wheel. We have charts which tell us when and where such Entrances materialise, where they are likely to lead and so on. Since they are both regular and predictable, we would not define them as magical. Does the definition make sense to you?'

'Perfect sense, madam.' Von Bek raised his eyebrows. 'Though whether I could convince even Albert Einstein of the existence of this tunnel, I am not sure.'

His references were meaningless to her, yet she smiled. There was no doubt that Alisaard found von Bek to her liking. With me she was much warier and I could not really understand why, unless she, too, believed the stories of my crimes and betrayals. Then it came to me! These women wanted Sharadim, my twin sister. Did they plan to offer me, a wanted outlaw, in return for her help? They were used, after all, to bartering males. Was I merely an item of currency?

But all these thoughts were driven from my mind as suddenly the ship began to whirl. We were flung back against the timbers as she spun round and round, never so rapidly as to fling us out, and then gradually began to lift into the air. It seemed that the tunnel was drawing us up, sucking us through into the next dimension! The ship tilted and I was convinced we would be hurled into the water, but somehow our gravity remained the same. Now we were sailing down the tunnel just as if we followed the swift current of a river. I half expected to see banks on either side, but there was nothing save the glittering rainbow colours. Again I found myself close to weeping, but this time for the beauty and the wonder of it.

'It is as if the rays of more than one sun have all been focused together,' said von Bek, coming to stand beside me. 'I am curious to learn more of these Six Realms.'

'There are, as I understand it, dozens of differently constituted groupings in the multiverse,' I told him, 'just as there are different kinds of stars and planets, obeying a variety of physical laws. To most of us on Earth these are not readily perceptible, that is all.

Why that is so, I do not know. Sometimes I think our world is a kind of colony for an underdeveloped or crippled race, since so many others take the multiverse for granted.'

'I would happily live in a world where such sights as these are familiar,' said von Bek.

The ship continued to travel rapidly along the tunnel. I noticed, however, that the helmswomen remained alert. I wondered if there were some additional danger.

Then the ship began to turn again and to shift her position so that she seemed to be diving down into pitch darkness. The crew shouted back and forth to one another, preparing for something. Alisaard told us to hang on tightly to the sides. 'And pray that we are come to Gheestenheem,' she said. 'These tunnels are notorious for shifting their bearings and stranding travellers until the following revolution!'

The darkness was so complete I could see nothing of my companions. I felt a peculiar surging sensation, heard the timbers of the ship creak, and then, very slowly, light returned. We were bobbing on ordinary water again and were still surrounded by the bright columns, though these were fainter than when we had first seen them.

'Steer through! Steer through!' cried Alisaard.

The ship bucked and jerked forward, heading between the columns with the helmswomen throwing all their weight on the oars. Another wave and we were through, rushing on the crest, towards a distant shoreline which reminded me, for a vague reason I could not identify, of Dover's chalky cliffs, topped with a lush and rolling green.

Here golden sunlight fell upon blue water. Little white clouds hung in a blue sky. I had almost forgotten the sheer pleasure of an ordinary summer landscape. It had been, I thought, several eternities since I had looked upon such sights. Not since my parting with Ermizhad, in fact.

'My God!' exclaimed von Bek. 'It is England, surely? Or Ireland, perhaps?'

These words were without any meaning to Alisaard. She shook her head. 'You are a compendium of alien names, Count von Bek. You must have travelled very widely, eh?'

At this he was forced to laugh. 'Now you are the unwitting naïve one, good lady. I assure you my travels have been very tame compared to what you take for granted!'

'I suppose the unfamiliar always seems more exotic.' She was enjoying the breeze in her hair and had stripped off more of her ivory armour, as had the others, in order to feel the sun on her skin. 'A gloomy world, the Maaschanheem. All that shallow water makes it so grey, I suppose.' She was looking ahead now. The cliffs were parted here and formed a great bay. Within the curve of the bay was a quay and behind that a town whose houses crowded upwards on three sides above the sea.

'There's Barobanay!' Alisaard spoke in some relief. 'We can be ourselves again. I hate these charades.' She rapped her knuckles on her ivory breastplate.

There were many other sailing ships of all types moored along Barobanay's quaysides, but there was none like ours. I guessed that the white ships were part of the trappings which the 'Ghost Women' used to keep other folk at a distance.

The ship tacked in, oars were shipped, ropes were swung out to young men and women who stood by to receive them and secure them to capstans. The women were clearly of Eldren blood while the men were equally obviously human. Neither sex seemed to possess the demeanour of slaves. I mentioned this to Alisaard.

'Save that they are not allowed certain specific rights,' she told me, 'the men are happy enough.'

'You must have some who have wanted to escape, no matter how pleasant their lives?' said von Bek reasonably.

'First they must have the knowledge of our Entrance Tunnel,' said Alisaard as the boat bumped against the wall.

We watched as a gangplank was laid from ship to quay. Then Alisaard led the way onto dry land, into a little cobbled square and up a steep, winding lane to where, some distance from the shore, a tall, somewhat Gothic, house stood. It had the air of a civic building.

The sun was warm on our bodies as we took the final few steps up to the building.

'Our Council House,' said Alisaard. 'A modest enough piece of architecture, but it is the hub of our government.'

'It has the unpretentious air of our old German town halls,' said von Bek with approval. 'And,' he added, 'it is considerably finer than anything we've experienced of late. Just think, Daker, what one of Armiad's Binkeepers would make of a Council House like this!'

I could only agree with him.

Within, the place was cool and pleasant, full of sweet-smelling plants and flowers. The floor was marble, but fine rugs were scattered everywhere, and there was nothing chilled about the green obsidian of pillars and fireplaces. On the walls were tapestries, mostly non-representational, and the ceilings were painted with elaborate and exquisite designs. There was an air of quiet dignity about the place and I found it harder still to believe that these Eldren women planned to use me for barter.

An older woman, with silver hair piled above a face which, typical of her kind, showed none of the less attractive signs of age we humans so frequently display, emerged from a small door on the right. 'So you were persuaded to come to us, Prince Flamadin,' she said warmly. 'I am most grateful.'

Alisaard introduced Ulric von Bek and explained a little of the circumstances. The older woman wore flowing red and gold. She welcomed us and said she was known as the Announcer Elect, Phalizaarn. 'But of course nobody has explained to you why we were seeking you, Prince Flamadin.'

'I had the impression, Lady Phalizaarn, that you wanted the help of my sister, Sharadim.'

She was surprised. She signed for us to go ahead of her through a door and into a conservatory full of the most magnificent blooms. 'How did you know of that?'

'I have a certain sixth sense in these matters, my lady. Is it true?'

She paused beside a purple rhododendron. I seemed to have embarrassed her. 'It is true, Prince Flamadin, that some of our number have tried – through unconventional means – to summon your sister to them, or at least ask for her help. They were not forbidden to do this, but in general it was disapproved by everyone, including the Council. It seemed an unlikely and barbaric means of approaching the Princess Sharadim.'

'These women do not, then, represent all the Eldren?'

'Simply a faction.' The Announcer Elect looked a little quizzically at Alisaard who dropped her gaze. It was clear to me that Alisaard was, or had been, one of those women who sought my sister by 'barbaric' means. Yet why had she rescued me from Armiad? Why had she sought me out at all?

I thought it fair to say something on Alisaard's behalf. 'I must tell you, madam, that I am used to such incantations.' I smiled at Alisaard who had looked up in mild surprise. 'It is not the first time I, myself, have been called across the barriers of the worlds. But what puzzles me is why I should have heard the call for Sharadim.'

'Because Sharadim is not whom we sought,' said Alisaard simply. 'I must admit that until yesterday I was prepared to insist that the oracle had misled us. I was convinced that no human male could have the rapport with the Eldren which was needed if we were to proceed. Of course we knew of you both. Knew that you were twins. We assumed the oracle had spoken of Flamadin in mistake for Sharadim.'

'There were many heated debates on the matter,' said Lady Phalizaarn gently. 'In this very hall.'

'The night before last,' Alisaard continued, 'we attempted once more to call Sharadim. We thought that there was no better place to do this than at the Massing Ground. We were aware of the power flowing in us by then. It was stronger than ever. We lit our fire, we linked arms, we concentrated. And for the first time we had a vision of the one we sought. You can imagine, I am sure, whose face it was.'

'You saw Prince Flamadin,' said Lady Phalizaarn, evidently trying to disguise the satisfaction in her voice. 'And then you saw him in the flesh…'

'We remembered that you had commissioned Helmswoman Danifel to approach Prince Flamadin if he was at the Massing. We went to her and admitted that we had been mistaken. Together, as you can see, we went to visit Prince Flamadin. We were forced to go secretly because of the nature of the Massing and the character of the brute who is Baron Captain of the particular hull where Prince Flamadin and his friend were guesting. To our complete astonishment we arrived to discover that Prince Flamadin and Count von Bek were in the process of attempting escape. So we helped them.'

'Alisaard,' said Lady Phalizaarn softly, 'did you think to invite Prince Flamadin to Gheestenheem? Did you give him the choice?'

'In the heat of the moment, I forgot, Lady Announcer Elect. I apologise to all. We thought we might be pursued.'

'Pursued?'

'By the bloodthirsty enemies from whom Alisaard saved us,' said von Bek quickly. 'We owe you our lives, madam. And, of course, we should have accepted your invitation had it been extended.'

Lady Phalizaarn smiled. She, too, was evidently charmed by my friend's old German courtesy. 'You are a natural courtier, Count von Bek. Or perhaps a natural diplomat is a better choice.'

'I would prefer the latter, my lady. We von Beks have never been overfond of monarchs. We even had one member of our family serve in the revolutionary French National Assembly!'

Again the words were meaningless. I could understand them but they were like a foreign language to the others. One day von Bek would learn, as I had learned, to carry on a conversation without reference to the existence of our Earth or its twentieth century.

'I still have no notion of what you want from me,' I said politely. 'I assure you, my lady, I am here most willingly, given that all others appear to be against me, but I will be frank with you. I have no real memory of being Prince Flamadin. It is only a matter of a few days since I first inhabited his body. If Flamadin has knowledge that you need, then I am afraid I'm likely to disappoint you.'

At this the Lady Phalizaarn beamed. 'I am most relieved to hear that, Prince Flamadin. The accuracy of our "oracle", as Alisaard insists it be called, is further confirmed. But you shall hear all when the full Council convenes. It is not for me to speak until I am given instructions to do so.'

'When does the Council convene?' I asked her.

'This afternoon. You are at liberty to explore our capital if you will, or to rest. We have chambers here which have been set aside for you. Anything you need in the way of food or clothing, please let us know. I am exceedingly pleased to see you here, Prince Flamadin. I had thought it almost too late!'

On this mysterious note we were dismissed. Alisaard showed us to the rooms which had been prepared for me. 'You were not expected, Count von Bek, so it will take a little while to make ready your accommodation. Meanwhile there are two adjoining chambers, with a couch large enough for even a man of your size.'

I opened the door. 'This is what I'm interested in,' I said delightedly. It was a huge bathtub, rather reminiscent of the old Victorian kind, though it had no obvious plumbing attached to it. 'Is there perhaps some way we can obtain hot water?'

She indicated something I had mistaken for a bell rope hanging to one side of the tub. 'Two tugs for hot,' she said. 'One for cold.'

'How does the water reach the bath?' I wanted to know.

'Through the pipes.' She pointed at a peculiar kind of plug near one end of the bath. 'And up through there.' She spoke to me as if I were some kind of barbarian being introduced to civilised amenities.

'Thanks,' I said. 'No doubt I'll soon learn how to work it.'

The soap she handed me was a kind of abrasive powder, but it softened well enough in the water. My first blast of hot water almost killed me. I learned that she had forgotten to tell me that it was three tugs for a mixture…

Von Bek had been talking to Alisaard while I bathed. She had left by the time it was his turn to use the tub. He had the benefit of my new wisdom where the water was concerned. As he soaped himself he rattled on cheerfully. 'I asked Alisaard if her race and humans can normally interbreed. She thinks it unlikely, though she can only speak from her own experience. Apparently this method they have isn't all that simple. She said that "a great deal of alchemy" is involved. Presumably they make use of chemicals, other agents. Some form of artificial insemination, perhaps?'

'I've no understanding of such matters, unfortunately. But the Eldren were always clever with medicines. What puzzles me is how the women came to be separated from the men and if these people are the descendants of those I knew or are they, perhaps, their ancestors?'

'Now I find you hard to follow,' von Bek admitted. He began to whistle some popular jazz song of his time (which was a few years before my own, as John Daker).

The rooms were furnished in much the same style as the rest of the Council House, with large pieces of carved hardwood furniture, tapestries, rugs. There was a great quilt flung across my bed which, by the workmanship, must have taken fifty years to make. More flowers filled the place and the windows looked down into a courtyard with a gravel walk, a green lawn and a fountain at the centre. The mood of tranquillity was thus maintained. I felt I could cheerfully settle amongst these people. But I knew it was not to be. Again came a pang of almost physical agony. How I longed for my Ermizhad!

'Well,' said von Bek later as he towelled himself, 'if I did not have urgent business with the Chancellor of Germany, I would find this Barobanay an excellent place for a holiday. Eh?'

'Oh, indeed,' I replied absently. 'However, von Bek, I think we'll be busy soon enough. These women seem to think it a matter of urgency, our coming here. I still find it hard to understand, however, why Sharadim was called and not me. Did Alisaard offer you any further explanation?'

'A matter of principle, I think. She did not wish to believe that a human male could be of any use to them at all! I suppose that's based on her experience. And then, of course, there was the business of the murder, or the probable murder.'

'What? The murder they say I attempted? Do they think now that I actually succeeded in killing my twin sister?'

'Oh, no, of course not.' Von Bek rubbed at his hair. 'Weren't you present when Alisaard mentioned that? Apparently Prince Flamadin is almost certainly dead. The story put out from the Draachenheem is the reverse of the truth. Flamadin seems to have been murdered on the direct instructions of Sharadim!' Von Bek found this amusing. He laughed and slapped me on the shoulder. 'It's a turning world, eh, my friend?'

'Oh, aye,' I agreed as my heart began to pound again. 'A turning world indeed...'

Chapter Two

'WE SHOULD FIRST tell you,' said the Lady Phalizaarn, rising from amongst the seated women, 'that we are in
grave danger. For many years we have been attempting to seek
out our own folk, the Eldren, and rejoin them. Our method of
maintaining our race is, as I am sure you can imagine, distasteful
to us. Admittedly our purchased males are well-treated and given
almost all the privileges of the community, but it is an unnatural
business. We would rather procreate through union with those
who had a choice in the matter. Of late we have embarked upon
a series of experiments, designed to locate our people. Once we
have located them, we believe, we will find a means of rejoining
them. However, we have made a number of unlikely discoveries.
What is more, we have been forced to compromise and, finally,
some of our number have taken a wrong direction. Now, for
instance, your sister Sharadim knows a great deal more than we
would have revealed, had we understood her character.'

'You must illuminate me as to that,' I said. Von Bek and I were
seated, cross-legged, in front of the women, most of whom were
of a similar age to Phalizaarn, though some were younger and
one or two older. Alisaard was not present. Neither were any of
the others who had rescued us from Armiad's hull.

'We shall,' the Announcer Elect promised. But first she
intended to describe briefly her people's history; how as a handful
of survivors they had been driven further and further into hiding
by the numerous forces of barbarian humans. Eventually they
decided to escape into another realm where the Mabden could
not follow. There they would begin life again. They had explored
certain other worlds. Yet they wished to find one where humans
had not settled. They devised a means of reaching such a world.

Earlier explorers had brought back with them two great beasts whose own curiosity had led them to follow the explorers. It was already known that these beasts had some means of returning to their own world – of creating a new gateway through to it between the barriers. The Eldren planned to release the beasts and then follow them through. The creatures were not antagonistic towards the Eldren. Indeed, there was a kind of mutual respect between them which was hard to define. The Eldren felt they would have no difficulty living in the same world as the beasts. So it was that one party followed the male beast through the gateway it made. The second party, of women, were to follow a little later, when the men had made certain it was safe. So they waited and, hearing of no danger, they sent the female beast through. However, they were following in her wake when suddenly she vanished. There was a sense of struggle, a sense that the beast was trying to warn them of something, and then they had found themselves in this world. Somehow the beast which was to lead them to safety had either lost her way or been abducted.

'Somehow the gateway had shifted. The multiverse intersects like cogs in a clock. One tick of the pendulum and you find yourself in an entirely different world, perhaps many times removed from the one you sought. That is what happened to us. Until recently we never knew what became of the beast who was supposed to lead us through. In order to survive we were forced to use our knowledge of alchemy so that we could breed with males who had wandered here from human dimensions. At length we discovered we could buy such males from various traders in the Six Realms. Only at the Massing do all the realms intersect. At times, however, it is not difficult to visit perhaps one or two others whenever we choose. Meanwhile we have devoted ourselves to a study of what constitutes the multiverse, of how and when certain realms cross one another's orbits. By means of our psychics, the same as those who contacted you, mistaking you for Sharadim, we have communicated very occasionally with our menfolk. It became clear that the only way to reach them was to find the beast which had intended to lead us through in the first place. Then a further disturbing problem came a few years ago. We discovered that the herbs we use in our alchemy to perpetuate ourselves were becoming rapidly scarcer. We do not know why. Perhaps a simple climatic change. We can grow plants very similar to them in our special gardens, but they do not have exactly the same properties. Therefore we have very few sources of supply left to us. We have almost no children. Soon we shall have none. Our race will perish. That is why our quest for help grew more urgent. Then came one to us who said that he knew where our beast could be found, but that only one creature in the whole multiverse was both fitted and fated to find her. He called this creature the Champion Eternal.'

Another woman spoke from where she sat on the floor. 'We did not know if it were male or female, human or Eldren. All we had was the Actorios. The stone.'

'He told us we should find you by means of that stone,' said Phalizaarn. From a pouch at her hips she drew it out, displaying it on the flat of her hand. 'Do you recognise it?'

Something within me knew the stone, but no memory would come to me. I made a helpless gesture.

Phalizaarn smiled. 'Well, it seems to know you.'

The jewel, all smoky darkness, full of restless, nameless colours, seemed almost to writhe in her palm. I felt a great need for it. I wanted to reach out and take it from her but I restrained myself.

'It is yours,' said a voice from behind me. Both von Bek and I turned. 'It is yours. Take it.'

No longer in black and yellow, but in enfolding purple, the black giant Sepiriz looked down at me with a kind of amused compassion. 'It will always be yours, wherever you see it,' he continued. 'Take it. It will help you. It has served its turn here.'

The stone was warm. It felt like flesh. I shivered as I held it in my fist. It seemed to send a thrill of energy through me. 'Thank you.' I bowed to the Announcer Elect and to Sepiriz. I placed the stone in my belt purse. 'Are you their oracle, Sepiriz? Do you bind them about with mysteries as you do me?' I could only speak with affection.

'That Actorios will one day sit in the Ring of Kings,' said the giant. 'And you shall wear it. But for now there is a more immediate game to play. A game, John Daker, which could earn you at least part of what you most desire.'

'Not a very specific promise, Sir Knight.'

He accepted this. 'It is only in certain matters that I dare be specific. The balance is singularly fine just now. I would not tip it. Not at this stage. Did my Lady Phalizaarn describe their lost she-beast?'

'I can remember the incantation very clearly,' I told him. 'It was a firedrake. A dragon. And it is held prisoner, I take it. They seemed to want me – or Sharadim – to release the creature. Is it trapped in some world which only I can visit?'

'Not exactly. It is trapped in an object which only you are entitled to handle…'

'That damned sword!' I stepped backward, violently shaking my head. 'No! No, Sepiriz, I will not bear it again! The Black Sword is evil. I do not like what it makes of me.'

'This is not the same sword,' he said calmly. 'Not in this aspect. Some say the twin blades are the same. Some say they have a thousand forms. I do not believe that. The blade was forged to accept what we would call a soul – a spirit, a demon, whatever you like – and it was by unhappy coincidence that the she-dragon became trapped there, filling the vacuum, as it were, within the blade.'

'Those dragons are surely monstrous. And the blade –'

'Simple matters of Space and Time are scarcely relevant to the forces of which I speak and of which you must know something,' said Sepiriz, raising his hand. 'The sword had but lately been forged. Those who had made it had not quite finished their work. The blade was, as it were, cooling. There was a massive movement throughout the multiverse. Chaos and Law even then fought for possession of the blade and its twin. Dimensions were warped, whole histories were altered in a space of moments, the very laws of nature were changed. It was then that the dragon – the second dragon – attempted to fling herself through the barriers between the realms and burst through to her own world. It was an unaccounted-for coincidence. As a result of those huge disturbances, she became trapped within the sword. No incantation could release her. The blade had been designed to be inhabited. Once possessed it could only release that which dwelled within it under certain portentous circumstances. And only you can release the dragon. It is a very powerful object, even without you. In the wrong hands it could damage everything we value, perhaps destroy it for ever. Sharadim herself believes in the sword. She heard the voices calling her. She asked certain questions and received certain answers. Now she would own that thing of power. Her plan is to rule all Six Realms of the Wheel. With the Dragon Sword she could easily have her way.'

'How did you learn that she was evil?' I asked Sepiriz. 'Amongst the folk of the Six Realms – or at least most of them – she is regarded as a paragon of virtue.'

The Lady Phalizaarn spoke. 'That is very simple. We made the discovery recently, after a trading expedition to the Draachenheem. We bought a batch of males, all of whom had been employed at Court. Many were nobles. To silence them, Sharadim had sold them to us. It frequently happens – since we are supposed to eat the men we buy – that we become a convenient means of disposing of unwanted people. Some of those men had actually witnessed Sharadim poisoning the wine she offered you on your return from whatever quest it was you had been on. She bribed some of the courtiers to side with her. The others she had arrested as conspirators, henchmen of Flamadin, and sold to us.'

'Why did she want to poison me?'

'You had refused to marry her. You hated her cunning and her cruelty. For years she had encouraged you to go adventuring abroad. This suited your temperament and she assured you that the kingdom was safe with her. Gradually, however, you began to realise what she was doing, how she was corrupting everything you believed noble in order to prepare the Draachenheem for war against the other realms. You swore you would tell all at the next Massing. Meanwhile she understood something of what the Eldren women had said. She realised that it was you they really sought. She had several motives for murdering you.'

'Then how am I here now?'

'That is puzzling, I agree. Several of the men here saw you in death. Stiff and bloodless, they said.'

'And what became of my corpse?'

'Some believe Sharadim still has possession of it. That she practises the most disgusting rites upon it…'

'That leaves the question "Who am I?"' I said. 'If I am not Prince Flamadin.'

'But you are Prince Flamadin,' said Sepiriz. 'All agree on that matter. What they cannot decide is how you escaped…'

'So you wish me to seek out this sword? And what then?'

'It must be brought to the Massing Ground. The Eldren women will know what to do.'

'Do you know where the sword may be found?'

'We have rumours only. It has changed hands more than once. Most who have attempted to put it to their own purposes have died quite terrible deaths as a result.'

'Then why not let Sharadim find it? When she is dead, I can bring the sword to you…'

'Your jests were never your strength, Champion,' said Sepiriz almost sadly. 'Sharadim may have some means of controlling the blade. She may have devised a method by which she can make herself invulnerable to the sword's particular curse. She is neither stupid nor ignorant. She will know how to make the best use of the sword once she finds it. Already she has sent out her minions to gather information.'

'She knows more, then, than you do, Lord Sepiriz?'

'She knows something. And that is more than enough.'

'Am I to try to reach the sword before she does? Or am I to stop her by some means? You are unclear as to what you expect of me, my lord.'

Sepiriz could tell that I was resisting him. I had no wish to set eyes on another sword like the Black Sword, let alone put a hand upon one.

'I expect you to fulfil your destiny, Champion.'

'And if I refuse?'

'You shall never know even a hint of freedom for eternity upon eternity. You shall suffer more terribly than those whom your self-ishness will consign to everlasting horror. Chaos plays a part in this. Have you heard of the Archduke Balarizaaf? He is a most ambitious Lord of Chaos. Sharadim is negotiating with him, offering an alliance. If Chaos claims the Six Realms it will mean nothing but hideous destruction, frightful agony for the conquered peoples, Eldren or human. Sharadim cares only for power, whereby she can indulge her perverse whims. She's a fitting medium for the Archduke Balarizaaf. And he, better than she, understands the significance of the sword.'

'So this is a matter between Law and Chaos?' I said. 'And I am chosen to fight for Law this time.'

'It is the Will of the Balance,' said Sepiriz with a note of unwonted piety in his deep voice.

'Well, I trust you as cheerfully as I trust any of your ilk,' I told him. 'I can do very little else. But I will do nothing unless you tell me that what I do will aid these Eldren women, for it is to the Eldren, not any great cosmic force, that I feel my greatest loyalty. If I succeed, will they be reunited with their men?'

'That I can promise you,' said Sepiriz. He seemed impressed by my statement rather than resentful of it.

'Then I shall do my best to find the Dragon Sword and release its prisoner,' I agreed.

'I have your oath on that now,' said Sepiriz with satisfaction. He seemed to be making a mental note. He also seemed somewhat relieved.

Von Bek stepped forward. 'Forgive this interruption, gentlemen, but I would be much obliged if you could tell me if I, too, have a preordained destiny or if I am to do my best to make my own way home?'

Sepiriz placed a hand on the Saxon count's right arm. 'My young friend, matters are far simpler where you are concerned and I can speak plainer. If you continue with this quest and aid the Champion to fulfil his destiny, you will, I promise, achieve what you most desire.'

'The destruction of Hitler and his Nazis?'

'I swear it.'

It was difficult for me to remain silent. I already knew the Nazis had been defeated. But it then occurred to me that perhaps they might have succeeded, that it had been von Bek and myself who had been responsible for the destruction of the fascists. I had some faint understanding, now, of why Sepiriz was bound to speak in mysteries. He had more than a knowledge of the future. He had a knowledge of a million different futures, a million different worlds, a million ages...

'Very well,' von Bek was saying, 'then I shall continue with this, at least for the time being.'

'Alisaard will also go with you,' said the Lady Phalizaarn. 'She has volunteered, since she was one of those responsible for revealing too much to Sharadim. And, of course, you will take the men.'

'The men? Which men?' Foolishly I looked about me.

'Sharadim's exiled courtiers,' she said.

'Why should I want them with me?'

'As witnesses,' put in Sepiriz, 'since your first task is to go at once to Draachenheem and face your sister with an accusation and your evidence. If she is ousted from power, it will make your task considerably easier.'

'You think we could do that? Three of us and a handful of men?'

'You have no choice,' said Sepiriz gravely. 'It is the first task you must accomplish if you would find the Dragon Sword. There is no better beginning. By confronting your evil twin, Sharadim, you will set the pattern for the rest of your quest. Remember, Champion, we forge time and matter as a consequence of our actions. That is one of the few constants in the multiverse. It is we who impose logic, for our own survival. Make it a good pattern and you shall come a step closer to achieving the destiny you most desire…'

'Destiny!' My grin had no humour in it. For a moment I rebelled. I almost turned and walked from the hall, telling Sepiriz that I would have no more of it. I was sick of his mysteries and his destinies.

But then I looked into the faces of those Eldren women and I saw, hidden beneath the grace and dignity, both anguish and desperation. I paused. These were the people I had elected to serve against my own race. I could not refuse them now.

For my love of Ermizhad, not for Sepiriz and all his oratory, I would take the road to Draachenheem and there give challenge to evil.

'We shall leave in the morning,' I promised.

Chapter Three

T HERE WERE TWELVE of us in the small boat as it entered the
columns of light and was drawn back into the tunnel
between the worlds. Alisaard, again in her ivory armour, steered
while the rest of us clung to the sides and gaped. The other nine
were all nobles of Draachenheem. Two of them were Land
Princes, rulers of whole nations, who had been abducted the night
Flamadin was apparently murdered. Four others were elected
Sheriffs of great cities and three had been squires at Court who had
seen the poison administered. 'Many others are dead,' the Land
Prince Ottro, an older man with heavy facial scarring, told me.
'But she could not make everyone a corpse, so we were sold to the
Gheestenheemers. Just think – we shall be the first to return.'

'Though sworn to secrecy,' young Federit Shaus reminded
him. 'We owe these Eldren women more than our lives.'

All nine agreed with this. They had taken an oath to say nothing of the true nature of the Gheestenheem.

The boat raced on through the weird rainbow light, occasionally bucking and swerving, as if it had struck resistance, but never
slackening her speed. Then quite suddenly we were bobbing on
blue water again, surging between two columns and then the wind
had caught our sail and we were upon an ordinary salt ocean,
with a clear sky overhead and a good strong breeze behind us.

Two of the Draachenheemers consulted a map with Alisaard,
giving her some idea of our position. We were going straight to
Valadeka, land of the Valadek, home of Sharadim and Flamadin.
Some of the Draachenheemers had wanted to return to their own
lands, to gather up their armies and march against Sharadim, but
Sepiriz had insisted we go directly to Valadeka.

Now a coastline came in sight. We saw great black cliffs framed against the pale sky. They were almost like the cliffs in my dreams. We saw spray and rocks and very few places where a boat could land.

'It is Valadeka's great strength,' Madvad of Drane, a black-haired fellow with enormous eyebrows, informed me. 'As an island she is virtually invulnerable to sea-attack. Her few good harbours are well guarded.'

'Must we land in one of them?' von Bek wished to know.

Madvad shook his head. 'We know of a small cove where, at certain tides, it is possible to land. That's what we seek now.'

It was almost nightfall by the time we were able to land on the cold shingle of a narrow beach surrounded by black granite crags and overlooked by the ruins of an ancient castle. The boat was dragged into a cave and one of the squires, Ruberd of Hanzo, led us through a series of secret openings and up a flight of old steps until we were standing amongst the crumbled stone of the abandoned fortress.

'One of our noblest families once lived here,' Ruberd said. 'Your own ancestors, Prince Flamadin.' He paused as if in embarrassment. 'Or should I say simply "Prince Flamadin's ancestors"? You say you are not yourself, my lord, yet I would still swear you are our Chosen Prince…'

I had seen no point in deceiving these honest people. I had told them as much of the truth as I felt they could comprehend.

'There's a village nearby, is there not?' asked old Ottro. 'Let's get there quickly. I could do with some victuals and a jug of beer. We plan to rest overnight, do we not, and continue on horseback in the morning?'

'The early morning.' Gently I reminded him of our plan. 'We must reach Rhetalik by noon tomorrow, when you said Sharadim is to have herself crowned Empress.' Rhetalik was the capital of Valadeka.

'Certainly, young quasi-prince,' he assured me. 'I'm well aware of the urgency. But one thinks and acts better if one is fed and rested.'

With myself and Alisaard swathed in cloaks so that we should not excite the villagers' curiosity overmuch, we found a tavern large enough to accommodate our party. Indeed, the innkeeper was delighted at this unseasonal bonus. We had plenty of the local money and were generous with it. We dined and slept in great comfort and had our pick of the best horses the next morning. Then we were riding again for Rhetalik. We must have made a strange enough sight to the Valadekans with myself in the leathers of a marsh-hunter, von Bek in a shirt, jacket and trousers roughly resembling what he had worn when I first saw him (made for him by the Eldren who had also furnished him with gloves, boots and a wide-brimmed hat), two of the Draachenheemers in the full, multicoloured silks and woollens of their clans, four others in borrowed ivory armour, and three wearing a mixture of clothing selected from the store offered by the Eldren. I rode at the head of this strange little band, with von Bek on one side and Alisaard on the other. She was wearing her helm almost as a matter of habit. The Eldren rarely showed their faces to people from other realms. They had made a banner for me to carry on my lance, but this was presently furled and covered. I also took pains to pull my cloak's cowl over my head whenever we met others on the road. I had no intention of being recognised at this stage.

Gradually the earthen track began to widen. Next we discovered that it was paved with great stone flags. Now more and more people were joining us, all heading in the same direction. They seemed in holiday mood and were drawn from all walks of life. I saw men and women evidently of a monastic disposition and others who were as plainly secular in their tastes. Men, women, children, all in their best, all in brightly mingled shades. These Draachenheemer were fond of rich plaids and patchworks and thought nothing of wearing a score of different colours. I found their taste attractive and began to feel extremely dowdy in my dull leather gear.

Soon the road began to be lined on both sides with great gilded statues, of individual men and women, of groups, of beasts of every persuasion, though with a preponderance of those large lizards I had first seen at the Great Massing. These beasts were plainly not in common use. For the most part the horse, the ox and the donkey were the ordinary beasts of burden, although here and there was a large piglike creature which people rode upon and carried goods on by means of a sturdy wooden saddle.

'See!' Land Prince Ottro said to me as he came riding up. 'It is the best time to arrive unnoticed in Rhetalik, as I said.'

The city was surrounded by very high walls, of warm, reddish sandstone topped by huge spikes of rock, similar to the crenellations on a medieval castle but of an entirely different shape. Each of these spikes had a hole at the centre and I guessed a man could stand behind the spike and shoot without much chance of being hurt himself. The city had been built for war, though Ottro assured me there had been peace throughout Draachenheem for many years. Within it consisted of similarly fortified buildings, of rich palaces, market arcades, canals, temples, warehouses and all the other varied buildings of a complex trading city.

Rhetalik seemed to slope inwards, all her narrow streets leading down towards a central lake at her centre. There, upon an artificial island of some age, stood a great palace of slender marble, quartz, terracotta and limestone: a palace which glittered and shone in the sunlight, which reflected a score of exquisite colours from the tall obelisks marking the island's perimeter. From the palace's central turrets there flew a hundred different banners, every one of which was a work of art. A curving, slender bridge crossed the moat to the delicately carved stonework of the gateposts which were guarded by sentries in elaborately inefficient armour of the most fanciful design. The baroque effect of this armour was further increased by the hulking beasts which, in harness and trappings to rival that of their masters, stood beside the guards and were equally stiffly at attention. These were the giant riding lizards I had seen before; the dragons which had given this world its name. Ottro had explained how, in ancient times, these creatures had been plentiful and his people had to fight them for the land.

We brought our horses to a halt beside a wall which over-looked the lake and the castle. All around us the streets were filled with bunting, with scintillating banners and little mirrors, with polished shields and plates so that the entire place seemed ablaze with silver light. The people of Valadeka were celebrating the coronation of their Empress. There was music everywhere, crowds of jubilant men and women, feasting in the twittens and lanes.

'Innocent enough, this festivity,' said von Bek, leaning forward in his saddle to ease his back. It had been several years since he had ridden a horse. 'Hard to believe that they celebrate the elevation of one who is supposedly the personification of evil!'

'Evil flourishes best in disguise,' said Ottro grimly. His companions nodded in assent.

'And the best disguise is simple,' said the youth, Federit Shaus. 'Honest patriotism. Joyful idealism.'

'You're a cynic, lad,' von Bek smiled at him. 'But sadly my own experience would support your view. Show me a man who cries "My country right or wrong", and I'll show you one who'd cheerfully murder half his own nation in the name of patriotism.'

'I once heard someone say that a nation was merely an excuse for crime,' said Ottro. 'In this case I might find myself in agreement. She has misused the love and trust of her people. They have made her Empress of this whole realm because they believe she represents all that is best in human nature. Moreover she now has their sympathy. Did not her brother try to kill her? Has it not been proven she suffered for years to try to preserve his reputation, letting people think him noble and good when all the while he was the very essence of self-indulgence and cowardice?' Ottro spoke bitterly.

'Well,' I said, 'since her brother is supposedly dead and you his victims' (that had been the tale put out) 'think how overjoyed she will be to discover that she was not wrong in trusting him!'

'She'll kill us on the spot. I still say it.' Von Bek did not believe our plan could work for a second.

'I doubt if even Sepiriz, with all his plots and cunning, would have sent us to certain death,' said Alisaard. 'We have to trust his judgement. It is based on more than we can know.'

'I have no relish for feeling myself a pawn in his mighty chess-game,' said von Bek.

'Nor I.' I shrugged. 'Though you would think I'd grow used to it. I still believe that individual will can achieve at least as much as all these alliances of men and gods Sepiriz speaks of. It has occurred to me more than once that they have become so engrossed in their game, in their cosmic politics, that they have lost sight of any original goal.'

'You have little respect for gods and demigods, then,' said Alisaard with a quick movement of her fingers to her face, as if she had forgotten she wore her visor beneath her cowl. 'I must admit we do not think much of such creatures in Gheestenheem. Too often what we hear of them sounds like the activities of little boys at play!'

'Sadly,' said von Bek, 'those little boys care more for power than most of us. And when they achieve it, they can destroy all those of us who don't wish to join in their games.'

Alverid of Prucca pushed his cloak away from his shoulders. He was more taciturn than most of the others. His principality was in the far west, where the people had a reputation for saying little and judging much. 'Be that as it may,' he said. 'We should get on with this business. It will soon be noon. Do we all remember the plan?'

'It is not a difficult one,' said von Bek. He jerked at his steed's reins. 'Let's get on with it.'

Making slow progress through the happy crowds we eventually came to the bridge. On this side it was also guarded by dismounted lizard-riders who saluted us as we approached.

'We are the invited delegation from the Six Realms,' said Alisaard. 'Come to pay our respects to your new Empress.'

One of the guards frowned. 'Invited, marm?'

'Invited. By your own Princess Empress Sharadim. Shall we

wait here like trinket sellers or shall we proceed to the tradesman's entrance? I had expected a warmer greeting from a sister...'

They exchanged looks and somewhat sheepishly let us pass. And because the first guards had admitted us, the others let us through without any form of challenge.

'Now follow me,' said Ottro riding ahead. He was most familiar with the palace and with protocol. He urged his horse forward, under a high arch which must have been twelve feet across and some six feet thick, of solid granite. This led us into a pleasant courtyard of turf surrounded by gravel. We crossed this, again unchallenged. I looked around me. The high walls of the palace reached up everywhere, ending in beautiful, almost ethereal, spires. Yet I felt I was entering a trap from which escape was impossible.

Under another arch, then another, until we came upon a group of young men in green-and-brown livery which Ottro recognised. 'Squires,' he cried. 'Take our horses. We are late for the ceremony.'

The squires ran forward to do his bidding. We dismounted and Ottro now marched without hesitation through a central door and into what was plainly a private apartment, though unoccupied. 'I used to know the lady whose rooms these are,' he said by way of explanation. 'Hurry, my friends. We've had luck with us so far.'

He opened a door and we were in a cool corridor with high ceilings and more of the colourful wall hangings enjoyed by these people. A few boys in the same green-and-brown livery; a young woman in a white-and-red gown, an old man in fur-trimmed plaid, looked at us with casual curiosity as we walked purposefully in Ottro's wake, turned a corner, then another, mounted three flights of marble stairs and eventually came to a heavy wooden door which he opened carefully, then signed for us to follow him.

This chamber was dark, unoccupied. Shades were drawn across all the windows. Cloying incense burned here. Great thick-leaved plants grew in profusion, giving the place something of the air of a huge greenhouse. There was the same sticky humidity, reminiscent of the tropics.

'What is this place?' asked von Bek shuddering. 'It is so different in atmosphere from all the rest.'

'It is the room where Prince Flamadin died,' said one of the squires. 'On yonder couch.' He pointed. 'It's evil you can smell, sir.'

'Why should it be kept in darkness?' I wanted to know.

'Because they say Sharadim still communicates with the soul of her dead brother...'

It was my turn to feel a chill. Did they refer to the soul of the body I now inhabited?

'I heard she keeps his corpse in these chambers,' another said. 'Frozen. Uncorrupted. Exactly as it was the minute the last breath went out of him.'

I grew impatient. 'These are mere rumours.'

'Aye, your highness,' said a squire in swift agreement. Then he frowned. I felt a sympathy for him. He was not the only one who felt confused. I had been murdered in this room, by all accounts – or, at least, something which was almost myself had been murdered. I put my hand to my head. My senses seemed momentarily to leave me.

Von Bek caught me. 'Steady, man. God knows what this can mean to you. It's bad enough for me.'

With his support I was able to collect myself. Now we followed Ottro through the chambers, every one as dark and as unwholesome as the last, until we came to another outer door. Here he stopped.

We could hear sounds from the other side of the door. Music. Shouts. Cheering.

I understood our plan, but I still found it hard to believe we had already gained so much. My heart began to pound. I nodded to Ottro.

With a sudden movement the old man drew back the bolts from the double doors and kicked them outwards with a crash.

We stared into a sea of colour, of metal and silk, of faces already turning towards us in curiosity at the sound.

We stared into the great, vaulted ceremonial hall of the Valadek, at lances and banners and armour and every kind of finery, a predominance of rose-red and white, of gold and black. From the huge windows set at both ends of this hall poured great shafts of sunlight, half-blinding us.

Mosaics, tapestries and stained glass contrasted magnificently with the pale, carved stone of the hall and seemed to be designed to lead the eye towards the very centre where, from a throne of blue and emerald obsidian, a woman of astonishing beauty was rising, her glance meeting mine the moment I reached the first step down the wide staircase which ended at the dais on which her throne was set.

Flanking her were men and women in heavy robes. These were the religious dignitaries of the Valadek, also married siblings as had been our custom for two thousand years. She wore the ancient Robe of Victory. It had not been settled on a member of the Valadek for centuries. We had never wanted to wear it again, for it was a War Robe, a robe signifying conquest by force of arms. She had offered it to me and I had refused it.

She held in her hands the Half Sword, the old broken blade of our barbarian ancestors, said to have killed the last of the Anishad bloodline, a girl of six, establishing the reign of our family until the reformation of the monarchy, when princes and princesses were chosen by the people. Sharadim and Flamadin had been chosen. We had been chosen because we were twins and this was thought a perfect omen. We should marry and bless the nation. The nation knew we would be lucky for them. They had not understood how much Sharadim had wanted this chance at power. I remembered our arguments. I remembered her disgust for what she saw as my feebleness. I had reminded her that we were elected, that any power we had was a gift of the people, that we were answerable to parliaments and councils. She had laughed at this.

— For three and a half centuries our blood has waited to be revenged. For three and a half centuries our family spirits have held their peace, knowing the moment must come, knowing that the fools would forget – knowing that if they had wished to see the last of their rightful masters, the Sardatrian Bharaleen, they should have done what we did to the Anishads and killed every last one of them, to the most distant cousins. We are fully of that blood, Flamadin. Our people cry out for us to fulfil our destiny...

'NO!'

Her eyes widened as, slowly, I began to descend the steps.

'No, Sharadim. You shall not come so easily to this power. Let the world know, at least, by what foul means you achieved it. Let them know that you will bring disorder, horror, bloody torment to this realm. Let them know that you plan to ally yourself with the darkest powers of Chaos, that you would conquer first this realm and then make yourself Empress of the Six Realms of the Wheel. Let them know you are even prepared to let down the barriers which hold back the forces of the Nightmare Marches. Let this great assembly know, Sharadim, my sister, that you feel only contempt for them because they had thought our old blood mellowed when actually it had gained a fierce intensity for being constrained so long. Let them know, Sharadim, who sought first to seduce me and then to slay me, what you think of their simple enthusiasm and their good will. Let them know you aspire to be immortal, to be elevated into the pantheon of Chaos!'

I had planned for the huge effect my words would have in that vast hall. My voice boomed. My words were knives, each one going directly to its target. Yet, until that moment, I had not known what I was going to say.

The memory had come to me suddenly. For a little while, it seemed, I had possessed Flamadin's mind, his own recollection of his sister's statements to him.

I had thought to make some revelation before the gathered nobles of a dozen nations. But I had not for a second suspected that it would be so specific or so accurate! I had begun by possessing the body of Prince Flamadin. Now Prince Flamadin had taken possession of me.

'Let them know all your thoughts, my sister!' I began a further descent. Now I waded through heaped roses, red and pink, and their sweet perfume filled my nostrils almost like a drug. 'Tell them the truth!'

Sharadim flung down the Half Sword which, a moment since, she had caressed like a lover. Her face was alight with hatred and, at the same time, a kind of exultant joy. It was almost as if she had rediscovered an admiration for her brother which she had long since forgotten.

Some rose petals drifted lazily in the great shafts of light from the stained glass. I paused again, my hands on my hips, my whole body challenging her. 'Tell them, Sharadim, my sister!'

Her voice when at last she spoke held not a trace of uncertainty. Indeed, it bore a cold and horrible authority. It was contemptuous.

'Prince Flamadin is dead, sir. Dead. And you, sir, are a crude imposter!'

Chapter Four

I HAD LEFT it until now to throw off my cowl. From every part of the hall there came a murmur of recognition. She backed away in fear, as if I were a ghost; others pushed forward to see me better. And out of the crowd near the dais, at Sharadim's signal, came half a hundred men-at-arms, with ceremonial pikes in their hands, to surround her and the throne.

I pointed behind me. 'And if I am an imposter, who are these? My lords and ladies, do you not recognise your peers?'

Ottro, Land Prince of Waldana, came to stand beside me. Then Madvad, Duke of Drane; Halmad, Land Prince of Ruradani and all the other nobles and squires.

'These are the men you sold into slavery, Sharadim. You must wish now that you killed them when you killed the others!'

'Black magic!' cried my twin. 'Phantoms conjured by Chaos! My soldiers will destroy them, never fear.'

But now many more nobles were rushing forward. One tall old man in a high crown made of coloured shells raised his hand. 'No blood is to be spilled here. I know Ottro of Waldana as if he were my kin. They said you went adventuring, Ottro, to look for fresh gateways to the other Realms. Is that so?'

'I was arrested, Prince Albret, as I tried to take ship to my own land. The Princess Sharadim ordered the arrest. A week later all whom you see here were sold to the Ghost Women as slaves.'

Another wave of murmuring from the crowd.

'We bought these men in good faith,' said Alisaard, still wearing her visor. 'But when we learned of their circumstances, we decided to release them.'

'There's your first miserable lie,' cried Sharadim, seating herself upon her throne again. 'When have the Ghost Women cared about the source of their slaves or of their circumstances? This is some plot hatched between rebellious nobles and foreign enemies to discredit me and weaken the Draachenheem...'

'Rebellious?' Prince Ottro took a step or two further until he was standing below me. 'Pray, madam, what do we rebel against? Your authority is purely ceremonial, is it not? And if it is not, why do you not reveal that fact?'

'I spoke of common treachery,' she said. 'To all our Realm and its nations. They disappeared not because they were captured, but because they sought an alliance with the Gheestenheemers. It is they who seek to corrupt our traditions. It is they who hope to gain power for themselves over us all.' Sharadim's face was the picture of outraged virtue. Her fair skin seemed to glow with honesty and her large blue eyes had never seemed more innocent. 'I was elected to be Empress of the Realm by the suggestion of various barons and land princes. If it brings disruption rather than added unity to the Draachenheem, I shall of course refuse the honour...'

There was considerable approval of her speech and many cried for her to ignore us.

'This woman deceived almost the entire Realm,' Ottro continued. 'She will bring ruin and black misery to us all, I know it. She is a mistress of deception. See this boy?' He brought young Federit Shaus to stand by him. 'Many must recognise him. A squire in the employ of Prince Flamadin. He saw Princess Sharadim place the poison in the wine with which she intended to murder her brother. He saw Prince Flamadin fall...'

'I murdered my brother?' Sharadim turned astonished eyes on the assembled nobles. 'Murdered him? I am confused. Did you not say that this was Prince Flamadin?'

'I am he.'

'And you are murdered, sir?'

There was laughter in the hall.

'The attempt failed, madam.'

'I did not murder Prince Flamadin. Prince Flamadin was exiled because he attempted to murder me. The whole world knows that. Every one of the Six Realms knows that. Many thought I should have killed him. Many thought me too lenient. If this is Prince Flamadin returned from exile, then he is breaking the Law and should be placed under arrest.'

'Princess Sharadim,' I said. 'You were too quick to judge me an imposter. Any normal response would have been for you to have assumed I was your brother returned…'

'My brother had his weaknesses, sir. But he was not evidently a madman!'

This drew further approving laughter from the crowd. But many were wavering.

'This will not do,' cried the old man in the crown of shells. 'As Hereditary Master of the Rolls I must use my authority in this matter. All must be put to Law. Let everyone be given the proper opportunities to speak. One day is all it will take, I am sure, for everyone to be heard. And then, if everything is still in order, the Coronation can commence. What do you say, your majesty? My lords and ladies? If the matter is to continue to the satisfaction of us all, let us call a Hearing on it. In this Hall at mid-afternoon.'

Sharadim could not refuse and, as for us, it was better than we had hoped for. We agreed at once.

I cried: 'Sharadim! Will you grant me an audience in private? You and three chosen companions. I and three of mine?'

She hesitated, looked over to one side of the hall as if in quest of some guidance. Then she nodded. 'In the antechamber in half an hour,' she said. 'But you cannot convince me, sir, that you are my exiled brother. Surely you did not think I would accept you as my own flesh and blood?'

'Then what am I, madam? A ghost?'

I watched as she and her guards left the hall in a billowing wave of silks and bright metal while the Master of the Rolls signed for us to accompany him through another side door and into a cool chamber, lit by a single large round window above. Once he had closed the door, he sighed. 'Land Prince Ottro, I had feared you slain. And you also, Prince Flamadin. There have been uncomfortable rumours here and there. For me, your words today confirm what I suspected of that woman. Not one of the nobles who voted to make her Empress is the kind I'd willingly invite to my own house. Ambitious, self-serving, foolish fellows all, who believe themselves deserving of greater power. That must be what she offers them. Of course, other, more innocent people followed suit out of ordinary, if misguided, idealism. They see her as a kind of living goddess, a personification of all their highest dreams and hopes. Her beauty, I suppose, has much to do with that. However, it did not need your melodramatic declarations of today to convince me that we are a whisker from complete tyranny. Already she speaks (albeit sweetly) of those in neighbouring realms who envy us our wealth, how we should protect ourselves more thoroughly…'

'Women are always underestimated by men,' said Alisaard, a note of satisfaction in her voice, 'and this enables them sometimes to gather far more power to themselves than the men suspect. I have noticed this in my own studies of history, in my own travels about the realms.'

'Believe me, madam, I do not underestimate her,' said the Master of the Rolls, closing the door behind him and motioning us to be seated at a long table of polished oak. 'You'll remember, Prince Flamadin, that I warned you to be more cautious. But you would not believe in your sister's schemes, her perfidy. She treated you like a favourite child, a wild son, rather than as a brother. And this enabled you to go scampering hither and yon in search of adventure while gradually she amassed more and more allies. Even then, you would have scarcely guessed the level of her evil had she not lost patience with you and ordered you to marry her, to consolidate her position. She assumed she could control you, or at least keep you a good distance from Court. Instead, you objected. You objected to her ambitions, her methods, her very philosophy. She tried to persuade you, I know. Then what happened?'

'She tried to kill me.'

'And put it about that you were the would-be murderer. That you were the one who stood against all our ideals and traditions.

It is as if she is a reincarnation of Sheralinn, Queen of the Val-adek, who regularly filled the moat out there with the blood of those she considered her enemies. I had guessed much of what you said today, but I had not realised she consciously sought to re-establish your dynasty as Empress of the Draachenheem. And you say she seeks the aid of Chaos? Chaos has not entered the Six Realms since the Sorcerers' War, more than a thousand years ago. It is contained within the hub, in the Nightmare Realm. We swore we would never let it through again.'

'I have heard she is already in communication with the Archduke Balarizaaf of Chaos. She seeks his help in fulfilling her ambitions.'

'And what would an archduke's price be, I wonder?' The Master of the Rolls was now even more concerned.

'A high one, I would guess,' said the Land Prince Ottro quietly. Deliberately, he folded his arms across his chest.

'Do such creatures really exist?' von Bek wished to know. 'Or do you speak figuratively?'

'They exist,' said the Master of the Rolls gravely. 'They exist in uncountable numbers. They seek to rule the multiverse and would use mankind's folly and vice to that end. The Lords of Law, on the other hand, seek to use mankind's idealism against Chaos, and to further their own schemes. Meanwhile the Cosmic Balance seeks to maintain equilibrium between the two. So much is commonly understood by those who recognise the existence of the multiverse and who travel, to some degree at least, between the realms.'

'Do you know of a legend concerning a sword?' von Bek asked. 'And a creature said to slumber within it?'

'The Dragon in the Sword. Aye, of course I have heard of the Dragon Sword. It is a terrible weapon, by all accounts. Forged by Chaos, they say, to conquer Chaos. The Lords of Chaos would give much for that…'

'Could that be the Archduke Balarizaaf's price?' von Bek suggested.

I was impressed by how swiftly he came to understand the logic by which we now lived.

'Indeed,' said the Master of the Rolls, his eyes widening, 'it could be!'

'And that's why she wants it. And that is why she was so glad to hear of it from us!' Alisaard clenched her ivory fists. 'Oh, what dolts we were to tell her so much. We should have guessed that the person we really sought would not ask so many questions.'

'You communicated with her that successfully?' I was surprised.

'We told her all we knew.'

'And doubtless she had information of her own to add to yours,' Ottro said. 'But surely you do not want the Dragon Sword in order to strike a bargain with Chaos?'

'We wanted it so we might rejoin our own people in a far realm. The Eldren have no truck with Chaos.'

'Is there anything else I should know?' asked the Master of the Rolls. 'We must call a Hearing and we must try to prove Sharadim evil. But if we cannot, if the vote goes against us, we must consider other means of stopping her.'

'Surely our evidence will sway the Court?' said Alisaard.

Von Bek looked at her almost as if he envied her innocence. 'I have but lately come from a world,' he said, 'whose rulers are masters at turning lies to truth and making the truth seem the foulest lie. It's easily done. We cannot expect to be believed simply because we know we do not lie.'

'The problem is,' added the Master of the Rolls, 'that so many wish to believe Sharadim the paragon they all desire. Often people fight hardest of all to preserve a delusion. And they will frequently persecute those who challenge that delusion.'

We debated the matter further until the Master of the Rolls told us that the time had come for our meeting with Sharadim. Alisaard, von Bek, Land Prince Ottro and myself left the chamber and were escorted through the now deserted hall, still full of rose petals, and up a short flight of stairs into a series of rooms, some of which formed a kind of aviary, and finally to a circular room whose windows overlooked flower gardens and formal hedgerows and lawns, the inner courtyard of the palace. Here the Princess Sharadim sat.

On her right was a long-jawed fellow with thin, unkempt light-coloured hair. He wore a surcoat of orange and a jerkin and breeches of yellow. On her left, leaning a little on her large chair, was a bulky, plump creature whose tiny eyes were never still and whose jaw moved slowly, like a goat chewing cud; he wore a mauve surcoat and dark blue underneath. The last was a youth of such decadent appearance I could hardly believe my eyes. He was almost a grotesque parody of the type, with thick wet lips, drooping eyelids, pale, spotted unhealthy skin, twitching muscles and fingers, and reddish curly hair. They announced themselves in a sulky, challenging manner. The first was Perichost of Risphert, Duke of Orrawh in the distant west; then Neterpino Sloch, Commander of the Befeel Host, and lastly Lord Pharl Asclett, Hereditary Prince of Skrenaw, but better known as Pharl of the Heavy Palm.

'I know of you all, gentlemen,' said Ottro with poorly disguised disgust as he introduced us. 'And you know Prince Flamadin. This is his friend Count Ulric von Bek. Lastly Alisaard, Legion Commander of Gheestenheem.

Sharadim had waited impatiently through all this. Now she rose from her chair and, pushing through her companions, walked straight to where I stood and looked up into my face. 'You are an imposter. You can admit it here. You know, as do most of those who came with you, that I slew Prince Flamadin. True, his body is not corrupted and lies even now in my cellars. But I am lately come from where I left that body. It is still there! I know you for the one called the Champion, who those foolish women called to, mistaking myself for you. And I can guess what you are attempting by this essay into play-acting...'

'They hope to get to the sword before we do,' interrupted Pharl, scratching at his palm. 'And make their own bargain with the Archduke.'

'Be quiet, Prince Pharl,' she said contemptuously. 'Your imagination is notoriously poor. Not everyone holds identical ambitions to your own!' Ignoring his flushing features, she continued: 'You either wish to oust me from the throne and rule in my place,' she said, 'or you merely wish to bring my plans to an end. What? Do you all serve Law? Are you employed to give battle to Chaos and his allies? I know a little of your legend, Champion. Is that not your function?'

'I'll allow you your speculations, madam, but you cannot expect me to confirm or deny them. I am not here to give you more power.'

'You are here to steal what I have, eh?'

'If you would give up your schemes, if you would refuse any further dealings with Chaos, if you would tell us what you know of the Dragon Sword, then you will receive no further conflict from me. If, as I suspect, you do not accept my terms, then I shall have to fight you, Princess Sharadim. And that fight would almost certainly bring about your own destruction...'

'Or yours,' she said calmly.

'I cannot be destroyed.'

'I had heard otherwise.' She laughed. 'This disguise, this flesh you assume, that can be destroyed easily enough. What you love can be destroyed. What you admire can be corrupted. Come now, Champion, it is unworthy of either of us to mince words when we know exactly what we are dealing with!'

'I offered you a fair bargain, madam.'

'I have been offered better elsewhere.'

'The Lords of Chaos are notoriously treacherous. Their servants have a tendency to die in horrid circumstances...' I shrugged.

'Servant? I'm no servant of Chaos. I am in alliance with a certain party.'

'Balarizaaf,' I said. 'He will cheat you, lady.'

'Or I him.' Her smile was all pride. I had seen many like her in the past. She believed herself cleverer than she was because it suited others to let her maintain that delusion.

'I speak sincerely, Princess Sharadim!' I was more urgent now. I should have felt less fearful if she had been a little more clever. 'I am not your brother, it is true. But I have something of your brother's soul mixed with mine. I know that you lack the strength to counter Chaos when it turns against you.'

'It will not turn against me, Sir Champion. Besides, my brother knew little of my dealings with Chaos. You have gathered that information from elsewhere.'

This set me back a little. If I was not tapping her brother's memories, then I must be receiving my knowledge by some other means. Then it occurred to me that I was in some sort of telepathic communication with Princess Sharadim. That was how I had known what she meant to do. I found the thought unpleasant.

Flamadin and Sharadim had been twins, after all. I inhabited a body which was the exact counterpart of Flamadin's. Therefore it might be possible that communication existed between us. And if that were so, Sharadim was as much party to my secrets as I was to hers.

What further disturbed me was knowing that a corpse identical to me was still stored in Sharadim's cellars. I was not sure why I found this so distasteful, but it made me shudder. At the same time I had a sudden image: a wall of pale red crystal, and within the wall a sword which seemed to glow green and black and which at other times seemed to be on fire.

'How will you cut the crystal, Sharadim?' I said. 'How will you tear the sword from its prison?'

She frowned. 'You know more than I guessed. This is foolish. We should consider an alliance. They will all believe Flamadin restored. We shall marry. The folk of the Draachenheem will be overjoyed. What celebrations! Our power would increase immediately. We would share equally everything we gained!'

I turned away. 'These are the self-same proposals you made to your brother. When he refused, you killed him. Now that I refuse will you kill me, Sharadim? On the spot? Here and now?'

She all but spat in my face. 'Moment by moment I gain in strength. You shall be swallowed up in the storm I shall release. You shall be forgotten, Champion, and all who are with you. I shall rule the Six Realms and with my chosen companions shall indulge my every whim. That is what you refuse – immortality and an eternity of pleasure! What you have chosen is prolonged agony and certain death.'

She was foolish and because she was foolish she was exceptionally dangerous. I recognised that. I was afraid, as she had hoped I
would be afraid, but not because of her threats. If she allied herself with Balarizaaf there was no anticipating the danger we faced
in our search for the sword. And if she were thwarted, I thought,
she was the kind who would willingly drag all down with her as
she went. I preferred a more knowing foe.

'Well,' said von Bek from behind me. 'We shall see what the
Hearing brings. Perhaps the people will decide this issue.'

A look of secret calculation crossed Sharadim's face.

'What have you done, madam?' cried the Land Prince Ottro. 'Be
careful, Prince Flamadin. I can see the meanest treachery in her eyes!'

At this Prince Pharl of the Heavy Palm uttered a peculiar snigger.

Then there came a hammering on the door of our chamber
and I heard a voice cry from the other side: 'My lady Empress! My
lady. A message of the utmost urgency!'

Sharadim nodded and Perichost, Duke of Orrawh, stepped forward to draw back the bolt.

A frightened servant stood there, one hand to his face. 'Oh,
madam. Murder has been done!'

'Murder?' She displayed horrified surprise. 'Murder, you say?'

'Aye, madam. The Master of the Rolls, his wife and two young
pages. All cut down in the Silver Auditorium!'

Sharadim turned to me with a look of exultation in her huge
blue eyes. 'Well, sir, it seems that violence and terror accompany
you wherever you go. And they visit us only when you – or the
one you resemble – come amongst us!'

'You have killed him!' cried Ottro. He made a motion to his hip
before he realised that he, like the rest of us, was without weapons. 'You have killed that fine old man!'

'Well?' asked Sharadim of the servant. 'Do you have any idea
who was responsible for these crimes?'

'They say it was Federit Shaus and two others. That they
obeyed the Land Prince Halmad of Ruradani.'

'What? The ones who came with the rest of this party?'

'That is what they say, madam.'

I was furious. 'You planned this. Within an hour you have spilled further blood in pursuit of your appalling lie. Neither Shaus nor Halmad nor any of our companions was armed!'

'Tell us,' said Sharadim softly to the servant, 'how did that good man and his wife come to die?'

'By the ceremonial blades kept in the Auditorium,' said the servant, darting bewildered glances at myself and my friends.

'We had no reason to kill Prince Albret,' bellowed Ottro in perplexed outrage. 'You killed him to silence him. You killed him to provide yourself with a motive for destroying us. Let us continue with the Hearing. Let us speak our evidence!'

She spoke softly and triumphantly. 'There'll be no Hearing now. It is obvious to all that you came here on a mission of assassination, that you had no other motive.'

It was at this moment that von Bek sprang for Sharadim and seized her from behind, his arm across her windpipe.

'What good can that do?' cried Alisaard, confounded by all this villainy. 'If we use violence, we resort to their methods. If we threaten her, we prove her case against us.'

Von Bek did not loosen his grip. 'I assure you, Lady Alisaard, that I do not act thoughtlessly.' As Sharadim struggled, von Bek forced her to be still. 'I have had enough experience of such plots to know that everything is already planned. We will not receive a fair hearing. We will be lucky if we are able to leave this room alive. As for leaving the palace alive, I think we have only the poorest of chances now.'

Her three lieutenants were moving uncertainly towards von Bek. I stepped between them and my friend. My head had grown muzzy. I had a series of images, of emotions, which I knew were not mine. They were doubtless coming from the captured princess. I saw the crystal wall again, the entrance to a cave. I heard a name which sounded like *Morandi Pag*. More fragments of words. Another that was complete – *Armiad* – then *Barganheem*...

Ottro came up beside me, then Alisaard. The three made feeble motions in our direction but did not dare advance. Noticing Neter-pino Sloch slip one hand beneath his surcoat, I moved suddenly forward and struck him hard on the jaw. He went down like a stunned pig. I bent over him as he moaned and drooled on the ground. I tore back his surcoat, revealing a knife some nine inches long set between the double row of buttons on his jerkin. I pulled the blade free.

Next I inspected the other two. They glared and objected, but did not resist. I found two more knives.

'What contemptible creatures you are!' I handed a knife to Ottro and another to von Bek. 'Now, Sharadim, you'll tell that poor servant who currently bangs on your door to fetch those of our friends that remain alive. Bring them here and leave them here.'

Almost choking, she did as I ordered. Von Bek carefully placed a knife point at her side and relaxed the tension on her throat.

A few minutes later the doors opened. In came Federit Shaus, looking dazed and frightened, followed by all the others who had accompanied us to Rhetalik.

'Now send a message to your guards to search in the Eastern Wing of the palace,' I said. Scarlet with fury, she issued the command.

To my companions I said, 'You must return to the courtyard and have our horses saddled at once. Tell them you seek fleeing assassins. Then wait for us or, if you think your chances are better, head for wherever you think you'll be safest. Try to convince your own people of Sharadim's evil ambitions. On her instructions, Prince Albret and his wife were murdered, to silence him and create a crime for which she can blame us. Armies must be raised against her. Some of you must succeed. Prepare your people for what she plans. Resist her. Ride away from here at once, if you desire. We'll follow in a short while.'

'Go,' said Prince Ottro in agreement. 'He is right. There is no other way. I shall stay with them. Pray that at least some of us are successful.'

When they had disappeared, Prince Ottro looked quizzically at me. 'But how long can we hold off all the forces of the Valadek? I say we should kill her now.'

She uttered a great groan and tried to break free again, but felt von Bek's knife at her ribs and thought better of it.

'No,' said Alisaard. 'We cannot resort to her methods. There is no justification for cold-blooded murder.'

'True,' I agreed. 'By acting as they would act, we become what they are. And if we are what they are, then there is little point in resisting them!'

Ottro frowned. 'A fine point, but I do not think we have time for such niceties. We'll be dead within the hour if we do not act soon.'

'There's nothing for it,' I said. 'We must use her as our hostage. We have no other choice.'

Sharadim moved her body against von Bek's, trying to draw back from the knife. 'You would do best to kill me now,' she said fiercely. 'For if you do not, I will hound you through the Six Realms, and when I find you I shall...' Whereupon she uttered a series of intentions which chilled my blood, made Alisaard look as if she were about to vomit and turned Prince Ottro white as a Ghost Woman's armour. Only von Bek seemed unmoved. He had, after all, witnessed much of what she threatened, as an inmate of Hitler's camps.

I made a decision. I drew a deep breath. 'Very well,' I said, 'we shall probably kill you, Princess Sharadim. Perhaps it is the only way to ensure that Chaos shall not conquer the Six Realms. And I think we can kill you as imaginatively as you would dispense with us.'

She looked hard at me, wondering if I spoke the truth. I laughed in her face. 'Oh, madam,' I said, 'you have no idea what blood is already on my hands. You cannot possibly begin to guess what horror I have looked upon.' And I let her find my mind. I let her know something of my memories, my eternal battles, my agonies, of the time when, as Erekosë, I had led Eldren armies in the utter destruction of the human race.

And Sharadim screamed. She began to collapse.

'She has fainted,' said von Bek in bewilderment.

'Now we can leave,' I said.

Chapter Five

S PEED AND DESPERATION were our only allies. We left Sharadim's henchmen bound and gagged in a large chest. We took
the insensible princess with us. I held her in my arms as I might
hold a loved one. Every time we came upon a guard we would call
out that she was sick and that we were hurrying her to the hospital wing of the palace. And very soon we were back in the
courtyard, running for our horses.

Sharadim was now bundled into a cloak and slung over Prince
Ottro's saddle. We had crossed the bridge and were galloping
through the town within minutes. Still there was no pursuit.
Doubtless they were still shocked by the murder of the Master of
the Rolls and it had not yet registered that their princess had been
kidnapped.

Through the town, and now she was waking. I heard her muffled protests. We ignored them.

And then at last we were on the open road again and heading
for where we had hidden our boat. We looked back all the time,
but none came after us. Von Bek grinned, 'I had thought us as
good as dead. There is something to be said for experience!'

'And quick thinking to make use of it,' I pointed out. I, too, was
surprised that we had managed to get away before a hue and cry
was raised. Apart from the murder of Prince Albret, the other factor in our favour was that the entire palace had been geared for a
peaceful celebration. Most ordinary guards were on ceremonial
duty. Many strangers were coming and going all the time. By now
they would have found Neterpino Sloch, Duke Perichost and
Prince Pharl and would be attempting to discover what had happened to Princess Sharadim. These people seemed to have no
sophisticated methods of long-distance signalling. If we could

reach the boat in time, we had every chance now of getting completely clear of Valadeka.

'But what of our captive?' said Prince Ottro. 'How will we dispose of her? Take her with us?'

'It would prove an unwelcome encumbrance,' I said.

'Then I suppose we shall have to kill her,' said Ottro, 'if she is of no use to us. And if we are to save this realm from Chaos.'

Alisaard murmured an objection. I said nothing. I knew that Sharadim was now awake again and could hear our conversation. I knew, too, that I had frightened her sufficiently – if momentarily – to make a little further use of her.

Two hours later we had released our horses into a field and were climbing down the cliffs to where we had left our boat. Sharadim was over von Bek's shoulder. Ottro led the way. Eventually we stood on the shingle. The sky was grey now and the whole beach seemed dead. Even the ocean had a lifeless quality to it.

'We could take the body with us,' Ottro argued, 'and dump it in the sea. That would be the end of her for ever. The nobles would pick up the pieces soon enough.'

'Or would they seek revenge on my murderers, I wonder?' She was on her feet, shaking out her lovely golden hair. Her eyes were blue flints. 'You could bring our realm to civil war, Prince Ottro. Would that be what you want? I promise unity.'

He turned away from her, untying cords from the mast and settling it in the centre of the boat.

'Why did you not go yourself to Barganheem and try to take the sword?' I asked her. I was bluffing. I was using the few words I had found in her mind.

'You know as well as I why that would be folly,' she said. 'I can enter Barganheem at the head of an army and take what I want.'

'Would not Morandi Pag object?'

'What if he did?'

'And Armiad?'

She drew her beautiful brows together in another glare. 'That barbarian? That parvenu? He will do what he is told. If he had

493

come to us a few hours before the Massing we could have settled this once and for all. But we had not known where you would be.'

'You sought me at the Massing?'

'Prince Pharl was there. He offered to buy you both, dead or alive, from Armiad. So he would have done, had not the Ghost Women found you first. Armiad is a poor ally, but so far he is the only one I have in the Maaschanheem.'

I realised now that her schemes already extended beyond her own realm. She was gathering accomplices everywhere she could. And Armiad, of course, in his hatred for me, was perfectly willing to be of service to her. Now I knew, too, that the Dragon Sword was probably in the Barganheem, that someone called Morandi Pag knew its exact location, or was its protector, and that Shara-dim felt he was powerful enough for her to require an army to aid her against him.

Federit Shaus, Alisaard and Prince Halmad by now had readied the boat and were preparing to push it into the water. Prince Ottro drew out the long knife I had taken from Neterpino Sloch. 'Shall I do it? We must get it over with.'

'We cannot murder her,' I said. 'She's right in one thing. A civil war could result from that. If we leave her, some will realise we're not the killers she says we are.'

'Civil war's inevitable now,' said Prince Ottro feelingly. 'More than one country will refuse to acknowledge her as Empress.

'But many others will accept her. Let our actions be witness to our humanity and honesty.'

Prince Halmad and Alisaard were both in strong agreement.

'Let her be brought to Law,' said Alisaard. 'I for one shall not descend to her methods. Flamadin is right. Now many will suspect her. Her own people might insist upon a trial...'

'That last I doubt.' Von Bek spoke soberly. 'Or let us say that those who do insist on a hearing will be silenced soon enough. There is a monotonous pattern to the rise of tyrants which, I suppose, is reflected in the general pattern of human folly. Depressing though it is, we must accept the fact.'

'Well, she'll be resisted now,' said Ottro with satisfaction. 'Come, we must set sail at once for Waldana. There, at least, I will be believed.'

Sharadim was laughing at us as we shoved off into the water. Her wonderful hair whipped in the wind and her cloak snapped and flapped as she clasped it around her body. I stood in the stern, looking back at her, staring into her eyes, perhaps trying to will her to put a halt to her evil. But her laughter grew stronger. I could still hear it when the boat rounded the headland and she was lost from sight.

I think that some big schooners came after us. We saw them on the second day but happily they did not see us. By then we were almost at the coast of Waldana. We let Ottro and the others ashore in a small fishing harbour, at night. The prince saluted us. 'I go to rouse my people. We, at least, shall oppose the Princess Sharadim.'

We had no time for rest.

'North,' said Alisaard. She had a kind of compass on a thong about her neck. 'But quickly. By morning it will be gone.'

We sailed north, the black of the ocean gradually turning to pewter as the sun rose, and then, on the horizon, we saw the entrance. Already it appeared to be fading. Expertly, Alisaard moved the sail to catch the full benefit of the breeze. The boat tugged forward. It seemed to bring von Bek and myself alive again. Eagerly we stared at the great columns of soft light which plunged from an unseen source and descended to an unseen destination.

'I'll have to risk a more rapid approach,' cried Alisaard. 'It's now only seconds before the eclipse is over.' And with that she directed our little boat between two of the columns which had grown so close together that I thought we must be crushed by them. The whole temple of light was contracting, the columns moving to form a single faint beam.

But we were through and even though this tunnel was considerably narrower than the last, we knew we were safe. For a moment we knew a little relief on tranquil water, then the ship was tilting, moving along the corridor at enormous speed.

'We are taught to know where and when to find all the gateways between the realms,' Alisaard informed us. 'We have charts and calculators. We can anticipate when one gateway opens and another closes. We know exactly where one will lead and another will not. Never fear, soon we shall be in Barganheem. We shall arrive about noon.'

Von Bek was weary. He fell back in the boat, a weak smile on his face. 'I have to trust your judgement, Herr Daker, but I'm blessed if I know how you decided we should find this sword in Barganheem.'

I told him how I had come by the knowledge. 'I have the advantage over Sharadim that I can consciously read something of what is in her mind. She can only guess. That is, she has the same power but she does not know how to use it. I was able to let her see my whole mind for a moment –'

'And that was why she fainted so suddenly? Aha! I am glad you do not let me enjoy such a privilege, Herr Daker!' He yawned. 'But this means that if she ever learns the secret Sharadim will be able to read something of your thoughts, also. She will have the same advantage.'

'Even now she could well be determining which of her intuitions she should trust. There's every chance she'll pick the right ones.'

The boat shivered. We looked forward. Ahead was a bright green mass of light, almost a ball, like a sun. Slowly it turned to blue and then to grey. Then the corridor seemed to narrow dramatically and we found ourselves ducking. There was a noise like wind-chimes, random yet musical, and we were jerking painfully, the whole boat bumping up and down on what, evidently, was no longer water.

Below us were clouds. Above was a blue sky and a sun at zenith. The columns had disappeared. We were not on water at all, but in a soft, green mountain meadow. A little way from us, in another field separated by a drystone wall, three black-and-white cows were grazing. Two of them looked with mild curiosity in our direction. Another made a noise as if to indicate she had no interest in us whatsoever.

In all directions were these same steep meadows, walls and mountain peaks. It was impossible to see anything of the land below the clouds. There was a strange, pleasant quietness here. Von Bek put his leg over the boat and smiled at Alisaard. 'Is all of Barganheem so peaceful, my lady?'

'Much of it,' she said. 'The river traders tend to be quarrelsome, but they never bother to climb so high.'

'And what of the farmers? Will they object to finding a boat in one of their fields?' Von Bek spoke with his usual dry humour.

Alisaard was removing her visor completely. Once again, as she shook out her long hair, I was struck by her resemblance to my Ermizhad, both in mannerisms and looks. And again I felt that pang of jealousy when she gave von Bek an answering smile which held, I was sure, at least a hint of an emotion that was stronger than casual friendship. I controlled myself, of course, for I had no right to feel as I did. I was committed to Ermizhad. I loved Ermizhad more than I loved life. And this, I reminded the childish creature whining within me, was not Ermizhad. If Alisaard found von Bek sexually attractive and my friend reciprocated her feelings, it should be an occasion for me to feel pleased for them. Yet still the little nagging devil remained. I would have cut him from me with a white-hot knife if that had been possible.

'You'll notice that the farmers have placed no livestock in this particular field,' said Alisaard. 'They are as aware as any that this is, in their terms, a magic place. They have had cows disappear when the Pillars of Paradise materialise! They've seen stranger things than boats. However, we cannot expect them to be of much help to us, either. They have no experience of travelling between the realms. They leave such adventures for the traders of the river valleys far below.'

'How shall we begin to look for Morandi Pag?' I asked, break-ing rather curtly into her speech. 'You said you could guess, by the name, where we should begin looking, Lady Alisaard.'

She looked at me curiously, as if she sensed an emotion which had something to do with her. 'Are you in pain, Prince Flamadin?'

'Merely anxious,' I told her briefly. 'We cannot let Sharadim gain another minute…'

'You don't think we have made time for ourselves?' Von Bek reached down and wet his hands on the lush grass. He patted at his face and sighed.

'Gained some and lost some,' I reminded him. 'She must either consider bringing an army into Barganheem or she must plan fresh strategy. If she's as impatient for power as I believe, she will now be willing to risk more than she ever did in order to get to the Dragon Sword before we do. So, Lady Alisaard, where would you think it wise to begin looking for Morandi Pag?'

Silently, she pointed down the steep hillside towards the clouds. 'Unfortunately we must descend to the river valleys. That name has an unhuman ring to my ears. But be warned – when we reach the valleys you must allow me to speak. They have traded with the Gheestenheemers for several centuries and we are the only people who have not at some point offered them violence. In as much as they trust any outrealmer, they'll trust me. They will not trust you, however, for a moment.'

'A xenophobic race, eh?' said von Bek cheerfully, readying him-self for the long walk down.

'Not without reason,' said Alisaard. 'You Mabden are the unlikeliest of evolved species. Most of us learn to enjoy and understand the differences between cultures and races. Your his-tory appears to be a long tale of persecution and destruction of anything not like yourselves. Why is that, do you think?'

'If I had that answer at this moment, my lady,' said von Bek with some force, 'I do not believe I would be here discussing the problem. All I can assure you is that a few of us "Mabden" are as concerned by the truth you state as anyone. I sometimes think we are born of a monstrous nightmare, that we live perpetually with the horror of our hellish origin, that we seek to silence any voice which reminds us of what ill-formed intelligences we are!'

She was evidently impressed by his passion. I merely wished that I had said as much and been as eloquent. I forced myself to take a keen interest in the surrounding view as we tramped rapidly downhill towards the calm plateau of cloud.

'Once below that layer,' said Alisaard, 'we shall no longer be in the territory of the farmers. Look, there's one of their houses...'

It was a rather tall, conical building, with a chimney and thatch almost to the ground. I saw two or three figures nearby, going about the ordinary business of farming. However, I was struck by the oddness of some of their movements. Our descent took us closer to the farm. The people did not look up as we went by, though they had plainly seen us. Evidently, they preferred to pretend we did not exist. As a result I could stare without much rudeness at them. They seemed oddly bent. At first I attributed this to the nature of their work, to some unusual cut to their clothing, but it soon became obvious, from the glimpse I had of their faces, that they were not human at all. I was reminded at first of a kind of baboon. And now I understood a little better what Alisaard had meant. Another close glance and I saw large, solid cloven hoofs where the feet would be on a human. What else were these quiet, harmless farmers but devils from the superstitions of Daker's world? 'Why,' I said with a laugh, 'I do believe we are marching through Hell, von Bek.'

My friend offered me a sardonic glance. 'I assure you, Herr Daker, that Hell is not nearly as pleasant.'

Alisaard called out a greeting in her clear, sweet voice. It was as if a beautiful songbird had suddenly begun its call. Hearing it the farmers looked up. Their strange, wizened faces beamed in recognition. Now they waved and shouted something to us which was in such a thick dialect I could barely understand a word. Alisaard told me they were wishing us good fortune 'below the sea'. 'They think of these layers of cloud as an ocean and the people beneath it possess almost a mythological character to them. They have, of course, never seen a real sea. There are large lakes below, but they will not go beyond their own shores. So this is the sea.' And it was at that point that I began to realise we had entered the clouds, that visibility was rapidly growing less. I looked back. Already I could barely see the farmhouse. 'Now,' Alisaard told us, 'we had best link hands. I shall continue to lead. The path is marked by cairns, but frequently animals will destroy them. Be wary, too, of the smoke snakes. They are predominantly dark grey and frequently cannot be seen until they are at your feet.'

'What do they do, these smoke snakes?' Von Bek stretched his hand out to Alisaard. He put his other hand in mine.

'They protect themselves if you step on them,' she said simply. 'And since we have no weapons save the knives we must be more than usually careful to avoid that. I shall watch for the cairn. You two watch the ground. Remember, they are of a darker grey.'

In all that white and grey, with rocks and the remains of abandoned walls sometimes emerging from the fog, I wondered how anyone could spot such a creature. Nonetheless I scrupulously did as she had instructed me. I had come to trust Alisaard both as a comrade and as a guide. This fact increased my misery on one level, particularly when it seemed to me she gave von Bek a further admiring glance.

The going was slower and slower, yet I continued to concentrate on looking for the dark grey of a smoke snake. From time to time I saw something moving; something which curled lazily upwards like a snake and then sank down again, which seemed to possess a vast number of coils, like the old pictures of sea-serpents on mariners' charts. I thought I heard a faint noise, too, like the rise and fall of surf on a gentle beach.

'Are those the sounds the smoke snake makes?' I asked Alisaard. I was astonished at the echoing effect of the fog. My voice sounded completely unreal in my own ears.

Ahead, concentrating on finding the next cairn, she nodded.

It had grown very cold and our clothing was either soaked or running with water. I could not imagine it would be much warmer when we emerged from the fog, since it was thick enough to blot out most of the sunlight. Von Bek, too, it seemed was feeling the chill, for he appeared to be shivering.

I looked ahead, wondering if Alisaard's ivory armour offered her any protection at all from the fog. As I did so, I saw a great grey coiling shadow rise up not three feet from the Ghost Woman. I cried out in warning. She did not respond, but stopped. The three of us watched as the thing writhed slowly into the fog. I had still not made out any features. 'They are not to be feared when they poise themselves like that,' Alisaard told me. 'They are merely looking at us. If they can see us then we are in no danger. It is only the young ones, and usually only when they are disturbed in sleep, who strike. But I remind you – do not step upon a smoke snake. They react violently when startled. These old fellows have seen many travellers and know they are not in danger. Am I clear?'

She sounded almost impatient, as if she dealt with a slow-witted child. I apologised for my panic. I said I would remember what she said and keep my concentration only on the ground ahead of me.

Von Bek understood that I had received a mild reprimand. He turned to look at me just as we started off again. He winked.

And it was at that moment that I saw his foot stepping directly upon the tip of a grey coil.

'Von Bek!'

He looked at me in horror, realising what I had seen. His eyes widened further in pain. 'My God,' he said softly, 'it has my calf...'

Then Alisaard was flinging herself downwards, knife poised, left hand stretching full ahead of her.

The dark grey coils were moving slowly but surely up von Bek's leg. I could see no head, no mouth, no eyes, yet I knew the creature was crawling up his body, seeking the upper parts, the head and face. I reached out to try to tug the thing off and there came a savage metallic hiss from somewhere within the beast. Another coil seemed to detach itself from the main body and cling to my wrist. With my knife I cut at it, trying to slice it, but somehow the knife made no impression at all. Von Bek also used his knife. And with equal impotence. I saw Alisaard's figure very dimly through the fog. She was still on the ground, growling to herself, cursing in frustration, as if she sought something she had lost. I heard the ivory armour clattering against rocks. I thought I saw her arm rise and fall. And still the smoke snake continued to climb my arm and von Bek's leg at the same time. I was close to being sick with the horror of it while von Bek's face was paler than the mist surrounding it.

I looked at the tip of the coil, where it was almost at my shoulder. Now I thought, somewhere within the creature, I saw the faintest suggestion of features. It darted at my face then, as if in outrage at my discovery. I felt a sharp pain in my cheek. I felt blood begin to run down my chin. Almost at once the smoke snake's head revealed a scarcely visible but distinct mouth full of long, thin teeth, of vibrating nostrils, the suggestion of a tongue.

And, thanks to my blood, the head now glowed a delicate and horrifying pink.

Chapter Six

WITHIN SECONDS THE smoke snake had begun to turn a darker red. Its other head reached von Bek's face and struck, as it still struck at mine, taking tiny, almost dainty, bites of my flesh. I knew it would continue to bite in this way until my head was nothing but a white skull on my body. I believe I screamed something, but I cannot remember the words. It was a prospect of death all the more terrifying because it would not be quick. I waved my knife in front of the head, which now displayed glaring crimson eyes, hoping somehow to distract it. But it had a strange kind of patience. It was as if it waited until it perceived a gap in my defence then it would dart through again. And again my face would sting from a further wound. I remembered scars on a traveller's face at the Great Massing. I remembered wondering what had pocked him so. And I yelled again. At least, I thought, it was possible to escape the smoke snake. That man had done so, though it had cost him an eye and half his face.

Von Bek was yelling, too. There was an appalling inevitability about the creature's attack. As our arms grew more tired, as it became steadily more and more visible, thanks to our blood, it merely waited, maintaining its grip on our limbs and occasionally giving vent to that awful metallic hissing.

What made the experience worse for me was that the creature no longer seemed angry. It was a simple enough organism, I supposed. It only reacted when it believed itself attacked. When it had its coils about something, that something was then tasted. If the taste was good, that something simply became the smoke snake's ordinary prey. It probably could not even remember its initial reason for attacking von Bek. It had no reason to hurry now. It could take a leisurely meal.

I tried to stab the fanged maw with the knife again. All logic suggested that the creature which could inflict such wounds must therefore be able to receive such wounds. But it was not so. My knife, cutting and slashing wildly, found only the tiniest resistance and a faint, pinkish dust seemed to surround the head like a halo for a moment before being reintegrated back into the bulk of the animal.

All this, of course, in a matter of seconds.

Meanwhile, Alisaard continued to curse and shout. I could not see her at all. I could only hear, as if in the back of my mind, her rattling armour and her animal-like grunts and howls of frustrated action.

Von Bek's face looked as if he had been weeping tears of blood. Streamers of blood ran down his cheeks. Part of his left ear had been torn away. He had a bite, swollen with blood, in the very centre of his forehead. He drew rapid, sobbing breaths. His eyes spoke not so much of a fear of death but of the horror and pointlessness of the manner of his death.

Then I heard Alisaard's cry change. It was almost a howl of triumph. A kind of ululation. I still could not see anything of her, save a white hand grabbing for the insubstantial main body of the smoke snake. She uttered a sort of prolonged groan. I saw her knife dart out of the fog and her other hand seemed to strike at the identical spot.

The smoke snake reared back. I was sure it would take one of my eyes. I brought my hand up to shield myself. Unable to see the snake I might easily have believed the thing did not exist, save in my imagination. It had virtually no weight. Yet it held me tight.

I heard von Bek give vent to a huge roar. I thought the thing had struck some vital spot and, still without looking, threw myself forward, even while I knew I was incapable of saving him. But there would be some value, I remember thinking, if one died in such an attempt. There is consolation for certain souls, even in the moment of the most hideous and violent death.

I felt two arms embrace me. I opened my eyes. The smoke

snake's coils no longer writhed around half von Bek's body. I wondered if he and I were already dead. If this were some anodyne illusion of safety as our lifeblood bloated the belly of our antagonist.

'Herr Daker!' I heard von Bek say in some surprise. 'He appears to have fainted, my lady.'

I lay on the ground. I saw my friends staring down at me. There was amusement as well as anxiety there. I looked at them. I felt tremendous relief that they lived. And I felt again that demeaning pang of jealousy as I saw their heads come together above mine. 'No,' I murmured. 'You must be Ermizhad. Be Ermizhad if only for a moment while I die...'

'That is the name he spoke before,' said Alisaard.

I thought them rather unconcerned that their friend was dying. Were they already dead?

'It is the name of an Eldren woman, like yourself,' I heard von Bek say. 'He loves her. He has sought her across the aeons; he has searched for her in so many realms. He thinks you resemble her.'

Her features softened. She removed a glove and touched my face. I moved my lips and said for a second time: 'Ermizhad, before I die...' But already reality was returning and I knew I hovered on the edge of play-acting, willing to pretend I was still in a swoon if I could prolong that moment, that feeling of receiving good-hearted and honest sympathy, such as I had once received from Ermizhad and which, I hope, I had given in return. Then I made a great effort and said firmly: 'Forgive me, my lady. I am recovered. My senses are about me again. Perhaps you would be good enough to tell me how Count von Bek and myself are still amongst the living!'

Von Bek helped me into a sitting position. The fog did not seem quite so dense now. I thought I could see some distance down the hill, to where wide, silver water awaited us.

Alisaard had seated herself upon a rock. She had something small and unlovely at her feet, placed on a flat shard of flint. It, too, seemed to possess thousands of coils, but these were tiny and of no possible danger, unless they were poisoned. She poked at the little black thing with her knife point. It seemed completely lifeless. Indeed, beneath her knife it began to crumble. Parts of it rapidly turned to fine, black dust.

Unbelievingly I said: 'Surely that cannot be the remains of the smoke snake?'

She looked up at me, sucking in her lower lip, raising her eyebrows. She nodded.

Von Bek stared down at the fragments. 'It was defeated by the commonest of substances in the hands of a most uncommon woman.'

She was pleased by his praise. 'I know only one way of killing a smoke snake. You must find its centre. Cut it, and you create as many new creatures as there are fresh pieces. You must make it bleed and kill it at the moment before it can divide. The blood carries that which you use to destroy it. Happily I remembered that. Happily, too, like all Gheestenheemers I travel with my own supplies.'

'But what killed it, Lady Alisaard? How did you save our lives when our weapons had no effect on the thing?'

Von Bek interrupted her. He was laughing. 'You'll see the humour of it, when she tells you. Please, Alisaard, let him not stay in suspense any longer. The poor man's exhausted!'

Alisaard showed me the palm of her left hand. It had a faint crust of white near the centre. 'Salt. We always carry salt.'

'The thing responded as swiftly as any ordinary garden slug!' Von Bek was exultant. 'As soon as she found that core – and that was where her courage was unbelievable – she had to strike with her knife to draw blood and apply the salt at the exact same second. The core shrivelled immediately. And we were saved.' He dabbed at the little scabs on his face. The wounds were already healing. They would leave few marks. I supposed myself as lucky. 'Nothing to show for it,' my friend added, 'but what appears to be the remains of a bad case of acne.'

He helped me to my feet. I presented myself to the Lady

Alisaard. Now she resembled my Ermizhad even closer than she had at first. 'I thank you from the bottom of my heart, Lady Alisaard. I thank you for my life.'

'You would have given yours trying to save Count von Bek,' she said gently as she flipped the dead core out into the mist. 'Luckily I had a little more knowledge of these things.' She looked with a mixture of merriment and sternness at von Bek. 'And let us hope a certain gentleman does better at watching his feet rather than his comrade if he comes this way again.'

Chastened, von Bek became an exemplary German nobleman. He drew himself upright and at attention. He clicked his heels and bowed in acknowledgement of what he regarded as a just condemnation of his folly.

Both Alisaard and I found it difficult to hide our amusement at his sudden adoption of formal manners.

'Come,' she said then, 'we must make haste to reach the lower slopes. There we shall be out of the domain of the smoke snakes and can rest without much fear of any further attacks. It is too late now to approach the city, for it is their custom to refuse all visitors after dark. But in the morning, refreshed, we can go there and hope they will agree to help us find Morandi Pag.'

With the mist at last above us and twilight bringing further chill, the three of us drew close together for warmth as we stretched out on the springy and rather comfortable turf of the slope. I remember looking down into the valley where it widened out into a kind of bay overlooking the lake. In this bay and along the riverbank for some distance inland I could see lights winking, fires blazing. I thought I heard voices, although these could have been the sounds of flocks of jet-black carrion birds as they crowded home to their nests in the upper crags. I wondered at the city. I could see no buildings of any kind. I could see no ships, though I thought there were some quays and piers at the water's edge. Further along the shore of the lake there grew a deep, thick wood whose trees primarily resembled oaks. From this, too, now emerged some lights, as if foresters made their way homeward.

Again I looked in vain for buildings. I wondered vaguely as I fell into a deep and exhausted slumber if, like the smoke snakes, the city and its residents were invisible to the human eye. I remembered something of another people who had been called 'ghosts' by those who refused to understand them and I tried to bring the memory into sharper focus. But, as often happened with my over-crowded brain, I could not quite grasp the full recollection. It had something, I thought, to do with Ermizhad. I turned my head. In the last of the light I looked directly into Alisaard's sleeping face.

And in the privacy of the night I believe I wept for Ermizhad before sleep came to fling me into further torment. For I dreamed of a hundred women: a hundred who had been betrayed by war-like men and heroic folly, by their own deepest feelings of love, by their romantic idealism. I dreamed of a hundred women. And I knew each of them by name. I had loved each of them. And every one was Ermizhad. And every one I had lost.

At dawn I woke to see that near the horizon of the lake the clouds had parted and great red-gold waves of sunlight were pouring through, staining the water where they struck. Elsewhere this explosion of light stood in heavy contrast to the black and grey of the surrounding mountains and waters, giving them an added dramatic value. I half-expected to hear music, to see the people of the river valley come rushing out into the morning, cheering in that magnificent dawn. But the only sound from the settlement below us was the occasional clank of domestic pots, the yap of an animal, a thin voice.

I could still not see where the city itself was. I supposed these people to be cave-dwellers who camouflaged the entrances to their houses. This was a common enough custom in all the realms of the multiverse I had visited. Yet I was somehow surprised that the traders who risked the journey through the Pillars of Paradise to barter with neighbouring realms did not live in what I would think of as more civilised buildings.

Alisaard smiled when I voiced this puzzle. She took me by the arm and looked into my face. She was more youthful than

Ermizhad and her eyes were a subtly different colour, as was her hair, but again it was almost painful to be so close to her. 'All the mysteries will be solved in Adelstane,' she promised. Then she linked her arm in von Bek's and, like a schoolgirl on a picnic, led us down the grassy hill towards the settlement. I paused for a moment before following. For a moment I had lost any notion of where I was or, indeed, who I was. I thought I smelled cigar smoke. I thought I heard a double-decker bus in the nearby street. I forced myself to stare at the blossoming dawn, the huge tumbling clouds on the far side of the lake. At last my head cleared, I remembered the name of Flamadin. I remembered Sharadim. A tiny shock went through my body. And then, for my present purposes, I was whole again.

I caught up with my friends when they were almost at the bottom of the hill, passing through a gate in a low wall and looking back as if they realised for the first time that I was not with them.

We walked together down a winding track to where the water was shallow, forming a ford. I could see now that this weir had been artificially built to do away with the need for a bridge which could be easily seen from above. I wondered at this strange precaution even as we waded through the cold, clear water and eventually stood on the other bank, staring up at a series of mighty openings in the cliff face, each one of which had been cunningly fortified and then disguised as natural rock. Now I was beginning to realise that these people were not bereft of architectural and building skills.

Alisaard had replaced her visor. Now she cupped her hands and called up. 'Friendly visitors here to throw themselves upon the mercy of Adelstane and her lords!'

There was a sudden silence. Even the tiny sounds of cooking could no longer be heard.

'We bring news in the common interest,' called Alisaard. 'We have no weapons and we are neither loyal to nor serve any of your enemies.'

This had begun to sound like a formal declaration; a matter of necessary courtesy, I supposed, if we were to be granted an audience with the troglodytes.

All at once the silence was broken by a distinct thud. Then another. Then a louder sound, as if metal struck metal. Then the long booming note of a gong came rolling from the higher entrances of the cave system.

Alisaard lowered her arms as if in satisfaction.

We paused. Von Bek made to speak but she motioned him to hold his tongue.

The note of the gong died away. Next came a kind of breathy roaring as if a giant failed to find a note on a monstrous trumpet. Then part of the nearest cave entrance seemed to fall inwards, revealing a dark, jagged opening; it might have been a natural fissure in the rock.

Alisaard led us forward and, with an easy movement of her body, slid herself through the opening. Von Bek and I followed, with rather less grace and some complaint.

And then we were turning and looking in awe at what was next revealed to us.

It was perhaps the most graceful city of spires and slender architecture I had ever seen in all my wanderings. It was white, glistening as if the moon shone upon it. It was stark against the surrounding semi-darkness of the vast cave. Above we heard the breathy noise again, then the booming, and we realised that the sounds had been created through natural acoustics in the cave which had to be more than three miles in circumference and whose roof was lost from sight. It was so delicate, that city, with its traceries of marble and quartz and glittering granite, that it seemed a breeze would waft it away. It had the fragility of a wonderful illusion. I felt that if I blinked it might not be there when I looked again. I had been right to be suspicious of apparent primitivism, but I had been wrong to think for a moment that the river traders were barbarians.

'It's like a city made of lace,' said von Bek almost in a whisper. 'A thousand times more beautiful even than Dresden!'

'Come,' said Alisaard, beginning to walk down the large, polished steps which led to a road which in turn led to Adelstane. 'We must now proceed without a hint of hesitation. The lords of this city are over-quick to detect spies or scouts from an enemy.'

Behind us little fires were burning in the rocks. I saw white faces peering from the shadows of crude shelters. These people shuffled and scuffled and muttered to themselves before gradually returning to their interrupted tasks. I found it very difficult to associate such obvious savages with the people who dwelled in and had built the city.

I asked Alisaard who the people of the walls were and she apologised for not telling me more. 'They're Mabden, of course. They are afraid of the city. Afraid of almost everything. And being permitted no weapons with which they can attack what they fear, they are reduced to what you see. It seems the Mabden can only kill or run away. Their brains are of no use to them.'

Von Bek was sceptical. 'They look to me like the useless economic units of some over-rigid political system, driven out here so that they will not be a burden on the others.'

Alisaard frowned. 'I cannot follow you.'

Von Bek was smiling, almost to himself. 'You have great experience of magic and scientific marvels, Lady Alisaard, but it appears there are very few economically complex civilisations in the whole of the multiverse!'

She appeared to understand him. Her brow cleared. 'Ah, of course! Yes, your assumption is more or less accurate. This is not the right sector for those societies.'

I looked with private pleasure on von Bek's face as he realised that not only had he been guilty of intellectual arrogance, he had been put in his place by someone who was undoubtedly his mental superior.

Von Bek looked at me and saw that I had recognised his response. 'It's odd how easily we slip into the assumptions and follies of our own cultures when we are faced with the alien and the inexplicable. If ever I come through this and am successful in my ambition; if Germany is ever free of war and insane terror, I have it in mind to write a book or two on the subject of mankind's reactions to the novel and the unlikely.'

I clapped him on the back. 'You are avoiding one trap and falling into another, my friend. Never fear, when the moment comes you'll decide against those treatises and get on with the business of living. It's example and effort which improve our lot, not any number of learned volumes.'

He took what I said in good part. 'You are truly a simple soldier at heart, I think.'

'There are probably few simpler than me,' I told him. 'Few more ordinary. It baffles me why I should have become what I am.'

'Perhaps only a fundamentally sane creature could accept the amount of experience and information you have accumulated,' said von Bek. His voice was almost sympathetic. Then he cleared his throat. 'However, there's a danger in too much sentimentality as well as too much intellectuality, eh?'

We had arrived at the glowing, circular gate of the city. A ring of fire, it seemed to me, burned steadily and without heat. It shone so brightly that we were half blinded, unable to see beyond the gateway into Adelstane herself.

Alisaard did not pause but walked directly up to the mighty circle and stepped through it at the point where it touched the rocky surface. We could do nothing else but follow her example. Closing my eyes I stepped into the fire and immediately found myself on the other side, unscathed. Von Bek was next. He found the whole thing, he said, remarkable.

Alisaard said: 'The fire burns cold only for friendly visitors. The Lords of Adelstane have extended to us their most trusting welcome. We can feel flattered.'

Now we saw about five figures ahead of us on the white road which still reflected the firelight behind us. The figures were dressed in billowing robes, heavy weaves of sober colours, lighter silks and lace to rival the exquisite complexity of the city's architecture. Each figure held a staff on which a small, stiffened linen banner stood. Each banner was a finely detailed picture in its own right. The pictures were extremely stylised and I could not immediately recognise the subjects. My attention was quickly drawn away from the banners, however, by the faces of the waiting five. They were not human. They were not even the eldritch faces of Alisaard's people. I had not realised that Barganheem was the realm dominated by those strange beasts, the Ursine Princes. These people resembled bears, though it was plain there were many differences, particularly about the hands and legs. They stood upright with no difficulty whatsoever. Their black eyes were like rainwashed ebony, yet they did not threaten.

'Be welcome in Adelstane,' they said in chorus.

Their voices were deep, vibrant and somehow to me they were also comforting. I wondered at those who had made themselves this people's enemies. I felt that I could trust any one of them to do exactly what they claimed. I stepped forward, extending my arms in greeting.

The bearfolk moved back a step, their nostrils quivering. They attempted to recover themselves and it was plain they thought they had been discourteous to us.

'It is our smell,' said Alisaard softly in my ear. 'They find it revolting.'

Chapter Seven

I HAD EXPECTED to find myself and my friends in some vast receiving room, an auditorium where guests could state their business and be seen by all the Ursine Princes and their retinues. Such ceremony would have been suitable for the city.

Instead we were led by the five dignified creatures through streets of exceptional cleanliness, filled with buildings of astonishing beauty, until we came to a small domed hall which, in its simplicity, reminded me somewhat of an old Baptist church. Within we found warmth, comfortable chairs, a library – all the accumulated treasures which, say, a university don might come by in a lifetime of quiet appreciation of the world.

'This is where we live much of the time,' said one of the bearlike people. 'We have domestic quarters, of course. We conduct our business from this place. I hope you will forgive the informality. Will you have wine? Or another drink?'

'We appreciate your hospitality,' I said awkwardly. I was going to add that we were rather anxious to see the great princes as soon as they could spare time to see us when Alisaard, doubtless anticipating me, interrupted.

'We all appreciate it, my lords. And we are honoured to find ourselves in the company of those who are called the Ursine Princes throughout the Six Realms.

I was surprised, even while I was grateful to her. It seemed completely wrong to my expectations that such a wonderfully decorative city should not indulge the most elaborate of ceremonies. And I had thought we were to be inspected by a whole host of noble bears. Now I could only presume that these were the only ones. Certainly the only ones we should meet.

The large room was heavily perfumed. From the fireplace in

the centre of the left-hand wall great gusts of incense billowed. I realised that our odour must be inconceivably disgusting to them for them to go to such pains.

'Ah, that,' said one of the Princes, seating himself and his complicated arrangement of clothing in a great armchair, and pointing at the fire with his pole, 'that is our custom. I trust you will forgive our fads. We are all somewhat old and set in our ways. I am Groaffer Rolm, Prince of the North River, successor to the Autuvian family which, sadly, ceased to produce issue.' He rubbed at his snout and sighed. The closer I came to them, the more I realised they only superficially resembled bears. It seemed to me this species had existed long before the advent of the bear. 'And this is Snothelifard Plare, Prince of the Big South River and the Little East, hereditary head of the Winter Caravan.' A wave of silk and lace at the creature beside him. 'Over there is Whiclar Hald-Halg, Prince of the Great Lake Spill, last bearer of the Flint. Glanat Khlin, Prince of the Deep Canals, Bat Speaker. And lastly, my wife Faladerj Oro, Prince of the Shouting Rapids and Regent of the Western Seasonals.' Groaffer Rolm made a small, polite grunting noise. 'I am, I'm afraid, the last male Prince left.'

'Are your people so depleted by aggressors?' von Bek asked sympathetically, after we had returned the introductions. 'Is that why you were so cautious, lord prince, to admit us here?'

Prince Groaffer Rolm paused, raising a hand. 'I have misinformed you, it seems. Until lately, this realm knew peace for century upon century. We grew used to persecution, certainly, and we built our cities away from the envious eyes of Mabden and others. But we have so successfully hidden ourselves from enemies we have only the habit of caution left!' He pretended to turn his head and inspect the fire. Actually he was inhaling more of the incense.

His wife, Prince Faladerj Oro, spoke. 'Most of what we mine is too precious, too beautiful, to trade. You see before you five decadent old creatures in the decline of their race's age. We have lived without stimulus for too long now. We are dying.'

'Though,' said one I took to be younger, Whiclar Hald-Halg, 'we have seen four full cycles of the multiverse come and go. Few others survive one.' She spoke proudly. 'There are few with histories as long as those you call the Ursine Princes. We call ourselves Oager Uv. We have almost always been a river people.' She began to seat herself, fluffing her lace and her heavy wools as she did so.

Prince Groaffer Rolm waited with attentive stillness until Whiclar Hald-Halg had completed her speech. 'There you have us,' he said. 'We have a few family left, but that is the sum of our race. We had expected to end our days in peace. The Mabden offer us no trouble. Sometimes they trade one of their young for whatever it is they have decided they need from us. We, in turn, pass the boys on to Gheestenheem, where we know no harm will come to them. But then came news of this army of liberators, apparently sworn to release the Mabden from imprisonment here. Is it this you would warn us of?'

Alisaard was puzzled. 'I know nothing of such an army. Who leads it?'

'A Mabden. I cannot remember his name. They are coming through on the Eastern Banks, apparently, in large numbers. Of course, it is many years since we were there ourselves. If all they wanted were those shores, we would have given them up. We want nothing but this city and tranquillity. But, thanks to a Mabden more honourable than most, we learned of this invasion in time. And so our allies will arrive here shortly, to defend us in our last years. It seems an unlikely irony. And, moreover, it is a familiar one, eh? The remnants of an ancient aristocracy defended by those who were once their fiercest enemies?'

I was suspicious as, I could see, were Alisaard and von Bek.

'Pardon, Prince Groaffer Rolm,' said Alisaard. 'But when did you learn of this holy war against you?'

'Not thirty breaks since.'

'And do you remember the name of the honourable Mabden who has offered to help you?'

'That I can remember easily, aye. Her name is the Princess

Sharadim of Draachenheem. She has become a good friend to us, and asks nothing. She understands our principles and our customs and she has made it her business to learn much of our history. She is a good creature. It is a blessing for us that all our other cities are long since abandoned. She only has the one to defend. We anticipate her soldiers during the next conjunction.'

Alisaard flushed. Like me, like von Bek, she did not know how best and with what formal manners, to disabuse the Ursine Princes.

At last von Bek said brutally, 'So she deceives you also. As she deceives so many in her own land. She means you ill, my lords, and that is certain.'

There came a considerable snuffling, throat clearing and not a little cracking of joints.

Alisaard spoke passionately. 'It is true, my princes. This woman plans to league herself with Chaos and destroy the barriers between the realms, turning the Worlds of the Wheel into one vast and lawless place where she and her allies of Chaos shall establish a perpetual tyranny!'

'Chaos?' Prince Glanat Khlin waddled to the fire and breathed in the smoke. 'No Mabden can league themselves with Chaos and survive – not in their original form, at any rate. Or does she hope to be made a Lord of Chaos herself? That is sometimes the ambition of such people…'

'I would remind my Sister Prince,' said Snothelifard Plare, 'that we have only heard charges from this trio. We have been offered no evidence. I have, for my own part, an instinctive trust of the Mabden female Sharadim. I have a way of understanding her kind. These emissaries could be from those who march against Adelstane!'

'On my word,' cried Alisaard, 'we are not your enemies. We serve neither Sharadim nor the jihad you speak of. We came to you for help in our own quest. We seek to stop the spread of evil, to halt Chaos and its schemes for our realms. We came to you because we hoped to find Morandi Pag.'

'There you have it!' Snothelifard Plare pulled back her muzzle and clicked at her teeth with her nails. 'There you have it!'

Alisaard looked from face to face. 'What do you mean?'

Groaffer Rolm inhaled an enormous mouthful of smoke. Even as he spoke the fumes began to escape from his nostrils and add to those already in the room. 'Morandi Pag has gone mad. He was one of us. An Ursine Prince, you would say. Prince of the South East Rushers and the Cold Ponds. A great trader. Always his own steersman. Friend. Oh!' And Groaffer Rolm raised his snout to the painted ceiling and gave a mournful groan.

'His childhood friend,' explained Faladerj Oro as she stroked her husband's wrinkling head. 'His great sharer.' And a little whimper escaped her mouth. 'Yes. He is with them, we are informed. We sent for him. Urgently. We told him we must see him in Adelstane, so that he could tell us he does not serve the Mabden. But he did not come. He did not send a message. Amongst our people that is a statement that what is rumoured is true.'

'Morandi Pag has an odd mind,' said Glanat Khlin. 'Always an odd mind. Took action, he did. Always action following his delicate and unreadable logic. As a trader he was the last of the true River Princes. As a seer he had trained himself to look into a thousand times and places. As a scientist his theories were of exquisite intricacy. Oh, Morandi Pag was what our ancestors were. An odd mind which could foresee unimaginable possibilities. So he left for his crag at last. But we did not know he disapproved of our treatment of the Mabden. He had only to make it clear. We do merely what the Mabden say they want. We offered them one of our loveliest cities for themselves. They refused it. If we are guilty of obtuse reasoning, we should be told. We would change. If the Mabden want to return to a Mabden realm, we can take them. But they would not consider any of our suggestions. Now this comes. We did no wrong, I think.'

'Perhaps we did wrong,' said Snothelifard Plare. 'If so, Morandi Pag of all the Princes could have told us how. Yet that is done. We have a barbarian force marching against us. It means killing. We cannot defend ourselves entirely without employing death. These other Mabden know death and how to deal it. We are without resources in the matter of tools, even.'

'Aye,' agreed Groaffer Rolm, recovering himself slowly. 'No weapons, and Sharadim has the means of finding these. She defends beauty, she says. That, we think, is worth defending. But we could not easily kill. Mabden can easily kill, as we all recognise here, I think. Ah! Morandi Pag. He will not send even writing to us. No. We do not want the Mabden. They are fleas. Ah!' And he turned his head into the fireplace, leaving his wife in great confusion, offering us a glance of apology for her husband's description of those she considered our kind.

'They are worse than fleas, Prince Faladerj Oro,' I said quickly. 'They are perhaps the worst sort of flea, at any rate. Wherever they bite, they leave disease and ruin behind. But I suspect both Mabden armies to be commanded by Sharadim. She uses one to frighten you, one to reassure you. We know she planned to bring an army here. But we thought she marched against Morandi Pag. If so, how can she be in league with him?'

'Someone should visit that crag, as I said.' Groaffer Rolm puffed smoke from his nostrils again. 'If he is dead or ill, then much is explained. And I agree with these Mabden, fellow Princes. Sharadim cannot any longer be trusted. I suspect we waited so long to find Mabden whose morality we could respect that we deceived ourselves...'

'The Princess Sharadim is an honourable creature,' said Prince Snothelifard Plare. 'I know it in my bones.'

'Why did you not send someone to this crag before?' I asked. 'If you suspected Morandi Pag to be ill.'

Groaffer Rolm's snout grew wet and he sniffled. He coughed and pushed his head so far into the fireplace it almost disappeared. 'We are too old,' he said. 'There is none can make the journey.'

'Is the crag so far away?' Von Bek's voice took on a new urgency.

'Not so far,' said Groaffer Rolm, re-emerging from the incense. 'About five miles, we used to reckon.'

'You could send nobody five miles?' Von Bek began to sound contemptuous.

'It is across the lake,' Glanat Khlin spoke defensively. 'The lake he himself explored, looking for the mythical Central Passage which is said to pass permanently through all realms at once. All he found, they say, was his crag. But there is often a maelstrom there. And often big winds. We have no boats for it. Nothing made. And we can make nothing ourselves now.'

'You, the great River Princes, have no boats? I have seen your ark at the Great Massing.' I could not believe they were lying. 'You do have boats.'

'A few. The ark is mere trickery so that no Mabden will look greedily on our artefacts. The Gheestenheemers have similar strategies, which is why we have always been allies. A few little boats left, yes. But we are too old.'

'Then lend us one of those,' said Alisaard. Hesitantly she put her hand on Groaffer Rolm's massive arm. 'Lend us a boat and we will cross the lake to find Morandi Pag. Perhaps we shall find that he does not work against you. Perhaps the Mabden lied in this as in everything else?'

'The Princess Sharadim has psychic gifts,' growled Snothelifard Plare. 'She knows Morandi Pag schemes our finality.'

'You will let them prove this.' Groaffer Rolm rose up from his chair in a great hissing and whispering of fabric. 'You will let them prove it, lord prince. What bad can that bring us?'

Snothelifard Plare bent with fastidious slowness towards the fireplace and drew in the fumes by means of a long, loud sniff.

'Take the boat, but be careful,' Faladerj Oro said, sounding almost like a mother to her children. 'The crag lies beneath the sun. It is hot and the water acts strangely. Morandi Pag went there for solitude, to study. But he stayed. Only he knew the exact way the sea runs. It was one of his golden strengths. We watched him as young females, scenting for the currents lying in the deepest reaches. Then he would take his rafts and race through. Half our charts were drawn before the birth of Morandi Pag. Half our charts have been drawn since he came to us. And even a long-lived people like ours do not pass through four full cycles of the multiverse. He was our last great pride. If he had been a leader, I think we should have survived even a fifth cycle.' She did not seem greatly upset by the prospect of her race's extinction. 'Morandi Pag has derived his knowledge from the whole of the multiverse. Compared to him the rest of us are ignorant and parochial. We have boats below. They can be floated up to the old mole. Will you wait for the boat there? We shall give you charts. We shall give you provisions. We shall give you messages of friendship and concern for Morandi Pag. And then, if he lives, he will reply.'

Not an hour later we stood in the grey light beneath those massive cliff walls, on a worn stone quayside, watching as, from the depths, there drifted a pale golden boat, with a mast all ready and a sail wrapped against the wet; with oars and little watertight boxes full of sweet pastes and grains, the water pouring from her as she rocked beside the stone mole, ready to receive us.

'I have seen these boats of theirs once before,' said Alisaard, stepping confidently into it and arranging a seat for her comfort. 'They cannot fill with water. It is a system of vents and valves, but so cunningly hidden in the design that they cannot be discovered by anyone save their makers.'

The boat was much wider than the last one we had used. This boat was plainly designed to accept the weight and bulk of the bearfolk. But the boat responded with subtle ease to the tiller and the breeze.

We saw no more of the Ursine Princes as we set off towards the vent in the clouds, where light still poured, almost violently, upon water which, as we approached closer, was evidently foaming furiously and sending up occasional geysers of steam.

'Scalding water,' said von Bek wearily. He seemed ready to accept defeat. 'That's what defends Morandi Pag's crag. Look at the charts, Herr Daker. See if there are alternative means of approaching.'

But there was none.

Soon, picked out by that vast funnel of sunlight, we saw through the steam and the foam a tall spike of rock, rising at least a hundred feet above the turbulent waters. Upon this spike, just visible now, was a building resembling those we had just left behind. It might even have been a natural formation, worked by thousands of years of elemental forces, but I knew it was not. It could only be Morandi Pag's house.

We slowed our boat's progress, heaving to before we were caught up in the swirling currents. The steam was so hot that we were soon all of us perspiring. There were other crags, other vicious spikes of rock surrounding Morandi Pag's, but none was so tall. We stood upright in the boat and waved in the hope that he had some means of guiding us in. There was no sign of life from the white lace palace on the crag.

Alisaard had the charts beside her. 'We can go through this,' she said pointing. 'It is a slab of rock which the sea has worn through. It offers the best protection from the geysers. Once through that we have to steer between the crags, but the water, according to the chart, is cooler there. At Morandi Pag's crag, there is a small bay, apparently. This is what we must reach before we are crushed against the rock walls. We seem to have only this choice. Or we can return to Adelstane and tell them we were unsuccessful. We can wait until Sharadim comes with her army. What shall we do then?'

She had answered her question. We would go forward. She scarcely waited for us to agree before, the chart in her teeth, one hand on the tiller and the other on the boom cords, she was driving towards the roaring, unsettled heat.

I hardly knew what happened to us in those few minutes while Alisaard steered our boat. My impression was of wild, dangerous waves, hurling us back and forth so that we rocked as we surged up and down, of sharp rocks passing an inch from the hull, of the wind tearing into the sail and of Alisaard singing a strange, ululating song as she took our craft towards the crag.

The black opening of the sea-worn tunnel came in sight and

we were swallowed at once. The sea boomed and screamed at us. The boat scraped first one wall and then the other. Alisaard's song continued. It was a beautiful song. It was a defiant song. It was a challenge to the entire multiverse.

And then we were on a fresh current, being drawn out of the tunnel and towards Morandi Pag's towering shard of rock. I looked up. The intense sunlight seemed to have been concentrated by some cosmic lens. At its strongest point it shone directly upon the white palace, revealing whole parts of it to be utterly ruined.

I was furious. I slammed my fist against the side of the boat. 'We have risked all that for nothing. Morandi Pag is dead. Nobody has lived in that place for years!'

But Alisaard ignored me. With the same delicate precision she steered the dancing boat towards the crag. And there, suddenly, we saw a pool of placid water, surrounded by high walls, with only a single narrow entrance. It was through this that Alisaard aimed our boat. It was in this little enclave of tranquillity that we at last found ourselves. The boat rocked gently against the harbour wall. Beyond that wall we could hear the roaring water, the screaming geysers, but it was muffled, seemingly a long way distant. Alisaard finished her song. Then she stood up in the boat and she cheered.

And we cheered, too. Never has anyone cheered so thankfully.

The adrenaline was still running through us. Even Alisaard showed no sign of exhaustion. She clambered rapidly up the rungs of the harbour wall and stood watching as we left the boat more carefully and eventually joined her.

'There,' she said, indicating a flight of steps and an opening beyond, 'we are at the entrance to Morandi Pag's castle.'

Ulric von Bek looked out to where the sea still foamed. He said quietly: 'I pray this Pag has devised a better way of leaving his stronghold. I am already feeling anxiety about our return voyage!'

Alisaard strode ahead of us, her ivory armour shedding the last of the sea water. She began to call Morandi Pag's name.

Von Bek laughed suddenly. 'She should tell them we're from the funeral company. That old bear has been dead for years. Look at the condition of this place.'

Alisaard began to speak a version of the same proclamation she had made outside the caves of Adelstane. 'We are peaceful travellers, enemies of your enemies. We shall enter your home, knowing that you have not forbidden us that privilege.'

She paused. There was no response.

Together the three of us passed through the cracked and mildewed entrance which, to our surprise, led immediately upon a set of steps going downwards into the rock.

The steps crept steadily down. Outside we could hear the distant groaning and murmuring of the waves. The place had a musty smell. I thought I detected a snuffling sound, of the kind Groaffer Rolm had made. It came from below.

And then, all at once, I grinned. My grin was shared by my companions.

For from the darkness at our feet there began to curl a thick, greenish smoke, its perfume so strong we were almost sickened by it.

'I think an Ursine Prince makes ready to bid us welcome.' It was von Bek who expressed this. Alisaard chuckled appreciatively. I thought her response excessive.

Through this voluminous cloud we now progressed until we had at last reached a small archway. From the other side of this we made out tables, other furniture, books, ladders, instruments of all kinds, several different orreries, strange light from odd-shaped lamps. And emerging slowly with a rolling, energetic kind of shuffle, came the huge bulk of Morandi Pag himself. He wore few clothes – a little decorative lace and embroidery – and was almost entirely white. His fur had once been black, I suspected. Now there was only grizzled black hair on his head and down the middle of his back.

His large, dark eyes held an alert, perhaps sardonic, curiosity missing in his peers. Yet there was also a strange light in them, a tendency for his gaze to wander away from what he had begun to look at, to focus on sights invisible to us. His voice was deep and comforting, though vaguer and richer than those of the other princes. His manner was, in short, evidently absent-minded. It was, however, as if he deliberately fostered this in himself; as if he feared to let his mind cohere. This was a great intelligence, but one which had received an enormous blow. I had seen such looks on the faces of survivors from a thousand different forms of out-rage. Von Bek, also, noticed this. We exchanged a glance.

Morandi Pag seemed amiable. 'More Mabden explorers, is it? Well, Mabden, be welcome. Do you chart these waters, as I once charted them?'

'We are not merchant adventurers, my lord,' said Alisaard calmly. 'We are here because we hope to save the Six Realms from Chaos.'

There was a flash of awareness in those mild eyes. Then it was gone. Morandi Pag mumbled a tune through the remains of his teeth. He shuffled back towards his books and retorts. 'I am old,' he said, without looking at us. 'I am too old. I am probably half-crazed with knowledge. I am not of use to anyone.' He turned very quickly, almost glaring at me. And it was at me that he shouted. 'You! It will come to you. It will come to you yet. My poor little Mabden.' He leaned against a bench on which a dozen burners had been placed. It was these which gave off the heavy perfume. 'Knowledge ceases to be wisdom when one has no method for making sense or use of what one learns. Eh? It was probably inevitable. Eh?'

'Prince Morandi Pag,' said Alisaard urgently. 'Our mission is what we say it is. Against Chaos and all that brings. Surely you would not hide something from us? Something crucial to our quest!'

'To protect,' he said, moving his snout up and down in con-firmation of his own statement. 'Only that. Yes.'

'Do you know where the Dragon Sword is?' von Bek asked him.

'Oh, yes. That. Of course I know. You may see it, if you wish.

Below.' He sighed deeply. 'Is that all? The old hellsword itself, hm? Yes, yes.' But his eyes had already wandered to a jar of blue glass on his table. Within it, some sort of firefly seemed to be dancing. The noise Morandi Pag made was one of gentle pleasure.

After a moment, he turned that enormous head towards us again. He seemed to deliberate for almost a minute. Then he said soberly, his voice quavering a little with age, 'I am extremely frightened by what is happening. How can you three not be afraid, also?'

'Because, Prince Morandi Pag, we have yet to confront anything,' said von Bek. He spoke very softly indeed, as if he were gentling a horse.

'Ah!' said Morandi Pag, as if he found the explanation satisfactory. 'Ah, you cannot imagine, cannot imagine...' He became distracted again. He began to murmur names, scraps of equations, lines of verse, much of it in languages we could not begin to understand. 'La, la, la, la. Would you three share a little of what I have? Food was never the problem, as you may have heard. But...' He scratched at his left ear. He looked at us enquiringly.

'The Dragon Sword, Prince Morandi Pag,' Alisaard reminded him.

'Yes. You wish to see it? Yes. It is below.'

'Will you take us to it? Or shall we go ourselves?' she asked slowly. 'What shall we do, Prince Morandi Pag?'

'See what you think.' He had forgotten our conversation already. He tapped at tubes and bottles. 'La, la, la, la.'

Von Bek motioned towards a door on the other side of the room. 'We must see what is through there. I am sorry to seem impolite, but we have little time.' He strode through parchments and tomes, abandoned instruments and piles of jars, each of which contained a mysterious substance, and put his fingers out towards the handle. He paused, looking enquiringly at Morandi Pag.

Eventually the old bear spoke. Again his voice was controlled, full of wise awareness. 'You may go through there to look for it, if you wish.'

We had joined von Bek by the time he had begun to turn the handle. The door was not made of wood but of pock-marked rock, like pumice, multicoloured. There were designs carved into it. The designs were in the same style I had seen on the banners at Adelstane. I could not quite make out what they represented.

Without a creak or a protest, the door opened smoothly. The room beyond was small and circular, virtually a cupboard. Lamps flickered from within it. On shelves were packets, scrolls, boxes, jars, strawbound bottles and a number of objects whose function was obscure.

However, it was what hung from the central beam by means of a big brass hook which drew our attention. It was an ornamental cage, which, judging by the droppings on its sides and bottom, had once been used to hold an enormous bird.

But it no longer held a bird. Instead the captive who stared at us through the narrow bars was a small man. Dressed in what closely resembled medieval motley, he seemed thankful that we had come. There was no telling how long he had been there.

From behind us, Morandi Pag's voice had grown vague again.

'Ah yes,' he said. 'Now I remember where I hid the little Mabden.'

Chapter Eight

T HE MAN IN the cage was Jermays the Crooked. He recognised me almost at once and laughed aloud. 'Well met, Sir Champion! I am glad to see you.'

Morandi Pag came shuffling up to fumble at the complicated lock. 'I put him in there when I sighted your boat. That way any enemy would think him a slave or pet and not necessarily wish to destroy him.'

'Put me in there, I might add,' said Jermays without malice or anger, 'against my protests. That's the fifth time you've had me in that damned cage, Prince Pag. Don't you ever remember?'

'Have I put you there before?'

'Almost every time you've spotted a boat.' Jermays clambered with his usual agility from the cage and dropped to the floor. He looked up at me. 'Congratulations, Sir Champion. Yours is the first to get through undamaged. You must be a skilled helmsman.'

'The credit is all the Lady Alisaard's. She is an expert at the tiller.'

Jermays bowed to the Gheestenheemer. The young dwarf, on his bandy legs and with his thin, ginger beard, managed a certain dignity. She seemed charmed by him. Next he presented himself to Ulric von Bek. The two exchanged names.

'You already know my little Mabden?' said Morandi Pag in tones of absolute normality. 'It will be wonderful for him to have others of his kind for company. You're the Champion, I know. Yes, I know you are the Champion. Because...' And his eyes became strangely blank. He stood with his muzzle gaping, staring into the middle distance.

Jermays darted forward and took the old bear's arm, leading

him back to his chair. 'He has too much in his head. Sometimes this happens.'

'You know him well?' asked Alisaard in some surprise.

'Oh, indeed. I have been his sole companion here for almost seventy years. I had no choice. In my present circumstances I do not seem to be able to roam through the realms at will, as I sometimes can. I have found every day stimulating, I must say. Now, you were looking for something.' He helped Morandi Pag slowly resume his seat. 'I should like to assist.'

'Morandi Pag said he would show us the Dragon Sword,' von Bek told him.

'Oh, so he has spoken of the Scarlet Crystal? Yes, I know where that is to be found. Well, I can easily lead you down there, but we shall have to take Morandi Pag with us. For I am useless where spells are concerned. Will you give him a while to rest?'

'We are upon a desperate quest,' said Alisaard softly.

'We shall go now!' Morandi Pag rose suddenly, full of energy. 'At once! It is urgent, you say? Very well. Come, you shall see the Dragon Sword!'

There was a narrow doorway at the back of the cupboard room where we had found Jermays. Morandi Pag led us through it, down two more spiralling flights. Now we could hear the sea booming and crashing all around us. It was so violent that we felt it must break down the rock walls and come flooding through.

Jermays the Crooked lit a brand and by means of the light from this he bent and with his long-fingered hands pulled on a chain set into the damp floor. He had opened a manhole. Misty light now came from below. Jermays disappeared down the hole, having signed for us to follow.

Morandi Pag said: 'Go first. It will take me longer because of my age and my bulk.'

I saw von Bek hesitate. He suspected a trick. But Alisaard urged him forward. I followed her down the somewhat slippery ladder.

The ladder descended directly into a cave which was actually a hollow pinnacle of rock. We stood on a long slab overlooking a swirling and foaming pool of water formed by rushing streamers which poured from what looked almost like windows set at fairly regular intervals above us. The water seemed to leave by an unseen series of vents at the bottom. It was a marvellous natural sight and we looked at it in silence for some while, wondering where we could possibly go from here.

I felt the bear's paw upon my shoulder. Turning, I saw that his eyes were melancholy. 'Too much knowledge,' he said. 'It will happen to you, unless you take action. Our minds are finite in their capacity to accept information. Yes?'

'I suppose so, Prince Morandi Pag. Is the sword likely to do me harm?'

'Not yet. The harm it has done you and the harm it will do are not part of your current destiny, I think. But actions can change courses, naturally. I am not sure…' He cleared his throat. 'But you would see the sword, eh? Then you must look down there, into that pool.'

'They'll not see it, Prince Pag,' said Jermays the Crooked, speaking loudly over the sound of the ocean. 'Not without your incantation.'

'Ah, yes.' Morandi Pag looked disturbed. He scratched at his white chest. He patted reassuringly at my arm. 'Never fear. It is a peculiarly complicated arrangement of logic. A mental equation I must form. It helps me if I sing something. You'll forgive me?' And he raised his snout and gave vent to a singular kind of wailing and grunting, a musical howling and a series of sharp barks.

'Has he gone crazy again?' asked von Bek.

Jermays pushed at his back. 'Go to the edge. To the edge. Look into the waters. Think of nothing. Quickly. He is making the incantation!'

Now all four of us stood at the very end of the slab, peering through the spray into the swirling grey-green water as it poured relentlessly into the pool. The water had an hypnotic effect. It almost immediately captured our attention and held it. I felt myself swaying, felt little Jermays reach out and steady me. 'You must not fear falling,' he said. 'Simply concentrate on the pool.'

With some trepidation I did as he ordered. I could hear Morandi Pag's voice blending with the sound of the sea and the sound seemed to form an image, something substantial. Gradually the waters began to glow with a crimson lustre. Outside the tower the wind howled and the sea continued to assault the rocks. But within the spray was hardening, turning to tiny fragments of quartz fixed in space, and the crimson ocean had become an entire chamber of crystal. And suddenly I no longer heard Morandi Pag's voice. I no longer heard the natural sounds beyond those walls. A mighty stillness had fallen.

Now we looked through the crimson crystal to where something green and black seemed frozen, embedded deep within the rock, like a fly in amber.

'It is the Dragon Sword,' murmured Alisaard. 'It is exactly as it was in our visions!'

Black blade, green hilt, the Dragon Sword seemed almost to writhe in its prison of crystal. And I thought I saw a tiny yellow flame moving deep within the blade, as if something else were imprisoned in the sword, just as the sword was imprisoned in the crystal.

'Can you let me hold it, Morandi Pag?' asked Alisaard in a whisper. 'I know the spell to release the dragon. I must bear it back to Gheestenheem.'

The Ursine Prince was as rapt as the rest of us. He seemed not to have heard her. 'It is a thing of great beauty, I think. But so dangerous.'

'Let us take it, Morandi Pag,' begged von Bek. 'We can make good come out of it. They say the sword is only as evil as the one who bears it...'

'Aye, but you forget. They say it instils evil into whoever takes hold of it. Besides, it is not for me to say if you should or should not have the Dragon Sword. It is not mine to give.'

'But it is in your cave. Surely it is in your possession?' Alisaard began to look suspicious.

'I can summon it to this cave, because of our location. Or what do I mean? I mean that I can bring the shadow…'

Quite suddenly Morandi Pag slid down onto the stone and seemed to fall into a peaceful sleep.

'Is he unwell?' said Alisaard in alarm.

'He is tired.' Jermays stood over his friend. He placed a hand on the bear's wrinkled head, another near his heart. 'Simply tired. He is these days in the habit of sleeping more than half the day as well as the night. He is naturally nocturnal.'

Von Bek shouted urgently. 'The sword! The sword is fading. The crystal wall is disappearing!'

'You said you wanted to see it,' said Jermays, standing upright as best he could. 'And see it you did. What else?'

'We need to release the dragon from the sword,' Alisaard told him. 'Before the blade can be forced to serve Chaos. The dragon seeks only her homeland. Keep it there, Jermays. Give us time to break it free of its prison! Please!'

'But I cannot. Neither could Prince Pag.' Jermays seemed genuinely baffled. 'What you saw was an illusion – or rather a vision of the Dragon Sword itself. The wall of crimson crystal is not in this cave any more than the sword can be found here.'

The crimson glow had faded. The spray had become ordinary moisture again. The sea thumped and pounded and roared. Jermays begged us to help him get Morandi Pag to his feet. The old bear began to revive as we helped him as far as the ladder.

'But we had understood from you that it was physically here.' Von Bek spoke in an aggrieved tone. 'Morandi Pag said it was here.'

Alisaard corrected him. For a moment there was a sardonic smile on her features. 'He said we could see it,' she told von Bek. 'That was all. Well, that's better than nothing. Now perhaps, when he revives, he'll tell us where we must go to find it.'

Morandi Pag mumbled something as Jermays put his shoulder under the bear's rump and tried to push him up the ladder. Quickly I climbed up on the other side, then swung over so that

I could take the old prince's paw and haul him from above. Eventually we got him back into the chamber, by which time he seemed to have grown alert again. He it was who seized the flambeau and led the way up the stairs. 'Here!' he cried. 'Follow me. This is where we go.'

When we had all rejoined him in his main chamber he had already reached his armchair, fallen into it and was sleeping, as if he had never left.

Jermays looked down at him affectionately. 'He'll sleep for a whole day now, I think.'

'Shall we have to wait that long before we can continue with our search?' I asked.

'It depends what you want,' Jermays said reasonably.

'You told us we had been granted a vision of the sword. But where is the crimson crystal wall? How can we get to it?' Alisaard wanted to know.

'I think we had assumed you knew the whereabouts of the sword,' said Jermays. 'And that you had decided not to pursue it.'

'We had not the merest clue,' Alisaard told him. 'We do not even know which realm it is in.'

'Ah,' said Jermays, apparently illuminated by this information. 'That explains much. What if I were to tell you that the Dragon Sword is held in the Nightmare Marches, that it has been there almost as long as the Gheestenheemers have dwelled here? Would that alter your intention of seeking it out?'

Alisaard put her head in her hands. The news had not merely confounded her. Temporarily, at any rate, it had robbed her of her resolve. 'What chance have three mortals of finding anything there? And what chance have we of surviving?'

'Very little,' said Jermays in a matter-of-fact tone. 'Unless, of course, you had an Actorios. Even then it would be extremely dangerous. You are welcome to remain here with us. For my own part I would be glad of the additional company. There are few interesting card games for two players. And Morandi Pag tends to lose attention these days, even in a game of Snap.'

'Why should the possession of an Actorios stone give us an advantage in the Nightmare Marches?' I asked him. Even as I spoke I was reaching into my belt pouch and touching the warm, fleshlike stone of the Actorios which had been given me by the Announcer Elect Phalizaarn in Gheestenheem and whose destiny, according to Sepiriz, was intimately linked with mine.

'It shares something in common with a runestaff,' Jermays said to me. 'It can have an effect on its surroundings. To some slight extent, of course, compared with other more powerful artefacts. It will stabilise that which Chaos has touched. Moreover it has a certain affinity with those swords. It could help lead you to the blade you want...' He shrugged his crooked back. 'But what good would that do you? None, I suspect. And since it will be a good few ticks of the cosmic pendulum before you have an Actorios in your possession, Champion, there's no real point to this discussion.'

I took out the pulsing, writhing stone and showed it to him on the flat of my palm.

He stared at it in silence for a while. He seemed suddenly subdued, almost frightened.

'Well,' he said after a bit, 'so you do have such a stone. Aha.'

'Does that alter your estimate of our chance in the so-called Nightmare Marches, Master Jermays?' asked von Bek.

Jermays the Crooked darted a look at me that was oddly sympathetic. He turned around, pretending to interest himself in Morandi Pag's collection of alchemical glass. 'I could do with a pear,' he said. 'I get a craving. Or a good apple would do at a pinch. Fresh food's scarce here. Unless you like fish. I have a feeling I'll be able to pick something for myself soon. The Balance is wavering. The gods wake up. And when they begin their play, I shall be tossed about as usual. Here and there. But what will become of Morandi Pag?'

'There is an army on its way,' said Alisaard. 'It plans either to torture information from him or to destroy him, we are not absolutely sure. Princess Sharadim will lead the army.'

'Sharadim?' Again Jermays looked directly at me. He had turned round in a flash. 'Your sister, Champion?'

'Of sorts. Jermays, how can we enter the Nightmare Marches?'

He waved his unnaturally long arms and went to stand beside the sleeping Ursine Prince. 'Nobody's stopping you,' he told us. 'It is not usually a question of the Nightmare Marches refusing visitors. Most visitors to those Marches are to say the least unwilling. The place is ruled by Chaos. It is where Chaos was exiled in the old battles of the Wheel, so many centuries ago that almost everyone has forgotten. It could have been at the very beginning of this cycle. I can't remember. The Nightmare Marches lie at the very hub of the Wheel contained by the self-same forces which maintain the Six Realms, almost as if compressed by a kind of gravity. Is it not Sharadim who will seek to release those forces? Who will attempt to free the ruler of the Nightmare Marches, Archduke Balarizaaf? Why go to him? Soon he could come to you.' And Jermays shuddered.

'You know of Sharadim's movements?' asked Alisaard eagerly. 'You can predict what she will do?'

'My predictions are never accurate,' Jermays said. 'They are useless to anyone. I dart from place to place. I see a little of this, a little of that. But I haven't the mind or the temperament to fit anything together. That could be why the gods permit me to travel as I do. I am a shadow-creature, lady, for the most part. You see me at present in one of my most solid rôles. And it cannot last too long. Sharadim has huge and evil ambitions, I know. But nothing I can say will help you counter this. The pattern, such as it is, could already be set. She seeks the Dragon Sword, eh? And by means of it will bring the Chaos Lord to his fullest power, perhaps. Aye...'

Then suddenly Morandi Pag was grunting in his sleep, shaking his huge head, fluffing his whiskers and, lastly, opening wide, intelligent eyes. 'Princess Sharadim leads an army against my kind. That is what you have to tell me, eh? She threatens what? Adelstane? The other realms? Chaos involved? I can hear her.

Where is she? — *Now, Flamadin, my false brother, you shall not defeat me. My power increases by natural momentum as yours declines.* Does she believe me still in Adelstane? It seems so. She'll storm our gates. Will she break through? Who knows? My sisters are there! My brother. My old friend Groaffer Rolm is there! Did they send you to find me?'

'They sent a message, Prince Morandi Pag, that they are concerned for you. And that they are in danger and need your help. Mabden attack them. More Mabden than they know.'

'Not you?'

'For better or worse, Prince, we are your allies against a common enemy.'

'Then I must think what to do.'

And he had closed his eyes and was asleep again.

'You know how we can reach the Nightmare Marches, Jermays?' von Bek asked. 'Will you tell us?'

Jermays the Crooked nodded absently and rummaged about on Morandi Pag's bench. Then he went under the bench and began to throw old pieces of parchment about, willy-nilly. Then he crawled across the floor and opened a chest. Within the chest were dozens of neatly rolled parchments, numbered as far as I could tell. He looked down on these and beamed. Then, very delicately, he selected one, being careful not to disturb the others. 'These are Morandi Pag's charts. Charts of so many realms. So many configurations and complexes, conjunctions and eclipses.' He unrolled the parchment. 'This is the table I hoped to find.' He began to run his finger down it. 'Aye. It seems there's a gateway about to open in the north-west. Near the Goradyn Mountain. You could go that way. It will take you into the Maaschanheem. From there you would have to travel to The Wounded Crayfish and wait for the gateway which will take you into the Realm of the Red Weepers. Good. From there, within the volcano they call Tortacanuzoo, you will find a direct route into the Nightmare Marches. Or so I believe. However, if you wish to wait five days, seven hours and twelve seconds, you could go from near Adelstane itself, into Draachenheem, through Fluugensheem, and still be near The Wounded Crayfish at almost the same time you arrived from Goradyn. Or you could return to the upper mountains, wait for the Sedulous Urban Eclipse, which is rare enough anyway and worth experiencing, then go directly to Rootsenheem by that method.'

Alisaard silenced him at last. 'When is there a direct gateway from Barganheem?'

He paused, studying the tables for all the world like a man of the twentieth century looking up the train timetables. 'Direct? From Barganheem? Another twelve years...'

'So we have no choice but to make for The Wounded Crayfish anchorage?' she said.

'It seems not. Though if you were to travel to The Torn Shirt...'

'It seems in your world as in mine,' said von Bek dryly, 'it becomes increasingly difficult to get into Hell.'

Alisaard ignored him. She was committing Jermays's words to memory. 'Wounded Crayfish – Rootsenheem – Tortacanuzoo. That's the shortest route, eh?'

'Apparently. Though it seems to me that Fluugensheem should be crossed, if only briefly. Perhaps it is bypassed. There is said to be a cross-warp around there. Did you ever discover it?'

Alisaard shook her head. 'Our navigating is fairly simple. We do not risk the swift-leaping journeys. Not since we lost our menfolk. Now, Master Jermays, can you tell us where to find, in the Nightmare Marches, the Dragon Sword?'

'At their very core, where else!' This was Morandi Pag, heaving his bulk from his chair. 'In a place called The World's Beginning. This is the heart of the Nightmare Marches. And that sword sustains them. But it can only be handled by one of the blood, Champion. One of your blood.'

'Sharadim is not of my blood.'

'She is enough of your blood to serve Balarizaaf's purpose. If she only lives long enough to drag the sword from its crystal prison, that will suffice.'

'You mean none can remove it from the crystal?'

'You can, Champion. And so can she. Moreover, I would guess she knows the risk she takes. Which is not a simple death for her. She might succeed. And if she does, she ascends to immortality as a Lord of Hell. As powerful as Queen Xiombarg or Mabelode the Faceless or Old Slortar Himself. That is why she risks so much. The stakes are the highest she can imagine.' He put his paws to his head. 'But now the ages all congeal into one agonising lump. My poor brain. You understand, I know, Champion. Or you will. Come, we must leave this place at last. We must return to the mainland. To Adelstane. I have my duty. And, of course, you have yours.'

'We can use the boat,' said Alisaard. 'I believe I can steer a course out of the rocks.'

At this Prince Morandi Pag chuckled with genuine humour. 'You will let me take the tiller, I hope. It will do me good to sniff the currents again and guide us clear to Adelstane.'

Chapter Nine

'SOME SAY THERE are no more than forty-six individual folds in the configuration of the waves,' said Morandi Pag as he seated himself heavily in the boat. 'But that is a statement made by those who, like the feudal islanders of the East, honour simplicity and a kind of unholy neatness over complexity and apparent disorder. I say there are as many folds as there are waves. But it was once a matter of pride that I could smell them all. Waves and multiverse are, I would agree, one. However, the secret of steering any course, no matter where you are bound, is to treat each aspect as fresh-minted and utterly new. To formalise, in my view, is to perish. The folds are infinite. The folds have personalities.' His nostrils quivered. 'Can't you sniff the currents again? And all the intersecting realities, all the thousands of realms of the multiverse. What a wonder it all is! And yet I was not wrong to be afraid.' With that he gave the sign for Alisaard to slip the rope, turned the sail a touch, made a small motion with the tiller and we were riding the roaring waves again, heading for the hollow rock by which we had entered.

There was never a moment when any of us felt in danger. The boat danced lightly across the enormous, threshing waters. She turned as gracefully as any bird in flight, sometimes upon the crest of the waves, sometimes in the gullies, while sometimes she seemed to lie sideways onto the great breakers. Spray and wind attacked our faces as we surged through the opening and into semi-darkness. Morandi Pag was roaring with laughter, almost enough to drown the sound of the waves, as he guided us through and out into the relative calm of the ocean proper.

Jermays the Crooked hopped up and down in glee. He was in

the prow, capering and shouting his approval at every minor shift in the boat's direction.

Morandi Pag moved his muzzle in a peculiar expression, as if expressing satisfaction with his skill. 'It has been too long,' he said. 'I have not the youth for this. Now we shall go to Adelstane.'

We crossed the ocean rapidly, seeing the great black mountains rising all around us. The little harbour was reached and the boat tied up. After that it was a matter of a few minutes to walk to the opening where we had first been admitted.

Not a quarter of an hour later we stood once more in the comfortable library, filled as usual with incense, while the Ursine Princes greeted their long-lost peer. It was a most tender sight. All of us were forced to wipe away tears. The creatures had a wonderfully gentle way of behaving with one another.

At length Groaffer Rolm, still very emotional, turned from thanking us for restoring his long-lost brother to him, and said: 'We have heard from the Princess Sharadim. Her army awaits only the opening of the gateway. Whereupon it will enter our realm, not a mile from Adelstane itself. The other army, we are told, also marches, using our old canal paths, and will be here within the day.

'I take it, Morandi Pag, that you agree with these Mabden. Sharadim means us harm.'

'These Mabden speak truth,' said Morandi Pag. 'But they must be about their business. They have to reach the Maaschanheem. From there they must go via Rootsenheem and Fluugensheem to the Nightmare Marches.'

'The Nightmare Marches!' Faladerj Oro was genuinely horrified. 'Who would volunteer to venture there?'

'It is a matter of saving all Six Realms from Sharadim and her allies,' said von Bek. 'We have no choice.'

'You are heroes indeed,' said Whiclar Hald-Halg. She laughed to herself. 'Mabden heroes! Now there's a pretty irony...'

'I will take you to the first gateway myself,' Morandi Pag told us.

'But what of Sharadim and her armies? How shall you deal with them?'

Groaffer Rolm shrugged. 'We are all together now. And we have our ring of fire. They'll be hard put to enter that. And should they breach Adelstane's defences, they must find us. There are many ways we can delay them.'

Jermays the Crooked helped himself from a jug of wine. 'But she infects all the realms,' he said. 'She can alter her personality to appeal to any culture she encounters. What is happening in this realm also happens, in a different way, elsewhere. How shall that be countered?'

'It is not our business and neither do we have the capacity to fight the wars of the other realms,' said Groaffer Rolm. 'We can only hope to hold her off in Adelstane. But if Chaos breaks through and makes itself her ally, then we are doomed I think.'

We made our farewells to the Ursine Princes and Morandi Pag took us along the ancient canal banks of the great, slow river, climbing slowly into the heavy shadows cast by mountain walls on all sides. Here at last he paused and was about to speak when it seemed the very mountains shivered and the darkness began to fill with a white radiance which, as it gathered in strength, could be seen to contain all colours. Gradually there formed in that clearing beside the river a set of six pillars which formed a perfect circle and had the appearance of a temple.

'It's miraculous,' said von Bek. 'I am always amazed.'

Morandi Pag passed a white paw over his old brow. 'You must make haste,' he said. 'I can sense that the Mabden armies close on Adelstane. Will you go with them, Jermays?'

'Let me remain here,' Jermays said. 'I have to see if my old trick of travelling has returned. If it has, I will be of greater use to you. Farewell, Champion. Farewell, beautiful lady. Count von Bek, farewell.'

Then we had stepped into the space between the pillars and almost at once were looking upwards. Then we were moving in the direction we faced.

The sensation of movement was stranger still without the apparent solidity of a boat. We were not entirely weightless. Instead it was as if we were borne on a current of water, though water which did not threaten to drown us.

Ahead I could see a misty grey light. My head began to spin and for a few seconds my body felt as if it had been plucked up by a gigantic and gentle hand. Seconds later I was on firm ground though still surrounded by the pillars of light. Alisaard stood beside me and, nearby, a fascinated von Bek. The German count shook his head in wonderment again. 'Why are there not gateways like this between my own world and the Middle Marches?'

'Different worlds have gateways which take different forms,' Alisaard told him. 'This form is native to the Worlds of the Wheel.'

We stepped out of the circle of light and found ourselves in the familiar, overcast landscape of the Maaschanheem. Everywhere was coarse grass, reeds, pools of water, glinting marsh. Pale waterbirds flew overhead. As far as we could see there was only flat ground and shallow water.

Alisaard reached into her pouch and drew out a small book of folded charts. She squatted to consult one of these charts, spreading it on the relatively dry ground. 'We must seek The Wounded Crayfish anchorage. This is The Laughing Pike. We have no choice but to try to walk there. A way is possible, according to this map. There are trails through the marsh.'

'How far is The Wounded Crayfish from here?' asked von Bek.

'Seventy-five miles,' she said.

In somewhat depressed spirits, we began to trudge northwards.

We had not gone more than perhaps fifteen miles when we saw ahead of us on the low horizon the dark outline of a great travelling hull. It seemed to be making rather more smoke than was usual, yet it did not seem to be moving. We guessed that it might be in difficulties. I was for avoiding the vessel, but Alisaard felt that there was a small chance we could get some sort of help from them.

'Most peoples are inclined to trust Gheestenheemers,' she said.

'Have you forgotten what happened aboard the *Frowning Shield*?' I reminded her. 'In helping von Bek and myself you infringed the most sacred codes of the Massing. My guess would be that your folk are not at all welcome anywhere here. What diplomatic harm you did was doubtless made use of by Sharadim, who would have done all she could to win allies here and poison minds against you. And as for us, we are probably fair game for any party of Binkeepers who happens to spot us. I would be disinclined to hail that vessel.'

Von Bek was frowning as he peered ahead. 'I have a feeling it does not represent danger to us,' he said. 'Look. That's not smoke from her funnels. She's burning! She's been attacked and destroyed!'

Alisaard seemed more shocked than either von Bek or myself. 'They war amongst themselves! This has not happened for centuries. What can it mean?'

We began to run over the soft, uneven ground, heading for the ruined hull.

Long before we reached it, we could see what had happened. Fire had gone through the entire vessel. Blackened bodies in every posture of agony lay against the charred rails, upon the smoking decks. They hung like broken dolls in the smashed timbers of the yards. And from everywhere came the stink of death. Carrion birds swaggered amongst this wealth of flesh, fat as domestic pets. Men and women, children and babies, all had died. The hull lay half on her side, beached, looted.

About fifty yards from the remains of the great hull we saw a few figures rise up from the reeds and begin to move away from us. Several were blind and had to be helped by the rest and this is why their progress was so slow. I called out to them:

'We mean you no harm. What hull was that?'

The survivors turned scared, white faces towards us. They were in rags – wrapped in anything they had been able to salvage from the wreck. They looked half-starved. Most were older women, but there were a few girls and youths in the group.

Alisaard now wore her ivory visor, as a matter of habit. She lifted it, saying softly: 'We are friendly to you, good folk. We would offer you our names.

One tall old woman said, with surprising firmness: 'We know you. All three. You are Flamadin, von Bek and the renegade Ghost Woman. Outlaws all. Enemies of our enemies, perhaps, but we have no reason to think you friends. Not now the world betrays everything we value. Princess Sharadim seeks you, does she not? And also that bloody-handed parvenu Armiad, her most ferocious ally…'

Von Bek was impatient. He started forward again. 'Who are you? What has happened here?'

The old woman raised her hand. 'You are not welcome here. You brought the evil into our realm. The evil we had thought exiled for ever. Now there is war again between the hulls.'

'We have met,' I said suddenly. 'But where?'

She shrugged. 'I was Praz Oniad, Consort to the Snowbear Defender. Co-captain and Rhyme Sister to the Toirset Larens. And what you see is all that is left of our home hull, the *New Argument*, and all that is left of our families. There is a second War between the Hulls, led by Armiad. And although you did not begin that war, you were part of its excuse. By breaking the rules of the Massing you brought in every kind of uncertainty.'

'But we cannot be held responsible for Armiad's ambition!' cried Alisaard. 'That existed before we did what we did.'

'I said "excuse",' said Praz Oniad. 'He claimed that other hulls had aided the Ghost Women in the raid on his hull. He claimed that. And next he argued that he must protect himself. So allies came from Draachenheem. Hardened fighters who knew how to kill, how to make war. Before long he had allies, of course, amongst other hulls who feared his strength and did not wish to be destroyed as we and so many more have been destroyed. Armiad now commands thirty hulls and they defile the Massing Ground, turning it into an armed camp, their stronghold, together with their Draachenheemer allies. Now all other hulls must pay tribute and acknowledge Armiad King Admiral, a title which we abolished hundreds of years since.'

'How could this have happened in so short a time?' murmured von Bek to me.

'You forget,' I told him, 'that time passes at somewhat different rates in different realms. In relation, that is, to one another. It seems several months have gone by since we left the Great Massing.

'We hope to put a stop to Princess Sharadim and her allies,' I informed the old woman. 'Her plans and those of Armiad were made long before we knew of them. They would destroy us because we know a way of defeating them.'

The old woman looked at us sceptically, but a little hope showed in her worn features. 'It is not revenge we of the *New Argument* seek,' she said. 'We would gladly die if it meant a stop to this terrible war.'

'War threatens all Six Realms.' Alisaard stood beside her now and gently took her hand. 'Good lady, this is Sharadim's doing. When her brother refused compliance, she blackened his name and outlawed him.'

The old woman looked suspiciously at me. 'They say this is not Prince Flamadin at all but a doppelgänger. They say he is in reality the Archduke Balarizaaf of Chaos, assuming human form. They say Chaos must soon erupt throughout all the Realms of the Wheel.'

'Part of what you have heard has substance,' I said. 'But I assure you I'm no friend to Chaos. We seek to conquer Chaos. And we hope, in that conquest, to bring peace back to the Six Realms. To that purpose, we are on our way to the Nightmare Realm…'

Praz Oniad voiced a sharp, bitter laugh. 'No human willingly ventures into that realm. Are these more lies? You would not survive. Your mind would melt. The illusions of that realm cannot be perceived by mortals without those mortals going mad.'

'It is our only hope of defeating Sharadim and all her allies,' said Alisaard. 'Those allies, it is true, include the Archduke Balarizaaf.'

The old woman sighed. 'What hope is there?' she said. 'This is no more than desperate folly.'

'We journey to The Wounded Crayfish to find a gateway,' von Bek said. 'What anchorage is this, good lady?'

'This is The Fountain Overflowing,' she said. 'Anchorage of the *Imaginary Fish*, also destroyed by Armiad's fire-flingers, the same he got from Sharadim. We have no weapons. He now has many. The Wounded Crayfish is miles from here. How do you travel?'

'On foot,' said Alisaard. 'We have no choice, good lady.'

The old woman frowned, making some sort of calculation for herself. Then she said: 'We have a punt. It is of no use to us. If you speak truth, and I would guess you do, then you are our hope. Poor hope is better than none. Take the punt. It will be possible to use the shallows and be at The Wounded Crayfish by tomorrow.'

They dragged the flat-bottomed boat from out of the burned hull. It stank of the fire and the destruction, but it was undamaged and floated easily on the nearby water. We were given poles and instructed how best to use them. And then we left the pathetic little party on the bank while we shoved our punt on towards The Wounded Crayfish.

'Be careful,' cried the Lady Praz Oniad, 'for Armiad's raiders are everywhere now. They have ships of the Draachenheem pattern which can easily overtake one of ours.'

Warily we continued our journey, taking turns to rest as we poled on through the night. And then at last Alisaard consulted her charts and pointed ahead. In the dawn we detected a shimmer of white light.

The gateway was already there.

But between us and it loomed the huge bulk of another hull. And this one was by no means incapacitated. She flew all her colours.

'There's a vessel ready for battle,' said von Bek.

'Could Armiad or Sharadim have wind of our journey and sent this hull to intercept us?' I asked Alisaard.

She shook her head dumbly. She did not know. We were already exhausted from poling the flatboat and had no means of fighting the huge hull.

All we could do was to beach our boat and make a dash for the pulsating gateway. This we did, stumbling and flailing as we forced ourselves on, up to our knees in marsh, falling when our feet became trapped by clumps of weed. Slowly the gateway came closer. But we had been seen. There were shouts from the hull. I saw figures landing on the headland close to the gateway. They were dressed in dark green and yellow armour and bore swords and pikes. Without weapons, we had virtually no chance against them.

Still we floundered on towards the gateway, hearts pounding, hoping for some stroke of luck which would allow us to reach the gate before the heavily armed warriors who now called to each other, spreading out as they ran towards us.

Within moments we were surrounded. We prepared to fight with our bare hands.

I had seen no armour like theirs in the Maaschanheem. To me it resembled Draachenheemer war-gear. When the leader stepped forward, awkward in all that restraining metal and leather, and removed his helmet, I knew why I had thought as I did.

The sweating, unwholesome head which was exposed was familiar enough to me. I had expected Armiad or one of his Bin-keepers. Instead I faced Lord Pharl Asclett, whom we had left bound in Sharadim's chambers when we made our escape from her palace. His face was twisted in a kind of snarling grin.

'I am very glad to see you again,' he said. 'I have an invitation from the Empress Sharadim. She would be pleased to have you attend her forthcoming wedding.'

'So she's Empress, eh?' Alisaard cast around her for a weakness in their surrounding ranks.

'Did you expect her to fail?' Prince Pharl's face bore a look of sly superiority.

'And who does the lady marry?' Von Bek also played for time. 'Yourself, Pharl of the Heavy Palm? I had heard you had no predilection for the fair sex. Or any, for that matter.'

The Prince of Skrenaw glared. 'I would be honoured to serve my Empress in any capacity. Even that. No sir, she marries Prince Flamadin. Hadn't you heard? There are celebrations in Fluugensheem. They have elected the Empress and her consort to rule over them since the King of the Flying City crashed his command while drunk. Will you come with us, back to our hull? We have waited here for you these past five days...'

'How did you know where to find us?' I asked.

'The Empress has powerful supernatural allies. She is also a great seer in her own right. Besides, she has stationed captains at many gateways of the Maaschanheem and Draachenheem. This was considered one of those you would be most likely to choose, though I must admit I expected you to appear from the gateway...'

He paused as he detected a sound like distant thunder and, turning his horrible head, gasped at what he saw.

We craned for a glimpse. The great hull was attempting to go about, but it seemed to be tangled in an all-encompassing web. I saw a ball of sputtering fire go up from a deck and be flung back as it struck the net. Now I could see a number of sprightly sailing ships, reminiscent of those I had seen in Gheestenheem, surrounding the hull. It was these which had attacked the vessel. The noise had been from the charges used to shoot the tangle of nets across the entire hull.

Before Prince Pharl could voice an order a wave of warriors suddenly rose up from the ground and attacked our captors. They were led by a small figure who wore only a marsh helmet and breastplate, who carried a gaff twice his height and who capered on the fringe of the fight, waving his weapon and urging on his men, all of whom were in the grey-green armour I had first seen in the Maaschanheem. The figure grinned at me. It was Jermays the Crooked.

'We, too, anticipated the enemy!' he called. He chuckled as his fighters closed on Prince Pharl's men and swiftly overwhelmed them. Pharl himself was captured. He glared in fury at us all.

When the warriors pushed up their visors to reveal in their ranks the faces of Ghost Women as well as native Maaschanheemers, he was close to tears.

Jermays came panting up like a happy dog. 'Peoples of several realms now band together against Sharadim and her minions. But we are badly outnumbered. You must go swiftly now. The gateway will soon be useless to you. Sharadim rules in Draachenheem. Ottro was killed in battle. Prince Halmad still fights against the Empress. Neterpino Sloch failed to win the Battle of Fancil Sepaht and paid the price. He is now legless. Sharadim has sent Mabden from this realm into Gheestenheem and battle now threatens the Eldren. Meanwhile she seeks to consolidate gains in Fluugensheem and all Rootsenheem, such as it is, is hers. Her creatures lay heavy siege to Adelstane, since the Ursine Princes failed to succumb to her trickery. Much depends on you. Her power is almost great enough for her to summon Chaos, to blend her conquered realms with theirs! Swiftly – swiftly – through the gate!'

'But we go to Rootsenheem!' I cried. 'If she rules there, how can we succeed?'

'Give false names!' was Jermays's rather unlikely advice.

And so we ran again, plunging between the columns of light, letting them draw us through into another tunnel. Through this we flew, feeling the elation birds must know when they soar on the air currents, and then at last we saw blinding yellow light ahead of us. Within seconds we stood on warm sand, looking towards a massively constructed ziggurat which seemed, in its carved stones, older than the multiverse itself.

Alisaard spoke softly. 'We are, indeed, in the Realm of the Red Weepers. You are Farkos, from Fluugensheem. You, Count von Bek, are Mederic of Draachenheem. I am Amelar of the Eldren. No more speaking. They come.' And she pointed.

Already an opening had appeared in the base of the ziggurat. From it came a party of men in strange gear similar to that which I had first observed at the Great Massing.

Heavily bearded, wearing peculiar costumes – a kind of fine

silk stretched on wide frames so that their skin was touched hardly at all, large gauntlets, helmets of some light wood supported on a kind of yoke across the shoulders, they stopped a few yards from us, raising both arms in greeting.

I was half-expecting another attack, but the men spoke with sonorous gravity. 'You have come to the Realm of the Red Weepers. Do you cross the threshold by accident or by design? We are the hereditary guardians of the threshold and must ask these questions before we allow you to proceed.'

Alisaard stepped forward. She introduced us by our false names. 'We come by design, noble masters. But we are not traders. We humbly ask permission to pass through your realm to the next threshold.'

I could now more clearly see the men's faces. Their eyes were wide and staring, rimmed entirely in red. Their helmets shaded their faces but I could now see that under each eye on a kind of wire frame was suspended a small cup. With a frisson of nausea I realised that the eyes were constantly exuding a viscous red fluid, a kind of mucus, and that the men themselves stared blindly at us.

'What business, then, are you upon, noble mistress?' one of the Red Weepers asked her.

'We seek knowledge.'

'For what purpose shall that knowledge be used?'

'We are charting the pathways between the realms. The knowledge will be for the good of all Six Realms, I swear.'

'You will do us no harm? You will take nothing from this realm that is not willingly offered?'

'We swear.' She signalled to us to echo her words.

'Your heartbeats suggest fear,' said one of the other Weepers. 'Of what are you afraid?'

'We have but lately escaped Maaschanheemer pirates,' Alisaard told them. 'There is great danger everywhere these days.'

'What danger threatens?'

'Civil war and the conquest of our realms by Chaos,' she told them.

'Ah, now,' said another speaker. 'Then you must go quickly about your business. We have no such fears in the Rootsenheem, for we have our goddess to protect us, may she bless you all.'

'Let the goddess bless you all,' they chorused piously.

I was struck by an instinctive suspicion. 'Pray, noble masters, whom do you call your goddess?' I asked.

'She is called Sharadim the Wise.'

Now we knew why war and disaster had failed to touch Rootsenheem. Sharadim had no need to promote either here. The realm was already conquered and had doubtless been hers for many years. It was easy to imagine how easily she had deceived this ancient, near-senile people. When she offered the Realm of the Red Weepers up to Chaos, few, I guessed, would protest or even know what was happening to them.

This knowledge, however, gave our mission additional urgency. Alisaard said: 'We seek the place you call Tortacanuzoo. Where shall we find it, noble masters?'

'You must cross the desert, travelling due west. But you will need a beast. We will have one brought to you. When the beast is no longer needed, it will return to us at its own volition.

And thus, on a huge wooden platform fixed to the back of an animal roughly the size and shape of a rhinoceros, we began our crossing of the great desert.

'Soon Sharadim must control all the realms save Gheestenheem,' said Alisaard soberly. 'And even Gheestenheem could fall, her power increases so. She commands millions of warriors by now. And it seems she has revived the corpse of her murdered brother so as to impress the people of Fluugensheem.'

'That I could not understand,' I said with a shudder. 'Do you know what she plans?'

'I think so. Fluugensheem's legends and myths have much to do with themes of duality. They look back to a Golden Age when a Queen and a King ruled over them and all their cities flew. Now only one has that power and it grows old, for they have lost the knowledge of building new ships. They, too, it seems, came originally from another realm. If Sharadim has been able to force an imitation of life into the body of Flamadin then this also means her Chaos-borrowed power is greater than it has ever been before. She has doubtless, through her skill at politics, convinced the Fluugen-sheemers that the stories they heard of Prince Flamadin's being outlawed were false. She is skilled at answering the needs of all she seeks to manipulate. She presents an entirely different face to each of the Six Realms – whatever they would most wish to see in their idealism and their secret yearnings for order and peace...'

'She is in other words a classic demagogue,' said von Bek, cling-ing to the side of the platform as the beast lurched for a moment before correcting itself with a great blustering exhalation of ill-smelling breath. 'It was Hitler's secret that he could seem one thing to one group and an entirely different thing to another. That is how they rise so swiftly to power. These creatures are bizarre. They can virtually change shape and colour. They have an amorphous quality and yet at the same time they have a will to dominate others which is unrelenting, almost their only consist-ent trait, their only reality.'

Alisaard was impressed by this. 'You have studied your histo-ries?' she asked. 'You know much of tyrants?'

'I am the victim of one,' said von Bek. 'I am to be the victim of another, too, it seems, if we are unsuccessful!'

She reached out to take his hand. 'You must keep your cour-age, Count von Bek. It is considerable and has stood you in good stead already. I have known few as brave as you.'

I watched as his hand folded hers in turn.

And again I knew that terrible, unjustified, unwanted pang of jealousy, as if my Ermizhad showed affection to a rival. As if that rival courted the only woman I had ever really loved!

They saw that I was disturbed and became concerned about me. But I dismissed their questions. I claimed that I was affected by the heat of the old, red sun overhead. I pretended to be tired and, putting my face in my arms, tried to sleep, to dismiss the appalling thoughts and emotions surging through me.

Towards evening I heard von Bek shout. I uncovered my eyes to see that his arm was now around Alisaard's shoulders. He was pointing to the horizon, where the sun had now dropped so that it seemed to be sinking into the sands of the desert, to be absorbed like blood. Against this scarlet half-globe was the black outline of a single mountain.

'It can only be Tortacanuzoo,' said Alisaard. Her voice was trembling, but I could not tell whether it was from the proximity of von Bek's presence or from anticipation of what we were about to encounter.

Lost in private speculation the three of us stared in silence at the gateway to the realm of the Archduke Balarizaaf. We were about to enter the Realm of Chaos and at last were struck by the enormity of our adventure, of how little chance we had of surviving it.

The beast continued to plod on towards Tortacanuzoo. Then, as if in greeting, the ancient mountain gave voice to an almost human roar. The beast stopped, lifting its head to answer. The sound was virtually identical. It was uncanny.

A flicker of flame rose suddenly from the summit, a few strands of grey smoke sailed lazily over the setting sun.

I felt a terrible sensation of terror in the pit of my stomach and I wished with all my heart that we had been captured by Prince Pharl at the gateway into Rootsenheem, or been killed in our fight with the smoke snake.

The others had no direct experience of Chaos. Indeed, as far as I could recall, I had never encountered Chaos as directly as we now intended. They, however, were innocents compared to myself. I at least had some knowledge of the warping, mutating power of the Lords of Disorder, the supernatural entities who on John Daker's Earth would be called Arch-Demons, the Dukes of Hell. I knew that they made use of our most treasured virtues and most honoured emotions. That they were capable of almost any illusion. And that all that was keeping them from pouring forth from their stronghold to engulf so many other realms of the multiverse was their caution, their unreadiness or unwillingness to war against the rival powers of Law. But if we humans invited them to our realms, they would come.

They would come when they had been offered proof of human loyalty to their cause. Proof which Sharadim was even now presenting with every victory she made.

I shivered as the old volcano muttered and fumed. It was not hard to see the mountain as an entrance into the bowels of Hell.

Then I had forced myself to action. I clambered off the platform and began to wade through ankle-deep sand towards Tortacanuzoo.

I called back to the lovers, who hesitated behind me.

'Come, my friends! We have an appointment with the Arch-duke Balarizaaf. I see no advantage to keeping him waiting.'

It was von Bek who answered me, his voice puzzled. 'Herr Daker! Herr Daker! Can you not see them? Look, man! It is the Empress Sharadim herself!'

Chapter Ten

IT WAS SHARADIM.

She was on horseback, surrounded by a group of brightly dressed courtiers. They looked for all the world like a party of aristocrats on a picnic or a hunting spree. They were riding up the mountain ahead of us. Now, above the voice of the volcano, I could hear snatches of conversation, laughter.

'They have not seen us!' Alisaard called softly, beckoning me back towards the animal. She and von Bek crouched beside one of its massive thighs. Understanding their caution, I rejoined them.

'They are euphoric in their power and cannot believe themselves under threat in a realm where Sharadim is worshipped as a goddess,' said Alisaard. 'When they round that bend and are lost from sight again, we must make haste to reach those steps you see, cut into the foot of the mountain.'

It was growing darker. I saw the sense of her strategy and nodded agreement. A short while later the last of Sharadim's gaily clad party turned the corner and was gone. Following Alisaard we dashed for the steps and had reached the protection of the mountain long before Sharadim emerged on the other side. Cautiously, we began to mount the steps, following in the wake of our most dangerous enemy.

As we came round to the other side I saw some costly tents pitched below. A servant was feeding pack animals. It was almost a village in its own right. This was Sharadim's camp. But surely she did not intend to go directly into Hell! Even in her pride and her conquests she could not believe herself so invulnerable as yet!

The pace of the horses grew slower as they approached the summit, while we, creeping on the stairs above the trail, were able to move with relative swiftness until we were slightly ahead of Sharadim and her party, but virtually within hearing distance.

Their voices were louder now. I recognised Baron Captain Armiad of the Maaschanheem, Duke Perichost of the Draachenheem, a couple of courtiers from the palace. Also among the group were thin-faced Mabden with the wolfish look of barbarian raiders, men in outlandishly padded black livery. There seemed to be representatives of all the cultures of the Six Realms, save for the Eldren and the Ursine Princes.

I began to guess at Sharadim's intent. This was to be a demonstration of her power. A means of ensuring that her allies were convinced by her threats and promises.

One I did not recognise rode beside her, in a cowled cape. He had the look of a priest. She was in holiday spirit, laughing and joking with all around her. I was impressed again by her unlikely beauty. It was not difficult to see how she was able to convince so many of her angelic disposition. Indeed, she had even convinced the blind Weepers that she was a goddess, and they had never looked on her face.

We emerged now into a kind of wide amphitheatre which was the top of the volcano. Out in the very centre of the crust was a red, glowing, unstable substance which from time to time gave off a thin shoot of flame and some smoke. The volcano seemed to be at its cooling stage rather than about to erupt, so I felt no danger in this. I was fascinated, however, to see that a great tier of stone seats had been erected on one side. This was reached by a causeway, also of geometrically cut stone. Along the causeway, almost like voyagers about to take ship, Sharadim and her party rode.

With a wave of her hand, Sharadim ordered her courtiers to dismount and take seats in the tier. She remained mounted and, leaning over, put a restraining hand on her cowled companion, making him draw up his horse beside hers.

Above the grumbling of the volcano, Sharadim now began to speak.

'Some of you have expressed doubts that Chaos can aid us in the final stages of our conquests. You have required proof that your rewards will be almost limitless. Well, soon I shall summon one of the most powerful nobles in all Chaos, the Archduke Balarizaaf himself! You will hear from his lips what you refused to believe from mine. Those loyal to Chaos now, who do not flinch from deeds which lesser creatures deem vile and cruel, shall be raised above all others, save myself. You shall know the expression of every whim, every secret dream, every dark desire. You shall know a complete fulfilment which the weak can never begin to taste. Shortly you shall look upon the face of Balarizaaf, Archduke of Chaos, and you shall know what it means to be strong. I speak of strength capable of reshaping reality to the individual will. Strength which can destroy whole universes if it so desires. Strength which brings with it immortality. And with immortality shall come the realisation of even the most fleeting of whims. We shall be gods! Chaos promises an infinity of possibilities free from the petty constraints of Law!'

Now she turned with upraised arms towards the volcano. Her voice sang out, sweet and perfect in the still evening air:

'LORD BALARIZAAF, ARCHDUKE OF CHAOS, MASTER OF HELL, YOUR SERVANTS CALL YOU! WE BRING YOU THE GIFT OF WORLDS. WE BRING YOU OUR TRIBUTE. WE BRING YOU MILLIONS OF SOULS! WE BRING YOU BLOOD AND HORROR! WE BRING YOU THE SACRIFICE OF ALL WEAKNESS! WE BRING YOU OUR STRENGTH! AID US, LORD BALARIZAAF. COME TO US, LORD BALARIZAAF. LEAD CHAOS THROUGH AND LET LAW BE FOREVER IN DEFEAT!'

A flicker of scarlet light at the centre of the volcano seemed to respond. She continued to chant in this manner and soon her courtiers were joining in with her. The entire night was infected by their voices as the sun finally set and the only light came from the volcano itself.

'Aid us, Lord Balarizaaf!'

Then, as if bursting through an unseen ceiling, came first one beam of light and then another. These were not white as the gateways we had used hitherto. These seemed to reflect the scarlet of the flame. They glowed. They resembled pillars composed of living, bloody flesh.

One by one these pillars grew in width and intensity until at last thirteen of them were poised between the sky and the volcano and it was impossible to see where they began and ended.

Her face and hands scarlet in the light from the pillars, Sharadim crooned and sang. She called out obscenities and imploring promises. She offered her god anything he might desire.

'Balarizaaf. Lord Balarizaaf! We invite you into our realm!'

Now the volcano shook.

I felt the ground shifting under my feet. Alisaard, von Bek and I looked at one another in uncertainty. The gateway was open. It led to Chaos, without question. But what would happen to us if we tried to enter it now?

'BALARIZAAF! LORD OF ALL! COME TO US!'

All around us there was a wind whistling. Lightning began to crackle upon the brink of the crater. Again the mountain trembled and we were almost thrown off our staircase to the causeway below.

The columns of scarlet light pounded as if they were living organs. An unholy yelling began to sound, far away, and I knew it came from the pillars.

'BALARIZAAF! AID US!'

The yelling became a scream, the scream turned into chilling laughter, and then, blazing with black and orange fire, his unstable features writhing, changing shape with every second, stood a creature no taller than a man but from whose lips there now escaped a deafening voice: 'IS IT YOU, LITTLE SHARADIM, WHO CALLS BALARIZAAF FROM PLAY? IS THE TIME COME? SHALL I LEAD YOU TO THE SWORD?'

'The time is almost here, Lord Balarizaaf. Soon we shall have conquered the entire Six Realms. This whole realm shall then become one. A realm of Chaos. And my reward shall be the Sword and the Sword shall give me —'

'Infinite power. The right to be one of the Sword Rulers themselves. A Lord of Chaos! For only you or the one called the

Champion may wield that blade and live! What more must I repeat, little Sharadim?'

'No more, lord.'

'Good, because it is painful for me to stay in this realm until it is truly mine. The Sword shall make it truly mine. Come to me soon, little Sharadim!'

It seemed to me that Lord Balarizaaf gave poor guarantees. But so blinded by the prospect of unchecked power were these people that they were prepared to believe anything they were told.

Balarizaaf was suddenly gone.

Below us, Sharadim's courtiers murmured amongst themselves. There was no doubt of their complete loyalty to her now. One or two were already on their knees.

Sharadim reached towards her cowled companion, beside her on his horse, and she pushed back his cape. She revealed a face which was all too familiar to me!

It was a grey face, a lifeless face, with eyes the colour of pewter staring directly ahead of it. It was my face. I was looking at my doppelgänger.

And even as I stared at it, its dead eyes met mine. They began slowly to fill with something approximating energy. The lips moved. A hollow voice said:

'He is here, mistress. What you promised me is here. Give him to me. Give me his soul. Give me his life…'

Alisaard was howling at me. Von Bek was tugging at me. They were pulling me with them down towards the causeway. At the far end of this, by the tiers of seats, heads were beginning to turn.

We dashed over the causeway, down smooth rocks, onto the crust of the volcano itself. And then we were running towards the pillars of blood.

'Flamadin!' I heard my pseudo-sister cry.

They were howling like jackals as they came in pursuit of us. Yet they were reluctant to approach too close to the gateway, for they knew it led directly into Hell.

The three of us reached the scarlet pillars and hesitated. Sharadim and her courtiers were still behind us. I saw the puppetlike motions of her creature. 'Its life is mine, mistress!'

Von Bek was panting. 'My God, Herr Daker. That is the nearest thing I have ever seen to a zombie. What is it?'

'My doppelgänger,' I said. 'She has revived the corpse of Flamadin with the promise of a new soul!'

Then von Bek had dragged me back into the circle of the pillars and we stood looking down into the bubbling core of the volcano.

Slowly the crust seemed to widen, revealing pulsing, violent heat, a smell at once sweet and repellent. And then we were being drawn down into it. Drawn through the gates of Hell and into a realm whose supreme ruler was Lord Balarizaaf, the creature we had just seen.

I think we were all screaming by the time we were passing through the tunnel of flame. The descent seemed to last for ever as the yellow and red fires went past us in every direction.

Then I felt firm earth beneath my feet again. I was deeply relieved to see that it looked anything but abnormal. It was ordinary turf. It did not undulate. It did not burn. It did not threaten to swallow me. And it smelled like ordinary turf.

On the other side of the columns of light, which had now turned a kind of delicate pink, I made out blue sky, the weight of a forest, and I heard birdsong.

Together with my friends I walked slowly out of the columns and into a glade whose grassy mounds were covered in daisies and buttercups. The forest consisted primarily of large-boled oaks, all of them in their prime, and a little silver river ran through the glade, adding its music to that of the exotically plumaged birds which flew across a peaceful sky or came to perch on nearby branches.

We were like wondering children as we looked around us. Alisaard had begun to smile. I contented myself with breathing in the sweetness of the blossoms and the grass.

We seated ourselves beside the little river. We smiled at one another. This was an idyll from our most innocent dreams.

Von Bek was the first to speak. 'Why!' he exclaimed in delight.

'This is not Hell at all, my friends. This truly is the most perfect Paradise!'

But I was already suspicious. When I looked behind me the pillars of blood had gone. I saw instead a scene which was almost exactly the same as our own. I turned and retraced my steps, looking for the gateway. It had not been there long enough, I felt. My suspicion increased. There was something strange about the atmosphere of this place, something unnatural. Instinctively, I stretched out my hand. It struck a smooth, hard wall – a wall which mirrored this paradise but which did not reflect our images!

I called out to my friends. They were laughing and talking, engrossed in their own intimate obsessions. I was impatient with them. This was not the time for my allies to become mooning lovers, I thought.

'Lady Alisaard! Von Bek! Be wary!'

At last they looked up. 'What is it, man?' Von Bek was irritated by my interruption.

'This place is not merely an illusion,' I said. 'I suspect it is an illusion to hide something far less pleasant. Come and see.'

Reluctantly, hand in hand, they ran towards me over the soft Arcadian grass.

Now that I was close to the wall I thought I could see behind the illusion to the other side where dim shapes moved, hideous faces beseeched or threatened, misshapen hands stretched out towards us.

'There are the true denizens of this realm,' I said.

But my friends saw nothing.

'It is your own mind showing you what you fear is there,' said von Bek. 'As much an illusion as the other. I will admit this place is an unlikely one and doubtless is artificial. Nonetheless, it is very pleasing. Surely Chaos is not all terror and ugliness?'

'By no means,' I agreed. 'And that is part of its attraction. Chaos is capable of marvellous beauty of all kinds. But nothing in Chaos is ever just one thing. It is ambiguity. It is illusion disguising illusion. There is no true simplicity in Chaos, only the appearance of simplicity.' I drew the Actorios from my purse. I held it up so that its strange, dark rays struck out in all directions. 'See?'

I directed the Actorios towards the reflecting wall and quite suddenly the illusion cleared, displaying what had lurked behind the barrier.

Von Bek and Alisaard both stepped back involuntarily, their eyes widening, their faces pale.

Creatures neither beast nor human shambled and slouched amongst filthy huts which seemed to be made of fused flint. Some of them pressed grotesque faces to the wall in attitudes of despairing melancholy. The others merely moved about the village, performing various tasks. Not one of them did not walk without a limp or drag a distorted limb.

'What are these people called?' murmured von Bek in horror. 'They are like something from medieval paintings! Who are they, Herr Daker?'

'They were once human,' said Alisaard softly. 'But in giving their loyalty to Chaos, they accepted the logic of Chaos. Chaos cannot bear constancy. It is changing all the time. And what you see is the change Chaos has wrought in humankind. That is what Sharadim offers the Six Realms. Oh, indeed, some of them may come to experience enormous power for a while. But in the end this is what they always become.'

'Poor devils!' murmured von Bek.

'Poor devils,' I said to him, 'is an exact enough description of them...'

'Would they attack us, if the wall did not keep them back?' von Bek asked.

'Only if they thought we were weaker than themselves. These are not the warlike creatures Sharadim commands. These merely put themselves in servitude to Chaos because they thought it would benefit them somehow.'

Alisaard turned away. She drew a deep breath and then expelled it suddenly, as if she had realised the air were tainted.

'This was folly,' she said. 'This was the greatest folly. We were told to seek out the centre and there find the sword. But we are in Chaos. Since nothing is constant, we have no way of knowing in which direction we must travel.'

Von Bek comforted her. I stood back, again having to force myself to take hold of my emotions. Jealousy had come flooding back again.

'We should count ourselves fortunate,' I told them, 'that Archduke Balarizaaf is as yet unaware of our presence. We should press on. We should get as far from this gateway as possible. Into those woods.'

'But if Balarizaaf rules here, he will find us as soon as he decides to look,' said Alisaard.

I shook my head. 'Not necessarily. He is virtually omnipotent here, but he is not omniscient. We have a small chance of reaching our goal before he seeks us out.'

'This is true optimism!' Von Bek slapped me on the back and laughed, his eyes avoiding the dimming vision of the village. Soon, as we moved away, the reflection had returned.

'I've a mind to be wary of those woods now,' said von Bek to me. 'But I suppose we have no choice. It's thick, eh? Like one of those old forests from German legend. I suppose if we're lucky we'll find a woodcutter who will direct us on our way and perhaps allow us three wishes, too.'

Alisaard smiled, her spirits rising. She linked arms with him. 'You speak so strangely, Count von Bek. But there's a kind of music to your nonsense which I like.'

For my part, I found his whimsy merely facile.

The oak wood had an atmosphere of permanence, as if it had stood here for a thousand years or more. In the cool, green shadows, we saw rabbits and squirrels and there was an air of tranquillity about the place which was thoroughly enchanting. But even without recourse to my Actorios, I knew that it was bound to be something other than it seemed. That, after all, was one of the few rules in Chaos.

We had only gone a yard or two into the wood when we saw,

standing behind a beam of dusty sunlight, a tall, armoured figure. It was clad entirely in metal of black and yellow.

At first I was relieved to see Sepiriz here. And then it came to me that this, too, might be an illusion. I stopped. My friends also came to a halt beside me.

'Is that you, Sir Knight in Black and Yellow?' I asked him, folding my hand over the Actorios. 'How came you to Chaos? Or do you, too, serve Chaos now?'

The armoured man advanced into the light. His bright livery seemed to glow with its own radiance. He lifted his helm and I saw the impressive ebony features which could only belong to Sepiriz, the servant of the Balance. He was amused by my suspicion but not dismissive of it.

'You are right to question everything in this realm,' he said. He yawned and stretched himself in his metal. 'Forgive me, I have been asleep. I slept while I awaited you. I am glad you found the entrance. I am glad you had the courage to come. But now you must call on even greater courage than before. Here in the Nightmare Realm you may find horrible torment or salvation for the Six Realms – and more! But Chaos has many weapons in her arsenal and not all of them are obvious. Even now Sharadim prepares her creature to accept your soul, Champion. Do you understand the implications of that?'

He could see that I did not.

He hesitated and then continued: 'The corpse she has animated will be able to take the Dragon Sword – if it possesses your lifestuff, John Daker. Sharadim controls this quasi-Flamadin and so it will be her cat's-paw. She risks far less than if she were to take hold of the sword herself.'

'Then she seeks to deceive her ally, Archduke Balarizaaf, who believes that she will handle the sword for him?'

'He cares not which of you eventually lays claim to the blade – so long as you use it for his purposes. He would therefore prefer you as an ally rather than as an enemy, Champion. That is worth remembering. And remember this, also – death is not what one must fear in the Nightmare Realm. Death as such hardly exists here, but to be immortal in this world is the worst fate of all! And you must also remember that you have allies here. A hare will lead you to a cup. The cup will show you the way to a horned horse. The horned horse will take you to a wall. And in the wall you will find the sword.'

'How can such allies exist in a world dominated by the tyranny of Chaos?' Lady Alisaard asked him.

Sepiriz looked down at her and his smile was gentle. 'Even in Chaos there are some whose purity and integrity are so complete they are untouched by anything which surrounds them. It is in the very heart of Chaos that those most able to resist her often choose to dwell. This is a paradox enjoyed by the Lords of Chaos themselves. It is an irony which even the grave Lords of Law take pleasure in.'

'And is it because you possess this purity that you are able to come and go in the Nightmare Marches, Lord Sepiriz?' asked von Bek.

'You are right to question me, Count von Bek. No, my time in this realm is limited. If it were not, why I should doubtless seek the Dragon Sword myself!' He smiled again. 'As an emissary of the Balance I am allowed more freedom of movement than most creatures. But it is by no means unchecked, that freedom. The time comes for me to leave. I would not attract Balarizaaf to you. Not yet.'

'Will Sharadim find a way of telling the Chaos Lord that we are in his domain?' I asked.

'She does not communicate with her ally at will,' Sepiriz said. 'But she could choose to enter the Nightmare Marches herself. And then you would find yourselves in the greatest danger.'

'Then we can expect to find no allies here,' said von Bek soberly.

'Only the Lost Warriors,' said Sepiriz. 'Those who wait on the Edge of Time. And their help can be called upon only once. And only then if you have no other recourse. Those warriors may fight once in a cycle of the multiverse. When they unsheathe their swords there are inevitable consequences. But you know this already, eh, Sir Champion?'

'I have heard the Lost Warriors,' I agreed. 'They have spoken to me in my dreams. But I can remember little else.'

'How shall these warriors be summoned?' asked von Bek.

'By breaking the Actorios into fragments,' said Sepiriz.

'But the stone cannot be broken. It is virtually indestructible.' Alisaard's voice rose in outrage. 'You play tricks upon us, Lord Sepiriz!'

'The stone can be broken. By a blow from the Dragon Sword. That is what I know.'

And Sepiriz reached up and closed his helm.

Von Bek uttered a desperate laugh. 'We are truly in Chaos. There's a paradox for you! We can only summon allies when the Dragon Sword is already ours! When we have no need of them!'

'You will decide that when the time comes.' Sepiriz's voice was hollow and distant, as if he faded from us, though his armour was as solid as ever. 'Remember – your greatest weapons are your own courage and intelligence. Go swiftly through this wood. There is a path which the Actorios will show you. Follow it. Like all paths in Chaos it leads eventually to the place they call here The World's Beginning…'

Now the armour began to dissipate, to fade, to join with the dancing motes of dust in the sunbeams.

'*Swiftly, swiftly. Chaos gathers territory with every passing hour. And with that territory she gains a host of souls sworn to her service. Your worlds shall soon be little else but a memory unless you find the Dragon Sword…*'

The armour vanished entirely. All that remained of the Knight in Black and Yellow was an echo of a whisper. Then that, too, was gone.

I took out my Actorios and held it before me, turning this way and that.

Then, to my relief, I stopped. Very dimly at our feet there stretched, for a few yards only, a faintly shimmering ghost of a pathway.

We had found the road to the Dragon Sword.

Book Three

Hither, hither, if you will,
Drink instruction, or instil,
Run the woods like vernal sap,
Crying, hail to luminousness!
    But have care.
In yourself may lurk the trap:
On conditions they caress.
Here you meet the light invoked
Here is never secret cloaked.
Doubt you with the monster's fry
All his orbit may exclude;
Are you of the stiff, the dry,
Cursing the not understood;
Grasp you with the monster's claws;
Govern with his truncheon-saws;
Hate, the shadow of the grain;
You are lost in Westermain:
Earthward swoops a vulture sun,
Nighted upon carrion:
Straightway venom wine-cups shout
Toasts to One whose eyes are out:
Flowers along the reeling floor
Drip henbane and hellebore:
Beauty, of her tresses shorn,
Shrieks as nature's maniac:
Hideousness on hoof and horn
Tumbles, yapping in her track:
Haggard Wisdom, stately once,

Leers fantastical and trips:
Allegory drums the sconce,
Impiousness nibblenips.
Imp that dances, imp that flits,
Imp o' the demon-growing girl,
Maddest! whirl with imp o' the pits
Round you, and with them you whirl
Fast where pours the fountain-rout
Out of Him whose eyes are out;
Multitudes of multitudes,
Drenched in wallowing deviltry:
And you ask where you may be,
*   In what reek of a lair*
Given to bones and ogre-broods:
*   And they yell you Where.*
Enter these enchanted woods,
*   You who dare.*

– George Meredith,
'The Woods of Westermain'

Chapter One

WE HAD GONE perhaps five miles when the greenwood on all sides began to rustle urgently, as if threatened. We had only the shadow path to guide us. Steadfastly, in spite of the rapidly increasing agitation, we continued to go forward in single file. Alisaard was immediately behind me. She whispered: 'It is as if the forest senses our presence and becomes alarmed.'

Then, one by one, the oak trees turned to stone, the stone became liquid and, in an instant, the entire landscape was transformed. The path remained visible, but we were surrounded by monstrous green stems and at the top of these stems, far above our heads, were the yellow bells of gigantic daffodils.

'Is this what lies behind the illusion?' said von Bek in awe.

'This is as much reality as it is illusion,' I told him. 'Chaos has her moods and whims, that's all. As I told you, she cannot remain stable. It is in her nature to be forever changing.'

'While it is in the nature of Law,' Alisaard explained, 'to be forever fixed. The Balance is there to ensure that neither Law nor Chaos ever gain complete ascendancy, for the one offers sterility while the other offers only sensation.'

'And this struggle between the two, does it take place on every single realm of the multiverse?' von Bek wanted to know. He looked around him at the nodding flowers. Their scent was like a drug.

'Every plane, on some level or another, in some guise or another. It is the perpetual war. And there is a champion, they say, who is doomed to fight in every aspect of that war, for eternity...'

'Please, Lady Alisaard,' I interrupted, 'I would rather not be reminded of the Eternal Champion's fate!' I was not altogether joking.

Alisaard apologised. We continued in silence along the path for about another mile, until the landscape shuddered and changed for the second time. This time in place of giant daffodils were gibbets. On every gibbet swung a cage and in every cage was a scabrous, dying human creature, crying out for help.

I told them to ignore the prisoners and keep to the path. 'And this? Is this mere illusion?' shouted von Bek from behind me. He was almost in tears.

'An invention, I promise you. It will vanish as the others vanished.'

Suddenly the prisoners were gone from their cages. In their place were huge finches squalling for food. Then the gibbets disappeared, the finches flew away, and we were surrounded by tall glass buildings for as far as the eye could see. These buildings were in a thousand different styles yet were unstable. Every few moments one of them would fall with a great crashing and tinkling, sometimes taking one or more of the neighbouring buildings with it. To follow the path, we were forced to wade through shards of broken glass which set up a great clatter as we advanced. Voices sounded now, from within the buildings, but we could see that the houses were empty. Shrieks of laughter, wails of pain. Horrible sobbing sounds. The moans of the tortured. The glass gradually began to melt and, as it melted, took the form of agonised faces. And those faces were still the size of buildings!

'Oh, this is surely Hell,' cried von Bek, 'and these are the souls of the damned!'

The faces flowed up into the sky, turning into great metal blades in the form of fern leaves.

And still we made our way slowly along the shadow path. I forced myself to think only of our goal, of the Dragon Sword which could take the Eldren women to their homeland, which must not be allowed to fall into the hands of Chaos. I wondered what means Sharadim would use in trying to defeat us. For how long could she maintain a semblance of life in that corpse, my doppelgänger?

A wind howled through the metallic leaves. They clashed and jangled and set my teeth on edge. They offered us no direct danger, however. Chaos was not in herself malevolent. But her ambitions were inimical to the desires of both human and Eldren as well as all the other races of the multiverse.

Once, in that iron jungle, I thought I saw figures moving parallel to us. I lifted the Actorios. It could easily detect creatures of ordinary flesh and blood. But if someone had been trailing us, they were now too far away for the stone to find them.

In seconds the ferns became frozen snakes; then the snakes came to life. Next the living snakes began to devour one another. All around us was a great swaying and writhing and hissing. It was as if a tangled hedge of serpents lined both sides of the shadow path. I held tight to Alisaard's trembling hand. 'Remember, they will not attack us unless directed. They are hardly real.'

But though I reassured her, I knew that any of Chaos's illusions were real enough to do harm in the short span of their existence.

But now the snakes had become country brambles and our path was a sandy lane leading towards the distant sea.

I began to feel a little more optimistic, in spite of knowing how false my security was, and had begun to whistle when I rounded a turn in the path and saw that our way was blocked by a mass of riders. At their head our old enemy Baron Captain Armiad of the *Frowning Shield*. His features had become even more bestial in the time since we had last seen him. His nostrils had widened so much that they now resembled the snout of a pig. There were tufts of hair sprouting from his face and neck and when he spoke I was reminded of the lowing of a cow.

These were Sharadim's retainers. The same we had left behind when we dashed for the gateway into this realm. Evidently they had lost no time in following us.

We were still without weapons. We could not fight them. The bramble hedges were solid enough and blocked flight in that direction. If we wished to flee, we would have to run back the way we had come. And we would easily be ridden down by the horsemen.

'Where's your mistress, Baron Porker?' I called, standing my ground. 'Was she too cowardly to enter Chaos herself?'

Armiad's already narrow eyes came closer together still. He grunted and sniffed. His nose and eyes seemed permanently wet.

'The Empress Sharadim has more important business than to chase after vermin when there is the greatest prey of all to hand.'

Armiad's remark was greeted appreciatively by his fellows who gave forth a great chorus of snorts and grunts. All of them had faces and bodies transformed by their espousal of Chaos's cause. I wondered if they had noticed these changes or if their brains were warped as thoroughly as their physical appearance. I could barely recognise some of them. Duke Perichost's thin, unpleasant face now bore a distinct resemblance to a starved hamster. I wondered how long, in relative time, they had been here.

'And what's the greatest prey of all?' von Bek asked him. Again we were talking in the hope that the next change in the landscape would be to our advantage.

'You know what it is!' shouted Armiad, his snout twitching with rage and turning red. 'For you seek it yourself. You must do. You cannot deny it!'

'But do *you* know what it is, Baron Captain Armiad?' said Alisaard. 'Has the Empress allowed you into her confidence? It seems unlikely when the last time she spoke of you she complained that you were poor material for her purposes. She said you would be disposed of when your turn was served. Is it served now, do you think, Lord Baron Captain? Or have you been given what you most desired? Are you respected by your peers at last? Do they cheer their King Admiral whenever his hull passes by? Or are they silent, because the *Frowning Shield* is as filthy and disgusting as ever, but is now one of the last hulls still rolling in the Maaschanheem?'

She mocked him. She goaded him. And all the time she was testing him. I could see that she was finding out what Sharadim's instructions had been. And it was becoming plain, from Armiad's restraint, that he had been ordered to take us alive.

His tiny eyes glared Murder, but his hands twitched on his saddle horn.

He was about to speak when von Bek broke in. 'You are a foolish, stupid, greedy man, Baron Captain. Can you not see that she has rid herself of unwanted allies? She sends you into Chaos. Meanwhile she continues her conquest of the Six Realms. Where is she now? Fighting the Eldren women? Wiping out the Red Weepers?'

Now Armiad lifted a triumphant snout and voiced something close to laughter. 'What need has she to fight the Eldren? They are gone. They are all gone from Gheestenheem. They have fled before our navies. Gheestenheem is absolutely ours!'

Alisaard believed him. It was plain he did not lie. White and trembling she yet controlled herself. 'Where have they fled? There is nowhere, surely, they could go.'

'Where else but to sanctuary with their ancient allies? They have gone into Adelstane and crouch with the Ursine Princes behind their defences while my Empress's army lays siege. Their defeat is inevitable. A few fight on, with the pirates of my own realm, but most huddle in Adelstane awaiting slaughter.'

'They have used the gateway between Barobanay and the Ursine stronghold,' murmured Alisaard. 'It is their only possible strategy against such forces as Sharadim commands.'

Again Baron Captain Armiad lifted his snout in a kind of laugh. 'Conquest has been swift across all the Six Realms. For years my lady made her plans. And when the time came to put them into action, how wonderfully she was able to achieve her ambitions.'

'Only because few rational people can ever begin to understand such a lust for power,' said von Bek feelingly. 'There is nothing more puerile than the mind of a tyrant.'

'And nothing more frightening,' I added under my breath.

The bramble hedges began to curl upwards, forming spirals of gauze in a thousand colours.

Without a word, Alisaard, von Bek and myself dived from the path and into the tangle of rustling linen while at our backs charged the yelling, clumsy pack, made clumsier still by the grotesque distortions of their bodies. Yet they were mounted and had the advantage of us.

We had lost the shadow path. We darted from one piece of cover to the next. Baron Captain Armiad and his companions blundered in pursuit, hooting and bellowing. It was as if we were chased by a pack of farmyard beasts.

There was nothing comical, however, about our terror. All we had was an idea that Sharadim had ordered us taken alive, but in their blind stupidity these creatures might easily kill us by accident!

Desperately I sought for another shadow trail, holding the Actorios out before me.

The streamers of gauze became great fountains of water, shooting high into the sky. It was between these that we now ducked and dodged. Then Duke Perichost had sighted Alisaard and with a triumphant snort had drawn his sword and was bearing down on her. I saw von Bek turn and try to reach her. But I was closer. I flung myself upwards, grasping the Draachenheemer's wrist and twisting the sword from a hand which now more closely resembled a paw. Alisaard dropped down and picked up the blade even as I threw my whole weight against the duke and forced him off the horse and onto the ground.

'Von Bek!' I cried. 'Into the saddle, man.' I thrust the Actorios upon Alisaard who took it, looking baffled. Now more of the Chaos creatures had sighted us and were charging in crowded formation towards us.

Von Bek swung up and helped Alisaard seat herself behind him. I ran for a while beside the horse yelling for them to go ahead of me and try to find a new trail. I would do my best to find them.

Then I was turning to face the charge of a Mabden barbarian whose lance was aimed directly at my groin. I sidestepped the lance and grasped the haft, dragging it down and to the right, hoping the Mabden was fool enough to hang on to it.

He came off the saddle as smoothly as if it had been greased. And now I had his lance.

In seconds I had taken the barbarian's place on the horse and was riding after my friends. Both von Bek and myself were more proficient horsemen than the warriors who came in our wake. Darting in and out of the great fountains we gradually escaped Baron Captain Armiad and his pack. Then another reflecting wall came between us and them. We dimly saw them on the other side. There was no particular reason for the wall to compose itself at that particular point. It was merely a random whim of Chaos. But it proved lucky for us as, sweating, we slowed our pace.

I saw von Bek turn in his saddle and kiss Alisaard. She responded enthusiastically to this. She flung her arms around him, the Actorios stone clutched in one beautiful hand.

And it was Ermizhad who kissed my friend. It was Ermizhad who betrayed me. The only betrayal I had thought impossible!

Now I knew for certain it was she. All along she had deceived me. I had slain whole peoples because of my love for her. I had fought in a thousand wars. And this was how she returned my loyalty?

What was worse, von Bek, whom I had believed a comrade, had no scruples in the matter. They flaunted themselves. Their embraces mocked everything I held dear. How could I have trusted them?

I knew then that I had no choice but to punish them for the pain they now caused me.

Steadying my horse, I lifted up the lance I had taken from the Mabden. I weighed it in my hand. I was skilled in the use of such weapons and knew that one single cast could pierce the pair of them, uniting them in death. A fair reward for their treachery.

'Ermizhad! How is it possible!'

Now my arm went back as I prepared to throw. I saw von Bek's cowardly eyes grow big with disbelieving horror. I saw Ermizhad begin to turn, following the direction of his gaze.

I laughed at them.

My laughter found an echo. It seemed to fill the whole realm. Von Bek was shouting. Ermizhad was shouting. Doubtless they were pleading for mercy. I would give them none. The laughter grew louder and louder. It was not merely my own laughter I heard. There was another voice.

I hesitated.

A tiny shout came from von Bek. 'Herr Daker! Are you possessed? What is it?'

I ignored him. I had come to realise how he had tricked me, how he had deliberately courted my friendship, knowing that he was to keep a liaison with my wife. And had Ermizhad helped him plan the deception? It followed logically that she had. How had I failed to guess all this? My mind had been clouded by other, less important issues. I had no need of a Dragon Sword. I had no loyalty to the Six Realms. Why should I let myself be distracted by these problems when my own wife dishonoured me before my eyes?

I ceased to laugh at that point. I poised the lance for the throw.

And then I realised that the laughter was continuing. It was not my laughter.

I looked to one side and saw a man standing there. He wore long robes of black and dark blue. There was a familiarity about his face I could not place. He had the look of a wise, well-balanced statesman in middle years. Only his wild laughter denied this impression.

Now I knew that I looked upon the ruler of this realm, at the Archduke Balarizaaf himself.

And without thinking I flung the lance directly at his heart.

He continued to laugh, even as he looked down at the haft which protruded from his body.

'Oh, this is fine amusement,' he said at last. 'So much more interesting, Sir Champion, than conquering worlds and enslaving nations, don't you think?'

And I realised, just barely, that I was victim of this realm's hallucinatory influences. I had almost killed my two best friends in my madness.

Then the Archduke Balarizaaf had vanished and Alisaard was

crying out to me to look. With the Actorios she had found another shadow path, dimly visible ahead of us. But of still greater interest was the large brown hare which loped along it.

'We must follow it,' I said, even as I began to tremble in reaction to what I had almost done. 'Remember what Sepiriz told us. The hare is our first link with the Sword.'

Von Bek offered me a wary glance. 'Are you yourself again, my friend?'

'I hope so,' I told him. I was riding ahead now; riding after the hare which continued, with characteristic insouciance, to lead us along the shadow path.

Soon the track had narrowed and the horses were stumbling on loose rocks. I dismounted, leading my mount. Von Bek and Alisaard followed my example.

The hare appeared to wait patiently for us. Then it moved steadily on.

At last the beast stopped at a point where the trail appeared to go through solid rock. We could see a wide valley below us, a river which looked as big as the Mississippi, a massive fortress seemingly all made of silver. Still dismounted, we approached the hare and the wall of rock. I reached out for the beast, but it hopped away from me. And then, quite suddenly, I was falling into blackness, falling through the melancholy emptiness of the cosmic void. And it seemed to me I heard Balarizaaf's laughter again. Had we allowed ourselves to be trapped by the Archduke of Chaos, after all?

Were we consigned to limbo for all eternity?

Chapter Two

I FELT THAT I had fallen for months, perhaps years, before I realised the sensation of movement was gone and I was on my feet on firm ground, though still in utter blackness.

A voice was calling to me: 'John Daker, are you there?'

'I am here, von Bek, wherever here may be. And Alisaard?'

'With Count von Bek,' she said.

Gradually we managed to grope our way towards each other and link hands.

'What is this place?' von Bek wondered. 'Some trap of the Archduke Balarizaaf's?'

'Possibly,' I said, 'though I was under the impression that the hare led us here.'

Von Bek began to laugh. 'Aha, so like Alice we have fallen down a rabbit hole, yes?'

I smiled at this. Alisaard remained silent, plainly baffled by the reference. She said: 'The realms of Chaos have many places where the fabric of the multiverse has worn thin, others where worlds intersect at random. They cannot be charted, as we chart our own gateways, yet sometimes they exist in one place for centuries. It could be that we have fallen through one of those gaps in the fabric. We could be anywhere in the entire multiverse…'

'Or nowhere, perhaps?' said von Bek.

'Or nowhere,' she agreed.

I still maintained the view that the hare had led us here intentionally. 'We were told to find a cup, that the cup would lead us to the horned horse and the horned horse would lead us to the sword. I have faith in Sepiriz's powers of prediction. I think we are here to find that cup.'

'Even if it were here,' von Bek argued, 'we could hardly see it, could we, my friend?'

I bent down to touch the floor. It was damp. There was a mildewy smell about the place. As I ran my hand further I confirmed my guess that we stood on old, worn flagstones. 'This is manmade,' I said. 'And I would guess we are in an underground chamber of some sort. Which means there must be a wall. And in the wall, perhaps, we'll find a door. Come,' and I led them slowly across the floor until at last my fingers found a slimy block of stone. The stuff was unpleasant to the touch, but I soon confirmed that this was, indeed, a wall. So we followed the wall, first to one corner, then to another. The chamber was about twenty feet wide. Set in the third wall was a wooden door with iron hinges and a huge old-fashioned lock. I took hold of the ring and turned it. Tumblers clicked with surprising smoothness. I tugged. There was light beyond the door. Cautiously I pulled it open another inch or two and peered into a corridor.

The corridor had a low, curved ceiling and seemed as old as the chamber. Yet at intervals along it there ran what I recognised at once as ordinary twentieth-century light bulbs, strung on visible flexes, as if placed there for temporary use. The corridor ended on my right at another door, but on my left it stretched for some distance before turning a corner. I frowned. I was deeply puzzled.

'We seem to be in the dungeons of a medieval castle,' I whispered to von Bek, 'yet there's modern lighting. Take a look for yourself.'

After a moment he pulled his head back in and closed the door. I heard him breathing heavily, but he said nothing.

'What's the matter?' I asked him.

'Nothing, my friend. A premonition, call it. We could be anywhere, I know, yet I have a feeling that I recognise that corridor. Which is, you'll agree, unlikely. One such place is much like another. Well, shall we explore?'

'If you feel ready,' I said.

He uttered a faint laugh. 'Of course. My mind's somewhat disturbed by recent events, that's all.'

And so we stepped into the corridor. We made a peculiar sight, Alisaard in her ivory armour, myself in the heavy leather of a marsh warrior and von Bek in his imitation twentieth-century costume. We proceeded cautiously until we reached the turn in the passage. The place seemed deserted, yet plainly was in use, judging by the lights. I peered up at the nearest bulb. They were of an unfamiliar pattern to me, yet clearly operated according to the usual principle.

We were so engrossed in exploring this corridor that we were too late to look for cover when one of the doors opened and a man stepped out. We stood there, ready to challenge him as best we could. Although there was a faint imprecision to his form, he seemed solid enough. The sight of his costume was, moreover, enough to shock me, and as for von Bek, the man gasped aloud.

We were face to face with a staff officer of the Nazi SS! He was engrossed in some papers he carried, but when he looked up it was to stare full in our faces. We said nothing. He frowned, stared again, visibly shuddered and then, muttering to himself, turned away. As he walked in the opposite direction he rubbed his eyes.

Alisaard chuckled. 'There is some advantage to our situation,' she said.

'Why didn't he speak to us?' von Bek asked.

'We are shadows in this world. I have heard of such things frequently, but never experienced it. We have only partial substance here.' She laughed again. 'We are what the Eldren have always been called in Six Realms. We are ghosts, my friends! That man believed himself to be suffering from a hallucination!'

'Will everyone here think the same?' von Bek asked nervously. For a ghost, he was sweating badly. He, better than I, knew the implications of being caught by these brutes.

'We can hope so, I suppose,' she said. But she could not be sure. 'Sight of that man has terrified you, Count von Bek! It is he who should have been afraid of you!'

'I can understand something of this,' I told her. 'And I believe Sepiriz may have found a way to keep his pledge to Count von Bek whilst also having his own purposes served. You said you thought you recognised this place, von Bek. Now do you recall where you may have seen it before?'

He bowed his head, rubbing at his face with his hands. He apologised for his condition, then straightened his back, nodding. 'Yes. A few years ago. A distant cousin brought me here. He was an ardent Nazi and wished to impress me with what he claimed to be the resurrection of ancient German culture. We are in the so-called hidden vaults of the great castle at Nuremberg. We are at the very centre of what the Nazis consider their spiritual stronghold. Of course it would be impossible for an outsider to come here now, but then their numbers were fewer, they were less respectable, they had less power. These vaults are said to be as old as the first Gothic builders, who were here before the Romans. They lie under the main hillside on which the castle is built and were excavated in fairly recent times. When I came here there was much talk of their discovery of the "foundations" of the true Germany. But I was used to that kind of nonsense by then. I found the place disturbing largely because of the value my Nazi relative placed on it. Very soon after I had visited it, I heard, it was forbidden for anyone but the highest of the Nazi hierarchy to come here. Why, I do not know. There were the usual rumours, of Hitler's black magic rites and all that, but I didn't believe them. My theory was that a secret military installation of some kind was being built here. In those days it was still necessary for the Nazis to pretend to be honouring the Armistice agreements.'

'But Sepiriz said the hare would lead us to a cup,' I said in some bafflement. 'What sort of cup are we expected to find in Nuremberg?'

'I am sure we shall discover that in good time.' Alisaard had become impatient with this talk. 'Let us continue. Remember that much still depends on us. We have the fate of the Six Realms in our hands.'

Von Bek looked about him. 'I remember that there was a main vault. A kind of ceremonial chamber which my cousin seemed to believe had some kind of near-mystical importance. He called it the hub of the Germanic spirit. Some such nonsense. I must admit I was almost as bored as I was sickened by his talk. But perhaps that is what we should look for?'

'Do you remember the way?' I asked him.

He considered for a moment and then pointed. 'It is where we were going. That door at the far end. I'm fairly sure that it opens onto the main chamber.'

We followed him now. Two other Nazis passed us, but only one saw us, out of the corner of his eye, and again it was plain he did not trust his vision. If this time was contemporary to von Bek's I could imagine that most of these people were short of sleep and had become fairly used to hallucinations of one kind or another. Indeed, if I had been a member of the SS, I too would probably have been seeing all kinds of ghosts.

Von Bek paused outside a door which was evidently of recent workmanship, though in the Romanesque pattern of much of the rest. 'I think this is the chamber I mentioned,' he said. He hesitated. 'Shall I open it?'

Taking our silence for assent, he reached towards the large iron ring and tried to turn it. It refused to move. He put his shoulder to the oak of the door and pushed. He shook his head. 'It's locked. I suspect there are modern locks on the other side. It hardly gives.'

'Could it be that since our substance is, as it were, somewhat diffuse on this plane, we cannot exert enough force on the door?' I asked Alisaard.

She had only a little knowledge of the phenomenon. She suggested that all we could do would be to wait to see how others opened the door. 'There could be a trick to it.'

Accordingly, we drew ourselves in to a nearby alcove and, hidden in the shadows, watched as various Nazi officers came and went in the corridor. There were no armed soldiers here, which led us to suppose that the Nazis felt themselves secure at this level.

We had waited perhaps an hour and were growing impatient with this plan, when a tall grey-haired man in black-and-silver robes which resembled the uniform of the SS turned the bend in the corridor and advanced towards us. He looked like some kind of officiating priest, for he carried a small box in his hand. Pausing at the door to the chamber, he opened the box and produced a key which he inserted into the lock. This was turned. We heard various tumblers moving. The door swung open. A musty scent came from the chamber beyond.

Immediately we followed quietly behind the grey-haired man. Plainly he was preparing the chamber for some rite, just as a priest might prepare the church. He lit tapers and with these he ignited large candles. The stones of the vault were certainly ancient. The roof was supported by dozens of arches so that it was impossible to tell its actual dimensions. The flames sent shadows flickering everywhere. It was not difficult for us to hide. When the officiary had completed his task he left the chamber, closing and locking the door behind him.

Now we were free to explore. We realised that the place had been designed fairly recently as a temple of some kind. At the far end was an altar. On the wall behind the altar was the black, red and white of the Nazi hooked cross, surrounded by insignia of equal barbarity, versions of ancient Teutonic symbols. Upon the altar itself was a stylised silver tree and beside it the figure of a rampant bull in solid gold.

'This is the stuff which some Nazis wished to put into our churches,' whispered von Bek. 'Pagan objects of worship which they claim are the symbols of a true German religion. They are almost as anti-Christian as they are anti-Semitic. It is as if they hate every system of thought which in any way questions their own mish-mash of pseudo-philosophy and mystical claptrap!' He stared at the altar in disgust. 'They are the worst kind of nihilists. They cannot even see that they destroy everything and create nothing. Their invention is as empty as any inventions of Chaos I have seen. It has no true history, no concrete substance, no depth, no quality of intellect. It is merely a negation, a brutal denial of all Germany's virtues.' Again he was close to tears. Alisaard took his hand. She knew little of what he spoke, but she felt deeply for him.

'Try to consider our purpose here,' she murmured. 'For your own sake, my dear.'

It was the first time I had heard her use such a term. And the stabbing jealousy came again. Oh, how I longed for the consolation of such a woman, someone so close to being my own Ermizhad that I might easily have pretended it was she. But I was able to gather my senses once more. I remembered the madness which had come over me such a short time ago. I was in constant danger from such delusions.

Von Bek was grateful for her concern and her reminder of his purpose here. 'A cup – the Grail – is frequently part of this cult's paraphernalia,' he said. 'But I cannot see it anywhere.'

'The Grail? Weren't you telling me, when we first met, that your family has some connection with the Holy Grail?'

'A legend, that's all. Some of my ancestors were said to have seen it. Others were said to have held it in trust. But the story became too fanciful, I think. One legend even said that we held it in trust not for God but for Satan! I read all this when I was seeking a means of discovering what I thought were old passages to lead me secretly out of Bek without the Nazis realising. That was how I came upon the maps and books relating to the Middle Marches...' He stopped as we heard a sound from the corridor. Swiftly we withdrew into the dark shadows of one of the arches.

The door opened once more, sending a shaft of electric light into the gloom. Three figures now stood there. None was particularly tall and we could not see their faces because of the high, stiffened collars which framed their heads. The cloaks looked like those worn by certain orders of warrior-priests, such as the Knights Templar, and indeed these men carried great broadswords in their gauntleted hands while under their arms were heavy iron helmets which looked as if they had been forged in the Dark Ages.

There was a look of barbaric strength about the three figures which was entirely the result of their chosen costume. As they moved forward towards the altar, closing the door behind them and bolting it, I saw that one was very thin and walked with a limp; another was rotund and wheezed a little as he made his way beneath the arches while the other moved with a peculiar, artificial stiffness, his shoulders set back in the manner of a short man who wished to appear taller than he was. I put out my hand to hold von Bek's arm. He was trembling. I was not surprised.

There could be very little doubt that we were in the presence of three of the twentieth century's arch-villains. The three men were Goebbels, Göring and Hitler and everything I had ever read about their bizarre mystical beliefs, their faith in supernatural portents, their willingness to accept the strangest and most unlikely notions, was here proven at last.

Believing themselves unobserved they began to chant lines from Goethe. In their mouths I felt the words were defiled and horribly abused. As with so many other romantic notions, they perverted the German poet's ideas to their own miserable purpose. They might as easily have chanted the incantations of a Black Mass or defiled a synagogue with their filth, the effect was somehow the same.

> *Allen Gewalten*
> *Zum Trutz sich erhalten,*
> *Nimmer sich beugen,*
> *Kräftig sich zeigen,*
> *Rufet die Arme*
> *Der Götter hierbei.*

'All powers are granted to souls undaunted, when self-reliant, firm and defiant, then shall the gods be helpful to thee!'

They abused these words as they abused all words, all the finest ideas and feelings of the German people, turning them into tools to build their own pathetically inadequate ideology. I would not have been surprised to find the ghost of Goethe standing beside me, ready to take revenge on those who so badly misused his work.

Now Goebbels stepped forward to light two huge red candles on either side of the altar.

I could sense von Bek beside me, barely restraining himself from lunging at these creatures. In silence, I held him back. We had to wait. We had to see what would be revealed to us. Sepiriz had wanted us to come here. He had sent the hare to lead us here. We must wait for the ritual to proceed.

I was astonished how banal their own words were. Full of entreaties to ancient gods, to Wotan and the spirits of Oak and Iron and Fire. The light from the candles illuminated their faces – Goebbels, a mask of twisted ratlike glee, like a bad schoolboy relishing his own wickedness; Göring, plump and serious, plainly believing everything he said and, moreover, evidently drunk or drugged into near-oblivion; and Adolf Hitler, Chancellor of the Third Reich, his eyes dark mirrors, his pale face full of an unwholesome luminosity, willing all this to become reality as, no doubt, he sought to will the rest of the world into acceptance of his hideous insanity.

It was a powerful scene and one which I hope never to witness again. This was human perversity which had little to do with even the worst examples found amongst the followers of Chaos. This was so much closer to my own experience, my own time, that I could sympathise with von Bek who struggled with himself like a chained dog who seeks only to kill, who had seen at first hand the horrors this trio had brought to his nation, whose whole original purpose in linking his fate with mine was concerned with destroying them, of saving his world from their evil.

I looked at Alisaard. Even she sensed the ugly power of these creatures.

'Let the powers of our ancient tribal gods, the gods who lent strength to the conquerors of Rome, be granted to our Germany in these, the hours of her destiny, the hours of decision.' This was Goebbels, plainly not really believing what he was saying, but well aware that both Hitler and Göring were by no means as incredulous. 'Let us be granted the mystical might of the great gods of the Old World, filling us with that dark, natural energy which defeated the enfeebled followers of the Judaeo-Christian would-be conquerors of our ancient land. Let our blood, which is the pure, undiluted blood of those fearless ancestors, flow again through our veins with the same sweet thrill it knew in the days before our honest, guiltless forebears were corrupted by alien, oriental religions. Let Germany know a return to her full, untrammelled selfhood!'

More of this nonsense followed, with von Bek growing increasingly restless and Alisaard and I becoming gradually bored and impatient.

'Now we summon the Chalice, the vessel of our spiritual essence, the Chalice, which is that same cauldron Parsifal sought; the Chalice of Wisdom, which the Christians stole from us and incorporated into their own mythologies, calling it the Holy Grail!' Goebbels chanted, shifting his weight from one foot to the other; fidgeting like some malformed dwarf. 'Now we summon our Chalice so that we might partake of its contents and be filled with the Wisdom we seek!'

These words were echoed now by Hitler and Göring.

'Now we kneel!' cried Goebbels, evidently relishing every moment of his power over the others.

Obediently the two Nazi leaders went down on their knees, leaving only Goebbels standing, his arms spread as he addressed the altar.

'Here in this most ancient of all places, where the Chalice has resided since the beginning of Time, let us be granted a vision. Let us drink that wisdom. Let us be granted the power of our old gods, the knowledge of our old blood, the certainty of our old strength. We must know which way to go. We must know if we are to concentrate our forces on releasing the power of the atom or upon conquering the threat from the East. We must have a sign, great gods. We must have a sign!'

I shall never know if Goebbels was merely putting on a theatrical act for his less sceptical comrades or if he actually believed the rubbish which fell from his thin lips. I do not know if his incantatory speeches had any part in what occurred next, or if von Bek's presence in the vault was the cause of the phenomenon. His family was associated with the Grail, just as I, in all my guises, was associated with the Sword. And that, perhaps, is why fate had drawn us together, since it was a great and important fight we presently fought. How much of a rôle Sepiriz played and how much he knew, I still do not know entirely, but it is obvious his powers of perception and prediction had been used to ensure that we would be in that exact place at an exact time.

For now there began a phase of the ritual which, I could tell, took all three by surprise, most of all Goebbels. We heard the sweetest music fill the vault. A scent like roses accompanied it. The music was almost choral. It was in direct contrast to the dark heaviness of our surroundings, to the pagan paraphernalia of the Nazi hierarchy. And then came a white and blinding light. A light of such loveliness that we could after a moment stare into it without suffering. For at the centre of that white light, the source of the music and the perfume, was a simple chalice, a golden bowl, the like of which I had seen only once before.

This is what Christian legends called the Holy Grail and what the Celts had called the Cauldron of Wisdom. It had existed for all time, under many names, just as the Sword we sought had existed, just as I, the Eternal Champion, had existed. Beyond the radiance I perceived Goebbels, and Hitler, and Göring, all upon their knees now, looking in utter astonishment at the unexpected vision.

I heard Hitler muttering over and over again some mindless oath. Göring seemed to be hiccuping and trying to raise his fat body to its feet. Goebbels had begun to grin, again like an evil schoolboy who had made a wild discovery. He was almost laughing.

'It's true! It's true!' Goebbels screamed now, addressing himself, his own doubts. 'It's true. We have a sign! What shall we do? Must we dispose of the threat from the East before we concentrate our forces on building an atomic bomb or should we attempt to consolidate our gains while putting our energies at the disposal of our scientists? How long can it be before Russia attacks us? Or America and England invade us? What shall we do? Our conquests came so rapidly we are hardly able to think. We need guidance. Are you truly a sign from the old gods? Will they truly direct us onto the right path to ensure Germany's dominance of the world?'

'The cup cannot speak to us, Herr Doktor!' Adolf Hitler was suddenly contemptuous, sensing his Minister's uncertainty in the face of this actuality. 'It must be held. Then the truth will be revealed. Surely that is what it means?'

'No, no, no!' Göring finally lumbered to his feet, panting heavily. His eyes were red, his nose ran, and thin lines of spittle fell from his lips. He drew a great, shuddering breath. 'There is a maiden, surely. A maiden who guards the Grail. A Rhinemaiden, eh? I know. From Wagner, eh?' And he giggled.

I could scarcely believe that these were the men who had done so much to influence the course of my own world's history. It now seemed obvious that all of them were drugged in some way. They were acting like silly children. And yet I suppose I should have realised that it is in the nature of all such creatures to be at heart infantile. Only children believe they can achieve enormous power over the world without paying a price for that power. And the price so often is the sanity of the one who seeks it. In a way these three men were even more like grotesque caricatures of the people they had once been than those poor distorted things of Chaos who had pursued us earlier. Did they realise it? And did that realisation actually further their willingness towards their own corruption and descent into utter madness?

'Yes,' said Adolf Hitler with a display of almost ridiculous self-importance. 'Rhinemaidens. Valkyries. Wotan himself. This chalice merely signifies their presence.'

This ludicrous debate continued for a few moments. I believe they had never wanted this vision. The rituals they performed were a kind of reinforcement of their need to believe in the rightness of their actions. This vault in the depths of the Nuremberg castle, the robes, the incantations, were all a means of revivifying their flagging, drug-dependent energies, a way of making themselves believe in their mystical destiny.

And now it dawned on me that the Grail had not appeared in answer to Dr Goebbels's summoning. It had appeared because we were there – or, specifically, I guessed, because von Bek was there. I looked at my friend. His face was rapt as he gazed upon the Grail. Plainly it had not occurred to him that the golden cup had a special affinity with him, in spite of his family's legends.

Now Hitler stepped forward, his strange little face suddenly sober as he stretched shaking hands towards the Grail. The radiance from the cup emphasised the horrible pallor of his skin, the unhealthiness of his appearance. I could not believe that such a corrupted being would be allowed even to look upon the Grail, let alone touch it.

Those clutching fingers, which already had the blood of millions upon them, reached towards the singing cup. The eyes reflected the glow, glittering like little stones; the moist lips parted, the features twitched.

'You realise, my friends, that this is the source of energy we seek. This is the power which will allow us to defeat every enemy. The Jews as usual look in the wrong direction for the means of creating an atomic bomb. We have found it, here in Nuremberg. We have found it at the very core of our spiritual stronghold! Here is energy to destroy the entire globe – or to build it again in any image we desire! How paltry is the thing they call science. We have something far superior! We have Faith. We have a Force greater than Reason! We have a wisdom beyond mere knowledge. We have the Holy Grail itself. The Chalice of Limitless Power!' And his hands seemed like black claws reaching into that pure light; reaching towards the Grail; about to despoil something of such wonderful holiness I felt sick at the very thought.

But now the Cup was singing louder. It was almost shrieking

its alarm at Hitler's intention. The note changed to one seemingly of warning. Yet still the dictator made to grasp it. His fingers touched the glowing gold.

And Adolf Hitler's shriek was louder than the cup's. He fell backwards. He sobbed. He stared at his fingers. They gleamed black as if the skin had been fused to the bone. Then, like a little child, he put the fingers into his mouth and sat down suddenly on the flagstones of that ancient vault.

Goebbels frowned. He reached out, but more cautiously. Again the Grail sounded its warning. Göring was already retreating, covering his face with his arm, screaming: 'No, no! I am not your enemy!'

In tones of placatory reasonableness Joseph Goebbels said: 'It was not our intention to violate this thing. We merely sought its wisdom.'

He was frightened. He looked around him as if he sought a means of escape, as if he had grown appalled at whatever it was he had accidentally brought there. Meanwhile his master remained upon the floor, sucking his fingers, staring thoughtfully at the Grail and from time to time murmuring something to himself.

Afraid that the cup would now disappear as readily as it had appeared, I reached forward to grasp it. In the light I understood suddenly that they could see me. Hitler in particular had focused on me and was shading his eyes to try to get a clearer view of me. I thought better of taking the cup. I said to von Bek: 'Quickly, man. I am certain that only you will be able to set hands upon it. Take it. It is our key to the Dragon Sword. Take it, von Bek!'

The three Nazis were advancing again, perhaps fascinated by the shadowy figures they saw, still not absolutely certain that what they observed was real.

Now Alisaard stepped between them and the Grail, raising her hand. 'No further!' she cried. 'This cup is not yours. It is ours. It is needed to save the Six Realms from Chaos!' She spoke to them reasonably, having no knowledge of what they represented.

Plainly Hermann Göring at least believed he had seen his

Rhinemaiden. Hitler, however, was shaking his head as if trying to rid it of a hallucination, while Goebbels merely grinned, perhaps convinced and fascinated by his own insanity.

'Listen!' Göring cried. 'Do you recognise it? She's speaking the old High German! We have summoned an entire pantheon!'

Hitler seemed to be biting his lower lip, trying to come to a decision. He looked from us to his fingers and back again. 'What shall I do?' he said.

Alisaard could not understand him. She pointed towards the door. 'Go! Go! This cup is ours. It is what we came here for.'

'I would swear it is High German,' said Göring again, but it was plain he could understand her hardly any better than she could understand him. 'She is trying to tell us the correct decision. She is pointing! She is pointing to the East!'

'Take the cup, man,' I said urgently to von Bek. I had no idea what would happen to us if we remained much longer. The Nazis were not stable. If they fled from the room and locked the door behind them we would be thoroughly trapped. It was even possible we would die in that vault before they dared open it up again.

Von Bek responded to my cries at last. Very slowly he reached out his hands towards that beautiful chalice. And the thing seemed to settle into his palms as if it had always been his. The voice grew sweeter still, the radiance subtler, the perfume stronger. Von Bek's own features were illuminated by the chalice. He looked at once heroic and pure, exactly as the true knights of the Arthurian legends might have seemed to those who accompanied them on their quest for the Grail.

I led both him and Alisaard past the uncertain Nazis and towards the door of the vault. We took the chalice with us. They did not attempt to stop us, yet they were not sure whether to remain or to follow us.

I spoke to them as I would speak to a dog. 'Stay,' I said. 'Stay here.' Alisaard drew back the bolt.

'Yes,' Göring murmured. 'We have our sign.'

'But the Grail,' said Hitler, 'it is to be the source of our power...'

'We shall find it again,' Goebbels reassured him. He spoke dreamily. It seemed to me that the last thing he wanted to do was to set eyes on either the Holy Grail or ourselves ever again. We had threatened the strange power he had over his fellow Nazis, especially over his master, Hitler. Of the three men in that vault, only Goebbels was truly glad to see us go.

We closed the door behind us. We would have locked it if we could.

'Now,' I said, 'we must return as quickly as possible to the room we were first in. I suspect that is the way back to Chaos...'

As if entranced, von Bek continued to hold the cup in his two hands, moving with us, though his attention remained fixed on the Grail.

Alisaard looked at him with a lover's eyes, holding him gently by the arm. And now, when SS men approached us, they fell back, blinded. We reached our destination without difficulty. I turned the handle of the door and it opened onto blackness. Cautiously I entered, then Alisaard followed, leading von Bek, whose eyes had never left the Grail. An expression of rapt sweetness was on his handsome face. For some unknown reason I was faintly disturbed by it.

Then Alisaard had closed the door and the Grail's radiance filled the room. We were all dark shadows in that light.

Yet now I counted three such shadows, besides my own!

The smallest of these now drew its little body closer to mine. He grinned up at me and saluted.

Jermays the Crooked no longer wore his marsh armour. Instead he was clad in more familiar motley. 'I note that you've lately experienced what's common for me.' He bowed. 'And know the power as well as the frustrations of being a ghost!'

I took his offered hand. 'Why are you here, Jermays? Do you bring news of the Maaschanheem?'

'I am presently in the service of Law. I bring a message from Sepiriz.' His face clouded. He added slowly: 'Aye, and news from the Maaschanheem. News of defeat.'

'Adelstane?' Alisaard came forward, pushing loose hair away from her lovely features. 'Has Adelstane fallen?'

'Not yet,' said the dwarf gravely, 'but Maaschanheem is completely reduced. The survivors, too, have rallied to the Ursine stronghold. But now Sharadim sends even the great hulls through the Pillars of Paradise in pursuit of them! No realm is free of invasion. Each is violated. In Rootsenheem the Red Weepers are enslaved, swearing loyalty to Chaos or they are slain. This, too, is true of Fluugensheem and, of course, the Draachenheem. Only Sharadim's forces occupy Gheestenheem now. All humans are defeated. The Eldren and the Ursine Princes continue to resist, but they cannot hold Adelstane much longer, I fear. I have just come from there. The Lady Phalizaarn, Prince Morandi Pag and Prince Groaffer Rolm send you messages of good will and pray for your success. If Sharadim or her creature reaches the Dragon Sword ahead of you, it cannot be long before Chaos breaks through and Adelstane is engulfed. Moreover, the Eldren women will never be reunited with the rest of their race...'

I was horrified. 'But do you know anything of Sharadim and her dead brother?'

'I've heard nothing, save that they returned to Chaos on unfinished business...'

'Then we must try to return to Chaos, also,' I said. 'We have the cup Sepiriz told us of. Now we seek the horned horse. But how can we get back to Chaos, Jermays, can you say?'

'You are here,' said Jermays the Crooked in some surprise, and opening the door he revealed daylight, a rich, exotic smell, dark fleshy leaves and a trail which disappeared into what was apparently a tropical forest.

And, when we had passed through the archway, Jermays had gone, together with the door and any sign of the Nuremberg dungeons.

It was at this point that von Bek lowered the chalice, an expression of dismay on his face. 'I have failed! I have failed! Oh, why did you let me leave!'

'What is it?' cried Alisaard in surprise. 'What is the matter, my dear?'

'I had the opportunity to kill them. I did not take it!'

'Do you think you could have killed them in the presence of this cup?' I asked him reasonably. 'Aside from the fact that you had no weapon?'

He calmed a little. 'But it was my single opportunity to destroy them. To save millions. I surely will not be given a second chance!'

'You have achieved your ambition,' I told him. 'But you have achieved it obliquely, according to the methods of the Balance. I can promise you that now they will destroy themselves, thanks to what happened in that vault today. Believe me, von Bek, they are now as thoroughly doomed as any of their victims.'

'Is this truth?' He looked from me to the chalice. The golden cup no longer glowed, but although it was plain, it still possessed enormous power.

'It is the truth, I swear.'

'I did not know you possessed the power of prediction, Herr Daker.'

'In this case I do. They can last only a short while longer. Then all three will die by their own hands and their tyranny will collapse.'

'Germany and the world will be free of them?'

'Free of their particular evil, I promise you. Free of everything save the memory of their cruelty and barbarism.'

He drew a great, sobbing breath. 'I believe you. Then Sepiriz kept his word to me?'

'He kept his word in his usual way,' I said. 'By ensuring that your ambition and his own coincided. By gaining something which serves his own mysterious ends and which in turn serves ours. All our actions are linked, all our destinies have something in common. An action taken in one plane of the multiverse can achieve a result in quite a different plane, perhaps millennia (and who knows what kind of distance?) apart. Sepiriz plays the Game of the Balance. A series of checks, adjustments, fresh moves, all designed to maintain ultimate equilibrium. He is only one such servant of the Balance. There are several, to my knowledge, moving here and there through all the myriad planes and cycles of the multiverse. Ultimately we cannot any of us know the full pattern or detect a true beginning or an end. There are cycles within cycles, patterns within patterns. Perhaps it is finite, but it seems infinite to us mortals. And I doubt if even Sepiriz sees the whole Game. He merely does what he can to ensure that neither Law nor Chaos can achieve a complete advantage.'

'And what of the Lords of the Higher Worlds?' asked Alisaard, who already knew something of this. 'Can they perceive the entire scheme?'

'I doubt it,' I said. 'Their vision is perhaps in some sense even more limited than our own. Frequently it is the pawn who perceives more than the king or queen, by virtue of having less at stake, perhaps.'

Von Bek shook his head. Quietly he murmured: 'And I wonder if there will ever be a time when all those gods and goddesses and demigods will cease their warring? Will cease to exist, perhaps?'

'There may be such periods in the cyclic histories of the myriad realms,' I said. 'There could be an end to all this, when the Lords of the Higher Worlds and all the machinery of cosmic mystery shall be no more. And perhaps that is why they fear mortals so much. The secret of their destruction, I suspect, lies in us, though we have yet to realise our own power.'

'And do you have a hint of what that power may be, Eternal Champion?' said Alisaard.

I smiled. 'I think it is simply the power to conceive of a multiverse which has no need of the supernatural, which, indeed, could abolish it if so desired!'

And at that point the jungle heaved once, turning itself into a flowing ocean of molten glass which somehow did not burn us.

Von Bek yelled and lost his footing, keeping hold of the chalice. Alisaard grabbed him and tried to help him up. A noisy wind was blowing. I made my way to my companions. Von Bek was up again. 'Use the Actorios!' I cried to Alisaard, who still had the stone in her keeping. 'Find the shadow path again!'

But even as she reached into her purse to find the stone the Grail had begun to sing. It was a different note to the one we had first heard. It was softer, calmer. Yet it held an astonishing authority. And the glassy undulations slowly subsided. The smooth hills of obsidian grew quite still. And we could see a path leading through them. Beyond the path was a sandy beach.

Holding the chalice before him, von Bek led us towards that shore. Here was a force, I realised, far stronger than the Actorios. A force for order and equilibrium able to exert enormous power upon its surroundings. It dawned on me that much of what had happened up until now had been engineered by Sepiriz and his kind. I had already seen that von Bek had an affinity with the Grail the way that I had a similar affinity with the Sword. Von Bek had been needed to find the Grail. And now he was bringing it into this realm, close to the place called The World's Beginning. Was there significance in this action?

We had reached the shore. Above us were grassy dunes and beyond that an horizon. We tramped up to the dunes and stood looking out over a plain which appeared to be without end. It stretched ahead of us, an infinity of waving grasses and wild flowers, without a tree or a hill to break the flatness. There was a subtle scent all around us and, when we turned, the ocean of glass had gone. Now the plain stretched away in that direction also!

I saw a man approaching us. He strode with a leisurely gait through the tall grass. The light wind tugged at his robes. He wore black and silver. I thought for one wild moment that Hitler or one of his henchmen had followed us into this realm. But then I recognised the grey hair, the patriarchal features. It was the Archduke Balarizaaf. Almost as soon as I noticed him he stopped, raising his hand in greeting.

'I will not advance much closer, if you'll forgive me, mortals. That object you carry is inimical to my particular constitution!' He smiled, almost in self-mockery. 'And I must admit I do not welcome its presence in my realm. I have come to strike a bargain with you, if you'll listen.'

'I make no bargains with Chaos,' I told him. 'Surely you understand that?'

He chuckled. 'Oh, Champion, how poorly you understand your own nature. There have been times and there will be others when you know loyalty only to Chaos…'

I refused to be drawn. Obstinately, I said: 'Well, Archduke Balarizaaf, I can assure you that I possess no such loyalty at this moment. I am my own creature, as best I can be.'

'You were always that, Champion, no matter what side you seemed to serve. That is the secret of your survival, I suspect. Believe me, I have nothing but admiration…' He coughed, as if he had caught himself in a moment of discourtesy. 'I respect all you say, Sir Champion. But I am offering you the chance to alter the destiny of at least a full cycle of the multiverse, to change your own destiny, to save yourself, perhaps, from all the agony you have already known. I assure you, if you pursue this present course, it will bring you further pain, further remorse.'

'I have been told it will bring me at least some peace and the possibility of being with Ermizhad again.' I spoke firmly. I resisted his arguments, for all their apparent sense and certainty.

'A respite, nothing more. Serve me, and you will possess almost everything you desire. Immediately.'

'Ermizhad?'

'One so like her you would come to forget any difference. One even more beautiful. Adoring you, as no man has been adored before.'

I laughed at him then, to his evident surprise.

'You are truly a Lord of Chaos, Archduke Balarizaaf. You have no real imagination. You believe that all a mortal seeks is the same power as you possess. I loved an individual in her complexity. I have come to understand that even more since I have suffered the delusions this place imposes upon the human brain. If I cannot know again the woman I loved, I want no substitute. What do I care if

I am adored by her or not? I love her for herself. My imagination delights not in control of her, but in the fact that she exists. I had no part in her existence. I merely celebrate it. And I would celebrate it for eternity, though I be parted from her for eternity. And if I am reunited, even for a brief while, that is more than justification for the agony I suffer. You have stated, more concisely than I, what Chaos stands for, Lord Archduke, and why I resist you!'

Balarizaaf shrugged and seemed to accept my statement in good humour. 'Then perhaps there is something else you would want from me? All I ask of you is that you take up the Dragon Sword in my name. The Eldren women are virtually finished. Sharadim and Flamadin rule the Six Realms of the Wheel. If you serve me in this one small thing, so that I may consolidate this little fragment of the multiverse under my control, then I will do everything I can to return you to your Ermizhad. The game is over here, Sir Champion. We have won. What more can you do? Now you have the opportunity to serve yourself. Surely you cannot wish to be Fate's fool for ever?'

The temptation was great and yet I had little difficulty resisting him the moment I looked at Alisaard's desperate face. It was from loyalty to the Eldren that I fought, that I played this turn of the game. If I denied that loyalty, then I denied all right to being united again with the woman I loved. So I shook my head, saying instead to Count Ulric von Bek, 'My friend, would you be so good as to take the chalice a little nearer to the Archduke so that he may inspect it?'

And with a shriek, a ferocious, malevolent and terrific noise which denied all the sweet reason of his earlier tone, the Archduke Balarizaaf fell backwards, his very substance beginning to change as von Bek approached him. His flesh seemed to boil and transmogrify on his bones. In a matter of moments he revealed a thousand different faces, very few of them even remotely human.

And then he had gone.

I fell to my knees, shuddering and weeping. Only then did I realise what I had been resisting, how much I had been tempted by his invitation and his promises. My strength had gone out of me.

My friends helped me up.

The cool wind flowed through the grass and it seemed to me that this was not a production of Chaos at all. This was, temporarily at least, the result of the Grail's influence. Once more I was impressed by the cup's power to bring order even in the heart of Chaos!

Alisaard was speaking softly to me. 'It is here,' she said. 'The horned horse is here.'

Trotting towards us through the grass, its head lifted as it uttered a whinny of greeting, came a beast whose coat flashed sometimes silver, sometimes gold. From its forehead there grew a single horn. Like the Grail it bore a strong resemblance to something from my familiar earthly mythology. Alisaard was smiling in delight as the beast came up to her and nuzzled her hand.

From behind us a voice came. It was a familiar voice, but it was not the voice of the Archduke Balarizaaf.

'I will take the cup, now,' it said.

Sepiriz stood there. There was something in his eyes which suggested pain. He reached out his great black hand to von Bek. 'The cup, if you will.'

Von Bek was reluctant. 'It is mine,' he said.

Sepiriz displayed a rare flash of anger. 'That cup belongs to nobody,' he murmured. 'That cup is its own thing. It is a singular object of power. All who attempt to own it are corrupted by their folly and their greed. I had not expected you to say such a thing, Count von Bek!'

Chastened, von Bek bowed his head. 'Forgive me. Herr Daker says that you made it possible for me to initiate the self-destruction of the Nazis.'

'That is so. It is now woven into the pattern of their destiny, by your courageous actions here and by what occurred when you sought out the Grail. You have achieved much for your own people, von Bek, I can assure you.'

And with a great sigh, von Bek handed Sepiriz the Grail. 'I thank you, sir. Then what I meant to accomplish is done.'

'Aye. If you wish, you can return to your own plane and your own time. You have no obligation to me.'

But von Bek looked tenderly at Alisaard and he smiled at me. 'I think I will stay to see this thing through, win or lose. I have a mind to see how this particular phase of your game ends, Lord Sepiriz.'

Sepiriz seemed pleased with this, though his eyes still spoke of some secret fear. 'Then you must follow this horse,' he said. 'It will lead you to the Dragon Sword. The forces of evil are gathering even greater strength now. It will not be long before the Realms of the Wheel collapse completely, reduced to the stuff of Chaos. For this particular realm is stabilised, to the extent that it is stable at all, by those which surround it. If they are consumed, then pure Chaos will be the result. A mass of horrifying obscenity at which these Nightmare Marches merely hint. Nothing will survive in anything like its previous form. And you will be trapped within it for ever. Forever prey to the whims of a Balarizaaf a thousand times more powerful than he is at present!' He paused, drawing in a great breath. 'Do you still elect to remain here, Count von Bek?'

'Naturally,' said my friend, with characteristic and almost comical aristocratic aplomb. 'There are still a few Germans in the world who understand the nature of good and evil and where their duty lies!'

'So be it,' said Sepiriz. He folded the chalice into his robe and was gone.

Not knowing what we must face when we got there, we followed the unicorn. Already the influence of the Grail was fading. The grass first turned a peculiar shade of yellow, then of orange, then of red.

The unicorn now waded across a shallow lake of blood.

Waist-deep in this, and shivering with horror, we pressed on.

It was as if we walked through the blood of all those who had died thus far in service of Sharadim's lust for a perverse and immortal power.

Chapter Three

THAT HORRIBLE LAKE stretched in all directions, filling all our horizons. Save for the unicorn leading the way and the three of us, there were no other occupants, it seemed, in the entire Realm of Chaos.

For some reason I could not rid my mind of the idea that we were, indeed, wading through the blood of countless murdered souls. It seemed to me, as time went on, that perhaps this was not blood shed by Sharadim or the Lords of Chaos. It could as easily be blood which I had spilled as the Eternal Champion. I had slaughtered Humanity. I had been responsible for the deaths of so many others, in all my myriad guises. I felt that even this vast plain of blood was only a fraction of it.

Again my two friends had linked arms, like lovers. I was slightly ahead of them, still following the unicorn. I began to see reflections in the red liquid. I saw my face as John Daker, as Erekosë, as Urlik Skarsol, as Clen of Clen Gar. And the action of that cool wind seemed to bring words with it.

'You are Elric, whom they shall call Womanslayer. Elric, who betrayed his race, just as Erekosë betrayed his race. You are Corum, killed by a Mabden woman, whom you loved. Remember Zarozinia? Remember Medhbh. Remember all those you betrayed and who betrayed you. Remember all the battles you fought. Remember Count Brass and Yisselda. You are the Eternal Champion, eternally doomed to fight in all mankind's wars and in all the Eldren's wars, just and unjust. What meaningless actions are yours! The noble become the ignoble. The impure become the pure. All is malleable. All changes. Nothing remains constant in the schemes of Man or Gods. Yet you go on down the aeons, through plane after plane of existence, allowing yourself to be used as a pawn in a pointless cosmic game…'

'No,' I told myself, 'there is a point to it. I must do positive penance *in my remorse. I must redeem myself. And in that redemption I shall discover peace. And in peace, at last, I shall find my Ermizhad. I shall know some small freedom…'*

'You are Ghardas Valabasian, Conqueror of the Distant Suns, and you have no need of anyone…'

'I am the Eternal Champion, bound by cosmic chains to a duty still undone!'

'You are M'v Okom Sebpt O'Riley, Gunholder of the Qui Lors Venturers, you are Alivale and you are Artos. You are Dorian, Jeremiah, Asquiol, Goldberg, Franik…' And the list of names went on and on and on. They rang in my ears like bells. They beat in my head like drums. They clashed like weapons of war. Weapons of war, filling my eyes with blood. A million faces assailed me. A million murdered creatures.

'You are the Eternal Champion, doomed always to fight, never to rest. There is no end to the battle. Law and Chaos are relentless enemies. There can never be reconciliation. The Balance demands too much of you, Champion. You grow weak in its service…'

'I have no choice. It is what I am destined to do. And all of us must fulfil our destinies. There can be no choice. No choice…'

'You can choose whom you fight for. You can rebel against that destiny. You can alter it.'

'But I cannot abolish it. I am the Eternal Champion, and I have no doom save this doom, no life save this life, no pain save this pain. Oh, Ermizhad, my Ermizhad…'

The rhythm of my wading legs seemed to be the same as the rhythm of the words in my head. I was speaking aloud now. 'I am the Eternal Champion and I pursue a Cosmic Doom. I am the Eternal Champion and my destiny is set for me, my destiny is war and death, my destiny is fear…'

The voice which spoke to me was my own voice. The voice which answered me was my own voice. There were tears streaming from my eyes, but I brushed them aside. I waded on. I waded through that terrible lake of blood.

I felt a hand on my shoulder. I shook it off. 'I am the Eternal Champion. I have no life, save that. I have no means to alter what

I am. I am the Champion. I am the hero of a thousand worlds and yet I have no true name of my own...'

'Daker! Daker, man! What is happening to you? Why are you mumbling so?' It was von Bek's voice, distant and agitated.

'I am pursued by destiny. I am the toy of fate. The Chaos Lord spoke truth in that. Yet I shall not weaken. I shall not serve his cause. I am the Eternal Champion. My remorse is complete, my guilt is so great, my doom is already set...'

'Daker! Take hold of yourself!'

But I was lost in my monomaniacal self-absorption. I could think of nothing but the dreadful irony of my predicament. I was a demigod in the Six Realms, a legendary hero throughout the multiverse, a noble myth to millions. Yet all I knew was sadness and terror.

'My God, man, you are going thoroughly mad! Listen to me! Without you Alisaard and I are completely lost. We have no means of knowing where we are or what we are supposed to do. The unicorn leads us to the sword. Which only you among us can bear, just as only I could take hold of the Grail!'

But the war-drums continued to sound in my ears. My mind was filled with the clash of metal. My heart was consumed by melancholy at my own dreadful fate.

Von Bek's voice broke in again. 'Remember who you are, man! Remember what you are doing! Herr Daker!'

I saw only blood ahead of me, blood behind me, blood on every side.

'Herr Daker! John!'

'I am Erekosë, who slew the human race. I am Urlik Skarsol who fought against Belphig. I am Elric of Melniboné and I shall be so many others...'

'No, man! Remember who you really are. There was a time you told me about. A time when you had no memories of being the Champion. Was that some kind of beginning for you? Why are you still called John Daker? That is your first identity. Before you were called, before they named you Champion.'

'Ah, how many long cycles of the multiverse have passed since then.'

'John Daker, pull yourself together. For all our sakes!' Von Bek was yelling, but his voice sounded still very far away.

'*You are the Champion who bears the Black Sword. You are the Champion, Hero of the Thousand-Mile Line...*'

The blood was lapping about my chest. Somehow I was sinking deeper and deeper into it. I was about to drown in all that blood I had spilled.

'Herr Daker! Come back to us. Come back to yourself!'

I could no longer be sure of any identity. I had so many. And yet were they all the same? What a poor, unfulfilled life it was to fight so. I had never wanted to fight. I had never known the sword until King Rigenos called me as Defender of Humanity...

The blood was at my chin. I grinned. Why should I care? It was only fitting.

A cold, small voice spoke to me. 'John Daker, this will be your only real betrayal, if you betray that identity. That which is truly yourself.' It was von Bek speaking again. I shrugged him off.

'You will die,' I heard him say, 'not because of your human weakness but because of your inhuman strength. Forget that you were the Eternal Champion. Remember your ordinary mortality!'

The blood lapped against my lips. I began to laugh. 'See! I drown in this concrete reminder of my own guilt!'

'Then you are a fool, Herr Daker. We were wrong to trust you as a friend. And so were the Eldren women. And so were the Ursine Princes. And so was Ermizhad foolish to trust you as a lover. It was John Daker she loved, not Erekosë, the monstrous tool of Fortune...'

The blood was in my mouth. I began to spit it out. I rose gasping. I had been on my knees. The level of the lake had not risen. It was I who had fallen. I stood up, staring blankly for a moment at Count von Bek and Alisaard. They were holding me, shaking me.

'You are John Daker,' I heard him say again. 'It was John Daker whom she loved. Not that relentless sword-swinger!'

I coughed. I could still hardly understand him. But then gradually it dawned on me that what he said had meaning. And as the meaning grew clearer, I thought that perhaps he spoke the truth.

'Ermizhad loved Erekosë,' I said.

'She might have called you that, for that was the name King Rigenos gave you. But the one she really loved was John Daker, the ordinary, decent mortal who was caught up in a web of hatred and appalling destiny. You cannot change what happened to you, but you can change what you have become, John Daker! Don't you see that? *You can change what you have become!*'

It seemed to me at that moment these were the wisest words I had heard for many a year. I wiped the liquid from my face. It was not blood at all. I shook the drops from my eyes, from my hands.

Ahead of us, the unicorn waited patiently. I realised that once again I had lost my grip on reality. But now it was clear I had somehow lost a little of my real identity in all my cosmic adventurings. I had been discontented as John Daker. My world had seemed grey to me. But in some ways it had been richer than all the wild, fantastical spheres I had visited...

I reached out and shook von Bek by the hand. I was smiling at him. 'Thank you, my friend. You are the best comrade, I think, that I have ever had.'

He, too, was smiling. The three of us stood there in that crimson lake and we hugged one another while overhead the sky began to boil and smoulder and turn as angry a red as the waters below.

Then it seemed to us that the ocean of blood rose up to meet the falling sky, forming a single vast wall of glittering crimson crystal.

We looked around us for the unicorn, but it had vanished. Now ahead was nothing but the vast crimson cliff. And then I remembered the vision we had been shown at Morandi Pag's. And staring into that wall I saw it, embedded there, like an insect in amber, a green-black blade in which a tiny fragment of yellow flickered.

'There it is,' I said. 'There is the Dragon Sword!'

My friends were silent.

It was only then that I realised the liquid had solidified completely. Our legs were as perfectly set in crystalline rock as was the sword. We were trapped.

I heard the sound of hoofbeats. The rock in which my legs were encased trembled as the horses grew closer. Twisting my body round I looked over my shoulder.

Two figures rode towards us on identical horses. On bright, black horses. They were dressed in gaudy finery, matching surcoats and cloaks, matching swords and banners. And one was Sharadim, Empress of the Six Realms. And the other was her dead brother, Flamadin, who sought to drink my soul and make it his own.

Now, standing at the base of the great red cliff, the Archduke Balarizaaf, again in the guise of a sober patrician, folded his arms and waited. He was smiling. He disdained to look at me. He called instead to Sharadim and Flamadin. 'Greetings, sweet servants. I have kept my promise to you. Here are three little morsels, stuck like flies on a paper, for you to do with as you will!'

Flamadin threw back his gaunt, grey head and a hollow laugh escaped it. His voice was, if anything, more lifeless than when I had last heard it, on the edge of the volcano in Rootsenheem. 'At last! I shall be complete again. And I have learned to be wise. I have learned that it is folly to serve any master save Chaos!'

I looked for a sign of real intelligence in that poor, dead face. I saw nothing.

Yet I still felt that I looked into my own features. It was almost as if Flamadin were a parody reminding me what I as the Eternal Champion was in danger of becoming.

I felt sorry for the creature. But at the same time I was deeply afraid.

The two slowed their horses and advanced towards us at a walk. Sharadim looked at Alisaard and she smirked. 'Have you heard, my dear? The Eldren women are driven from their own realm. They hide like rats in the warrens of the old bearfolk.'

Alisaard looked back at her with a firm eye. 'That news was offered by your lackey Armiad. When I last saw him he had grown to resemble the pig he always was. Do I detect a similar coarsening in your own features, my lady? How long can it be before your affinities with Chaos begin to show?'

Sharadim glared and urged her horse on. Von Bek smiled at Alisaard. Plainly she had struck a good blow. He said nothing, merely ignoring the two riders as best he could. Sharadim snorted and rode towards me.

'Greetings, Sir Champion,' she said. 'What a world of deception it is! But then you would know that best of all, since you posed as my brother Flamadin. Do you know they already have a legend in the Six Realms, amongst those few who remain unkilled or uncaptured. They think Flamadin, the old Flamadin of the stories, will return to help them against me. But Flamadin is now at last at one with his sister. We are married. Had you heard? And we rule as equals.' She smiled. It was a dreadful and it was an evil smile.

Like von Bek I chose to ignore her.

She rode up to the crystal wall and she peered into the rock. She licked her lips. 'That sword shall soon be ours,' she said. 'Are you looking forward to holding it in your two hands, brother?'

'My two hands,' said Flamadin. His eyes were empty. He was staring upwards at nothing. 'My two hands.'

'He is hungry,' Sharadim said in pseudo-apology. 'He is deeply hungry, you see. He lacks his soul.' And she looked with vicious, smiling cruelty directly into my eyes. I felt as if knives had been driven into my sockets. Yet I forced myself to stare back at her. I thought: *I am John Daker. I was born in London in 1941 during an air raid. My mother's name was Helen. My father's name was Paul. I had no brothers. No sisters. I went to school...*' But I could not remember where I went to school first. I tried to think. I had an image of a white, suburban road. We had moved after the Blitz, to South London, as I recalled. To Norwood, was it? But the school? What was the school's name?

Sharadim was puzzled. Perhaps she could tell that my mind was elsewhere. Perhaps she was afraid I had some hidden power, some means of escape.

She said: 'I suppose we need waste no more time, Lord Balarizaaf.'

'Your creature,' he said, 'it must contain the Champion's essence, if only for a short time. Failing that, Sharadim, you must keep your word to me, and take the Sword yourself. That was your bargain.'

'And your bargain, my lord, should I be successful?' For a little while, at least, she had some kind of power over this god.

'Why, that you should be elevated into the pantheon of Chaos. To become one of the great Sword Rulers, replacing one who has been banished.'

Balarizaaf looked at me, as if he regretted my failure to accept his offer. It was obvious he would prefer me to do what was needed. 'You are a powerful enemy,' he said reminiscently, 'in any guise. Do you remember, Lord Corum, how you fought my brothers and my sisters? Do you remember your great War against the Gods?'

I was not Corum. I was John Daker. I refused all other identities.

'You have forgotten my name, I believe, my lord,' I said. 'I am John Daker.'

He shrugged. 'Does it matter what name you choose, Sir Champion? You could have ruled a universe by any of your many, many names.

'I have only one,' I said.

This forced him to hesitate. Sharadim, too, had become curious as to my meaning. Thanks to my recent experiences and the help of my friends I was able to speak with authority. I was determined to consider myself a single individual and an ordinary mortal. I felt it was the key to my own salvation and that of those I loved. I looked into Balarizaaf's eyes and I peered into the abyss. I turned my gaze from him to Sharadim and saw in her face the same emptiness which possessed the Lord of Chaos. Flamadin's poor, blank stare was as nothing compared to what I beheld in their faces.

'You will not deny, I hope, that you are the Eternal Champion,' said Sharadim sardonically. 'For we know that you are.'

'I am only John Daker,' I said.

'He is John Daker,' said von Bek. 'From London. That is a city in England. I do not know what part of the multiverse, I fear. Perhaps you would be able to discover that, Lady Sharadim?' He was reinforcing me and I was grateful to him.

'This is a nonsensical pastime,' Sharadim said, dismounting from her horse. 'Flamadin must feed. Then he must take the Sword. Then he can strike the blow which will set Chaos free upon the Six Realms!'

'Should you not wait, my lady,' said von Bek coolly, 'so that your retainers should witness this. You promised them a spectacle as I recall...'

'Those cattle!' She was dismissive. She grinned as she directed her remarks at Alisaard. 'They proved themselves useless here. I have thrown them against Adelstane. There they are happy, running at the walls. Soon those who survive will be having their way with your kinswomen! Now, Flamadin, dear, dead brother. You will dismount. You remember what you must do?'

'I remember.'

I kept my eyes upon him as he got off his horse and began to shamble towards me. I saw Alisaard hand something to von Bek, who was closest to me. Sharadim had not noticed. Her whole attention was on the resurrected corpse of the brother she had murdered. As he drew closer I detected the stink of corruption about him. Was this the body my soul was expected to inhabit?

Von Bek's hand touched mine. I opened my palm and accepted what he gave me. It was the pulsing warmth of the Actorios stone. It was the only shield we had against sorcery in this realm.

Flamadin's dead fingers reached my face. I threw up my arms to defend myself, still unable to pull free of the solid rock encasing my lower legs. There was a peculiar, meaningless grin on Flamadin's lips, more like a rictus of death than an expression of humour. The breath from his mouth was foul.

'Give me your soul, Champion. I must eat it and then I shall be whole again...'

Unthinkingly I brought up the Actorios and smashed it against that half-rotten forehead. It seemed to sear into the flesh. There was a stink of burning. Flamadin merely stood where he was, making a kind of gulping noise. There was a blazing mark in his head where the stone had struck him.

'What's this? What's this?' shrieked Balarizaaf in a voice of frustrated malevolence. 'There is no time for delays. Not now! Hurry. Do what you must do!'

Again Flamadin reached out for me. I prepared myself to strike a second blow, but then it occurred to me to try something else. With the writhing Actorios I drew a circle around myself in the red crystal.

'No!' cried Sharadim. 'Ah, the Actorios. He has an Actorios! I did not know!'

The rock around me began to bubble and heave, giving off a pinkish vapour. I pulled myself free and stood upon the solid crystal. I threw the Actorios to von Bek, telling him to imitate what I had done, and I began to run towards the crimson wall. Behind me lumbered Flamadin while Sharadim screamed: 'Lord Balarizaaf! Stop him! He will reach the Sword!'

Balarizaaf said reasonably: 'It matters not to me which one of you reaches it, so long as it is used for my purposes.'

This gave me pause. Was I inadvertently falling into a trap set by the Lord of Chaos? I turned. My friends were running towards me, but Flamadin was ahead of them. His fingers again reached for my face. 'I must feed,' he told me. 'I must have your soul. No other will do.'

This time I did not have the Actorios. I pushed at his cold body, trying to keep him away. But with every touch I felt something of myself ebbing out, being drained by him. I tried to move back, but I had reached the crystal wall.

'Champion,' said Flamadin greedily. His eyes had begun to take on a semblance of life. 'Champion. Hero. I shall be a hero again… I shall have what is my right…'

Even as I fought with him my energy was being sucked from me. My friends reached us. They tried to pull him back, but he was stuck to me like a leech. I heard Sharadim laughing. Then Alisaard pressed the Actorios against Flamadin's throat. He gave a great choking roar and tried to throw her off him. Fire seemed to burn my own neck. I was horrified by the degree of symbiosis I now experienced. I was sobbing as I still struggled to free myself from him.

Flamadin's ruined flesh was glowing with my life. I felt my vision dimming. There was a flickering sight of myself from Flamadin's viewpoint.

'I am John Daker!' I cried. 'I am John Daker!'

I managed to restore something of myself by this reminder. But wherever, in her panic, Alisaard applied the Actorios, I still burned.

At last I fell to the ground, completely weakened. My friends tried to drag me further away from the Chaos creatures, but I begged them to stop Flamadin. Even now he was flattening himself against the crystal near where the sword was embedded. I could see that inch by inch he was himself being absorbed by the rock. Then he had gone completely into it. I felt that I, too, was wading through the crimson crystal. I saw my own hand reaching out for the hilt of that great black-and-green sword with its rune-carved blade, its flickering yellow flame.

Meanwhile, through John Daker's eyes, I saw Balarizaaf smiling. He was content with what was happening and made no move to interfere.

Only Sharadim was uncertain. She could not tell how much of my substance had been sucked into the doppelgänger. My own point of view shifted back and forth. Part of the time I was Flamadin, reaching still for the great blade. Part of the time I was John Daker being helped up by my friends who looked wildly about them for some means of escape, or at least a weapon of defence. We had the Actorios. It occurred to me that neither Balarizaaf nor Sharadim was overeager to move against us while we had that stone.

Inch by inch Flamadin waded through the crystal. I was in intense pain. I murmured over and over again that I was John

Daker and only John Daker. Yet my decrepit fingers reached for a sword and proved that I was also Flamadin. I groaned. I wanted to vomit. There was a kind of whispering echo in my head which I came to believe was Flamadin's mind struggling for life, recalling some argument which perhaps his sister had tried to instil in him before she resorted to murder.

The Sword can cure the evil at source... The Sword can bring harmony... The Sword is an honourable weapon... But not in the wrong hands... The Sword used in defence is actively good...

'No!' I cried, addressing whatever vestiges of the original Flamadin remained. 'It is a deception. The Sword is still a sword. The Sword, Flamadin, is still a sword! Touch that blade, Prince Flamadin of the Valadek, and you are condemned for ever to limbo...'

I heard Sharadim urging him on. With John Daker's eyes I saw her take a step further towards the crystal cliff. Flamadin's hands were almost upon the Sword's hilt now.

Within that ghastly body I struggled to hold back the hand. But there was a desperate will at work. What had been Flamadin was greedy for life, greedy for the rewards it had been promised.

All around me the red light glowed. All around me were shards, fragments, reflections. I thought I could see a thousand versions of myself.

I was weakening.

'I am John Daker,' I moaned. 'I am only John Daker...'

Flamadin touched the Sword. The blade moaned a little, as if in recognition. He clasped the hilt. It did not resist him. It did not give him pain to touch it. Now I was almost entirely Flamadin, exulting in this power, this strange version of life I had achieved.

I drew the Sword up. I displayed it to those who peered through the crystal, watching me.

As John Daker I was slowly dying as the last of my soul began to merge with Flamadin's.

I wrenched myself from that mind. I was whimpering and crying as I reached out for the Actorios which Alisaard still held. 'I am John Daker. This is my reality.' The same hand which enfolded the

Dragon Sword now also enfolded the Actorios. I heard screaming. It was myself. It was Flamadin. It was John Daker. I was both of them. I was being torn into two.

Now John Daker made one huge effort to pull his soul free from the body of Flamadin. I recalled my childhood, my first job, my holidays. We had rented a thatched cottage in Somerset, not far from the sea. Which year had that been?

Flamadin was weakening a little. His viewpoint became hazy while John Daker's grew stronger. In recalling my common humanity, by rejecting the rôle of hero, I had the chance to free myself from the burden which had fallen upon me. And in freeing myself, I might possibly help others.

I was sure that John Daker was winning the struggle, but now Sharadim was joining in the fight, and Balarizaaf, too. I heard them urging Flamadin to use the Sword, to do what he had sworn to do.

I fought against him. But his arm swung back. I tried to stop him, even then. His arm came forward, the Dragon Sword slicing into the stuff of the crystal wall. He was carving a gateway for Chaos!

I moaned in my weakness as John Daker. Having dragged my soul back from Flamadin, now I sought to return, so that I could put a halt to what he did.

The Dragon Sword rose again. It struck the crystal wall again. Rosy light flared. Rays burst in all directions. And through the rent made by the Sword I saw darkness. And in the darkness was another world. A world in which I glimpsed white towers gleaming. A familiar world.

They had planned this exactly! The gateway into Chaos would be the gateway into the vast Adelstane cave, where Sharadim's army laid siege to the last defenders of the Six Realms!

I shouted out my horror. I heard Sharadim's laughter. I turned, as John Daker, and saw Balarizaaf seem to swell to twice his height, an expression of sublime satisfaction on his features.

'He is cutting an entrance into Adelstane!' I told my friends. 'We must stop him.'

Whatever now animated Flamadin was not my soul. I had reclaimed it all. But even as my strength returned I saw the red crystal flow and dissipate, filling the sky again, turning to liquid again. And that unholy radiance was pouring through into the gigantic cavern.

Without thinking, I ran after Flamadin, still seeking to stop him. But he had passed through the narrow gateway he had carved. I saw him striding to where, on the floor of the cave, Sharadim's armies were camped. There were stone huts now and tents, and here and there were the massive Maaschanheemer hulls, pressed into service against Adelstane.

Alisaard and von Bek were with me as we clambered down rocks to the cave. Flamadin was shouting something to the warriors, many of whom had plainly been touched by Chaos already. They had the warped, bestial features I had seen on Armiad and the others.

'For Chaos! For Chaos!' cried Flamadin. 'I have returned. Now I shall lead you against our enemies. Now we shall know true victory!'

I half-believed that Flamadin was animated by the Sword itself!

The armies were both dazzled and baffled by the crimson light suddenly flooding into the cavern. Sharadim and Balarizaaf were not yet through. I knew that soon the gap must widen further and allow the whole of Chaos to come through, to infect, mile by mile, gentle Barganheem and, eventually, the whole of the Six Realms. And I could see no way now of stopping this encroachment.

'WE ARE THROUGH! OH, WE ARE THROUGH!'

This was Sharadim's voice behind me. She had remounted her black charger. She had drawn her own sword. She was riding after us.

Flamadin, flailing and stumbling like a scarecrow, was making for the nearest hull. A terrible stink came off the vessel. The smoke which curled from its chimneys was if anything even more foul than before.

My only thought was to reach him before Sharadim caught up

with him, to wrest the Dragon Sword from him and try to do what I could to save those who survived in Adelstane. I knew my friends shared my ambition. Together we began to climb up the hull, choking back our nausea at the stench. All around us now the hosts of Chaos were beginning to stir, grunting, yelling, pointing. Then, as Sharadim rode out of the crimson glare, a great cheer went up.

I looked towards Adelstane and her fiery ring, which still held, her delicate lacy white towers, her superb beauty. I could not let this be destroyed, not while I still had life. As the three of us reached the rails we saw on the main deck the Baron Captain Armiad himself, lifting his own sword to salute Flamadin. Whether by chance or by destiny, we had arrived back on the *Frowning Shield*!

So engrossed in their triumph were they that they did not see us come aboard. We were horrified at the condition of the vessel. The few inhabitants who remained were in a wretched state, evidently enslaved to do the work of war. Men, women and children were in rags. They looked starved. They looked beaten. Yet I saw more than one face which held hope when they saw us.

We were able to run for the cover of one of the houses. Almost immediately we were joined by a bony wretch whose dirty features still bore the traces of youth and beauty. 'Champion,' she said, 'is it you? Then who is that other?'

It was Bellanda, the enthusiastic young student we had first met aboard this vessel. Her voice was cracked. She looked close to death.

'What is wrong with you, Bellanda?' whispered Alisaard.

The young woman shook her head. 'Nothing specific. But since Armiad declared war upon those who opposed him we have been made to toil almost without rest. Many have died. And we of the *Frowning Shield* are considered fortunate. I still cannot believe how swiftly our world changed from one ruled by justice to one dominated by tyranny...'

'Once the disease takes hold,' said von Bek gravely, 'it spreads so rapidly that it can rarely be checked in time. I saw this happen to my own world. One must be forever vigilant, it seems!'

I watched Armiad lead Flamadin to the stairway of the central deck. Flamadin continued to hold the Dragon Sword above his head, displaying it to all. I looked across the floor of the cavern and saw Sharadim riding towards the hull, calling out to Flamadin, who ignored her. He was enjoying his own strange triumph. The corpse's features were twisted in a hideous parody of mirth. He swung up from the central deck into the rigging of the mainmast, so that he could be seen by all those gathered below.

I knew that I had a few minutes to get to Flamadin before his sister. Without further consideration, I began to climb, planning to use the network of spars and ropes to reach him, just as I had once used them as a shortcut when moving about the ship.

Hand over hand I went up the spiderweb of greasy ropes, then swung myself closer to the central deck.

Flamadin stood upon a platform now so that he could again display the Dragon Sword. His poor, ruined flesh seemed about to fall from his bones. The gesture, as he raised the blade, was almost pathetic.

'Your hero,' he cried in that bleak, dead voice of his, 'has returned.'

Even as I worked my way towards him I could not help but see him as a telling parody of what I myself had become. I did not like the picture. I continued, while I crawled along a spar over the heads of the gathered warriors, to remind myself that I was John Daker. I had been a painter of some description, I seemed to recall, and had had a studio overlooking the Thames.

Flamadin sensed me even as I made to drop down on him. His corpse's eyes looked up. He had the appearance of a startled child whose new toy was about to be taken from him.

'Please,' he said softly. 'Let me keep it a little while. Sharadim wants it, too.'

'There's no time,' I said.

I let myself go. I dropped beside him. Holding the Actorios before me I reached for the Dragon Sword. I could see the yellow flame flickering at its heart, behind the runes.

'Please,' begged Flamadin.

'In the name of what you once were, Prince Flamadin, give me that blade,' I said.

He winced away from the Actorios.

I heard a commotion below. It was Armiad. 'There are two of them. Two the same! Which is ours?'

My hand closed on his wrist. He was far weaker now than he had been. The Sword's strength no longer filled him. Indeed, it was as if the blade called back its energy and took what was left of Flamadin's also.

'This sword is not evil,' he said. 'Sharadim told me it is not evil. It can be used for good...'

'It is a sword,' I told him. 'It is a weapon. It was made to kill.'

A crooked, miserable smile came on his corrupted features. 'Then how can it ever do good...'

'When it is broken,' I said. And I turned his wrist.

And the Dragon Sword fell free.

Armiad and his men were climbing up the rigging. All were heavily armed. I think they understood at last what was happening. I looked back into the cavern. Sharadim was almost at the hull and there was an army following her.

A peculiar sobbing sound came from Flamadin as he watched me retrieve the Dragon Sword. 'She promised me my soul back, if I bore the blade for Chaos. But it was not my soul, was it?'

'No,' I said, 'it was mine. That was why she kept you alive. In that manner you deceived the Dragon Sword.'

'Can I die now?'

'Soon,' I promised.

I swung around. Armiad's men had reached the platform. The Dragon Sword was shouting in my two hands. In spite of all I had gone through, all I had decided for myself, I found that I was joining in its song, that I was filled with a wonderful wild glee.

I lifted the blade. I sheared through the necks of the first two raiders. Their headless bodies fell onto others below them and all tumbled down to the distant deck in a tangle of gouting blood and jerking limbs.

With the sword in one hand I reached for a trailing rope and swung out over my antagonists, slashing at them as I went. I slid down to the deck, behind Armiad, who had been one of the last into the rigging.

'I believe you wished to settle an account with me,' I told him, laughing.

He looked in horror at my sword, at my face. He mouthed something as he shrank back against the mast. I stepped forward, then placed the tip of the Dragon Sword into the wood of the deck. 'I am here, Baron Captain. Settlement is due, I'm sure you'll agree.'

Reluctantly, his pig snout twitching, he returned to the deck. All his men were watching now. Their bestial faces were intent on the scene.

Suddenly there was a monstrous roar from behind me. I glanced over my left shoulder. The crimson light was flaring still brighter. The gap was growing wider. I saw movement behind it: huge grotesque figures mounted on even stranger steeds. Then I had to return my gaze to Armiad.

Sword in hand, he reluctantly advanced. I thought I could hear a kind of whimpering coming from his fluttering snout.

'I'll kill you quickly,' I promised him. 'But kill you I must, my lord.'

And then I felt a heavy weight land squarely on my back. I fell sprawling, the Dragon Sword flying from my grasp. I struggled to get up. I heard Armiad give a great snort of startled glee. I felt cold lips on my neck. I smelled foetid breath.

Looking up I saw Armiad and his men begin to close around me. I tried to reach the Dragon Sword but someone kicked it away.

And Flamadin, still straddling my back, said through rotting lips: 'Now I shall feed again. And you, John Daker, will die. I shall be the only hero of the Six Realms.'

Chapter Four

O N FLAMADIN'S ORDERS, Armiad and his men seized me.
With his strange, awkward movements my doppelgänger
walked towards the Dragon Sword and picked it up again.

'The Sword will drink your soul,' he said, 'and then it will in
turn invigorate me. I and the Sword shall be one. Immortal and
invincible. I shall know the admiration of the Six Realms once
more!'

He seemed to wince as he grasped the blade, staring at me
almost with regret. It was impossible for me to understand what
terrible, cold fragments of a soul still moved him, how much of
the original darling of the Worlds of the Wheel remained. His
sister had been able to stay the progress of his body's corruption,
but now he was disintegrating before my eyes. Yet he hoped for
life. He hoped for my life.

Armiad grunted with pleasure. His clammy hands now held
my arm. 'Kill him, Prince Flamadin. I have so longed to be witness
to his death, ever since he first impersonated you and brought
upon me the mockery of my fellow captains. Kill him, my lord!'

On the other side of me was something I dimly recognised as
Mopher Gorb, Armiad's Binkeeper. Now his nose had elongated
and his eyes had grown closer together so that he resembled some
kind of dog. His grip on my arm was tight. Saliva flecked his muzzle. He, too, was enjoying my anticipated death.

Flamadin drew back his arm until the point of the Dragon
Sword was a few inches from my heart. Then, with a kind of sob,
he made to thrust.

The entire cavern was a mass of noise and moving warriors, all
bathed in that same crimson light. Yet I heard one sound above
the others. A sharp, precise crack.

Flamadin grunted and paused. There was an inflamed hole in his forehead. From it oozed a substance which might once have been blood. He lowered the Dragon Sword. He turned to look behind him.

There stood Ulric von Bek, Count of Saxony, with a smoking Walther PPK .38 in his hand.

Flamadin tried to stagger towards this new assailant, the Dragon Sword still half raised. Then he had fallen to the deck and I knew the final vestiges of life had deserted him.

Yet Armiad and his men still held me. Mopher Gorb produced a long knife, plainly intending to slit my throat. He gave a strange little grunt and dropped the knife. Another wound blossomed, this time in the side of Mopher Gorb's head.

Armiad dropped his hold on my arm. The rest of the ghastly crew began to back away. But now Alisaard had leapt forward, snatching up Mopher Gorb's sword, and she was thrusting, thrusting at the Baron Captain, who defended himself both ferociously and well against the Ghost Woman, but was no match either for her grace or her skill with a sword. She had pierced his porcine heart in moments, then turned her attention on the others. I, too, fought with a borrowed sword. There were too many between me and Flamadin's corpse. I fought as best I could, trying to reach it. And von Bek, too, had a sword. The three of us were at last standing together.

'Bellanda kept your gun for you, I see!' I cried to von Bek.

He grinned. 'I now don't regret asking her to look after it. I thought I'd never see it again! Unfortunately, there were only two shells left.'

'Well used,' I said gratefully.

Suddenly we realised that we were surrounded entirely by dead men. All Armiad's disgusting crew were defeated. A few wounded crawled here and there, attempting to escape. Von Bek uttered a cheerful yell of triumph, but this was swiftly cut short by a scream from Bellanda for, making an impossible leap on her great black stallion, there came the figure of Sharadim, landing full on the central deck, the hoofs pounding like battle-drums above the corpse of her brother, the Dragon Sword still in his hand.

I began to run then, trying to reach the blade before she could dismount. But with a great billowing of her cloak she was off the back of the snorting beast and had reached down to wrest the Dragon Sword from her brother's deathgrip.

As she took hold of the Dragon Sword, she gasped with pain. She was not meant to hold it. Only by an effort of will did she lift it. Yet lift it she did, and she maintained her hold upon it.

I continued to be struck by her extraordinary beauty. As she carried the Dragon Sword back towards her horse, apparently unconscious of any who observed her, I thought she resembled more than any woman I had ever seen the goddess it was her ambition to become.

I stepped forward. 'Princess Sharadim! That sword is not yours to carry!'

She had reached her horse now. She looked round slowly, frowning in irritation. 'What?'

'It is mine,' I said.

She put her lovely head on one side and stared at me. 'What?'

'You must not take the Dragon Sword. Only I have the right to bear it now.'

She began to climb into her saddle.

I could think of no other action but to take out the Actorios and hold it up before me. Its pulsing, writhing light made my hand glow black, red and purple. 'In the name of the Balance, I claim the Dragon Sword!' I told her.

Her face clouded. Her eyes blazed. 'You are dead,' she said slowly, through gritted teeth.

'I am not. Give me the Dragon Sword.'

'I have earned this blade and all it stands for,' she told me, pale with rage. 'It is mine by right. I have served Chaos. I have given the Six Realms to Lord Balarizaaf to do with as he will. At any moment he and all his kind will come riding through the gateway

I, by my actions, created. And I shall receive my reward. I shall be made a Sword Ruler with dominion over my own realms. I shall be immortal. And as an Immortal I shall hold this sword as the sign of my power.'

'You will die,' I said simply. 'Balarizaaf will kill you. The Lords of Chaos do not keep their promises. It is against their nature to do so.'

'You are lying, Champion. Go away from me. I have no use for you as yet.'

'You must give me that sword, Sharadim.'

The Actorios pulsed with stronger light. It was almost wholly organic as it sat in the palm of my hand.

I stood beside her now. She clasped the blade to her. I could tell that everywhere it touched it gave her intense pain, but she ignored the pain, believing that soon she would never experience physical agony again.

I could see the little yellow flame flickering back behind the runes carved into the black metal.

The Actorios began to sing. It sang in a small, beautiful voice. It sang to the Dragon Sword.

And the Dragon Sword murmured a response. That murmur became a strong, powerful moan, almost a shout.

'No! No! No!' cried Sharadim. Her skin, too, reflected the peculiar, writhing light. 'Look! Look, Champion! Chaos comes! Chaos comes!' And laughing she swept the blade round so that the Actorios was struck cleanly from my hand. I dived towards it, but she was swifter. She had raised the blade, yelling in her pain as it burned her hands.

She meant to destroy the Actorios.

My first instinct was to dash forward and save it at all costs, and then I remembered something Sepiriz had told me. I stepped back.

She grinned at me, the loveliest wolf in the world. 'Now you realise there is no defeating me,' she said.

She brought down the blade with incredible ferocity, striking accurately at the shining stone which lay there, pulsing like a living heart.

She screamed as the blade connected with the Actorios. It was a scream of complete triumph which turned, all in the space of a second, to bafflement and then to anger and then to nothing but agony.

The Actorios was shattered. It burst into fragments. It exploded in all directions.

And each fragment now contained an image of Sharadim!

Each fragment of the Actorios was bearing part of Sharadim away into limbo. She had thought to make herself all things to all people. Now it was as if each persona had separated and was imprisoned in a splinter of that peculiar stone. Yet Sharadim herself still stood there, frozen in her final act of destruction. Gradually her expression of enraged pain changed to one of terror. She began to shiver. The Dragon Sword moaned and wailed in her hands. Her flesh seemed to boil on her bones. All that astonishing beauty was vanishing.

Von Bek, Bellanda and Alisaard made their way towards me but I gestured for them to go back. 'There is great danger still to come,' I shouted. 'You must go to Adelstane. Tell the Eldren and the Ursine Princes what is happening here. Tell them they must wait and watch.'

'But Chaos comes!' said Alisaard. 'Look!'

The figures I had seen in the redness were larger than before. Grotesque riders led by Balarizaaf himself. The Lords of Hell were riding to claim their new kingdom.

'To Adelstane. Hurry!' I told them.

'But what will you do, Herr Daker?' asked von Bek. His face was full of concern for me.

'What I must. What has become my duty.' I thought he would understand those words.

Von Bek inclined his head. 'We shall await your presence in Adelstane.' It was clear that all three of them thought themselves as good as dead.

The huge rent in the cosmic fabric was growing wider still. And the black riders waited patiently for it to become large enough to admit them.

I stopped and picked up the Dragon Sword. It made a small, sweet sound, as if recognising a kinsman.

All around the blade the fragments of the Actorios were whirling, like planets around a sun. In some of those fragments as they went by, I saw one of Sharadim's many faces staring out, with the same expression of horror she had worn just before her body collapsed.

I looked down at her shrivelled corpse. It lay across that of her brother. One had represented the evil of the world, the other the good. Yet both had been defeated by pride, by ambition, by a promise of immortality.

I watched as von Bek, Alisaard and Bellanda disappeared over the side of the hull. The camps of Sharadim's army were in confusion now. They seemed to be awaiting their leader's command. There was a fair chance that my friends could reach Adelstane unhindered. They had to go there. They could not, I knew, survive what was yet to come.

Now I lifted up the sword and I set my mind into a particular pattern. I remembered Sepiriz telling me what I must do when the Actorios was shattered, what power I could call upon. I could hear them chanting in the back of my brain. I could hear their despairing voices as I had heard them a thousand times in my dreams.

'We are the lost, we are the last, we are the unkind. We are the Warriors at the Edge of Time. And we're tired. We're tired. We're tired of making love...'

'NOW I RELEASE YOU! WARRIORS, I RELEASE YOU! YOUR MOMENT HAS COME AGAIN. BY THE POWER OF THE SWORD, BY THE DESTRUCTION OF THE ACTORIOS, BY THE WILL OF THE BALANCE, BY THE NEED OF HUMANKIND, I SUMMON YOU. CHAOS THREATENS. CHAOS SHALL CONQUER. YOU ARE NEEDED!'

Now, on the far side of the cavern, above the wonderful white city of Adelstane, I saw a cliff. And on that cliff was lined rank upon rank of men. Some rode horses. Some were on foot. All were armed. All were armoured. All stared fixedly towards me as if in sleep.

'*We are the shards of your illusions. The remains of your hopes. We are the Warriors at the Edge of Time...*'

'WARRIORS! YOUR TIME HAS COME. YOU MAY FIGHT AGAIN. ONE MORE BATTLE. ONE MORE CYCLE! COME! CHAOS RIDES AGAINST US!'

I ran to Sharadim's stallion which panted and snorted near the corpse of its mistress. It did not resist when I climbed into the saddle. It seemed glad of a rider. I turned it towards the rail of the hull and galloped forward, leapt clear over the side of the vessel and landed on the rocky floor of the cave where Sharadim's soldiers came forward in a flood of flesh and metal to cheer me. I had thought them my enemies. I was baffled for a moment until I realised with a kind of ironic delight that they knew only of Flamadin and Sharadim. They thought me their Empress's brother and consort! They were waiting for me to lead them against Adelstane in the name of Chaos.

I looked backward. The huge crimson wound was swelling larger and larger. The grotesque black shapes were growing.

I looked towards Adelstane.

'Warriors!' I cried. 'Warriors, to me!'

The Warriors at the Edge of Time had awakened. They were pouring down from the cliffs above Adelstane, running along invisible paths towards me.

'Warriors! Warriors! Chaos comes!'

There was a wind howling now. A crimson wind. It blew upon us all.

'Warriors! Warriors of the Edge! To me! To me!'

The stallion reared under me, hoofs flailing. It uttered a great snort of pleasure as if it awaited this moment, as if it lived only to gallop into battle. The Dragon Sword was alive in my right hand.

It sang and it glowed with that dark radiance I had known so many times before, in so many different guises. And yet it still seemed to me that there was a quality in it which was not quite the same as any I had known before.

'Warriors! To me!'

They came in their thousands. In all manner of war-gear. With every strange weapon it was possible to conceive. They marched and they rode and their faces had come to life, as if they, too, like the stallion, understood only battle.

I felt that I, too, was never more truly alive than when I bore my blade in war. I was the Eternal Champion. I had led vast armies. I had slaughtered whole races. I was the very epitome of bloody conflict. I had brought it nobility, poetry, justification. I had brought it heroic dignity...

Yet within me a voice insisted that this must be the last such fight. I was John Daker. I did not wish to kill in any cause. I wished merely to live, to love and to know peace.

The Warriors of the Edge were forming ranks around me. They had unsheathed their many weapons. They were yelling and animated. They knew joy. And I wondered if each of these had once been like me. Were they all aspects of heroic warriors? All aspects, even of the Eternal Champion? Certainly many of their faces had a certain familiarity for me, so much that I dared not look at them too closely.

The Princess Sharadim's soldiers were now in confusion. The Warriors of the Edge turned hard, killers' eyes upon them, yet they did nothing. They awaited my orders.

Now one of Sharadim's generals came riding through the ranks. He was very fine in his dark blue armour, his plumes, his spiked helm, his full, black beard.

'My lord Emperor! The allies you promised us. Are they all assembled?' His face was bathed in crimson light. 'Does Chaos come to aid us in our destruction? Is that our sign?'

I drew a breath and then I sighed, poising my sword. 'Here is your sign,' I said. I swung the blade in a single movement which sheared off his head so that it fell with a heavy clanking to the ground. Then I cried out to the assembled army which Sharadim had raised to conquer the Six Realms.

'There is your enemy! In fighting Chaos you stand some small chance of salvation. If you stand against us, you will perish!'

I heard a babble of questions but I ignored them. I turned my black stallion towards the widening crimson wound. I lifted my sword in a sign to all who would follow me.

And then I was charging at full gallop towards the Lords of Chaos!

There was a sound behind me. A mighty yell which could have been a single voice. It was the battle-shout of the Warriors at the Edge of Time. It was an exultation. They had come to life. They had come to the only life they knew.

Now through the crimson gateway the massive black figures rode in. I saw Balarizaaf, powerful in armour which flowed about his body like mercury. I saw a creature with the head of a stag, another which resembled a tiger, while many others bore no likeness at all to anything which had ever walked or crept upon any realm I had visited. And from them came a peculiar stink. It was both pleasant and horrible. It was both warm and cold. It had an animal quality about it, yet it could also have been the smell of vegetation. It was the pure stink of Chaos, the odour which legends said rose always out of Hell.

Balarizaaf reined in his scaly steed as he saw me. He was stern. His voice was kindly. He shook his huge head and when he spoke his voice was a booming reverberation. 'Little mortal, the game is over. The game is over, and Chaos has won. Do you still not understand? Ride with us. Ride with us, and I will feed you. I will let you have creatures to play with. I will let you remain alive.'

'You must go back to Chaos,' I said. 'It is where you and your kind belong. You have no business here, Archduke Balarizaaf. And she who made a bargain with you is dead.'

'Dead?' Balarizaaf was disbelieving. 'You killed her?'

'She killed herself. Now all the different women who were

Sharadim, who deceived so many of her kind, are scattered through limbo for ever. It is a harsh fate. But it is deserved. There is no-one left to welcome you, Archduke Balarizaaf. If you enter this realm now, you disobey the Law of the Balance.'

'How do you see that?'

'You know it is true. You must be called, whether there be a gateway or no.'

Archduke Balarizaaf made a noise in his huge chest. He put a hand the size of a house to his face. He scratched his nose. 'But if I enter, what can stop me? The invitation was there. A mortal prepared the gateway. Those realms are mine.'

'I have an army,' I said. 'And I wield the Dragon Sword.'

'You spoke of the Balance? It is a fine point, I think. I do not recognise your logic. And I believe that the Balance would not recognise it. What does it matter to me if you have raised an army? Look at what I bring against you.' And he swept his monstrous arm to show not only his immediate liegemen, lesser nobles of Chaos, but a seething tide which could have been animals or humans or neither, for their form was hardly constant. 'This is Chaos, little Champion. And there is more.'

'You are forbidden to cross into our realm,' I said firmly. 'I have summoned the Warriors of the Edge. And I wield the Dragon Sword.'

'So you persist in telling me. Am I to praise you? Or how must I be impressed? Little mortal, I am an Archduke of Chaos and I was summoned by mortals to rule their worlds. That is enough.'

'Then it seems we must do battle,' I said.

He smiled. 'If that is what you wish to call it.'

I pointed my Dragon Sword forward. Again came the great shout from my back.

I was riding resolutely into the teeth of Chaos. There was nothing else I could do.

The rest was battle.

It was like all the battles I had ever fought made into one. It seemed to last for eternity. Wave upon wave of belching, whining, barking, squealing, stinking things were thrown against me; some with weapons, some with teeth and claws, some with imploring eyes which begged a mercy they could never return. And yet, all about me, like an impervious wall of hardened flesh, of muscle and bone which seemed tireless, I saw my allies, the Warriors of the Edge. Each of these fought as skilfully as I. And some fell, engulfed by the creatures of Chaos. But there were more to replace them.

The tide of Chaos came, wave after wave, upon us. And wave after wave it was repulsed. Moreover, some of the humans fought with us. They fought with a will, glad to be no longer in Shara-dim's service. They died, but they died knowing that they had, in the end, not betrayed their own kind.

The Lords of Chaos had kept back from all this. They disdained to fight mere mortals. Yet it grew plain, as the hours wore on, that their creatures could not defeat us. It was as if we had been destined for this one great fight, trained in every arena of war the multiverse could provide. And I knew that in some sense this was my last fight, that if I succeeded in this, I might know peace, if only for a while.

Slowly the ranks of Chaos were growing thinner. My blade was encrusted with their lifestuff (it did not seem the same as blood) and my arm grew so tired I felt it would fall from its socket. My horse bled from a hundred different cuts and I, too, had received several wounds. But I hardly noticed them. We were the Warriors at the Edge of Time and we fought until we were killed. There was nothing else for us to do.

Now Archduke Balarizaaf came riding through his forces again and he was not disdainful. He did not laugh. He was grim and he was fierce. He was angry, but he no longer mocked me with his gaze.

'Champion! Why fight so hard? Call a truce and we'll discuss terms.'

This time I turned my horse towards him. I summoned energy for myself and my sword. And I charged.

I charged into the face of the Archduke of Chaos. I flew, my horse's hoofs galloping on air, straight towards that huge and supernatural bulk. I was weeping. I was shouting. I wanted only to destroy him.

Yet I knew I could not kill him. It was, indeed, likely that he would kill me. I did not care. In a fury at all the terror he had brought to the Six Realms, at all the misery he had sown and would always sow, at the wretchedness he had created wherever his ambitions took him, I hurled myself and my sword at his face, aiming at his treacherous mouth.

From behind me I heard again that great exultant battle-shout of the warriors. It was as if they recognised what I did and encouraged me, celebrating my action, honouring whatever it was that moved me to attack the Archduke.

The point of the Dragon Sword touched that suddenly opened maw. I felt for one moment that I must be swallowed by him, falling into his red throat.

The saddle of my horse was no longer under me. I sailed directly at Archduke Balarizaaf's head.

And then it had vanished and I felt earth beneath my feet. The crimson wound was closing before me. I looked and saw the piled corpses of our enemies and the corpses of our allies. I saw the bodies of ten thousand warriors who had died in that battle whose memory was even now fading from my mind, it had been so terrible.

I turned. The Warriors of the Edge were sheathing their weapons, wiping blood from their axes, inspecting their wounds. They had expressions of regret upon their faces, as if they had been disappointed, as if they wished to continue the fight. I counted them.

There were fourteen still alive. Fourteen together with myself.

The crimson wound in the cosmic fabric was healing rapidly. It was now hardly large enough to accept a man. And through it stepped a single figure.

The figure paused, looking back to watch the gap close and vanish.

It was suddenly cold in the cavern of Adelstane. The fourteen warriors saluted me, then marched into the shadows. They were gone.

'They rest until the next cycle,' said the newcomer. 'They are allowed battle only once. And those who die are the fortunate. The others must wait. That is the fate of the Warriors at the Edge of Time.'

'But what is their crime?' I asked.

Sepiriz removed his black-and-yellow helm. He made a small gesture with his hand. 'Not a crime exactly. Some would call it a sin, perhaps. They lived only to fight. They did not know when to stop.'

'Are they all former incarnations of the Eternal Champion?' I asked him.

He looked thoughtfully at me, sucking his upper lip. Then he shrugged. 'If you like.'

'Surely you owe me some more substantial explanation, my lord,' I said.

He took me by the shoulder. He turned me towards Adelstane and we began to walk over stone slippery with the blood of all those dead thousands. Here and there the wounded were tending to one another. The hulls and the tents and the stone shanties were full of the dying now.

'I owe you nothing, Champion. You are owed nothing. You owe nothing.'

'I can speak for myself,' I said. 'I have a debt.'

'Would you not say it is fully paid now?'

He stopped. He opened his mouth and he laughed at my confusion. 'Paid now, Champion, eh?'

I bowed my head in acceptance. 'I am weary,' I said.

'Come.' He walked on through all those corpses, all that ruin. 'There is work still to do. But first we must take news of your victory into Adelstane. Are you aware of what you achieved?'

'We fought back the encroachment of Chaos. Have we saved the Six Realms?'

'Oh, yes. Of course. But you did more. Do you not know what it was?'

'Was it not enough?'

'Possibly. But you were also responsible for banishing an Arch-duke of Chaos to limbo. Balarizaaf can never rule again. He challenged the Balance. Even then he might have won. But your act of courage was decisive. Such an action contains so much that is noble, so much that is powerful, so much that affects the very nature of the multiverse, that its effect was greater than any other. You are truly a hero now, Sir Champion.'

'I have no wish to be a hero any longer, Lord Sepiriz.'

'And that is doubtless why you are such a great one. You have earned respite.'

'Respite? Is that all?'

'It is more than is allowed to most of us,' he said in some aston-ishment. 'I have never known it.'

Chastened, I let him lead me through the fiery ring of Adels-tane and into the arms of my dear friends.

'The fight is over,' said Sepiriz. 'On all of the planes, in all of the realms. It is over. Now the healing and the changing must begin.'

Chapter Five

'WE SHALL KNOW a better peace now,' said Morandi Pag, 'for those who remain in the Six Realms. There must be building, of course, and replanting. But rather than withholding our ancient knowledge and retreating into our caves, we, the Ursine Princes, will do our best to help. So, too, shall each of the races give their special skills to the common good.'

The white city of Adelstane was tranquil once more. The remains of Sharadim's army, who had fought with us against Chaos, had returned to their different worlds, determined to ensure that their future would never again allow the rise of a tyrant. Never again would they be deceived by such as Sharadim into making war upon one another. New councils were being formed, drawn from all the races, and the time of the Great Massing would not now be merely a time for trading.

Only the Lady Phalizaarn and her Eldren women had not returned to Gheestenheem which, we had heard, had been razed by Sharadim's warriors. They were making specific preparations for their own departure.

Bellanda of the Maaschanheem had gone back with her people, aboard the *Frowning Shield*, promising us that if we should ever return to the Maaschanheem we would experience better hospitality than any we had previously known. We bade her farewell with special affection. I knew that if she had not kept the gun in trust for von Bek all those months I for one would probably not be alive.

Alisaard, Phalizaarn, von Bek and myself were guests in the comfortable study which the Ursine Princes used for their own conferences and gatherings. Again the clouds of incense filled the fireplace and drifted throughout the room as, discreetly, the bear-like people did their best to disguise their distaste for our smell.

Morandi Pag had already declared his decision not to return to his sea-crag, but to work with his fellows towards the improvement of communication between the Six Realms.

'You have done much for us, you three,' said Groaffer Rolm with a wave of his silken sleeve, 'and you, Champion, will be remembered in legends, that is certain. Perhaps as Prince Flamadin. For legends have a habit of mingling, transforming and becoming something new.'

I inclined my head, saying politely: 'I am honoured, Prince Groaffer Rolm, though for my own part I would be glad to see a world free of heroes and legends. Especially heroes such as myself.'

'I do not believe that is possible,' said the Ursine Prince. 'All one can hope for is that the legends celebrate what is noble in the spirit, what is honourable in deeds and ambitions. We have known ages when the legends have not celebrated what is noble, when the heroes were self-serving, clever creatures who improved their own situation against the interests of the rest. Those cultures are usually ones which are close to decay and death. Better to praise idealism than denigrate it, I think.'

'Though idealism can lead to acts of unspeakable evil?' asked von Bek.

'That which is valuable is always in danger of being devalued,' said Morandi Pag. 'That which is pure can always be corrupted. It is our business to find the balance...' He smiled. 'For do we not echo, in our domestic actions, the war which rages between Chaos and Law? Moderation is, in the end, also survival. But this is what we learn in middle age, I suppose. Sometimes the proponents of excess must triumph, sometimes the proponents of restraint must win. That is the way of things. That is what maintains the Balance.'

'I do not believe I have much of a care for the Cosmic Balance,' I said, 'nor for the machinations of Law and Chaos. Nor for gods and devils. I believe that we alone should control our own destinies.'

'And so we shall,' said Morandi Pag. 'And so we shall, my friend. There are many cycles yet to come in the great history of the multiverse. In some of them the supernatural shall be banished, just as you banished Archduke Balarizaaf from this world. But our will and our nature is such that at other times those gods, in different guises, will return. The power is always ultimately within ourselves. It depends how much responsibility we are prepared to take…'

'And that is what Sepiriz told me, when he said I should know respite?'

'It seems so.' Morandi Pag scratched at his grizzled fur. 'The Knight in Black and Yellow travels constantly between the planes. Some even think he has the power to travel through the megaflow, through Time, if you like, between one cycle and the next. Few have such great power or such terrible responsibility. Occasionally, it is said, he sleeps. He has brothers, according to what I have heard, all of whom share with him the duty of maintaining the Balance. But I understand little more of his activities, for all my own studies in the matter. Some say he even now sows the seeds for the salvation of the next cycle as well as for its destruction, but perhaps that is too fanciful a notion.'

'I wonder if I shall see him again. He said his work was done here, and that mine was almost done. Why should there be such a peculiar affinity between certain people and certain objects? Why is it that von Bek can handle the Grail and I can handle the Sword and so on?'

Morandi Pag made a grunting noise at the back of his throat. He put his muzzle into the fireplace and took a deep breath of the fumes, then he sat back in his armchair. 'If certain schemes are set at certain times, if certain functions are required to ensure the survival of the multiverse, so that neither Law nor Chaos shall ever gain full command of it, then perhaps certain creatures must be matched to certain powerful artefacts. After all, every race has legends concerning such things. These affinities are part of the pattern. And the maintenance of the pattern, of Order, is of paramount importance.' He cleared his great throat. 'I must look into this further. It will be an interesting way of passing my final years.'

The Lady Phalizaarn said gently, 'The time for leaving has

come, Prince Morandi Pag. There is one last great action to be taken, then this particular stage in the eternal game is completed. We must go to rejoin the rest of our people.'

Morandi Pag inclined his head. 'The ships we hid for you are ready. They await you in our harbour.'

Von Bek, Alisaard and I were the last to go aboard the slender Eldren vessels. We remained, almost reluctantly, making our final farewells to the Ursine Princes. Not one of us said anything of meeting again. We knew it was never likely to be. And so it was with a special regret that we parted.

We three stood on the high aft deck of the final ship to sail out of the harbour, leaving the massive cliffs of Adelstane behind us, sailing beyond the whirlpool crags where Morandi Pag had lived for so long.

'Goodbye!' I cried as I waved to the last of that noble race. 'Goodbye, dear friends!'

And I heard Morandi Pag call to me. 'Goodbye, John Daker. May your rest be all you desire.'

We sailed for a day until we came at length to a place where great beams of light pierced the clouds and stroked the rolling sea: rainbow light forming a circle of great pillars, a kind of temple. We had come again to the Pillars of Paradise.

The triangular sails of the Eldren vessels filled with wind as, one by one, the clever sailors drove their ships between the columns. One by one they vanished until we were the last ship remaining.

Then Alisaard took the helm. She flung back her head and shouted her song. She was full of joy.

It seemed again to me that Ermizhad stood there, as she had stood beside me in all our adventurings so long ago. But the man whom this woman loved was not Erekosë, the Eternal Champion. It was Count Ulric von Bek, nobleman of Saxony, exile from the Nazi obscenity, and that he returned her love was clear. I no longer knew jealousy. That had been an aberration brought about by Chaos. But I knew a deep loneliness, a sadness which could never, no matter what befell me, be dismissed. Oh, Ermizhad, I mourned for you then as the Pillars of Paradise drew us inwards and upwards and out into the glorious, sun-filled seas of Gheestenheem.

We sailed now, our convoy of ships, towards Barobanay, the old capital of the Ghost Women.

The women who crowded the decks and worked the ships were still dressed in their delicate armour of engraved ivory, though they no longer wore the helmets which had once disguised and protected them by means of instilling fear in potential enemies. When we sailed at last into the burned and wasted harbour and looked upon the black ruins of that town which had once been so lovely, so secure and comfortable and civilised, many of those women wept.

Yet the Lady Phalizaarn stood upon the pitted stones of the quay and she addressed the Eldren women. 'This is a memory now. It is a memory we must always keep. But we should not grieve, for soon if the promise of our legends is true, we shall at last be going to our true home, to the land of our menfolk. And the Eldren will become strong again, in a world which is theirs, in a world which cannot be threatened by savage barbarians of any ilk. We begin a new story for our race. A glorious story. Soon, just as we are united with our men, the she-dragon will be freed and come together with her male. Two strong limbs of the same body, equally powerful, equally tender, equally able to build a world even lovelier than the one we knew here. John Daker, show us the Dragon Sword. Show us our hope, our fulfilment, our resolution!'

At her orders I pushed back my cloak. There on my hip was the sheathed Dragon Sword, where it had been scabbarded since the fight outside Adelstane. I unhooked the scabbard from my belt and held the Dragon Sword up for all to see, but I would not draw it. In my debates with the Lady Phalizaarn we had agreed that I should draw the blade again only once. And then, I swore, I should never draw it again.

If I could, I would have handed it over to the Announcer Elect and let her do what was needed. But it was my fate to be the only one who could handle the poisonous metal of that strange sword.

The Eldren women were disembarking, streaming into the broken buildings, the ashes, the fire-darkened timbers, of Barobanay.

'Go!' cried Lady Phalizaarn. 'Bring us that which we have kept throughout our long exile. Bring us the Iron Round.'

Von Bek and Alisaard came to stand beside me on the quay. We had already discussed what had to be done. Morandi Pag had offered to try to help von Bek return to his own world, but he had elected to stay with Alisaard, just as I had once been the only human to remain with the Eldren, with my Ermizhad. They linked arms with me, offering me comfort, aiding me in my resolution, for I had made a pact with myself, with John Daker, and I was determined not to break it.

Soon the Ghost Women, their ivory smeared with black dust, came staggering from out of the ruins. They had with them a large oak chest, borne on poles slipped through brass loops set into brass bands binding the wood. It was an ancient chest, plainly, and spoke of a different age altogether. It was like nothing else the Eldren owned.

To one side of me the sunshine continued to glint on the blue ocean; to the other the breeze stirred the smoky ashes of the razed town. On the quay itself, and on their slender ships, the Eldren women gave me their full attention as the oak chest was opened and out of it was taken the thing they called the Iron Round.

It was a kind of anvil. It was almost as if a section had been cut from a tree trunk and placed upon a pedestal, then the whole turned into heavy, pitted iron. It was like a small table, yet I could see from its surface that generations of smiths had worked their metal upon it.

Into the base of the Iron Round were carved runes and these runes resembled many of those I had seen upon the blade of the Dragon Sword.

They brought the anvil and they placed it at my feet.

Each of those faces held expectation and hope. This was what they had lived for all those generations, breeding as best they could from the poor stock provided them, resorting to an artificial way of life which they found distasteful, yet maintaining their dream that one day the cosmic mistake which had cost them their menfolk and their future would be corrected. It was for this day, too, that I had striven. All else had been secondary. Out of love for the race which had adopted me, the woman I had loved and who had loved me with such intensity and depth, I had sought out the Dragon Sword.

'Unsheath it, Champion,' cried Lady Phalizaarn. 'Unsheath your sword so that we may all look upon it for the last time. Unsheath that power which was created to be destroyed, which was forged for Chaos to serve Law, which was made to resist the Balance and to carry out its destiny. Unsheath your powerful blade. Let this be the last act of that hero called the Eternal Champion. In redeeming us, let him also be redeemed. Unsheath the Dragon Sword!'

And I took the scabbard in my left hand. And I took the hilt of the sword in my right. And slowly I slid the sheath away so that black radiance began to pour out of the green-black metal carved with so many runes, as if the sword's entire story was written there.

In the bright air of the Gheestenheem, before the assembled women of the Eldren, I held the blade up high. I let the scabbard fall. I took the Dragon Sword in my two hands. I raised it so that all might look upon it, upon the dark, living metal, upon the little yellow, flickering flame within.

And the Dragon Sword began to sing. It was a wild, sweet song. It was a song so ancient it spoke of an existence beyond Time, beyond all the concerns of mortals and of gods. It spoke of love and hate and murder, of treachery and desire. It spoke of Chaos and of Law and of the tranquillity of perfect balance. It spoke of the future, the past and the present. And it spoke of all the myriad millions of worlds of the multiverse, all the worlds it had known, all the worlds which remained to be known.

And then, to my astonishment, the Eldren women also gave voice. They sang in perfect harmony with the blade. And I found that I, too, was singing, though I knew nothing of the words which left my lips. I had never believed myself capable of such wonderful song.

The chorus built and built. The Dragon Sword throbbed with an ecstasy of its own, an ecstasy reflected in the faces of all who witnessed this ceremony.

I lifted the blade above my head. I cried out, yet I did not know what it was I said. I cried out, and my voice held all my own dreams, all my longings, all the hopes and fears of an entire people.

I was trembling with exquisite delight, with awe and with something akin to fear, as I began to bring the blade down, in one clean, sweeping motion, upon the Iron Round.

The anvil which had been all that these women had possessed to remind them of their destiny now seemed to glow with the same strange light given off by the Dragon Sword.

The two parts met. There was a huge sound. A sound like the breaking of every planet, every cosmic barrier, every sun in the entire multiverse. A monstrous sound, yet a beautiful sound. It was the sound of fulfilled destiny.

And now the sword, which had been heavy for so long, was light in my hands. And I saw that the blade was broken, clean in two, that for a moment one part of it was embedded in the Iron Round, while the other remained in my grip. And I shuddered at the incredible sensation of delight which permeated my entire body. And I gasped and I continued to sing my song, the song which the women sang, the song of the Eldren, the song of the Dragon Sword and the Iron Round.

And as we sang, something like flame erupted from the anvil, something which had been released from the sword and yet which, for a short while, had also inhabited the round. It curled and it writhed and it, too, was singing. And the singing became a roar, echoed in the throats of all those women, and the flame grew fiercer and stronger and it began to take shapes to itself, and colours to itself, and it seemed to me, as I fell away from its enormous might, that this was altogether a more powerful force than any I had witnessed before. For this was the force of human desire, of human will, of human ideals. It grew and grew. The shard of the sword fell from my hand. I was upon my knees, looking up as the presence took form, roaring still, curling and writhing still, blotting out the sun.

It was a huge beast. A dragon whose scales rippled in the glow of the sun. A dragon whose crest burned with the richest colours of the rainbow. A dragon whose red nostrils flared and whose white teeth clashed, whose coils rose skyward with exquisite grace, whose wings spread wider and wider, beating strongly as the beast ascended into the clear, blue sky.

Yet still the song went on. Still the dragon and the women and I all sang. Still the anvil sang, though the sword's voice grew fainter now. Up, up, it beat, that wonderful creature; up until it turned, weaving and diving, skimming the waters, spearing up again into the sunlight, rejoicing in its strength, in its freedom, in its pure animation.

Then the dragon roared. And her breath was warm upon our faces, bringing us, too, fresh life. She opened her vast mouth and she clashed her teeth in an orgy of release. She danced for us. She sang for us. She displayed her power for us. And we knew a complete rapport with her. I had known this only once before and the memory of that time was gone from me. I wept with the pleasure of it.

Then the she-dragon was turning. Her multicoloured wings, like the wings of some enormous insect, began to beat with a different purpose.

She turned her long, saurian head and she stared at us from out of wise, tender eyes, and again the breath steamed suddenly from her nostrils, and she was calling to us, calling us to follow.

Von Bek took my hand. 'Come with us, Herr Daker. Come with us through the Dragon Gate. We shall know such happiness there!' And Alisaard clutched my arm. She said: 'You will be honoured by all the Eldren now. For ever.'

But I said sadly that it was not to be. 'I know now that I must find the Dark Ship again. That is my duty and my destiny.'

'You said you had no further desire to be a hero.' Von Bek was surprised.

'That is true. And I will be a hero, will I not, in the Eldren world? My only hope to rid myself of this burden is to remain here. I know that.'

All the women were now aboard their vessels. Many were already putting out to sea, over the white-tipped waves, in the wake of the she-dragon. They waved to me as they left. And still they sang.

'Go,' I told my friends. 'Go and be happy. That will console me for any loss, I promise you.'

And thus we parted. Von Bek and Alisaard were the last to go aboard the final ship which left the harbour. I watched as the wind filled their triangular sail, as the slender prow made a cleft in the gentle waters.

The great she-dragon, which had been released at last, according to legend, described a complete circle in the sky overhead, seemingly for the sheer joy of flying.

But where she had gone the circle remained. A blue and red disc which gradually widened until it touched the waters below. The colours became more complex. Thousands of rich, dark shades shimmered above the water. And through this circle now passed the great she-dragon, vanishing almost at once. Then came the ships of the Eldren. And they, too, were swallowed up. They had rejoined their kind. The dragons and their mortal kin were reunited at last!

The circle faded.

The circle vanished.

I was alone in a deserted world.

I was alone.

I looked down at the two halves of the sword, at the anvil. Both seemed to have sustained enormous forces. It was as if they had melted yet held their shape. I was not sure why I had this impression.

I stirred the hilt of the sword with my foot. For a moment I was tempted to pick it up, but then I turned aside with a shrug. I wanted no further business with swords, or magic, or destiny. I wanted only to go home.

I left the harbour behind me. I walked amongst the miserable ruins of the Eldren town. I remembered such destruction. I remembered when, as Erekosë, Champion of Humanity, I had led my armies against a town similar to this, against a people called the Eldren. I remembered that crime. And I remembered another crime, when I had led the Eldren against my own folk.

Somehow, however, the pang of guilt I had known since then was no longer present. I felt that all was now redeemed again. I had made amends and I was whole.

Yet I still knew the loss of Ermizhad. Would I ever be united with her?

Later, towards evening, I found myself again on the quayside, looking out towards the setting sun. Everything was silent. Everything was calm. Yet it was a solitude I did not relish, for it was the result of an absence of life.

A few seabirds wheeled and called. The waves slapped against the stones of the quay. I sat down on the Iron Round, again contemplating the two shards of the Dragon Sword, wondering if perhaps I should have gone with the Eldren, back to their own world.

And then I heard the sound of horses behind me. I turned. A single rider, leading another steed. A small, ill-formed fellow, all in motley. He grinned at me and saluted.

'Will you come a-riding with me, Sir Champion? I would relish the company.'

'Good evening to you, Jermays. I trust you have not brought me further news of destiny and doom.' I climbed into the saddle of the horse.

'I never cared much for those things,' he said, 'as you know. It is not my business to play an important part in the history of the multiverse. These past times are perhaps the most active I have seen. I do not regret it, though I should have liked to have witnessed Sharadim's defeat and the banishment of Chaos. You performed a mighty task, eh, Sir Champion? Perhaps the greatest of your career?'

I shook my head. I did not know.

Jermays led the way from the quay and along the shore of the sea, beside the white cliffs. The sun made the sky a wonderful deep colour. It touched the sea. It made all seem permanent and unassailable.

'Your friends have gone now, have they?' he asked as we rode. 'Dragon to dragon, Eldren to Eldren. And von Bek, what sort of dynasty will he found, I wonder? And what sort of history will come out of all that went on here? Another cycle must begin before we shall get any hint of the fate of Melniboné.'

The name was familiar to me. It stirred the faintest memory, but I dismissed it. I wanted no more of memories, whether they be of past or future.

Soon it was night. Moonlight was pure silver upon the water. As we rounded a headland, with the tide rolling at our horses' feet, I saw the outline of a ship at anchor in the little bay.

The ship had high decks, fore and aft, and its timbers were carved with all manner of baroque designs. There was a broad, sweeping curve to her prow and her single mast was tall, bearing a single large, furled sail. I could see that on each of her raised decks the ship had a wheel, as if she could be steered from stern or prow. She sat lightly on the water, like a vessel awaiting fresh cargo.

Jermays and I rode our horses through the shallows. I heard him cry: 'Halloo, the ship! Are you taking on passengers?'

Now a figure appeared at the rail, leaning on it and apparently staring out over our heads towards the cliffs. I saw at once that he was blind.

A red mist had begun to form in the water about the ship. It was faint and yet it seemed to stir not with the movements of the sea itself, but with the movements of the dark vessel. I looked out across the ocean, but the moon was hidden behind clouds and I could see little. It seemed that the red mist was growing.

'Come aboard,' said the blind man. 'You are welcome.'

'Now we must part,' said Jermays. 'I think it will be long before we meet again, perhaps in another cycle altogether. Farewell, Sir Champion.' He clapped me on the back and then had turned his horse and was galloping back through the water to the shore. I heard the hoofs thumping on sand and he had vanished.

My own horse was restless. I dismounted and let him go. He followed Jermays.

I waded through the water. It was warm against my body. It had reached as high as my chest before I could catch hold of a trailing ladder and begin to climb aboard. The red mist had grown thicker now. It obscured all sight of the shore.

The blind man sniffed the air. 'We must be on our way. I am glad you decided to come. You have no sword now, eh?'

'I have no need of one,' I said.

He grunted in reply and then called out for the sail to be unfurled. I saw the shadows of men in the rigging as I followed the blind captain to his cabin, where his brother, the helmsman, waited for us. I heard the sail crack down and the wind tug urgently at it. I heard the anchors raised. I felt the ship pull suddenly and roll and swing out to sea and I knew that once again we were sailing through waters which flowed between the worlds.

The helmsman's bright blue eyes were kindly as he indicated the food prepared for me. 'You must be weary, John Daker. You have done much, eh?'

I stripped off my heavy leathers. I sighed with relief as I poured myself wine.

'Are there others aboard tonight?' I asked.

'Of your kind? Only yourself.'

'And where do we sail?' I was reconciled to whatever instructions I might be given.

'Oh, nowhere of any great importance. You have no sword, I note.'

'Your brother has already remarked upon that. I left it broken on the quayside in Barobanay. It is useless now.'

'Not quite,' said the Captain, joining me in a goblet of wine. 'But it will need to be reforged. Perhaps as two swords, where it was once one.'

'A new sword from each part. Is there enough metal for that?'

'I think so. But that will not concern you for a while, at any rate. Would you sleep now?'

'I am tired,' I said. I felt as if I had not rested for centuries.

The blind captain led me to my old, familiar bunk. I stretched myself out and almost immediately I began to dream. I dreamed of King Rigenos and Ermizhad, of Urlik Skarsol and all the other heroes I had been. And then I dreamed of dragons. Hundreds of dragons. Dragons whom I knew by name. Dragons who loved me as I loved them. And I dreamed of great fleets. Of wars. Of tragedies and of impossible delights, of wizardry and wild romance. I dreamed of white arms locked around me. I dreamed again of Ermizhad. And then I dreamed that we had come together again at last and I awoke laughing, remembering something of that dragon song which the Eldren women had sung.

The blind captain and his brother the helmsman stood there. They, too, were smiling.

'It is time to disembark, John Daker. It is time for you to go to your reward.'

I got up, then. I was dressed only in a pair of leather breeches and boots. But it did not feel cold. I followed them out into the darkness of the deck. A few yellow lamps gleamed here and there. Through the red mist I saw the suggestion of a shoreline. I saw first one tower and then a second. They seemed to be spanning a harbour.

I peered through the darkness, trying to distinguish details. The towers looked familiar.

Now the helmsman called to me from below. He was in a small boat waiting to carry me to land. I bade farewell to the Captain and I climbed down to the boat, seating myself on the bench.

The helmsman pulled strongly on his oars. The red mist grew dimmer still. It seemed close to dawn. The twin towers had a bridge spanning them. Elsewhere were thousands of lights gleaming. I heard the mournful hoot of what I thought at first was a great water-beast. Then I realised it was a boat.

The helmsman shipped his oars. 'You are at your destination now, John Daker. I wish you good fortune.'

Cautiously I stepped onto the slippery mud of the shore. I heard a drone from above me. I heard voices. And then, as the helmsman disappeared back into the red mist, I realised that I had been in this place before.

The twin towers were those of Tower Bridge. The sounds I heard were the sounds of a great modern city. The sounds of London.

John Daker was returning home.

Epilogue

M Y NAME IS John Daker. I was once called the Eternal Champion. It is possible I shall bear that name once again. For now, however, I am at peace.

By summoning up this identity – the original, if you will – I was able to resist and ultimately defeat the powers of Chaos. My reward for this action is that I am allowed to resume my life as John Daker.

When called by King Rigenos to be Humanity's champion, I had been discontented with my life. I had seen it as shallow, without colour. Yet I have come to realise how rich my life actually is, how complex is the world I inhabit. That complexity alone is worthy of celebration. I understand that life in a great city of my world's twentieth century can be just as intense, just as satisfactory as any other. Indeed, to be a hero, forever at war, is to be in some ways always a child. The true challenge comes in making sense of one's life, of imbuing it with purpose based on one's own principles.

I still have memories of those other times. I still dream frequently of the great battle-blades, the chargers, the massive fighting barges, the weird creatures and the magical cities, the bright banners and the wonder of a perfect love. I dream of riding against Chaos, of bearing arms against Heaven in the name of Hell, of being the scythe which cut Humanity down... But I have discovered an equal intensity of experience in this world, too. We have merely, I think, to teach ourselves how to recognise and to relish it.

That is what I learned when I faced the Archduke Balarizaaf, Princess Sharadim and Prince Flamadin at The World's Beginning, when we struggled for the Dragon Sword.

It is ironic that I saved both myself and those I cared for by recalling, at the crucial moment, my identity as an ordinary mortal. There are subtle dangers to the rôle of hero. I am glad I no longer have to consider them.

So John Daker has returned home. The cycle is complete; the saga finds a form of resolution. Somewhere, doubtless, the Eternal Champion will continue to fight to maintain the Cosmic Balance. And in his dreams, if nowhere else, John Daker will recall those battles, as he will sometimes recall a vast field of statues, all of which seem to bear his name... For the present, however, he need take no further part in battles, nor wonder at the significance of that field.

I still long, of course, for my Ermizhad. I shall never love anyone as I loved her. I believe I must surely find her, not in some bizarre realm of the multiverse, but here, perhaps in this city, in London. Does she look for me, even now, as I search for her? It surely cannot be very long before we are reunited.

And when that time comes there is no sword forged, in this world or any other, which will divide us!

We shall know peace.

Though our span of years be those of ordinary human beings, they will be our own years. We shall be free of all cosmic designs, free of destinies and grandiose dooms.

We shall be free to love as we were always meant to love; free to be the flawed, finite, mortal creatures which from the first was all we ever wished to be.

And, for those years at least, the Eternal Champion will be at rest.

MICHAEL MOORCOCK (1939–) is one of the most important figures in British SF and Fantasy literature. The author of many literary novels and stories in practically every genre, he has won and been shortlisted for numerous awards including the Hugo, Nebula, World Fantasy, Whitbread and Guardian Fiction Prize. He is also a musician who performed in the seventies with his own band, the Deep Fix; and, as a member of the space-rock band, Hawkwind, won a platinum disc. His tenure as editor of NEW WORLDS magazine in the sixties and seventies is seen as the high watermark of SF editorship in the UK, and was crucial in the development of the SF New Wave. Michael Moorcock's literary creations include Hawkmoon, Corum, Von Bek, Jerry Cornelius and, of course, his most famous character, Elric. He has been compared to, among others, Balzac, Dumas, Dickens, James Joyce, Ian Fleming, J.R.R. Tolkien and Robert E. Howard. Although born in London, he now splits his time between homes in Texas and Paris.

For a more detailed biography, please see Michael Moorcock's entry in *The Encyclopedia of Science Fiction* at: http://www.sf-encyclopedia.com/

For further information about Michael Moorcock and his work, please visit www.multiverse.org, or send S.A.E. to The Nomads Of The Time Streams, Mo Dhachaidh, Loch Awe, Dalmally, Argyll, PA33 1AQ, Scotland, or P.O. Box 385716, Waikoloa, HI 96738, USA.